AMBITIONS END

by
Mike Upton

Bloomington, IN Milton Keynes, UK

authorHOUSE™

AuthorHouse™
1663 Liberty Drive, Suite 200
Bloomington, IN 47403
www.authorhouse.com
Phone: 1-800-839-8640

AuthorHouse™ UK Ltd.
500 Avebury Boulevard
Central Milton Keynes, MK9 2BE
www.authorhouse.co.uk
Phone: 08001974150

This book is a work of fiction. People, places, events, and situations are the product of the author's imagination. Any resemblance to actual persons, living or dead, or historical events, is purely coincidental.

First published by AuthorHouse 2/9/2006

ISBN: 1-4208-9163-4 (sc)

Printed in the United States of America
Bloomington, Indiana

This book is printed on acid-free paper.

Ambitions End is dedicated to several people.

Firstly to my wife Brenda for her quiet but continuous support to me during the tortuous process of writing and re-writing this book and for proof reading the manuscript. Secondly to my daughters Catherine and Victoria for their belief in me. Lastly to Daniel Cooke of AuthorHouse Publishing for his enthusiastic encouragement and positive help in taking me from manuscript to finished printed book.

To all of them I say thank you.

It is also dedicated to all those cynics, doubters and others who didn't believe that I could or would do it.

To all of them I say - read it - enjoy it - and there you are - I did it!!!

He who would rise in the world should veil his ambition with the forms of humanity.

Chinese proverb

CHAPTER 1

The thick tyres of the big Jaguar swished quickly along the wet road, the wipers making their monotonous constant movement across the windscreen. It was a cold dark windy moonless northern night typical of late autumn and signalling the forthcoming onset of winter and the sort of night where people hurried to be indoors or the pub or anywhere except outside.

Inside the car however it was warm and quiet and a marked contrast with the unfriendly outside. The driver and two passengers were all fully occupied but in their different ways. Classical music played quietly.

Mark Watson Chief Executive of Lovells a large multinational company sitting in the right hand side rear seat looked up from the sheaf of papers he'd been studying for the last hundred miles and was wondering if anything had been left to chance, if anything could go wrong at this last moment. He stared at the back of his driver's head seeing his hair just starting to curl over his white collar his mind was on the coming meeting. The prize for which he had worked so hard for so many years was within his grasp. It was all nearly his.

Glancing over to the other side of the rear seat he looked at Sam slumped in the corner. While letting his mind continue to think about the coming meeting he stared at the sleeping young woman and thought of the sex they enjoyed, sometimes hurried and frantic, other times slow and tender. Those romantic images though were quickly excluded by thoughts of the meeting tonight a meeting that consumed him, worried him, excited him. It was hard to believe that when he walked in and signed the agreement tonight it would at last be all over. He was going to win after all this time.

'Won't be long now Mark' Graham said softly. He'd been his driver for many years and knew about Mark's frenetic work rate, his passion for business, his fiery temper and his occasional amazing acts of thoughtfulness or kindnesses which were so unexpected that they were all the more effective.

Graham knew when he could call him Mark, when to use the deferential term sir, and when to use his surname Mr. Watson.

'You've made good time in spite of the weather' replied Mark as he turned back to the documents.

'You can never tell with the bloody motorways' grumbled Graham. 'Sometimes they're alright sometimes they're a real bastard. Tonight we were lucky. No accidents, no hold-ups, no silly sods trying to carve everyone up, and no bloody cops trying to make a name for themselves by booking a few speeders.'

Graham was a fast driver and had to be as Mark never left enough time to get from one meeting to another. Still he paid well but in return expected not only absolute dedication and commitment but also absolute discretion.

'What do you want to do?' he continued. 'Go straight to your meeting? You'll be at least three quarters of an hour early or do you want to go to the Hotel and kick yer heels there for a bit?'

'Hotel' snapped Mark.

'Okey dokey, hotel it is. I'll come off at the next exit and we'll be there in no time.'

Picking up the in car phone Mark quickly punched in a number drumming his fingers on his knee while he waited impatiently for the call to be answered.

'Caroline Burton' said a quiet cultured voice, which was deep and slightly husky.

'All fixed?' asked Mark.

'Apart from the on going major issue of Sir Charles's continued intransigence then there are just a few minor issues to resolve'.

'What minor issues?' he demanded instantly, his antenna alert straining to pick up any clue from her voice as to whether they were really minor or whether they might be more serious.

'Wait a minute let me move to a quiet corner of the room'.

He waited.

'Look apart from Sir Charles there's nothing that looks like a deal breaker' she said softly, 'but there are a few unresolved points. We're working on all of them and I am sure we can fix them if we are left to do so without being interrupted, so Mark just fuck off and let me get on and do what you pay me to do'.

He smiled to himself. Caroline was the best corporate lawyer he had ever known and he knew that she would sort out whatever were the remaining minor legal points. She was also the only one of his staff who not only would dare to tell him to fuck off but would also get away with it, except Sam of course.

'OK Caroline, but you know how important this particular deal is to me and we are so close to it now. I want it Caroline, I really want this one'.

'Go away and leave me to finish. We all know that this is important to you. Wait for me or Steve to call' said the soft voice. There was a click and the line went dead.

'Is everything OK' asked Sam stretching and rubbing her eyes. 'I must have dropped off. What's the time?'

'Yes you dropped right off. We're about three quarters of an hour early so we're going to the hotel first' replied Mark packing his papers back into his brief case. 'We'll check in then I'll make a couple of calls and Steve will give us a shout when they're ready'.

Soon the Jaguar pulled up in front of the Grand Hotel which although old was still be best hotel in the City. Graham drew to a halt, jumped out and had Mark's door open before the hotel doorman reached the car.

'Bags in the boot' said Graham and the doorman moved smoothly to reach them out of the car. Sam walked quickly up the steps and marched straight to reception while Mark stretched his six foot frame before following her.

'You have three rooms booked for us, a suite for Mr. Mark Watson, an adjoining room for Miss Peters and a separate room for Mr. Graham Field.'

'Let me just check that for you Madam' smarmed the trim little receptionist who was proudly displaying two badges pinned to her slightly old fashioned uniform jacket. One indicated her name was Val and the other told everyone she was employee of the month.

'Yes that's right, if you could each fill in a registration form'.

'I'll do it for us all' said Sam. 'Get someone to take Mr. Watson up to his room now while I do this please'.

'Well really the forms have to filled in first' said Val knowing quite clearly what the rules were regarding check in. No form. No room.

Looking up Sam smiled. 'I'm sure you have your procedures but Mr. Watson's had a long journey and really needs to have a rest before an important meeting that he's going to later tonight'.

'Well' hesitated Val looking at Mark.

'He's tired, he doesn't have much time and I'm sure you can make an exception on this one occasion can't you? Also can you get some coffee organised now please'.

Val looked over at Mark who was now speaking urgently into his mobile phone and saw an attractive tall man in his forties. Looking back at Sam and being employee of the month took her decision without referring to her supervisor. 'That will be quite alright' she said with sudden authority.' The boy will take Mr. Watson to his room. 'Jim' she called in a shrill bossy tone, 'take this gentleman to The Yorkshire suite on the first floor right away'.

Jim looked surprised at Val's tone of voice but ambled over and muttering 'this way sir' led the way to the lift. Mark briefly fixed Val with his piercing blue eyes, quietly thanked her then swept over to the lift where the young porter waited.

The ancient lift clanked into action. 'Sod it' exclaimed Mark as his phone cut out. 'Why can't hotels have lifts that don't cut off mobile phones?' he snapped at Jim.

'Dunno, nothing to do with me' replied Jim sulkily and then added 'sir'.

Sam stayed with Val who'd almost had a funny turn when Mark had stared into her eyes, and dealt with those essential details that were necessary at hotels, sorting out payment arrangements, having credit cards swiped, checkout times, room service for what she thought Mark might need, and the myriad of minor details that were such a part of a hotel receptionist's life.

Reaching the first floor Mark followed Jim to the designated suite as he opened the door with a flourish, walked in and started his practiced routine of explaining how the television, light, shower and other fittings in the room worked. Ignoring him Mark started to tap numbers into his phone then looked up 'Yes yes' he snapped 'I can work all that out thanks just leave the bag and that's all'. He pressed the "call" button on his phone.

'Right ho sir' said Jim and stood looking expectantly at Mark.

'Hang on a minute' grumbled Mark into his mobile and then looking at Jim he snapped 'Now what do you want? Oh a tip I suppose. Well see Sam she'll sort you out. Now just get out'.

He paced around the room mobile phone to his ear as he listened to an update of the negotiations not from Caroline who he really couldn't bring himself to chase again, but from one of her support team involved in the negotiations. It really was going to be all right except for the Sir Charles issue, but then he had the ultimate solution to that if the old man continued to be intransigent.

The door opened and sulky Jim came back in carrying a large suitcase followed by Sam who in one smooth movement motioned Jim to put the bag down, slipped a five pound note into his hand and gave him a lovely smile which cheered him up no end and ushered him out.

Studying Mark carefully trying to gauge his mood she knew from past experience he could be volatile and extremely tetchy at times like these. She had to judge just what he wanted. Sometimes it was silence, sometimes he wanted to talk, or drink coffee, or put his feet up and relax, or sometimes like tonight he just paced like a caged animal. It wasn't sex that would happen later.

'Coffee?' she queried softly.

'No' he snapped. 'We've got to get this just right. I want to bury that bastard once and for all tonight........sorry yes coffee would be great but we haven't got much time.'

At almost the same moment there was a soft knock at the door and Sam walked quickly over, opened it and ushered in Jim who was outside holding a tray with a pot of coffee.

'Thank you' she said and gave him another stunning smile.

'Is there anything else Madam?' queried Jim who would now do anything for Sam although he wasn't taken with her grumpy bloke. He wondered what the relationship was. She wasn't wearing a wedding ring he'd noticed as he prided himself on being quick to spot things like that. Boss and secretary and he guessed they were shagging each other. Nice he thought. I wouldn't mind shagging something like that especially with legs and a figure like that.

'No thanks. You've been most helpful. If we need anything we'll ring down'.

Ushering him out she turned again to Mark who'd already poured himself a cup of coffee. He took a sip. 'Shit that's hot' he exclaimed and went into the bathroom, turned on a tap and added cold water to cool the drink.

Sam thought about commenting that of course the coffee was hot as it had just been poured out but deciding that silence would be better poured her own cup added some milk and then got the laptop out of its case plugging it into the appropriate wall sockets for telephone line and power. After the obligatory short wait for it to warm up she quickly entered passwords and logged on to her office so as to be ready to access any file that Mark might want, or to word process any documents. It was only the work of another couple of minutes to connect up the small printer and everything was ready for whatever Mark required. After all that was what she was employed for, to be his ever ready secretary and personal assistant.

Oh yes and also to sleep with him whenever he wanted.

Smiling to herself she knew there was no love there from his side, tenderness sometimes but not love. She fulfilled a need for him and had realised long ago that even though she adored him and was desperately in love with him there was no chance of it being reciprocated. He loved his wife, his family and his baby not her, but when he needed her as he so often did, she would dream and hope one day, then maybe just maybe, one day he might love her even if just a little.

Mark's mobile phone rang and he snatched it up and peered at the tiny screen.

'Caroline what's happening?' he asked loudly.

'I think you've about got yourself a deal, except for Sir Charles' said the soft voice at the other end. 'You could start to make your way over here. Will you be long?'

'I'm on my way. Have we really done it? Are there any points remaining to be settled?' queried Mark urgently worrying that there were still problems to be resolved.

'There's really only that one major issue to be sorted' Caroline replied soothingly 'and that's the position of Sir Charles. He's being really sticky and is still maintaining that he won't vote for the takeover. The rest of the Board are either with us, or at least neutral. It's yours Mark except for Sir Charles'.

Mark chuckled 'Is that really the only problem remaining?'

'Yes. Everything else is resolved. How much we're paying for his business up front, how much after 3 months and final payment after six months. Ownership transfer, share allocations, executive authority, day to day operation, integration into your business, redundancies including those senior people who are affected and will be going and terms applicable for them, trademarks, due diligence queries, production continuity. It's all there except for Sir Charles and without him you haven't got a deal'.

In spite of Caroline's rapid briefing Mark still had a number of questions and he fired them at her thick and fast down the phone as he strode to the door. 'Come on Sam' he yelled over his shoulder. 'Stop hanging about. We've got a deal to do' and he was off and down the corridor.

Sam quickly logged off the laptop, grabbed her handbag, ran out of the door giving it a slam and just got to the lift as the doors opened to let Mark in.

Arriving in the lobby Mark walked quickly to the swing doors. Outside Graham was in conversation with the doorman having immediately on arrival established an easy rapport with him in the way that chauffeurs and hotel doormen do so easily. Seeing his boss barging through the glass swing doors of the hotel Graham ran down the steps opened the nearest rear car door for Mark while Sam trotted around to the other side. Quickly closing the door he slid behind the wheel and fired up the engine as Mark said 'You know where we're going? Are you sure you know the way as I don't want to waste time cruising around trying to find the damn place'.

Graham calmly 'Yes no problem we'll be there in about ten minutes' and set off at a fast pace. He'd carefully checked with the doorman while waiting for Mark so that he knew the quickest way to get to DGH Chemicals as he still remembered the time years ago that he hadn't known the way to one of Mark's destinations and had frantically stopped at a newsagent to ask the way and still got lost. Finally a policeman on traffic duty gave the correct directions. Mark had roasted him and he'd vowed never ever again to not know how to get Mark to where he wanted to go.

Soon through the drifting rain, the name DGH Chemicals shone out brightly lighting up the gloom of the night and casting a bright pool of light onto the fence and shrubs that made up the perimeter of the site. Swinging off the road into the entrance Graham slowed as he approached the red and white barriers that barred the way into the complex. Pulling up at the security gatehouse he lowered the window and was about to speak to the security guard when a figure stepped out of the shadows nodded to the guard and leaned into the car past Graham.

'Hi Mark, can I hitch a lift and update you'

'Yea sure' grinned Mark 'how's Caroline done?'

Steve Thomas who was Caroline's assistant retuned the grin, got into the front passenger seat, quickly furled and stowed his umbrella between his legs, brushed his hair off his forehead and turning gave a cheery thumbs up. Twisting his head back to the front he told Graham to drive up to the main entrance of the offices which were about five hundred yards up the impressive driveway then turned round to again face Mark before replying.

'She got 'em by the balls. Magic to watch. She's one hell of an operator you know. Everything that they put up she countered or demolished but in such a way that they didn't really realise that she was destroying them. When we started I thought that their team was really tough and we would have a really shit time. But she's dynamite. Her only problem is Sir Charles. He's an awkward old bastard and stubborn as glue. How the hell we're going to persuade him to vote over his shares I just don't know'.

'Leave Sir Charles to me Steve. Are there any other problems?'

'No that's about it. Do you think that you really can make him change his mind?'

'So we've done it'.

'Well no not until we persuade old Charlie boy'.

'I told you leave him to me. I'll deal with him'.

Steve looked at Mark and saw in his eyes something triumphant and yet at the same time chilling. He'd seen that look before where Mark smiled but his eyes turned to ice and shivering involuntarily knew that Mark really was confident that he'd beat the old sod.

The car stopped in front of the office entrance. Graham jumped out and held the door open for Mark who got out slowly and then stood and looked up at the still imposing edifice that was represented by the Head Office of DGH Chemicals. The night time darkness and the rain obscured the fact that the building was old and scruffy. In daylight it looked very tatty but now at night it seemed large and impressive. In it's heyday it must have been stunning and overpowering with its six floors, most of which were brightly illuminated even at this late time. Mark, Sam and Steve moved into the main reception area. Steve acknowledged the ex army security receptionist as the three walked to the lifts.

'We're going to the top floor. They know we're coming so no need to ring through to anyone' commanded Steve curtly.

'Right sir' replied Dave. Cocky bastard he thought. He'd had been in charge of night security at DGH for nearly eighteen years. He knew like many others that things had not been good at the firm for some time and the rumours had been around for months that the business was going bust, or would be taken over, or some other complicated financial arrangement these top highflying financiers might dream up. He worried about it because at fifty eight he knew he'd never get another decent job and as his pension wasn't that good he needed to work for another few years yet.

Mind you the Chairman had always said that he'd look after the older employees, but you never knew did you? Still he mused there was sod all he could do about it, so he smiled at the visitors and hoped that it would all be all right in the end. There had been a lot of late night and early morning meetings recently and the press had been full of speculation about a takeover. Something was going on it. Well he'd find out soon enough he thought.

The lift rose smoothly. A disembodied electronic voice announced that they had arrived at the sixth floor and the three visitors walked out with Steve leading the way down a corridor leading off to the left and after about twenty yards stopped by a door, paused, turned the handle and walked in holding it open for Mark and Sam.

Inside, it was clear that this was a working room but no one was in there at the moment. Documents, various papers, files, folders, a couple of laptop computers, together with several empty coffee cups and a nearly empty plate of sandwiches now curling at the edges all showed that this had been the subject of a great deal of hard work.

'I'll let Caroline know we're here' said Steve and he slipped away.

Mark paced restlessly while Sam sat quietly on one of the easy chairs. A few minutes passed and then the door opened as Steve and Caroline walked in.

Caroline was tall with dark blonde shoulder length hair which although usually immaculate was now somewhat dishevelled showing that she had been running her hand through it many times, something she did when stressed. Her dark grey business suit was also a little crumpled and she looked tired.

Mark realised that she had been leading his negotiating team arguing with the other side on his behalf for a couple of days and most of last night. She'd probably had enough of it and of his constant phone calls to check progress.

'OK Caroline tell me where we're up to' he said quietly as his eyes bored deeply into her which even now after the several years that they had worked together surprised him each time by their startling blueness.

Propping herself part on and part off the edge of a table which took up most of one end of the room she paused furrowing her brows as she sought to assemble the key facts in a cohesive and concise way oblivious of the fact that her pose was causing her skirt to ride up exposing a considerable length of thigh to which Mark's eyes flicked like a magnet. She gave him a quick yet thorough briefing on the way the negotiations had gone. The problems and how they had been overcome. The way that some of the DGH directors had sought to protect their own interests in trying to negotiate special severance deals if they knew that their services wouldn't be retained, or favourable amendments to their existing contracts of employment if they were to have a place in the new company formed following the merger of DGH and Mark's company, Lovells.

She continued with the details of supply contracts, banking arrangements, customer contracts, profitability, relationships with the trades unions, staff numbers, proposed details of the timing of an announcement and how close DGH was to breaching its banking covenants.

Pausing she thought rapidly. Had she forgotten anything that was important before Mark went into the main conference room to eventually sign the deal providing Sir Charles Houghton could be persuaded to sign on the dotted line?

She understood that for Sir Charles it was the end of his company that he had built up over many years from the business originally started by his father David George Houghton, hence the abbreviated set of initials DGH known everywhere as Houghtons. But her job was to negotiate the legal points for Mark and his Company. It was Mark who paid her, and very well at that. A big enough salary for her to be able to afford the enormous mortgage on a large apartment in London's Docklands, a flashy Porsche car, and two sometimes three exotic foreign holidays a year. Caroline was paid well, and lived well.

Single, since she had divorced Tom, their marriage having lasted only three years as she'd realised after the first year that although he was good in bed and a really nice man, he was entirely without ambition and content to trundle through life taking things as they came along. Driven by a desire to get to the top in the corporate legal field she was now well on the way to doing it. Tom would have held her back.

Sometimes she thought with affection of the little cottage outside Melton Mowbray that was their first and only home together but Tom couldn't cope with her ambition and constant desire for more. He realised that he could never hold her as what he wanted from life and made him content, were so different from her ambitious needs that it was inevitable they would grow apart. Money, power, influence and a big job in the City of London was what she'd wanted but he'd wanted none of these.

'What about Sir Charles then what reason does he give for not signing?'

Mark's question jerked her back to this evening and the final instalment of the long takeover battle that was about to be played out.

'He changes tack Mark. Earlier today it was that the terms weren't good enough. Then it was that he was unhappy about the plan to close the GM research unit. It's always something different. I think he just doesn't want to sell out. He still thinks that he can lead the business out of the mess it's in, and Mark it is in a hell of a mess. You are going to have a field day sorting this out. There's millions to save through reorganisation and restructuring. The rest of their Board are up for it, at least those that are staying are. As for the others, the ones on your "out" list they're happy with the severance packages we've organised. He's stubborn though. I've tried everything. I've cajoled him, argued till I'm blue in the face, sworn at him, threatened him but nothing seems to shift him. I won't say I give up because you know that I never do, but frankly Mark I'm totally at a loss to know what else to try?'

'Thanks Caroline. You've done a great job. I'll just have to see if I can shift the old bugger..........and I think I know just what will do it'.

Caroline was puzzled but when she saw Mark's expression she knew he had a trump card up his sleeve but what that the card was she had no idea.

'Go and ask if I can see Sir Charles on his own for a few minutes please Steve' he said quietly.

Steve left the room leaving Mark, Caroline and Sam alone.

'Tough couple of days huh?' queried Mark. Caroline nodded. 'Never mind, as I said you've done a great job and it's nearly over now'.

The three of them sat quietly waiting for Steve to return with an answer. Sam noticed that Mark had relaxed. Until now he'd been like a knotted piece of string but now he obviously thought that he'd won in spite of the major shareholder Sir Charles Houghton refusing to sign the deal. She wondered that would happen if Mark couldn't make him change his mind. Would the deal collapse maybe? She'd seen other deals of Mark's fail. He didn't always win in spite of the media hype about his golden touch.

The door opened and Steve returned. 'He says it's highly unusual and irregular and.....'

'Bollocks' interrupted Mark. 'Just go and tell the old sod that I have something to discuss with him in relation to this deal. Now Steve. Now'.

.........'but if it's important he will meet with you in his office' continued Steve while Mark paused for breath.

'Oh great thanks' and then quietly 'sorry Stevie boy'

'No problem. Shall I show you the way?' said Steve quite unconcerned by Mark's little outburst as he opened the door.

Picking up his briefcase he walked after Steve. A quick turn to the right took them past the Board Room and a little further on there was a door with Chairman's Office on a brass plate on the door. Steve knocked and entered. Firstly they went into a small office which was normally occupied by a secretary, a real Scottish terror of a woman known as May. Mark had had a few cross words with her in the past and often thought of her as "may or may not".

They moved through May's office to the other side where Steve knocked on a further door. Almost immediately it opened and there stood Sir Charles. Tall, fat, powerful, his whole presence intimidating to most people something he used to advantage. Basically he was a bully.

Well thought Mark, time for you to get clobbered.

'OK Steve thanks. I'll talk with Sir Charles alone'. He waited till he heard the door shut then staring hard at his opponent, the man he'd hated for so long said quietly 'Well Charles I know it's sad but this is the end of the line for you and your business. It has no future. You've run out of cash, the banks will foreclose on you, your employees will be thrown onto the scrapheap, your competitors including us will pick over the wreckage piece by piece. On the other hand I am offering a fair price for the business and we'll keep the best parts and build or integrate them into my Company. Most of your employees will have their jobs secured and the combined business will have a great future'.

'You mean you'll asset strip my great company started all those years ago by my father, flog off the bits you don't want, and exploit the bits that you do. No Mark, we'll fight on. My fellow Board Directors and I will make a fight of it. Even if they waver and agree to your terms, remember that I own or control sixty percent of the business and if I won't sell there is damn all you can do about it so you can forget it'.

'Charles face facts. You're finished. Utterly washed up and finished. Go out on a high. Sell the business to me and leave with your head up. The alternative is a very rapid collapse. Think carefully Charles' Mark said earnestly as he leaned towards the fat man opposite him. 'You don't want that to happen. If the banks take it over' he paused 'no not if, when they take it over and put you into receivership hundreds of your people will lose their jobs. The banks really will break it up and asset strip it. What about Belinda? How do you think she would feel?'

Sir Charles Houghton knew in his heart that Mark was right. The banks would destroy everything. His wife Belinda, a great socialite would be devastated. His employees would be on the scrap heap. He was letting his father down. After all they'd been in tight corners before and somehow got out of it surely he could do it again couldn't he? He looked at Mark and slowly shook his head. He had to battle on.

'Mark the answer is no. We'll fight on. Maybe we'll lose but we'll fight you. My Board will stay with me'

'No they won't' snapped Mark keeping his anger and hatred under control. 'They're with us. Everyone is with us. The banks are with us. The Institutions are with us. Your key people are with us. Give up now'.

'No damn you, no' snarled Sir Charles.

Mark looked at him very intently. 'Is that your final word?' Receiving an affirmative nod he sighed, sat down in a chair on the opposite side of Sir Charles's desk and said 'I hoped I wouldn't have to do this Charles but you leave me no option. I want your Company and I'm going to have it'.

He reached into his briefcase and took out a large brown envelope. Looking again at Sir Charles he dropped it onto the highly polished desk and pushed it towards him.

'Take a look'.

'What the hell is it?' replied the older man as he tilted his large swivel black leather chair forward.

'Look and see' said Mark very quietly and sat back but didn't take his eyes off Sir Charles's face.

Slowly the fat man picked up the envelope, ripped it open and tipped its contents onto his desk. A sheaf of photographs tumbled out. He snatched them up and as he looked at them his face went white. His hands started to tremble as he slowly leafed through the dozen or so pictures that he held.

'Where? How? I......'

He paused.

'I..........'

He paused again his mind racing. 'Your boat' he muttered very quietly and looking up at Mark he was disconcerted to see the younger man's eyes boring into him. 'You bastard. You fucking bastard'. He leapt up and leaned forward slamming his hands on to his desk as he continued much more loudly 'You had me filmed. You set me up. Stay and relax for a while you said. Think about my offer you said. I'll send you some nice friendly company you said. All the time you had it in mind to film and then blackmail me. You won't get away with this I'll go straight to the police'.

Sir Charles stood up straight to his full height wagging his finger at Mark as his voice rose to a yell. 'You jumped up little shit. Think you can pull a stunt like this you lousy little fucker well you can't. I'll sue you through every court in the land. It won't be me that loses his business it'll be you. How do you think the media will take to knowing what a conniving, smarmy, underhand, blackmailing sod you are? Eh! What do you think of that mister clever dick? Mister darling of the City'. He leaned forward again his face red with anger and flecks of spittle flew out of his mouth as he raged at Mark.

Mark remained sitting absolutely still and continued to stare intently at the man on the other side of the desk who was now incandescent with rage. Speaking calmly and quietly he asked 'And what will Belinda, your children and grandchildren think when the pictures and allegations come out in court? Should make excellent copy for the News of the World, The Sun and the Mirror. Humping Houghton. Tycoon's randy romps in Mediterranean. Houghton bonks while business collapses. I can see it now, can't you? Oh and while we're talking about bonking does Belinda know about the house in Paddington?' He passed over some more prints. 'Does she.......Charles? And what do you think the serious papers will make of it eh, The Times, Telegraph, The Guardian. How will they react to this news? Then there's your other directors and your employees. How do you think they'd take to these sorts of antics when the business is in such desperate trouble? Well?'

Sir Charles Houghton stared at Mark for a long time then slowly sank back to his chair. He visibly crumbled as he looked at the younger man opposite who he now knew had won. Business wise he'd won. Financially he'd won. Emotionally he'd won. Won his Company. Won everything.

'What do you want from me? What do you want to destroy these?' he croaked pointing at the photographs.

'Simple' replied Mark. 'Sign the deal and make your sixty percent of the shares over to us. Do that and these will never see the light of day. I give you my word. There's no benefit to me in having these pictures come to light. Like all deterrents they are only of power if they don't have to be used. I have no wish to expose this about you or hurt you, Belinda or your family. I want the business not your public humiliation.

Now why don't you think about it for a few minutes?' He paused and looked at the large clock on the wall 'say ten minutes and by the way if you are thinking of tearing those up I've got other copies of course and video film'.

He stood and made to leave the room and had just reached the door when Sir Charles growled at him.

'Wait.' he paused 'I need to be sure that you'll keep your word and that these pictures and any others you have are destroyed. Belinda couldn't bear.......and my children and the grandchildren' he broke off and gulped ….. 'I have to think about that before agreeing to sell my shares in this business to you. Leave me for a while to think. I'll call you shortly'.

'Charles, I gave you my word. Now no more chances. No more prevaricating. No more delays. Your business is finished. You're finished. It's over. Sell to me tonight. This is my final offer, my very final offer'.

He closed the door firmly and walked away with a grim expression on his face. The deal was so nearly done and in his heart he felt great satisfaction that his long quest that had taken years to achieve was so nearly complete. It was a pity that that Sir Charles Houghton hadn't been persuaded by business logic alone and that this unpleasant photographic business needed to be used still if that's what it took, so be it he thought.

Ten minutes to go and then he'd know if he'd won.

As he walked back into the other room to join the others he realised that it was going to seem a very long ten minutes.

CHAPTER 2

Mark was born in Dulwich Hospital in South London on 30th July 1960 during a thunderstorm. He was the first and as it transpired the only child of Christopher and Betty Watson aged twenty five and twenty four respectively. The fierce Sister in charge of the maternity unit at the hospital terrified Betty but had been quite kind during the painful process of giving birth.

As she handed the crying bloody little bundle to Betty she remarked that she expected that Betty's new son would make his mark in the world as he'd arrived with a bang. At the final moment of birth there had been a terrific clap of thunder which shook the whole building and made Betty jump and contract so violently that Mark had slid out straight into the waiting arms of the nurse who was helping.

Betty and Christopher like all expectant parents prior to the birth had spent hours trying out various names for the expected arrival. Betty thought Michael or Colin would be nice, while Christopher favoured Stanley, which was his Father and Grandfather's name, or William. They had never really considered girls names, because Betty had always been certain that she was carrying a boy. In her mind there was never any doubt. Many times in later life she was asked why she was so certain and she could only ever answer that she just knew it was a boy.

When Christopher visited that night to see his son for the first time, although normally a fairly unemotional man he was overcome with joy and happiness at the sight of his little man.

'Christopher' said Betty quietly 'how about Mark as his name'

'Mark but I thought you wanted Michael or Colin and you know I'd thought of Stanley or William. What makes you want Mark?'

'It was something Sister Murphy said. What do you think? I like it, Mark Stanley Watson'. She paused. 'It sounds right don't you think?'

'Mark Stanley Watson. Well maybe'. He gently pulled back the shawl and looked again at his new son's face. 'Hello Mark Stanley Watson. Do you like that? Are you a Mark? Do you know' he said looking at Betty 'I think it suits him very well. Mark Stanley Watson it is'.

And that was that. Mark had arrived and Sister Murphy was right. He was destined to make his mark in the world in the years ahead.

Ten days after the birth Betty proudly took Mark home to the little ground floor flat where they lived in Tulse Hill which was an area of south London that had around the turn of the century been somewhat genteel, but now was starting to become a little run down.

Christopher worked in London as a junior buyer for Rogerson Limited one of the many import, export and wholesale companies that at that time abounded in the City. Travelling each day by bus and underground his journey took about an hour. He was a quiet man who worked diligently to support his wife and their new addition, was careful over money and at the end of each month after he and Betty had finished eating supper, while she washed up he would sit down at the dining room table and open a small brown paper covered book which he had taken out of a drawer in the sideboard. This was his accounts book and into it he carefully entered his monthly outgoings, rates, rent, and other household expenditure items including the weekly cash that he gave Betty for the following week's housekeeping.

His little book also contained their income details consisting of his small and Betty's even smaller salary for her work as a typist to a solicitor. He would carefully add up his expenditure and income columns and see whether they had balanced the book for that month. Because he was a careful man then he did manage to balance the two sides of the equation and there was a small surplus each month. Often this was only a few shillings or so but at least they were not beholden to anyone and he was able to put his surplus into a National Savings Post Office savings account.

He had a great fear of being in someone else's debt and he was looking forward to a day ahead when maybe he would be in a position to be able to consider buying a flat or house. That was his dream but now at the end of the first month that the Watson family comprised three not two, he saw with a shock the effect of Betty no longer working. She had struggled into work until eight weeks before her confinement into hospital which was unusual in those days but she had been determined to continue to help provide her financial part for the family for as long as she could.

For the first month ever Christopher saw that there was no surplus but a deficit. Looking across at Betty sitting knitting by the fire he thought about the implications of not being able to cover his outgoings. Betty sensed him looking at her.

'What's the matter?'

'Nothing' replied Christopher quietly 'I was thinking about Mark and what sort of a life he'll have ahead of him'.

'I don't know but I expect he'll do all right. We'll bring him up well and teach him to be a good boy'. Betty didn't like to dwell on unpleasant thoughts.

'Yes you're right' said Christopher reassuringly and was pleased to see Betty relax, pick up her knitting and to watch the needles clicking away again.

But nevertheless he did worry. Now there were three of them and baby Mark would soon start to cost money. Clothes, food, heavens knows what and no money coming in from Betty.

Most of their small savings had gone on baby things. A cot, some baby clothes, nappies, powder, creams and what seemed a whole host of things that cluttered up the tiny second bedroom of their little flat.

Christopher realised that he would have to find a job that paid more money than he was earning as a buyer for Rogersons. It wouldn't be easy as he had no real qualifications except for an ability to work hard and honestly and to apply common sense to the normal run of business.

He dreamed of the far away places around the world from where the various products that his firm imported came from and started to keep postage stamps from letters that referred to the different locations. This was the start of a hobby of stamp collecting that lasted him all his life and by the time he died at ninety-nine he had a room at their home with shelves floor to ceiling, filled with stamp albums. It was a collection of several million stamps and worth a fortune, but to him it wasn't the value that mattered but the years of enjoyment that he'd had in creating the collection.

So time went by. Every weekday Christopher got up, had a piece of bread and margarine and a cup of tea for breakfast before leaving to catch the bus to go to work. He'd used to enjoy a boiled egg but a small economy that he decided to make was to save the coppers that an egg cost and just make do with a piece of bread. He bought a cup of tea and a bun for lunch and really just had one main meal a day which was the one Betty cooked for him each evening when he got back from work.

By March all their savings were gone and so Christopher plucked up courage to ask Mr. Smithers his boss if he could possibly see his way to a small raise in his salary. Mr. Smithers couldn't and said that he was disappointed to have been asked such a thing as after all Christopher was still only a junior buyer and had much yet to learn.

On his bus that night going home he continued to worry about money.

'Cheer up, might never happen' said a cheery voice. Christopher saw Lionel Anderson a salesman from one of their suppliers who called on him at the office, plump down on a seat in front of him.

'Hello what are you doing here?' replied Mark.

'I'm off to celebrate'.

'Why won the pools have you?'

'No. I'm going to start me own business. Buying and selling. Saved up some money and I've rented a little warehouse. Gave in me notice and start tomorrow'.

'But that's Saturday' exclaimed Christopher.

'Yes, sure is. If I'm paying for the warehouse I want to get started. No point in paying for something and not getting any benefit is there? I think I can make a load of money. I'm going to buy for, say a pound and sell for one pound five shillings. That's twenty five percent profit. Easy money eh?'

'Well not quite' said Christopher seeing his monthly accounts book layout in his mind. 'After all you've got to pay yourself something and then there's the rent on your warehouse, and you'll have to pay the electricity. Will you have anyone else working for you? If so you've got to pay them too. All that's got to come out of your five shillings profit. What's left is your real profit. In fact even that isn't, because you've got to buy new stock, send out invoices, pay suppliers, have stationery printed. Are you sure five shillings is enough?'

Lionel looked at him. 'Hope so. See I'm an ideas man. I reckon I can live on me wits buying and selling but I suppose I need to think a bit more about it. Still I've rented this warehouse so I've got to get started'.

'Whereabouts is it?'

'I'm off there now. Want to come and look? It's sort of between Brixton and Tulse Hill under a railway bridge'.

He nodded and was pleased at Lionel's quick grin. They chatted for a while until at one of bus's interminable stops Lionel jumped up excitedly saying 'Here we are come on' as he ran down the stairs.

They walked back a little way from the direction that the bus had come then turning right down a side street came to a long brick railway viaduct beneath which most of the arches were converted into small business units. A few were empty but others held car repairers, a wireless business and a furniture storage warehouse. A couple were closed with large metal doors making it impossible to see inside but at the end next to one of the empty units was one with two wooden doors that looked somewhat the worse for wear. Within one of the larger doors was a small door which had a large padlock through a rusty hasp.

'This is it. What do you think? Neat eh?' Lionel was bursting with excitement which rubbed off a little bit onto Christopher. 'Come and have a look' he said struggling with the padlock until he got it open.

Christopher stepped gingerly inside and looked around by the dim light of a couple of fly spattered light bulbs hanging from the ceiling that flickered into life. It was surprisingly large but dingy. No dirty would be a better description, and it smelt musty.

'I know it needs a bit of fixing up but it's cheap and it'll do me for a start'.

'Yeah' said Christopher looking around not sure whether he was impressed or frightened by Lionel's bold, maybe foolhardy venture. 'But what are you going to buy and sell?'

'Anything that I can that's legal. Nothing dodgy. Nothing that's fallen off the back of a lorry if you know what I mean. No this is going to be straight and legit. I'll build a little office over there' he said pointing to the far corner where some old sacks and assorted rubbish were piled up against the wall. Christopher was sure that he saw something move over there. Mice, or rats probably.

'I'd get a cat if I was you. Bound to be mice here'.

'Good idea. Well what do you think? I know it's a shit tip but imagine decent lighting, goods stacked properly in rows, lorries loading and unloading. I might take over the next door empty one. I might take over the whole row eventually'.

Christopher looked at the other and saw his eyes shining with excitement and couldn't help but feel a twinge of jealousy.

'How are you going to get started?'

'I've done me first deal. I've sold a load of soap to a little wholesaler in Streatham. Now I've got to buy some for less than I sold it. That's what I'm going to do. Buy and sell. Sell and buy. I'm a good salesman but I don't know if I'm any good at buying?.

Shivering as it was cold in the warehouse Christopher looked at his watch and said that it was time he was going. Shaking hands with Lionel he wished him good luck and walked back to the bus stop. He didn't have long to wait and he was back in his flat in Tulse Hill with Betty and Mark only a little later than usual.

He didn't say anything to Betty about where he'd been but later that evening he lay awake in bed and couldn't get Lionel's enthusiasm for his warehouse out of his mind.

For the next three weeks Christopher continued with his daily routine. He would get up early each morning so that he could be with Betty while she fed baby Mark. He loved to watch the bond that was fast developing between mother and baby and he made Betty her breakfast of porridge, toast with a scraping of butter and some jam and a cup of tea. For him just a slice of bread, some margarine and occasionally he treated himself to a thin scraping of jam with a large cup of tea. Then he would kiss his wife and baby good bye and with a cheerful 'See you both tonight' stride briskly down the road to the bus stop.

His day at the office was filled with meetings with various suppliers' representatives or commercial travellers as many were known in those days all trying to sell him their wares. Christopher was a good buyer and not inclined to rush into decisions. He'd found by experience that sometimes when the traveller returned next time a better price would be offered to close the deal, and sometimes it was so that he could refer to his boss Mr. Smithers.

Reginald Smithers had been in the firm a long time. Now fifty four years of age as head buyer he held a position of some importance and was generally held in some awe by the junior buyers. There was a standing instruction that if the total value of a deal exceeded a certain sum of money, a figure which he seemed to change at random and without explanation to the junior buyers then he had to be consulted before the arrangement was finalised.

Christopher often asked why this was necessary but always received the same reply 'Because that's the way this business is run'.

At the end of each day he would return to home and make out that he'd had an interesting day when in reality the continued worries about money, Mr. Smithers overbearing way of running the buying office and a curiosity about how Lionel was getting on all contributed to an increasing feeling of dissatisfaction.

One night he stopped off on his way home to see how Lionel was making out. He guessed that by now there might be a few cases of groceries in that dank old railway building but what he saw really surprised him.

Pushing open the little door he was amazed at the transformation. The building was more than half full. On the right hand side there were boxes of tinned vegetables, biscuits, cordials, pickles, sacks of salt, drums of pepper, crates of tea and coffee beans, while down the left hand side were ranged soap powder, washing powders, bleach, caustic soda, floor and furniture polishes and assorted other non food items such as boxes of candles, greaseproof paper, and ant powder. At the far end there was a wooden construction which was unfinished but he guessed would eventually be some sort of office.

The whole building was much cleaner and brighter. New light bulbs had replaced the two flyblown ones he'd seen hanging from the ceiling on his first visit and several new ones had been added. In the three week's since he'd been here last the place had turned from an old tatty building into a proper store. 'Hello, are you there Lionel?' Christopher called out loudly.

'Who's that? Pete you're back real quick ain't yer?' and Lionel looked out from his uncompleted office with a puzzled expression on his face, then seeing Christopher he broke into a smile.

'Cor fancy seeing you ere. I thought it was Pete who does me deliveries. Hey it's real good to see yer. What do you think eh? Bit different from when you was here last in't it? Brighter and I done what you said and put up new lights and cleared out all the old rubbish. You was right you know. Loads of mice under them old sacks. Ran all over the bloody place they did when I chucked the sacks out but I got myself some mousetraps and borrowed my mum's cat and I ain't seen none for a week now. What do you think then? I've done loads of deals and I've even got a couple of regular customers now who've given me repeat orders'.

His face was shining and his enthusiasm was obvious as he explained that he'd got an arrangement with a chap from round the corner who had an old Bedford lorry and would deliver Lionel's orders to his customers for a reasonable charge. Lionel went out in the morning and did the selling, and then in the afternoon he came back to his warehouse, as he liked to call it and pack the orders ready for delivery the next day.

'Mind you' he went on 'if the work goes on building up, then I'm going to 'ave to get meself some 'elp. Bloody knackering it is doing everything. And as for me paperwork, well you'd never believe what a bugger's muddle that's in. Still I suppose it'll sort itself out eventually. It'll 'elp when I've got this office finished and set up'.

Christopher looked slowly around the part built office and his eyes took in the piles of papers scattered on the bench. There were copies of orders, delivery sheets, and some invoices. In short a complete muddle of paperwork.

'This is no good' exclaimed Christopher. 'You need a proper system otherwise how will you know where you are, what you've sold, what money you are owed and most importantly how much profit you've made? How do you get paid now?'

'Some customers pay me cash when I call to collect it after they've ad delivery. With others I send out a bill and then call round a couple of days later to get me money. It's getting tricky to keep it all under control. See, I'm good at selling and I'm learning fast about the buying side but I ain't so hot on all the paperwork stuff'.

'I can see that. Well you'll have to sort yourself out or you'll get in a right mess'.

'Yeah I know that, but I've no idea how I'm going to do it. Wish I had someone like you to do it for me..........hey that's an idea. Why don't you do me paperwork? You could come in at weekends or an evening or two and sort it all out. I'll pay you for doing it. What do you say?'

Christopher felt the stirrings of an interest. What it needed was a system and it probably wouldn't be too difficult to set one up. After all he had a good system at home for his own household accounts and this was the same really only a bit bigger and he'd get paid for doing it which would be a godsend

'All right I'll set you up a system and get you sorted out. I don't want to do it at weekends though because I like to spend time with Betty and baby Mark but I could stop off on an evening on my way home from work. I'll come in tomorrow and make a start. You just make sure you keep all this lot safe' he said gesturing around the half built office at the muddle of papers. One thing though Lionel' he paused now feeling embarrassed. 'You said you'd pay me. How much did you have in mind?'

'Well how about a couple of quid to sort it all out, and then ten bob a week to keep it going? See how it goes and how much there will be to do'.

'Fair enough I'll come in tomorrow and make a start'.

'Great, see you tomorrow then'.

'Yes, see you' said Christopher feeling that he'd been in some way dismissed, but nevertheless happy at the thought that he'd be getting some money to help his financial situation. Two whole pounds to sort out the muddle and then ten shillings a week would make a big difference. Walking to the bus stop he wondered what Betty would think.

He got up early the next Saturday morning and arrived just as Lionel was opening up the doors. 'Thought I'd make a start today' he said cheerfully.

'I didn't think that you wanted to do this at weekends what with the baby an all?'

'Well I don't as a regular thing, but I felt I'd need a good go in the day time to see how bad it all is. Then I'll do what we agreed and come in on a couple of evenings a week'.

What he didn't want to say was that he desperately wanted the two pounds that Lionel had agreed for sorting it out and the quicker he got that done the quicker he'd get the money so he made his way to the part built office at the back, found a chair and went around finding as many pieces of paper as he could which were tucked in old cardboard boxes, shoved in the one drawer of the old desk and some on the floor under a half brick.

He started to make piles by type of item. Copies of orders went on the right hand side of the desk, delivery notes went on the left, invoices went in the middle, and any other items went into a cardboard box at the side of the desk.

Gradually order emerged from the chaos and by about eleven thirty he had finished sorting the muddle and started to implement his system. He was so engrossed in his work that he didn't hear Lionel come in.

'Lunch time fancy a pint and a sandwich?'

Christopher who wasn't used to spending money on himself for lunch thought quickly how much it might cost and decided that he couldn't really afford it so making the excuse that he wanted to get on with what he was doing he declined. Alone in the office he continued working to establish a system and gradually his logical mind started to identify activities which could be made to link together into a working method for the buying, selling, delivery and invoicing process. His biggest worry was that there didn't seem to be a proper track of deliveries linked to invoices.

Certainly Lionel had sent out several invoices but Christopher quickly established that there were plenty of deliveries that had been made for which he couldn't find a matching copy invoice. In his mind's eye he could see that a proper set of ledgers would be required and resolved to buy some so that accurate records could be kept. After all he thought you can't have a proper business without proper records.

Returning from the pub Lionel asked how things were going and somewhat to Christopher's surprise he seemed genuinely interested in the progress that had been made. By mid afternoon Christopher knew his system would work and enable the whole business to be carefully tracked and controlled. His estimate was that Lionel was as much as three hundred pounds short in revenue from having not sent out invoices for deliveries that had been made. He also thought that invoices should be typed and not sent out hand written as Lionel had been doing. 'Looks more professional' he said.

'Maybe, but I can't type' retorted Lionel sharply.

'I can so I'll do it for you. You can look on me as your office manager, invoice clerk, query sorter. I'll put you in a system and run it then you'll know exactly where you are at the end of each week. I'll set up proper ledgers and we'll have a proper business under way.' He stopped and realised that he'd said "we'll have", and not "you'll have" but Lionel didn't seem to have noticed.

'Now look' said Christopher sternly. 'Copy orders go in this box, copy delivery notes go in this one' and he diligently explained the basics of his system. Lionel listened carefully and promised to follow the procedure. With that assurance Christopher said that he'd finish for the day and get himself off home.

He had to wait nearly half an hour for a bus to come along, but didn't really notice the passing of time as he was excited about what he'd done and what was to come working for Lionel. His enthusiasm was clear when he got home and Betty saw a change in her husband as he talked animatedly about what a muddle it had been at the warehouse and how he'd sorted it all out.

They spent the rest of the day quietly together and when Mark needed feeding or changing they did it together with Christopher delighting in his son who was growing fast. 'Fantastic isn't it' he said. 'Look how fast the little chap's growing. You really are an excellent mother to him Betty and a fine wife to me too'. She beamed broadly and for her life was complete and content.

On Monday he went to his job in London and during his lunch hour walked to a stationery supplier who had the books that he wanted although they were more expensive than he'd expected. Accordingly he decided that he could only afford two of them and not the four that he'd originally planned to buy. Being sure to ask for and obtain a receipt he paid and walked back to his buying office.

At the end of the day he went home and after dinner quickly helped Betty clear the table before setting out his new ledgers which he then proceeded to rule out with columns and sections that he thought would suit Lionel's business. He could have bought books already lined out but those that he had purchased were one shilling cheaper and it was only the work of a few minutes to make the necessary columns.

He returned to Lionel's business on Tuesday evening and straight after work got off the bus and made the now familiar walk to the warehouse. Lionel was there looking tired but cheerful. In fact thought Christopher he had never seen Lionel looking anything but cheerful.

Lionel watched him rummaging though the boxes and when a much relieved Christopher turned he saw Lionel grinning at him. 'See, I done wot you asked. All in the right place. Bit of a bloody nuisance remembering where to put em but there you are all shipshape'.

Christopher agreed that it was and then settled down to enter the information into his new ledgers. He worked carefully and by half past nine had completed the task. Lionel was sitting the other side of the office looking at a map of the local area, planning where he was going to go tomorrow to sell his goods.

'When are you going to call it a day for tonight' asked Lionel smiling at his own confusion of day and night. 'I'm ready to lock up and get meself a beer at the local'.

'Oh well if you want to go I'll pack up now. I'll come back on Thursday and do some more. There's just one thing though. I'd really like to buy another couple of ledgers, some paper clips, a spike to keep things waiting to be dealt with and one and one or two other bits and pieces that I think will make a real difference to the office here'.

'Yea well you get whatever you think we want Chris old man'.

Now Christopher was embarrassed as he explained that he was a bit short of ready cash and wondered if Lionel could advance him, say one pound from the two pounds that he'd promised for sorting out the paperwork mess. 'I'll use it for the things that we want in the office here, it's not for me' he said defensively. Lionel laughed and said here was three pounds, the two that he'd promised him and another pound to get the stationery items that Chris needed.

Protesting that he only wanted a pound as he wasn't entitled to the two pounds because he hadn't finished bringing everything up to date Lionel wouldn't hear of it and said that if they were going to work together then they had to trust each other but he insisted that they went to the pub for a beer.

Betty who had been getting worried that Christopher was later than she'd expected was relieved when he came in and listened attentively to his description of his evening's activities. It sounded exciting but she was worried that he was now doing two jobs and what would Mr. Smithers say if he found out. Christopher told her to stop worrying and be happy that he'd found a way to make some more money. Betty supposed he was right, but it didn't stop her worrying.

Twice a week Christopher stopped off at the warehouse in the evening and did the books. Betty made him a sandwich which he took to work and then would eat during his evening's work. Lionel had installed a kettle in the office and there was usually some milk and a tin of biscuits with which he supplemented his sandwich. He was content and thoroughly enjoyed what he was doing. The business was getting bigger and Lionel had got some helpers to do the heavier humping and lifting in the warehouse. He was a good salesman. He'd sell hard to prospective customers but was careful to listen to their needs and never sold them a duff deal, or loaded them with stock they didn't want. His preference was to sell them what they needed and then take a repeat order rather than lumber them with stock they didn't need and leave them high and dry.

This careful approach soon established a reputation for honesty and straight dealing and as a result the business expanded rapidly. Lionel decided that he needed someone else to help him do the selling so he put an advertisement in the evening paper and a few days later several letters arrived which he and Christopher settled down to read. Some were discarded straight away but three were invited for an interview. Christopher typed the interview invitations on their recently acquired second hand Olivetti typewriter and Lionel signed and posted them.

The office was now much tidier and looked "proper" as Lionel put it with its glass windows looking out on the warehouse. They wanted a telephone and called in at a Post Office to obtain the necessary forms which were completed and sent off after being advised that it would take a few weeks before installation would occur.

Christopher produced a trading statement after his first month and Lionel was relieved to discover that he'd made a very handsome profit. In fact 'bloody 'ell' had been how he'd greeted the figures.

'I knew this would be a good business and now you've proved it Chris my lad. This calls for a celebration let's go and have a beer' but Christopher declined and said that he wanted to talk seriously to Lionel.

'Look' he said. 'Yes you've made money and turned a profit but you could make a lot more. You need to increase your selling prices on these items' and he handed Lionel a long list of products where he thought that there was an opportunity to improve the profit margin, 'and decrease your selling price on these items which if they were more competitively priced would enable you to sell more' and he handed Lionel a second list.

Lionel took the handwritten notes from Christopher and studied them carefully. He took his time as he looked through the points that Christopher had made. 'This is really good stuff Chris, very useful. Now let's go and have that drink and talk about your ideas' and so they went to the Flying Eagle a noisy pub which had the advantage of being not too far away.

While Christopher found a small table in the corner Lionel marched up to the bar and ordered a couple of pints. Returning he listened carefully as Chris expanded on his ideas. He was flattered that Lionel was taking notice of his thoughts and outlined other thoughts and plans which he proposed to Lionel.

'Pity you're not part of the business Chris. We'd do real well you and me. 'Ave you ever thought of leaving Rogersons?'

Yes I have. You see I find it hard to make ends meet at the moment what with Betty not working and little Mark growing up. It all costs money, and so yes I have been looking for another job that pays more than old Smithers does but so far I've not landed anything. Still I expect something will turn up soon. Hope so' he added fervently.

On his next visit to the warehouse as soon as he walked in Lionel said that he wanted to talk to him and suggested that they both sat down in the office. There was only one chair which Lionel took so Christopher pulled an old wooden crate in from outside and perched on that.

'Now then Chris I've been thinking about what you said the other night. I'm only scratching the surface of this business and I can expand it but I need someone to 'elp me with the thinking out of the future and things like that. That's where you come in. Why don't you leave Rogersons and join me? I'll make you a partner and we'll call the business Anderson and Watson, or A and W for short'. He then outlined how he saw Christopher running the office and doing the "thinking bit" while he continued with the selling and customer side.

Lionel instinctively knew what made customers happy and what didn't. He also knew that he wasn't good at the clerical side and so if he could get Chris to join him then he'd have the best of both worlds. He offered to increase Chris's present salary by twenty percent which nearly made Christopher fall off his wooden crate.

'Come on Chris we'll make a great team. What do you say?'

'Let me think about it and talk it over with Betty. I'll let you know by the weekend'.

He then settled down to the books but this time he saw them differently. Now they could be his books not just the books, or Lionel's books. He stopped working earlier than usual and set off home to talk to Betty. He knew that she would worry about such a radical change but the extra money would be very useful. I could even start to save some money again he thought and started to dream of one day buying a house and a car.

He was right. Betty wasn't at all sure it was a good idea and she asked lots of questions about what if it all went wrong? How well did he know Lionel? What would Mr. Smithers say? If they needed more money wouldn't it be better to keep looking for another proper job rather than throw in his lot with an untried and risky business with Lionel?

Christopher patiently explained why he thought it was the right thing to do. He never got cross with her but quietly and carefully answered her questions. In the morning as he was getting ready for work she continued to question whether it was the right thing to do but if he had any doubts they were dispelled when Mr. Smithers who had been in a foul mood all morning bawled him out in front of the whole office for a small error that he'd made.

In reality it was only a minor mix up over two suppliers who both thought they'd got an order for a particular type of biscuit which could have been easily put right if only Mr. Smithers hadn't sought to make such a mountain out of it.

'Sheer incompetence' he said loudly. 'Sort of error a first day starter might make' and he had continued in similar vain finishing with 'If it happens again you'll be for the sack Watson, do you hear me?

That made up Christopher's mind. 'You won't have to sack me, I'm resigning right now and I'll leave at the end of the week if you please Mr. Smithers'.

Smithers was stunned. This wasn't what he wanted. He'd just meant to bully the lad because that was his only method of managing people.

'Resign. What do you mean resign? Nonsense. Junior chaps like you don't resign. You don't mean it at all'.

'Yes I do. I'm going to another firm that wants me and will value what I have to offer. I'll write out my resignation right now' and he went to his desk and quickly scribbled the appropriate note which he handed to Mr. Smithers who took it without a word.

Christopher stopped at Lionel's warehouse on his way home. 'You did mean what you said about me joining you and calling the firm Anderson and Watson didn't you'.

'Yea why?'

'Well I've chucked in my job and I'm joining you' replied Christopher grinning and holding out his hand. Lionel shook it warmly, surprised that Christopher had actually done it.

Friday came and went. Everyone in the office said goodbye to Chris except Mr. Smithers who ignored him and at five o'clock Christopher made his way home from Rogersons for the last time.

On Saturday morning he got up early and was waiting at their warehouse for Lionel until the other arrived. They shook hands again and when they'd finished mutually congratulating each other and telling each other how good it was going to be and what they would achieve together they turned to their respective areas of work.

Christopher installed himself in the office and Lionel went off to chivvy up the lads he'd got helping him load and unload lorries. Well thought Christopher 'I've done it now and so I'd better make a go of it'.

And he did.

CHAPTER 3

So a new chapter opened in Christopher's life. Betty remained sceptical and worried about this new venture but she was reassured by Christopher's confidence in what he was doing.

They had discussed whether to have more children but Christopher warned that they were having difficulty with making ends meet now with just the three of them so if they had more children their difficulties would increase further.

'After all it's not just the cost now but wait till they grow up and want bicycles and bigger clothes, then what?' said Christopher wisely so they decided that Mark would be their only child.

At work Lionel focussing on selling and with Christopher quietly guiding in the background the business started to grow substantially. Now two delivery lorries were needed to take out the goods that Lionel had sold and to support that they needed additional loaders in the warehouse.

One evening Christopher suggested that rather than paying to hire lorries and drivers it would be more economical to have their own vehicles and drivers.

'Our own lorries' exclaimed Lionel with his face beaming. 'We could have Anderson and Watson written on the sides couldn't we eh? I'll get me mind round where we can pick up a couple of old lorries'.

'Not too old' warned Christopher. 'Don't want them breaking down or being unreliable do we?'

'Leave it to me' replied Lionel and within a few days he announced that he'd 'sorted out the transport' returning later that day driving a Bedford truck. Christopher duly added it to his "Assets". A few days later a second truck joined the first and two drivers also joined the business.

A telephone had been installed and it proved a real boon as once customers got to know that A and W were on the phone they started to phone their orders in rather than Lionel having to go out to create the demand. He still used his considerable selling skills when customers did phone in, suggesting new products to them, or increasing their orders in return for a better price.

The business grew over the next six months and the amount of storage room they needed on some days started to exceed the floor space that they had available. As the unit next door was vacant Christopher went to see the landlord and negotiated a two year lease on the extra premises. This meant they had to re-organise the warehouse and so they put food items in one warehouse and non-food products in the other.

Their warehouse staff numbers increased to six and they recruited a warehouse foreman called Sid Franks a surely looking man but he seemed capable of organising the work in the two warehouses and sorting out the routing for the lorries. Christopher didn't like him, but Lionel thought he'd do.

Following their earlier advert Andy Lomax had joined the business to work as a salesman under Lionel's direction and control.

Andy had proved a good choice and their order book expanded. 'Remember' Lionel used to tell him each morning before he set out on his selling calls 'we want repeat business. No conning people into buying what they don't want. Push 'em to their maximum but don't push them over. We've got a good reputation for fair trading and I'm not having it mucked up, see?'

Andy was a quick learner and following Lionel's philosophy soon became a key member of the business. He was particularly good at dealing with the shopkeeper's wives or grown up daughters as he had a cheeky smile, a naughty wink, slicked back hair and the sort of face that made women just want to talk to him. Once they did he exploited it to the full and could easily sell them a range of goods.

So as A and W expanded and sold its goods all over south London their reputation for fair dealing and quality service spread. They were so successful that they decided to expand north of the Thames so Lionel bought a second hand Vauxhall car to enable him to cover more territory and recruited another salesman to look after their south London trade while he and Andy explored the north.

Christopher recruited a book-keeper an earnest middle aged lady called Flo who was a real treasure. She diligently kept the increasingly complicated records and information up to date. The office had been extended to take Christopher, Flo and Lucy that they'd also brought in as a junior. Not overly bright she was a willing soul who made tea, tidied up and generally did what Flo or Christopher wanted for what was really a mere pittance of a weekly wage but she was happy enough and in her own way was another factor in helping the enterprise work smoothly.

A and W found a ready market north of the Thames and rapidly established their reputation for fair dealing, good prices and excellent customer service.

Lionel also realised that if he provided Andy with a car as well as himself they could increase even further the territory that they covered as currently they met at the warehouse at half past seven each morning and then travel together to the north side of London where Lionel would drop Andy off at the end of a high street for him to start to work his way down the street calling on as many food and non-food shops as he could picking him up later in the day.

A and W's product range expanded. They recruited two more salesmen, one to work in the south and the other to work in the north. Lionel also started to travel further outside London and was pleased to discover that what A and W offered found just as much favour in the leafy suburbs of Hertfordshire or Surrey or Kent as it did in London itself.

They formally made A and W a Limited Company, a process which was simple to complete and it made them "correct" as Lionel saw it. They designed a new layout for their headed notepaper and company sign and gave all the salesmen business cards with the new logo imprinted on it. Their small fleet of lorries were properly sign written to reflect the new design and all in all they felt that their business was now really going places.

Mark was growing up fast and was a cheerful happy little boy. He loved to play with his father at weekends but Christopher was disappointed that he didn't see much of him during the week. A brief chat and possibly a quick play together first thing in the morning but by the time he got back from work Mark was in bed and fast asleep.

Christopher's finances were now secure and although he continued his practice of completing his personal accounts book he'd realised a couple of years ago that they were now sufficiently sound financially that it wasn't necessary any more. Yet he couldn't bring himself to stop doing it. In fact he thought that instead of paying rent it was time they thought about buying a house of their own and he went to his bank and discussed a mortgage with them. He found the process of applying, signing the forms and waiting for an answer interesting but decided to complete it all without involving Betty as she would only worry about it.

To his delight one morning a letter arrived from the bank confirming

> "We are prepared to advance the sum of £ 1,500 pounds for the purpose of a house purchase and they awaited his kind instruction to proceed".

There was a lot more in the letter and attached sheets of paper warning of dire consequences if he failed to maintain the payments correctly but none of that could diminish his joy on that morning.

That night when he returned from work he said 'Betty I've got something to tell you. We're going to buy our own house. No more living in this flat and paying rent to a landlord. We're going to have our own place. What do you say to that then?'

Immediately concerned about this sudden potential change in her life but she listened carefully to Christopher's explanation of what was involved and found herself joining in his excitement and enthusiasm. He asked her to visit some estate agents and obtain details of houses for sale at the sort of price that they could afford. So she happily spent the next few days trudging around various estate agents specifying what they wanted and to her great pleasure found there were several properties within their price range.

They pored over the details in the evenings making lists of those they wanted to see based not only on the price but also the location, ease of getting to the office for Christopher and location of shops and schools for when Mark would go to school.

On the Friday evening, Christopher who'd passed his driving test recently asked Lionel if he could borrow his car for the weekend and explained why he wanted it. Lionel was more than happy to lend it to him but promptly commandeered one of the salesmen's cars for himself.

Getting up early on the Saturday morning they set off to look at the half a dozen houses they'd listed as worthy of viewing and Betty enjoyed the luxury of Christopher driving them around. At the end of the day they decided that the third house they'd seen was one they would like to go back and see for a second time, as it seemed to be the right one for them.

It was just on six o'clock in the evening when they pulled up again in Warlingham Road, Thornton Heath for the second time that day. The house for sale was a mid terrace property identical to the ones on either side and indeed to the ones all down both sides of the road and was typical of the huge amount of early 1900's solid but boring house building that had taken place around London.

Mark was getting fractious but a bar of chocolate kept him happy while he waited in the car and Christopher and Betty knocked on the door. The owner was a bit surprised to see them again but agreed to let them in for another look around. Betty thought that was kind of him, but as Christopher said to her later 'Don't think he's doing us a favour he wants to sell his house'. They looked round it again, went out into the small back garden and decided that it was just what they wanted. The owners a shy couple called Forbes wouldn't discuss a selling price and said that must be done with the estate agent.

Christopher and Betty spent Sunday irritated that estate agents were closed and hoped that there weren't any other people looking around "their house" as that was how they thought of it now. Still having the car they decided on an outing and picnic and went to a park where there was a boating lake so Christopher treated the family to a ride on a motor boat which chugged around the lake quite slowly but they enjoyed it and talked about it all the way home. After tea which they had together as a family a routine that Betty liked for Sundays, Christopher played with Mark for a while before settling him down for the night. Neither parent could sleep well that night as they were both excited and nervous about whether the Forbes would accept their offer which was a little less than the asking price.

On Monday Christopher went straight to the estate agent rather than the office and had a brief discussion with the pompous man in charge who agreed to contact the vendors and put Christopher's offer to them. In fact he knew that the offer would be accepted as the Forbes were very keen to sell as they wanted to move to Devon to be near their only daughter who had married and moved down there, but he felt that estate agents had to be seen to be doing their job and promised to contact Christopher at his office 'if there was any news'.

The call came just after lunch and Christopher learnt that his offer was accepted and all matters relating to the sale would now be put in hand. A quick phone call to the bank set that part of the process in action and then Christopher rang a solicitor recommended by the bank to act on his behalf.

Eight week's later the Watson family moved out of their flat and into their first home using one of the firms lorries to transport their limited belongings.

At A and W Ltd., they had outgrown their existing under the railway units in Tulse Hill and needed to find larger premises. Expecting that it would be difficult they were pleasantly surprised to find that several empty premises were available. The task of moving was enormous and they closed for business on a Friday, and worked all through that day, Saturday and Sunday and by around midnight on Sunday they had managed to shift most of the stock and all the records. Fortunately the new telephone was already connected.

In the moving enterprise Betty came to help, Lionel's wife Amy worked like a Trojan, Andy and the rest of the salesmen, together with the warehousemen and lorry drivers all pulled together to achieve the move over to Croydon which was their new location. Andy spent quite a bit of time eyeing up Amy who had nice legs and several winks flew from him in her direction whenever he could catch her eye.

The new building was very different from the one they left. It was much bigger covering nearly twenty thousand square feet and was taller meaning that goods could be stacked higher than before. They ordered some racking which would enable them to really optimise the use of space. There were several offices upstairs and a proper yard, despatch area and three loading bays.

'Phew' said Lionel when he arrived on the Monday morning as he walked around the vast warehouse now only half full. 'Do you think we'll ever fill all this Chris?'

'Yep we will but remember it's not stock in the warehouse that matters, its cash in the bank. Stock sitting here is just money tied up. We need to keep turning the stock over. Get it in from our suppliers, get it out to your customers, get it invoiced, and get the cash in. Do that and we'll be alright. You must make sure that all your sales people sell the profitable items and at the right prices. I'll personally check all the cost and selling prices and we'll produce a proper price list. We'll have some special offers every two weeks so we control our overall prices and hence profit margin. Also we'll incentivise the salesmen to sell the lines we want sold not just those that the either find easy to do, or that they like selling'.

Lionel nodded his understanding and acceptance of Christopher's ideas and was glad that Christopher had joined the firm five years ago as without him he would probably have gone bust because he didn't understand enough about cash flow, pricing and what Christopher had started to call their business strategy.

The two partners also decided although in reality it was Christopher's idea which he subtly persuaded Lionel to accept, a practice which he adopted frequently, that they needed to recruit a professional buyer to see the various manufacturer's representatives that were calling on A and W selling their goods for A and W in turn to sell on to the retail outlets and shops of all types. At present Christopher or Lionel tried to fit in time to see them and negotiate prices but this wasn't getting them the best deals.

They advertised in the Croydon Advertiser and soon they were reading through the piles of letters that had arrived in the office. Many were wholly unsuitable and they got a swift "no thank you" but there were six letters that attracted the attention of the two proprietors who read and re-read the applications. Eventually they whittled it down to four and wrote inviting them for an interview.

They used Christopher's office and on the day in question four individuals duly presented themselves at their designated times to see whether they had what it took to join A and W Ltd.

Lionel and Christopher interviewed together. Lionel's style was to get them to talk and chat generally about their past and what they wanted for the future, while Christopher's was much more incisive and challenging and he probed hard on their understanding of pricing, profit margins and control of costs. At the end of the day they decided that two should be invited back for a second interview. The problem was that Lionel felt one of the candidates was better than the other while Christopher had the opposite view.

For the second interview they decided that they would interview them alone and compare notes at the end of the sessions so this is what they did and eventually agreed on a candidate, so a job offer went to Mr. David Peacock and a letter of regret went to the other candidate. David Peacock or Cocky as he became known made his mark straight away.

The big supplier's representatives found themselves dealing with a tough negotiator who squeezed them for better prices but offered them big deal opportunities and rapidly influenced the way that buying and therefore the crucial input side of the business was run. He was a likeable man who soon became popular with the rest of the staff and Christopher relaxed that they had made a good choice. Cocky understood what the business strategy was about and realised that provided he could keep the goods coming in at competitive prices then Lionel and his team would be able to sell profitably.

The new pricing strategy succeeded with control established from head office and the salesmen selling to specified campaigns and designated guidelines. Although initially sceptical the salesmen soon got used to the new method of working and were cheered by the size of the bonuses they earned.

Both proprietors were spending long hours in the business but had the satisfaction of seeing it grow and expand profitably and they'd got into the habit of meeting on a Monday morning to review the previous week's results and consider their plans for the coming week. One morning Lionel raised his favourite subject, expansion.

'I reckon we ought to expand outside London and the Home Counties' he said. 'I don't see why we shouldn't be selling up to Birmingham, over to Norwich, down to Brighton and perhaps along as far as Bournemouth. What do you say Chris?'

Christopher thought for a minute and then replied pensively 'Well we could, but we'll have to put the infrastructure in place first. We'll need more salesmen, we'll have to get some additional lorries, I'll need at least one if not two extra clerical people here for the invoicing and book keeping, and we must be sure that our formula of good service and fair dealing is what's wanted in these potential new areas. Tell you what, why don't you take a trip up to Birmingham and prospect around for a day or so, come back and lets talk about it.

CHAPTER 4

Lionel set off for Birmingham looking forward to the prospects as he thought that customers up there would want good prices, reliable service, and an efficient supplier.

He knew from the various trade magazines which customers he wanted to contact and at the end of the day he felt from the contacts that he'd made that there was ample opportunity for their business there. Several potential customers had complained about their existing suppliers and the complaints seemed to cover just about everything. Poor service, high prices, lack of interest.

However Birmingham was a big city and he thought that he ought to have another day sounding out the trade so finding a rather scruffy little pub which did bed and breakfast he booked himself in for the night and then borrowed their phone to call Christopher and explained that he was going to stay for another day to make certain of the opportunity.

The pub didn't do meals except for breakfast, and so he wandered around for a bit until he found a little café that did him a rather good fish and chips supper with bread and butter and a pot of strong tea. He walked back to the Green Man where he was staying and fighting his way through the crowded bar he ordered a pint and found a corner to sit and slowly consume it. His thoughts rambled over the past few years and how big the business was now compared to that first deal of a load of cheap soap in that old warehouse under the railway in south London. Not rich by any means but he and Christopher were each able to take a not insignificant salary out of the business and were living quite comfortably. He liked working with Christopher and knew that their skill sets were complimentary to each other.

Yes, all in all Lionel was pretty satisfied with his life and if he could get the expansion going up here and then down to the south coast he felt that their future and the business would be very secure indeed.

Next day he was convinced that he was right and that they should expand up here and so he set off back to Croydon where driving into the car park he saw a Rover car that he didn't recognise. Walking in he asked their receptionist Joan whose car it was and was surprised to learn that it belonged to Mr. Watson. Running up the stairs two at a time, he went into Christopher's office and grinning asked him about the car.

'Well I thought it was about time I had a car and as we're doing ok at the moment I decided to buy one.

'Looks a nice motor. Hope you and the family enjoy it. Now then Chris, Birmingham's great. There's loads of business up there for us to take' and he gave a detailed account of his trip concentrating on the dissatisfaction of customers with their existing wholesalers. Christopher asked lots of questions but after a while agreed that it was probably worth them starting up there and so he worked out the logistics during the rest of the day and by the time he was ready to go home he had a workable plan.

However for reasons that he couldn't define he also had a strange sense of foreboding.

He and Betty were happy in their little house. It was brick built and part pebble dashed, painted cream, had three bedrooms but the one that they kept as a spare was really a small box room and just about big enough to fit in a small single bed but theirs at the front and Marks at the back were of a reasonable size. A small bathroom completed the upstairs while downstairs leading off the hallway there was a front sitting room, a rear dining room and a small kitchen. Outside at the back was a small garden and Betty discovered a pleasure in planting and caring for flowers and shrubs which remained with her for the rest of her life. She worked hard in her little garden and Christopher made a garden shed out of spare bits of timber which he collected from work and brought home in the boot of the car which he now used to commute each day to the office.

Mark loved the garden and like all small boys ran about on the little lawn, played with his toys and developed his imagination by playing "lets pretend" games. He was quite an advanced little chap and was well ahead of his age with his reading but what particularly struck Betty was his quite amazing memory for strange things. 'He's an odd'n she'd say to Christopher. 'He forgets some quite simple things but other things he remembers from years ago'. This memory was a strength that stayed with Mark all his life and when he grew up he could read something and later recall it almost word for word, or remember faces astoundingly well but he was always dreadful with people's names which never seemed to stick in his mind.

Mark had started junior school and settled comfortably into the routine and progressed quickly finding the learning not too difficult and consequently doing quite well in the year end tests. His results were satisfactory but not outstanding and he moved up class by class each year.

The dreaded eleven plus exams were looming in just over a year and Mark was not looking forward to them. Christopher was concerned as to what sort of secondary education Mark should have as he wanted to be sure that his son had better chances than had had himself and so he applied for Mark to have a place at Whitgift College, a public school on the other side of Croydon and at ten years old Mark sat the common entrance exam.

Betty took him on the bus to the school set in its wonderful grounds and left him there. Although slightly overawed by the masters in their gowns and what seemed like miles of dark wooden panelled corridors Mark thought that he'd done quite well in the written papers and also the verbal interview which he'd been given by Mr. Henry one of the senior masters who remained in Mark's memory by continually talking about rugby. Mark said that yes he thought he'd like to play rugby but at his present school they only played football. He and the other aspiring hopefuls were allowed to leave the school around three thirty in the afternoon and taking a bus back to Thornton Heath then walking home he felt quite happy with his day as he told his mother all about it. Betty asked him about how the day had gone and what tests or exams he'd had to complete and seemed pleased.

Christopher came home full of enthusiasm and asking lots of questions said he was sure Mark had done his best and now they'd have to wait and see what the masters marking the papers thought about it. In fact Mark's English papers were above the pass level, his Maths and Mental Arithmetic papers attracted outstanding marks and his essay showed great promise so his application went onto the "invite back for final interview" pile.

Betty was delighted when the letter from the school arrived inviting Mark for a second interview and on the day in question he returned to the great building for more Maths and English papers, another Mental Arithmetic paper which he found quite simple and he had to write two essays. He felt quite confident about what he wrote.

He wasn't so sure about the interview with an elderly master who asked how he thought he'd get on learning Latin. Mark said that he didn't know but was quite happy to give it a go. Old Mr. Winkler smiled and said good 'That's the ticket. Now have you learnt any French or German at your present school?' Mark said that 'no he hadn't but if he was lucky enough to get into Whitgift he was sure that he'd be able to learn the foreign words'.

So the day came to an end and he made his way home wondering if he'd get into the school. Again Mark's essays held him in good stead supporting his Maths papers and three weeks later a letter arrived at their home offering

> Master Mark Watson a place at Whitgift commencing in September, subject to payment of the appropriate fees which were fully detailed in the enclosed prospectus.

Christopher and Betty were delighted. The next weeks were filled with visits to school outfitters to buy the huge amount of uniform and equipment that was required and eventually on the 15th September 1970 Mark Watson entered the hallowed portals of Whitgift School and was allocated to class A1.

Expansion of A & W into the Birmingham area was straightforward.

'Smoove as silk' said Lionel. Christopher's logistic planning had been thorough and their first orders were taken and delivered satisfactorily much to the pleasure of their new customers. The lorry drivers were happy about the longer runs that they were now making but Christopher started to think that if the business in the north really took off then they might have to think about opening a depot up there to save the cost of trucking the goods from Croydon to Birmingham. Flushed with his success in opening up the northern territories Lionel next ventured to the South Coast and he and Andy spent a week travelling from Bournemouth to Margate. After the first day they decided to stop canvassing and started to take actual orders which they posted back to Christopher who anxiously waited for Lionel to phone in.

When he did Christopher angrily grabbed the phone and yelled 'What the hell do you think you and Andy are doing? We've not sorted out how we are going to deliver down there, you can't just go and set us off with a whole bunch of new customers without planning it properly. The reason Birmingham worked well was because we planned it properly. You'll balls everything up if you just bung in a load of new customers and orders. We've built the business on good service, sharp prices and attention to detail. You're putting all that at risk by rushing us into the south'.

'Bollocks' replied Lionel down the phone. 'You'll sort it Chris, don't make such a fuss about a few extra orders and by the way I've put an ad in the local papers down here for some salesmen. We'll 'ave one in Kent and one in 'Ampshire. That'd do it I reckon. They can split Sussex between 'em. I'll come back down in a couple of weeks and interview them'.

'Lionel, we're not ready for this yet. Let's consolidate what we've got and plan any expansion into Hampshire, Sussex and Kent properly, not just rush in. We need to do it properly'.

But there was no changing Lionel's mind and he slammed the phone down on Christopher and went back to his car where he drove quickly to the next potential customer and just for the hell of it sold in an enormous amount of stock and then phoned the order into A and W's order department. 'Stick that up your bum Chris' he thought. 'Planning be buggered there's a gold mine here and we're going to dig it'.

Christopher was right the business couldn't cope. The orders flooded in from the south coast especially from the two new salesmen that Lionel had insisted on recruiting and soon there were delays in delivery that affected not only the new areas of the business but also put problems into the established trade in Greater London, the Home Counties and Birmingham.

Complaints started to be received of wrong deliveries, late deliveries, missed items off the loads and worst of all one or two customers said that they'd take their business to a competitor of which there were several.

Lionel washed his hands of the matter and told Christopher sharply 'That it was up to him to sort out the problems. He and his salesmen were doing their part getting the orders in he couldn't understand why Chris didn't sort out the warehouse and drivers. Don't bleat to me about too much business, just get it sorted' he'd say.

What he failed to understand was that he was overwhelming the capacity of the business. The only way out of the mess that was being created was to either scale back for a while until they could re-organise themselves or undertake a massive expansion of the infrastructure which would involve not only a warehouse in Birmingham but also one in the South. They would need more staff in the new depots but also at Head Office and this would cost a considerable sum of money, more than they could afford and would involve substantial bank borrowing to fund the expansion. Christopher wasn't opposed to borrowing from the bank but wanted to do so in a controlled way not a headlong rush as was happening now.

He and Lionel moved from arguing to really falling out over the future strategy of the business and the rows became heated and more frequent.

For the first time since they started to work together Christopher found that he disliked certain aspects of Lionel and his attitude to work. He tried to make him see sense, but to no avail. Lionel was obsessed with the success that they'd had so far and felt that it was a magic formula that he could just repeat. A distance started to be generated between them.

One morning Lionel breezed into Christopher's office and announced that he'd been to see the bank manager who'd agreed, subject to seeing a proper business plan to advance the money they needed to acquire more warehouses.

'No problem at all in getting him to part wiv the money' he said. 'You just write up the plans in language that he'll like and there we are. Easy.'

Christopher worked over the weekend and against his better judgement put a proposition together which he and Lionel took to the bank the following week. They answered the many questions from the bank manager and then were told that it was probably going to be alright but that they'd have to wait as it would be a few days before they'd hear one way or the other.

When they did it was yes. The bank would advance the loan that they required but the payment terms were far more onerous than Christopher had been expecting.

'Look Lionel, we've got to make this work otherwise we are going to be in serious difficulty. These repayments are fierce you know and if we fall behind then heaven knows what will happen. We could finish up losing the business. Banks are fine when you want to borrow money but once they've got you in their clutches you've had it. We've always managed by being careful. Now it's different so for goodness sake let's at least agree that there will be no more expansion until we've got all this lot sorted. I reckon it'll be a least two or three years before we can start expanding again, so bear that in mind'

Lionel gave him a strange look but seemed to nod acceptance of his partner's advice.

They opened their warehouses in Birmingham and Southampton and for a while all went well. They recruited staff, trained them in their method of business operation. Cocky ordered lots of stock which manufacturers duly delivered to their new buildings and they got both outlying parts of the business up and running.

A and W Ltd., appeared to recover from its near crisis. Service in its original area was back to normal and most of the customers that had deserted them came back, but some didn't. The Company established itself in the new areas and its criteria of service and good prices started to bring in business but in the south the competition was much stronger than anything they had experienced before and so the prices at which they could sell were lower, hence affecting their profit margins. It was a problem but not desperately serious as long as the original trading areas of London and the Home Counties retained the ability to sell at higher prices.

But they couldn't as competition increased in those areas as well.

Several competitors were snapping at A and W's heels. Some were small but others were bigger firms. Lionel wasn't too worried and thought that they'd see them off by giving their customers low prices and lots of special offers until the competitors gave up and left A and W alone. Christopher took a different view and felt that they were now in for a long battle of attrition from which there would be definite casualties. He hoped they wouldn't be one of them.

One of their most persistent competitors was a northern based company called Houghtons Ltd., that had started as a wholesaler in Leeds but over time had spread south to Birmingham and more recently into London and the Home Counties, and then into Essex, Surrey, Sussex, Kent, Hampshire and Dorset. Not only had they spread out geographically but they had also diversified and instead of just concentrating on wholesaling Grocery items they'd established a very profitable secondary business supplying Chemists with drugs, prescription items, toiletries, and the myriad of items sold in chemist shops. This provided Houghtons with a powerful income stream of revenue as at that time chemist prices were fixed and not subject to price cutting so they were able to use the money they made in this sector of their business to ruthlessly undercut any of their grocery competitors. They also saw the future power of the supermarkets and set up a division to supply that demanding sector. Over time this became the biggest part of Houghton's business and in later years they expanded into manufacturing their own products with factories in Europe and America as well as the UK.

David George Houghton the founder had started the business using most of the capital given to him on his twenty fifth birthday by his father who had made his money, as had his grandfather before him, from coal mining in the Yorkshire area. In those days coal was the great black gold and through a policy of ruthless exploitation of their workers coupled with a sharp business brain the Houghtons had managed to become very rich indeed. They enjoyed a luxury lifestyle in the North of England.

Given his inheritance David shunned the idea of running coal mines and instead started in a similar way to Lionel but many years earlier. It was he who'd seen the opportunity to supply Chemists and he'd also set up two another businesses, one supplying liquor to off licences in the north and the other supplying requirements to ironmonger and electrical shops. Houghtons grew rapidly and became a very profitable, powerful business.

His son Charles had been conceived by mistake after a one off sexual encounter at a Christmas party with a pretty young girl called Sarah. Both families were shocked to learn that Sarah was pregnant and as far as they were concerned there was only one thing for the two wrong doing young people to do and that was to get married as quickly as possible. The forced wedding took place in April. There were plenty of knowing looks and wagging tongues at the event but with two such wealthy families it was passed over. Much to everyone's surprise the marriage lasted and David and Sarah lived happily together in considerable luxury.

Five months after the forced wedding, Charles the first of their eventual three children, was born in Leeds Infirmary.

As he grew up he was sent away to Prep and then Boarding School but he wasn't interested in University wanting instead to get into the family business so Charles had been brought permanently into the business at the age of eighteen although David had forced him since the age of ten to work every school holiday in the warehouses, on the lorries, or in the office so that he learnt the business from the bottom up. He was a hard unforgiving taskmaster who drove himself, his employees and especially his son hard.

Charles inherited his father's bombastic manner which he used without compunction never being afraid of reminding people that he was the boss's son. He unashamedly exploited his position firing people he didn't like and much to his father's delight showed great aptitude for business so much so that at age twenty one David handed over the running of the business to his son Charles.

The ruthless strategy of their business worked well and many of their smaller competitors folded or in some cases were taken over by Houghtons. When he knew that he had brought a competitor to its knees Charles would ring up the owner and invite him to a meeting over lunch in the best hotel in the appropriate area. He had a tried and trusted formula whereby he waited and just talked small talk until the main course had been served and then he would explain that he knew his opponent couldn't survive and so why didn't they sell out to him. He'd offer a fair price for the business, although as his victims discovered Charles's view of a fair price and theirs was often quite different.

He pressed hard during the lunch and then returned to his office to await events. More often than not he received a phone call agreeing in principle, but wanting to discuss the finer details. If his target refused then he simply attacked every one of their customers for the next few months with amazingly low prices and special loyalty bonuses if they switched their trade to Houghtons, until either his victim capitulated or went broke.

So eventually and inevitably, Houghtons and A and W started to compete head on for the same sets of customers. Every time Anderson and Watson dropped their prices to match those of Houghtons then they found to their horror that their ruthless competitor undercut them again. Not only were they using their chemist and off licence revenue streams to fund their low price strategy but once they had seen off a competitor in their established areas they put their prices back up again. Whatever A and W did they were out priced by Houghtons.

Christopher was alarmed that their volume of trade was dropping worryingly which was leading to the first elements of a cash flow crisis. He looked at their cost base and tried to see if they could make cuts but although he worked out that they could afford to let a few of their staff go it wouldn't be enough to enable them to get their prices down to sufficient levels to compete with Houghtons. They were boxed in and couldn't see a way out.

Added to his worries was the concern that he Betty and Mark had recently moved from the little house in Thornton Heath to a big Victorian three storey house with cellars and a huge attic in Wallington, a Surrey town on the edge of the countryside. To do this Christopher had taken on a bigger mortgage from the bank which he had been able to arrange without difficulty as his re-payment record for their first house was excellent.

Even Lionel's irrepressible "it'll be alright" approach to life started to falter and the two proprietors found that month by month the financial returns of A and W were showing losses.

After six months it was very serious because Houghtons showed no sign of giving up and Christopher started to contemplate the awful possibility that they may not be able to trade their way out of their problems. Their financial resources were now so weak that they had to be careful with paying bills and had to prioritise which of their suppliers could get paid and when, and which couldn't. In the past they had prided themselves on always paying their suppliers on time but now they were unable to do so and they were continually robbing "peter to pay paul" as the only way to eke out their cash.

They approached the bank to try and re-negotiate the terms of their loan but this was curtly refused and Lionel was reminded of Christopher's warnings when they took out the loan about banks being happy to lend you money when things were going well, but unforgiving and unhelpful when you wanted their help.

They dismissed several members of staff at Head office, in the warehouses, and from the sales force but still they couldn't compete against Houghtons. They decided to withdraw from Birmingham and so closed their warehouse there and put it up for sale. They advised their Birmingham customers that they could no longer supply them, apologised for this and thanked them for their past business.

Charles Houghton heard about this and rang his father gleefully to say that he thought that they'd really got A and W on the run now and that if they kept up the pressure they'd soon see them off completely. Old David Houghton although pleased to learn of the continuing success of the business nevertheless was concerned at the apparent delight with which his son was predicting the demise of yet another competitor.

'There are people in that business thou knows' he cautioned reverting to native Yorkshire dialect as he often did when stressed. Charles ignored it and thought that his father was going soft in his old age. He couldn't remember him or his grandfather worrying about people in the coal mine businesses. They used them, exploited them and chucked them out if they were too old or infirm to work. No, he'd keep on what he was doing.

Betty saw that Christopher was worried and although he tried to keep the problems from her she knew that things at work were not going well. He was leaving even earlier in the morning, working very late into the night and even going to the office on Saturdays and sometimes Sundays as well. He wasn't sleeping and was tetchy with her, something that he'd never been before.

Mark also noticed an atmosphere at home and although he was enjoying life at Whitgift he found the work hard and had disappointed his parents at the end of the first year by slipping down a grade and going into class 2B and not 2A. Still he shrugged there was next year to get better and he threw himself into the excellent facilities that the school offered and became a key member of the junior rugby team and showed great promise at cross country running, squash and cricket. He excelled at swimming and was like a fish in the water capable of all strokes but outstanding at front crawl and butterfly.

His academic work in the next year was sufficient to keep him in the B stream but not good enough to move back into the A stream so in September at the start of his third year he moved up into class 3B.

It was a lovely June evening when Christopher drove up the leafy street in Wallington where their large house stood, got out of the car and paused before opening the gate to their short front driveway. Betty who was in the front garden watched him as he opened the gate and stood looking up at the solid façade of the building. She thought that either the car was giving problems as he looked so sad and worried or perhaps there was worse. A further look at his face though sent a shiver through her. He looked distraught.

'Chris whatever's the matter?'

He followed her into the house and they went into the dining room that looked out onto the large rear garden that was full of flowers.

'It's the firm' he said sadly. 'I don't think we can survive. We expanded too fast and now the competition is killing us. Whatever we do they beat us. If we drop our prices they drop further. If we put a price up because our costs have gone up they just hold their price where it is. I warned Lionel that we were growing too fast. We haven't enough money coming in to pay our debts. We've been delaying and delaying to ease the cash that's coming in before paying it out, but frankly we've run out of rope. I'm going to see the bank again tomorrow but if they won't advance us more money or increase our overdraft then we've had it. It's as simple as that. All that hard work gone up in smoke just because I couldn't stop Lionel's great expansion plans.'

Betty didn't know what to do to comfort him and so she went into the kitchen and took his dinner out of the oven. She had eaten earlier with Mark who was full of the fact that he was playing rugby for the Colts First Fifteen on Saturday afternoon as scrum half about which he was very excited.

Christopher got up from the table and called upstairs to Mark 'First fifteen I hear, well done lad' and then he returned to the table to finish his meal. It tasted of nothing. Not Betty's fault. Just the way he felt right now.

After dinner he went to the sideboard and got out his little book and started to update their own personal income and expenditure position, much as he used to do before when they were poor and hadn't a spare halfpenny.

He worked away quietly and then turned to Betty. 'We'll be alright if it all goes pear shaped. We'll keep the house as long as I can keep up the repayments on it that is, and we've got some quite considerable savings so there's no immediate panic. Mark can stay on at school but we'll skip a holiday this year I think'. Seeing Betty looking so worried he went over and stroked her hair. 'Cheer up, something will come along. I can always get another job I guess' and he was pleased to see that her worried face eased and she looked much calmer. Although he slept surprisingly well that night she didn't, wishing she understood more about business and how difficult it all seemed to be.

Next morning at the office he read through the revised financial predictions that he had prepared. Cocky informed him that yet another three suppliers had refused to supply any more goods to A and W until they got their outstanding accounts paid in full. Also another solicitor's letter had arrived threatening to sue the firm if their client's outstanding accounts were not settled within seven days.

He went into Lionel's office where his partner was talking earnestly on the phone to someone, apologising that their delivery was only half of what was ordered but explaining that they had been let down by their suppliers and he was sure that it would all get sorted out in the next day or so. Yes he knew that they had been famous for the service and low prices, and yes he understood that Houghtons were now offering better prices and prompt service, but please would they just bear with him while he sorted out the problem. From his expression the person at the other end of the phone obviously was not going to bear with him.

Slamming down the receiver Lionel yelled at the instrument 'Well go and fuck yourself then'. He looked up at the other man and said 'He won't but it made me feel better'. Then he grinned and said 'Come on Chris let's go and sort out the fucking bank. Shit or bust today eh'.

The journey to the bank took only a few minutes and at five minutes to ten, the two men were sitting on a hard wooden bench in a corridor away from general view outside the office of the bank manager Mr. Gilchrist.

At exactly ten o'clock Mr. Gilchrist's secretary Olive, an ugly woman with mousy straggly hair, several long facial whiskers, of chubby medium build and indeterminate age but probably around fifty, appeared as if from nowhere and bade the two gentlemen to follow her as Mr. Gilchrist was ready for them. They were surprised to see three people in the room not just Mr. Gilchrist who introduced the two other men. One was tall and thin with a neck that was too thin for his collar, a slightly stooped posture and an expression of misery and doom. He would have been well suited to be an undertaker. The other was much younger and clearly in some awe of the other two. It transpired that he was there to make notes of the meeting but not to take any part in the discussions.

'Coffee gentlemen' asked Olive and she spent the next few minutes filling cups, handing round milk and sugar and generally dealing with things such as ensuring that Mr. Gilchrist and the other bank officials had clean paper pads on the table and sharpened pencils.

'Thank you Miss Walters that will be all. No interruptions now please' said Mr. Gilchrist quietly. 'Gentlemen let me introduce my two colleagues. Mr. Sharp from the Bank's debt recovery department', at which the undertaker nodded slowly in the general direction of Christopher and Lionel, 'and Mr. Evans one of our under managers. Let us be seated and begin'. He gestured towards a large solid oblong table that took up about one third of the room. 'Do you have any good news for us concerning the financial situation of your business and especially the situation regarding the Bank's exposure to that position?'

'Erm, yes' began Lionel 'I think that the worst is probably over and we should be able to stabilise things now and then get back onto a growth path again. I', he paused and corrected himself, 'We're quite confident about that aren't we Chris?'

'Well......' but before he could add that he wasn't nearly so sure about that as Lionel, Mr. Gilchrist interrupted.

'What is the evidence for this optimism Mr. Anderson?'

'A general feeling about the business you know. I know my way around this trade and I can smell an improvement around the corner'.

'The Bank will require far more than a smell around the corner Mr. Anderson to even consider continuing with any financial support. Oh yes indeed. We need firm evidence. Do you have any?'

Christopher, worried about Lionel letting loose on unsubstantiated wild thoughts and ideas decided to try and take control of the meeting. Leaning forward he interjected 'Look things have been really rough and they are going to continue to be so but I have re-done all our financial projections and if the Bank can see its way to continuing to help us then I think that there is a reasonable chance that we can, firstly survive, and secondly start to build back some of our former trade. We've put up our Birmingham warehouse for sale and that should realise us a good price, and we propose to also sell the Southampton warehouse as well and consolidate our position back into our original heartland of London'

'Consolidate, or retreat Mr. Watson?'

'No not retreat. Consolidate and capitalise on our strong original base'.

There was a silence as Christopher handed over the folder of information that he had spent most of yesterday finalising. He handed a second copy to Mr. Sharp who took it without a word or acknowledgement of any kind, but simply took his glass case out of his top pocket, removed his small lensed spectacles, flicked past the several pages of narrative and carefully studied the figures that made up the last few pages of the document. As he worked his way through the information he made pencil notes in the margins of several pages, sometimes seeming to write many figures down and then checking back at previous pages. Mr. Gilchrist had started to read from the first page. The young Mr. Evans sat immobile but he did flick a small smile to Christopher who looked from one to another of the three Bank personnel. Lionel fidgeted in his chair.

There was silence in the dark wooden panelled room broken only by the sounds of slow ticking clock, the muffled noise of traffic outside the window and somewhat incongruously a blackbird could be heard singing. Flecks of dust floated and glinted in the air. Mr. Sharp sniffed from time to time.

Mr. Gilchrist slowly read each page of the narrative. Mr. Sharp looked up at Lionel briefly, sniffed loudly and then continued to study the figures. His expression remained inscrutable but foreboding. Christopher's heart started to drop. He looked at Lionel and shrugged sadly.

After what seemed an age Mr. Gilchrist came to the end of the written commentary and briefly having looked at the figures closed the folder, placed it on the table in front of him and sat upright with his hands clasped together in his lap. He looked at Mr. Sharp who was frowning as he continued to study the figures before he turned to the front of the folder and started to read the narrative, checking certain points back to the pages of figures. Finally he too completed his perusal of the document and placing his folder in front of him looked firstly at Lionel and then at Christopher, sniffed again then turned to Mr. Gilchrist.

'I am unconvinced by the written arguments and more so by the figures he said slowly and quietly. Quite unconvinced. What is your view Wilbur?'

Christopher realised that up to that minute they had no idea that Mr. Gilchrist's christian name was Wilbur. Wilbur Gilchrist seemed somehow appropriate for a dull bank manager.

'I have to say that I am inclined to agree' replied Wilbur Gilchrist.

Sharp then asked Christopher a few questions about the figures and projections and made detailed notes about what was said to him.

Gilchrist outlined his thoughts about what he had read. 'I fear that there is too much hope and expectation and insufficient definite cause for belief in the action plan to correct the situation. The Bank needs hard facts to work on but what you have given us gentlemen, are your hopes'. He looked across at the two worried businessmen. 'We at the Bank cannot and do not work on hope. We work on facts, financial facts. However I suggest that you leave Mr. Sharp and I to consider the matter in further detail and I will telephone you tomorrow morning with our views. I have to say though that regretfully it does not look promising gentlemen.' He finished and turned to Mr. Sharp for confirmation 'Does it?'

'Decidedly not. I see no cause for optimism'.

'Look is there anything else we can tell you to help you come to a favourable decision? Lionel asked earnestly.

The two Bank men exchanged glances. 'Is there anything else you have to tell us?' queried Mr. Sharp.

Christopher pursed his lips and said softly 'No. It's all there in that folder'.

There was nothing else. They weren't just in trouble they were desperate. Without the bank's help they were finished and they had nothing to assist the bank make a favourable decision.

'Very well then until tomorrow. Good day gentlemen'. Mr. Gilchrist led the two crestfallen businessmen towards the door and out into the corridor. 'Thank you for coming to see us. I will telephone you tomorrow. Good bye'. He shook them both briefly by the hand and turned back to his office. The interview was ended.

Not knowing quite what to say to each other, Lionel and Christopher walked disconsolately back to their car and drove back to their offices.

'That's it then' said Lionel. 'All fucked up and finished. The bastards. They are not interested in helping us are they? That miserable git Sharp. He'd made up his mind before we started. I don't fink anyfing we could have said would ave changed that bastard's mind. He's a bloody weasel. A jumped up nobody......'

'But he's got the power of life or death over our business' interrupted Christopher. 'Whether we like it or not, whether we like him or not he and Gilchrist can destroy or save us and there's nothing we can do about it. If they say no tomorrow morning then that's the end of Anderson and Watson'.

They both passed the rest of the day in a sort of daze going mechanically through the motions of business until they went home.

Seeing how depressed he was Amy took Lionel to bed early but even her undoubted skills there failed to cheer him up. Christopher tried to read a book but when Betty went up to bed he remained sitting downstairs for a long while before making them some cocoa and walking wearily up to bed.

The day of reckoning dawned, wet, miserable and dull. An unhopeful sign thought Lionel as he drove to the office. When he arrived Christopher was already there looking drawn and haggard.

The morning dragged slowly by until just before twelve o'clock the telephone on Christopher's desk rang and their switchboard operator advised him that Mr. Gilchrist's secretary from the bank was on the line. He asked her to put the call through and to call Lionel.

'Mr. Watson?' queried Olive.

'Yes speaking'.

'I have Mr. Gilchrist for you' and following a brief silence and a couple of telephonic clicks the male voice spoke just as Lionel barged into the room.

'Good morning Mr. Watson. At our meeting yesterday I committed to contact you this morning. I will come straight to the point as I know you will be anxious to learn the results of our deliberations. I am afraid that I have bad news for you. It is my duty to tell you that the Bank finds itself unable to continue to support you with any further extension of funding and indeed now requires the repayment of all outstanding monies immediately. In other words we are calling in the overdraft Mr. Watson'.

'In other words you're killing us off' shouted Christopher down the phone. 'We haven't got any money to pay back the overdraft. You know that. Asking us to do that will finish us. We just need some time. We explained all that yesterday. Look we can pull this business through. We'll go to another bank. Come on don't push us down. Just give us a little more time.......please Mr. Gilchrist'.

Gilchrist who was used to these sorts of reactions from businesses or individuals when faced with the stark reality of the bank calling in its loans waited calmly for Christopher to pause in his tirade and then responded gently.

'Mr. Watson I do understand your disappointment but losing your temper with me will not help the situation. Mr. Sharp and I spent a considerable time yesterday studying your financial position to see whether we could find any way to assist you. We also took advice from higher authority in the bank to see if that would help. We have not come to our decision lightly but it is final Mr. Watson, quite final. Therefore it would be best if you and Mr. Anderson came into the bank today so we can finalise matters. As for going to another bank Mr. Watson forget it. As soon as they see the state your business is in they will simply not entertain any financial help for you. Now I have booked three o'clock in my diary to see you both. Will that be convenient for you?'

Christopher thought of the irony of Gilchrist asking if it was a convenient time for him to destroy their business. 'Yes that will be alright'.

'Until three this afternoon then. Goodbye'.

Lionel knew from hearing Christopher's half of the conversation that they were finished. 'So what happens now Chris?'

'I guess they'll put a Receiver in and sell off everything they can to recover their money. Oh what a mess'.

That afternoon Mr. Gilchrist opened the meeting by formally handing each of them a letter stating the bank's demand for immediate repayment of the overdraft. It confirmed that the original terms of the overdraft which had been increased, extended and amended several times enabled the bank to demand immediate repayment ay any time and that failure to comply with this demand would result in the bank taking all legal steps that it considered necessary to recover its money.

He asked them to confirm whether they understood what was being asked and when they said that they did he then formerly asked for the immediate repayment of the overdraft.

Receiving their acknowledgment that they were unable to do that, he lifted his telephone and asked for a Mr. Brandon to join them. This new individual was introduced as the person from the bank that would handle the winding up the business and would be the primary liaison with the Receivers who would arrive at A and W tomorrow morning. Their authority was absolute and they would explain to the two owners, the procedure and consequence of putting a business into receivership. He finished by advising that Mr. Brandon would return with them to their offices and that they were no longer empowered to make any decisions about any aspect of the business. Some forms and documents were then signed to formally put the process into operation.

And that was that. It was all over in twenty minutes.

At their offices Bill Brandon asked to see around the entire building nodding and listening carefully as he was shown the premises.

'That's fine then thanks a lot' he said as they returned to Christopher's office. 'You two might as well go home now and leave it to me, the Bank and the Receivers. We'll want to see you both tomorrow morning but there's nothing for you to do today. You both have company cars I assume. Please be sure to bring them in with you tomorrow as they will be among the first assets to be sold' and with that he sat down at Christopher's desk and opened his briefcase to remove some folders and papers.

'I've got some personal things in my desk' said Christopher quietly. 'I'd like to take those please'.

'Of course. I'll give you half an hour to tidy up and clear out personal items' and so saying he stood up and walked out of the door.

Lionel and Christopher cleared their offices then called all the staff, warehouse crew and those lorry drivers that were back from their deliveries together and explained what had happened, shook them all by the hand thanking them for all that they'd done for the business. To the oft asked question "what's going to happen now" or the equally worried "what will happen to me" they were unable to give answers but made as many reassuring noises and responses as they could.

They returned the next day to answer several hours of questions from the Receivers. At the end of that first day the two sad and disillusioned proprietors of A and W handed over their car keys and various documents to the Receivers and then called a taxi which took Lionel home first before dropping Christopher at his house.

The Receivers were a small team of people from one of the major accounting firms in the City of London who took charge of the business. Their powers were absolute. Over the next few days they contacted a number of A and W's competitors to see if they wanted to take over the business or merge in some way but the only one that showed any interest was Houghtons who sent a small team to look around and then made a derisory offer for the stock which the Receivers accepted.

Christopher sat in the garden and thought about how it had all started so well, how it had grown, expanded too fast and finally collapsed. He didn't blame Lionel. After all he could have been firmer and stopped Lionel but he had also believed in the dream and now it was all over. He was still sitting there later in the afternoon when Mark came bounding home from school.

'Hi Dad, you're home early today. Guess what happened in school. Dad you're not listening. What's up?'

'It's the firm Mark. Anderson and Watson. My firm. Well mine and Lionel's firm. It's ....' he paused and swallowed hard. 'It's in trouble. In fact it's had it. We're finished. Bust. The end'. He looked at Mark's shocked face.

'What do you mean Dad? Can't you make in right? Surely you can sort it out can't you? What about us? Can I stay on at school? Will that be alright? What will we do for money?'

The questions flooded out from Mark's young lips as he struggled to comprehend what had happened. Christopher answered them as honestly as he could but in a way that he thought that a fifteen year old would understand. Mark listened and asked more questions and then wandered in to the house to seek out his Mother. He asked a whole lot more questions of her but she was unable to answer most of them having never understood business.

'You'll have to ask your father' she'd reply to most of them.

So Mark did. He pumped questions at his father most of the rest of the evening until eventually Christopher wearily said 'Look I'm tired. No more questions tonight there's a good chap. Now go and do your homework because if you study hard you'll get good exam results and then a good job with a sound firm and you won't be in the mess that I'm in now'.

'You know Dad when I grow up I'm going to go into business and I'll get that man Charles Houghton for you. I'll pay him back for you'.

Christopher laughed at his son's earnest expression but saw something in the boy's eyes that he'd never seen before. They'd turned piercingly cold and it made his father shiver.

'We'll see, but thanks Mark' and he ruffled the boy's hair and turned on the television to watch the news.

'I mean it Dad, really I do. One day you'll see'.

The weeks passed. Most of the office staff and salesmen were dismissed. Occasionally Christopher or Lionel were summoned either to the Bank or to A and W to answer questions. There were mountains of forms to fill in and the whole exercise was depressing in the extreme.

They started to think about the future. Lionel decided that he might start up again somehow and wondered if Chris would like to join him. Christopher thought about it but decided that he wouldn't. It wasn't that he blamed Lionel for their problems it was just that he couldn't bring himself to go through all the problems of starting up a business again. No he would get a job working for someone else. Let them have the worry.

He studied the Daily Telegraph and The Express as well as some of the local papers and wrote off for a number of jobs. He was disappointed that from his first batch of applications he either received no reply or letters regretting that he would not be called for interview.

Now ultra careful he recorded every transaction of expenditure matching it against his calculation of the meagre income from their savings into his accounts book. In order to survive until he got another job they were having to use their savings but Betty was careful when shopping and bought the poorer cuts of meat, cheaper quality vegetables, and fruit that was a little past its best and had been marked down in price. She retained absolute faith in Christopher to sort out the problems that they were in.

Nearly three months had elapsed since the collapse of Anderson and Watson and Mark had been shocked to see the way his father had deteriorated. To Mark's young mind it was terrible. His father had become withdrawn hardly speaking and taking no interest in anything. He'd get up but sometimes not bother to shave or dress properly, morosely study the papers spending hours poring over the job sections. Then he'd sit down and write letters. Often he received no reply but sometimes the replies would invite him to an interview but following the meeting a few days later the "regret" letter would arrive pushing him into greater depression. His only relaxation seemed to be his stamp collection.

Summer turned to autumn and Christopher was really worried. More than half their savings had gone and with the winter coming there would be higher expenditure for the coal, electricity and gas.

Mark had started his new term at Whitgift and was playing rugby with skill and flair. As scrum half he had a crucial position in the team and was brave, quick and quite ruthless when pounding down the opposition. He threw himself into tackles with tremendous effort and established a reputation as a first class player. Betty worried about the kicks, knocks and bangs that he received resulting in him limping home from school sometimes with great bruises but he laughed it off and told her to stop fussing.

His various masters noticed a sudden dramatic change in his attitude and he now worked extremely hard at his academic studies and his grades improved significantly.

Without any enthusiasm Christopher attended yet another interview with a pleasant man who was in charge of a small import and export business trading mainly with Africa. Brian Thompson was looking for an experienced business man to take control of the office side of his business leaving him to deal with the negotiations with the African exporters. It was a well established business and the present incumbent was approaching retirement hence the need for the recruitment of a replacement.

Christopher enjoyed his meeting but was surprised when Brian said after about half an hour's discussion 'Look I hope you don't mind me mentioning this but although you are clearly well qualified for this job you don't seem terribly enthusiastic about wanting it'.

Christopher somewhat taken aback realised that probably he had been answering the questions mechanically and not trying to sell himself to the man the other side of the desk. Maybe that's why all the other opportunities had failed to materialise, so he found himself explaining how he hated the interview process.

He told Brian in detail all that had gone wrong with A and W., about their hopes and dreams as they built the business, the fun and the challenges, the successes and failures, long hours, the early mornings and late nights, the fight for survival, the unrelenting pressure from Houghtons, the dogged refusal of the bank to help them out at the end and hence the eventual collapse. He spoke of the degrading process with the Receivers, of the stock being sold cheap, the staff being got rid of with no compensation and how he felt that he'd let everyone down.

He spoke about how for months now he'd worried about what he could do to help himself get a proper and decent job to support Betty and Mark but with no real formal qualifications no-one seemed to want him especially when they heard about the collapse of his business.

He was speaking strongly and passionately until he suddenly stopped himself in full flight, paused and said softly 'I'm sorry to have wasted your time Mr. Thompson. Thank you for seeing me. I'll make my own way out. Goodbye'.

'Where the hell do you think you are going?'

'Erm well back home. I've nothing else to do now'.

'You may not have right now but from next Monday you do. You've a job here. You might not be the ideal candidate but you've the experience that I need and if you stop feeling sorry for yourself and get rid of that chip on your shoulder then you've work to do here'.

Christopher could hardly believe it. 'Do you mean it?' he asked feeling tears come to his eyes.

'Yes I do' smiled Brian and seeing the emotion welling up in the interviewee diplomatically looked away for a few moments to read some papers on his desk while the other got his emotions under control.

'Thank you. You won't regret it, I promise you'.

'I know that. Now lets talk about the terms and conditions for the job' which they did for a few minutes then shaking hands Christopher made his way home. He felt elated and stopped twice on his journey, once to buy a bottle of wine and a bar of chocolate, and the second time to buy a bunch of flowers.

Arriving home Betty saw as soon as he entered the house that here was her old Christopher again. He hugged her, gave her the flowers and asked her to put the wine in the fridge for them to have a glass each as a treat with their dinner that night. The chocolate he gave to Mark when he came home from school and the boy was also glad to see his father back in his old form.

Christopher reported for duty at his new firm on the next Monday. He stayed there for a little over twenty years running the office, no longer harbouring any great ambitions just doing a good job until he retired aged sixty five.

CHAPTER 5

Mark had loved Whitgift and when it came to thinking about a career he seriously considered going into the forces but as he had promised Christopher that he would get even with the man who had brought down his father's company he decided to go into business which was something of a problem for the career's masters at school.

They were used to guiding pupils into university, teaching, the military or Government service such as the Home Office or the Foreign Office. Mark though was adamant. He rejected the reasoning that he should go to university and leaving at the end of the sixth form term with six "O" levels and two "A" level passes in his exams, started to write to various companies offering his services.

He received several replies inviting him for an interview and soon developed a standard set of responses to the questions as to why he didn't want to go to university explaining that he wanted to build a career to make his father proud of what he would achieve in the future.

He was offered three positions, all in London. One was from a shipping agent whose offices were near London Docks. It was a small shabby firm and although it meant he would be frequently going into the docks themselves, finding the ships and checking their cargoes and manifestoes something which sounded quite exciting, he rejected that as having insufficient opportunity to build a career. The second was from a parcels delivery company, part of a bigger group but he was unhappy about their lack of commitment to training and helping him with his career.

The third offer was from the London Office of a major international corporation Thompson and Smith Ltd., in which they invited him to join their management trainee programme, starting in their London offices in Bedford Square just off Tottenham Court Road but with a career path which extended across their many businesses. They also had overseas operations which appealed.

Mark accepted their job offer and with some trepidation but enormous enthusiasm on the first Monday of October 1978, started work in the Bedford Square offices.

He met a couple of other young men of his own age. Malcolm had been with the firm for about a year and the other, Rob for about two years. Both were on the management trainee programme although Mark was puzzled as to why Rob didn't seem to have progressed any further than Malcolm, even though he had been there twice as long. There were several other men in the offices, all much older, and a sprinkling of female clerks. The telephonist was Debbie and she was pretty with nice hair but scatty, frequently putting calls through to the wrong person, or forgetting to get calls that she had been asked to do. Both Malcolm and Rob claimed to have slept with her and they winked and said that she was known as the company bike. This puzzled Mark until they explained that it meant that anyone that wanted a ride on her could have one. Mark thought about that and filed the information away for possible future use.

The whole of the London office operation was run by a very upright although slightly deaf ex army major known as Mr. Dunson, whose secretary Miss Trowse was a fearsome dragon of a woman.

Mr. Dunson called Mark into his office on his first day to painstakingly and after he'd been at it for a couple of hours, boringly, explain the entire company history right back to the time in the mid eighteen hundreds when two men, a Mr. Smith and Mr. Thompson had started their respective businesses independently of each other, but both making a range of cleaning chemicals and polishes. Their businesses grew and expanded in this country and abroad. Finding that they were increasingly competing against each other they eventually merged to become Thompson and Smith Ltd., quoted on the London Stock Exchange with offices and factories all over the world.

By mid morning when the office Manager moved onto product knowledge he could hardly remain alert but he continued to listen carefully until Mr. Dunson said that he had finished the history and thought that for the remainder of the day Mark should introduce himself to the others in the building.

At lunch time Rob and Malcolm collected him and took him to a pub around the corner where they had a pint of beer and shepherds pie. They quizzed him on whether he could remember old Dunson's history lesson and grinning said they hoped he had. 'Very important to know the company's history' they intoned together in a passable imitation of Dunson, 'for from lessons of the past we can plan the opportunities of the future'. Mark joined in the laughter happily.

Returning to the offices which were delightful having been created inside one of the many classic Georgian buildings that formed Bedford Square Mark continued going around meeting as many people as possible. They were a mixed bunch but most were friendly and wished him the best of luck.

Day two started with Mr. Dunson walking into the general office where Miss Trowse, Rob, Malcolm and Mark had their desks just after nine and asking Mark to spare him a few minutes.

'Sit down' he said kindly when Mark had entered his office. 'How did day one go?'

'Fine thank you'.

'Good and what did you learn?'

'Well of course I had your excellent lesson about the company to start me off'. He thought a bit of flattery would go down well and observing Dunson's face detected a small flicker of pleasure. 'Then I did as you suggested and spent time meeting the other people here'.

'Do you have a good memory?'

'Yes I think so, why?'

'Imagine I am in the position that you were yesterday just joining this great company. Now tell me the history of the company if you please. We'll see how good a listener you were and how good a teacher I am'.

Oh shit. Mark thought furiously as the laughing comments of his two compatriots at lunch in the pub came back to him about how well he had learned the history. They'd known this would happen the rotten bastards.

Looking straight at Mr. Dunson he smiled confidently even though he didn't feel it at that moment. 'In eighteen fifty three' Mark started, paused, and then found that his memory clicked into action and for about ten minutes he held the older man spellbound with a summary of the history. In those few minutes he condensed over three hours teaching from yesterday into the key facts. He spoke clearly and without pause until at the end he stopped and said 'I think that's about it sir. Did I miss anything that matters?'

Dunson was extremely impressed. He confirmed that Mark had covered the salient points well and bade him remember that 'From the lessons of the past we can plan the opportunities of the future, and don't you forget that. Well done. Right get back to your desk. Miss Trowse will set you off on your work today'.

Mark was a quick learner and soon grasped the rudiments of what the London office of Thompson and Smith did. Essentially it housed the sales function for the major customers such as the large supermarket and wholesale companies. His, Rob's and Malcolm's jobs were to co-ordinate the orders received during the day into totals for the various factories around the country, type up the totals onto special forms and post them each night to the appropriate factory. They also dealt with the myriad of queries that came from the factories and from customers. Many of the brands and products which the company manufactured in their various factories were advertised on television or in the press. Mark learnt that this was called marketing and it sounded interesting.

He worked diligently and got through a great deal more work than either Rob or Malcolm who seemed to spend a great deal of time chatting about last night's exploits, their latest girlfriend or where they were going tonight.

They all had to be careful talking about girls when Miss Trowse was around.

'We don't want that sort of dirty talk going on in this office thank you' she'd exclaim whenever the subject of sex arose. She controlled almost every aspect of the three young men's working day but she soon noticed that Mark although the newest was clearly the best of the three. He worked harder, arrived earlier in the morning, stayed later and asked intelligent questions. He often questioned Mr. Dunson about the company's advertising campaigns and was not afraid to voice his opinion on what he thought about them. What Mr. Dunson liked was not the fact that Mark was prepared to discuss the subject but that his views were thought out and unlike so many people who criticise without adding a positive alternative Mark always explained why he thought something could be improved and how.

Mark found Rob and Malcolm irritating as his view was that they were just idle. They for their part thought Mark was a pain as he never seemed to want to stop working. When five o'clock came each evening, they wanted to get out of the office as soon as they could. Mark on the other hand would stay and ensure that he had completely finished his day's work and then spend time reading trade magazines or the company's promotional literature.

Miss Trowse regularly reported unfavourably on Malcolm and particularly Rob, while her reports about Mark were full of praise.

Mark had a good social life outside work much of which revolved around sport. He still played rugby on Saturday's for the Old Whitgiftians and he went to team training on Wednesday evenings. He was also captain of the O W's swimming and water polo teams and trained in the school swimming bath with the rest of the team on Thursday evenings. He went out drinking in local pubs with other friends of his and his £100 purchase of an old V W Beetle car gave him the mobility he needed. It frequently broke down and he became a dab hand at fixing it sufficient to limp back home where he would spend hours at weekends crawling under it or delving into it's old engine.

He took a few girls out in it and enjoyed the mutual fumbling and groping but didn't persuade any to have sex with him. His friends constantly talked about sex and some had probably done it but he thought most of it was just talk, however he was curious to discover what sex was all about.

If he was to lose his virginity which he was increasingly keen to do, then Debbie the company bike might be the one to do it with as he guessed she knew a lot about it. She was attractive with short curly brunette hair, pretty and slim with a nice but quite small figure.

It was after another frustrating evening, this time with a dark haired girl called Natasha that he decided he really needed to see if he could get it together with Debbie.

On his third date with Natasha they'd gone to a pub near Leatherhead and after a couple of drinks found a quiet little clearing off the main road often used by courting couples . She willingly got into the back seat of the car and they started kissing. Allowing him to undo her blouse but not her bra she let him play around with her breasts but when he ran his hand under her skirt she immediately stopped his exploration.

'No Mark don't do that' she muttered.

No amount of pleading succeeded so seething with frustration he unzipped himself and pushed her hand into his open fly but she just gave him a quick squeeze and then thought that it might be best if he took her home.

Nothing could make her change her mind so zipping himself up while she re-fastened her blouse he started the car, slammed it in gear and drove her home where she lived with her parents. They kissed briefly in the car outside her parent's house and she said that she was sorry and hoped it hadn't spoilt things as she really liked him but she "wasn't that sort of girl".

He said he liked her too and that they must meet up again but as he drove off said out loud 'Bloody women what do I have to do to get it then? Right' he continued 'I'll take Debbie out and see if I can crack it with her'

Pleased with his decision he drove along singing all the songs he knew about bikes eventually arriving home around mid-night.

The next day he thought about how he could put his master plan with Debbie into action. He wondered how many times he'd have to take her out before he could ask her to do it with him and whether she'd expect to go to expensive restaurants or shows in the West End. He hoped not as he didn't have much money since Thompson and Smith didn't pay very high salaries to its junior staff. Success though came surprisingly easily.

During the morning he stopped by the switchboard and talked to her about pop music and what sort she liked. She chattered away to him and he felt sufficiently relaxed to ask the question.

'I wonder whether you'd like to come out for a drink, or go to the cinema or something one evening with me'.

'That'd be nice' she smiled. 'Yes I'd like that.'

'Great. What about tonight?'

'No I can't tonight, but I'm free tomorrow if that's all right for you?'

Alright for me, you bet it's all right for me he thought and grinning broadly he said tomorrow would be fine.

The next day he drove his old car to London rather than taking the train and just after five o'clock he cleared his desk top. Mr. Dunson had a clear desk at the end of the day policy and would grumble if anyone left papers or files out on their desks at night.

'Tidy desk, tidy mind, tidy people, tidy business' he'd say to any recalcitrant untidy desk owner.

Miss Trowse was surprised to see Mark rushing off, something he didn't usually do. He walked to the pub where he'd agreed to meet Debbie. It was quite crowded and he worried that he might not see her so he wandered round both bars and then just as he was getting concerned a tinkley voice said behind him 'Looking for someone?'

'Not any more' he replied gratefully as he turned to see Debbie smiling at him.

'Sorry I'm a bit late, but I had to change and the ladies loo at the offices is a rather cramped and it took a bit of time. Still here we are now. So what are we going to do this evening then?'

What he really wanted to say was that he didn't care what they did as long as it didn't cost too much and they finished up having sex. 'Oh I thought we'd have a drink here and then we could go to the cinema, or a restaurant, whatever you like really'.

'There's a nice Italian restaurant in Soho. We could go there. It's cosy and not too expensive' suggested Debbie.

So that's what they did. They had a couple of drinks then walked into Soho passing various restaurants and bars until they came to the one Debbie had in mind. It was as she had described it, cosy and not yet busy so the waiters fixed them a table in a corner. Music played quietly, the tables had bright red and white tablecloths and the place had a wonderful smell of Italian cooking. So far the evening was going alright he thought and the menu prices weren't too expensive.

Debbie was easy to talk with and their conversation ranged over a wide spread of subjects. He learnt that she had one older sister and a younger brother, that she had left home a couple of years ago and now lived in a flat of her own in Hampstead. It wasn't really Hampstead she said, but Belsize Park which was near Hampstead, it's just that Hampstead sounded nicer than Belsize Park. Also it was just one room not a proper flat but it had all the essentials including a large bed. She giggled as she said that adding that he wasn't to get any ideas, but the way she looked at him made make him hope that he probably could have ideas.

A little after ten o'clock Mark suggested that he could drive her home if she wanted or they could go to another pub. She looked at him and thought that a drive home in his car might be nice so they walked the underground car park where Mark had parked that morning. He apologised that it was only an old Beetle but she said that she didn't mind at all and thought it was sweet.

Not being familiar with north London he got lost a couple of times but eventually they came to the Hampstead area and Debbie took over directions for a while until arriving at Hampstead Heath she said that as it was a nice night why didn't they park up and look at the lights of London spread out below for a while.

This might be it he thought. He didn't want to blow his chances with her by being too forward but equally he didn't want her to think he wasn't interested in her.

In the event Debbie solved the problem for him because she said that she'd had a lovely evening and with that she loosened her coat and pulled his head towards her and kissed him gently at first, then more fiercely. Mark responded and soon they were indulging in deep passionate kisses that lasted longer than he'd ever kissed a girl before. He tentatively squeezed her jumper over the nearest breast and she snuggled a little closer, so starting a more daring exploration he undid the buttons of her jumper and ran his hands over her bra. Again she made no move to stop him as he reached around the back and struggled to undo the back fastening. 'Here let me' she giggled and twisting her arms behind her unclipped the back strap. The bra fell loose to his touch and he was able to take her breasts in his hands. Squeezing them he realised they were a lot smaller than Natasha's who was the only other girl whose breasts he'd felt.

'Shall we get in the back of the car?' he whispered hopefully. 'It's more comfy'.

'I don't mind getting in the back but don't think you are going to screw me there. It's too bloody cramped and I like a bit of comfort. Besides it's also risky in case someone comes along and sees us. The police keep a look out for that sort of thing up here you know'.

Mark's heart jumped. She hadn't said that he couldn't screw her just that he couldn't do it in the back of the car. Now what was he to do? Pondering on this problem of what to do next he kissed her again and continued to fondle her small breasts. She responded with deep kisses and her hand stroked his trouser crotch several times. After a little while she leaned away from him and suggested that they could go back to her little place for a coffee and to get to know each other a bit better and as she said it she gave his crotch a very firm squeeze.

Mark couldn't believe his luck and as he started the car she buttoned up her jumper. Following her directions they drove to a somewhat dingy road in Belsize Park which as she had said wasn't really Hampstead but was near it.

'You'll have to be ever so quiet' she cautioned him doing up her coat as he pulled up and parked the car. 'Take your shoes off on the front step before we go in. Mrs. Ray is a nosy old cow and we're not supposed to have any visitors in our rooms after ten and especially no one of the opposite sex. You creep upstairs quickly and quietly while I make a bit of noise in the hall then but with a bit of luck she'll miss you'.

It all sounded a bit precarious but the plan worked well. Debbie opened the street door after Mark had taken off his shoes on the front porch and sneaking in quietly she pushed him towards the stairs and signalled that he should make his way up while she banged the street door shut and dropped her handbag on the hard lino floor. Sure enough the downstairs flat door opened and Mrs Ray a large fat woman stuck her head out coughing through a haze of cigarette smoke.

'Hello Mrs. Ray, whoops butterfingers' she trilled kneeling as she picked up the bag and started scooping up the few items that had scattered. Glancing out of the corner of her eye she saw that Mark had made it up the first flight and disappeared round the corner and was now out of sight. 'Well goodnight Mrs. Ray see you' and having retrieved all the dropped items she walked slowly towards and then up stairs knowing her landlady was watching her retreating back. At the top of the first flight she turned and saw Mrs. Ray's door closing. Mission accomplished she thought but putting her finger to her lips she took Mark's hand and led him along the upstairs landing to a second flight of very narrow stairs which led up to the top floor on which her room was located. Unlocking her door she pushed him inside, turned on the lights and pulled the curtains.

'There that's alright then' grinned Debbie. 'Now put the kettle on. I need to go to the bathroom which is on the floor below. Don't go away will you?'

While Debbie trotted downstairs he had a look around her abode. It was as she'd said just one room but it was quite large with a few bits of old cheap furniture. There was a table and three wooden chairs, a couple of worn armchairs, a large wardrobe, a double bed and a bedside table. In one corner was an alcove in which there was a sink and a couple of gas rings and he guessed that this did as her kitchen. He looked through her record collection on the bookshelf and taking out a Rolling Stones LP took it over to the record player. He'd just taken off his jacket and tie when she came back in the room.

'That's better' she muttered going over to the kettle and reaching up to a small curtained off area above the sink which hid a couple of shelves, took down a jar of coffee and spooned the powder into two mugs. In no time the kettle boiled. 'Black ok as I haven't got any milk?' she queried walking slowly over to hand him his coffee. 'You can put that record on if you like but keep the sound down'.

He set the record playing, sprawled onto an armchair and wondered how to rekindle the flames of passion. Debbie sat on his lap so he kissed her while running his hands over her breasts. She responded by pushing her tongue deep into his mouth until after a little while she stood and pulled him to his feet. Smiling, she leaned back to undo his shirt buttons before slipping it off his shoulders and down his arms. Kissing his bare chest her tongue travelled down towards his waist where kneeling in front of him she deftly undid his trouser belt and zip and in one smooth movement rolled trousers and pants down to his ankles. His prick stiffening rapidly stretched upwards.

'My you are a big boy aren't you' she said admiringly and with that she took the end of his penis into her mouth and sucked gently. Mark rocked back on his heels as she worked on him and felt he was in heaven as he'd only ever dreamed of this happening to him.

Releasing him she stood up. 'Come on then there's a bed over there' and with that she turned and led him to the other side of the room. As his trousers and pants were still round his ankles he kind of hopped and hobbled which made his prick jerk about in a very undignified way until they both collapsed on the bed in a heap spending the next few minutes giggling, kissing, groping and undressing. Eventually it was all sorted out and the two naked young people were ready. 'Have you got anything for this?' she asked stroking his erect penis gently. He looked puzzled. 'You know Durex' she continued.

Panic stricken he remembered that he'd left the packet that he'd bought in a state of great embarrassment in the barbers shop yesterday lunchtime in the car. 'I erm, I err sort of thought that you'd be on the pill or something' he muttered worriedly.

'Well I might be or I might not be lover but don't worry I've got some' and reaching into the little bedside cupboard she extracted a pack of condoms opened it and removed one of the foil wrapped contents. She asked if he wanted to put it on or would he like her to do it.

As nonchenently as he could, never having handled one before, he asked her to do it so she slit the foil with her fingernail and expertly rolled the slippery rubber down his now extremely erect prick before lying on her back and holding out her arms to him. He climbed awkwardly on top of her and tried to push himself into her but sensing he was having difficulty she took hold of him and helped him enter her. Immediately he started to thrust furiously in and out.

'Woa there boy, slow down a bit' she squeaked. He did for a moment but then started to pump away quicker and quicker. 'Here you have done this before haven't you?' she queried buckling under his onslaught.

'Yea loads of times' he gasped continuing to pound into her until suddenly with a great grunt and exhalation of breath he climaxed and collapsed onto her.

'Hey you haven't bloody well come already have you?' she exclaimed angrily. 'You have haven't you? You bastard? I hadn't even started to get warmed up. Shit it was your first time wasn't it? Bloody hellfire. You pratt. Why didn't you tell me you hadn't done it before? I'd have helped you and made it special…..and got myself to come off too. It really was your first time wasn't it? Wasn't it?' She'd raised her voice, clenched her fists and thumped his chest in frustration and some not inconsiderable anger.

'Yes sorry' he admitted sheepishly. 'I thought if you knew that I'd not'.……..he paused embarrassed. 'Well if you knew I hadn't done it then you might not want to do it with me. I'm sorry' he repeated again and with that he clambered off her and laid face down by her side feeling totally distraught. He knew he'd made a complete mess of things but he'd just got carried away. At school all the boys had ever talked about was doing it with a girl, except the poofy ones of course. Same at the rugby club but no-one ever talked about how to do it. Where did you learn he wondered?

'Ah well I guess it's not the end of the world' sighed Debbie calming down. 'Look it'll be alright' she added more kindly. 'Let's take that off shall we' and with that she felt beneath him and part rolled part pulled the used condom off his now rapidly deflating prick quickly tying a knot in the open end before dropping it on the top of the bedside cupboard.

'Now then Mark Watson you've a lot to learn and you need to because with a big dick like that you'll give a lot of pleasure to women if you do it right. Coo I know loads of girls who'd give a month's wages to have a shag with a dick like that. Now listen to me and I'll tell you about making love to a woman'.

At twenty two Debbie was only three years older than Mark but she was light years ahead of him in sexual experience having had her first full intercourse six years earlier on her sixteenth birthday with a spotty youth called Rodney who lived in the next street. They'd fumbled around for a while up in Rodney's bedroom while his parents were out and then they had finally done it. Not terribly successfully as it was a first time for them both but nevertheless Debbie had enjoyed it enough to decide that it was something that warranted further investigation. She'd then embarked on a wide ranging quest of sexual experiment with a varied selection of boys and young men and over the years had learnt to be a very competent lover.

Talking quietly to Mark about a woman's needs during lovemaking she made him examine her body closely and carefully. She told him about how to pace himself and how he should start slowly and then gradually build up speed and strength of thrusts. Mark listened, looked, learnt and after about half an hour was anxious to try again but she made him wait and teased him by insisting that he played with her small breasts. He learnt to stimulate her nipples then she made him sensuously massage her shoulders, neck, legs and buttocks. She made him examine her clitoris and pussy and taught him how to arose her there. Eventually seeing how desperate he was becoming she reached for another condom, rolled the protective onto him and invited him to practice what she'd taught him.

'Remember start slowly and build up. It's about us both getting enjoyment out of it' she warned as she helped him enter her for the second time that evening.

This time though it was entirely different. Debbie had turned it from an act of shagging into lovemaking and he realised what a difference there was. He took time trying to remember what she'd taught him and with her whispering in his ear encouraging him to go faster or slower, harder or more gently he felt himself slowly rising on a tide of passion towards his second climax. 'I'm nearly there' he gasped eventually and was relieved when she said that she was too. They both climaxed within seconds of each other and this time Debbie smiled up at him. 'There now wasn't that better?'

'Oh Debbie that was absolutely incredible. I just don't know what to say or how to thank you' he babbled until she put her finger over his lips.

'Schh it was good for us both' she smiled taking the condom off him when he slid down by her side. Again a quick knot and it joined the first one on her bedside table. 'Come on now my big lover boy it's time for some sleep' and with that she pulled the sheets, blankets and eiderdown over them and put her arms around him. Mark lay awake listening to Debbie's soft breathing. He felt totally fulfilled and marvelled at what lovemaking had been all about. Eventually he dropped off and slept soundly until Debbie woke him by poking him in the ribs.

'Its quarter to seven and I leave for the office around eight. There's one rubber left in the packet and it seems a shame to waste it' she grinned at him slowly fondling his balls.

Mark needed no second asking and he lay there while she rolled the rubber onto him. He was surprised and delighted when she climbed on top guided him into her and started to ride him. Leaning forward she kissed him.

'Remember take your time and be gentle darling' she whispered in his ear as running his hands over her breasts he thrust up to meet her movements and before long she groaned quietly with her pleasure as he jetted his seed into its rubber prison.

Afterwards she climbed off him, unrolled the contraceptive off his prick and then delighted him by leaning forward and kissing his exposed member. Knotting this last rubber she put it with the other two then slid out of bed. Reaching over she picked up the three used condoms with his emissions sealed inside and taking his hand dropped them in it. 'There now you can get rid of these' she laughed.

He wondered aloud what to do with them.

'Well you can take them home with you as a souvenir or you can flush them down the loo but if you do that make sure you put plenty of paper down at the same time otherwise they might just float. Any rate we've got to get on now or we'll both be late for work. I'll go to the bathroom first and then you can have your turn. You needn't worry about the old bat downstairs this morning as she goes to work at seven and she'll be gone by now'.

Placing the three used condoms on a small table by the door Mark started to worry about other things though as he found his pants and pulled them on. His shirt and suit trousers were all crumpled up on the floor where they'd fallen after the rather excited undressing session last night and he needed a shave. He was trying to wipe out the creases in his shirt when Debbie came back and wondered what he was doing. When he explained his problems she told him to go to the bathroom and she'd sort out his clothes. He didn't argue and gingerly picking up the three rubbers he went off to find the bathroom on the first floor landing.

Fortunately it was unoccupied so after a long and satisfying pee he tore off several sheets of paper and alternating paper and condom he soon had the three rubbers covered. Crossing his fingers he flushed the handle hard. For a moment he panicked as he thought that the bowl was going to block up with all the paper but giving a strangled gurgle it all disappeared although he did have a heart stopping moment when one of the condoms floated free and swirled around on the top of the water for a while before being sucked down. He met no-one returning to Debbie's room.

She was now partly dressed in a pretty little pink mini skirt with her legs encased in tights but as yet no bra or top on. However she had an iron in her hand and was running it over his shirt. When he asked if she had a spare razor she said no but he could use the one she used to shave her legs. Putting down the iron she went to another cupboard and handed him a plastic disposable razor. By the time he had scraped his stubble away cutting himself in a couple of places with the blunt razor and none too hot water that emerged from the sink tap, she'd restored some semblance of style back into his shirt and trousers.

The kettle was singing and he made them both a cup of coffee while she popped a couple of slices of bread under the little grill for some toast. Going to her dressing table she took out a black bra and after waggling her breasts at him she grinned then fastened the bra before pulling on a dark grey blouse to complete her dressing. Eating her toast she put on her eye makeup leaving her lipstick till later.

Just after eight o'clock they left her flat to go to their office. He dropped her off nearby then went and parked the car in the underground car park before strolling to the office well pleased with life.

During the morning, he slipped up to Debbie's cubby hole on a couple of occasions until he found a time when she was free to thank her for last night and wondered if they could go out again soon, perhaps even tonight.

She said she'd enjoyed it especially when she'd found what a good pupil he was but he wasn't to expect that she'd iron his shirt and trousers next time and yes she'd like to go out again but not just yet. Seeing his crestfallen face she assured him that it wasn't that she didn't want to see him or sleep with him but she didn't want to get serious and felt it best if they left it for a while. He was partly reassured by this but even more so when with a quick glance over his shoulder to make sure no-one was behind him she leant forward grabbed his crotch and grinning lewdly said that she definitely wanted to meet up again with what he had in there. Mark returned the grin and went back to his desk a happy man.

Over the following months he acquired new confidence with women and as well as regularly sleeping with Debbie he also broke his duck elsewhere and soon he had slept with half a dozen different girls including the dark haired Natasha who finally succumbed to him although continuing to protest that "she wasn't that sort of girl".

His work continued to be very good. One day Mr. Dunson suggested that he went to a conference that the company was giving for its sales and marketing departments. 'Marketing is the future my boy. It's time you went and learnt about it'.

So he did.

CHAPTER 6

From that first day when he went to that conference he was enthralled.

It was the Marketing men who devised the strategy for the sales force to implement with their customers. This was very different from the business which Mark's father Christopher and his partner Lionel had run. There they had to reply on their selling skills and relationships. Here, whilst selling skills were vitally important and relationships helped, it was a professional highly structured package of negotiations and deals linked to the enormous marketing support that enabled Thompson and Smith's sales force to compete against their competitors such as Beechams, Reckitt and Colman, Unilever and other huge conglomerates that also had marketing and advertising to support their own brands.

The conference started at ten o'clock and during the morning several different speakers spoke from the platform. There were presentations, speeches, slides and films of forthcoming TV commercials, detailed explanations of where the company's competitive advantages lay in comparison to its competitors, and where opportunities existed to grow its market share or distribution. There was information from the market research department about consumer purchasing habits, trade strengths and weaknesses, and a whole raft of phrases and information which frankly Mark didn't understand. However he made careful notes in the semi darkness on the conference pad he'd been given on entering the room and determined to find someone later on to explain it to him.

At the lunch break he sought out the Marketing Director Nick Davis, who was clearly in charge of proceedings and plied him with questions from the points he'd noted on his pad. When questioned as to who he was Mark explained when he'd joined the Company and what he did in the London office and said that he'd found the morning sessions extremely interesting. Nick answered Mark's questions for a while and then said 'Look why don't you and I get together at lunch and we can continue this conversation then. In the meantime I've got to check on a couple of things for this afternoon's sessions so you'll have to excuse me right now'.

Realising he'd been sidelined he wandered off to talk to other people until lunch was called and the milling throng numbering a couple of hundred made their way into the next door room already set out for the meal. Not knowing anyone Mark found a space at a table at the back. Sitting down he started on the pre laid out first course of melon and grapefruit listening to the conversation but not feeling able to contribute. Suddenly a hand gripped his shoulder.

'Ah there you are. I've been looking all over for you. I thought we had a conversation to finish'. Mark looked round and standing behind him was Nick Davis.

'Yes, but I thought that you'd be too busy to spend time talking to me'

'Not at all. Come on I've saved you a place next to me' and with that Nick strode confidently through the room until he reached a table near the front of the room. 'Here you are' he said pointing to one of two chairs that were unoccupied 'Sit there, fire away and we'll see if we can help you'.

He addressed this latter remark generally to the other people at the table who looked up puzzled until Nick explained. 'This young man works in our London office and has a number of questions about this morning's presentations. I seem to recall one of your questions is how we know that consumers are more likely to buy our new product in its new packaging than they were with the old pack? Seems a fair question to me. We may all know the answer but if we haven't explained it properly we need to do better. Now Raymond what's the answer to that eh?'

Realising that Nick had passed the question to the head of market research who had been another of the morning's speakers he listened carefully to the reply. 'Well the reason we know is that we went out and asked consumers what they liked and didn't like about our previous product pack and from that we were able to design new packaging and perfumes that more effectively fitted what the consumer was looking for'.

'Do you just go up to consumers in the street and ask?'

'Hardly' Raymond replied a little tetchily. 'We set up structured groups of consumers, called focus groups in various locations around the country and using a highly trained moderator we ask carefully designed questions to elicit the information we need. It's a very sophisticated process and is used by most major companies in the consumer market'.

'But how do you know that you've got the right answers and that these consumers aren't just giving you a load of old bullshit?'

Nick Davis roared with laughter. 'Often they do. The skill of the Market Research department and the Marketeers, Brand Managers and Marketing Managers is to interpret the data and make informed judgements. We can then test ideas either on a small scale or on a wider test market basis. At the end of the day that's what I'm paid for. To work with my team and make correct judgement calls. To decide what's bullshit in your terminology and what's real hard data. It's a combination of skill, science, art and a good dose of luck. Now does that make sense?'

'Yes and it sounds really exciting. I think I'd like to get into marketing'.

'Well maybe you will' replied Nick. 'Now eat your lunch as we'll be back in the conference soon'.

Mark ate but continued to ply those around him with questions until one by one they left the table and there were only a few people left in the lunch room and the conference was about to start again.

'Enjoy the afternoon sessions and never stop asking questions. Searching for the truth is what Marketing is all about' smiled Nick and shaking Mark's hand he too left the room followed by a very thoughtful young man.

The afternoon sessions were just as fascinating and at the end of the day Mark went home having had one of the most interesting days of his life.

The next day he asked Miss Trowse if he could see Mr. Dunson and she said she'd try and fit him in later in the morning. Around eleven Mr. Dunson rang Mark and said that he was free if he wanted to come in now. 'What can I do for you? Did you enjoy the conference?'

'Yes very much. That's what I wanted to see you about Mr. Dunson. I'd like to get into marketing. It's right at the heart of the Company's strategy and that's where I want to be. At the centre where the action is and the policy is made. I can see now where I want to go with my career'.

'I had a phone call from Nick Davis this morning about you. You made quite a hit with him yesterday. Well we'll have to see what we can do. No promises mind and for now get back to your desk and continue to do a good job with what you have at present'.

Mark walked back to his desk and worked like a fury on all his tasks that day. Several weeks went by and nothing materialised and he wondered if Dunson had forgotten. He mentioned it to Miss Trowse and asked her if she could remind him, but she said that she was sure that Mr. Dunson had matters in hand and to be patient.

But waiting was hard for Mark. More months went by and he was entering into his third year with the Company with still no sign of a move into Marketing. He distanced himself from both Rob and Malcolm who he saw were not career minded in the way that he was and he found that he didn't mind being a loner in the office.

He took Debbie out from time to time and occasionally slept with her but he also expanded his repertoire of other women that he persuaded to go to bed with him. He continued his rugby and swimming sports and enjoyed driving his old Beetle even though it seemed to break down more and more often nowadays but he couldn't afford to replace it and realised that it would just have to do for some time to come.

There was still no sign of any move and he started to wonder if he ought to think about changing Company when one morning as he worked at his desk Miss Trowse said that Mr. Dunson wanted to see him.

'What for?' he queried.

'Well you'd better go and find out hadn't you'.

Mark walked the short distance to Dunson's office, knocked and entered. 'You wanted me sir?'

'Ah yes my boy, come and sit down' replied the older man indicating an upright chair in front of his large mahogany desk. 'Now it's time we had a bit of a career talk. Careers are a joint process that we have to manage between us, you and the Company. When our two founders' he paused and looked almost reverently over to the photographs on the wall of the ancient starters of the business 'when they started to build their businesses all those years ago they didn't consider careers and ambition. No, their desire was to succeed and those that follow them like you and I who strive to continue their great work must look to the future, always remembering the lessons of the past. We learn from the past Watson to plan the future'.

Mark nodded sagely although really he hadn't a clue what the old man was on about.

'Lessons of the past, and opportunities in the future. That is business life Watson. The future. We have to grasp that future with both hands and exploit the opportunities that come our way. Sometimes of course we have to make our own opportunities whether that be in products, home environment, marriage or' he paused 'got a girlfriend have you? Any thoughts of marriage?'

'Yes, um no, I mean I've no regular girlfriend but I like girls and do go out with them', and a vision of Debbie with his prick in her mouth last week flashed into his mind. 'I've no thoughts of marriage, not yet at least' he added quickly in case Dunson thought he was queer, 'but in due course I'm sure I'll meet the right girl and settle down'

'Yes good that's the idea. Now then where were we?'

Oh fuck thought Mark. What the hell had the old goat been on about before he suddenly asked him if he was married but his extraordinary memory jumped to action and he smiled as he prompted Dunson, 'Er you were telling me about grasping opportunities Mr. Dunson in various spheres of life such as........'

'Exactly. That's it you see' interrupted Dunson. 'There we have it. That's what life is about. Opportunities. Now I expect you are wondering what lies ahead for you don't you? Well I would if I was in your shoes standing on the edge, on the very threshold of a great lifetime career. Do you realise Watson what lies ahead of you?' Mr. Dunson leaned forward and his voice became louder. 'A career that could lead you in time to the very top of this business. An opportunity eventually to become a Director. Well what do you say to that? Exciting prospect I'd say. Well?'

'Yes absolutely. Very exciting'. Now what was he going on about wondered Mark looking straight at Dunson?

'It's all in front of you. Everything. Work hard, be successful and it could all come your way in the future'. I know about these sorts of things' he said tapping the side of his somewhat veined nose. His voice was strong and quite loud and he had part risen from his chair.

'Well thank you Sir'. What Mark wanted to know was how Mr. Dunson thought that all these opportunities would come to him and while he was at it what about his request to go into marketing that he'd made several months ago.

'We'll miss you here Watson. You've done well and formed some firm foundations for your career' continued the older man as he sat back down in his chair.

Hang on a second did he say he'd miss him? Where was he expecting him to go he wondered? Surely he wasn't being sacked not after all that stuff about career and so on. This was crazy and muddled. Dunson smiled and stroked his white bristly moustache as Mark asked why he thought he'd be missed.

'What? Because you are leaving here to go into marketing that's why. Career move for you. First step on the ladder. Onwards and upwards. Big opportunity. From next Monday we're transferring you to Head Office in Leicester. You are on your way to great things'.

At last a move into marketing. His mind roved around the possibilities and the question of moving to Leicester however Dunson jerked him back to the present as he continued in a solemn voice.

'So remember laddie, learn from the past and build the future, yours and the Company's. Best of luck to you. Miss Trowse will give you all the details of where to go, who to report to and such like but I should like to thank you for all you've done here. I will be watching your future career with close attention. Good luck Mark' and with that he stood, walked round the desk and shook Mark's hand firmly.

Mark was quite touched and especially by the use of his Christian name. He'd never known old Dunson call anyone by their Christian name. It was always surname for men sometimes prefixed by Mr if it was one of his superiors or no prefix if it was someone of junior rank. In the case of women it was always Miss or Mrs, never their Christian name. 'Thank you sir, I'll do my best and try not to let you down'

'Better not damn you. Now off you go'.

Mark walked back to his general office in a bit of a daze but was pleased when Miss Trowse came over smiled and said 'Jolly good, richly deserved and I'm sure you'll go far', then turning to Rob and Malcolm she announced Mark's move. The reaction from the other two young men was interesting. Malcolm said congratulations and that he'd buy

Mark a pint at lunch time, but Rob just muttered that it was alright for some and carried on reading the morning paper, not having really started to do any work yet.

The rest of the week went by slowly but on Friday he was quite moved when Miss Trowse told him that she had brought in a cake which she had baked herself and with the afternoon tea she cut him a large slice and smaller slices for the others. She gave him a card which everyone in the office had signed.

Most had written a few words of good luck or encouragement. He particularly liked Debbie's which said, *"Love and kisses and don't forget what you've learnt!!"*

Even Rob shook his hand, admittedly a little reluctantly. Just before five o'clock as Mark walked round saying good bye to everyone he felt that he was on the verge of an important change in his life and was pleased and somewhat surprised by the real feelings of warmth with which people wished him luck and said to keep in touch. When he got to Debbie having checked that non-one else was around she pulled him into her little cubby hole to give him a hard kiss with her tongue teasing into his mouth.

'Anytime you want a bit of fun especially with that big dick of yours you know where to come' she giggled pressing her crotch against him. 'Come. Get it?' and she went into peals of laughter. 'Go on away with you and good luck lover'.

He packed his briefcase, looked at his grey metal desk for the last time, checked that he had emptied everything personal out of the drawers, picked up the thick brown envelope which contained all his instructions and rail tickets to get to Leicester next week, and finally on an impulse went over and gave Miss Trowse a kiss on her cheek. He noticed her quite pronounced dark moustache and somewhat leathery skin but grinned at her startled confusion, and giving a cheery wave, walked out of the old building, down the marble steps and walking quickly with all the rest of the Friday evening rush hour crowds to Tottenham Court tube station, made his way via tube and British Railways, home to Wallington in Surrey where Betty asked if his last day in London had been alright.

Yes he had said. It had been fine.

CHAPTER 7

Miss Trowse had given him a rail voucher so setting off on Sunday afternoon he travelled from Wallington to London Bridge then caught the tube across to St Pancras Station where he waited for nearly an hour until there was a train going to Leicester. It was a slow journey and the train seemed to stop everywhere but eventually around seven thirty he arrived and took a taxi to the hotel into which he'd been booked.

The hotel restaurant was closed so he wandered along the streets until he found an Indian restaurant whose owners were pleased to serve him and he enjoyed a medium curry and a couple of pints of lager before returning to the hotel for an early night.

The next morning he was awake early, washed, shaved, and made his way downstairs where he asked the hotel porter to call him a taxi which arrived after about ten minute wait. The journey didn't take long to the Head Office of Thompson and Smith and Mark was suitably impressed with the building when he arrived.

He paused for a moment before entering reception where a pretty receptionist smiled and asked if she could help him.

'Yes, I hope so. I'm Mark Watson to see Nick Davis'.

'I don't think he's in yet. Hang on, I'll check for you' and she dialled a number. When it was answered she asked whoever was on the other end of the line whether Nick had arrived. She listened for a minute or two then looked at Mark before returning to the conversation. 'OK I'll send him up in the lift and you'll meet him will you? Right ho, bye'. Putting the phone down she said that he should take the lift to the fourth floor where Carol, Nick's secretary would meet him.

Getting out of the lift he was non-plussed to see no-one there. It seemed that the lift had dropped him off in the middle of the building however a sound of clicking heels on the hard surface of the corridor floor got steadily louder and from round a corner which he had not observed, a small petite smartly dressed young woman walked quickly up to him.

'Hi I'm Carol. I work for Nick. Sorry to keep you waiting. Come along and I'll show you around. Is this your first visit here?'

Following her he noticing how her backside moved nicely inside the rather tight black skirt she was wearing. Leading him though the

Marketing department which was largely deserted she explained that most of the marketeers arrived around nine fifteen but they tended to work late in the evenings.

Mark's eyes swivelled everywhere as he was walked through the department. He saw posters, advertising material, lots of the company's and competitor's products. Many of the walls were covered with graphs and charts. There were maps with parts of the country coloured in, and statements above such as **"Northern test market area"**, or **"Test Market – New Formula"**. Although not totally incomprehensible to him he realised that he had masses to learn.

Soon Carol stopped at a door which unlike all the other office doors that had plain glass so anyone could see in this one had frosted glass with just a tiny clear peephole. She opened it and led the way in. There was a quite large desk, a couple of chairs in front of it, a small round meeting table with another four upright chairs, a bookcase and on the walls several plaques, certificates and pictures of products, or audiences attending conferences.

'Nick will be here soon. Would you like a coffee while you wait? There's a Times newspaper on his desk. Have a read he won't mind' and with that she bustled out leaving Mark alone. He picked up the paper but couldn't concentrate and after sitting for a few minutes started to wander around when Carol brought in his coffee. 'Only dishwater slop from the machine at the moment I'm afraid. If you need me I'm just next door. Oh and by the way, welcome. You're going to be working here in marketing aren't you?'

'Yes and thanks for the coffee' replied Mark staring her in the eyes as he savoured the statement that he was going to be working in marketing. He continued to study the photographs, posters and other items on the walls when suddenly the door burst open and in strode Nick Davis.

'Hi there. You're an early bird. Afraid we don't start early but we do work late here. Now then Carol's fixed you up with coffee. Good'. He plonked himself down in his swivel chair and leaned back. 'What I thought we'd do is spend about an hour together and I'll tell you about the department, our objectives, what we're working on and so on. Then Carol will take you round and introduce you to the team, finishing with Keith Walters who'll be your mentor, boss, teacher, manager and pain the neck' laughed Nick. 'But he's good and you'll learn a lot from him. It won't be long before he gets promoted'.

'Lets start though with a few facts about you shall we. All I know is that you quizzed me at the conference and I have to say that you asked some very sensible questions. Mr. Dunson has given you an excellent reference' he said taking a file out of his drawer and putting it on his desk. 'He may be getting on, and a bit of an old stickler but he knows a good chap when he sees one.'

Mark looked at Nick and saw a young man probably a little over thirty, confident, well groomed, wafting of aftershave and obviously comfortable and confident with his role at work.

'You didn't go to University did you? Why was that? I'm surprised, as you went to a good school and I'd have thought that you'd want to go on to uni'.

'I wanted to get to work. I want to get to the top of a business and I didn't think that I needed to go to University to do that. I'm a quick learner and if you'll just give me the chance I'll prove to you that I can make it to the top. My father......' he paused but decided not to reveal the collapse of A and W. 'My father was in business and I want to do as well or better on my own' he finished a little lamely.

Nick studied him carefully and knew that there was more to what Mark had been saying then he had actually said but he let it go and didn't press the point. He'd also seen something in Mark's blue eyes that he couldn't quite place but it had looked as though they had turned very cold. It was a strange effect. 'Alright let's move on. So what did you think of the conference?'

He watched Mark's eyes carefully but whatever he'd seen had disappeared and they appeared quite normal again. He wondered if he'd imagined it. Odd.

'Oh it was great, but ....'

'Go on'.

'Well I thought that some of the messages to the sales force were a bit muddled. It might have been better if there had been some priorities allocated at the end. As far as I could see it was left to the salesmen and their managers to sort out the priorities. Surely some of the things presented and talked about were more important than others. You probably think differently but you asked and that's what I think. Overall though it was very good. It's just that I think it could have been better but I really enjoyed it. I've never been to anything like that before'.

'Nick looked at him smiled and said that his comments were helpful and he'd think about it. Forget about it you mean thought Mark.

The remainder of the hour went quickly with Nick explaining the role of marketing. 'Essentially it is to identify consumer demand and then provide products or services that satisfy that demand. You'll find lots of text book descriptions and loads of bullshit about marketing but at the end of the day that's what it's about'. He finished by running through the three main objectives that he'd set his department which were Innovation, New Product Development and improving Company profitability.

'Is profitability a problem then' queried Mark.

'Good lord no but my job, indeed the job of any executive in the Company is to improve margins and hence profitability. With increased profitability we can re-invest in the business in new equipment, new factories, more advertising to drive sales and increase revenue, fund more market research to find new wonder products or packaging, improve the dividend to shareholders and finally and most important of all pay ourselves lots more money. Come on I'll hand you over to Carole and she'll start you off on your rounds. Hey, don't look so worried. I'm sure you'll do alright. Mr. Dunson says that you are a quick learner'

He picked up the phone pressed a button and asked Carol to come in. 'Right off on the grand tour. Show him it, warts and all and I'd like him to sit in on this morning's review meeting at twelve'.

Inviting him to follow her she explained that marketing was spread over the whole of this fourth floor which was laid out like an H. She diligently took him from office to office, person to person and finished as instructed by introducing him to Keith Walters.

Keith was a big gangling sort of chap with overlong hair, dressed somewhat flamboyantly with a pink shirt, light grey suit and a loud blue and pink tie who Mark guessed was only a couple of years older than himself. 'Hello good to have you on board. We're bloody well snowed under here. Got a couple of recent new launches that we need to review and a complete re-launch coming up. Fucking mayhem it is so am I glad to see you. Know anything about marketing do you?' and seeing Mark's negative nod beamed at him.

'Good. Then we can get you on the right lines from the start. Now start by having a read of that' he said passing over a thick folder which was marked on the outside "PROJECT DOUBLE".

'We've got a meeting coming up this afternoon, well just after lunch in fact with the Sales Director Peter Feldman. Nick'll be there as well, as will some Agency people and no doubt a few hangers on. It's the plans for our aerosol range relaunch.

Now you're in the office next door to this one with Simon only he's on holiday at the moment. Bloody inconvenient. My other two guys are Doug and Jerry. Sound like a couple of cartoon characters don't they. Hi folks, it's the Doug and Jerry show' he said in an American accent. 'Mark and Simon sound much more businesslike don't they?' he laughed. 'Thanks Carol I'll look after him now. You've done your mother hen bit. Off you go back to Nick and keep him out of my hair this morning will you there's a love. Buy you a coffee this afternoon if you keep him away from me till after lunch'.

'Wow a whole cup of machine coffee. How could I refuse an offer like that? Alright you've got a deal' smiled Carol. By the way Nick wants Mark to attend the review meeting at twelve'.

'Whatever for?'

'No idea he didn't say. See you' and she walked off heels tapping along the corridor.

'Come on next door then' said Keith wincing as he got up and limped towards the door. 'Got a right thumping on Saturday and feeling it a bit today' he said ruefully then seeing Marks questioning look added 'rugby'

'Oh where do you play........prop forward I guess?'

'Know about the beautiful game do you?' and he listened with interest as Mark explained how he'd played at school and for the Old Whitgiftians.

'Great. Now here's where you'll be sharing with Simon' and he led the way into an extremely untidy office full of boxes, samples, leaflets, files and what seemed to be just piles and piles of papers and magazines. 'He's an untidy bugger and no mistake' grumbled Keith. 'I must have a word when he gets back. Make yourself at home there' he suggested picking up a great pile of assorted papers off the desk he indicated would be Marks. 'Stick 'em all on Simon's desk. That'll make him sort it out when he gets back. Now get stuck into that folder so you know something about it for the meeting this afternoon' and with that he hobbled back into his own office.

Mark settled down and started reading the folder. It explained the reasons for relaunching the aerosol air freshener range due to falling sales and a recent competitive launch of a product which had better designs, stronger perfumes and lasted longer. Now Thompson and Smith's technologists had come up with something better and the company was very excited about the possibilities for this innovative new product and was developing some creative advertising to explain the benefits to the consumer as the product was extremely effective and a real leap forward in aerosol spray technology.

Mark was fascinated by the cleverness of the invention and quite riveted to the folder when suddenly the phone rang and Carol was reminding him that it was nearly twelve o'clock and that he should not forget to go to the review meeting. She gave him directions as to how to find the meeting room in which the discussions were to take place so he made his way down two flights of stairs and along a corridor which had solid doors so he was unable to see who or what went on behind them.

He found meeting room four and knocking firmly walked in. There were several people there some of whom looked up at him and others just carried on chatting. Nick Davis sitting at the head of the meeting table looked over to him and smiled. 'Right guys I think we're all here, just Adam late as usual. By the way everyone this is Mark Watson who's joined us today'. Mark looked around him at the assorted people at the meeting and nodded. Some smiled, some nodded, and one or two said hello or welcome. 'Now then the fifth item on the agenda I'd like to move up and take first because I want Mark to have some input to it and then we can release him.' There were some looks of surprise around the table not least from Mark himself. Looking over his neighbour's arm to study the agenda he saw item five was headed "Aerosol Re-launch Conference".

'Mark was at a previous conference and has some interesting ideas as to how we can make conferences more effective, don't you?' announced Nick looking at him across the table. 'Felt things needed prioritising, wasn't that it?' he added helpfully.

Mark gulped as everyone's eyes were on him. Crikey. Nick had listened to him after all. He took a breath and was about to start when just at that moment the door banged opened and another person flustered his way in muttering 'Sorry I'm late' to Nick who pointedly looked at his watch. Mark wasn't sure if he was indicating displeasure that he hadn't started to respond to his question about the conference or whether he was niggled that this newcomer was late to the meeting. Deciding that it was the latter he refocused his mind to answer the question especially when he saw that Nick was looking at him.

'Err yes, that's right. There was so much information put across. I know that it was the first one I'd been to and also I know that I've not been in sales or marketing, but I did talk to some of the other people there and they felt a bit lost as to what was important and a priority, and what wasn't'.

He paused and looked around the table and to his surprise no-one looked hostile but were all looking intently at him and what he was saying, so feeling more confident and making his voice stronger he went on. 'Look during the day there were eight or nine speakers and at the end someone should have said that out of everything that had been presented, the key issues were so and so. That this item was the most important and that item was second, and so on throughout the programme. I think if you got the sales force organised with the priorities you want rather than leaving it to their sales managers to sort it out, you'd have a much more effective and cohesive plan of action across the country'. He paused and finished by saying, 'Well that's what I think anyhow', and he sat back and waited for the reaction.

'Well guys what do we think?' asked Nick. 'If we do it it'll be important to agree the priorities and if you lot can't do that amongst yourselves, then I'll sort it out with Paul. Sounds like it might just be worth a try. After all we've nothing to lose and possibly a great deal to gain. Everyone agree?'

There were several nods of assent from round the table, a few muttered "maybes", and a couple of "yea let's give it a go" type comments and Mark saw that his idea was to be implemented by them. Nick thanked him for his contribution and looked back down to the agenda. 'Now item one'.

Realising that he wasn't wanted any longer he walked out of the room to return to the chaotic office on the fourth floor that he was to share with Simon realising that Nick had not only listened this morning but had asked for his views in front of all the people in that meeting and then agreed to put his plan into action. He'd recognised some of the people as speakers at the conference so he guessed they all probably worked for Nick.

Returning to the folder that Keith had asked him to read he was still engrossed when Keith looked round the door. 'Lunchtime, hungry?'

Keith limped and Mark walked beside him down to the far end of the corridor where they got into a different lift from the one that Mark had ridden up in earlier that morning. 'Canteen's on the ground floor' explained Keith. 'Have you had a good morning?'

Mark explained about the meeting. Keith grinned and said that it was good that he'd started to make an impression already and that if Mark was that good he'd better watch his back or Mark would soon be his boss! 'Actually' he continued 'I think you're right. We do chuck an awful lot of stuff out at people at those conferences. Some sort of priority system would be a bloody good idea. Now here we are, it's not exactly the Ritz but it's OK'.

After lunch as they made their way back upstairs Mark asked as casually as he could as to who was the pretty redhead he'd noticed in the canteen and where she worked?

'Hey you're a fast worker aren't you? Only just arrived and after the crumpet already. Karen Parker and she's a supervisor in customer service and before you ask' he laughed 'customer service is on the second floor. Now about this meeting this afternoon with Nick and Paul on Project Double.

Paul will be looking for points of competitive advantage over the competition. That could be in price, product superiority, packaging, launch incentives to the trade in fact anything that will give us an edge in this market.

Nick on the other hand whilst understanding those needs will want to ensure that the products fit our overall brand image and are complimentary to existing products from the company'.

Later as they made their way to the meeting Mark realised that there was a lot of complex thinking as well as logic and science to this marketing business and he was interested to see how the meeting would go as they made their way to the conference room.

Inside a tall man in his fifties was propped against the edge of the large meeting table swinging his leg as he chatted to another younger man that Mark also hadn't seen before. The Market Research Manager sitting at the table nodded in a friendly way to him. Nick Davis soon joined them. 'Right shall we start?' asked Keith looking at Nick, who nodded.

'Paul you haven't met Mark Watson who's joined us in marketing today and he'll be working with me' said Keith looking at the Sales Director who flashed a quick smile at Mark muttered 'Hello' and picked up the sheath of papers that Keith slid across the table to each participant at the meeting. Emblazoned on the front page under a clear plastic cover was printed an entwined pair of A's symbolising Double Air, the name of the re-launch product.

Turning to his colleague he said in a stage whisper that everyone could hear 'Well the cover looks good, but let's see if the plans and contents inside are any good. Any fool can draw pretty pictures!' He looked up and smiled. 'Sorry, we're ready and waiting to learn what pearls of wisdom are about to fall upon the table' and as he spoke he held his hands out palms up in a gesture which Mark thought probably was intended to indicate openness but in reality was a challenge.

Keith launched into a detailed explanation of the latest version of the launch plans and product benefits which consumer research had shown to be a potential real winning idea with the public. He went through Paul's previous objections and the list of points he'd raised at the last meeting and showed how they had virtually all been dealt with satisfactorily. A couple were still to be resolved but dates were given by which they would be sorted out. Paul said nothing just listened intently.

Keith talked fluently for about ten minutes and Mark listened carefully to words that were like a foreign language to him. Phrases such as *"consumer propensity to purchase"*, which he later found meant "would they buy it". *"Substitution matrix"* – bought instead of another product. *"Ethereal appeal"* – generally liked. *"Mood styles"* – how did the public feel. *"Sensual stimulation"* – was it easy to hold. *"Emotional time segmentation"* – morning, afternoon or night time; and many more.

Some he worked out, others he made a mental note to ask Keith about afterwards.

Paul seemed happy enough so far and although Nick also asked some detailed questions he too seemed ok with the project.

'What margin are we going to get on this?' snapped Paul suddenly.

'Better than the existing range that it will replace'

'Have Finance passed these?' was Paul's next query.

'Yes they're fine with them'.

'Where's their formal approval? I can't see their authorisation sheet confirming the profit margin'.

'It'll be there when you get the final pack to sign off to confirm the launch. This is still very much work in progress paperwork' explained Keith. 'What I wanted to do today was just get everyone up to speed with where we are with the run up to launch'.

'OK now what about the impact on the production lines in the factory. Presumably you're going to pack this in our Manchester plant?' asked Nick.

'That's certainly the most likely location, but we are just finally checking out Southampton who are keen to have it. An outside runner, but worth a look'.

'Southampton?' snorted Paul. 'No chance. They never produce anything on time. Their customer service is crap. It'll be a balls up from start to finish. Abso-fucking-lutely no way' he finished aggressively sticking out his chin.

'Paul' chided Nick gently supporting Keith. 'We need to check it out. Their production costs are much lower and the benefit to the margin is tremendous. Could generate nearly a million pounds extra margin in the launch year'.

'You don't get any profit if you don't deliver product. This launch will be tough enough without Southampton buggering it up. I've told you Nick, no way, no way' he repeated tapping the table firmly and looking straight at Mark, Nick then finally at Keith.

Keith and Paul glared at each other in silence for a few moments.

'Well' interjected Nick 'either they sort it and damn quickly in which case I agree it should go to Southampton or' and he raised his voice over Paul's loud grunt. 'If they can't then we'll have to find a way of raising the margin out of Manchester. Now Keith where are we on advertising?'

'We're a bit behind on that I'm afraid'.

Why?'

'I guess it's just a clash of priorities but now Mark's joined us we'll get back on track quickly. The ad guys are here today to review progress with me later this afternoon'.

'You'll have to. No point in launching if we've no advertising support. Right now let's summarise. By Friday firstly I want the production location sorted. Second I want an update on where the ad's got to, and lastly I need to see Finance's sign off on Double Air.

Thanks everyone, sorry I've got another meeting to go to' and with that he got up and walked quickly towards the door where he paused, looked straight at Keith and said sharply 'Friday. This Friday, ok?' and with that he went out of the room. They went through a few further points before the meeting started to break up and the participants started to make their way out.

Paul called over to Keith 'Forget Southampton. I'll never agree so just bloody forget it and stick it into Manchester. Barry up there won't let us down unlike that other clown down south'.

Mark followed a clearly angry Keith back to their offices where he sat down crossly in his chair. 'That bloody Paul. We've got a real problem now he's made such a fuss about where it's produced'.

'Yes but why didn't Nick support you more strongly? He's your boss; shouldn't he have helped you out?

'Ah well it's all politics. You see Nick is very career conscious and didn't want to be seen to be arguing too strongly for a solution which might jeopardise this launch. He knows it's crucial that production is alright and that there are no screw ups. Nothing pisses off our customers and therefore the sales force more than being let down on supply.

If that happens Paul goes apeshit because he misses his launch sales distribution and brand share targets and not only does that not put him in a good light with the Managing Director who'll bollock him up hill and down dale, but he and his team miss out on bonus earnings.

You see part of the sales force earnings are related to how much they sell. The Company allocates additional bonus or commission payments to be earned during new launches and if for whatever reason their sales fall short it hits them in the pocket. That's part of what is behind Paul's aggro. The other part is a genuine desire to get this product launched effectively and not to let customers down. And of course to avoid getting kicked by Bill.

Now if Nick forces production to Southampton and it all gets screwed up then it would be him in the firing line when the launch reviews were undertaken of how badly it's all gone. He does have a problem though. We desperately need the additional profit margin that Southampton can give us, but we can't afford to short deliver product.

Welcome to the world of Sales and Marketing. Two functions that need each other, rely on each other, work with each other but continually fight with each other. It's like Sales and Production, they're always at loggerheads with each other, as are Marketing and Finance.

Business, at least our sort of business is a continual fight between departments and people to win internal battles, to score points, to enhance careers, to fight and climb up the ladder. Push rivals down or off the career ladder. To get promoted and hence more money, more responsibility and a company car; then get a bigger company car, more responsibility, more money, and battle all the way to the top. It's a rough tough world Mark and don't you ever forget it. We're all in the fight and there are fewer and fewer winners. And why do we all do it? Because we love it. We love the fighting, the in-fighting, the jockeying for position for power. We love to win and we love to see the other guy screw up. You might wonder why this Double Air launch is so important to me.

I don't give a flying fuck for it as a product. I don't give a stuff about its fancy nozzle. I don't even have a great desire to fragrance people's homes better. I simply don't care what happens to it in the long term. But what I do care about is getting it launched on time, on budget, and to support that launch with great advertising so we can gain market share. Ok it's a great product and does just what it's supposed to do. Kills smells immediately because of the special spray, and then fragrances the room for a long time afterwards because of the soft gel. It'll enhance the Company's reputation in this category and build up our business.

But for me none of that matters. What does matter is that I can score some great big ticks on my career ladder.

There's going to be some restructuring of the Company coming up shortly. Not just our Division but the whole lot and they'll be some big, yes real big marketing jobs up for grabs and I want one of those. I've worked for it, developed my career, done lots of good things and now I want the next promotion. I'm ready for it and if I don't get it here then I'll go elsewhere to another company to get it. So Mark, you see even I have a personal axe to grind in this launch plan'.

He paused grinned ruefully at Mark and then added 'Hey don't look so surprised. This is the big wide corporate world. The business world. Dog eat dog. Big fish eats little fish. Better marketeer clobbers lesser marketeer, and it's great. So come on lets work out what the hell we're going to do. Any ideas?'

Mark stared straight at him and said simply 'Sort out Southampton. Find out why they screw up and fix it. Or get Manchester to get their costs down. Seems to me you......we've got to get one or other done'.

'Ah ha what a simple answer. Why didn't I think of that?' queried Keith sarcastically. 'Look Manchester is a great plant but its labour costs are high, and its production efficiencies are low because they've got lots of old machinery, hence its costs are high. But it is reliable. Whatever the production plan is up there gets produced, on time regular as clockwork. Furthermore the Plant Manager is tough who doesn't stand any nonsense from the work force. They don't particularly like him but they do respect him and they keep to the Union agreements. You don't get wildcat strikes or walkouts up there. Not with Barry running the place.

Now Jack down at Southampton, nice bloke but promises the earth and always comes in short. Too nice if you ask me. Got efficient machinery and lower labour costs but never quite makes it happen on time. He'll get some product away on schedule but one variety will be late or short. Or the whole lot'll be a couple of days late. There's always some bloody reason why it doesn't happen like it should. With the tight timescales we and our customers work to that spells disaster. Much as I don't like it I think it'll have to be Manchester. We can't take the risk or Paul will chop my balls into small pieces'.

'Why don't we go talk to Southampton. See if we can plan things better. Maybe find out if they need some help. Isn't that worth a try?'

Keith said nothing for a few minutes while he scratched his untidy hair then he picked up his phone and dialled a number.

'Nick, it's Keith. I'm going to send Mark down to Southampton tomorrow. Let him talk to Jack and see if there's any chance of getting a sensible production plan out of there'. He paused and listened and then went on. 'Yes of course it's risky and I know that Mark's only just got here but he's been with the Company over three years, he's a bright lad and I'd value his thoughts'. He listened again. 'We've nothing to lose. In the meantime I'll prepare a plan for Manchester and get on with finalising the advertising. Can you and I talk about that later this afternoon by the way? Mark'll be back tomorrow night and we'll make a decision first thing Wednesday morning'. He listened some more and finished with an 'Ok see you at four thirty to talk ads. Thanks'.

Mark looked at his watch. An hour before the next meeting with Nick. Keith asked if apart from the production issue there was anything else that Mark wanted to talk about on Double Air. He answered the few general questions that Mark threw at him and then smiled when he was asked why the product was to have two holes in the nozzle.

'Ah now that is clever' replied Keith. 'Don't know why no-one's thought of it before. It provides what the Research and Development boys call

> "a more comprehensive yet diverging delivery of perfumed gas in a lateral spray pattern which generates greater effectiveness in odour masking performance".

He grinned. 'It means it sprays out more jollop and stinks the room out better. You see what happens with this new product is that unlike existing aerosol products which have just one jet of perfumed air shooting out to a normal distance of about twelve inches, with Double Air two jets fire out in diverging directions. This means that although they start with the two nozzle holes only an eighth of an inch apart by the time the jet of perfumed air has reached the end of its reach, which is still around twelve inches away from the can, the gas jets are then about ten inches apart at that point. As a result when the consumer presses the button the product is spraying over a much wider area. Coupled with the fact that most consumers wave an aerosol can around when they are using it the whole effect is to cover a much greater area of the room more quickly and so it gives a faster odour killing property.

Add to this the soft gel benefit which provides lasting room freshening then the advantage created by the quick odour kill is enhanced by the long term fragrancing of the room.

The final key to its potential success is its shape. As you can see it is designed to look like a candle. After all consumers are unlikely to leave an aerosol can around, but if it is attractive or different in design as this is, then there is a high probability that they will do just that. Look at the research on this point. It makes interesting reading. Overall we think that we've got a real winner here.

Only a couple of downsides though. One is that the double nozzle is made in Japan which is a bloody long way to get urgent supplies if we've screwed up the forecasts of likely sales, and secondly it isn't too easy to apply the special nozzle cap with the soft gel part. Still Southampton factory have been doing trials and fingers crossed they can do it. At least they say they can. I bloody hope so'.

They discussed it for a little while then made their way to yet another conference room where the two advertising men were waiting who outlined to Keith where they'd got to in developing the advertising support for Double Air. Again strange phrases came into play *"rate card"*, *"spot buy"*, *"fixed slot"*, and many more.

Mark listened carefully and was slightly surprised when the more senior ad man asked him that he thought of the advertising proposal. He answered with a phrase that over the years was to become one of his favourites when talking to advertising people. 'Well I'm not sure I really understand all that mumbo jumbo you've been talking but will your adverts sell our product? That's what seems to me to matter'.

There was silence. 'But this is going to be great advertising' replied Vic the senior ad man puzzled.

'Will it sell our product?'

'We're building a brand image here. This could be one of the great advertising campaigns. This could win awards' lisped the junior ad man.

'We're trying to sell a new product with considerable benefits to a sceptical consumer public. What we want isn't great advertising that wins awards but effective advertising that sells products' riposted Mark taking an instant dislike to the poof opposite.

Keith who had sat back amused and interested in Mark's intervention now joined in the discussion which flowed back and forth for a while until he said that they ought to go and discuss with Nick so they all trooped off to Nick's office. Carol saw the contingent arriving and walked into Nick's office and came out beckoning them in. As they filed past her she smiled at Mark and asked how he was getting on. He grinned and said that everything was great.

The meeting went on for nearly an hour with intense debate going over different issues and approaches. Nick and Keith challenged the ad men who in fairness to them stood their ground and argued the case for their primary creative approach rather than the alternatives which they also had brought with them. Eventually Nick turned to Mark and asked him what he thought.

'Well I don't know much about it but if it sells product I guess it's ok. If it doesn't......then I'd forget it'. The poof scowled at him.

Nick looked at him smiled and said 'I think it will and I think it will also create a strengthening of the brand franchise amongst our core loyal users out there together with generating trial amongst new users. Right guys, lets take it to storyboard and script stage. I need that by Thursday please.

The two ad men got up to leave and shaking hands walked out of Nick's office. The poofy one who Mark later found out was called Julian which he thought was highly applicable, continued scowling as he left.

'That should get 'em working their balls off. Thanks Nick' said Keith.

'No problem. It's what I'm here for. By the way I do think they have got the potential of a great campaign there and let's hope it sells lots of product eh Mark? Now you are going to Southampton? I think it's a lost cause, still see what you can find out. Maybe you'll strike lucky. Anything else Keith? No?. Ok then. See you later guys' and with that Mark and Keith were dismissed.

Keith went into the room on the other side of the corridor where Carol and several other secretaries and typists were located. Many were packing up for the day and clearly some had already gone but Carol was there reading back her shorthand and typing furiously. She looked up. 'Brought me my coffee Keith?' then laughed when he immediately looked guilty. 'I kept Nick off your back for you like you asked so where's my reward?'

'I'll get it' said Mark and he rushed down the corridor to the nearest coffee machine returning shortly with the hot cup of liquid 'White no sugar, is that alright?'

'Fine thanks. Now look I'm right up to my eyes. Nick wants this typed up for first thing tomorrow. What do you want?'

'A car for Mark. Got any spare pool cars he can have to go to Southampton?'

'Hang on I'll ring Fred' and she dialled a number. 'Fred darling its Carol, Nick's secretary. I know it's late and short notice but could you do me a really big favour' she paused and put on a wheedling voice. 'Please Fred it's ever so important and Nick will go loopy if I don't get a car for our new chap tonight. He's got to go to Southampton tomorrow. Can you help me, please Fred'. She listened for a moment and then turned to the two marketers giving a thumps up. 'Oh you are a sweetie. You've saved me from a fate worse than death. I'll get him to come down and collect it. Yes of course, immediately. He's called Mark by the way. Thanks again, Fred you are an angel. Bye'.

Following Carol's instructions to collect the car straight away and putting up with Fred's grumbling about 'You marketing blokes who think you rule the world', Mark kept his cool and thanked Fred for the car which was a fairly new Ford Cortina. He drove it carefully round to the company car park then returned to his office where he found a pile of papers, announcements, circulars, instructions, sales figures, market research data and assorted information had been placed on his desk.

He was fully engrossed when a cheery voice said 'Come on times up for tonight. The Woolpack beckons'. Turning he saw Doug, one of Keith's other Product Managers. 'Some of us usually have a couple of beers before we go home. Fancy joining us? What do you drink by the way?' Mark told him a pint of bitter would be great so Doug stuck his head out into the corridor and yelled to Jerry who was nearly at the lift 'Usual for me and Mark would like a pint'. Pushing into Keith's office he said 'Just initiating Mark into the nightly pint routine Keith. You coming?'

'No not tonight. Got to finish this and then I'm off home. Thanks all the same. Another night eh?'

'Ok another night it is' then turning to Mark he winked. 'That's the trouble with being newly married. Work hard all day and then home for a night of lust, lucky sod. His wife's a cracker. Works in the lab here. Come on then' and as they left Keith took a piece of discarded paper out of the waste paper bin, screwed it into a ball and threw it at his grinning subordinate.

Doug introduced Mark to several people in the pub and he found it easy to talk to them. Around nine o'clock people started to drift away so he walked back to the company car park and drove carefully to his Hotel where after parking cautiously as the car was quite a bit bigger than his little Beetle, he went into the dining room, ordered a steak and salad and another pint of beer.

Later he went to bed and set his alarm for five am so he could make a good early start for Southampton.

CHAPTER 8

Woken by the shrill ringing of his alarm he jumped out of bed straight away to avoid the risk of dropping back off to sleep, washed, shaved, dressed, made his way downstairs and let himself out of the hotel front door. The Cortina started first go unlike his old Beetle which was often temperamental.

He headed south wondering what he would find at the Southampton factory and how he would explain the purpose of his visit.

'Excuse me I've come to find out why you keep ballsing up your production?' Or 'Everyone says you can't keep to production schedules. Why is that?'

Maybe a more subtle approach would be better. 'I wonder if you could reassure me that if you are given this launch of Double Air we'll be able to rely on you producing what you say you will?'

Suppose they told him to bugger off. After all he had no authority, no official reason to be there except that Keith had said that he should go. Well it had been his idea which Keith had accepted but he had no idea how he was going to approach Jack the Factory Manager who would be much more senior in the company than he was. Passing Winchester he eventually came to the outskirts of the great seaport of Southampton. Keith had given him a map to find the factory taken from one of the Company manuals of site locations and after a few false turns he finally drove down a white concrete road alongside a green fence until he came to the main entrance which sported a large notice:

THOMPSON AND SMITH

SOUTHAMPTON FACTORY

He drove up to the gatehouse, explained who he was and said that he wanted to see Jack the Factory Manager. 'Is he expecting you?' asked the security man.

'I'm not sure but I have something important to discuss with him'

'Wait a minute' and he turned away and picked up the phone. Mark couldn't hear what was being said, but he noticed the security man looking at him from time to time as he spoke on the phone.

What on earth would he do if Jack wouldn't see him? He'd come all this way but he should have rung up yesterday and made an appointment. What a bloody fool he was and what would Nick, Keith and the others say and think about him. He could imagine the other marketers teasing him in the pub as the man who drove all the way down to Southampton to see the factory manager without an appointment, only to find that he wasn't there. Shit what a pratt he was.

'Drive down that road to the left, park in front of the building and go into reception. Someone will help with you, and drive slowly there's a five mile an hour speed limit on site'.

Mark did as he was told relieved that he'd not been turned away out of hand. Entering reception the girl behind the desk asked if he was the person who wanted to see Mr. Elvers? While she rang through to announce his arrival he studied the various notice boards. Some showed charts of production output in graph form with different colours to indicate performance this year, last year and their target. Mark observed that this year was above last year but often dropped below target. Other notices stated

CUSTOMER SERVICE IS THE KEY TO SUCCESS

QUALITY MUST BE RIGHT FIRST TIME AND EVERY TIME

LET'S MAKE TODAY ANOTHER ACCIDENT FREE DAY

There were several other charts showing absence levels, days worked without accident, photos of various factory workers at their work locations. There were pictures of new machinery with descriptions such as:

THE NEW RX 20B BEING CRANED INTO PLACE
and
FINISHED PRODUCTS COMING OFF THE NEW CONVEYER.

'Are you Mark Watson?' Mark wondering what an RX 20 B was, tuned to see a medium sized man wearing a white coat smiling at him. 'Hello there. I'm Jack Elvers, Factory Manager. Don't get you fellows from Head Office down here very often. In fact I can't remember the last time we had one of you, certainly not this year. Can you remember any Lisa?' he asked the receptionist.

'No Mr. Elvers can't say I do'.

'Right well come on this way. We'll go to my office and then you can tell me why you've popped out of the blue like a jack-in-a-box'.

He led the way through a door at the back of reception and into a corridor and immediately the quiet hum of machinery that Mark had noticed became much louder. Jack led the way through another door into one end of the factory. There was a walkway protected from the actual factory floor with stanchions and rails all painted white. The noise was tremendous and seemed to engulf him as he walked along behind Jack to a set of open tread metal stairs leading up to a mezzanine floor which went part way round the factory and had various glass walled offices leading off it. Entering the first one Jack glanced through the windows down onto the factory floor. 'I can see everything that goes on from here' he said with satisfaction. 'Nothing escapes my beady eye' and he twisted his head and winked at Mark. Except production targets thought Mark. 'So what can we do for you?'

'It's about the launch of Double Air'.

'Have you guys decided whether it's coming here or going to Manchester?'

'Well that's why I'm here today. We'd like to launch it out of here but I'm told that there are frequent production problems here and things are often late which causes problems for our customers. We need be sure if we launched it out of here that you won't let us down' finished Mark speaking strongly now as he'd got into his stride and looking straight at the factory manager.

'Oh don't worry about that. We'll make it alright for you. So when's the decision going to be made then? Can't just drop it on us at the last minute'.

'Tomorrow. Decision time is tomorrow and at the moment there seems to be a general desire to make it up north as people seem to feel more certain that production schedules will be met. There's a lot of concern about doing it here.' Mark remembered Paul Feldman's view expressed so strongly yesterday 'Why are there problems here so often by the way?'

'Oh it all gets exaggerated you know. Sure we've had the odd blip this year and last year for that matter, but we've got it all under control now. You fellas can give us Double Air and relax'.

'Looking at your production output graphs in reception you seem to have had more than the odd blip. Seven times I noted that your output had dropped below target this year' challenged Mark his eyes piercing into Jack.

'Ah but that's the target. Look at how we've performed against last year. No you can put Double Air here quite safely' replied the factory man wriggling in discomfort at Mark's stare.

'Last year is irrelevant. Production against current target isn't that what matters?' riposted Mark still staring straight at the production man opposite him. 'It's now that matters, and it's the now and Double Air that we're nervous about. You're going to have to convince us that you'll hit your production targets. I know that they were sent to you some time ago and I see in the file that you've committed to achieving what's required in production output without the need for additional overtime. Are you sure that you can do that? But what happens if you need overtime? Is that a problem to organise?'

Jack felt very uncomfortable as he looked at the young earnest man sitting opposite who was obviously concerned about the risk of the Southampton factory mucking up their precious launch. In his heart of hearts he knew that the planning at the factory was a problem. The company wouldn't allow him to recruit any new people in the non production areas, and yet as volume output had grown over the past five years he knew that his planning team were just not up to the task. But Jack was a kindly man and couldn't bring himself to sack them and replace them with other better people. That was his dilemma and in spite of his expressions of confidence at the ability of the Southampton factory to hit the production targets, he knew it would be a struggle.

But if he didn't push for and succeed in persuading people like this young Mark that his factory should get this important new product launch then there was a chance that other new launches in the future might not come here either and he would be left with declining volume.

The Company often talked about building a new factory as Manchester was completely full and incapable of further building extensions to enable production to be increased. Southampton was also getting towards capacity and although there was some room to expand, there wasn't a lot and it might make more sense to build a brand new factory elsewhere and shut both Southampton and Manchester to centralise all production in one new giant factory. The modern trend was to close smaller factories and focus everything into one big plant.

If that happened he'd be out of work and so would his workforce. They'd probably get other jobs, but for him it wouldn't be so easy. At fifty two he was the wrong side of the magic fifty age barrier. He'd be seen by potential new employers as too old and he was aware that it would be hard to get another factory manager's job. In reality he had quite a cushy number and that suited him.

'Look Mark lets have a look around the factory. Come and meet some of my team here and form a view. They're a good bunch. Hard working, committed, quality conscious, and they'd really throw themselves into Double Air'.

For the next two hours Jack took him all over the factory. Production lines were humming away producing cans of aerosol products. Mark spoke to various people doing different jobs and Jack smiled and nodded to his workforce as he accompanied the younger man around. In another production hall Mark saw jars of liquid polish and creams being filled, in another bottles of liquid floor cleaner were being filled, while finally in the fourth and last production hall he watched as soap bars which had been made in yet another area of the factory were rushing down four assembly lines to a machine which automatically slipped them into a paper wrapper, folded and sealed them. Wherever he went he spoke to people.

Some seemed pleased to talk but others were not interested but just grunted a greeting and got on with their work.

At the end of the factory tour they went into the canteen and Jack introduced him to a number of supervisors and a couple of his under managers. They all knew about Double Air which surprised Mark as it was supposed to be confidential.

Jack spoke openly about Mark being part of the decision making process on whether Double Air would come to Southampton or go to Manchester. He said that he'd told Mark that they'd cope fine with it and wouldn't let the company down and didn't they all agree? There was a general nodding of heads or comments of agreement, except for two supervisors who just looked at each other and raised their eyes to heaven. They didn't say anything and Jack didn't see them, but Mark did and it worried him. After they'd left and he'd finished his pie and chips, he asked Jack if he could just have a final wander around on his own and he went off to try and find the two supervisors. He thought that he'd seen them earlier that morning in the aerosol plant and so finding his way back there he scoured the factory floor until he saw one of them.

'Hi there. You don't seem as convinced about this place as Jack Elvers?' he asked. 'What's your name by the way?'

'Pat, and nor would you be convinced mate if you bloody worked here. Right fucking mess this place is. Looks alright to visitors but those of us who work here can tell you different. Don't know whether we're on our arse or our elbow most of the time. Rush rush rush. Get this out, make this. No stop doing that. Make this. No, change again and make that. I tell you mate it's total bleeding chaos. It's not the factory and production that's all fucked up. It's the planners. They're hopeless. Frankly mate it's lucky anything gets out on time here,' he paused and looked straight at Mark. 'Most times it don't. If you want your new products produced on time for your launch don't put 'em in here sonny. Put 'em anywhere but here', then looking around worriedly he added 'but for fuck's sake don't say I said it or I'll get fired. You won't say anything will you mate?'

Mark irritated at being called sonny nevertheless reassured him that he wouldn't say anything that would incriminate him but asked where the other supervisor that had been with him at lunch worked so he could talk to him. Pat directed him to where Ben would be and a few minutes later Mark had a very similar conversation to the one that he'd just had with Pat. Now he was more worried than ever about the possibility of putting Double Air into this plant.

On the other hand, these two were supervisors. Quite low down in the organisation and surely Jack knew not only more about things but also what was required. So who was he to believe?

He made his way back to Jack's office which was now full of people all talking animatedly about something. Jack saw him looking in and came out. 'Look I'm pretty tied up now and will be for the rest of the day so I'll wish you goodbye. Give us Double Air and we'll make it happen for you. Cheerie-oh', and with that he went back into his all window office and left Mark to find his way out of the factory complex and back to reception where he signed out, gave Lisa a broad smile and walked slowly out to his car. While he sat for a long time turning things over in his mind, she sighed and thought he was the most attractive man she'd seen in a long time.

As he drove back up the A 30 he went over and over the problem in his mind. If he recommended Southampton and it all went wrong where did that leave him? He remembered Keith's homily about climbing up career ladders and how people loved to see the other guy screw up. Would this be his screw up he wondered? The safe route would be Manchester. Higher costs, lower profit margins, but safe. Southampton would give lower costs, higher profit margins and risk. Well Mark, he asked himself come on then, which is it to be?

He arrived back at his hotel in Leicester around seven thirty, had a pint of bitter, ate the daily special of Shepherds Pie and chips, and tired after his long drives, the walking around the factory and the worry of what to do, went to bed.

Next morning he was in the office early and wrote up a report on his visit and his conclusions. However when it came to recommend which factory he didn't hesitate and plumped for Southampton. He prowled the corridor waiting for Carol or any of the other secretaries or typists to come in and start work and eventually a spotty rather plump girl called Fay arrived and agreed to type up his notes and recommendation straight away.

When she brought them to his office a little later Mark smiled straight into her eyes as he thanked her. She felt her legs go a bit weak and said slightly breathily 'Anytime' and beat a hasty retreat back to the typing area where she told the other girls as they came in that the new chap Mark was absolutely gorgeous. Some agreed, some professed not to have noticed, but all who had seen him generally agreed that he was alright.

Mark put a copy of his paper on Keith's desk, added a scribbled note

"ready to discuss wherever its convenient"

and went back to his own office to await developments. They weren't long coming as Keith burst in.

'Are you sure about Southampton? I mean really sure? You know Paul's view but you've also said that although Jack's confident some of his people don't share that confidence.

'Yes I'm sure we should go to Southampton'.

Right. I'm going to get a meeting set up with Nick and then you can talk him through your recommendation. I hope to God you're right though. You obviously believe in taking risks' he grinned.

Mark carried on with his work, making various phone calls, reading documents and immersing himself in his job but every now and then a vague doubt wandered into his mind. Why had he recommended Southampton? The easy course of action would have been to condemn it and let Double Air go to Manchester. Yet somehow he knew that the right answer was Southampton and that was that.

It was nothing tangible simply a feeling that he had. He'd backed his gut instinct and made his recommendation. Now he'd have to live with it. In the future there would be many times in Mark's career when he made decisions that seemed obtuse or illogical but he did it based on his judgement and usually he turned out to be right.

Around mid-morning, Nick appeared and said somewhat angrily Mark thought, 'I gather from Keith that you think we should put Double Air into Southampton. Well I hope you've got good reasons for coming to that view or you might find that your marketing career, which yesterday seemed promising, could come to a very short sharp end. Right let's see what Keith says shall we? Is he of the same crazy view?'

'We haven't really talked about it, at least not in detail. I think he was waiting to discuss it with you and me. I mean for us all to discuss it'

As they walked into Keith's office Nick opened the discussion.

'Keith. Have you any idea of the risk you, well we, would run putting Double Air into Southampton? Where's Marks paper?' Keith handed over a copy and they both watched as Nick frowned his way through the short four page document. He read slowly and carefully and was obviously taking in every word that Mark had committed to print. When he came to the end he looked up at Mark. 'You've made a powerful case I grant you that but it seems that not all Jack's team are as certain as he is. We all know that Jack's the eternal optimist. Who are the people that hold a different view and why?'

'I can't remember their names I'm afraid I met so many people there' replied Mark vaguely remembering his promise to the two supervisors. 'But that doesn't matter. What does matter is that it looks a good factory. It's clean, runs efficiently. I mean while I was there the production and assembly lines didn't stop once unless it was for a proper product change over and.............

'Mark' interrupted Nick. 'With the greatest respect to your enthusiasm, belief and praise of the factory can I just ask you how many factories you've visited before which qualifies you to make judgements on Southampton's efficiencies or otherwise?

'None' replied a crestfallen Mark.

'Exactly. Well don't come in here on your third day in marketing and tell Keith and me how to run a factory. You know bugger all about it'.

Mark knew that Nick was right but he decided to have one more go.

'Look I'm sorry. Of course I don't know about running factories. At least I don't at the moment but I will in the future I assure you. I've told you in my report that the problem at Southampton is their planning function. It's crap. It's not the work force, or the production lines, or the machinery or despatch or loading, it's the bloody planning department. Couldn't we help them sort that out and then they've got a real chance of making a success of Double Air? It's just planning that's got to be put right. Where else in the company is there a good planning department or good planning people? Couldn't we send some people down there to help this launch? Maybe I could go. I'm good at numbers and I've got a logical mind. It can't be that difficult to sort it out. What do you say?'

'Guys' sighed Nick 'Do you know what you are doing to me? Splitting my heart and my head. My head says don't risk it. Put it into Manchester take the profit hit and hope that the branding, advertising, and Paul's sales teams can fight it into a decent market share position. My heart says I'd love that extra profitability and so put it into Southampton. Oh fucking hell. Why is life always so bloody difficult, eh? I'll tell you why' he answered himself, 'because that's what we're paid to sort out, that's why. I'm going to talk to Bill on his own, quietly to sound him out. I may need you to present your paper to him so be ready for a shout from me Mark. Ok?'

'Yes' gulped a surprised Mark.

Are you sure you're up for this Keith?' queried Nick turning and pausing as he walked out of the room.

There was a pause as Keith looked firstly at Mark, then at the four page paper, then back at Nick. Taking a deep breath he said 'Yes Nick in for a penny in for a pound. Yes I'm up for it'.

Nick gave him a strange look as he walked out.

Keith leaned back in his chair. 'Now that's interesting. If Nick is going to have a quiet chat with the Managing Director he must be more than half way convinced that Southampton is the place to go. Or he's got some previous view from Bill that he wanted it in Southampton. Nick's careful. Generally he will back and support his team, in other words you and me and the rest of the guys and girls in the department but he's not a great risk taker and seldom goes out on a limb like this. Oh well we lesser mortals can but wait and see'.

Time passed quite quickly and Mark worked hard enjoying the whole of what was emerging as his role and responsibilities. Late in the afternoon he wondered if Nick had yet spoken to the Managing Director. He'd find out soon enough he supposed and he buried his nose in his work again. Around seven in the evening he popped into Doug and Jerry's office and found them packing up for the night. Jerry looked up and called over to his compatriot. 'Hey Douggie here's the man who's going to risk a new launch at Southampton' he teased.

'No not Southampton surely. Does he look mad? Let me see. He must have gone funny in the head. Three days in marketing and he's off his rocker' grinned Doug.

'Yes sad. Still it happens to some. Come in here full of bright ideas, get sent to Southampton for a day and boom. Gone completely potty. Sad to see it happen and to such a nice guy'.

'Ah well. We'd better let him buy us a drink tonight before the men in white coats come and take him away. By the way Jerry where do they put cracked up marketeers these days?'

'Douggie my friend they send 'em to the Manchester factory where they sit in a little room up in the roof space writing out one million times "I should have put Double Air in here" then they jump into the famous Manchester Ship Canal which goes right beside the factory and disappear forever. All that remains is a faint voice in the breeze moaning Southampton, Southampton'.

'Oh shut up you two. Very bloody funny I don't think. Come on do you want a drink or not?'

'Ah well now oh mad one that is an important question' grinned Doug. 'Yes we want a drink but is whatever has afflicted you likely to be contagious and send us daft as well?' and he ducked as Mark swung a mock punch at him. 'Yes of course we'll come with you' and the three went off along the corridor.

'I tell you what' went on Jerry, 'you've certainly stuck your neck out and no mistake. What the hell ever made you suggest Southampton?'

Before Mark could answer Doug said in a quiet but high pitched whining voice 'Southampton, Southampton'.

'Piss off' laughed Mark as they got in the lift.

When they walked into the pub Jerry called for people's attention. 'The drinks are on Mark as he's gone mad and may be certified tomorrow'.

Mark realised that there was nothing that he could do but put up with the banter and so joining in he pulled some faces in what he hoped would be taken as an expression of daftness but he was surprised how many people seemed to know about his recommendation. The evening passed pleasantly with lots of chatter about work in general, marketing and their own particular products, new jobs, the latest cockups, promotion opportunities, the newest gossip about the Company and rumoured reorganisations, girls especially who was going out with whom and who might have slept with whom. They were a happy motivated bunch, keen on their careers, enjoying their work and their play.

He found himself in conversation with a tall girl who introduced herself as Tammy from Market Research. He learned that she too was quite new into the Company having been there for just over a month. She was nice if a bit gushing he thought but she certainly had a striking figure and lovely teeth and he enjoyed talking with her. They parted at closing time after agreeing that it might be nice to meet up for a drink sometime.

Deciding that as it was a dry fine night he would walk back to his small hotel he wandered along going over in his mind the factory visit yesterday, his paper which had started such a debate, the meetings today and then he grinned at the fun and leg pulling from Doug and Jerry and the rest of the others in the pub. He also thought about Tammy.

Thursday dawned raining, dull and miserable and he got wet walking to the office in spite of an umbrella which he borrowed from the hotel receptionist. As he approached the offices he felt his spirits drop and he walked with much less enthusiasm to his office today than he had on Monday and Wednesday. On his desk was a note:-

Give me a call when you arrive
Nick

He picked up the phone and rang Nick's number. There was no answer. Damn he thought and put down the receiver. He walked down the corridor to Nick's office and looking through the peep hole in the door window he saw that Nick was in deep discussion with some people that he didn't recognise. Undecided he hovered for a moment and then knocked and walked in.

'Nick just letting you know that I'm in and ready to talk whenever you're ready'.

'Ok. I'll be about ten minutes come back then' and he turned back to his discussion.

Mark asked Keith if he knew what Nick wanted. He guessed it was about Southampton but what? He soon found out.

'Sit down chaps' invited Nick when Mark and Keith returned. 'I had a good chat with Bill last night. It's often a good time to catch him you know at the end of the day. Occasionally he's all bloody minded but sometimes, and last night was one of those occasions, he enjoys a chat about the business. He's not opposed to Southampton. That doesn't mean he's wholly in favour but I reckon he's more on the side of Southampton than he is on the side of Manchester. He knows about Southampton's planning issues and agrees with your suggestion to sort planning out down there. Do that and we have a good chance with Double Air. He's asked Gordon to send two of his financial planners down there'.

'Gordon?' queried Mark.

'Finance Director. Sharp as a razor and tough as hell. If he'll do that we really might have a chance. I'm seeing him at eleven and if I can persuade him to help we'll meet again and talk through the finer points. If not then I don't see how we can go to Southampton and I think I'm going to support Manchester'.

'What about Paul?' Keith wanted to know. 'Who the hell is going to get him on side?'

'I guess we'll have to gang up on him. You two, me and Bill' laughed Nick. 'I'll call you later this morning when I've seen Gordon'.

As Mark was discovering, business was often about quite a lot of waiting for the outcome of meetings and decisions that required the involvement and support of other people and departments. He waited impatiently but when his phone rang at twenty past eleven it made him jump. He snatched up the receiver and heard Nick's voice say 'Gordon's agreed. He'll send two planners down south next week. You could be in business young man. Still want to produce down there?'

'Yes I do' yelled Mark. 'Thanks Nick. You won't regret it. I'll make this the most successful launch ever. You see if I don't'.

'You'd better Mark. You had surely better make it a real humdinger of a launch'.

Keith smiled when he heard the good news. 'Nick's done it then? Great. Now your hard work begins. Right this is what we need to do' and he explained the procedures and paperwork that needed to be completed to make the launch happen. Mark listened carefully making lots of notes then going into Doug and Jerry's office said in a moaning voice 'Southampton, Southampton', stuck two fingers up to each of them, laughed and said 'so there, Southampton it is' and walked out leaving the other two young marketers speechless.

CHAPTER 9

Keith was right. The hard work did begin then and for the next few months Mark was totally committed to working on Double Air every day and often late into the evening.

He had many meetings with the advertising agency who soon realised that they were dealing with a person who not only found himself comfortable with challenging them especially on words and phrases, known as ad copy, to be used in the finished ads but who forced them to work extremely hard to produce good advertising. He quickly grasped the principles of advertising but also seemed to have an instinctive knack of being able to interpret the lessons from consumer research into meaningful concepts that could be translated into advertising.

Initially Keith sat in with him but gradually he left Mark to manage the meetings on his own, his only stipulation being that Mark must discuss final copy, layout and design with him and Nick before final approval. Nick though also realised that Mark had a natural talent in this area.

He also made several trips to Southampton to ensure that Jack and his team understood what was required of them. Certainly the two planners which the Finance Director had despatched there had made a terrific difference and when Mark found Pat and Ben in the canteen they agreed that there had been a big change and things were much better organised. 'Might even get your precious launch right' grinned Pat to a worried Mark.

The first briefing to the senior sales managers went well after Paul had been mollified. He'd called into Keith's office one evening for an update on progress.

'Do I hear that you have decided to launch Double Air from Southampton?' queried Paul incredulously. 'Is that really what you've decided?

He was working himself into a real temper, pacing up and down, and when Mark hearing Paul ranting away joined the meeting the Sales Director lambasted the two marketeers.

'In all my life I don't think I've ever heard of something so bloody stupid. Well I've told you once and I'll tell you again it'll be an unmitigated disaster. You must be out of your tiny minds'.

He was boiling with rage until Mark quietly said that he understood Paul's reaction. Paul stopped in mid flight and shouted 'What?'

'I said I understand your reaction to our proposal. No not proposal our decision. If I was in your shoes with the past record of Southampton I'd feel exactly the same as you.

The problem down there was their planning function. I don't know why no-one's seen it before or if they had why they've not done anything about it. However Nick persuaded Gordon to release a couple of financial planners and just you look at Southampton's performance now. Their customer service and order fulfilment rates are as good as Manchester's. You must see that? Look I know I've only been here a little while but I am sure that Southampton won't let you, me or the Company down'.

Paul slowly relaxed as he listened to the very persuasive argument put forward with such conviction by Mark. 'Are those planner guys going to stay there?'

'Up to and beyond the launch yes. They're doing two things. To start with they're working with Jack and his team to plan every detail from the factory side for the launch. In addition they're overhauling the whole planning operation down there so it's not just a short term fix but a real long term solution. That's got to be good. It's what Southampton needs'.

Paul looked at Mark. 'Do you really believe in what you've just said about them getting it right?'

'Yes absolutely'. Mark stared back and held Paul's eyes without wavering.

'Well I hope you're right young man. Two things. Firstly I want Jack to come to the launch conference and secondly don't say I didn't warn you when' he paused 'alright not when but if, it all goes wrong. Good night' and he left remembering Mark's staring eyes that had been piercing deep into him.

'I thought he was going to explode. Stupid sod. No need to get that worked up about it but he calmed down at the end didn't he? Good that we've got him on side now isn't it?'

'For now, but I warn you laddie if Southampton fucks it up you'll hear the explosion on the other side of the world' laughed Keith. 'You did well. You were totally convincing. I just hope Jack and his lot don't let you down'.

'So do I Keith' mused the champion of Southampton. 'So do I'.

Work for the launch increased tempo in all departments. Sales managers made sure their plans to sell in to the various customers were properly thought out. Finance double checked the costs and expected production rates. Market research re-estimated expected sales. Transport was alerted to the probable need for extra deliveries. Regional distribution depots allocated space for the awaited stocks of the new products. Customer service were put on standby to be ready to cope with additional orders and to ensure they had sufficient extra staff available if required to handle the expected additional orders that all had to be checked, coded, entered into the computer system, aggregated and transmitted to production planning at Head Office and Southampton, as well as to the Sales teams and especially to Paul who would pore over the daily sales like a hawk.

The pace was fast, furious and fully absorbing and Mark loved it. Several people commented that this guy seemed something special. Not only was his work rate phenomenal but he was able to cope with all the last minute challenges that kept cropping up. Although he kept Keith updated, more and more he replied on his own judgement and made decisions without referring to anyone else, often well in excess of his levels of authority.

He made a few mistakes but when these were pointed out he'd thank the person who'd raised the matter and sort it out quickly and with good humour.

The raw materials that were needed for production of Double Air were ordered from various suppliers and delivered to Southampton who started to produce the required quantities. There were three fragrances and two were produced ahead of schedule which gave everyone confidence. Quality was fine, labelling was good and everyone started to relax until late one afternoon Mark got a phone call from Jack.

'We've got a major machine breakdown Mark. It's the high pressure gas part of the aerosol production unit which serves all four production lines filling product. We have had to shut down'.

He went on to admit that they didn't know how long it would take to fix and to add complication the machinery was Italian. He said that they'd work on it themselves with their own engineers all night and agreed to ring Mark in the morning and update him.

Mark felt sick. It was everything he'd feared but had hoped wouldn't happen. He felt helpless and could envisage Paul shouting 'I bloody told you so'.

Should he drive to Southampton and see for himself? He got hold of his emotions and thought logically about the issue. What could he do down at the factory? Nothing. So why go? No he was best staying here working on the implications. First he briefed Keith who went white at the shock, and then he decided to go and tell Nick and finally Paul.

Nick looked downcast and asked to be kept informed of developments.

Mark had expected Paul to blow his top but he simply asked 'So what are your contingency plans? You've still got a bit of time as I believe before this balls up they were ahead of schedule and had fully completed launch quantities of two variants. Well it's your problem at the moment' he growled slowly. 'If you don't get it fixed and the launch is fucked up then it's a problem for us all. So….. get….. it….. sorted' he yelled.

Mark confirmed he was working on contingencies and would keep Paul advised of progress. He wasn't sure if Paul's 'thank you' was said sarcastically or genuinely but shrugging his shoulders he went back to his office. Sod it he thought. It was all going so well. Now what the hell was he to do?

Doug looked in and didn't gloat or laugh simply asked if there was anything he could do to help. Mark replied that he didn't think there was.

'Ok well the offer's there if you need it. By the way I believe that Manchester's a bit slack at the moment, short of volume. Just thought you'd like to know'.

It took a moment or two for the implications of this comment to sink in then the penny dropped. Mark smiled gratefully, said thanks and dialled the factory manager at Manchester, introduced himself and explained his problem.

'So why are you telling me' queried Barry who had been just packing up for the night.

'If we are stuck and can't get Southampton fixed quickly could you produce some of the launch quantity for us?'

'No we couldn't'. Mark's heart dropped. 'Not 'cos we don't want to but we haven't got the kit to handle and apply the twin nozzle and gel applicator onto the pack. Sorry. If it was just a straightforward aerosol then we could have helped you out. Good luck' and he rang off.

Shit, now what. He rang Jack again and it took a long time to locate him. 'How's it going?' he asked when Jack came breathlessly to the phone.

'Not good Mark. It looks real bad. The main drive shaft of the gas filling unit linked to assembly has gone and it's buggered up some other parts in the process. Look I really need to be down there with the others. I'll call you tomorrow'.

Mark spent a miserable evening and after he went to bed he tossed and turned for ages thinking about the problem. Somehow he was not going to let this launch get screwed up. But what else could he do? Was there anything that Manchester could do to help? They couldn't apply the gel applicator but could fill aerosols. Well what about filling them in Manchester and then driving them down in their part completed state to Southampton to apply the gel applicator and cap? Would that work? Why wouldn't it he pondered? The cans were sealed when the gas was injected. They wouldn't leak. It might just work and with that thought he finally dropped off to sleep.

He was up very early and in the office before anyone else. He rang the Distribution department who worked round the clock to support the company's fleet of heavy vehicles on their various journeys. They listened with some incredulity to his questions but agreed to work out a cost and get back to him. He tried to think through the logistics of getting materials from Southampton to Manchester for the part completion of the production task before transporting them back down south for completion. He worked quickly and soon his desk was covered with notes, calculations, thoughts and crucially a time plan which showed that it might just be a workable solution.

The one thing he couldn't do was delay the launch. Not only was the sales conference booked, but appointments had been made with the company's major customers to present the new products. It would look very bad if they had to be postponed or cancelled. He simply had to get it fixed.

Just after eight Jack rang. He sounded tired and dispirited. 'It's not good Mark. We need new parts from the manufacturers in Italy. We've spoken to them this morning. They're time is an hour ahead of us remember and they are going to check and get back to us'.

'Did you stress to them the urgency of this Jack?'

'Yes of course we bloody did but they're Italians. They have a different view of urgent from us. We've got the machine stripped down, cleared out the broken parts and as soon as the new bits arrive we can fit them. That shouldn't take more than half a day at most, well maybe a little longer. When I know what they say I'll call you again. I'm sorry about this really I am as we were doing so well. The new planning system is working a dream. I'll call you when I know something more' and he rang off.

Mark rang Barry at Manchester. 'Look I've got an idea. I know it's crazy but hear me out. Southampton's breakdown is towards the end of the line, past the actual filling and labelling sections. So could you do that part, fill and label then send them to Southampton for them to finish by applying the spray nozzle and gel cap. That way we'd get product produced and still meet the launch window. We'll send you everything you need. Could you help like that?'

'Well you are right about one thing, it is crazy to part produce up here and then ship down south to complete. But it might just work. Give me half an hour. I'll get my team together and we'll see what we can do'.

Mark went and briefed Nick and Keith on the extent of the problems at Southampton but didn't mention his Manchester idea. Not long after he returned to his office Barry called him. 'Look we need to know the following' and he reeled off a list of questions mainly to do with logistics, supply of materials, scents, and items of that nature.

'But can you do it' asked Mark desperately. 'I mean if I get you these things can you do it?'

'Oh yes we can do it alright but you'd better be aware of the costs involved. You'll have double handling, extra transport, inevitable damage and losses from unsealed boxes and we'll have to produce most of it on overtime which has a high cost penalty. If you can stand the costs of all that lot, then yes we can do it for you'.

'I'll get you the information you want, but thanks. Thanks very much indeed. You might just have saved my life......and the launch' and he rushed off to tell Paul first who admitted that it was an ingenious solution to the problem. Nick and Keith were equally pleased, and Doug had the good grace when he heard the plan to say 'What a bloody good idea to use Manchester. Well done in thinking that one up Mark' and gave him a wink.

Mark called various people together and soon got the logistics issues under way. Then Jack rang with the news that the Italians had good news and bad news. The good was that some of the required spare parts were in stock in their Turin warehouse. The bad news was that the main drive shaft would have to be specially re-manufactured and that would take a couple of days provided they could find a production slot to fit it in.

Mark told him of the contingency plan and Jack cheered up realising it was a very clever solution to the problem. He said he'd liaise with Barry in the north and that between them they'd sort it out.

They did and the remaining aerosol variant was produced in a joint venture between Manchester and Southampton. During that process the various parts that were required arrived from Turin and eventually the southern plant was able to go back into full production again before the launch conference.

That was an exciting affair held on a Monday in one of the huge conference rooms of the very smart London Carlton Hotel in Knightsbridge.

From the stage Paul in a very determined manner spoke of the huge opportunity that Double Air offered to the company. Nick spoke excitedly about the brand and how this launch would strengthen their whole share of the market. There were other speakers including the senior advertising man and the company Market Research Manager Raymond that Mark had quizzed so long ago at his first conference. The room reeked of the new fragrances and film of the planned television advertising was showing continuously on tv screens around the conference room. Copies of the intended poster advertising that would appear on hoardings all over the country were also on display. It was clear at the lunch break that the sales force were motivated and eager to sell the new products. They also seemed pleased with the priority plans that were given to them and Mark was flattered to see his idea in action.

Lunch was served to the conference attendees in another large room that adjoined the conference room and as the meal was coming to an end Paul stood and with a microphone in hand called for quiet as he said that he had a couple of announcements to make.

'Firstly' he boomed 'I want to congratulate young Mark Watson for his hard and dedicated work in bringing this product to the point of launch. There have been many challenges that he's had to overcome, but he's tackled them with determination and succeeded. Well done Mark. Come on guys, he's sitting over there. Let's give him a big hand' and the room erupted in clapping and table thumping as everyone turned to look at him.

Paul allowed it to go on for a little while and then raised his hands for silence. 'The other person I want to thank is Jack Elvers from Southampton, the plant that used to give us problems but thanks to a new planning system and Jack's own brand of magic is now running like clockwork. Jack thanks for getting all the launch product ready on time. Let's hope we keep you busy with lots of repeat orders. We're in your hands, and I know that you won't let us down. Now then everyone lets have a big hand for Jack. Come on Jack and Mark come up here in front of everyone and take a bow'.

He smiled and patted Jack on the back when the production man had joined him having walked somewhat self consciously up to Paul's table where Mark was already standing. They all shook hands warmly and were to all intents and purposes three colleagues pleased with a joint venture and success.

However Mark realised what Paul had subtly yet very publicly done.

He'd identified the two people in the company primarily responsible for this launch out of Southampton. He'd put them out in the open as cannon fodder if anything went wrong. Had he lined them up in front of a firing squad and told everyone to get ready to fire he couldn't have been more pointed. If Southampton ballsed up then there were the two of them out in the open, completely exposed, devoid of cover and protection, ready to be shot.

Keith's speech on Mark's first day came back to him about people scoring points, fighting for power, pushing others off the promotional ladder. Well he'd just seen a raw example of that power in action, but done so cleverly. If all went well with the launch out of Southampton then what Paul would have been seen to have done was congratulate in advance the two people most closely associated with it. If it went wrong well then they were already hung out to be destroyed.

It was a lesson that Mark noted and in a way admired but also feared. No, not feared he thought that was too strong. Concerned. Yes that was about the measure of it. Well you devious bastard he thought, Jack and me will make sure you don't get the chance to skin us. You'd better hit your sales target and quotas because you won't be able to blame us if you don't. I'll remember what you've done today Paul he muttered very quietly to himself. I won't forget this.

Jack didn't see it like that. After lunch as the sales force which operated in a series of regions corresponding to the various television regions of the country, went into their various team meetings in different small rooms to plan the finer points of the sell in to their trade customers he went up to Mark and said happily 'Hey wasn't that decent of Paul to thank us like that? Really nice of him I thought. Didn't expect that at all'.

Mark didn't disillusion him and let him enjoy his accolade. 'Well Jack' he said 'I've done my bit by getting you the production and helped you out when your machinery broke down. Now it's up to you. Please don't, whatever you do, screw this up' and he looked deeply into Jack's eyes with such intensity that Jack felt transfixed and the hairs on the back of his neck stood up.

'No Mark. I know what we've got to do'.

Mark now felt a great sense of being emotionally drained. For the last few weeks his whole life had been focussed solely on getting Double Air launched on time. Now that it had happened it was up to Paul and his sales teams. The company was in their hands for the success or failure of the launch.

Now they had to wait for the results to come in to find out whether customers would like and thus buy the new air freshener concept that Double Air embodied. He wandered around the conference room reliving his first product launch.

There'd been various other non sales people who'd also attended who were starting to leave, but he was touched when Mr. Dunson came up and said 'Well done my boy. Knew you had it in you. I think this will be a great success and another good step in your career. Jolly glad I thought of pushing you into marketing' and with that he wandered off to talk to some others.

Pushing me into marketing mused Mark? I asked to go into marketing. Was this was another example of power and jockeying for position. Did even old Dunson indulge in it? Was he really trying to claim some glory if Double Air succeeded? Would he be saying to some of the Directors 'Well of course I could see the boy had talent. Had a career chat with him and pointed him in the direction of marketing'.

Oh well we'll see and he started to think about getting the train back to Leicester when a female voice said 'Hi there. Remember me. I'm Tammy. We met in the pub weeks ago. I work in market research. I've done a lot of the background consumer research on Double Air and Raymond my boss said that I could come to this launch. I think it's a great product. You've been really frantic with the launch haven't you as I've not seen you in the pub very much'.

Mark did remember her and she looked really pretty today. Her fair hair was tied back in a pony tail and she was wearing a tight black jumper and quite short dark green pencil slim skirt with matching shoes. He smiled and said of course he remembered her and they chatted about today's launch. He looked at his watch and said that as it was now three o'clock there was no chance of getting back to the office tonight to do some work so why didn't they have a wander around London and perhaps have an early meal before getting a later train back to Leicester. 'I feel like celebrating and apart from you I've no-one to celebrate with'. Seeing her frown he roared with laughter. 'Look I didn't mean it like that. What I meant was..........'

'I know what you meant' she said quietly. 'Yes let's do that it sounds lovely'.

They caught a tube to Park Lane, walked to Oxford Street which they wandered along slowly looking at the shops and enjoying the hustle and bustle of the big London street. They went into Selfridges then continued until they turned into Bond Street. Tammy was enthralled by the expensive ladies clothes shops and eventually they found themselves in Regent Street which in turn led them to Piccadilly Circus where they stood and looked at Eros for a while and speculated on what the statue might be thinking about all the people passing by him. From here they meandered along Shaftsbury Avenue and on into Soho.

The mixture of charm and seediness was intriguing and exciting. They marvelled at the juxtaposition of restaurants, newsagents, film companies, coffee bars, nightclubs which weren't open till later in the evening, but strip clubs and nude peep shows that were, office equipment showrooms, dirty book shops, offices, and open doorways with little notices inviting passers by to go in and visit the "model" plying her prostitution trade from dingy one room flats within. It was fascinating, slightly risqué and they thoroughly enjoyed it.

Feeling hungry Mark led the way to the little Italian restaurant to which he'd taken Debbie on their first date. They chose from the menu of the day and ordered a bottle of red wine which was definitely on the rough side of enjoyable nevertheless they had a pleasant evening and chatted about their lives, their upbringing, their childhoods and their careers so far. Mark told her about his ambition to eventually head a major company and although Tammy initially thought it was a combination of wine and male bravado talking, she soon saw the intense determination that he had.

Finally they finished their meal and took a taxi to St. Pancras station where they caught the train back to Leicester. Sitting side by side she snuggled into him resting her head on his shoulder and soon she was asleep in which state she stayed until he gently shook her awake as the train approached their destination. They shared a taxi to their respective lodgings arriving at hers first . He walked her to the door. They told each other that they'd had a lovely time and leaning forward he gave her a quick kiss before returning to the taxi and giving directions to his digs.

The Indian taxi driver told Mark that he had 'Very pretty girlfriend'. He replied that she wasn't really his girlfriend, at least not yet and tonight had been their first date. He relaxed against the back seat wondering if he might want her as a girlfriend. She was quite sweet and as they'd got to know each other she'd become less gushy.

When he'd first moved up to Leicester to work at Head Office the company paid his hotel bill for the first month but after that he'd searched the local papers until he'd found this large old house in a reasonable area that had been converted into flats, and he rented one of those.

As he paid for the taxi he decided to invite her out again. Making his way upstairs he remembered the time when he crept up to Debbie's flat and his introduction to sex. Yes he thought Tammy was pretty, seemed like fun, easy to talk to and he'd really quite like to get her into bed. It was some time since he'd had sex and maybe Tammy would be the one to change that for him. Now that was something to work on he grinned to himself as he poured a beer and flopped into an easy chair thinking about the conference, the launch, the time wandering around London with Tammy, the meal and the train journey back.

Next morning in the office he waited for news of the sell in by the sales force. It wasn't long in coming and by lunch time Customer Service department had taken several orders. At the end of the day he went down again and spoke to the pretty redheaded supervisor Karen, who had a list of the day's sales of Double Air.

'Reasonable but nothing remarkable. It's usually like that with new products for the first day or so. You need to wait for the big supermarkets and wholesalers to start to place orders. That's when sales can go through the roof, or if we don't have enough stock when the shit will hit the fan big style'.

'That'll be in about two weeks time I guess'.

'Yes. Should start to see it take off then. If it doesn't we've got a problem'.

'Oh it'll take off alright. The research was extremely positive and we believe that it'll not only enhance our share of the market but:......'

'Hey hold on Mark. You don't have to sell it to me you know. I work here remember. I'm just as keen as you for it to work'.

'Sorry it's just that it's my first big launch and I'm really excited about it. There's a lot riding on it', not least my first big step on the career ladder he thought.

'Look I'll call you lunch times and end of the day if you like to save you coming down and fill you in on how it's going'.

'Thanks but I'd prefer to come down. It's where the action is at the moment and besides' he smiled looking straight at her, 'it gives me the chance to see you'.

'Go on off with you. Leave me to pack up for the night. I'll update you tomorrow'.

Mark walked back upstairs to his office and then called Tammy. 'Fancy a drink?' and they arranged to meet at seven in the main reception.

'Where are we going?' she asked when they met. 'Not the Woolpack with all the others I hope'.

'Don't you like it there?'

'Oh there's nothing wrong with it but it's noisy and with everyone there we won't get any time on our own. I thought when you rang and asked me out for a drink you meant just the two of us'.

'I did' he said instantly changing his plans and they walked for a little while until they found a different pub with none of the other office people in it and sat talking easily together as young people do when they find a number of common interests.

She was strongly interested in left wing politics and women's lib issues and had been on a few protest marches. Her views were therefore totally opposite to his strong conservative view of life, nevertheless although they argued vigorously about their opposing political scenarios they found much in common in other matters.

They went on from the pub to a snack bar and chatted continuously through the poorly cooked and somewhat greasy meal until Tammy looked at her watch and said that as it was nearly eleven o'clock she ought to be going.

He briefly considered making an attempt to get her to come back to his flat but decided that he didn't want to rush things and possibly turn her off him so they found a taxi again dropping her off first. This time though they kissed properly. She blended her body into his as they were locked together on her doorstep until after a couple of minutes she pulled back and said 'Thank you for a really nice evening........ even if you are a stuffy old Tory' and giggling she went indoors leaving him with the smell of her perfume and the taste of her lips to savour on the ride back to his flat.

For the next three weeks his routine at work didn't change. Every lunch time and end of day he'd go down and see Karen and get an update on sales which were still just on target. He'd hoped that they'd have been above target but he knew that the target gradually increased week by week as the sell in progressed and the volume of orders now being sent into the company were considerably higher than those of the first few days.

Tammy and he went out a few times, sometimes to the cinema, sometimes to a cheap restaurant and sometimes just to a pub of which there were plenty in Leicester. He wished he had his own car as while kissing and cuddling on her doorstep or in the back of a taxi was alright and a couple of times he'd even managed to squeeze her breasts nevertheless he missed the intimacy and opportunity provided by his old Beetle. I must do something about getting a car of my own up here he decided as if not his love life was going to seriously suffer.

Nick told him that he was pleased with the launch progress and with the way Mark was handling things. Mark phoned Southampton twice a day and was reassured each time Jack told him that the plant was running well and that there were no production problems.

Paul was also pleased with the results of Double Air so far. He generated performance through his driving management style which with a combination of bullying and encouragement brought outstanding results. He pushed hard and demanded good performance from his people. Five supermarket chains had agreed to stock the new products and several more were considering the position. None had rejected Double Air yet. The wholesalers around the country were also being very supportive and all in all he was happy with the way things were going.

'A couple more weeks and then you'll see some real volume' he told Mark one evening when they met in a conference room to review progress. Keith had told Mark that these post launch reviews could be very acrimonious especially if sales were below the target with recriminations flying wildly around the room. However he thought that as Double Air was doing well this would be an easy meeting. It was.

One day Mark had a company car again as he had to visit an external market research company and returning to the office at nearly five thirty in the afternoon he decided to keep it overnight. Collecting Tammy when she finished work they drove out of Leicester to a pub in a little village where they had a couple of drinks and a bar meal. Tammy had scampi and salad while Mark tucked into a huge steak and chips.

After they left the pub they found a quiet little lane by the edge of a wood where he parked and turned off the lights. Leaning towards her they kissed and she didn't object when he reached under her jumper and started to play with her breasts which were nicely shaped, firm, and reasonably large. She for her part unzipped his flies and gently felt around inside until she could release his prick which as a result of her fumbling had hardened up making it difficult to get free. Finally managing to extract it she exclaimed softly 'Oh wow, now that's what I call a cock'.

She stroked his erection as they kissed deeply while he moved his hand down from her breasts to start sliding slowly up her long legs. She wriggled down on the seat to make room for him and he slowly found his way past the elastic waistbands of her tights and panties and eased his fingers inside the warm close fitting underwear to start playing with her pussy which quickly became wet. When he suggested that it might be more comfortable if they went back to his flat she pulled her face away from him murmured softly 'Umm lovely' and gave his prick a firm squeeze. 'Well what are you waiting for?' she whispered.

That was all the encouragement he needed. Sitting up and with some difficulty pushing his stiff prick back inside his clothes he very carefully zipped himself up and drove quickly back into Leicester parking in the street outside the old house that contained his flat. They ran in and scampered up the stairs into Mark's flat. 'Like a drink or something? I've got some beer' he asked as soon as the door had shut.

'No thanks I don't want anything to drink let's go to bed, after all that's why we've come back here isn't it' she said. Kicking off her shoes she lifted her jumper over her head and dropped it on a chair, unclipped her bra which also went on the chair, unzipped and slid off her skirt which joined the other clothes on the chair then sitting down on the bed peeled off her tights and panties.

Mark was amazed. He'd never seen a girl get undressed so quickly because it seemed only a few seconds ago that she had been fully clothed and now she was starkers. She'd made no attempt to undress sexily for him simply stripped off and now sprawling naked on her tummy on the bed crooked her finger beckoning him to her.

'Hurry up'.

Mark undressed as quickly as he could but still took considerably longer than she had. As he cuddled her she said she was on the pill so there was nothing to stop them making love straight away but would he please be careful how he entered her seeing he was so well endowed.

They were good with each other and Mark quickly realised that Tammy was not inexperienced in bed. She for her part enjoyed not only his size but also his skill, expertise and consideration towards her. It was rare in her experience for a man to be concerned about her enjoyment and fulfilment but Mark certainly was and she relished it as they took their time and enjoyed each other.

Much later they made love again and afterwards she said he had a choice. Either he'd have to take her back to her digs now or if she was going to stay the whole night he'd have get up early and drive her back so she could change for work as she wasn't going to turn up wearing the same clothes two days running. It would be a definite giveaway that she'd slept away from her own place and was the sort of things all the girls at the office would notice immediately. He willingly agreed to get up early and so she stayed the night.

Early next morning they tried various penetrative positions before he pulled her to the end of the bed and standing firmly on the floor holding her ankles tightly lifted her legs in the air and thrusting into her revelled in her cries of satisfaction until they both climaxed.

Afterwards she put back on what she'd worn yesterday while Mark just pulled on a tracksuit to drive her back to her digs. She sat curled up against the passenger door looking at him all tousled, unshaven and early morningish and liked what she saw. When they got to her digs they kissed before she pushed him away saying softly 'See you at the office later. I've had a lovely time and I'm glad that even though you're a stuffy conservative by nature you're very liberal in bed' then ran indoors laughing.

Mark drove back to his flat with a great feeling of elation. He was back in business for sex and it was on that short return drive that he realised how much he'd missed it but he'd been so busy with Double Air that it simply hadn't really entered his thinking. Now however it was right at the front of his mind and he determined that he wasn't going to go for long without it again, especially as Tammy was really nice, had great legs and was good in bed.

Arriving back at his flat he showered, shaved, dressed properly and drove the car to the office car park arriving just after Fred who was in a temper because one of his precious fleet of pool cars wasn't back when it should have been last night.

'It's not right. You had it booked out for yesterday only, not for overnight' he grumbled. 'There's day bookings, and there's overnight bookings and they're different. See. How can I keep things properly organised when people don't do what they're supposed to eh, answer me that young man? Here you haven't pranged it have you? That's not why it's late back is it? It's needed for eight thirty this morning you know'.

'No it's not pranged and I'm sorry to have mucked up your system. I'll remember next time. Look I've got to go. Thanks again' and he went into the office block leaving a muttering Fred to walk suspiciously around the car.

He'd been caught before by these young marketing guys but finding no damage he took a chamois leather and cleaned the windows so the vehicle was ready for his next user.

CHAPTER 10

Orders flooded into the company and sales at last exceeded the ambitious targets which the company had set. Mark was pleased but slightly nervous. They had plenty of stock which had been produced ahead of demand but if sales continued to come in at this rate then those stocks would soon diminish.

Now was the time to balance demand, production and stock holding. Get it right and all would be alright. Get it wrong and orders would not be fulfilled, customers would start to complain, sales and profit would be lost and Paul would go apeshit. Mark rang Jack and warned him that as sales were shooting through the roof he'd better get ready to produce more stock. Jack said that the he and planners were aware of the position and were carefully monitoring the situation and not to worry.

But he did. It was eight weeks after the launch and next week the television advertising would start and then consumer demand should move into yet an even higher gear but because their sales were now higher then planned then available stocks were below the level at which everyone would feel comfortable, especially if there was a further surge in demand.

Jack put the plant onto twenty four hour working and output increased substantially and for the next few days production not only kept up with sales but managed to exceed it putting extra stock into the company's warehouses and depots around the country.

The day of the first tv adverts finally came, and Keith, Mark, Carol, Raymond, and Tammy were gathered in Nick's office at lunch time to watch television for the commercial break in which they knew the first Double Air ad would appear. Mark positioned himself not only to be able to see the tv but also so that he had a good view of Tammy's legs clearly displayed in a short mini skirt. He winked at her and she smiled back. The two of them were now going out two or three times a week and most times they finished up sleeping together.

His mind and gaze reverted to the tv which was already switched on and quietly chattering to itself in the corner of the room. It wasn't as if they didn't know what the ad would be like. They had worked and argued over it, agonised and challenged, written and rewritten the scripts and story boards until they and the agency were in agreement. But now it was going on air live, for real.

It was a simple story of a housewife whose home suffered from smells, caused by her dog, her cat, the kitchen, the bathroom and finally from cigarette smoke in the sitting room. Nothing she had used before solved these problems.

Now there was this great new product Double Air looking like a large candle, which not only killed the smells immediately because of its special double spray nozzle but would if left in the room, thanks to the gel pad which was re-impregnated every time the aerosol was used, provide the on-going benefit of pleasantly fragrancing her home for several hours afterwards.

The commercial break which was in the middle of a popular lunch time programme suddenly arrived and Nick turned up the sound. The room went silent. First ad was for Lloyds Bank, the next was for Coca Cola but suddenly on screen their housewife demonstrated her problem and the magical solution of the twin spray and gel that Double Air provided. The final shot showed the product in close up as a strong off-screen reassuring male voice said

> "New Double Air spray and gel. Double fresh, double quick, double good. New Double Air, available now….. Double Air"

It was followed immediately by an ad for headache tablets. Nick switched off the set. 'Well there it is everyone. Came over fine I thought. Let's hope it does the business. On three more times today isn't it Mark?'

'Yes, in the middle of Coronation Street, during the evening play and in the middle of the nightly news bulletin. The agency bought good fixed spots and they'll be supplemented by random spots. Heavy tv campaign in first three weeks, then lighter over the next two. After that there's a four week pause and then a further three week medium weight burst. Press ads start next week. Outdoor posters and hoardings start during the four week tv absence. We're really in the campaign now'.

'Good. Just keep an eye on Southampton. Right thanks everyone' and with that Nick dismissed the assembled group who filed out and went back to their respective places of work.

Sales really rocketed now the advertising was creating the consumer demand. Stock that had been sold in to customers in anticipation of the expected sales soon ran out and Southampton although running twenty four hours a day, seven days a week struggled to keep up. They brought some more production lines into operation by stopping production of other products which were in turn switched to other factories in the Thompson and Smith Group as Double Air was seen as the priority and everything that could be done to support it, was done. Warehouses worked flat out to load the company's trucks which in turn made many additional deliveries.

Mark was both elated but very concerned. If sales continued at this rate then there would come an inevitable point where demand would simply outstrip their capacity to make the product. That would be a disaster. Somehow they had to find more production availability. The problem was the application of the special twin nozzle and gel cap. If a way could be found to do that at Manchester then the problem would be solved. But how? He rang Barry and explained his problem. The machinery at Manchester could not apply the special cap automatically and some modification to their plant would be required. Barry rang Bill the Managing Director to get authorisation to spend the money on the new kit and receiving immediate approval flew to Italy. In discussion with the Italian manufacturer he persuaded them to modify another piece of standard equipment which would then fit the Manchester machine. They thought that it would take a couple of days to make the temporary solution but they agreed to airfreight it to Manchester as soon as it was ready to save the three day lorry journey that would be taken if it came by road.

'Two days to make, one day to fly it here and another day to fit and test it. We'll work through the weekend if necessary. We could be producing your Double Air on day six from now provided the Italians do what they have to on time' Barry told Mark on his return from Italy.

Could they survive for six days without the additional production from the north? Mark watched sales, stocks and production daily and saw that it was going to be tight as stocks were going down too fast. Soon they only had two days cover.

The next day Barry rang to say that Turin had pulled out all the stops and found modifying a standard piece of kit less difficult than they'd imagined and so the required part was on its way.

Mark was elated and to celebrate bought a car as he wanted something more reliable than his old Beetle. He'd seen a Ford Fiesta advertised in the local paper at the sort of price he thought that he could just afford and so at lunch time he made his way to the garage and after a bit of haggling put down a deposit, signed some forms for a hire purchase loan and agreed to collect it on Saturday, then rang his father and asked him to sell the old car.

Sales continued at a high level for the next few days but Barry brought Manchester on stream on day four from the request for his help although at that point most of the company's warehouses around the country were virtually out of stock and so shortages were being made to customers. Paul introduced a short term rationing system whereby whatever orders customers placed, were automatically halved. He also delayed for a month in store cut price promotional activity to further calm demand.

Fortunately with the Manchester additional output stock levels began to improve and Paul ceased rationing demand. Everyone breathed a sigh of relief but it had definitely been a very close run thing.

Double Air continued to break all records and established a much higher market share for itself than had been expected as consumers took to its unique benefits. For Mark it had been a fantastic learning exercise and everyone agreed that he had handled the whole thing with great skill and determination showing an ability far in excess of his relatively short experience.

As the months went by sales dropped back from the heady days of the launch to a more comfortable level which Southampton alone could manage so Manchester stopped producing. Mark sent Barry a letter to thank him for his help.

Mark continued to manage Double Air and at the end of the year he was promoted from Product Assistant to Product Manager. There wasn't a great deal of difference except that his salary went up slightly, he had some more products to look after, and Tammy cooked him a meal in his flat that night to celebrate and then they made love on the floor in front of the electric fire. She regularly stayed overnight now and it was well known at the office that they were becoming a couple.

Soon after the announcement of his new position, Mark received a hand written letter from old Dunson in the London Office which he found touching.

Dear Mark,

I thought that I'd drop you a line to say how pleased I was to read in the internal notices that you've been promoted to Product Manager.

Your promotion is richly deserved and it pleases me that I can claim a small amount of credit for getting you on the first rung of the marketing ladder. I am glad that I was able to help you on your career path which will no doubt be long and stony at times, but with determination and conviction, supported by the "will to win" and lots of hard work, will enable you to defeat all obstacles.

There is no doubt in my mind that you will go a very long way in the Company. Indeed I see no reason at all why you cannot in due course become a member of the Board of Directors. I told you that when you were coming to the end of your time here and I still hold to that view.

I shall myself be retiring in a couple of years from now, so I hope to see you promoted further before I finally go. This is a great Company and you are a worthy member of it.

Work hard my boy, learn well and remember that we always learn from the past. That is what guides our opportunities for the future.

Good luck to you, and best wishes,

Charles Dunson.

He put the letter in his desk drawer and thought about his time in London which in some ways seemed not so long ago, but in others it was a lifetime away. He let his thoughts wander around the old London offices seeing in his mind's eye the various people including Miss Trowse and Debbie. He grinned at the thought of Debbie and concluded that he must pop down to London and see her again some time.

He mentally compared Tammy and Debbie but they were so different that it was really an examination of opposites. Debbie was a free spirit, fun, fairly empty headed and just out for a good time. Tammy was serious, deeply interested in left wing politics, a believer in women's rights and getting clingy.

He didn't want that. There was no way he intended to settle down yet. Others of his age were getting married and settling, but not for him. There was his career to build and just too much in front of him to be tied down to one girl, pretty though she was. He thought that he'd better cool it a bit with Tammy as she was definitely getting possessive. Last night for example.

They'd been at the pub with several others from the office and he'd spent some time chatting to Angela who had just joined the business to be one of the marketing secretaries. She was single and quite fun and he'd enjoyed talking with her but he had no intention of asking her out. However in the car Tammy didn't really talk just grunting monosyllabic answers to his chatting. When he'd asked what was wrong she'd snapped 'nothing' and slumped into silence for the rest of the short journey.

'Look what's up?' he queried when they were inside his flat.

'Nothing'.

'Yes there is. Come on. What is it?'

'Well if you must know I thought from the amount of time you spent with Angela you seemed to be more interested in her than me. You hardly spent any time with me tonight but you were all over her. Do you fancy her? After all I suppose she's quite pretty in a tarty sort of way?'

'Oh don't be so ruddy stupid and I don't think she's at all tarty. She's a nice girl and we were talking about pop music and where we were both brought up. Funnily enough she was born quite near where I was'.

'Bully for her and how can you say she's not tarty with that low cut jumper and her tits on display every time she leant forward. It's pathetic the way you men drooled over them'.

'Don't be so bloody silly or bitchy. Yes she's pretty, got a nice figure and she was fun to talk to but there's nothing special or permanent between you and me is there? We're just..........'

'Bitchy? Nothing special?' Tammy raised her voice. 'We go out together don't we? I sleep with you don't I? Doesn't that mean anything? I don't sleep with just anybody you know' she snapped angrily.

'Yes of course it does. It's marvellous, you're marvellous but I don't want to be tied down at this time. Not by you or by anyone. It's not you, it's me. I have my career and my life in front of me and I want to make that happen in whatever way I can to achieve my long term goals. I am going to get to the very top of industry and I need to be free to do that. Free to manage my career and free to go wherever that career takes me. Tammy if that's not ok for you then I'm sorry but that's the way it is. We can stay as we are if you like but don't get all possessive on me. I won't have it. It's not what I want'.

Looking at him she saw a determination burning in his eyes that she'd never seen before and at that moment she thought that possibly no woman, but certainly not her, would ever come in front of that career ambition.

'I need to think about that and what you want from your life. I thought perhaps we could be more than just boy, girl and sex, maybe something more permanent but now that you've explained what you want then I don't know. I'll have to think about it. It might be best if you took me to my digs. I don't think I want to stay with you tonight'.

He drove her home in silence. Getting out of the car she muttered 'Goodnight' and with her head bowed walked slowly into the house.

Mark drove back to his flat. If she couldn't put up with a casual affair then so be it but he wasn't going to put his ambition to lead a major company and get even with Charles Houghton at some time in the future in jeopardy by having his hands tied down with a mortgage, maybe kids, and scrimping and scraping his way through life.

He wanted to get to the top. Have lots of money. Power. Responsibility. A big house, expensive cars. Yes that's what he wanted but above all, over and above everything else he wanted to get Charles Houghton. He'd promised his father and he would keep that promise and the best way to do that was to get to the head of a major business. Then he would find a way to destroy the man who'd brought so much heartache to his father. For Mark it wasn't a question of if he'd do it, only when.

His career moved rapidly. The affair with Tammy finished as she was unwilling to just have a casual relationship. Also she was suspicious that he was interested in Angela. He wasn't as she'd made it clear that she was happy with her current boyfriend, but she did become his secretary.

However he did sleep with Karen from customer service, twice.

After a further eighteen months he was promoted to Marketing Manager and now had responsibility for something approaching forty percent of the Company's product range and his first company car, a Ford Granada. He also moved from his small, comfortable but slightly dingy flat to somewhere larger and smarter.

In the business he made his impact felt everywhere. He worked tirelessly and established a reputation for being tough with his people but prepared to back and support them against other departments. He loved the interdepartmental warfare and was good at it. He sought alliances where needed, manoeuvred people into agreements, enlisted help from other senior people and established his power base.

Most evenings he avidly read books about business strategy borrowed from the company's excellent selection of such works, or from the main library in the city. He also read biographies of successful people, not only business men, but leaders in history and tried to discover what had made them successful. He particularly admired Hannibal for having the courage to go the way everyone said was impossible and hence outthink, outflank and outfight his opponents.

He developed a wider circle of friends in the area and relied less on colleagues from work. This was partly of his own volition but also they were consciously drawing away from him and his driving career ambitions. He wasn't bothered by it. He saw it as their problem, not his.

There were a number of male friends with whom he'd sink a beer or play squash and he always enjoyed the company of pretty young women many of whom were strongly attracted not only to his good looks, but also to the sense of power that he exuded. He slept with some of them and they instantly they became a subject of envy among the others. That jealousy became more inflamed when they found out from the lucky ones how good he was in bed and especially how big he was in the cock department. Mark was aware of his attraction to women and used it to advantage when he felt the need to do so.

Knowing he'd be in London for a meeting with two of the several advertising agencies that he now used to cover the range of products and brands that came within his portfolio he'd rung Debbie who was delighted to hear from him.

'Fancy a night out for old time's sake?' She did. 'Meet me at eight tomorrow in the foyer of the Hilton on Park Lane. I'm staying there so bring your toothbrush'. She giggled and told him not to be so cheeky.

Having finished his meeting with the second agency he made up his mind. As their creative work wasn't up to scratch and their response time to his demands was too slow he'd split their work. Some would go to the first of the two that he'd been with that morning and who'd been a company agency for years, and he'd pass the remainder to a new hot-shot up and coming ad agency that was rapidly building a reputation for innovative advertising work.

That decided he went back to the Hotel showered and wondered about Debbie. He'd come a long way since her initiation of him into sex nearly four years ago. Although she wasn't the brightest or prettiest girl she was certainly the sexiest he'd experienced in bed so far. Or at least his memory of her was. Tonight would find out if that was still so or whether he'd just thought about it in rose tinted glasses as she'd been the one to help him lose his virginity.

At eight o'clock he was downstairs in the large and airy foyer that saw a continual movement of people. Right on time she came through the revolving doors handbag in one hand and a small grip type bag in the other. Walking straight up to him she stretched up on tiptoe to kiss him. When they broke apart she smiled hello said how nice it was to see him again, and that she'd brought her toothbrush. Holding hands they took a lift to the fifteenth floor. Entering his room she thought it was ever so posh and flung herself on the very large double bed and bounced up and down.

'I'm hungry but do you want to go to bed now and eat later?' she giggled.

'No come on let's eat. I'm starving as well and we've got plenty of time later especially as you've got your toothbrush and are staying' he grinned.

They went back to the lifts and pressing to go up soon stepped out at the marvellous restaurant called Windows that was situated right at the top of the hotel on the twenty eighth floor and gave a fantastic view of London from all directions. Debbie was fascinated at the fairytale sight that greeted them of the miles of street lights and buildings. They ordered drinks and later were taken through to the restaurant which surprisingly wasn't crowded and they had a table to the side to enjoy the view while they talked and ate.

She asked about his work and he talked about lots of things that he thought would amuse or interest her. He was careful not to talk about people at Head Office as he wasn't sure she would keep things to herself but the conversation and the wine flowed and after they'd finished their coffee he suggested it was time to try out the hotel bed.

On their way back down in the lift Debbie's hands were all over him and she smothered him in kisses. They wandered along the thickly carpeted corridor to his room and soon discovered that the hotel bed was extremely comfortable, very bouncy and perfect for their lovemaking which was prolonged, and varied between wild and sensual. Later when they lay side by side sated with sex for the time being she said that he'd obviously not forgotten what she'd taught him and indeed seemed to have passed into an advanced class.

It wasn't long after that as they were cuddled together that she licked him back to erection and climbing on top of him told him 'she was going to fuck the wax out of his ears'. He found her dirty talk very stimulating and later as he drifted off to sleep realised that this time she hadn't bothered with condoms.

They'd ordered breakfast in bed and so in the morning had great fun tipping the chilled orange juice onto different parts of each other's bodies and then licking it off. Debbie seeing that the honey was runny dripped it out of its little glass pot onto his penis and painstakingly licked off every drop. He reciprocated by smearing strawberry jam onto her nipples and took alternate bites of buttered croissant and then a lick of jam which made her nipples hard. She loved it when he poured some of the cream which was intended for their coffee into her pubic hair and then slurped it from her as it trickled greasily down towards her pussy. It was a natural progression for him to start making oral love to her and then they were soon locked into full intercourse.

All too quickly they had to think about leaving. The bed was a mess. Cream, jam, bits of croissant, toast crumbs and orange juice stains were liberally spread on it. They shared a bath, dressed and went downstairs where Mark paid the bill.

His car was in the underground car park and he gave her a lift to the Bedford Square offices before driving into the west end for a further meeting with KLT, the agency he was going to sack. He'd told them yesterday that he'd reflect on their future and return this morning with his decision.

Sitting with the Agency Director and Account Manager, Mark displayed another trait for which he was becoming well known. Getting straight to the point with no preamble he said that regretfully he had decided to rationalise the Company's agencies and that he was taking their billings and splitting them amongst two others.

They were shocked. Although they knew that their recent creative approaches hadn't met with his approval nevertheless they didn't expect to get sacked. It was a serious matter to any advertising agency to lose a client but one as important and prestigious as Thompson and Smith sacking them would reverberate around the tight knit world of advertising.

Mark made clear that his mind was made up and nothing would change it. In about ten minutes it was all over and he left and found his car which was on a meter with a parking ticket attached as he'd forgotten to put in any money. He drove back to Leicester where Bill the Managing Director had left a message with Angela, who'd been his secretary for some time, that he wanted a word with Mark when he got back.

'Bet I know what that's about' he groaned picking up the phone.

'I've had a call from John Broughton head of KLT. He says you told their people you've sacked them. Is that right?'

'Yes, they've had enough warnings. Their work's crap and not getting any better so I've split their billings between Youngmans who've got a big chunk of our ad budget already and are doing good work, and a new hot shot outfit called Fly whose work is very impressive'.

'I've heard of them. Beats me though why advertising agencies have to come up with such bloody stupid names for themselves. Fly, I ask you. What the hell does that symbolise? No don't let's waste time on that but get back to talking about you dumping KLT. Don't you think that you should have talked to me about it first? Ultimately as Managing Director I'm responsible for our advertising and I think common courtesy would have dictated that you should discuss this sort of thing with me'.

'Why?'

'I've just said. Didn't you listen? Have you discussed it with Nick?' Bill snapped.

'Not exactly. I told him last week that I wasn't happy with KLT's work and that we might need to part company but if you mean did I ask his permission then the answer is no. They're my brands. I'm responsible for them. I made and stand by the decision. Bill if you want to be consulted in future I'll do that but for now the decision is made and it stands'.

There was a long pause. 'Mark come down to my office will you. Let's talk about this face to face'.

When he entered Bill's plush office he was invited to sit in one of the easy chairs that were in the corner of the room. Bill took the other. He gazed at Mark for some time and then leaned back rested a hand along the arm of the chair, crossed his legs and folding his hands into his lap started to speak.

'Mark you are a very competent marketer. Your career is going well. You've established a reputation for skill, toughness and hard work that is head and shoulders above your peer group. That's why you've been promoted so quickly. It's clear that you have flair not just for the advertising side of marketing but for developing business strategies and new routes forward for the company. I've read your appraisals, watched you at work and in many ways I admire you.

But you can't always ride rough shod over others. You can't always just use people. You need to work with them, to enlist their help and support and ensure that you've got everyone in the business on side. If you go out on a limb too often, if you drive forward only ever listening to your own views then one day you are going to fall smack bang on your face and when that happens they'll be no-one to mop you up. If you go on using some people while trampling on those that don't fit your pattern of need then when you fall, as one day you will, those that you've upset, hurt or destroyed will seek to get their own back. And you'll have only yourself to blame. I'm a lot older than you. When I was your age I too had a great ambition to succeed and climb the corporate ladder and I've done it. But the difference between us is that I worked with people, fostered teamwork and built my career thoughtfully. You don't'.

'Bill with respect you're wrong. I do work with people. I work in and with teams but yes I admit I'm demanding and tough…..like you'.

'I can be tough when needed. In fact it's a useful weapon in the management armoury but don't use it all the time. Management is a skill that is part taught, part learnt and part intuition. If you are intending to get to the top you have to realise that you can't do it alone. You need people to support you and work with you…… not because they are afraid of you. Human beings make mistakes, need help, have fears and feelings, but will generally try and do their best. Help them and you help yourself'.

Mark looked at the director and said coldly 'Thanks. Now what about KLT? Are you going to back me?'

Bill sighed. 'Of course I am. As you said on the phone they're your brands, you're responsible and it's your decision. That's what I told John when he rang. It would however have been nice to have known beforehand. Did you think I'd overrule you? Management is about backing your subordinates. If they make mainly right decisions they'll go far. If the majority of decisions are wrong or poorly judged then they'll fail and have no job'.

'I know that and I make bloody sure I make more right decisions……... a lot more right decisions than wrong ones. Bill I'm going to get to the very top of industry. That is my mission in life, my goal and nothing will deflect me from it. I appreciate your taking the time to share with me your philosophy of management and I understand what you say and indeed agree with some of it, but not all of it. My way is and will remain to drive hard for performance and eliminate those that perform poorly or fail. Thanks for backing me with KLT by the way'.

'Ok. Mark soon you're going to need to move to another job in the company, maybe in another Division to get you ready for your first really senior management role, running one of the smaller businesses. I'll talk with Corporate Personnel and get back to you. Hey, don't look so worried, it'll be good news'.

'I'm not worried just interested as to where you'll move me' and giving Bill a grin he left and went back to his own more modest office to get on with the pile of work that was waiting for him.

Bill rang Nick Davies and asked if he could spare a minute. Nick knew that a request asking him to spare a minute meant get down there now, so he was soon seated in the seat recently vacated by Mark.

'What do you think of Mark?' began Bill. 'I don't mean his work which I know is damn good. No I mean him and his style. I don't think I've ever come across someone so driven by a desire to get to the top. Why is he so anxious to move up so far so fast? Have you ever looked into his eyes?'

'His eyes?'

'Yes. He sat there where you are now not ten minutes ago. I was talking to him about management style and trying to counsel him to go a bit easier on some of his own people and people generally around the business. He almost ignored my advice and told me he was determined to get to the very top of industry. I think there's no doubt that he will but he almost frightened me with that burning crusade and his eyes were seeing something in his mind that was driving his ambition'.

'I know what you mean. He is quite ruthless and I've also occasionally seen something in his eyes. I think once when he first started here he almost told me what it was that was driving him on fuelling his ambition, but he didn't and he never has since then. The strange thing is that those that are really good at their jobs and can survive his style will do anything for him. It is quite remarkable.

'I think it's time we got Corporate Personnel involved in his career. I'll talk to them'.

Making his excuses Nick left as he hadn't got time if Bill wanted to have a long chat about management development.

CHAPTER 11

Corporate Personnel were located in the basement of the building. The personnel Director, an Irishman by the name of Patrick O'Connell was ginger haired, short, wiry and known to be highly effective at identifying and developing potential high flyers in the business. He was also ruthless in helping management get rid of underperformers.

He'd been keeping an eye on Mark's career from a distance and although having checked with Bill and Nick about how he was getting on had not had a face to face career discussion with him. Now Bill had asked him to do that so he rang and fixed for them to meet.

At the appointed time Mark walked along the lower corridor to the staircase leading down to Personnel. He pushed open the door and was surprised at the bright appearance of the offices. Somehow he'd thought that a combination of personnel and the basement would have generated a dull boring set of offices. Not a bit of it. The people there were cheerful and looked happy and a young girl who'd always had a bit of a crush on Mark blushed and asked if she could help him.

'Yes please. I'm here for a meeting with Pat so if you just point me in the right direction I'll go and find him'.

The little personnel girl said that she'd take him and led off through the open plan office area to the far end where there were some individual offices. She stopped at one of those and knocked. Receiving a loud invitation to come in she opened the door and said that Mark Watson was here for his meeting. He smiled and thanked her. She blushed saying that it had been no trouble.

'Hi there Mark. Come on in, coffee?'

'Thanks that'd be great'.

'Could you do a couple of coffees Louise and see if you can rustle up some biscuits eh, there's a good girl'.

'Well now settle yourself down'. He indicated a couple of easy chairs. 'Now this is quite an informal chat just so we can get a bit more of a handle on what you want from your career. Bill tells me that you're very ambitious and he's sent me your review forms and appraisals. You've certainly made an impact here since you came and you've moved pretty quickly haven't you? Knocked a few people about too I see. In a

hurry are you? Ah Louise thanks, just put them over there on the desk'
he said as she returned with a tray of coffees and biscuits.

'Oh I'll bring them over for you. Black for you as usual Pat? Is white
with no sugar alright Mark? There's only some digestives, I hope they're
alright?'

When Mark looked straight into her eyes and smiled his thanks she
blushed again and nearly dropped the plastic cups but with an effort
managed to put them down on the coffee table that was between the
two chairs and then went and brought over the biscuits. Pat waited until
she'd left before picking up his cup and looking over the rim at Mark
as he opened the conversation.

'So what do you see as your long term career objectives?'

'That's simple. I am going to become the head of a major business.
This one, one of our competitors or one in another industry completely.
I don't mind, but get to the top I will. Not yet of course as I've still got
a lot to learn but in time I can do it, and not too much time either.
I make no secret of my ambition or my goal. Others have done it.
People like Charles Houghton for example. He's grown and built their
business from small beginnings when he took it over from his father
and turned it into a major company. I don't know if I'd want to run a
family business. Well I can't, my family don't have a business' he paused
and just stopped himself from saying 'any more not after that bastard
Houghton destroyed it' but he didn't and instead continued 'but get to
the head of a business, run it, grow it, make it highly successful and
provide above average returns for the shareholders that's what I want,
no not want, that's what I am going to do'. He was leaning forward
looking straight at Pat who saw the determination burning like a beacon
from him.

'I tink you moight well make it' replied the highly impressed
personnel man reverting to his native Irish brogue as he often did when
he was thinking quickly about how to handle an issue. 'Look Mark if
dat's what you want den our task is to help you develop to enable you
to achieve your dreams while at the same time harnessing your skills
and energy for the Company's benefit'.

'Not dreams Pat reality' and Mark's eyes burned deep into the other
man.

The conversation then went into detail as to what Mark had achieved so far, what he'd learnt, where he felt he needed more experience, what he saw as his next steps. They discussed, debated, argued and eventually agreed a mutual plan of action for Mark's career development. Pat warned Mark that it was a tough lonely road where mistakes were not expected or tolerated for long in those who were on the fast track to senior management.

After an hour the meeting was coming to an end Mark. Getting up Mark added 'I know what I want and when I want it. Timescale is not flexible for me. I look forward to seeing what you can, and are going to do'.

Leaving Pat's office he walked back through the main personnel department, paused to thank Louise for the coffee and went back upstairs to his own office leaving a thoughtful Pat, and a flustered Louise.

His work continued unabated for the next few months and he drove himself and his teams very hard. His results were good and he found himself spending more time with Paul Feldman and his senior sales teams.

The demands of their major customers for more information, more market research data, more complex business strategies were taxing the traditional skills of the senior sales people and increasingly they were calling Mark in to help present these new more complicated presentations to their customers.

Mark loved the cut and thrust of the negotiations. He was sharp, quick and good at it and even Paul had to admit that when Mark was firing on all cylinders then he was more than a match for any tough supermarket buyer.

So he frequently found himself working alongside Paul not fighting against him and although he never forgave him for potentially exposing him all that long time ago at the conference nevertheless he supported Paul because it meant that his products and brands would get the support from their customers. That was the reason why he did it, not to help Paul.

No he had decided long ago that one day he'd pay Paul back for what he had done, but he would pick his time. When he attacked it would be swift and effective so he waited patiently and worked alongside Paul.

But gradually relations between the two men deteriated. At meetings there was obviously an atmosphere between the two which everyone noticed but Mark ignored. 'Mind your own bloody business and get on with what you're paid to do' he'd snap at any of his team who questioned him about it.

One day a problem arose with one of the supermarket chains who announced that they were no longer going to support a particular Thompson and Smith product and instead were going to stock a competitor's product range. This was a big blow and meant that the company would lose a large amount of volume. Mark was furious and stormed in to see Bill the Managing Director accusing Paul and his team of incompetence and ineptitude.

It was strong stuff and whilst Bill privately thought that Paul ought to have seen the problem coming, to Mark he would only say that supermarket buyers were tough people and that it wasn't always possible to hold onto all the company's products in every one of them. But Mark wouldn't be placated and demanded that Paul be replaced. 'I could do a better job than him' he ranted. 'Come on Bill this isn't the first time that he's cocked up. I'm always bailing him out. Enough's enough.'

He then went on to cite specific instances and without saying anything that wasn't true he nevertheless managed to ensure that Bill realised that he'd had a lot more to do with many of the company's success with customers than had Paul. From that moment on Mark went on the attack whenever he could. He never missed an opportunity to damage Paul but was careful how he did it. Where it was an obvious point he'd attack in public. Where it was more subtle then he'd attack behind the scenes with Nick, Bill, occasionally the two together. Sometimes he'd write devastating reports on failures by the Sales department which he would circulate widely.

No-one knew whether it was the latest document that Mark had circulated citing various customer problems or if he was distracted by yet another row with Mark, or perhaps other issues were playing on his mind. The reason why it happened could never be established but what was certain was that Paul took a corner too fast on his way home one evening, skidded off the road straight into a tree and was killed instantly.

The police registered it as an accident caused by excessive speed and the coroner expressed sympathies to Paul's widow and family.

It was not said in public that the rows had caused it but behind closed doors there was much muttering and accusing. Mark didn't accept that he had anything to be sorry about and although he attended the funeral to pay his respects he left quickly afterwards and went straight back to work adding to his reputation as a hard man lacking in some feelings. This didn't bother him as he was becoming more and more single minded about climbing the corporate ladder and nothing was to stand in his way.

Another meeting took place between Bill and Pat O'Connell where they were deciding how best to replace Paul. There was no-one of the right calibre to promote. Pat had trawled through potential candidates from other Companies in the Thompson and Smith Group but no-one seemed quite right so he dropped his bombshell.

'Have you tought about giving it to Mark?' he asked with a disarming smile in his soft Irish brogue.

'Mark? Paul and his team were at daggers drawn with Mark. How the hell could he take over that team?'

'With some difficulty I grant you, but why not?. Tink about it. Poacher turned Gamekeeper. If he tinks he's dat bloody good then let him have a go. It'll oither be the making or the breaking of him and you know oi've got a sneaking feeling he'll make a go of it'

'Bloody hell I knew you corporate personnel types were devious but that's a real gem. Let me think about it'.

He did very carefully. It was a vital job and one for which the right person had to be found but the more he thought about it, the more slowly at first but then with increasing acceptance, he warmed to the idea. After all Mark himself had often said that he could do the job so why not let him? He was bright he'd proved he was a good negotiator and he was tough. Paul had certainly slipped a bit in the past year and was much less demanding on his teams than he'd been before. Maybe Mark's hard pushing style was what was needed.

Bill took a detour home that night and drove to the place where Paul had been killed. He stopped his car, got out and walked over to the tree that had ended Paul's life. There was a shocking scrape on the bark and various bits of car debris still scattered around. Broken glass, part of the bumper, assorted twisted small bits of metal where the fire brigade had cut the car apart to get Paul out. As he looked at this detritus he wondered if he would be doing Paul a dishonour by appointing Mark. Was he insulting the dead? What would Paul say if he could speak? Did it matter? Returning to the car he sat for some while looking at the crash site thinking deeply. Finally making up his mind he took a deep breath and drove away.

In the morning Mark walked to Bill's office wondering why he'd been summoned a few minutes earlier.

'Go in they're expecting you' smiled Margaret, Bill's middle aged secretary. Mark puzzled over the use of the plural wording until he saw Pat O'Connell in the room with Bill. Now why was the head of corporate personnel there?

Bill looked at him. 'Mark sit down. I'll come straight to the point. You need a career move and we've got Paul's job to fill. Put the two together and I think that's what we should do. I want you to take over as Sales Director. You're a bit young for it and you've still a lot to learn but we think it's the right move for you and for the Company. We're going to ship in someone from another Division to take over your responsibilities next week so you can get at the sales role almost immediately. You've often expressed your views on how the sales function could be improved. Well here's your chance to put it into practice. It's a big job but we think you're ready for such a challenge. What do you say?'

'Terrific. I'll show you that you've made the right decision Bill. Thanks'.

'We're all here to help' added Pat. 'Never be afraid to ask for help Mark it isn't a sign of weakness, it's a sign of strength. Remember that'.

Mark looked at him and then nodded slowly. 'Yep I'll remember all right, thanks Pat, and Bill thanks again. Terms and conditions?'

'Well put all that in writing to you today. Best of luck with it'.

Pat also held out his hand and shook Mark's firmly. 'Yes, good luck'.

Mark returned to his office and called his existing marketing team together to explain what was happening and then he called the senior sales managers together and introduced himself as their new boss.

The reaction showed on their faces. Some looked shocked, some worried, a few delighted, but all apprehensive. They knew his reputation and work rate and his pace of driving people but most of all they knew his requirement for excellence in all things work related.

Once he started Mark tore into the sales operation like a whirlwind. Those that he decided were below the required standard got fired. He restructured the operation and took out some layers of field management in order to improve accountability of his senior sales managers. He recruited the best salesmen and senior sales negotiators that he could find. Some came from their competitors and some from companies in different fields. He set new and more demanding objectives and visited every sales region in the country. He made sales calls with the salesmen as well as with their managers and immediately everyone who came into contact with him although somewhat intimidated were nevertheless highly impressed with the way he got things done and the undoubted ability he had to sell and negotiate. "Do it now" was his saying "Not tomorrow or next week, now".

The results were soon clear to see and sales started to climb. After six months he held a conference and the visitors from marketing, research, personnel and other departments could see a sales force which was sharper, brighter, and more confident in themselves and what they could achieve. They also revered Mark.

'They almost fucking worship the guy' whispered Pat to another colleague. 'Look at them'. It was clear that their respect was certainly higher than would be normally expected. 'He's sure got some charisma and style' he continued quietly. 'We made a good choice putting him into that job. They may not like him but they sure are supporting him. Oi reckon dat dey'd do anything for him you know'.

For the next two years Mark drove the sales results very hard and the company's market shares, distribution and volume of sales increased out of all recognition. However by the end of that time he was starting to get restless and thinking about the next bigger job as part of his path to the top and to Charles Houghton.

Three years after he'd become sales director one day Pat rang him.

'There's a great job going as Managing Director of our business located in Corby. Makes shampoos and that sort of stuff. Interested? The present incumbent is retiring. We think they need a bit of a bolshie bastard to stir things up. Could be right up your street. Like me to have a word?'

Mark said yes and so a few days later he went to the new business to meet Ted Boyd, the shortly retiring Managing Director.

The site was located on an industrial estate at Corby in Northamptonshire which had once been the centre of steel production but had been closed many years ago initially bringing tremendous unemployment and hardship to the men and their families who had worked there. But with Government help and incentives gradually new lighter industry had moved to the area and now it was a booming sprawling industrial estate populated by hundreds of different businesses, some large, some small. Thompson and Smith's plant was one of the larger units, established there five years ago replacing two older factories elsewhere. It was like many of the other factory units on the industrial estate a large shiny metal box, boring to look at but functional in use.

As soon as Mark arrived he saw that improvements were needed. The small reception area was untidy and the girl behind reception looked scruffy and took some time to acknowledge him.

'Can I 'elp you?' but she looked as though she couldn't care whether she could or not.

'Thank you I'm here to see Mr. Boyd. I'm Mark Watson by the way'.

Disinterestedly she picked up the phone, dialled a number and said 'Some bloke here to see Ted' and listening to the response at the other end looked at Mark and said 'What did you say your name was?'

'Mark Watson'.

'Says he's Mark Watson....... right ho'. She replaced the phone. 'Take a seat and someone'll come'.

'Thank you. Have you worked here long?'

'Two years' she replied in a tone that indicated that it was two years too long. Well if he had anything to do with it he'd soon solve that problem for her. He studied the walls which showed some photographs of the company's products but they were hardly up to date and clearly needed refreshing. As he looked around he saw that the carpet was dirty, the walls needed repainting and generally the place had a tired and uncared for look.

'Mark, hello there and welcome to Corby' announced a tall elderly thin man who had advanced part way down the stairs that ran up one side of the reception area and was now leaning over the metal banisters towards Mark. 'Come on up' and he met Mark half way holding out a thin hand but nevertheless shook Mark's hand firmly.

They went up to his office which was nicely furnished if in a somewhat old fashioned style. 'Coffee?' and he rang through to someone called Sam and ordered for them both. 'So, Pat tells me you're ready for your first MD's job. Well this would be as good a place as any to start. Nice business, got a few problems but not so big that it's always attracting the attention of the top brass. No, here you're very much your own boss. Well now tell me about yourself'.

So Mark talked about his life to date, what he'd done, his achievements and his ambition to get to the top of a major business and run it. His passion burned out of him and Ted was not only impressed but slightly frightened by the evident desire to get to the top. They talked for a long time and then Ted asked Sam to get Raj to come up. He explained that Raj Patel was the Production Director in charge of the factory and distribution.

When he came in Mark saw that Raj was a tall impressive Indian man who spoke softly and yet exuded a quiet determination. Introductions were made and Mark spent the next couple of hours being taken around the factory. In his mind he contrasted everything he saw with his first visit to Southampton years ago. Since then he'd visited lots of factories and could see if they were well run. This one was. It was clean, tidy and obviously efficient. Questioning Raj about his cost structure, labour relations, efficiencies, stock levels and despatch rates confirmed that here was a man who knew what he was doing.

So if the factory was fine, why weren't they making a lot more money than they were at present.

This business sold cosmetic style products, shampoos, hair care ranges, body lotions and a few other assorted products and a short discussion with Brad Pringle the Sales and Marketing Director soon identified where the problem lay. The products had been downgraded over the last couple of years and sold on a cheap price platform. The result was that sales volume hadn't increased but their revenue had gone down. The whole business had tilted towards what was often known as "value" which really meant cheap.

Ted confirmed that this had been the strategy which initially had worked well, but for the last twelve months it seemed to have failed. He thought a re-launch might be needed. The Finance Director Alan Wells was another quiet man but unlike Raj he struck Mark as quietly ineffective.

Returning to Ted's office Mark questioned him deeply for a further hour before thanking him for his time and taking his leave. He smiled at the disinterested receptionist who barely acknowledged his departure and returned to his car. Driving away he stopped at the first phone box he could find and rang Angela his secretary.

'Hi there' she responded cheerily 'have you had a good day? What were you doing in Corby by the way, you didn't say?'

'Nosey. I was having a look to see if there was anything to learn from them. Look can you ring me back as I'm in a call box and haven't got much money on me'.

'Was there?' asked Angela when she reconnected with him.

'What?'

'Was there much to learn?'

'Oh yes lots. Anyhow any messages'.

She outlined a few issues which they dealt with between them and then he asked her so see if Pat O'Connell was free. He was so she transferred the call.

'Mark me boy how did you get on up at Corby? Interesting visit oi dare say'.

'Pat it's a shambles. Not the factory. That seems ok and run by a good chap..........'

'Raj, yes he's one of our best Production Directors. We'll want him to move him out of there in a year or so as he'll then be ready for a bigger production job. He worked his way up from the shop floor you know. A real grafter, sort of chap you'll like and get on with'.

'Yes I do but as for all the rest, well that's a disaster. They've got the wrong strategy for price, wrong positioning of the product range and..........'

'So you'd be interested in replacing Ted then. Think you could handle it?'

'I know I could. It's right up my street. Sort out Sales and Marketing. The factory's ok for now. What I'd do is...................'

'Hold on' interrupted Pat. 'Don't tell me what you're going to do. All I want to know is do you want the job and do you think you can do it?'

'Yes and yes'.

'Right. I'll talk to the brass and get back to you. When are you next in here?'

'Tomorrow'.

' Leave it with me'

'Pat do you think I'll get it? Is someone else is in line for it? I can't be the only candidate'

'Your not but I think you're the best. I said leave it with me'.

Next morning he worked normally although Angela noticed a certain tension about him which was unusual. Around four o'clock he heard Pat's Irish brogue gently teasing Angela about her new hairstyle and then he walked into Mark's office and sat down. Mark felt tense as Pat's face gave nothing away.

'The usual procedure would be for a potential MD to be if not interviewed at least seen by one or two members of the Main Board of the holding company especially someone that they don't really know'. He paused and Mark's heart pumped strongly as he swallowed. 'In this case however there's to be a different approach to appointing the MD'.

Oh shit thought Mark, I've not got it. Who the hell has he wondered? 'Based on the recommendation of Bill and me and because it is felt that the main problems are marketing, sales and strategic positioning then they've decided to give it to you, sort of sight unseen'.

'Really? You mean I've got it?'

'Yes moi lad you have. Now two tings come to me moind. Firstly you owe me a large point of Guinness for me help in getting you the job. Secondly don't you let me or Bill down. Oh and maybe one other ting. When you become Chairman one day remember those that helped you get there eh!' and he grinned as he held out his hand to congratulate Mark.

So that was it. Mark had got his first Managing Director's job. Two week's later he had a quick last walk round and chat to his team, said goodbye to Angela who wished him the best of luck and he was on his way to Corby.

It wasn't a big business, it wasn't high profile, but it was his, and he was going to show them what he could do with it, and of course he reminded himself it took him another step nearer to Charles Houghton.

CHAPTER 12

He arrived early just after seven o'clock on his first Monday morning, having had a good quick drive over to Corby there being little traffic at that time of the morning.

The front door to reception was locked so he walked round the side of the building into the rear yard where a couple of trucks were waiting for drivers. The door into the despatch area was open. He went in vaguely remembering where he was from his recent site tour with Raj. He met and introduced himself to various people he came across but didn't explain what his role was to be as there hadn't been any announcements yet about him replacing Ted Boyd.

The workforce seemed cheerful enough and answered his questions quite happily. He couldn't get into the main factory from the despatch area but there was a small refreshment room off despatch with tea and coffee machines and getting himself a cup of coffee he sat down wondering why machine tea or coffee always tasted so awful.

A giant of a man came in wearing grubby overalls smelling of diesel. Plonking a small canvas grip onto one of the tables he went to the machine got himself a cup of something then made his way back where he reached into his bag and extracted a foil pack which when unwrapped revealed some thick sandwiches. He ate slowly slurping his drink at the same time. Looking at Mark he frowned.

'Don't see many of your types down here specially at this time of the morning mate' and looking suspiciously at Mark he went on chewing his sandwich.

'No I guess you don't. I'm Mark Watson by the way. I start work here today but I arrived early so I thought I'd have a look around. Seems quite busy here this morning'.

'Yep. I'm Joe by the way. I'm a driver, long distance and I'm taking one of them trucks to Salisbury. Full load'. He paused dipping his giant hand into his plastic box to retrieve another sandwich which he unwrapped and taking a mighty bite looked back at Mark. 'Am and pickle. That's what I like for me breakfast. The missus makes 'em, gets up and does 'em while I'm getting dressed. Always has, always will I guess. Answering your question though until recently we've been pretty quiet but things av picked up now. Still it's good that we're busy here

161

isn't it. Keeps us working class blokes in work. Terrible it was when the steel works shut. Terrible' and he sat for a few moments shaking his head at the memory.

'Have you worked here for a long time?'

'Since it first started mate. Used to be in the steel works. Horrible that was, dirty and dangerous driving them loads of steel but when steelworks closed there were no jobs around here then. Lots of us blokes on the dole. Shocking. Then companies started to move in 'ere including this one who advertised for drivers and I applied. There was a queue of people wanting jobs, any jobs. Guess I was lucky as I got one of the driving jobs and I've been 'ere ever since. It's alright here, much better than the steel job. Well must be off, see yer' and with that he gathered up his bag, scrunched up the wrapping paper from his sandwiches in his enormous hands and dropped it plus his cup in the rubbish bin.

'Look at this some blokes must live in a pigsty' he said picking up some empty cups and bits of paper from another table and put them in the bin as well. 'Bye mate' and wiping his mouth on the back of one of his giant hands while in the other he held his small canvas bag he wandered out to his truck which soon roared into life and drove out of the yard on its long journey to Wiltshire.

Mark looked at his watch and seeing it was ten to eight walked briskly round to reception which was now unlocked but unmanned. He went up the stairs and walked around.

A few people had arrived and were starting work but this included getting cups of tea or coffee, chatting about last night's football, or to which pub they'd been, or discussing the latest episode of a tv soap. They all seemed quite cheerful but somehow lacking in energy. Lethargic was the word that sprang to Mark's mind. He wandered from office to office introducing himself and explaining that he was going to be working there and what surprised him was that no-one asked him what he was going to do. Perhaps it had been announced already although he had understood that the announcements were to be made that morning. Still office and company grapevines were amazingly efficient. He thought the offices could also do with a coat of paint.

Making his way to Ted's office he sat in one of the easy chairs thinking. He left the door open and waited. Around half past eight Samantha, who he remembered was Ted's secretary, walked in to the outer office area, took off her coat then coming into Ted's office smiled as she held out her hand which he shook noting her firm grip.

'Hello I'm Samantha but please call me Sam. Welcome to Corby. I usually get in about now but if you want me to start earlier or later just say. I'm pretty flexible. Ted gets in about nine or thereabouts. Now can I get you anything?'

He asked her a number of questions and was pleased that even though she'd only been with the business for about a year she seemed to know what she was doing and how things generally went on around the place. They chatted until sure enough just after nine Ted walked in and added his welcome to Samantha's.

'Now' he said 'where shall we start? I've been here for a goodly long time and so much of it is second nature to me. You ask what you want'.

So he did. He spent the next two hours pumping questions at Ted and querying everything in the business. How, why, when and what. Ted found the interrogation quite unnerving however it gave Mark a thorough grasp of the fundamentals of the business in a very short space of time. This was a technique which as his career developed and he advanced up the ladder he used frequently and successfully when he wanted information or answers from his subordinates. They found the experience demanding and wearying but for Mark it was highly effective.

He then shocked Ted by asking when he was actually going to go as he felt that having the two of them around would be difficult and he thought it would be better if he took over straight away and Ted found himself something else to do until his retirement. Ted protested that three months working together was what he'd had in mind, but Mark was adamant and suggested that Ted busied himself saying good bye to customers, agencies, staff and other Thompson and Smith business heads.

Leaving Ted to think about that he asked Samantha to set up a meeting in the Board room of all heads of department and her which she did for eleven o'clock. She reminded him to call her Sam not Samantha.

Mark and Sam arrived four minutes before eleven. He seated himself at the head of the table and opened a folder. Just on eleven two people walked in followed in the next few minutes by two more and then one other arrived. Leaning over to Mark she said that everyone was present except Tom Chivers who was known for being late for meetings. He nodded said nothing and just sat looking around the room at the assembled company. His stare and silence made everyone feel uncomfortable. Finally the door opened and Tom came in muttering apologies for being late and sat down. Mark looked around the room before he started to speak.

'This meeting was scheduled for eleven o'clock. It is now seven minutes past eleven and finally everyone is here. That is seven minutes that everyone has wasted because some of you couldn't get organised to present themselves on time. There are eight of us here who have all wasted seven minutes each which by my mathematics is fifty six minutes, a fraction short of an hour. A whole hour's work wasted because some of you can't get to a meeting on time. To my mind slackness at arriving on time indicates slackness in the business. Now, you may have time to waste, I don't. In future if a meeting is scheduled to start at a particular time kindly ensure that you are all present promptly and ready to start at the designated time. That applies whether I am attending or not. Clear?' and he looked slowly around the room studying each of his team's faces one by one. There were various expressions of apology, acceptance or agreement.

'Yes look Mark I was tied up on..................'

Mark interrupted. 'I'm not interested in why you were late. You were late it's as simple as that. I'm not debating it with you, nor wasting any more time discussing it. In future get to meetings on time.

Now I believe that Ted told you, the senior team, last Friday that I have been appointed as his successor. That is effective from today. This is my first Managing Director's appointment and I am intending to make a great success of it. I'd like to work with you as a team but if you don't meet my standards which you'll find are high and I daresay a lot more demanding than Ted's then we'll be parting company. As I'm not leaving.........you will.

The rules are simple. Work hard, keep me informed, no nasty surprises and let's get the job done. This place has a great opportunity to grow and become a much more important part of the Thompson and Smith Group.

My initial view is that the strategy you've been following is wrong. We should be improving quality, upgrading packaging, developing new products and building the brands that we have. Your present plan of going down market is flawed and is not only failing now, but will continue to fail as you get clobbered from the top down by the big brands and squeezed from bottom up by the supermarket's own labels and other cheap brands. You're in no mans land, and losing.

We need to position ourselves upmarket and gain the benefits of higher prices and better margins that we can re-invest in the brand. When was the last time you did any advertising? Too long ago to remember I guess. Look we're in the fashion business. We're selling image and style not cheaply priced products. Now I want to see each of you separately today for some individual one to one sessions. Sam will fix times and then we'll get to know each other. If you need me anytime just come and see me. I work informally so I'll keep formal meetings down to a minimum. Any questions?'

There was silence so Mark said that the meeting was over and getting up he walked out closely followed by Sam leaving his team there. As soon as he'd gone there was a burst of conversation.

'Arrogant bastard' exclaimed Brad. 'Wrong strategy he says, well what does he know about it? He hasn't been here five minutes and already he's pontificating about changing strategy. I'll soon put him right on that and stop those grand ideas'.

'Yes, it's too soon for him to be making sweeping changes' added Alan Wells the finance director.

'Maybe we do need some change' chipped in David Levy the Legal Director. 'After all we've hardly been a great success in the past couple of years have we and we all know that Group HQ isn't enamoured with our results. I think it's only because Ted is so near to retirement that they've left us alone'.

'We've not got the resources to do what he wants. We've geared ourselves to value, not brand image and as for all that stuff about being late for meetings. He talks like a schoolmaster' chimed in Tom Chivers the technical director.

Their voices rose as they all started to discuss what Mark had said except Raj who sat silent until a pause occurred in the conversation when he said quietly 'He's right and you're wrong. I've told you guys before we're doing the wrong thing cheapening the product and going downmarket but you wouldn't take any notice. He gets my vote and support and if you'll excuse me I've got a factory to run'. He rose and started to walk out.

'Fucking creep' muttered Brad. 'Now it seems to me.........'

'Brad, Mark would like to see you now' said Sam who had quietly re-entered the room 'and this notice is going up on the notice boards at lunch time' she added handing them all a piece of paper.

ANNOUNCEMENT

This is to advise that Mr. Mark Watson has today joined this business to succeed me as Managing Director. His appointment is effective immediately.

Mark has been with the Company for over five years and has been working as Marketing Manager for our aerosol and polish ranges in the Leicester operation. He was responsible for the very successful launch of Double Air which is, now one of the Company's biggest brands.

I know you will make him welcome and give him every support to continue the progress that we've made here over the past few years.

TED BOYD
Managing Director.

'Shit' said Brad, 'I thought Ted had a few months to go before he left, Sam'.

'No. Mark's taking over today and Ted will spend the next few weeks on various projects and things'.

'Well he hasn't wasted any time has he? Bloody hell things are going to be different around here. What a pity. Old Ted was good as gold and easy to persuade. This guy might be a bit tougher'.

'A lot tougher I reckon' called Raj as he left for his factory.

Brad went back to his office had a quick flick through the mail that had arrived that morning, selected a range of documents and papers so that he could answer any questions that he thought Mark might throw at him and walked to Sam's office.

'So where's the great new man ensconced himself then?' he asked.

'Here behind you' called Mark from a small office that led off the area in which Sam's office was located. I'm here for today while Ted's moving out. Tomorrow I'll move in to his office'.

'Right. Well how can I help you. I really do think that you've got this strategy thing wrong you know Mark. Now let me tell you why'.

'Brad stop there. Let me explain the way that I see it. You're the one that's got it wrong and if you can't see that then there's not a lot of hope for us is there? You're getting killed out in the market place as it is and if you go on as you are, then you'll eventually get squeezed into nothing. No, we're going upmarket. New branding, new positioning, new packs, new products. So get used to it right now'.

But Brad didn't. He argued with Mark and was generally unhelpful until Mark realised that he'd no chance of changing Brad's views and therefore no chance of succeeding in changing the whole product positioning. He brought the meeting to an end and decided that the answer would be to get rid of Brad and find someone with views that not only fitted with his own but also believed in the need for change.

He had his individual meetings with the rest of the team and found that his Finance Director Alan Wells was hopelessly committed to avoidance of change; David Levy as Legal Director didn't seem to have a full time job and in any case Mark wondered why this small business wanted a legal director when all legal advice was available from the Group Legal centre in London; Tom Chivers seemed stubbornly wedded to the existing strategy; the only one who could see what Mark was talking about and supported him was Raj who Mark found had a refreshing attitude to change believing in the process of continuous improvement and that whatever was done could always be improved . He and his team constantly sought ways to do that.

At the end of his first day Mark called Sam in to see him. 'Look I know you've worked for Ted for a while but things are going to be very different with me. Do you think that you can cope with that? I need to know because if it's going to be a problem then you'd better tell me so I can find someone else'.

'I think with the amount of change it seems that you're going to create here you'd better have someone at your side who knows their way around the business and Group. Yes I'd like to stay and help you but I'd like to do more than just be a secretary. Ted is a lovely man but he was very traditional and sees me.........err, saw me just as a secretary. Open the post, get his phone calls, type his letters and make his coffee. I'd like to do more than that.'

Mark looked at her carefully. 'Tell me about yourself'. She did and as he listened he realised that she could perhaps be a right hand to him, not in any executive way but if she understood what he'd instinctively seen as wrong with the business, she could help him. At least he'd have two kindred spirits, her and Raj. He asked her about the team and her views accurately mirrored his own thoughts.

He also realised that she was extremely attractive. Tall with shoulder length pale blonde hair, a lovely figure, wonderful legs and a really charming smile which bordered on the sexy side.

'There's one other problem here you know Mark'.

'Only one' he laughed.

'Oh there's lots but one really big one. Who buys our products?'

'What? Well women I guess. After all most of them are for women so I guess they're bought by women'.

'Exactly and how many women are there in senior positions in this business? None. You're all men thinking about women's products. You've got a couple of juniors who are female in the marketing department but that's all. What you want is women creating products for women.

The whole business is male. The offices, the décor it's all very male orientated and as for that unhelpful cow down in reception she should be got rid of and quickly.' She looked at him and smiled. 'There you are that's a woman's logic for you'.

Mark stared at her and his eyes bored straight into her. She shifted in her seat but returned the stare for a little while until she could no longer hold his eyes and looked away. 'Sam you could be right. No not could be right you are right. Well I'm buggered. Sorry. But it's so obvious now you mention it. Well that'll create a stir won't it? Hey keep this to yourself but I've already decided to replace Brad and Alan and maybe David. Don't know about Tom Chivers. What do you think of him?'

'He's alright and a clever technical man but he needs different people working for him. He needs some.........'

'Women?'

'Yes some women' she laughed. He decided she had a delightful laugh which showed her perfect white teeth, exceedingly kissable lips and a very pink tongue.

'Sam you've already contributed more than a secretary. Work with me and together we'll blow the lid off this place. Look I'm intend to get to the very top of industry and I'd like you to help me do that. I am very ambitious you know.'

'I know'.

'How, we've only just met?'

'I rang Angela and asked her all about you as soon as Ted said you were coming here'.

'And what she did say about me?'

'Now that would be telling'.

'Oh come on tell me what she said' he wheedled.

'That's secretary to secretary information and that's how it will stay. My lips are sealed. Wild horses, new managing directors, nor force marching me naked through Corby will drag those secrets out of me'.

Looking at her twinkling eyes and sparkling smile he decided that Sam would be a great asset. She was clearly bright, obviously had a sense of humour, very pretty and as for the thought of her naked? Yes he thought he and Sam could go a long way together.

'All right I give in' he grinned 'but we have a lot to do'.

'We'll do it. You'll do it. I just know you will. I think you're just what this business needs, as long as you've got the balls to make changes and.........'

'And?'

'Get some women in'.

'Alright don't bloody keep on. Can you get me Pat O'Connell in Leicester on the phone please' and then you can go for tonight and I'll see you in the morning'.

He picked up some papers that she'd put on his desk and started to read while waiting for his phone call.

'Pat for you. Good night see you tomorrow' announced Sam crisply as she put the call through.

'Mark me boy how's your first day. Caused a revolution yet?'

'Pat I need some women'.

'Ah well don't we all. Now oi'm a happily married man meself so oi don't have the need if you follow me, but oi'd have tought dat you'd be able to foind yourself...........'

'Shut up' he snapped interrupting Pat's Irish brogue. 'I don't mean women like that I mean women for the business, at the top and near the top. I've got to make some changes to the team here and quickly and I want some women'.

He went on to speak enthusiastically about the opportunities in the business and Pat saw the logic behind what Mark was saying about needing a woman's view in the business. Mark said that he'd decided to split the position of Sales and Marketing Director into two separate roles and he wanted a tough Sales Director who could be a man as long as he realised they were in the fashion business but it was essential that he had a creative woman as Marketing Director and some women marketing managers.

'Well were not blessed with many women at senior levels in Thompson and Smith but I'll have a scout around the Group and see what we've got. If not you'll have to advertise. I'll get back to you tomorrow'.

Getting up he walked into Ted's office which now looked bare as all his personal effects, photographs and other assorted things were piled up in a couple of cardboard boxes on his desk. 'Ah here you are Mark. All cleared out for you. I gather you've started to create a few waves around here already'.

Mark looked quizzically at the older man who said that Brad had been in to see him as he wasn't happy with Mark's plans.

'Too fucking bad' snarled Mark as he helped a somewhat shocked Ted finish filling his cardboard boxes.

Pat didn't ring back next morning and it was Thursday afternoon before he called. 'Tough challenge you gave me but we've got several female marketers and I'll send through their details. For your Marketing Director though there's only one possible candidate in the Group and she's called Lizzie Montgomery. Thirty eight years of age, divorced, classically trained marketeer and currently marketing manager in our French business. She's been there nearly three years and is ready for a move. She could be your ideal candidate. Bit difficult to handle though. Want to meet her?'

They also discussed possible candidates for Sales Director and arranged that details of those candidates would be sent to him.

Mark reflected on the power and authority which he as Managing Director now had. Although he reported to what was called a Group Director who had several managing directors reporting to him, for the first time he was really alone and able to make decisions about his business and about his people on his own authority. He'd decided to get rid of three of his senior team and now the corporate wheels were in motion to make that happen. It was awesome and made him realise that he held the power of people's careers in his hands.

He realised that he'd been tough before and made the odd changes in his team but nothing like this. This was creating the team that he needed to enable him to change and build this business. This was all part of his climb to the top to avenge his father and get that bastard Charles Houghton.

Every day he scanned the papers for details of Houghton's business or information on Houghton himself and every article he saw whether he carefully cut out and put in a special file that he'd created.

He asked Sam to plan a redecoration of the reception area and replace "that cow" as Sam had described the unhelpful and scruffy girl that greeted visitors in reception. When Sam asked him what he had in mind for décor in reception he smiled at her. 'If we're going to be a fashion business then we need a woman's touch. I'll go along with whatever you decide. You're the great protagonist of women and women's ideas so get on with it. After all I'm only a man'.

She stuck her tongue out at him but secretly was pleased that he trusted her to fire and hire junior staff, well one at least and had asked her to create the change in reception.

Mark interviewed Lizzie and was impressed. She was an attractive woman who swept into his office, shook his hand firmly and sat down without being asked. Tall, well dressed, wafting expensive perfume with sunglasses pushed up into her beautifully coiffured dark hair which was tinged with auburn, Mark took to her straight away. He liked it when she described the business as looking awful and even more so when responding to his question as to what she thought of the current product range.

'Absolute shit. That's the only word for them. They are excruciatingly dreadful. Horrendous. I can find nothing to commend them at all. For a product range aimed at women they are cheap, utilitarian, unfeminine and frankly utter crap. If you want to improve things then we've got a long way to go'.

'Do you want to join me to do that?'

'Subject to the right remuneration package yes. It'd be great fun and a real challenge. I'll work with you to do it but you'll have to give me plenty of freedom. I can't stand being tied down with bureaucracy and petty rules and regulations. I'm a free spirit and I do creative, I don't do company politics or fitting in with pompous twits that want something done in a particular way.

You'll have to give me rope Mark and lots of it. If I hang myself well ok I'll have screwed up and you can get rid of me. If not, and I won't by the way, then I'll create you a range of cosmetic products that women, any woman, even me' she laughed loudly 'will be proud to buy and use because that's the business we're in. Giving women what they want'.

So the change in the business started. Lizzie arrived in a flourish and made sure that everyone knew she was there. Mark knew that Brad was going and soon, so with Pat's help he'd interviewed Kieran Doyle a potential replacement from another part of the Group after hours in a local hotel one evening and liked him immediately. He was smooth, polished and had in one part of his career, as was demonstrated by his occasional use of the word "sport", spent a couple of years in Australia. Thompson and Smith being a big international group sometimes moved their potential high flying executives around the world to build their experience and skills. At thirty two Kieran was one of the future stars of the company and Mark was glad to have got him.

As soon as he knew that he'd definitely got Brad's replacement secured then after one of their regular arguments which led to a huge bust up, Mark fired him. Brad was staggered and told Mark that he wouldn't be able to do without him.

Mark's eyes stared right into him as he replied quietly but with enormous menace 'I can do without anyone'.

Brad felt the hairs on the back of his neck prickle and stand out. He left within half an hour. The next day Kieran walked into the Corby business.

He and Lizzie hit it off straight away as Mark had surmised they would and he knew that he now had the start of a great team.

Alan Wells the Finance Director was the next to go. He was offered a transfer to another business at a lower grade, or a redundancy package. At fifty two he decided to take the money and retired to Southend with his wife Joan where using the severance money they bought a small guest house which would make them enough to live tolerably well for the future without the hassle of business. He was replaced by Harry Evans, a very bright accountant who immediately fitted in with the new team being created.

Lizzie not only got on well with Kieran and Harry, but also with Tom Chivers in Research who became committed to the business in a way that others had not seen for years. With Mark driving him for results and Lizzie throwing him challenges to think like a woman he started to contribute ideas and product concepts that fitted with Lizzie and Mark's ideas.

Mark increased the number of people he employed in the Marketing and Research departments and most of the recruits were female.

Sam enjoyed working for Mark. He was vibrant, dynamic, full of ideas, always challenging things, always asking how to improve results or reduce costs.

He'd congratulated her on her redesign of reception which was now painted in soft pastel colours, with concealed lighting playing on a few carefully chosen pieces of sculpture which were displayed on glass shelves. New settees in dark brown for visitors effectively contrasted with the pale apricot carpet which covered the area. The effect was stylish and improved the impact on visitors, especially customers as soon as they arrived in the building.

The effect was completed by a new receptionist who was charming, well spoken, pretty and went out of her way to be helpful.

Sam banned anyone from the factory walking through her new reception area with their dirty work boots and insisted that they went into the factory through a rear entrance from the yard. She masterminded a whole new soft feminine décor for the offices which was much appreciated by the many women who now worked in the business, but surprisingly also by the men.

Gradually the business seemed to come to life almost as if awakening from a deep slumber.

Lizzie fired the existing advertising agency and brought in one which she proudly told Mark had done some good work for other parts of the Group and would do a much better job for them. When she said that it was called "Fly" he grinned and congratulated her on her choice.

She drove her team of mainly women hard and was scathing if they screwed up or did things with which she didn't agree. Mark kept a careful eye on the Marketing and Research departments as these were key to their future development and although he believed in working people hard he didn't want them pushed over the edge. Not yet at least he mused one evening.

David Levy the Legal director was the last of Mark's original team that he fired. He called David in to his office one evening and told him that he didn't need a legal director and could see no need for the role as there was always plenty of legal advice available from the Group legal centre in London. David said that he understood and that he'd been thinking of going back into private practice for some time and having recently been sounded out by a local firm this might be the best way forward. He proposed leaving at the end of the month. Having achieved what he wanted which was a complete clear out of most of the team he'd inherited, Mark wasn't bothered when David left as long as it was soon and he nodded that yes the end of the month would be fine.

Pat rang Mark suggesting that a small dinner party to say farewell to Ted might be a good idea and if Mark wanted he'd be pleased to come and help the proceedings along.

Sam made all the arrangements and a small group of Raj, David Levy, Kieran, Lizzie, Harry, Mark and Pat had a quiet dinner in a private room at a local hotel. Pat made a speech to thank Ted for his long years of service, picked out some highlights of Ted's career and gave him a cut glass fruit bowl and a golf umbrella as leaving presents from the Company and read him a letter of good wishes from the Group Chairman.

Ted in his turn was gracious in his response and wished Mark and the new team every good fortune but there was perhaps just a note of sour grapes in the way that he said "new". However no-one picked up on it and when the evening finished and people had left Pat asked Mark to stay around for a while as they were both staying at the hotel for the night. When they were alone he suggested that they have a drink and a chat.

For a while it was just small talk then Pat asked how he was getting on and whether he was enjoying it. He reminded him that much was expected from the business and from the way he had implemented such sweeping senior personnel changes then he had better deliver the results that the Group required.

'Are you saying I was wrong to do what I've done?' questioned Mark.

'No of course not. You're the MD it's up to you. You asked for support in what you wanted to do and we've given that to you. Now you've got to deliver old son. It's a tough life at the top you know. Plenty of people are watching you. Some of those like me want to see you succeed, but there's plenty who would love to see you fail and fall off the ladder. You did a great job in Aerosols and Polishes Division which is why you've got this job but remember you're only as good as today. Yesterday gets you to here. Tomorrow is about how you handle now'.

Smiling Mark's mind went back to Keith's soliloquy on his first day and how it was a dog eat dog world. He also found old Dunson's voice floating into his memory. "From the lessons of the past we plan opportunities for the future".

'I know Pat and that's what I love about it. Do well and you go forward. Balls up and you're finished. Mind you it keeps you blokes in Corporate Personnel in a job doesn't it? Where would you be if us guys in the front line didn't keep wanting to create change eh?'

They both laughed and spent the rest of the evening chatting generally about the company but especially about Mark's business. He was so enthusiastic about the opportunities and what he was going to do with it that even Pat who had seen young dynamic career thrusters many times before realised he was in the presence of someone special who probably would create the change that was required.

They had a few more drinks and then went to bed, not drunk but certainly "well oiled" as Mark described it next morning to Sam when she brought in his morning coffee at ten to eight. She had taken to coming in earlier now in order to keep up with Marks' frenetic work rate.

Morale was good now and as Mark constantly spoke about the opportunities to build the business and how they were working on new products as fast as possible then the feeling that they were part of something exciting grew throughout all employees. But now that six months had elapsed since his arrival he was starting to get concerned at the length of time it was taking to get the new products developed so one evening he dropped into Lizzie's office to chivvy her along.

After a brief set of introductory questions he pressed her on what was causing the delays and sensing that she was giving him a bit of a run around and avoiding straight answers he thought that it might be time to apply some verbal pressure.

'Lizzie I just don't understand why it's taking so long? You've got enough people working on it, too many if you ask me. It's only fucking shampoo for God's sake'.

'Only fucking shampoo' she exclaimed loudly in response. 'Mark, I've told you it's a dream we're creating here. A dream for women who want a release from their daily drudge of life, of work, of grizzling kids. From husbands and boyfriends, from money troubles, from thinking what to get for tonight's supper for the family, from monthly period pains. If they're older release from worrying about lines around their eyes, wrinkles on their necks, boobs that are sagging, waists that are bulging, bums that are spreading and whether their husband or partner still finds them attractive. If they're young, release from agonizing about spots that might spoil their hot date and parents that don't understand them. They all, young or old want to be wonderfully, magically transported to a new gentle life of love, of being looked after where their cares are soothed sensuously away and they feel beautiful, relaxed, warm, loving and wanted for themselves as a woman. They want, no they yearn to be taken to that new wonderful fantasy life. That's what we're creating Mark and don't you bloody forget it'. She glared at him aggressively daring him to challenge her.

'So it's not just a bottle of shampoo then?' he laughed and then seeing that she was about to get really steamed up he held up his hands in a gesture of surrender.

'Hey only joking, but Lizzie I need results and fast. When can I see where you've got to so far to get a feel for when it's all going to come together? You can't continue to keep it to yourself. I want to be briefed and soon. In fact what about right now, that'd be good'.

She looked at him smiled. 'Actually we are making really great progress. OK you've been fair to me and left me alone to get this re-launch organised so I'll show you where we've got to. I think it'll blow your balls right out of your boxers, if you wear boxers that is, or are you a Y-front man? No don't tell me, I really don't want to know. Just go to the conference room and I'll be along in a few minutes with some of the team and we'll brief you. We were going to do it next week but if you want a feel for it now, well why not'.

Lizzie gathered her team who had been working on the re-launch. Apart from herself there was Sophie her senior assistant who had long dark hair that tended to drop onto her face when she leaned forward and was tall and thin as a rake, a bit like a human stick insect thought Mark. Jemma one of two junior assistants who was shorter with reddish brown hair but more normally shaped and Wayne the other junior assistant who was lanky and wore an anxious expression. They were all people Lizzie had brought into the company to work on the project.

As they all trooped into the conference room it was clear that Lizzie had rounded them up in a rush. They brought papers, files, mock up sample packs in boxes, rough draft advertising copy and anything else that they thought might be needed.

He smiled to himself as he could imagine what had happened after his sudden demand to see where she and the team had got to. She'd have gone back to her team and said something like 'Right everyone. Mark wants to be briefed on where we're up to with the project' and in response to questions of "when?" she'd have shocked them by answering 'Now so get everything together and meet in the conference room in five minutes'.

There would have been cries and complaints of 'we're not ready' and 'hang on that's too short notice' and no doubt other less complimentary comments about Managing Directors who suddenly wanted the world turned upside down but Lizzie would have cut the chat short and told them to just get on with it.

The whole team would have been close to panic at sudden exposure like this, even Lizzie with all her experience. This was her big moment when she had to show her boss whether she, and her team but essentially her, were any good at their jobs. Ideally she would have wanted to plan this presentation with more time and be fully ready but Mark was the boss and if he wanted to see it now, then now it would have to be.

He sat quietly and allowed them the time to get everything organised to present to him and then when the frantic activity settled down and they appeared ready he smiled charmingly at the assembled group.

'So come on then lets see if you can blo.......' he stopped realising that it may not be wise to repeat Lizzie's "blow your balls" statement. 'Err.…... enthuse me with your plans' and he sat back looking intently at each of them in turn. They all, including Lizzie, looked a little nervous but he said nothing more and waited.

Lizzie started by explaining in detail the research that they had conducted with female consumers of varying ages in different locations around the country which had identified the problems with the existing products. They established exactly what the consumer didn't like and hence what was wrong with their packaging and crucially the fact that being lower priced than competitive products they were perceived as cheap and nasty, which they were she added. They had also researched many competitor products and from all this information they had built a picture and therefore a potential proposition of how they could reposition their product to gain a revised position of a premium quality, stylish upmarket image.

To do this they would need better fragrances, classier packaging and especially improved performance. In other words as well as looking better, smelling nicer and changing consumer perceptions it also had to to wash hair better, or less harshly, or give more body, or less tangles or some or all of these characteristics.

"Stick insect" explained how they had carefully researched several different pack shapes for the new range and from those findings they now had a pack that was seen by their potential consumers as ideal and exactly in line with the premium image they were trying to create. They also developed different brand names and labels which had been extensively discussed with groups of women. Finally the proposed pack shape, label design and brand names were consumer researched together and it seemed that after all the weeks of work they had finally got something which was exactly right.

These results were shared with the advertising agency who carried out their own research to help them develop the advertising to support the new launch.

Slowly the two approaches from the Company and the Ad agency moved closer until eventually there was something that made sense to everyone.

Jemma covered the final area to be checked which was the pricing. How much more could they charge for the new improved product and would the consumer pay a sufficiently high price to cover all the costs including modifying machinery to make the new plastic containers, the research monies spent and the planned advertising support in addition to covering the costs of manufacture, buying the raw materials and packaging, paying for the overheads and people costs of the business, leaving sufficient profit to enable them to re-invest back into the business.

They decided that from their research they could command a price which would do all that was required but that it left them less of a profit margin than they would have ideally liked.

At that point Lizzie with a flourish produced the range of four products in final mocked up packs that looked to all intents and purposes just like the finished product.

'Mark we give you **_DREAMS OF LOVE_**'.

He was delighted and loved the brand name and the proposed bottle shape which was interesting, different and easy to hold. The whole thing was classy and upmarket. In short it was a stunning proposal.

'When we've got "Dreams of Love" shampoos away satisfactorily we can extend into deodorants, face creams and body lotions maybe even luxury soaps and bath foams. In short a whole category of women's beauty products in the future, all stemming from the shampoo start point. But shampoo must go first' finished Lizzie sitting back looking hard at Mark for his reaction.

The team working on "Dreams of Love" had clearly done a great job and now needed Mark's final approval and agreement. He had the ultimate responsibility for authorising the launch and the commitment of monies which could be in excess of one million pounds to support the launch.

History was littered with examples of Managing Directors who'd wrongly launched products that failed hence losing their company lots of money, pulled product launches or forced changes through that were wrong, or cancelled them at the last minute because they didn't think they were right, or simply because they lost their nerve.

It was also fact that in spite of tremendous amounts of work to produce the perfect juxtaposition of design and product benefit, nine out of ten new products launched failed. The reasons were many and varied but could include misinterpreting consumer intentions, aggressive competitive reaction and counter launches, failing to persuade the major customers to stock the new product or getting the pricing wrong.

Any of these could cause a failure. It was not a science. It was judgment and those that made good judgements succeeded and those that didn't failed.

Mark had listened carefully making several notes while the various members of Lizzie's team spoke. He asked several incisive questions and several times queried issues but the more he listened and questioned the more he was satisfied that Lizzie and her team had developed something that was going to give outstanding results. The problem though was the small profit margin. It simply wasn't enough.

He rang Sam and asked her to summon Raj as he wanted to see if there was any saving to be made in the Production area. There wasn't.

Next he asked for Research and Development to come in to query whether any of the ingredients could be cheapened without damaging performance. They couldn't.

Lastly he asked for Harry Evans the Finance Director to join them and he confirmed that his department had checked all the calculations and assumptions and that they were correct.

The talking stopped. There was no more to say and no apparent solution. Lizzie for the first time looked glum. She had known in her heart of hearts that this was the achilles heel of the whole project. Everything was great with the product but at the end of the day it simply didn't make enough money to justify the costs and advertising support without which the launch would fail.

Mark though could see a solution if he was brave enough. It was risky and required a key judgement call to challenge one of the research assumptions.

He felt the answer lay in how they decided to price the product. If they could charge more for it and all the other assumptions regarding how many consumers would buy it in the defined quantities and if they could still establish a substantial market share then it might just work. Turning to Sophie he asked for a calculator then beckoned Harry to sit next to him.

'Look' he said quietly. 'I think this is a potential world beater of a product but we simply mustn't strap ourselves with such a low margin. We'll be in a permanent bind. It doesn't make enough money to advertise and if we don't do that it'll be a crashing failure. However if we push the price up by another.......' he stopped and banged away on the calculator with one hand while with the other he flicked through pages of papers that he'd been handed during the presentation looking at various sets of figures until he found what he wanted and resumed banging on the calculator and scribbling notes on his papers. 'There look Harry' he continued still speaking quietly. 'Twelve percent higher selling price and we've got plenty of margin. The question is will we still sell the same quantities? If we do problem solved. If not it's doomed'.

He looked at Lizzie. 'Price, that's the key. You need to raise your price by twelve percent. That'll give us the margin we need won't it Harry?' He received the confirmatory nod he expected.

'Mark it won't stand that level of price. The price research has been very carefully done' exclaimed an alarmed Lizzie. 'What we've proposed is the optimum level. The correct interface of volume and price'.

Price volume research was a well established and extremely sophisticated technique which calculated a relationship between likely sales to be achieved at various levels of pricing. It didn't simply work out a straight line linear relationship that the higher the price the less sales. It took many factors into account. The product itself, its proposed price, competitive products and their prices and produced a set of results that enabled manufacturers to work out the best price to position their products. He knew the technique and had used it himself many times on other products.

But it wasn't an infallible process, and he was convinced that the "wow" factor the team had created had been underestimated which would secure them the higher price.

'It will Lizzie. I think you and the team have created something fantastic. It's just what we want. I believe in this so strongly that at the higher price which I'm certain it can take then we can even afford to increase the advertising behind the launch. Trust me I know what I'm talking about here. This is a real goer but only at that higher price. Be proud of what you've created and believe in it. I do and I'll back that belief. We'll launch Dreams of Love at the higher price and with the additional advertising. It'll be a fantastic success'.

It was.

Yet again his gut feeling and instinctive ability to get it right won through. It also marked yet another great step forward for Mark's career.

Over the next two years he totally revolutionised the business and established himself with a wide range of skills supported by great judgement.

He faced down the Trades Union when they demanded higher wage rates than he wanted to pay and there were some hard negotiations finishing with Mark chairing a bad tempered meeting with the Union District Official and the company's shop stewards. He called their bluff and challenged them to strike.

'You've had our final offer. That's it. It is final. Take it or bloody leave it but get out of my way I've got a business to run. If you want to call a strike go ahead'.

He walked out of the room taking his Personnel Manager with him leaving the union team to ponder their next move. They saw Mark was serious, the question was how serious. After nearly two hours discussion amongst themselves they gave in and advised him that they would after all accept the company's offer and put a recommendation for acceptance to the work force.

Mark thanked them for their co-operation but they couldn't work out if he was mocking them or genuinely thanking them. He didn't enlighten them, or his Personnel Manager who stopping in the corridor outside his office asked him if he'd meant that it was a final offer. Mark walking into his office turned, smiled and said very softly 'What do you think?' His eyes were like ice.

Other new products were launched in due course. The deodorants, body lotions and bath foams were all successes, the luxury soap less so.

Within three years from his arrival he had trebled the company's turnover and grown its profits by nearly six fold.

Pat O'Connell rang him from time to time and Mark was invited to senior meetings in the Thompson and Smith Group. He was interviewed by various trade publications and the local newspapers in the Corby and Nottingham areas. He even managed to make a few appearances on television news broadcasts when the company announced record results, investment in new machinery or the securing of some major new piece of business.

A good subject for television interviews he was articulate, good looking and success for the new generation of businesses on the old steel works site was still worthy news coverage in the local area.

He also started to come to the notice of others who watched his career from a distance and noted his increasingly high profile, and more importantly the stunning results that he was generating in his business.

CHAPTER 13

'Mark I've got some guy on the phone for you. Says it's important and personal. Do you want to talk to him?' asked Sam one morning.

'Did he say what it's about?'

'No he insists on speaking to you. Says it's personal. You've got time if you want to take the call as your next meeting isn't for half an hour'.

'Ok put him through'.

'Mark Watson?' queried a deep cultured voice.

'Speaking, how can I help you?'

'Well it's more how I might be able to help you. My name is Nigel Charlesworthy and I am a partner in the firm Wright and Charlesworthy. We're one of the leading firms in executive search'.

'Head hunters'.

'Well yes if you prefer and I'm interested in your head. I'm working on an assignment at the moment where I am looking for a Chief Executive of a large business and from what I've seen and heard about you I think you'd make an excellent candidate for the role. It would be an opportunity to run a much larger business than the Division for which you are currently responsible. Needs someone to really get it on a growth path, improve profitability, develop new products, close old inefficient plants, well you can imagine the sort of thing I'm sure.

Obviously at this stage I can't tell you the company involved but if you're interested then I'd be happy to meet with you and go into more detail. What do you think?'

Mark thought quickly. He'd been phoned by head hunters before and had usually thanked them for calling him but said that he wasn't interested in a move. On a couple of occasions he had met with whoever had called him and talked about the opportunity but then decided that he didn't want to take it any further. This time though was different.

He was conscious that he'd been with Thompson and Smith now for nearly ten years and he'd have to move at some time if he was to succeed in his ambition firstly to get to the top of industry, and secondly to get even with Charles Houghton. He knew that it was important to get experience in a range of companies and now with the successes of "Dreams of Love" and before that "Double Air" behind him, together with all the other good things that he'd done then it was time for a move. This might be the right opportunity.

'Well obviously I'm very happy here at Thompson and Smith and this role running what we now call the Beauty Division is in many ways a dream job' he laughed apologising for the pun and play on name "Dream".

'I might be able to offer you an even better dream job. Look why not come and talk to me about it. You've nothing to lose and possibly a great deal to gain. Do you want to think about it then get back to me?

'No I'd be happy to meet you. Hang on while I get my diary'. He rang through on his other line and asked Sam to bring his diary. They sorted out a date the following week which suited them both.

'By the way Mark what are you paid at the moment?'

He responded to the short series of questions about his remuneration package and smiled when the voice at the other end of the phone said 'Well you're certainly well paid for the role that you have but what I'm talking about is in another league altogether, a much bigger league but we can go into all that next week. I look forward to meeting you. Goodbye'.

Mark sat back and thought about the call. Yes it might very well be time to move on depending on what the job was and who the mystery company was.

Head hunting was said to have originated in America and eventually found its way over to the UK and Europe and then all over the world. It was a standard technique of people in that profession to be cagey about giving away very much detail in their first phone call. Discreetly they gave just enough information to tease and tempt their potential target but no more. They'd usually hint that the new role would pay considerably more. Next would be the meeting and interview, at which more details of the assignment including the client company for whom they were working would be disclosed, and the candidate's interest gauged along with an analysis of his or her suitability for the role.

If all was satisfactory at that stage and both parties decided to go further then the candidate would be short listed with anything up to three or four others for discussion with the potential employer where a further refining would take place then probably a couple of candidates would be invited to meet the client company. From them a preferred candidate would be chosen and a job offer made.

Mark put the meeting out of his mind and concentrated on his work for the Beauty Division. He had created this new divisional name for his business some month's ago and after a little reluctance from some of the most senior people in Thompson and Smith he had finally persuaded them especially as "Dreams of Love" and its subsidiary products were continuing to go from strength to strength.

He'd cut costs in the business and quite ruthlessly culled numbers in administrative and what he saw as non-core departments while continuing to support Sales, Marketing and Production which were what he called the wealth creating departments. All other departments he saw as cost causing and it was those that he cut.

In his mind business was simple. Build the wealth factors and reduce the cost factors. He pursued this strategy relentlessly and in so doing further enhanced his reputation for ruthlessness. Similarly with people. Those that were good at their jobs and worked hard he rewarded well. Those that didn't meet his demanding standards got no second chance. They were exited without compunction. To anyone querying such decisions he'd say 'They were holding the business back but more importantly they were holding me back'.

His ability to see through problems and find innovative solutions continued and often he amazed his people with his flair, dash and courage.

In negotiations with the Division's biggest customers he would fight them hard to resist giving additional discounts or promotional funding but he would demand greater shelf space, and in-store displays.

Careful never to overrule Kieran his Sales Director in front of customers he played a supporting role, but when reviewing progress if he felt negotiations were getting stuck or simply not moving fast enough then he'd pick up the phone to the top people in his customers and go into action down the telephone line, or demand an urgent meeting to see them face to face. Often he'd attack but sometimes he'd quietly use logic and sheer persuasive argument.

Kieran loved working with Mark and the two of them were a great team but even the experienced Sales Director sometimes thought that his boss had gone too far. Whether he did or not no-one knew because he always won the negotiations. His customers didn't particularly like him, but they did respect him both for himself and for the way he ran his business.

He established an export business which in spite of the paperwork and red-tape he liked because it was profitable and offered huge volume and having got the costs of the business cut to the bone then additional volume simply poured additional profit into the company's coffers. He made quick business trips overseas to visit their agents and foreign customers and he found himself comfortable in the export environment.

His overseas customers liked him as he dealt with them in an absolutely straight way and said a direct "yes" or "no". They also liked the fact that he was prepared to come to them unlike so many British exporters who were happy enough to turn up to annual overseas exhibitions, swill large quantities of gin and tonics, commiserate with each other how about tough exporting was, but rarely went to see their customers on their premises.

One thing that Mark always did whenever he went abroad was to send a postcard to Betty and Christopher from wherever he was. Betty would complain to Christopher about her son's dreadful writing and Christopher would carefully cut off the stamp and put it into his collection, but each in their own way were pleased that he thought of them even though they didn't quite understand why he kept going abroad.

The export business had grown so large and so quickly that Mark had to rent two additional warehouses on the Corby Industrial Estate to hold stocks of special export packs. Group Headquarters Finance Department wrote to ask him

> "why he had expanded his Division's premises without prior permission?"

He scribbled a handwritten response on their letter and sent it back to them.

Because my existing warehouses are full. Would you prefer me to stack my products in the street?

Next they'd asked him

> "why his redundancy expenditure was substantially in excess of his budget?"

He shot back a reply

Because I've fired several incompetent people !!

For Mark the final straw of what he saw as daft questions came when they asked him

> "If he was aware that the Group rules clearly state that major revisions to an agreed budget or forecast require a detailed written explanation outlining the reasons for the deviation from previously agreed numbers together with a personal presentation to the senior Finance Committee outlining actions taken and likely future implications for the business"

This time he sent a crisply worded typed reply.

> I assume from your ridiculous question that you would prefer that this business did not exceed or improve on the original budget profit expectations. We are producing significantly better results, which incidentally will IMPROVE on the original profit number by around 70%. Surely you only need all that explanation rubbish if results go down – not UP!!

He followed that with a letter to the Group Chairman advising him that Head Office was obviously overstaffed as there were people there with nothing better to do than ask daft questions which diverted him, and presumably others, from running their businesses. Sam asked him if he didn't think that it was a bit strong. He said no, send it.

Nothing happened except that requests dried up from Group Finance. A few days later day Pat O'Connell unexpectedly gave him a call and said that he'd like to drop in and catch up with how things were going. He arrived the following day and after making small talk for a little while leaned forward and looked straight at Mark.

'You're doing well me boy but the Chairman doesn't like what he calls "that cocky Corby bastard" poking him up the arse with a pointed stick. Now listen to me Mark. Stick to what you're doing, and doing well but don't overstep your power base'.

'Pat you haven't seen the daft fucking questions that those plonkers at Headquarters ask. They…….'.

He tailed off as Pat interrupted 'Mark learn about corporate politics and be careful. The Chairman didn't like your letter. He won't reply and he'll let the matter drop and I advise you to do the same for the future. Don't screw yourself up on these sorts of things it isn't worth it. Send Headquarters back the answers to their questions and get on and run your business.'

He stood and started to leave walking slowly to the door, where he paused and said with a grin 'One other ting. Dere's an interesting notice coming out tomorrow which oi tink you'll enjoy reading' and with that he was gone leaving Mark to ponder what he'd meant with his Irish accented last comment.

'What was that all about?' asked Sam when she came in.

'I think I've just had a bollocking but you know Pat he does these things so nicely. Mind you he says there's something interesting coming out in the internals tomorrow. Let me have it as soon as it comes in will you. By the way do you fancy dinner tonight?'

'Hey that's a bit sudden but yes great….. thanks. Shall I book somewhere? Fancy anything special?' Mark left it to her and returned to his pile of work. Later they went to a Chinese restaurant and had an enjoyable time as he was unusually relaxed. She asked him what fuelled his driving ambition but he wouldn't tell her. He drank very sparingly and at the end of the evening he leaned across the table and taking her hand looked deep into her eyes and said softly 'Sam come and spend the night with me'.

'Mark no. Don't spoil a lovely evening, but thank you for asking. Come on time to go home………separately' she grinned.

As they got to their respective cars she turned to him and said quietly 'Maybe one day but not tonight. It's just not quite right but I really have had a lovely time, thanks' and stretching up she popped a quick kiss on his cheek then opened her car door, got in, gave him a little wave and drove off.

He watched her go wondering why it was that on a whim he'd asked her to come and sleep with him but also why she'd turned him down.

He tried to remember exactly what she'd said, something about one day maybe. Ah well he thought as he too drove thoughtfully to his home where he drank a large whisky while listening to some jazz. Eventually he went to bed where he slept soundly till morning.

Sam mused as she drove. Why had she said no? She liked Mark as a man and she liked working for him. He gave her authority and freedom to act as his PA and she thrived on the power and responsibility that this gave her. He was very attractive especially when he was busy or hyped up in the middle of some deal where his cold ruthless streak always caused her stomach flutter. She didn't have a wide circle of friends and was currently single having broken up with a long term boyfriend some months ago. Although she'd had a couple of one off sexual flings after that it was quite some time since she'd slept with a man.

What had really stopped her though was the suddenness of his request. He'd taken her by surprise. Was it just a quick one off bonk he wanted or was it something more permanent that he was after? She knew little or nothing about his private life but she was conscious that he was single, unattached and very good looking.

Still turning the matter over in her mind when she got back to her flat in a small new tower block, instead of going straight to bed she poured herself a glass of cold white wine which she drank slowly while luxuriating in a deep hot bath filled with scented bath foam. She couldn't help thinking that if she'd said yes she might now be sharing a bath with Mark. Shrugging she swallowed the last of her wine, climbed out, dried quickly, put on a pretty pale yellow nightie and got into bed where she lay wondering what Mark would look like naked. Thinking of him in this way made her tremble slightly and her hands moved to her breasts which she gently caressed through the nightie imagining they were his hands. Smiling she slowly drifted off to sleep.

The alarm shrilled him awake in the morning. As he drove into the office he wondered how Sam would react to him this morning but to his surprise and relief she said nothing apart from thanking him for a nice meal and carried on entirely normally as if nothing had happened although he noticed that the jumper she was wearing was particularly low cut at the front . Later in the day she walked in waving the distinctive coloured paper on which Group internal announcements were printed.

'Look at this. Do you think it was following your letter to the Chairman?' He read the notice quickly.

> Following an examination of Headquarters costs, the Group Central Finance Department is to be significantly reduced in size. This will be followed by reductions in a number of other Headquarters departments. It is regretted that these cost saving measures have to be undertaken but they are essential in order to ensure that the Company is correctly structured for the future.

'Well well well, so he did listen then. Good for him. Hey what other ideas can I bang off to him Sam? Get me Pat on the phone and get this up on the notice boards here'.

He talked with Pat about the notice and whilst refraining from saying I told you so nevertheless he did remind Pat that his idea can't have been all bad. Pat agreed but said that Mark should think himself lucky that this time the Chairman had acted on the information instead of shooting the messenger.

Several days passed until the visit to the head hunter. He travelled to London by train and then took a taxi to the offices of Wright and Charlesworthy which were located near Piccadilly.

The building had originally been an elegant house in Regency times but was now converted into offices. He looked at the brass notice board listing the different businesses seeing that Wright and Charlesworthy were on the third floor. Exiting from the lift he walked into their reception area approaching a receptionist who smiled warmly and asked how she could help, then invited him to take a seat while she let Nigel know he'd arrived. Picking up a copy of the Financial Times from the selection of magazines and newspapers he waited until the voice he recalled from the phone call brought him to his feet.

'Mark hello, you found us alright then?' Nigel Charlesworthy who was six feet tall, slightly gangling in build and probably in his late fifties held out his hand and then after vigorously shaking Mark's led him into an office which was large and furnished with comfortable armchairs and settees in matching flowery print. On one side of the room against a wall was a small dining table with three upright chairs ranged around it. At the end of the room was a large old fashioned design walnut desk which was quite tidy with several files and papers neatly stacked on the left hand side, and a couple of "in and out" baskets on the right. Two telephones sat there. Overall the room gave an impression of style, comfort, and relaxed efficiency.

Mark sat in one of the armchairs as Nigel settled himself in another. The pretty receptionist hovered waiting until Nigel advised her about coffees for himself and Mark whereupon she promptly disappeared leaving the door a little ajar.

The two men made small talk for a few minutes chatting about the weather, the economy and the latest rumours about further tax increases that were said to be likely in the forthcoming Government budget until the door opened and the receptionist came back with a tray of cups, coffee pot, milk jug and plate of biscuits.

'Well now Mark you're obviously interested in what I might have to offer or you wouldn't have come to see me. Let's find out a bit about you shall we' and he poured them both some coffee before starting a rigorous and detailed probing of Mark's life to date.

He covered his schooling, his early career and his rapid rise in Thompson and Smith. Much time was spent on Double Air and the Beauty Division. Although he asked lots of questions it was obvious that he already knew a lot about Mark and what he'd achieved, which was the secret of a good head hunter. Get a clear brief from his client then research the available market carefully before making a few discreet phone calls such as the one that had enticed Mark along.

After an hour of questions and discussion he asked Mark what was his ultimate career aim? Mark looked him straight in the eyes as he said with grim determination that he was going to get to the very top of industry and manage a large business.

Nigel felt the intense power of the younger man's personality as he was transfixed by Mark's eyes before the younger man relaxed back into his chair and smiled his open charming smile which immediately put Nigel back at ease. Well almost, as Mark's determination had both impressed but also shaken him. This was a tough young business man in a hurry who would obviously go places.

He could be just what his client needed which was helpful as the two other candidates that he'd seen this week for the same role were not of Mark's calibre and both had disappointed him. Mark didn't.

He poured more coffee for them then returning to his chair surprised Mark when he said 'Lovells are looking for a Chief Executive and you might be their man'. He sat back watching the expression on Mark's face.

'Lovells well what do you know' replied Mark slowly. 'There have been rumours of course. I'd heard they needed a shake up but what's going to happen to their present Managing Director?

'Well confidentially he's going to leave but they're keeping it under their hats at the moment until they've found his successor. The plan is being steered by the non-executive directors who have become fed up with lack of improvement in the business. Frankly it needs a bloody good sort out and they've told the present incumbent Malcolm Bray that his days are numbered but his financial exit package depends on him keeping his nose clean and fully supporting the company until the day he leaves. No support. No payoff.

Yes thought Mark. This could be it. Build and grow Lovells then take over Houghtons. That would give him that bastard Charles Houghton. Once that thought had locked into his brain he was even keener to ensure that he got the job and said so.

Nigel said that he'd be talking to the Company shortly as he'd enjoyed the discussion and felt that Mark was an excellent candidate. Thanking Mark for coming he led the way back to reception where Mark made the receptionist's day when he smiled at her.

The next day Nigel rang and said that he wanted Mark to meet the non-executive directors and they checked dates that suited. The arrangements were made and Nigel wished him good luck.

The days went by quickly although his staff noticed that he was considerably more irritable than usual challenging and arguing more than usual.

Sam watched this and couldn't understand what was causing her boss to act in this way. He wasn't under any particular pressure from Group Headquarters. The business was performing above required targets for the year so far and the outlook was looking good. Staff generally were happy and the unions not causing problems.

Maybe his love life was causing him problems. The only person he hadn't gone for was her and she wondered if it was simply a matter of time before she felt the rough end of his tongue. Thursday was drawing to a close and Mark was still in a bad mood when she went into his office with a cup of coffee and asked if there was anything else that he wanted before she went home that night. He looked at her and said no and that he wouldn't be in tomorrow as he had a meeting off site.

'It's not in the diary Mark and although you said to keep the day free you didn't say you wouldn't be here so I've popped a couple of review meetings in for you. Do you want me to cancel them and where will you be if I need to get hold of you?'

He was about to tell her to mind her own business and then thought that what she had asked was perfectly reasonable and she was simply doing her job. She was a very efficient secretary that he trusted completely and he did want to talk to someone about Lovells in an informal manner.

In the few days since meeting Nigel he'd done a lot of research about them but he had no-one sufficiently close in whom he could confide on a personal level. No-one with whom he could talk openly and freely about his hopes and desires for his career, and why and what was driving him on.

'Sorry Sam but yes cancel them please and re-fix for next week. I've got a meeting in London which could take most of the day'.

'London? What on earth are you doing there?'

'Sam I've got something big on and I'm taking it a stage further tomorrow'.

'Is that why you've been such a miserable bugger for the past few days? You've been like a bear with a sore head and there isn't one of your team except me that you've not attacked, in most cases quite unfairly I'd say. It's so unlike you? This week you've been a right bastard to everyone and they don't like it you know'.

He looked at her and slowly his tense expression relaxed. Leaning forward and resting his head in his hands he looked up at her and she saw an expression in his face that she'd never seen before. Uncertainty.

Usually he was sure of himself, so certain that he was right and so confident in his abilities and decision making. Indeed he bordered on arrogance at times but managed to keep his approach to supreme confidence and didn't drop over that invisible line into conceit. Now though his expression was in a different part of the emotional spectrum and it was totally foreign on him. It was a part of him that she'd not seen before and she almost felt a need to sooth him somehow to take away whatever was troubling him.

Waiting for him to say something and sensing the turmoil that was going on in his mind she stayed quiet but smiled encouragingly at him. If only she could help she thought, and give him whatever reassurance he needed. Also surprisingly she felt some very strange emotions about him churning around.

'Confidentially Sam, and please keep this to yourself I've been sounded out for another job outside of Thompson and Smith. It's a much bigger job than this one and puts me on course to shoot a long way up the ladder in one fell swoop. I've had one meeting about it with Nigel Charlesworthy the head hunter. Tomorrow I'm meeting the non-executive directors of the company. It's Lovells'.

'Hey that sounds like a great opportunity. I know that you've been a bit frustrated here for the last few months and a new challenge like this is probably just what you need. I'll miss you........ we'll miss you of course. You've done great things here but I, err we, know you're ambitious and that one day you'd move on and this sounds as though it could be just what you're looking for.

Doesn't justify why you've been so horrid to everyone recently though', and staring at him the tip of her tongue peeped through her lips, an action which Mark had noticed before either when she was lightly teasing or mildly correcting him.

'No I know, sorry. I guess I ought to apologise hadn't I?'

'You apologising, now that'd shock them' she laughed. 'Might be nice though. Tell me all about tomorrow and Lovells'.

So for the next half an hour he spoke about Lovells and what he'd do if he got the job. She was riveted by what he said but realised that she'd really miss him but ignoring that she smiled encouragingly.

'It sounds great and best of luck for tomorrow. I'll reschedule the meetings I'd put in. Give me a ring to let me know how you get on. I'll be thinking about you. By the way, don't worry I won't say a thing to anyone'. She looked at her watch. 'Gosh is that the time? I must go I've got loads to do at home tonight. Bye and good luck' and she walked out of his office, cleared and locked her desk and went to the car park where she got into her little Fiat and drove home thinking about what Mark had told her.

He stayed at his desk for a long while getting his thoughts in order for tomorrow's meeting. He'd studied the business, felt confident that he knew its strengths and weaknesses and was ready to discuss his ideas for strategic change. His last act before leaving that night was to pull out a notepad and write several times

Sorry I've been such a bastard this week. Had a lot on my mind but thanks for all you and your department are doing, I very much appreciate it.
    Mark.

Walking round the now virtually deserted building he propped one of these notes on the desks of each of his direct reports so that they'd see them when they came in next morning then he too went home.

Sam was right. His team were surprised when they came in next day and saw their individual handwritten notes. Kieran rang Lizzie to ask whether she had got such a note and then expressed the view that perhaps Mark was going soft whereas Tom Chivers rang Harry to remark that perhaps Mark was human after all.

Next day he drove to London. Nigel met him and asked if he was all set and receiving a nod led the way to a large meeting room. 'Gentlemen may I introduce Mark Watson' he announced opening the door.

The assembled group of people stopped talking and looked at him. One detached himself and came over to shake him warmly by the hand.

'Mark hello. Thanks for coming in to see us. I'm Dan Lewis, non-executive Chairman of Lovells. Let me introduce you to the rest of the team. Firstly this is Ben Jacobs, Group Finance Director. He's the only member of the Lovells Executive Board that is aware of what is going on but as he was the one who first came and talked to me about his concerns concerning Malcolm the present incumbent we felt it only right that he was part of the replacement process. The rest of the team comprises Callum McCloud, William Owen, and Oliver Hartwell. Apart from Ben who as I've explained is an executive member of Board, the rest of us are all non-executive but we all have particular interests in part of the company's business.

Callum is an expert in overseas operations especially Europe. William has many years of experience in research in various industries and Oliver has built and demolished more factories and production units in large and small companies than you've had hot dinners. As for me, I just try and keep the show on the road which leads us nicely to the present situation.

The show is off the road. Sales are down, profitability has collapsed and the share price has plummeted. Key people have left and Malcolm won't listen to suggestions for change. The City is nervous and when they get nervous they write company values down. What we need is a new dynamic Chief Executive who can take the whole business by the balls and put it right. It won't be an easy task. In fact it'll be bloody difficult so let's sit down and find out what you might be able to do about it'.

He gestured to a seat at the end of the long table and the rest of the group arranged themselves around the remainder of it. Mark who was always keen to take control of situations felt he needed to make a small mark of assertion right at the start so he said 'Look before we start could I have a cup of coffee and perhaps a glass of water?'

It had the desired effect. Two of the interview team got up and one poured the coffee from the percolator on a side table that Mark had spotted and put it down in front of him while the other went to a small built in fridge asked 'Still or fizzy?' and then poured the requested drink which he took over to the candidate. Nodding his thanks Mark opened his briefcase, took out a file which he placed in front of himself, looked slowly round the group of people and smiled to indicate that he was ready to start.

Neatly done thought Dan Lewis who realised what Mark had been up to. It had been but a small set of actions but showed that he wasn't overawed by the assembled group. Dan had also liked the look of Mark as soon as he met him. He exuded confidence, was tall, good looking and his reputation for toughness could be just what they were looking for.

'Mark why don't you start by telling us why you are interested in this role?' asked Dan in an affable voice but he was watching the candidate very carefully. As well as being non-executive chairman of Lovells he held a number of posts in the City and although not far off retirement, was on the Board of several companies and chairman of three. He was shrewd and extremely experienced. He listened carefully to Mark's response which was less general than he had expected and seemed to be born of a real conviction that he could bring change to Lovells.

The questions went on for nearly two hours with each of the interview team questioning him. Sometimes they would ask only one question before handing on to someone else, at other times a particular individual would probe deeply into a particular line of enquiry and ask several questions before handing over to a colleague. Sometimes one of his interrogators would revert to a line of enquiry which had been pursued earlier by one of the others and although covering broadly the same area would nevertheless bring a slightly different slant to the question. It was a well known interview technique which could often trip up a less worthy candidate by exposing inconsistencies in what he'd said.

Mark though saw the traps that were laid, avoided them and handled himself well. Nothing seemed to trouble him and he answered clearly and competently with responses that were comprehensive and demonstrated the depth of preparation to which he had gone. Crucially it showed not only how much he had learnt about Lovells but his thoughts on what needed to be done to put it right and those thoughts were provocative and challenging. He also asked questions of the assembled group and challenged their answers so his questioners realised that in Mark they were dealing with a very able individual who filled them with confidence in his ability to deliver what he said he would.

Gradually the questions slowed and one by one his inquisitors sat back indicating that their particular set of points had been completed. The atmosphere started to relax and it was obvious that the process was coming to an end. Mark remained outwardly calm but internally he was tense as he waited for the killer question that someone would throw at him. It was often done like this. Get through the main part, complete the bulk of the questions and allow the candidate to relax and drop his guard when he thought that the ordeal was nearly over. Then someone would fire it at him.

It could be a complicated point perhaps to do with the financial structure of the company which would come at him like a speeding cannon shell, or a tricky people issue that would be floated at him but was spinning with booby traps for the unwary candidate. If answered unwisely it could blow apart the whole of the previous two hours. Many job interviews have been lost because of a crashing failure right at the end.

The Chairman leaned back, smiled and made "Well done it's nearly over" sort of comments then he looked around the table and asked 'Now then. Has anyone anything else they'd like to cover?'

'Well there's perhaps just one little point that might be worth a couple of minutes to explore if we've time Dan?'

Here it comes thought Mark as he turned towards Callum McCloud the overseas expert.

'You realise Lovells overseas operations are pretty important to the Company but all your experience so far has only been in the UK. How do you think you'll manage to run our overseas businesses because the markets and the people are quite different you know?'

Very clever thought Mark. They'd found and now had attacked him on the one weakness in his skill set for the job. It could be the fatal flaw in his candidature. It was also the one area for which he'd prepared least well.

'Of course the people are different, they're foreigners' and his face creased in a smile while he thought furiously. Callum didn't flicker but the rest of the group either laughed or smiled broadly.

'The principles though of what we have to do are the same. Identify the key strategic issues, establish a plan to fulfil those requirements and then implement with total efficiency. I cannot see any good reason why the overseas business should not perform to the same level of effectiveness as those in the UK. Some of your foreign businesses are doing alright but several from what I've read seem to be in need of a bloody good sort out. If that's not possible then get rid of them.

Sell them to someone else who can make more of them if they're a better strategic fit with them than us and utilise the funds generated from such disposals to build growth in other areas.

The balance sheet although showing some signs of weakening compared with the past, is still fundamentally strong and could support a much higher level of debt than we have currently. Given a clear long term plan which the City could accept we should be able to raise finance from them without difficulty to help fund growth provided they are convinced about a growth strategy.

Also remember that I have built a thriving and profitable export business in the Beauty Division of Thompson and Smith and that's a tough thing to do….. and that's overseas!

So to close on this point I don't see that my lack of current experience in running overseas markets is in any way a handicap. In fact in many ways it could be an advantage as I come to whatever issues there may be with a fresh set of eyes. What matters is my overall ability to take hold of Lovells, identify the changes that are required, build on the good, eliminate the bad and produce results for the City, the other shareholders and our employees that will stun the world.

I will make your Company the best there is with the finest set of financial results of which you could dream. I'll create a company that you'll be proud to be part of, that will be a leader in its field, that challenges the norm, that drives a change agenda and becomes a world beater'………he paused and looked straight at Callum 'here and overseas. If you want that done then give this role to me'.

He swivelled his glance to Oliver Hartwell. 'I'll want freedom to act to implement change as I see fit. I'll not be constrained. You'll have to trust me and back me'.

He turned to William Owen. 'Do that and I'll deliver the results'.

His voice had risen slightly. He looked around the table allowing his eyes to fasten on each of the people present for a brief moment. Without exception they all felt that he'd seen right into their very souls as he'd both challenged and warned them. Leaning forward, hands on the table clenched but with his index fingers projecting forward like a pair of gun barrels he continued.

'If you can't handle that then I'm not for you and this isn't the Company for me'.

He focussed his gaze straight at Dan Lewis at the end of the table who had found his words little short of electrifying. Folding his fingers back and laying his hands flat on the table top Mark said quietly but with enormous conviction and determination 'But I think you can handle it and that this…. is…. the Company…. for me'.

There was silence for a few moments and then Dan who was wondering just what he had or hadn't seen in Mark's eyes as they flashed at him with those final words said 'Thank you. I'm sure that completes the matter from our side. Now is there anything you'd like to ask us before we finish'.

He declined, said that he'd enjoyed the meeting and looked forward to hearing from them. Dan rose thoughtfully and went out of the room. While he was away the others asked time passing questions like "how had he travelled there today", "was his car parked far away", "where was he off to next" and so on until Dan returned with Nigel.

'Survived it then' boomed Nigel. 'Still in one piece?'

'Just' grinned Mark as he got up replacing his folder in his briefcase. He'd only referred to it a few times in the meeting. He walked round shaking hands with all present leaving the Chairman to last. Gripping his hand hard he looked him in the eyes thanking him for his time.

Nigel led him out of the meeting room and into his own office.

'Well how did it go? Still interested are you?' The two men spent a few minutes briefly chatting about the meeting. Mark confirmed that he was very interested and that now he'd met the non-executive team and found out more about the business he was even keener on the opportunity.

Making his way with Nigel to the lift he smiled at the receptionist as he passed which much to her surprise caused her a little flutter but then he was rather dishy she thought.

He walked the short distance back to the multi storey car park where he'd left his car. Finding his vehicle he sat and thought about how the interview had gone running through in his mind the questions and his answers. Much as he tried there wasn't anything that he felt he'd fluffed or been unable to handle satisfactorily. Yes he thought, all in all he'd done well even with that fast ball at the end about his lack of overseas experience. Time would tell though and he'd find out soon enough.

Starting the car he drove slowly down the winding ramps to the exit where a bored West Indian attendant in a scruffy uniform took his money and grudgingly gave him a receipt.

He realised that he was still hyped up from the interview and needed to relax and be on his own for a while and not embroiled in meetings, phone calls or people clamouring for his attention. However he did wish that he had someone to talk to about the meeting.

None of his friends outside work would provide the stimulus that he needed nor would his parents. He wanted to talk the interview through out loud, say what they'd asked him and how he'd replied. He needed complimenting on how he'd done and challenging whether he could have done better.

Damn he thought as he drove, with whom could he do that? Suddenly he knew and seeing a phone box pulled over to the kerb making the car behind brake sharply and hoot loudly. Raising his hand in apology he muttered 'Silly bugger shouldn't have been so close' then waited for a gap in the traffic before he could open the door to get out.

CHAPTER 14

Relieved the phone box wasn't broken he dialled his office asking the switchboard operator to get Sam to call him back on the number displayed in the flyblown notice board at the back of the box. He waited impatiently and then snatched up the receiver as soon as it rang.

'Hi it's Sam. How did it go?'

'OK I think. No, actually pretty well. Look I don't want to be alone tonight. I need to talk to someone. Can we meet up so I can tell you all about it?'

'Sure. Where do you want to meet? Here at the office? Shall I hang on till you get back? Or do you want to go out for a meal?'

'No not the office, nor a restaurant. I want to be quiet and somewhere on our own. Come round to my apartment. I'll cook us something. Won't be anything fancy probably just a ready meal in the microwave but at least we can talk'.

'Alright but forget the ready meal. I'll get something fresh and bring it round with me. About seven suit you?'

Mark drove a circuitous route back to his apartment so he could think arriving about five o'clock. Sam packed up from the office around the same time and drove to Sainsburys where she scampered around buying a selection of ingredients from which she would cook tonight's meal for them both.

Mark liked Italian food but as cooking was not a great skill of hers she decided on something simple so she filled her basket with a selection of Italian cold meats which she'd serve as a starter. Some fresh pasta and one of those jars of exotic sounding Italian sauces which tasted pretty good yet didn't take too long to cook, together with some ready prepared salad. She doubted if, like most single men, Mark would have any fruit in his apartment so she added a large ripe melon and finished the shopping with a long crusty French baguette She ignored wine being certain he would have plenty.

Frustrated by the long Friday evening queues at the checkouts eventually she got out of the store and drove home where she rushed indoors, stripped off, filled a bath with hot water scented with bath foam and laid there for about ten minutes.

Getting out she dried herself and wandered into her bedroom to get dressed. First she put on a pair of panties, white with red polka dots and a matching bra. Over these she went casually smart in a close fitting pale pink low necked blouse with white buttons up the front, a light grey mini skirt which not only hugged her bum but also showed to advantage her attractive legs which she encased in a pair of black tights. A pair of sling back medium heeled black shoes completed the outfit.

Checking in the mirror she ran a comb through her hair, carefully applied some lipstick, eye shadow and mascara finishing with a quick spray of perfume behind her ears and on her inside wrists which she rubbed together. Finally giving a quick squirt down her cleavage she ran back downstairs to her car and drove to Mark's apartment arriving just after seven.

After he had got home Mark was still hyper from the meeting. It wasn't just the two hour interview grilling which in fact he'd quite enjoyed, but he was excited about the prospects for Lovells. No it was more than that. He could see that the business was big enough to give him the opportunity to get close to Charles Houghton and eventually destroy him.

He mooched around the apartment, had a shower and then dressed in dark blue slacks, a pale blue short sleeved shirt and a pair of loafers. Switching on the tv he channel hopped for a while but finding nothing that interested him put on some music. Rock tracks irritated him and soft jazz did nothing to calm him so he turned the hi-fi off again. He went into the bedroom and lay down on the bed closing his eyes trying to relax but after a few minutes he got up again and wandered about. He disliked matters outside his control and that was the problem here.

He could do the job, and bloody well at that if only he could get to it, but the answer as to whether he'd get the chance lay in the hands of that bunch of non-execs and the Group Finance Director who must have found it strange to be part of a panel interviewing his future boss. Oh well shrugged Mark balls to him and balls to the lot of them. It was perfectly obvious that he was right for the job so why go through all this fucking waiting rigmarole when they could have said there and then "Well done Mark the job's yours when can you start?".

Constantly looking at the clock he hoped that Sam wasn't going to be late. Don't know why she needed to go shopping he thought. There was nothing wrong with a ready meal.

Picking up the phone he flicked through the list of numbers in his little phone book he dialled her home number. There was no answer and it just rang until an answer phone clicked in. He listened with curiosity as she announced to whoever was listening "That she couldn't come to the phone but please leave a message". He didn't and put down the receiver.

Going to the fridge he took out a bottle of chilled sauvignon blanc wine and extracting the cork with a satisfying pop poured himself a glass which he took into the sitting room and flopped down on the long red settee.

Calm down he told himself but it was no good and his mind just continued to churn round and round. So engrossed in his thoughts was he that when the doorbell rang he jumped and spilt some wine on the seat cushion but ignoring it he walked quickly to the door.

'Hi come in. Am I glad to see you. Here let me take those' and he took the plastic shopping bags from her and put them in the kitchen. 'Drink? I've got some white wine open or would you prefer red? Or maybe a gin and something?'

'White wine's fine thanks' and she followed him into the kitchen watching as he poured her wine. 'Umm that's a great way to finish the week' and she took a small sip. 'Now you said you wanted to talk about today. Shall I cook while you talk or do you want to eat first and then talk, or maybe talk first and then eat?'

'Talk first'.

They moved back into the sitting room and Sam looked around as this was the first time that she'd been inside Marks's apartment in Northampton and she was certainly impressed by it.

Originally the building had been a warehouse built on the side of the Grand Union Canal to serve the leather trade but as that industry had fallen into decline eventually the building became derelict until a building group bought it to convert into stylish apartments of varying sizes and shapes. Mark's was a big two bedroom unit with a large sitting room, dining area and kitchen. The whole apartment gave an impression of size and airiness and it looked as though there was a balcony which she presumed overlooked the canal. She guessed the bedrooms would also be large.

'Well now how did it go? You sounded very excited when you rang me. Have you got the job yet?' she asked as she allowed herself to sink into one of the red armchairs inevitably exposing long expanses of leg which Mark studied before looking at her face.

'I don't know Sam they didn't give any indication one way or the other. That's the trouble but I bloody want it. It's perfect for me. I can take Lovells by the balls give it a tremendous shake and turn it into something really great. There's so much that I can do there. They need me ....or someone like me who's not afraid to take it on. It's a sleeping giant and thus a tremendous opportunity'.

Looking at him she saw a vibrancy, nervousness and excitement that poured out of him in a way that she'd never seen before. He stomped around the room while he spoke, his words tumbling out non stop.

She'd seen his many different moods at the office, challenging, demanding, awkward, stimulating, exciting, angry, helpful, and each mood brought on particular actions from him but she'd never seen him like this. Even when he lost his temper at the office he was still in complete control of his emotions.

Now here this evening it was different. His emotions were exposed and she saw him in a different light. Worried, vulnerable and agitated. His whole body was like a taut spring. Every now and then he sat down but then as his words started again he'd jump up and walk around. Twice he wandered into the kitchen and refilled his wine glass and on neither occasion did he stop talking just raised his voice to be sure she could hear him. He didn't offer to refill her glass.

Listening to him she realised that she was both important but also irrelevant.

Important in that he was talking with her. No she mused he wasn't really talking with her he was talking at her and for that purpose she was important. However she was also at the same time irrelevant in that she was simply an object at the end of his words. She wasn't his secretary, or a woman, or indeed anything other than the recipient of his non stop flow of words. A sponge to absorb his thoughts, hopes, fears, desires and wants.

His self confidence still shone through and that was part of the conundrum that was on display before her. Mark's two extremes of his confidence and his vulnerability were colliding right in front of her and it was a weird experience to see it. Eventually he slowed down and his words came less quickly. He dropped back onto the settee and seemed to notice her again almost for the first time.

'Does all that make sense?'

'Yes very clearly and obviously you'd be perfect for the role but I don't see why you're so uptight? If you don't get this one there'll be other big jobs to come your way. What's so vital about this particular one?'

'Time Sam that's what is important. I need to move on now if I'm to keep control of my personal timetable and what I want out of life'.

He stopped and looked straight into her eyes. 'I have a goal and a time to achieve it and I can't allow myself to fall behind schedule'.

The burning ambition was there in his eyes. It shone out from him. What was it she wondered? There was something there that was eating away at him and driving him on to achieve. But what? Once before in the office she felt he'd nearly confided in her but the moment had passed and never arisen again. Maybe tonight it would.

He stopped speaking but continued to look at her or perhaps it was truer to say look through her with his amazing ability to look through people's eyes right into them. Several people had commented that he seemed to look into their very soul and he'd just done it to her. Shuddering involuntarily she got up and said that she'd make a start on supper. He nodded without saying a word. As she made her way into the kitchen looking back she saw that he was still sitting motionless staring at the space she'd just vacated.

She opened cupboards finding plates, glasses, knives, forks and started to put what was needed on one of the long work surfaces. It was a big fully equipped kitchen but being unfamiliar with where things were, it took a little while to find everything that she wanted but soon she'd got herself organised and had the pasta bubbling in a saucepan with the jar of sauce infusing it with "real Italian flavours and spices" and two plates with the selection of cold meats which she'd dressed with a little olive oil, lemon juice and black pepper. Peering into the living room she saw him still sitting there but he seemed more relaxed.

She didn't know where he wanted to eat. At the far end of the long living room there was a raised area on which stood a glass table and eight stainless steel chairs with high backed black leather seats, but in the kitchen was a breakfast bar with some high stools.

Where do you want to eat? In here or in there?'

'Wherever you like'

'In here then. More cosy'.

He said nothing just continued to sit looking straight ahead deep in his own thoughts.

'It'll be ready in a few minutes so go and wash your hands and do all the things that you men decide that you have to do just as it's time to sit down and eat'.

He made no reply so she shrugged and continued to busy herself tipping the salad into a glass bowl that she'd found, gave a stir to the saucepan which was now giving off delicious smells making her realise that she was hungry and getting another bottle of wine out of the fridge as the one Mark opened earlier was nearly empty. She'd only had the one glass that he'd given her when she arrived so he'd drunk at least four glasses but she knew that one of his many attributes was an enormous capacity to drink without getting drunk. Although she had never been on a boozing session with him she had overhead some of the men at the office talking about his capacity to hold his drink when they were entertaining or being entertained. He was known to be able to drink pretty well anyone under the table and still be bright and sharp the next morning.

'Are you ready to eat?' she called turning round towards the living room but was surprised to see him in the kitchen as she hadn't heard him come in.

'Have you washed your hands?' she asked wriggling up onto one of the tall bar stools trying to avoid exposing too much of her legs.

'Yes miss,' he grinned holding out his hands for inspection whilst his eyes roved over her legs. Seeming more like his normal self and being much taller than her he slid himself easily onto another stool, picked up a fork and speared a couple of pieces of the flat salami type meats. Putting them into his mouth he drained the remains of the first wine bottle which he'd brought in with him into his glass slurping it down in one gulp before refilling it from the new bottle. He ate silently and quickly and had cleared his plate before she was half way through hers even though she'd given him more than herself.

She finished hers quickly. 'You look as though you enjoyed that' and sliding off the stool couldn't avoid exposing her legs almost to the top of her thighs. On the other side of the kitchen the saucepan was bubbling furiously.

Later neither of them could remember exactly what triggered off the sex.

She recalled him saying 'Sam I can't tell you how much I want this Lovells job' and also remembered that when she'd turned to reply he was standing closely behind her. The haunted earnest look was back in his face but his eyes were alive and seemed to burn brightly. Moving closer to her he reached out and held her. 'I want Lovells and I want you. I need them both..... now' and he pulled her to him.

Trying to step away her back pressed against the work surfaces behind her so she was squashed between him at the front and the units behind. Leaning forward and down he lifted her chin and kissed her gently at first and then suddenly much more fiercely. For a second she froze before something melted inside her and she responded with equal fervour and their lips mashed together hard.

Their tongues fenced with each other, their kisses were strong and passionate and their breathing grew more rapid as she moulded herself into him. Their lips moved not just against each others lips but around each other faces. He kissed her nose and her closed eyes and his tongue teased into one of her ears and then traced its way down the side of her face back to her lips. She kissed his chin feeling the day's stubble rasp against her tongue.

'Sam' he gasped as his hands moved to the buttons of her blouse and he started to undo them as rapidly as he could. His face moved down and turned slightly to the side as he kissed her neck before moving further down to kiss the large amount of cleavage she was now showing.

'I need you. Can..........' but he didn't finish what he was saying as she completely enveloped him by simultaneously putting her arms tightly around his neck and kissing him while at the same time lifting first one and then her other leg and wrapping them around his waist.

'Yes' she gasped as her tongue plunged deep into his mouth again.

He carried her out of the kitchen across the sitting room and into another room where he groped around the wall eventually finding the light switch and she saw they were in his bedroom. Still deeply kissing he laid her on the bed and without removing his mouth from hers felt his way down to undo the remaining blouse buttons then reached round her back for her bra strap.

She in her turn was trying to undo his shirt and for the next few minutes they kissed and struggled to undress each other. When they were naked he pressed her onto her back and uncaring of her needs pushed his penis into her causing her to shriek loudly in surprise at his size. Fortunately because of the pent up feelings that he'd unleashed with his sudden kissing of her in the kitchen and her surrender by being carried into the bedroom together with their frantic mutual undressing she was wet and able to accommodate him.

Gasping and grunting at his size and the force of his thrusts in the almost violent way that he was making love to her although she could start to feel the beginning of her own waves of passion building it was clear that he was committed to his own pleasure and seemed for a while to be solely intent on satisfying his own needs. However he suddenly slowed and moved in her more slowly for a while until speeding up and pistoning extremely hard he groaned as he came and she felt his ejaculations erupting inside herself.

Sam too was now on the verge of climaxing so feeling him start to slow down she pleaded for him to keep going. Gritting her teeth she pushed herself against him while squeezing her pussy as tightly as she could around his still hard prick. Holding her breath and throwing her head back she clasped her hands around his buttocks and tried to pull him even more deeply into her while her legs that were wrapped around his waist clamped him ever more tightly. Although he'd finished he held on and continued to move even speeding up a little until with a gasp and several loud cries she too climaxed.

Slowly the two of them calmed down and moved apart before progressing to gentle kissing and stroking until in a while all movement ceased and they lay still together.

'Sam I ....'

'Don't talk, just hold me'.

Cuddling they said nothing just stroked each other letting their minds roam over what had just happened.

'Sam I just don't know what happened or what made me do that. Are you angry with me? Have I ruined things between us? You wanted it too didn't you?'

'Yes of course I did. No I'm not angry. It was wonderful and I'm glad that it happened and that I was here for you when you needed it.........needed me'. Don't try and rationalise it. There was a need, a huge need and we were able to fulfil that for each other. Shall I tell you something? I've always known that it would happen....... one day. For me it was never a question of whether it would happen, only when. Now it has. It'll happen again too on another day, another time, sometime'.

Kissing him softly she cuddled him savouring his manly smells. She felt calm and happy with him. Mind you she hadn't come here tonight for sex she'd come to listen to him and cook a meal. 'Oh shit the pasta' she suddenly yelled and leaping naked out of bed ran out of the room. Mark grabbed a towel and followed her.

In the kitchen she was holding the saucepan handle and peering in. An unpleasant burnt smell emerged from it and turning to him she said that it was ruined.

'Never mind. There's always a frozen ready meal which you may remember young lady is what I originally suggested we have'.

'But I wanted to cook you a nice real pasta dish'.

'Well that's had it hasn't it?' He tipped the ruined pasta into the waste bin, then opened the freezer and scrabbled around finally he held up a frozen pack of Spaghetti Bolognese. 'We can stay Italian with this'.

Sam wrinkled her nose then squeaked loudly when he suddenly pressed the frozen pack against one of her bare breasts. 'You rotter' she squealed. 'Alright ready meal spaghetti it is but let me go and put something on. I'm not cooking in the nude with you leering at me'.

'Spoilsport' he chuckled then exclaimed 'Hey' as she suddenly lunged forward and whipped the towel off him and held it behind her back. Putting her head on one side she looked at his penis which although flaccid was still an impressive size and larger than she'd ever seen before. 'Not bad I suppose' she giggled her tongue protruding from her lips.

'Not bad? You'll go a long way to find one as good as that my girl I can tell you' and as he slowly moved across the kitchen towards her she saw his prick was starting to twitch and elongate itself.

'No not again, well at least not yet. Down boy. Go on cover it up and get it under control' she laughed and throwing the towel to him fled back to the bedroom and into the en-suite shower room that led off it. Shutting the door she turned on the spray, adjusted the temperature to a nice warm level and then enjoyed the slight prickling sensation of the power shower she twisted and turned a trying to keep her hair out of the water.

Stepping out she took a towel off the heated rail and dried herself before tipping some of Mark's talcum powder onto her hands and flapping it under her arms, over her feet and into her pubic hair. Not wanting to get dressed yet fortunately there was a towelling dressing gown hanging on a hook in the corner of the little room so she took it down and wrapped it around herself. It was much too big but by tying the belt tightly and rolling up the sleeves she could make it do.

Moving back into the bedroom she saw Mark pulling on a pair of tracksuit trousers. He smiled at her. She noticed how all his tension and agitation had gone. He was relaxed and back to the Mark she knew.

'Come on then let's go and find out what your ready meal is like'. Re-entering the kitchen the microwave "pinged" so taking the ready meal out she tipped it onto two plates and with the salad she'd prepared earlier they had their Italian meal after all, which they washed down with more wine.

After they'd tidied the kitchen and had coffee and a glass of brandy in the sitting room they made love again this time starting on the settee but finishing on the floor with Mark flat on his back and Sam carefully, because of his size, sitting on him to ride him and herself to a wonderfully vigorous if rather noisy on her part, climax.

They dozed on the floor for a while then he suggested that as there was little point in her going back to her home now she should stay with him tonight. She agreed and later retiring to his bed they both thought that the best way to round off the evening would be to make love again.

They did but this time very slowly and taking lots of time.

Mark was the first to wake in the morning and he thought about Sam lying by his side. Hell, he'd forced himself on her last night not that she'd seemed to mind but it could have had a very different outcome. She was his secretary for crying out loud not his girlfriend, mistress or lover. How could things at work ever be the same again? Would she want to continue to work for him? Maybe she'd want to become a regular mistress? He needed her as his secretary as she was bloody good at that role. They were a team and worked well together, now he'd probably wrecked all that.

But she was certainly good at lovemaking. He remembered lying on his back feeling the sitting room carpet beneath his buttocks and shoulders with her moving up and down with increasing vigour which had made her quite large breasts bounce around until he'd pulled them down to his mouth to suck her nipples which had hardened rapidly under the ministrations of his tongue. An enthusiastic love maker she seemed to climax easily, if rather noisily. Thank God the walls of this old building were so thick or she'd have woken the immediate neighbours at least if not the entire set of residents.

Thinking about her and their lovemaking caused his penis to stiffen so he turned towards her and gently stroked her shoulder before starting to let his tongue trace its way down her spine towards her buttocks. He was just starting to kiss her two globes when she rolled onto her back and opening her legs said sleepily 'Not there, here. Kiss me here Mark.......please'.

Needing no second invitation he moved down so that his head was between her legs and lowered his mouth to her pussy. Softly he pressed his tongue to her clitoris and inside pussy lips as he started to work on her most secret areas soon hearing her moaning in satisfaction until she placed her hands on either side of his face and pulled.

Realising that she wanted him to move up the bed he responded immediately and quickly bringing his face level with hers he was just about to kiss her lips when she pushed him onto his back then swivelled herself around and slid on top of him so that they were in the classic sixty nine position. When they were entwined she took his prick into her mouth while simultaneously lowering her pussy down onto his face so that his tongue could re-start its attentions.

Then the telephone rang.

Lifting his head he wriggled out from between her legs and reached for the receiver while she continued to suck on his penis.

'Hello, Mark Watson speaking'.

'Good morning Mark. It's Nigel Charlesworthy. Hope I didn't wake you but I need to talk to you and I remember you saying that you're an early bird even at weekends'.

'Who is it' asked Sam quietly allowing his penis to slip from her mouth but she replaced it with her hand which she started to slide slowly up and down the wet and slippery member.

'No problem Nigel. I've been up for ages. What can I do for you?'

'Liar you've only just got it up' muttered Sam and she bit his penis surprisingly hard.

'Ouch'. He looked at her and pushed her away mouthing 'Stop it'.

'What was that? Did you say something?'

'Why? I was just starting to get into the swing of things' she whispered loudly taking his balls in her hand and gently pressing them together.

'No nothing Nigel. Just swallowed a mouthful of hot coffee'.

'Fibber' giggled Sam jiggling his balls around.

'Ah yes I see. Now look it all went well for you yesterday and the team are convinced that you're the man for the job.

'Terrific. Oh fuck'.

Just as he'd sat up and moved away from her to concentrate on the phone call Sam had sucked one of his balls into her mouth. A sharp pain shot through his left testicle which was squashed as it banged on her teeth while popping out of her mouth. He sat on the edge of the bed listening to Nigel but she slithered around and started to lower head into his lap.

Again he pushed her but this time it was a different kind of push, not soft or playful but hard and unfriendly as he moved away as far as the telephone cord would reach to stand and talk. Sam watched his prick deflate realising that he wasn't in the mood for playing games now. This was a serious phone call.

'What's up? Something wrong?'

'No nothing's wrong just banged something. Go on Nigel I'm listening'.

Nigel. Of course the head hunter he'd spoken about. 'Sorry' she muttered. No wonder he'd lost interest in her. He was standing with the phone wire at full stretch listening very carefully and uttering the odd comment such as 'sure' or 'right' or 'I agree' or 'yes we talked about that in great detail' and several times 'absolutely'.

His penis which moments before had been like an iron bar in her mouth had now completely wilted. She slid out of bed and made her way to the en-suite bathroom where she sat and peed. Wiping herself and then washing her hands she emerged pushing the en-suite door closed in response to Mark's frantic arm waving indicating that he wanted to avoid the noise of flushing being heard down the phone.

'I'll make some tea' she mouthed but he ignored her and in the absence of any response she went into the kitchen and put on the kettle which although not taking long to boil did give her time to start loading the dishwasher with last night's supper things that were still scattered around. She made a pot of tea and a cafetiere of coffee, filled a small jug with milk and could hear that he was still talking as she walked back into the bedroom.

Entering she saw him still naked, his back to her, his ear glued to the phone and for the first time she felt vulnerable being completely undressed. Odd she thought. He's naked and that seems alright but if he's not interested in me now, and obviously he's not, then it feels wrong for me to be wandering around his apartment without any clothes on especially if he was ignoring her as he was now.

She remembered seeing the bathrobe that she'd worn last night lying on the sitting room floor where it had been discarded during their lovemaking last night and went to retrieve it. Returning to the bedroom she moved into a position where she could catch his eye and silently mouthed 'Tea or coffee?'

He smiled and tucking the phone under his chin made the shape of a T with his two index fingers by putting one into a vertical position and the other balanced on it horizontally, so she poured out a cup of tea and took it over to him.

Pouring a coffee for herself she sat on the bed hunched up with her knees pulled up to her chin, one arm wrapped around them and the other holding her coffee as she listened to his side of the telephone conversation.

'Yes I can do that Nigel certainly. No problem at all. I've nothing arranged that can't be cancelled. Where's the meeting to take place?'

She watched as he listened for a few moments and then said 'Hang on I'll get a pen'. Putting the phone down he moved over to the dressing table from where he picked up a ball point pen and a small pad of paper. Taking up the phone again he continued 'Ok fire away' and made careful notes of what was being said to him. Every now and then he double checked something.

'You say that there'll be two of them?'

'Yes definitely two maybe three' Nigel confirmed 'There will be Martyn Simpson he's the key man from Scottish International Bank who are Lovells bankers, and Dominic Clegg who's big in the Fund Management world of finance. He's probably the lead Institutional investor and the Institutions need to be convinced that you're the man for the job. Remember their interest is solely in whether you can rebuild the business so the share price recovers and the value of their investments goes back up.

As you've not run a public company before their approval is vitally important. Don't underestimate them and the power they hold behind the scenes. You may think that managements run major companies. Well of course they do but they need to keep the Institutional shareholders and their bankers on side. Do that and they'll support the management. Screw it up, allow the value of the company to decline and they'll have your guts for garters.

Initially, the present incumbent had them on side but he lost his way. He got the strategy wrong, lost the Institutional support and when they'd had enough, through the non-executives they wielded their immense power and demanded that he be replaced by someone new. I hope it's going to be you.

You've certainly won over got the non-execs and the Finance Director. As far as that team are concerned you're the man for the job and following your meeting with them you can bet that there have been some pretty intense telephone discussions, probably even some meetings with the Banks and Institutions yesterday leading to them wanting to see you. The fact that they want to do it tomorrow on a Sunday shows you how desperate they are to replace the head of the business.

One point that they will want to press you about is how quickly you can get out of Thompson and Smith and start with them. They know you can't just walk out of there one Friday night and into Lovells on the next Monday but they don't want to wait too long. What sort of notice period are you on and what timescale do you think Thompson and Smith would be likely to agree to let you go?'

They discussed various alternatives and Nigel thought that one option if Thompson and Smith would let him go quickly would be for Mark to agree to only work overseas for a period before taking up the reins in the UK for the whole business. 'It would give you the opportunity to learn about their overseas operations especially as you've not run overseas businesses before and allow some time to elapse before you take the entire business under your wing. Also it's only in one or two areas overseas that Lovells, and Thompson and Smith are direct competitors.

But don't let's worry about all that too much as there'll be a way around it. In my experience there always is. So you just focus on tomorrow and good luck. Give me a call and let me know how you get on. I'll give you my home number'.

Mark picked up his pen again.

'Nigel that's great. Thanks a lot. I'll call you tomorrow. Goodbye'.

Replacing the receiver he punched the air with his clenched fist and shouted 'yes' before turning to Sam who was smiling at him. 'They want me to meet the Banks and Institutions tomorrow. I've just got this hurdle to get through and I'll have it'. His eyes were shining and still naked he walked back towards her as she sat still hunched up on the bed.

She could see the elation in his face, in his eyes and to her amazement also in his penis which was stiffening before her eyes. Not so long ago after they broke off from their oral lovemaking session she'd watched it collapse and shrink as he talked to Nigel. Now it was reversing that process right in front of her. It wasn't just sexual need that was making it happen but the adrenalin jolt that he was getting from thinking about his opportunity to get this big job and its route to fulfilling his career. Suddenly it came to her. This was what really turned him on, mentally, physically and obviously sexually. The rush of business and his career.

As he stood by the edge of the bed looking down at her his erection proud, challenging, demanding, she looked up at his face, smiled and uncurling herself leaned forward to take him deeply into her mouth. Soon he moaned softly as using just her lips and tongue she brought him to a climax.

Later they showered, had breakfast and sat quietly eating and drinking their coffee. She said that she'd masses to do and tried to kiss him as she left but he turned his lips away so she gave him a quick peck on the cheek and said that she'd see him in the office on Monday.

Driving home her mind went over their lovemaking last night and this morning. But he'd really hurt her by turning his lips away from her. Well what did you expect you silly bitch she thought? Did you think that he'd express his undying love for you? No get real. He screwed you, you screwed him and this morning you gave him a full blow job. It was all good but it was just sex, nothing more than that. He'd been as horny as hell last night and she'd been there. Probably any other woman who'd been there would have done just as well. OK it had been great sex. He was very well made and a good lover. Well the third time he was. Then he'd been considerate, kind, loving and as much concerned for her satisfaction as his own. That was the only time though as the other times including what she'd done orally for him this morning after the phone call had been pure selfish self satisfaction for Mark Watson.

Pull yourself together she thought arriving at her flat, where she spent the rest of the day tidying and cleaning, reading magazines and relaxing until it was time to have a bath, get changed and meet up with a couple of friends at the pub.

She put Mark out of her mind for the whole evening however later in bed he returned to her mind and she lay there for a long time thinking about him, eventually deciding that it had been just a one off.

Hadn't it?

CHAPTER 15

After she'd left he put on his track suit and ran to the gym where he pounded the equipment hard for over an hour before running back showering and dressing in casual clothes. Slumping into an armchair he read through some business papers which had been in his brief case since Thursday which he'd not yet had time to tackle.

Around one o'clock he walked to a nearby pub ordered a meat pie and a pint of bitter and sat eating and thinking about Sam. He'd enjoyed the sex with her but he didn't want to make anything serious of it. Good fun but not to be repeated. He'd make that clear on Monday. It was just a one off.

Back in his apartment he went over his thoughts for Lovell's business and how he would change it. No not just change it, transform it. If these City guys wanted their share price back up and improved dividends to pay out to the shareholders he'd do it for them.

Share price is driven by the view that the City takes of a company's future prospects as well as its current performance and the confidence they have in the management's ability to deliver performance. His track record was good and he understood the principles and practice of business. He could take risks, indeed he enjoyed doing that but realised that this would need careful positioning with the Bankers tomorrow not to frighten them off into thinking that he might be a reckless.

There was a fine line between calculated risk taking and recklessness. He was good at the former and didn't indulge in the latter.

By comparing the last three annual Report and Accounts for Lovells he'd been able to see where the business was making progress and where it wasn't. He also carefully read previous statements about their strategy and drew some conclusions as to the lack of success they were having.

The current Chief Executive Malcolm Bray hadn't been able to face up to the tough decisions that were needed and had failed to cut costs in the less profitable sectors, nor had he invested sufficiently in those that were growing or had the potential to grow. The result had been a slow decline in the financial results. Never spectacular now they were dire, culminating in the ultimate humiliation for any public company's management, a profits warning.

As this had taken the City by surprise they'd down rated the value of the company leading to an immediate dramatic drop in the share price. One thing the City hated was surprises in company results. They liked to feel that they were part of a company's strategy and understood what was going on.

The problem was that once surprised unfavourably unless they could see and understand that immediate action was being taken to solve the problems, they would go on marking down the value of the business and selling their holdings. It became a downward spiral. Because they were unhappy with the prospects they sold shares. This caused the share price to fall further, so they sold more shares which drove the price down further and so it continued. Price down, sell shares. Price down again, sell more shares. Down and down until either the company was taken over, went bust, or changed its management.

Mark didn't think he'd have a problem with either cutting costs or investing behind the successful parts of the business. In fact he didn't think he'd have a problem with any of it. He just wanted to get hold of it and show them what he could do.

Carefully he thought it all through. He worked out how he'd present his policy and strategy to them and once he was clear about that he started to make copious notes in the Lovells file that he'd created. The afternoon went by quickly and he finished his deep thinking around six o'clock.

He'd been invited out to dinner so checking his watch and with a final look through his notes he put them away in his briefcase. Now for this evening he thought as he ran a bath soaked for a while before getting out drying himself and dressing. As his hosts had said smart casual for the dress code he put on a blazer, dark grey slacks, pink shirt and no tie.

Walking down to the underground car park and getting into the Rover that was his present company car he drove the twenty odd miles to Lubenham where Maggie and Brian lived in a converted barn. They'd bought it as a wreck of a building and had now finished renovating it into a delightful home. There were several cars already ranged around the circular driveway but he found a space to park and then crunching across the gravel banged on the reclaimed solid oak front door.

'Ah here you are. Thought you'd forgotten or weren't coming' trilled Maggie as she opened the door.

'Sorry I'm a bit late. Been busy and sort of let time get away from me. Hope I haven't mucked up dinner or anything. Anyhow these are for you' and he handed over a bunch of flowers which he'd bought from a petrol station on the way. 'And this is for Brian'. He held out a bottle of wine.

'Oh Mark how kind of you. Look we're about ready so you'll have to make yourself known quickly and then we'll go eat. Brian' she called into the inner recesses of the house, 'Mark's here, get him a drink and introduce him while I start to serve'.

'Mark hello, made it at last I see. Good. Ah thanks that's kind of you' commented Brian taking the bottle of wine. 'Come along and I'll introduce you. Want a drink?' and he led the way down the wide hall way which had been re-floored in reclaimed old flagstones.

'Well if we're going straight in I'll wait and have some wine with dinner. Mustn't have too much as I'm driving tonight'.

'Yes real bugger isn't it. Not like the old days where if you were caught driving under the influence as they used to call it, provided you could stand up and if necessary walk down the white line in the middle of the road then you'd get away with it. Now then everybody' he announced as he flung open the door to a room that was a cross between an inner hall and a sitting room 'this is Mark Watson our last guest for tonight'.

There were seven other people in the room. He recognised one of the couples from a previous dinner party but the other two couples and a woman on her own were strangers to him.

Walking round he introduced himself shaking hands and smiling. The last person was the woman on her own, short with long dark hair but extremely attractive who spoke with a soft yet quite deep voice. In response to his introduction she replied 'Hello I'm Abi Stevens' and shook his hand firmly.

He smiled and stared briefly into her eyes before removing his hand and asking her if she'd known Maggie and Brian for a long time.

'Yes for ages. Maggie was my chief bridesmaid when I got married' she replied.

'Oh so where is your husband?'

'He died four years ago'.

'I'm sorry I had no........'

'Oh course you didn't. It's alright. You weren't to know and at least it shows that Maggie hasn't told you all about the widow woman and tried to pair us up' she grinned.

'Dinner's ready, come on everyone' announced Maggie as she came back into the room. 'Brian can you lead the way'.

They all trooped after Brian in an untidy gaggle into the next room. Mark stood at one end and waited for everyone to find their allotted place at the large table. He found himself positioned at one end and chatted briefly with another guest who was located on his right. The last to enter the room was Abi and as she made her way around the table peering at the place names he looked and saw that her name was on the little tag in the vacant space on his left. As she approached he could see that her yellow dress clung tightly to her highlighting her smallish waist and neatly sized breasts. It was high necked at the front but as she turned making her way down to his end of the table he saw it plunged low at the back.

'You're here' he said quietly.

'Thank you' she smiled. 'Seems that Maggie has paired us two singles up after all. You are on your own tonight aren't you?

'Yes single and fancy free' he laughed.

'So what's a good looking man like you doing at a dinner party like this on his own? No girlfriend..... or boy friend maybe?' she asked as he held out her chair for her to sit.

'No to both of your questions. It's simply that I've been too busy working to find anyone with whom I could settle down. One day perhaps I'll find someone special but in the meantime I have a number of friends whose company I enjoy' and he grinned at her.

'I bet you do and I imagine many of them are ladies. Right?' she teased.

'Some' he admitted.

'So what keeps you so busy that you can't find time for one special lady then?'

'Well, I run the Beauty Division of Thompson and Smith which doesn't leave me a lot of spare time'.

'That's sounds a big job. But surely all work and no play doesn't that make Jack.........or Mark a dull boy?' she teased again.

'No I don't think so' and he launched into the intricacies of his job and how he'd reinvigorated the business. She was fascinated listening to him as he obviously had a real passion for what he did and so engrossed was she in listening that when Maggie appeared to clear plates away she'd not even made a start on her first course of salmon and cucumber mousse.

'Sorry we've been talking. Hang on a minute. It does look delicious Maggie. Give me a moment and I'll eat it quickly'. She lifted some onto her fork and delicately put it into her mouth while Mark who'd eaten his starter in a couple of large mouthfuls watched her lips envelope themselves around the fork.

'Umm this is really divine isn't it? From the way that you scoffed yours I guess you must have enjoyed it' and once again that lovely smile and slightly teasing expression came to her face. 'Do you always eat that fast?'

Abi was really quite something he thought as he admitted that he always gobbled food quickly. Attractive, nice figure, lovely voice, clearly bright, intelligent, it looked as though she was going to be a good companion for the evening. Although outwardly very self confident, the one part of his makeup that caused him a problem was getting into small talk with people especially if he couldn't quickly find a subject or subjects of some mutual interest.

However he didn't think it was going to be a problem tonight.

It wasn't. They found it easy to talk to each other and their conversation ranged over a wide range of subjects. She was well educated, interesting, a good conversationalist and had written a couple of little booklets about local wildlife, together with articles and small feature pieces featuring

"life from a harassed single mother's point of view"

for local newspapers and magazines. 'Nothing grand' she explained. 'In fact I often think its rubbish that I write and it amazes me that it gets published, but it does and so helps pay for my teenage children's education. Mind you in many ways I'm lucky as I get a good widow's pension from Roger's firm and he had a pile of life insurance so I'm hardly on the bread line but two growing kids do seem to cost an awful lot'.

Mark flattered her that she didn't look old enough to be a mother of teenagers so she explained that she certainly was, bringing up on her own two daughters who went to a weekly boarding school. One was twelve and the other fourteen. She said that she was currently coping with all the growing problems of young daughters especially their hormonal transitional tantrums from childhood into teenagers.

Their conversation between each other stopped for a while as they both realised that they'd been neglecting their other seated companions and so for some time they avoided talking to each other and focussed on eating and chatting with others around themselves. Maggie was a good cook and the pork fillet served with garlic, apple and apricot was pronounced by all to be a masterpiece. Mark again cleared his with amazing speed but Abi ate more slowly and delicately. Every now and then he glanced at her and a couple of times noticed that she was also looking towards him. They smiled at each other and both felt pleasure that their glances had met nevertheless at the same time almost a shyness that they'd caught each other out looking at themselves.

Maggie was delighted that Abi and Mark were getting on well as she'd felt that Abi's period of mourning should be well and truly over now and that she needed a new man to look after her and the girls. Tragic though Roger's sudden death had been it was time to move on. Four years was a long time for an attractive woman to be without a man.

Maggie saw Mark as a very attractive man who was known to be highly ambitious but who would need a woman to settle down at some stage and fancying herself as a bit of a matchmaker she was delighted that her little plan of sitting them together seemed to be creating some chemistry between them. Rather than put them opposite or directly side by side to each other she'd arranged the seating plan so that they were next to one other but on each side of a corner which meant that they would find it easier to talk face to face. One or two of the other guests exchanged knowing looks as Abi and Mark once again plunged into deep conversation when the pudding was served.

After the puddings had been devoured and Maggie had been duly complimented, the cheese board made its way around the table. Mark was delighted to see Abi carve off a large piece of Stilton for herself. He'd always liked women who ate strong cheese and disliked those that whimpered they only wanted "a little piece of cheddar".

Coffee came and with it some guests drank brandy, port, or liqueurs. Mark having had a couple of glasses of wine with the meal stuck to sparkling water and he noticed that Abi had only drunk one glass of wine all evening.

When he asked if she wanted a liquor she'd replied 'No thanks. Roger my husband drank quite heavily at dinner parties and I got used to just having a glass of wine then driving us home. It's a habit that seems to have stayed'.

Later, some of the diners made "it's time we were going" comments but Mark and Abi made their way back to the inner hall and stood talking in the corner by the large open fire. They continued talking until just after midnight when Mark said that he was sorry but he had to go as he needed a clear head and a good night's sleep, because he had an important meeting tomorrow.

'What on a Sunday?'

'Yes 'fraid so. No rest for the wicked' and then on an impulse said quietly 'It is a very important meeting for me. Look I've enjoyed this evening immensely. Would you give me your phone number and I could call you? Perhaps you'd like dinner or a drink sometime?'

'That would be nice' and she gave him her home number which he wrote down on a scrap of paper that he found in his blazer pocket.

'Abi thanks very much. I've really enjoyed your company tonight. I'll call soon'.

'Yes do. I've also had a lovely evening, in fact possibly the nicest evening for a very long time. Thank you for being such a delightful dinner companion. Call me and don't leave it too long'.

He took her hand to shake it then used it to pull her gently towards him. Leaning forward he gave her a peck on the cheek. 'Thanks. I'll ring you soon........promise'.

He opened the street door and as it was pouring with rain grabbed an umbrella from the hallstand. Making a run for it to her car he ran alongside her holding the brolly over her so she was fairly dry although he got soaked. She scrabbled in her bag for her car key and then quickly opened the door and jumped into her Volvo enabling him to swing the umbrella over his own head.

'Goodnight and I'll call you soon'.

'Whenever it suits you. Goodnight Mark'.

He drove home thoughtfully. Abi was quite something. She was different from other women he'd met and he'd really enjoyed her company. He wondered if he should ring tomorrow and tell her the outcome of his meeting. Maybe I could ring, tell her and invite her out but on further reflection he thought that yes he would call her, but not for a few days.

Arriving home he poured himself a large whiskey and took it with him into the bedroom, gulped it down while undressing then turned out the light and slithered under the duvet. For a while sleep eluded him as he thought about Abi and tomorrow's meeting eventually he dropped off and slept quite well.

Abi went to bed thinking what a charming good looking man her dinner companion had been and lying there started to have some quite erotic thoughts about him before telling herself to calm down. Turning onto her side she soon slept.

He woke up with a start just after three o'clock from a dream in which Abi in a soaking wet yellow dress only just long enough to cover her buttocks was chasing a naked Sam who was brandishing his office diary while Nigel the head hunter was conducting an orchestra in which the pianist was Chairman Dan Lewis and the rest of the players whose faces were unclear were playing furiously but no sound came from any of their instruments. In his dream he could sense someone behind him and turning he came face to face with Paul Feldman lying bleeding in his wrecked car, his bloodied hands held out for help.

He shivered even though he was covered in sweat. Lying quietly he took several deep breaths and made himself forget the dream. Soon he dropped off again and slept until the alarm woke him at seven on Sunday morning.

Getting up he made himself breakfast of cereal and toast with a large pot of coffee. He wandered into his sitting room and picked up his notes from yesterday which he studied again. He couldn't see anything that he'd missed and so he sat at his computer keyboard and typed away quickly for a few minutes. Having checked what he produced he ran off half a dozen copies, double checked them then walked to the bathroom where he showered and thought about what to wear.

Being a Sunday lunch he didn't think it would be appropriate to wear a suit and yet if he was meeting some bankers and finance people then to be too casual wouldn't be right either. After looking through his wardrobe he settled for a sports jacket with cavalry twill trousers complimented by a pair of brown brogue shoes. A pale check shirt initially with a bright red tie which looked rather smart, but might make them think he was making a statement about being a prominent supporter of socialism so he changed it for one that was dark blue. Good and conservative, should appeal to a Bank.

The journey was uneventful and took about ninety minutes. He found his way easily from the directions Nigel had given him. The house was a large Victorian rectory but following considerable modernisation now made Dan Lewis and his wife Pat a comfortable home. He drove slowly up the shrub lined drive, parked, walked to the front door and rang the bell. It wasn't long before the door opened and Dan stood there holding out his hand.

'Mark nice to see you again. Come in and meet the others' and he led the way indoors down the wide hallway and into a room on the right hand side.

There were three men sitting in large comfortable easy chairs chatting easily with each other. Dan cleared his throat and said 'Well here we are. This is Mark Watson from Thompson and Smith'. The assembled group stood and one by one introduced themselves to Mark.

'Now come and sit here' continued Dan and indicated an armchair that had been set a little apart from the others. Bit like the "mastermind chair" where the contestant was put on the spot to answer a series of questions thought Mark as he sat down and smiled at the group ranged against him. They shifted their chairs so that they were facing him in a kind of semi circle with Dan sitting somewhat out of that grouping over to one side, clearly not part of the interrogation.

Martyn Simpson, tall and in his fifties, well dressed in a tweed suit spoke first. 'Mark thanks for coming to see us today. If I may I'll open the batting for our team. As you know Lovells is in a fair old mess and we have to be sure that the person we put in there is going to sort it out. We don't want to have to go through this again in a year of so. Therefore

I'd be interested in your views as to what you think has led Lovells to their present situation then perhaps we could discuss your thoughts as to what can be done to put it right'. He looked closely at Mark.

'Well you are right in your statement that Lovells is in a mess but I don't believe there is anything that cannot be put right. It might take some time and there will be a clear need to focus on priorities, which I may say is one of my strengths, but given commitment, the right team and a determination to achieve results it can undoubtedly be done'.

Looking straight into Martyn's eyes, Mark's passion and self belief shone through even at this early stage of the interview.

'Fine words Mark that anyone can say but let's explore how you are going to do it. After all if it was that easy the present incumbent would have done it'.

'Of course it's not easy I wasn't suggesting that but I think I can find the levers to pull the business round. Look what I've done in my career so far. Starting......'

He didn't get beyond the word "starting" when Dominic Clegg a short fat man with a red face who breathed noisily through his large nostrils and was from one of the big financial fund management groups who were major shareholders in Lovells, interrupted.

'We've looked and it's impressive I grant you but running a public company is different from running a Division of a public company'. He held up his podgy hands palms towards Mark and said ingratiatingly 'Not that you haven't achieved a great deal so far. It's just that we have to be certain that you have the experience to take on this challenge. After all it's not just Scottish and International Investment Bank or ourselves that are worried about the present position. There are many other Institutional shareholders, and of course thousands of ordinary people out there who hold shares in Lovells but all of them, large or small, private or Institution want the same thing........the company turned round and the share price back up'.

'Of course. I understand that extremely well and I can do that for you. Let me explain how I'll tackle the issues' and Mark took the papers which he'd prepared this morning out of his briefcase and handed round copies. 'These headings cover what I see as the main issues'.

He spoke fluently and without hesitation for the next twenty minutes without once referring to any notes but covering all the points on the pages that he'd handed out. In doing so he rapidly changed their scepticism, firstly into acceptance then into belief in him and his ability to do what they required. His eyes flashed and his voice rose and fell. He dominated without overbearing them. He excited them with his vision of change. He thrilled them with how he'd turn round the ailing fortunes of Lovells. He challenged them to find holes in his arguments. He probed them on whether he'd missed any key points. He cajoled. He pressed. He converted them. He forced them to the view that he was the man for the job.

Pausing he referred to his notes and smiled. 'Well that's how I'd start to tackle it and those are what I see as the key issues. There are of course others that I can't understand until I get in there but if we fix the issues I've outlined we'll be well on the way to sorting the business'.

The door opened at that moment and Dan's wife Pat came in with a large tray of cups and a silver coffee pot. 'Hope I'm not interrupting but I thought that you might like some coffee' she announced to the room in general. Putting the tray down on a side table she left Dan to pour and then turning to leave gave Mark an encouraging smile.

The discussion turned to some detailed points of finance funding and its effect on the company's results and then ranged over a wide range of subjects.

One man from the group of three who had not spoken but had been making careful notes was Oliver Bradley also from Scottish and International Bank. As questions from the other two dwindled he looked at Mark. 'How do you feel about the large numbers of people that may be affected by your proposed sell offs, closures or other disposal plans?'

'Naturally that is to be regretted. Much regretted in fact but my job is........will be to improve the financial results and if that means that we have to take some harsh decisions then so be it. You can't have it both ways you know. You can't expect Lovells to be sorted out and not affect the numbers of people employed. As I said earlier that is one of the biggest problems that they have. There are simply too many people employed. Just look at the way their head count has increased over the past year. We have to change that quickly. It will be unpleasant but best done rapidly then we can get on rebuilding morale'.

Oliver, who was in his late forties and wore a permanent frown nodded then turned as Dominic again took up the questioning and moved to the subject of acquisitions.

'Mark you've made a point of wanting to look at acquisitions. Why do you think that is an important element of your strategy?'

'Well it has to be part of the strategy of growth and profit improvement. Acquisition of other businesses is not the strategy in itself it is an element within the overall re-build strategy, alongside reducing costs, re-focussing the business into the core areas of expertise, getting out of non-core activities and simply re-energising the whole shooting match.

Within that there is a place for acquisition where adding something that is either complimentary to what we........or rather you are doing, or by getting into new areas quicker or at less cost than doing it ourselves then we shall achieve our goals that much faster. I'd say it is part of what we have to do, but only part. First and foremost is to sort out the mess that's there now'.

Martyn then re-took up the questioning and went over some of the ground covered previously but coming at issues from a slightly different direction and in so doing was, Mark realised, really probing him hard on what he'd said before and challenging his answers and proposed course of actions. However as Mark had such a good memory nothing tripped him up and when Dominic also chipped in with some very sharp and detailed questions again Mark was capable of handling what was being thrown at him. But he also started to look for an opportunity to take more control of the interview not just answer the questions that were being thrown at him from the three interviewers.

His chance came when Oliver Bradley said 'We've talked a lot about the job Mark, now let's talk about the man. In other words you'.

'Before we do that I'd like to ask some questions about the business and especially the rest of the Board, the role of the non-executive directors and how much involvement the Bank and Fund Managers have in the day to day running' commented Mark. 'Martyn how involved are you in the business day to day?'

Mark saw out of the corner of his eye that Oliver would have preferred to have had his own question answered but Mark stared hard at Martyn and held his gaze until the banker dropped his eyes uncrossed then re-crossed his legs then answered Mark's question.

He explained that as the Bank had become increasingly concerned with the Company's results then he had worked in close harmony with Dan Lewis but he wished for nothing more than to move to a back seat role when the Bank saw that the business was back under control. Mark pressed him on this and some other points and also hit Dominic hard with some incisive questions about his Fund Management's view of the industrial sector in which Lovells operated.

Eventually turning back to Oliver he smiled. 'Now what do you want to know about me, the man, as you put it?'

Sulkily Oliver asked about his interests outside work, his views on various life style subjects, where he went for his holidays, what he liked to spend his money on, all of which Mark answered happily. However when the question of why he wasn't married came up Mark snapped at him.

'Frankly I don't see that's any business of yours. I'm not gay if that's behind your question not that I see that should make any difference as to whether I can do the job but I've not yet found anyone with whom I want to settle down. Now what else do you want to know?'

Oliver looked for a moment as if he was going to challenge him but seeing the firm jut of the interviewee's jaw and noting that his expression sent out "get off this subject" vibrations he quietly said 'I think I've learnt all I need to know about you personally thank you Mark'.

Dan Lewis then stepped into the momentary silence. 'Chaps, you given Mark a pretty good grilling and he seems to have survived so as it's getting on for one o'clock I suggest we adjourn for some lunch. We can go on chatting over some food and a glass of wine. How does that seem, eh?'

'Sounds good to me' said Mark getting up and stretching his legs. The others also stood and made their way towards the door. He asked where was the nearest toilet and was directed down a side corridor at the end of which opened a small door. He found himself in an untidy room full of wellies, thick sweaters, outdoor coats of various types including several waterproof jackets, walking sticks, a couple of shooting sticks, empty bags for carrying cartridges, gun covers and various other accoutrements related to country living and shooting.

In the untidy floor pile could be seen a large and scruffy dog basket. On the wall were a couple of large steel cases which he guessed held a selection of guns. The room smelt musty and of leather, tweed and dogs. He made his way through to a further door at the back which when he opened it was indeed the lavatory.

Unzipping he stood and peed and while watching his liquid jet into the bowl he thought over the morning's discussions and felt that he'd done pretty well, certainly with Martyn and Dominic. He wasn't sure about Oliver to whom frankly he had taken a dislike but shrugging as he finished peeing he wasn't bothered. They'd have to take him as he was and if they didn't like, tough. With that sentiment in mind he made his way back into the gun room and washed his hands in a large stone sink which had just one tap with cold water. Finding a surprisingly clean towel he went back to find the others.

Following the sounds of talking he joined the group in another room of the house on the opposite side from the sitting room where he'd been interviewed this morning.

Dan came over and suggested that Mark sit between himself and Martyn while the others ranged themselves around the rest of the round table which was already laid with cutlery, table mats and glasses. It was a cosy room with a couple of well worn dark green leather settees, a fireplace in which a log fire was burning filling the room with a wonderful smell of wood smoke, a bookcase covered one side of the room and a television and video stood in the corner. Obviously some sort of snug or general purpose room and when he asked Dan about it he confirmed that this was where he and his wife tended to spend quite a lot of their time the other rooms in the house being lovely but large and cost a fortune to heat. He continued by explaining that originally this had been the rector's study where he would have seen his parishioners and spread the good word.

Pat pushed open the door and came in with a trolley laden with a large piece of roast beef and various dishes containing potatoes and other vegetables. 'Dan can you carve for your guests while I go and get the gravy'.

Her husband set about the meat and soon had plates of thickly sliced meat in front of everyone. 'Like good thick slices myself, none of this wafer thin rubbish. Now help yourselves to veg'. For a little while there wasn't much talk as dishes of carrots, sprouts, roast potatoes and peas were passed around together with mustard and horseradish. Pat returned with a large china gravy boat and then left the men to their lunch. Dan offered wine around but Mark asked for water as he didn't really like to drink at lunchtime because it made him sleepy and in any case he had a long drive back home.

The talk was general and flowed easily and later Pat returned, removed the plates and dishes replacing them with a home made apple pie and a pot of coffee. When they'd finished eating Dan asked Mark if he had any further points that he wanted to raise?

'Not really thank you simply to say that I've thoroughly enjoyed meeting everyone here today and it has confirmed for me that not only can I do the job but I would very much like to be given the opportunity to do so. Give me the chance and I'll deliver the results for you. That's it. I've nothing else to add'.

'Right ho. Well we've got some chatting to do. We'll get back in touch through Nigel. Thank you again for coming all this way at such short notice. Now let me show you out'.

Mark stood and shook hands with the other three who all, even Oliver, seemed friendly enough towards him then he walked with Dan to the front door.

The Chairman came outside with him and walked with him to his car. Holding out his hand he said 'Mark they're a tough duo are Martyn and Dominic but I think you are more than a match for them. Well done and I'm sure we'll be meeting up again. Goodbye, drive safely' and he watched as Mark slowly manoeuvred his way around in the driveway before moving off towards the road then, he walked back indoors to join the financiers.

Once on the main road Mark pressed his foot down and drove fast reviewing the meeting which overall he thought had gone well. Now he wanted someone to talk to about it. Although he first thought of Sam he rejected her on the basis that it was too soon after Friday night and they had to talk about that and how it might affect them both in their future relationship at work.

Then he thought of Abi but remembered her saying that she had to take her girls back to Boarding School on Sunday evenings so now excited about the interview but miffed that the two people that he'd like to talk to were not really available he slowed down and drove back to Northampton and his apartment where he wrote up some detailed notes on today's meeting.

He picked up the phone and dialled Nigel's number. A female voice answered and asked him to 'Hang on a minute' then Nigel's deep voice asked 'How did it go?'

'Very well I think. At least it seemed to from my side. Have you heard from them?'

'No but that doesn't surprise me. I imagine Dan will call me tomorrow but look if I hear anything this evening I'll ring you, but you were quite happy with everything were you? Still interested? Any worries come up or anything you're not happy about?'

'No nothing. It's perfect for me. I know I can do it and I just want the opportunity to do it'.

'All right. Glad it went well and I'll be in touch as soon as I hear something. Goodbye'.

Slumping in front of the TV Mark watched for a while then switching it off poured himself a whisky, got a chicken curry ready meal out of the freezer grinning as he remembered Sam's howl of protest on Friday when he'd pressed a frozen pack onto her bare breasts.

After he'd eaten he listened to music, had another whiskey then went to bed where he read a book about the Roman invasion of Britain until around eleven o'clock when his eyes started to droop so he turned out the light and slept like a log till morning.

CHAPTER 16

As usual Mark was in early and by the time Sam arrived at the office he'd cleared his "in-tray", dictated some letters into his portable dictation machine and was wondering how she would react to him this morning and what he should say to her. After all things could never be the same again but in many ways although he didn't regret what had happened he did need them to be unchanged as she was so much part of him in a work sense. They were a good team and he didn't want to train up another secretary to work for him. Sam had an instinctive way of knowing what he wanted and how he liked to get things done. Pondering on this his thoughts were cut short as she came in with his first cup of coffee of the day.

'Good morning' she said brightly. 'You've got a pretty hectic day I'm afraid as I've rather crammed meetings in, including those two that were cancelled at short notice as you were out Friday'.

'Thanks, I'm sure it'll be fine. Look.......'

'Raj needs a quick word before you get started today. Urgent he said'.

'Yes but can we......'

'He said it was important so shall I get him before you start your day?'

Giving up trying to discuss the two of them he nodded assent and soon the tall Indian Production Director put his head round the door to explain that he needed to make some urgent repairs to one of the production lines, which would be expensive and unfortunately wasn't budgeted. He continued that if the work wasn't carried out urgently then more serious problems would develop. Mark approved the expenditure but told the Production Director to save money elsewhere as he wasn't prepared to increase his annual total.

Raj started to protest then saw Mark had his fixed jaw expression and knew that not only was it a waste of time to argue but he'd just get Mark all riled up so muttering 'Sure' he went away to organise the work.

'Lizzie and the team are here for your update on marketing strategy' announced Sam through the open door. 'Shall I send them in?'

'Yes, but look I need to talk to you'.

'No time at the moment. You've got a really busy day. If you get behind on the schedule I fixed everything will go pear-shaped.

'OK but we must find some time. You and me. Alright?'

'Yes, okay some time later but here's Lizzie and team'.

So the day continued with meetings, more meetings, phone calls between meetings and great piles of papers to be dealt. Sam brought him a sandwich and a glass of freshly squeezed orange juice for his lunch but didn't hang around so he ate and read and made phone calls and drank coffee, and every now and then wondered about Sam. She had said nothing and just acted as if everything was normal except maybe she swung her hips a little more than usual.

Towards the end of the day he was reading some complicated papers when his phone rang and Sam spoke.

'I've got Nigel Charlesworthy on the line. He rang earlier but I explained that you were wall to wall and that I'd get back to him when you were free. I'll put him through now'.

'Mark, how are you today?'

'Fine thanks, never better'.

'Splendid, well I bring good news. They want you so well done. Lots to tie up of course, terms, package, start date, your exit from where you are now and so on but I've no doubt they can all be sorted. So I assume that subject to terms and package being right you're still up for the job?'

'Absolutely'.

'Right well this is what they have in mind as a package for you. Hear me out and then let's discuss it'.

Nigel outlined the details of the salary, bonus, share option scheme, private heath care, pension contributions and company car. The package was extremely generous and Mark was struck with a dilemma. Should he try and negotiate more and was that what they were expecting, or should he just accept what was offered? While he was thinking Nigel obviously thought that the offer wasn't good enough to tempt Mark away from Thompson and Smith. Knowing that he had some flexibility from Dan Lewis to negotiate he added 'Look if it helps you make up your mind I'm sure they'll go another fifteen thousand or so on the salary they've offered'.

'Make it twenty and you've got yourself a new Chief Executive'.

'Right. I'll get clearance for that and be back to you later'. He rang off pleased as he knew that Lovells were quite prepared to go to the higher figure which effectively doubled Mark's current salary and in so doing would increase his own fee which was based on thirty percent of the candidate's starting salary. The additional twenty thousand would bring him nearly seven thousand pounds extra.

The phone rang again. 'Got it?' asked Sam.

'Don't know we're negotiating. He's going to ring back. Sam can you come in for a moment please...... now'. This was it he thought. They couldn't just ignore what had happened and he had to sort it.

'Sit down. We have to talk about Friday night. We can't pretend nothing happened. We had sex for heaven's sake. We spent the night together. We.....'

'Yes we did and you're right we can't ignore it. I don't blame you for what happened. I could have stopped you but I didn't. We both wanted it, needed it, and we can't undo what happened. But it doesn't have to screw up' she paused and grinned, 'sorry bad choice of words but it doesn't have to cause problems between us.

You're the boss and I'm your secretary. After all it's not as if it's the first time in history that a boss and his secretary have slept together is it? We have our own lives to lead. Here at work we're a team and outside work, well we can go our own separate ways. I'm not sitting around mooning about Friday night like some love struck teenager. I'm a grown woman who knew what was happening, who enjoyed what happened and I have no regrets. I hope you don't either'.

'No I don't. None at all in fact and I'd really like us to go on as before. You're right we are a team and a bloody good one at that. Do you think that we can do that, go on as before?'

'Here in the office you mean? Yes, I do now let's forget it. No that's silly not forget it. We can never forget it but let's put it behind us and get back to work........ eh boss?' and with that she stood and walked out of his office back to her own outer area to get on with the rest of her day's work. He was sure she swung her hips more than usual.

Nigel's call came about half an hour later and he explained that he had agreement from Dan to the increased salary package. A formal letter setting out the details of the offer and a full contract would be posted that day to Mark's home. There was some discussion about timing of resignation and announcements and it was agreed that Mark would liaise with Dan directly on those.

'Well that's it Mark. My job is done. Congratulations and remember when you get there if you need to replace or recruit any one into your team give me a call'.

They said mutual good byes then Mark leant back in his chair.

'Well?' asked a smiling Sam from the doorway.

'Yes Sam, yes'. He raised both arms above his head and let out a big breath. 'You're looking at the new Chief Executive of Lovells. Now what do you say to that my girl?'

'Congratulations. So when are you going to resign?'

'Tomorrow. I'll draft the letter tonight and you can type it first thing in the morning. I'll go to Leicester and see Pat and if I can get to Graham the Group Director I will, but if not then Pat will have to handle the formalities'.

'Would you like me to stay and type it tonight?'

'No, I need to think carefully about it to get it right and rather than wasting your time I'll just sit here quietly and do it. Leaving will be a wrench but it's time to move on'.

'Alright if you're sure. I'll see you in the morning'.

'OK and Sam?'

'Yes?'

'Thanks'.

She smiled 'What for? I'm just doing my job…….. boss' and she walked out without looking back. She was definitely swinging her hips more than usual.

After she left it was all quiet so he settled down to write his resignation letter and he had several goes at it until he felt that he'd got the sentiment and tone right. When he had he dictated it onto his machine, put his papers away and walked out of the office to the car park.

Once home he showered, fixed himself a sandwich and a can of beer and sat down to relax until he remembered that he'd promised to ring Abi before too long. Looking at his watch he wondered when might be a good time to call so he waited until after eight thirty and then finding her number he picked up the phone and dialled.

It rang for some time and then her slightly flustered but still attractive voice came on the line.

'Hello there. This is Mark. We met at dinner last Saturday and you said I could call you. Is this a convenient time or are you busy? You know children and things'.

'No it's OK but just hang on a sec will you?' He heard her speaking to someone finishing with the words said rather firmly 'Now please' and then she came back on the line. 'Sorry about that but Emma's been sent home from school as she's not very well. I collected her today, some sort of flu but as they don't have a proper sanatorium she's better here at home but she'd come downstairs for a drink'.

'Look if it's inconvenient I'll call back'.

'No its fine I'm really glad to hear from you. How did your meeting go last Sunday?'

'Oh that, yes it went fine thanks. Look I wondered if you'd like to come out for a drink or maybe a meal? That's what I rang up to find out. I enjoyed talking with you on Saturday and I could tell you about my meeting and we could just get to know each other a bit. What do you say?'

'I say that would be lovely. When did you have in mind because as it'll be half term next week I'll have to sort out a child minder before I can go definite on a particular date?'

They settled on Thursday evening provided Abi could get someone to look after her children. Later she rang back confirming that she'd organised child minding and suggested that he pick her up around eight.

Mark went to bed feeling on top of the world. If he had but known it so did Abi who had been experiencing pleasant feelings about Mark ever since they'd met.

Next morning Sam typed up his letter of resignation and he rang Leicester to find out if he could see Graham Stoker the Group Main Board Director who was Mark's immediate boss. He couldn't. Graham's secretary explained that he had two meetings already booked for this morning and then he was off to Thailand on business and that he had no spare time at all.

Next he tried Pat who had been helpful to him in the past who said that if it was urgent then he'd squeeze Mark in just before lunch.

When he sat down in Pat's office just after twelve he took the envelope out of his pocket and pushed it across the desk. 'You'd better read that. Graham isn't available and so I guess you need to deal with it'.

Pat picked it up and before opening it looked at Mark. 'Resignation?'

Mark nodded and waited while Pat opened the letter and read carefully. 'I'm not surprised. Knew it would happen one day only a question of when not if. Where you going?'

'Lovells'.

'Holy fuck. The shit'll hit the fan in a big way when that becomes known. Which Division?'

'The lot. I'm going to be Chief Executive of the Company but if it helps the exit from here then I'll just work overseas for a period of time before taking over the whole Group.

'Holy Mother. That's a big job. You have done well. Congratulations. We'll be sorry to lose you but you were bound to move on sometime and this sounds a fantastic opportunity. When do you want to go?'

'As soon as possible. I realise that you'll have to sort out a replacement for me, and I hope we're not going to have a big hassle over me going to a competitor. Pat if you insist that I work my six month's notice I guess I'll have to but if you can broker a deal to let me go early I'd be very grateful. Just don't force me onto garden leave as sitting around doing nothing would drive me potty.

Garden Leave is a device used by major Companies to delay a key executive who had decided to leave from starting at the new company until the full period of their notice had expired. They were still paid by their existing employer but not required to come into work but also were unable to take up the new role. It meant that the executive sat at home doing no work hence the process had acquired the name garden leave.

Pat could understand that problem for someone as dynamic as Mark and although Thompson and Smith's policy was that notice periods should be served in full his own opinion was that when someone had decided to leave it was best to let them go as soon as reasonably practical.

'I'll see what I can do. No promises and the overseas route might be a solution. However nothing can happen until we've sorted out your successor. Give me a day or so and I'll get back to you. Graham being abroad doesn't help as I'll need to talk to him, when he gets to wherever he's gone'.

'Thailand'.

'Oh shit, hours away. Roit now piss off and let me extract your arse out of here as quickly as oi can'.

Mark thanked him for whatever help he could give and returned to the office.

Pat worked hard over the next couple of days. First he sorted out two potential replacements for Mark ready to discuss with Graham and then when he got through to the hotel in Thailand he had a long conversation regarding the various options. Initially Graham was all for putting Mark onto garden leave but Pat persuaded him that there wasn't really any benefit in that as whatever knowledge Mark had about the company would still be relevant in six months time and what was to stop him talking on the phone or having clandestine meetings with Lovell's people. No-one would ever know and nothing could ever be proved so why not get the succession sorted and let Mark go, especially as he was going to run their overseas operations to start with.

'What do you mean to start with? Where is he going to finish up?' came the demand from thousands of miles away?

'Well my bet is that he wouldn't have joined for just the overseas part. I wouldn't mind betting that he'll eventually finish up back here running the whole outfit'. He paused to allow that thought to sink in before adding 'Only a guess mind'.

So it was agreed. Get Mark's successor installed and then let him go provided he wasn't based in the UK during the time of his notice period. When Mark heard he told Pat that if he'd been a woman he'd have kissed him. Pat roared with laughter and reverting again to his Irish accent replied 'In dat case it's a bloody good ting dat oi'm a bloke'.

Sam had mixed feelings when Mark told her that he could go early. She was sorry that he was going but pleased for him, however when Mark asked her to go with him she was staggered.

'I've no idea what the secretarial situation is there but I don't care. I've told you before you're good for me and we make a great team. We can sort out Lovells together. What do you say eh? Come on Sam say yes. I need you and we'll have a lot of fun. Hard work too, in fact I imagine very hard work, but also fun. Pleeeeese'.

She thought quickly of the implications. She'd have to sell her flat and move. Her parents lived nearby and there was them to consider. All her friends were in this area and her sister lived only a few miles away. 'Well it will depend on the package I'm offered and whether I want to work for their new Chief Executive' she mused out loud. 'Do you think I'll like him?' and her tongue peeped out as it slid across her lips.

'Oh I hear that he's a really nice guy and I'm sure he'll sort out a good salary package' grinned Mark in response. 'Really Sam? Do you mean you'll come?' but he could see from her face that she meant it so he walked round the desk and gave her a hug and a quick kiss on the forehead. 'Thank you'.

Pat had to work hard because although he had a prime candidate to replace Mark, he had to extract him from his present Division, and then find a replacement for that man, and then a replacement for the replacement. In all he'd had to sort out a chain reaction involving four people including one move from overseas back to the UK but by the end of the week he'd rung Mark and explained who was to take over from him and when. Mark promised Pat a slap up meal at the restaurant of his choice for being so helpful.

The Irishman said it was nothing just part of what he was paid for but he would take up Mark on his offer naming an expensive restaurant in London to extract his bounty.

The next six weeks flew by as Mark tidied up loose ends and introduced his replacement, a studious sort of chap called Julian to the key people in the business, major customers, advertising agencies and suppliers.

He took Abi out several times, their first date having gone really well and they both enjoyed each other's company and found that they had much in common in their approach to life, general interests, politics, even the fact that they belonged to gyms, although different ones. Grinning he said 'I bet you look stunning in a leotard, we ought to work out together one day'.

'Maybe' was her soft reply.

He found himself becoming really attracted to her both not only physically but also intellectually? However he didn't want to rush and try to get her into bed as he thought that there might be the makings of a more meaningful and deeper relationship than simply a quick fuck.

Abi for her part was finding herself increasingly drawn to this man who exhibited such drive and passion for his work and was so challenging and demanding on himself that it was achingly attractive. She was worried about being drawn close to him when she knew that he was going overseas for months but nevertheless felt unable to stop having such feelings for him. He'd met her daughters and they seemed to like him and although he knew little about kids he got on well with them and showed a kind caring side to him that was charming and attractive.

Finally it was time for Mark to leave Thompson and Smith. There was a little ceremony in his office. He was given a card that lots of people had signed, a tie and a watch with the collection made on his behalf. He made a short speech and everyone shook hands then he walked somewhat sadly out of the building. Sam was waiting in her little Fiat and drove him home as he'd had to hand back the keys of his company car and didn't expect to get his new car until Monday when he started at Lovells. She refused his invitation to come in for a coffee or a drink and reminded him to call her on Monday.

She'd already resigned and had timed it so that there was only one week of her notice period still to serve when Mark left. This would enable her to ensure that Julian was properly settled in and then she'd join him.

Opening his front door there was the usual pile of mail comprising letters, bills, junk mail and a small package which he opened first. Inside, a note from Dan Lewis's secretary said she was enclosing some car keys for his new company Jaguar which should be parked in the car park and that she'd see him on Monday morning at their Crawley offices.

He couldn't help grinning as he rushed down to the basement car park and saw the gleaming "big cat" sitting there. Immediately he got in breathing the smell of real leather seats and walnut dashboard. Starting the engine he gingerly drove it up the steep ramp and out into the light. It was a beautiful car and for Mark his world was at that moment full of joy.

Saturday dragged by slowly but he cheered up in the evening as he'd arranged to take Abi out again this time to a small country house hotel which boasted an excellent restaurant to which people drove from long distances to enjoy the culinary delights of Marcel the chef. They had an enjoyable relaxed meal and he would have loved to have taken her upstairs to one of the large elegant bedrooms that were a feature of this establishment and spend the night making love with her but he hadn't booked a room and also he wanted to be careful not to rush things between them.

Over dinner they guessed that two of the couples in the dining room were probably having illicit weekends there. It was Abi who brought up the subject when she pointed out one couple where the man was in his late fifties and wearing a formal dark grey suit whilst his female companion was in her twenties and wearing a dress that was not only unbelievably short but the front was so low cut that her large breasts were practically falling out.

'She's his secretary, his mistress or a hooker but if she leans any further forward her boobs will drop into his soup…. and I bet they're full of silicone. God she'll eat him alive when they get upstairs' giggled Abi. 'Is your secretary like that or is she an ugly middle aged spinster? No, somehow I can't see you with an ugly secretary. I bet she's very pretty and dotes on you. Am I right?'

Mark admitted that Samantha was pretty but said that he didn't think she doted on him just gave him a first class secretarial support. 'We're a really good team' he finished.

Abi looked at him hard before directing his attention to her other suspect couple. They were both in their early forties and from a combination of their slight awkwardness with each other, occasional furtive glances around the room, continual stroking of hands and deep staring into each others eyes she suggested that although they were both wearing wedding rings they almost certainly were not married to each other.

'Another naughty pair having a dirty weekend away together' she grinned looking at him. He didn't feel the need to say anything but they both realised that in some unseen way by talking obliquely about sex they'd passed a point in their relationship, and were happy about having done so.

Later when they left the restaurant and were walking back to Mark's shiny new Jaguar they held hands for the first time. He opened the passenger door for her until she was seated before going round to his own side and sliding in.

'Mark that was a lovely meal and another really nice evening. Thank you'.

'It was you that made it special' he replied softly and leaning across stroked her face with both hands before pulling her gently towards himself. His kiss was soft and tender and she offered no resistance but responded with equal softness. When they moved apart she laid her head on his shoulder and sighed.

'Umm I hoped you'd do that' she said looking up at him. 'I've wanted to kiss you all evening, come here' and this time she kissed him more passionately and their tongues slowly at first and then more fiercely explored each others mouths. It was a long time before they moved apart again. Glancing at the dashboard clock she said 'I'm sorry to be a spoilsport but we're going to have to go. I only have a child minder until eleven thirty and the secret of being able to get baby sitters when you want, is never to abuse the time you say you'll be back. That way they're happy to sit for you.

Giving her a quick peck on the lips he started the car and drove her home arriving just before the eleven thirty deadline. Getting out he walked round to open her door.

'Mark I've really got to go. Thanks for a lovely night, call me soon' and she walked quickly to her door, opened it and turning to wave, blew him a kiss before going inside.

He drove back to his own flat only slightly miffed that she hadn't invited him in to continue their kissing but the feeling passed and he realised two things. Firstly he could still taste her lips on his own and secondly he was starting to have some really serious feelings for her. He floored the accelerator marvelling in the Jag's huge surge of power.

Sunday morning was taken up with a long phone call to Abi after he'd been to the gym and then he sat and read the Sunday papers, saving the business sections until later. He had a couple of beers and a steak for lunch at his local pub then in the afternoon he packed a couple of suitcases rang an hotel just outside Crawley to book in for the night, and with nothing more to detain him checked that all non essential electrical items were switched off in his flat and locking his door made his way to his new car to drive to Crawley. He went via his parent's house where he stopped for afternoon tea. Betty scolded him for not warning them that he was coming but for all that was pleased to see him.

Arriving at Crawley around ten thirty he had a couple of whiskeys, then went to bed where he spent a few minutes catching up with the business sections of the Sunday Telegraph and the Sunday Times.

The Times had a piece saying that Chief Executive Malcolm Bray and Lovells had parted company last Friday:-

> "by mutual consent following a restructure of the business in order that Bray could pursue his career in new directions and that until the appointment of a new Chief Executive then Chairman Dan Lewis would assume the vacant responsibilities in addition to his role as Chairman"

Anyone reading it knew it meant that he'd been fired. The paper speculated as to who might replace Malcolm Bray and dropped broad hints that new man Mark Watson who appeared to have been recruited to sort out Lovell's overseas operations may well be the new overall Group Chief Executive in due course. The Telegraph was more upfront stating that Mark was obviously to be the new Chief Executive of the Lovells Group and simply wondered why that hadn't been openly announced. Maybe, it hinted there was something in Mark's contract with Thompson and Smith that made that difficult.

Both papers also had articles featuring Charles Houghton's latest acquisition of a small company which was in financial difficulty.

Mark's eyes narrowed as he considered the implications of this and he guessed that it was probably another business that Houghtons had driven to the wall. 'I'm getting nearer to you Charles Houghton, and one day I'll play you at your own game, and you'll lose' he hissed angrily staring at his adversary's photo prominently displayed in the Sunday Times version of the story. He tore out the articles from both the Times and Telegraph and getting out of bed slipped them into his briefcase for eventual transfer to his Houghton file.

Lying on his back he forced himself to breathe slowly and deeply and soon he calmed down and let his mind drift onto other matters including Abi where he tried to form some objective judgement about his true feelings for her. He enjoyed her company and he'd love to get her into bed but was it more than that? Turning the question over in his mind he realised that it might be more than just fondness of her company. But what about Sam? He'd screwed her and it had been great but it had just been sex with her, that's all it was. Just sex. Wasn't it? So why had he asked her to uproot herself and come to Crawley? Just to be his secretary? Was it really because she was a brilliant secretary and worked well with him, or did he want her with him so he could develop a relationship? If so where did that leave Abi?

Muttering 'oh fucking hell' he turned over and slept until there was a knock on his door and a maid brought him in a pot of tea and told him it was six thirty.

CHAPTER 17

On the cold January morning he checked out of the hotel and drove to Lovells Head Office. It was one of the new glass office palaces that had sprung up all round Crawley, a thriving centre for major industrial conglomerates. They'd all been attracted by offers of low initial rentals or special deals on rates, the proximity of the M 23 motorway, the fast train service to London and of course the international airport.

A security guard poked his head out of the metal guardhouse and enquired if he could help.

'Hello I'm Mark Watson and I start work here today. I'm seeing Dan Lewis'.

'Oh yes sir I'd been told to expect you. If you'd like to park in front of the main building to your right and go into reception I'm sure someone will take care of you. By the way sir, welcome to Lovells'.

'Thanks and what's your name'.

'Grenville Smith sir but everyone calls me Graham'.

'Right Graham it is. See you' and with that he drove slowly to the indicated parking place. Glancing in the rear view mirror he saw Graham speaking into a phone and guessed the message was going round that the new boss had arrived.

He parked and walked into reception where a smartly dressed girl in her twenties with a badge indicating her name was Jane smiled and said 'Good morning Mr. Watson. I've let Mr. Lewis's secretary know you are here'.

Jane had obviously been one of the recipients of Graham's phone call he thought as he walked around the reception area which was mainly glass and stainless steel with an impressive marble staircase sweeping to an upper floor. The reception furniture was smart, modern and functional. Small coffee tables held a selection of quality business magazines including Venture, Manufacturing Today and Food Chain and there were modern impressionist paintings on the non glass walls. In the corner was a vase of fresh flowers.

Reception areas told a lot about a company and this one looked as though it belonged to a modern dynamic company that knew where it was going. But that wasn't true in this case as Lovells didn't know where it was going.

He heard female heels clicking their way down the stairs and turning saw a formally dressed woman in her late forties.

'Mr. Watson, I'm Martha Mr. Lewis's secretary. Will you come this way?' and she indicated that they should walk upstairs. Smiling his thanks to Jane who as soon as he'd gone picked up the phone and rang a friend to say that the new bass had arrived and he was gorgeous.

Martha continued as she led the way 'We thought that you might be early so Mr. Lewis is here already today. Normally he doesn't come in until much later on a Monday as he has a long drive from Gloucestershire. Can I get you some tea or coffee?'

'Coffee would be fine thanks'. She led him into Dan's office.

'Welcome. God do we need you. Things are not at all good I'm afraid and they've deteriorated since we last spoke, especially in America'.

'Well we'd better start to sort it out' smiled Mark confidently. He was sure that whatever mess the business was in he could put it right. Whoever or whatever had caused the problems they were not of his making so he could say what he thought and do what he wanted to correct matters. He'd demanded a free hand to do the job as part of his terms for accepting the role and they'd agreed. He meant to ensure that they stuck to their side of the bargain.

'Right. Update me Dan' and so began a detailed three hour briefing. Initially it was just Dan and then Ben Jacobs the Finance Director joined. Ben had prepared some documents outlining where the business was underperforming and giving the key statistics and information that would give Mark finger tip control of the important control measures.

Martyn Simpson from the Bank rang to welcome him and point out that the Bank wanted improvements of a substantial nature and quickly. Mark grinned as he put down the phone. He was going to enjoy this challenge.

The day was spent closeted in Dan's office. Various people were summoned in from time to time arriving somewhat nervously but several were even more so when they left. They were rattled by Mark's direct incisive questioning of why things were going wrong and why they hadn't taken action to correct the issues. He looked askance at some of their answers or other times he'd just stare at them without saying a word causing them mentally and in some cases physically to wriggle at the inadequacy of their answers.

Mark was shocked at the depth of the problems that he was encountering and this was just for the UK and European businesses. The overseas business located in America and Brazil appeared in an even worse state.

He demanded answers to questions and sent people away to prepare detailed responses to his queries or in some cases to the suggestions that he made.

In this not only did he disturb the equilibrium of the senior people but he also set down his marker for change.

Some of his suggestions were just plain obvious and fell into the "can't see the wood for the trees" syndrome in that Lovells people had got too close to the detail of the various problems so were unable to think themselves out of the difficulty. Other ideas were radical and at least two people made the major blunder of telling Mark that what he suggested couldn't be done. To each of them he'd replied 'Do you mean you can't, or you won't do it? No problem I'll get someone else in to do your job that can do what I suggest'.

He asked Dan who was in charge of Human Resources and finding out it was someone called Jim Myers rang him and asked him to pop up to Dan's office as he had a couple of things that needed doing urgently.

Jim walked in, smiled nervously at Mark but nearly fell through the floor when Mark named the two people who'd opposed his ideas and asked Jim to get rid of them immediately. 'Is there a problem with that' he enquired dangerously quietly when Jim spluttered that this was somewhat unusual and that there were procedures that were normally gone through in these sorts of circumstances.

'No doubt but I don't have time for that. Just get rid of them. Pay what you have to but I want them out today'.

Jim hesitated and looked at Dan and then back at Mark. He seemed to be about to say something else but when Mark waved him away and turned back to Dan, he realised that he'd been dismissed from Mark's presence and scuttled out quickly. 'Ring me to confirm when they've left won't you' called Mark to the retreating back of the Human Resources Manager.

'He'll have to go as well Dan. He's not strong enough for this job. We've got some major surgery to undertake and I need a real toughie in HR to help me sort it out. I'll ring Nigel Charlesworthy and get him started on finding replacements for those three. First of many I expect. We've spent the day so far on the UK and Europe so now let's have a look at North and South America and see what's what over there'.

'We need Chuck in here then' said Dan.

'Chuck?'

'Yes. He's about the only one of the Yanks who seems to know what he's doing. He's fought Malcolm Bray over strategy but no one took any notice of him and he's also at odds with most of the team in America. In fact I can't really think of anyone who sees eye to eye with him but at least he's over here at the moment'.

'Sounds like my sort of bloke' laughed Mark. 'Let's get him in'.

Immediately Mark met the American he liked the look of him. Short, stocky, slightly overweight, crew cut bullet shaped head and well fitting clothes.

'Hi there, glad to meet with you Mark. You gona to sort out this shit?'

'Yep, when I've found out what needs sorting'.

'Hell most of it does. I'm Chuck Grodzinski by the way. Raised in the Bronx. Granddaddy left Poland and settled in New York. I've done my spell fighting for my country in the US army and now I'm fighting most of Lovell's senior management and you know what, that's tougher than the army yes siree'. He held out his hand and shook Mark's firmly. 'Hopefully not you, sir'.

'So do I. Now what do you do Chuck?'

Chuck settled in one of the easy chairs crossed his legs and leaned back. He explained that originally his role had been to represent the American interests to the UK Main Board but they had progressively ignored any advice or ideas that he and to some extent the American Executives had put forward and insisted on implementing strategies which were European in concept and therefore bound to fail in North America. And fail they did. In response to Mark's query regarding Brazil and the rest of South America, Chuck just snorted and said 'Real bad shit man. Real bad'.

Dan looking at this watch said that he had a dinner in London to attend that evening and so he'd leave the two of them to their discussions. In fact they went on for nearly three hours at the end of which Mark decided that he needed to fly to America and Brazil as soon as possible. Irritated that Martha had gone for the evening without saying goodnight he declined Chuck's offer to find someone to book some airfares instead picking up the phone and punching in a number he knew by heart.

'Sam can you book three seats Business Class to New York leaving as soon as possible. Open return. Don't know when we'll be back'.

'Sure. What are the passenger's names? What do I charge them to and how's it going on day one?'

'Get them invoiced to me here. If that's a problem charge them to my personal Amex card. You've still got the number haven't you? Passenger's names are me, Chuck Grodzinski, err and you'.

'Me. But I haven't started yet. I can't join until next week when my notice expires and by the way how do you spell Chuck's surname?'

'Can't you take some holiday? No I guess you can't. Alright. Book yourself for Friday night flight and get there Saturday. Just get Chuck and me over there quickly'. He spelt the complicated surname. 'Book rooms at the Waldorf Astoria will you. Sorry to dump this onto you but all the secretarial help seems to have packed up here for the night. Oh and yes it's going great, right bloody mess though. Call me if there are any problems. Bye and thanks'.

'Come on Chuck. Let's go eat and you can continue to brief me'.

Chuck suggested a small Spanish restaurant that he knew and over a good meal Mark learnt about Lovells American problems. How their operations had been profitable and effective until Malcolm and his team started to think that they knew how to run business which patently they didn't and the results started to slide and got worse and worse.

Instead of realising that it was the strategy that was flawed they blamed the American and Brazilian Managements. Relations between the USA and the UK deteriorated and became increasingly acrimonious as blame and accusation flew back and forth across the Atlantic. Several American Executives were fired but the problems continued as long as the British Management tried to call the shots for strategy from this side of the ocean without understanding that the strategy that worked in the UK or Europe wouldn't work in America.

The Brazilian Management had fared equally badly and their once profitable business declined rapidly.

What Mark liked about Chuck was that he explained the issues in a clear non political way. He simply stated facts, wasn't at all fazed by Mark's direct and probing questions and gave his honest opinions as to what was wrong and what needed to be done to put it right.

Chuck for his part was impressed with Mark. He liked his aggressive punchy style and decided that not only could he work for someone like this but he'd like to do so. Having been on the point of resigning as he'd had enough of the previous management, but hearing rumours of the Chief Executive's likely demise he'd decided to hang on until the new guy arrived. He was glad that he had done so and thought that the two of them would get on. If Mark was as good at implementing change as he was at sniffing out the issues then it was going to be an exciting and bumpy ride which he'd enjoy.

Sam rang the next morning and said that she'd made all the bookings and who should she confirm it with at Lovells. Mark gave her Martha's name.

He spent the first part of the second morning chasing updates on the issues he'd raised the previous day. Several people in the business got the rough end of his tongue when he explained angrily that when he asked for something to be done that day he expected that it would be done in that designated timescale. Having to chase up for the information the next day wasn't good enough. "Do it and do it now" became a phrase of his that was heard around the business.

Martha came in and said that someone called Sam had rung and given details of some flights. Was that right, who was she and why was she making flight bookings?

He said yes it was right and that as she'd left last evening and he needed to get the flights booked he'd rung Sam to do it. Oh and by the way Sam would start work at Lovells next week as his secretary except that she wouldn't be at Crawley for a while but overseas with him.

'I beg your pardon. Do you mean that you are bringing in a new secretary and that she's travelling overseas with you?' exclaimed Martha with some incredulity.

'Exactly. Sam will be working with me. Nothing against you Martha but Sam and I have worked together for some time and we, well we just know how each other works. We're a team and I want her with me here'.

'Well it's all most irregular you know' huffed Martha.

'Get used to irregular things round here. I'm sure you'll have more than enough to do just working for Dan and if not you can always help Sam out if she gets snowed under with work. It's all part of the changes that I've been brought in to effect. Now here are two tapes which I've dictated. Could I have them as soon as possible please?' When he looked down at some papers Martha knew she was no longer required and walked stiffly back to her office. Tapes. It was a long time since she'd transcribed taped dictation but if that's what he wanted, well that's what he'd get.

First she had to find where a set of dictation transcription equipment was in the building and eventually locating one in the finance department after a few false starts she got the hang of it again and by mid afternoon she'd finished and took the work into Mark. He nodded and asked her to leave it in his in-tray. Soon he picked up the folder and read through the letters, memos and instructions that he'd dictated. They were alright but they weren't like Sam would have done them still soon she'd be with him and the "team" would be back in action.

It was gone nine o'clock when he left the office that night and as he drove out he stopped at the exit barrier. 'Hi Graham, how are you tonight? You work long hours don't you?'

They chatted for a couple of minutes and then he asked the security guard where was a good place to eat as he didn't fancy eating at the hotel.

Graham suggested a pub nearby. 'It does good nosh and the beer's alright too if that would suit you sir', and Mark agreed that yes it would suit him fine.

Before driving away he asked why Graham was on duty that night as he'd somehow assumed that he was on a day shift having met him in the morning on his first day. The guard said that shifts were often switched around at short notice and he was on nights now for a while having done a stint on days. He said he didn't mind as he was quite flexible but hoped sometime to do something more interesting than just being a security guard.

'Ah that explains it. Well maybe things might change for you one day. Good night' and he drove off leaving Graham with the view that the new boss seemed a good bloke and not all stuck up like some others that he could name.

The Leaping Trout was a bit tatty but the home made steak and kidney pie was good and the single pint of beer that Mark had was cool, dark and refreshing.

The third morning was hectic as lots of people clamoured for time with him to explain what they'd done about his requests or instructions. The departure of the two senior people he'd insisted were fired had sent a real shock wave around the business and not only had sharpened everyone's response time but eliminated the reply 'It can't be done'.

Nigel rang to confirm he was working on the three assignments Mark had given him, then at lunch time he and Chuck went to the airport and caught a Virgin Atlantic flight to New York. They both relaxed in the quiet comfort of "Upper Class" which lived up to its promises of being equivalent of other airline's First Class but at Business Class price. Chuck commented that other senior executives always flew first class and didn't seem bothered by the price but he was glad to see that Mark was more cost conscious. They discussed many aspects of the American business and Mark was looking forward to getting "stuck in" as he put it when he got there.

'Well go straight to the office and start work straight away' he said.

'Oh boy. That'll phase 'em as your predecessor would never go straight into action after a long flight. He'd go to the hotel and have a good night's sleep before turning up at the offices. Sometimes he'd delay for a whole day before starting work'.

'Time they got used to a change then' grinned the Chief Executive. 'There'll be plenty more changes coming along soon'.

'Yeah I guess there surely will', muttered Chuck. 'Holy hellfire. This is going to be some shake-up'.

Virgin had a limousine waiting for them at the airport and after the normal slow progress through American Immigration, who were probably the most unhelpful and unwelcoming border guards that Mark had ever met they eventually walked out into the crisp cold but bright air of a New York Kennedy Airport day to the car.

An enormous Korean driver held the doors open for them and soon they were being driven into the "Big Apple".

It was Mark's first visit to New York so Chuck avidly pointed out all the prominent landmarks as they proceeded into the centre of the city. Their speed varied from breakneck, to a slow crawl or stationary but eventually after about an hour they arrived at Lovell's American offices just off Fifth Avenue.

Chuck tipped the driver while Mark stood gazing up at the huge skyscraper that loomed upwards before him.

'We don't have the whole building' grinned Chuck, 'just the tenth to seventeenth eight floors'.

'I would hope not. Do we need all this and why here in the centre of New York. The rent must be astronomic. Couldn't we be out of town somewhere?'

'Sure we could but they'll give you a hundred reasons why we should be here'.

'What do you think?'

'Me? I'd go someplace else. Move just four or five blocks from here and the office rents drop. Still in New York City, not quite such a fashionable address but a lot cheaper. Yes siree if it was me that's where I'd go. Hell anyplace except right here'.

'Right. We'll find a new location. Now come on Chuck into battle'.

When they walked into reception and announced themselves the pretty black receptionist whose desk plaque indicated that she was called Sarah May phoned through to someone and said that Mr. Watson and Chuck were in reception.

She listened and then looking at the two visitors said 'Yes they were right here'.

Mark could barely contain his grin but managed to keep a straight face as he asked her if there was some sort of a problem? She replied that she was sure everything was fine and someone would be out to see them in a moment but in the meantime could they sign in. She smiled at Chuck but looked warily at Mark.

The doors at the back of reception opened and a tall man came through, running his hand through his somewhat tousled hair smiling nervously at the visitors.

'Hi there folks and welcome to New York. We kinda expected you'd be visiting with us tomorrow. Good to see you again Chuck'.

This latter comment was said in a way that indicated that not only was he not pleased to see him but thought that Chuck should have tipped them off that the new boss was arriving earlier than expected. Chuck ignored the sentiment, said that he was fine and introduced Mark to Tony Faber the head of Lovells American business who led the two recently arrived people into his office which was enormous, plush and reeked of cigar smoke.

Looking straight into the American's eyes Mark opened the discussion. 'It's good to meet you Tony. Now there are a number of things I don't understand. Firstly why is your business in such a mess? Second what have you personally done to put it right? Thirdly what have your team been doing to solve the problems that exist here, and lastly what are your long term improvement plans?' then he sat back and studied Tony intently who for the first time felt the power of Mark's eyes burning straight into him.

Tony shifted in his expensive chair and started to waffle about differences of opinion with England over strategy which made it difficult to manage the problems.

'From now on there will be no differences of opinion over strategy. You tell me what needs to be done and if I agree you'll get on with it. If not we'll sort out a different approach. So Tony what should we do?'

They began a long discussion. Certainly Tony had some ideas but they lacked depth of thought. They were superficial and didn't stand up to detailed challenge and Mark became worried about the American's ability to correct the mess the business was in. Mark asked for the rest of the management team to be brought in and after introductions started to fire questions then snap angry responses at them.

After a while he noticed a few of them looking at their watches, some subtly, some more openly and that made him all the more determined to make the discussion go on even later. Around nine o'clock he was feeling pretty shattered but didn't let on to the team, simply suggested they adjourn until morning when he was in the offices at seven well before any of the management team.

As was so often the case in business it was the management that was the problem and it was particularly true in this case. Certainly Malcolm Bray hadn't understood the strategic needs of for America but the US management had also not made it sufficiently clear as to what they felt should be done. They had spent their time moaning about what was being imposed on them instead of putting forward constructive alternatives.

By lunch time Friday his third day in America, Mark understood most of the American consumer business except the Electrical Division which being different he'd decided to leave till last. For the rest he was clear on what was needed as an immediate fix and when he unveiled it to the US team after lunch they were staggered by its boldness and incisive demand for action as well as the speed by which he'd conceived and developed it.

He also explained that Chuck would be the new head of the business as at an earlier meeting that morning he'd requested Tony's immediate resignation in which case his pension and health benefits would be preserved but if he didn't go straight away then Mark would fire him with a damaging effect on those important benefits.

Tony resigned but said that he'd be consulting his lawyers.

'Do that' Mark snapped in reply.

So it was mid Friday afternoon when he turned to the Electrical Division. This had been especially hard hit over the last four months by an aggressive price and promotional campaign from a particular competitor Saratoga Industries Inc., who seemed to have targeted all of Lovell's distributors.

'Who are Saratoga?' demanded Mark of Raul Frederico the Hispanic head of that division.

'Well they are part of a British outfit called Houghtons who seem to have set themselves on a path of dominating the small electrical appliance replacement parts market. Whatever we and others offer they undercut. I think they are sourcing components from the Far East where labor costs are much less. We just can't match them with US labor costs'.

When Mark heard the answer he felt himself go cold and breathed slowly and deeply to keep his emotions under control. Here it was. Unexpectedly the first chance to fight back and avenge his father. Houghtons were still using the same tactics. Undercut and destroy. Well for the first time they were going to lose. They were now up against him and he was going to show them what a real fight was all about.

'There is only one way to take them out of the picture and that is to fight fire with fire. Raul whatever price they offer better them by five percent. You have told me that price is the key determinant in this particular market. So undercut them and if.........no when they respond to that drop again, and if they respond to that, drop again, and again if necessary. Whatever you do beat them. Don't lose a single contract on price. I'll underwrite your profit hit in the short term. If manufacture is cheaper in the Far East we'll produce there but we'll cut the price now not wait until we get the cost benefit. Just get them for me Raul. Take them out once and for all. Stick to it and don't give up. Any problems or issues talk to me. I want them destroyed and I'll support you to do so'.

He could afford to do what he said because the Electrical Division was less than one third of the total American business and he knew that with Chuck running the whole operation there would soon be a major turnaround in the rest of the US Group which would generate profits above their budget. He could use a part of that to financially prop up the Electrical Division and support their aggressive anti Houghton competitive stance. At least that is what he planned but he realised that it was a high risk strategy because if Chuck couldn't quickly turn round the rest of the business he wouldn't be able to afford the price cuts in his electrical division that he'd just authorised. Only time would tell if the risk was justified and his strategy would work.

Raul was delighted. He'd long suggested moving production to the Far East but it had always been vetoed, firstly by the American Management who wanted to support American jobs, and secondly by Malcolm Bray and the holding company Board. After the meeting he agreed with Chuck that things really were going to be different round here.

'Yeah' replied Chuck 'And there's gonna be one other difference too'.

'What's that?'

'You deliver the results and that's fine. Screw up and you're out. He don't take no prisoners this guy. So Raul old buddy get your ass in gear and deliver, that's my advice to you. If you don't it won't be only him after you, it'll be me as well'.

Next morning was Saturday and just before seven o'clock there was a loud knocking at Mark's suite door in the Waldorf Astoria Hotel.

'Room service'.

'I didn't order room service. You've got the wrong room. Go away'.

The knocking continued so getting angrily out of bed Mark strode across the room stark naked to the bathroom from where he grabbed a towel before re-crossing the room to the door, removed the safety chain and wrenched it open. 'Look no room service I told..............'

Sam stood there looking tired, dishevelled and holding a tray with two cups of coffee and a grin on her face.

'You may not have done but I bet you're glad to see me aren't you?' and she saw his still sleepy face break into an enormous smile. He flung his arms around her and dragged her into the room managing to spill most of the coffee in the process.

'Sam. Fantastic. Welcome. Hey do I need you. We've so much to do. Oh it's great that you're here, really great. Come in. Have you got a room?'

'Yes on the next floor down. I wanted to let you know that I'd arrived before I go and get some sleep. You don't want anything done today do you?'

'No. Yes. Well lots actually. Look sit down I need to talk to you'.

'Mark I'm shattered. The only way I could get here overnight was in economy class. I haven't slept a wink. I must go to bed and sleep. I'll be fine by tonight. Let's meet for dinner and then you can brief me on what you want done but you must let me rest today'.

His excited face softened and his enthusiasm for telling her all about the business could wait.

'Sure. Let's meet in the bar at six this evening. Go and rest now and I'll see you later'.

'Thanks'. She looked at his powerful almost naked body and for a moment wondered about pulling the towel off him but really she was here to do a professional job and the sex that they'd had was a one off. Wasn't it? In any case she was really too tired to do anything but go to bed and sleep so smiling her thanks to him she agreed to meet later and went back to her room. Stripping off she quickly washed her hands and face, brushed her teeth, drank a glass of water, hung the **"do not**

disturb" notice on the outside door handle and slipping into the large double bed was asleep in minutes.

They met as arranged. Sam revived having had around ten hours sleep listened as Mark spoke about the issues. He continued over cocktails and during dinner in the quiet but very expensive restaurant located on the ground floor of the enormous hotel.

They went to bed in their separate rooms. He went straight to sleep but she lay for some time thinking about his body naked that morning except for just a towel.

Sunday was spent sightseeing together and generally taking it easy although Mark never stopped talking about his ideas and plans. They ate in a small diner just off Sixth Avenue.

The new price strategy for the Electrical Division went into effect on Monday and within days sales shot up and several supply contracts that had been precarious were now saved. Houghton's products were delisted from many outlets and Lovells started to rebuild their position. Mark demanded improvements in existing products and insisted that someone from Raul's team went to Korea and Taiwan to source the existing products at much cheaper prices and find new innovative products to add to the range.

Sam organised an office for herself and within a couple of hours was again acting as Mark's right hand. His diary was organised and she arranged for his calls to be routed through to her.

He gave her a list of people he wanted to see or to talk to on the phone, appointments to be made, production or office locations that Lovells had scattered across the USA he wanted to visit, and by lunch time he felt that they had always worked together in the USA business. That was what he liked about her, she really was a part of his business self. She organised two short term letting apartments, one for herself, and one for him. They were in different buildings and separated by several blocks of streets.

His office saw a steady stream of visitors. Some came from within the company some from outside, and already the American team were starting to see the enormous work rate that for him was the norm but which left others exhausted by the sheer relentless pressure that he applied to himself and all those around him.

By the end of the month he'd fired several people, organised replacements, bludgeoned a new outline medium term strategy through which had the support of most of the American management but those that didn't agree joined the list of departees. He agreed new investment programmes, changed two advertising agencies, and set up discussions with a couple of smaller rival businesses with a view to acquiring them. He knew that it would take months to conclude those deals so the sooner he started the quicker he'd get a result.

He was careful to keep Dan Lewis back in the UK advised of what he was doing and although he didn't tell Dan any untruths he was economical with the full extent of what he was up to. The job, the pace and the challenges excited him and he loved it.

It was late one Monday night about two months since he'd arrived in America when he'd finished a hectic day of negotiations with some of their key suppliers to force reduced cost prices out of them. He insisted Sam should type up the notes and minutes of all the discussions and meetings that evening. While she was doing that he spent time on the phone, some were calls to the UK ignoring the fact that it was nearly midnight in England.

Around ten o'clock when both he and Sam were done he offered to buy her a pizza from a little restaurant around the corner from the office. As they stood in the long queue waiting for a table he turned to her and she saw that needing look on his face.

'Sam I hate waiting like this. Let's get a takeaway from the take out section over there and go back to my apartment and eat it there. It'll be a lot quicker judging by how long it's taking to get a table here and I'm hungry. The take out section seems to serve people quickly'.

She agreed and a few minutes later clutching two pizza boxes they hailed a cab and as they got in Sam gave the driver her address. 'Nearer than yours and we don't want these to go cold do we?' she queried with a raised eyebrow and her tongue peeping through her lips.

Arriving at her apartment building Mark paid the driver, walked up the steps through the swing doors, nodded to the night doorman and then they were in the lift.

'Sam'.

'I know' she smiled softly and handing him the pizza box kissed him gently on the lips before starting to rummage around in her purse for her keys. The lift clunked to a halt and he took her hand as she led the way down the carpeted corridor to her door.

Once inside they simply fell into each other's arms and kissed deeply, hungrily and passionately. Their hands moved around each other's bodies and he eased himself back so that he could undo her jacket buttons which left the garment gaping open. He ran his tongue down her neck and chest. Reaching behind herself she unclipped her peach coloured bra and pulled his face towards her exposed breasts where he fastened his lips onto first one nipple and then the other. Their breathing was getting louder as reaching down she found and undid his trouser belt and zip. Slipping her hands inside the elastic of his pants she pushed them and the trousers down freeing his erect penis.

He jerked her skirt above her waist, hooked his thumbs into the waistband of her panties and tights and pushed them down to her knees, which was as far as he could reach. Realising his problem she let go of his erection and with some difficulty got her underclothes off one leg and foot leaving them tangled around the other. Holding his penis tightly she spread her legs and rubbing his knob end against her pussy which instantly moistened, grasped his buttocks and grunting at his size pulled him into her.

They moved with each other. 'Yes come on' she exclaimed as he started thrusting into her. Leaning back against the hallway wall behind and wrapping her non underwear encumbered leg round the back of his legs she pushed hard against him. It wasn't long before she felt herself building towards a climax so squeezing his penis with her pussy muscles she heard him murmur and then piston into her with a real fury until with a final gasp and a series of hard deep thrusts she felt him spending inside her. His timing was perfect as this was the trigger that released her own orgasm and her gasps and moans were loud and prolonged.

Gradually they stopped moving and disengaged from each other. Sensing that the tension had eased out of him in much the same way that his semen had squirted and drained out of him she kissed him softly. They muttered 'thank you' to each other then separated to straighten their clothing, he pulling his trousers and pants back up while she eased her skirt back down, re-fastened her bra, buttoned her jacket then bent down to untangle the tights and panties from her left foot rolling them into a small bundle which she put on a hall table where he'd put the pizza boxes. With her tongue peeping through her lips she grinned 'We don't have to stay in the hall you know'.

'Why it's very nice here'.

'Like quick stand up kneetremblers do you then?' she queried with a cheeky expression on her face.

'They have their moments' he replied picking up her light hearted and teasing mood. 'Some of my best......' but before he could say any more she pressed her forefinger to his lips.

'I don't want to hear about your former sexual exploits thank you. Come on let's go and do something with these shall we' she bantered pointing at the food box. 'Or would you like a drink first?'

'Drink please. What do you have?'

'Not a lot I'm afraid. Wine and maybe some vodka. You choose'.

He settled for white wine and handing him a cold bottle out of the fridge and a bottle opener she sat on the floor watching him fill two glasses after which he joined her on the floor. Conversation flowed easily between them but they avoided mentioning their recent intense lovemaking.

'I was going to warm up those pizzas wasn't I? There must be something about you and cooking. Last time we were eating we got interrupted if you remember? I'll go and put them on' and getting athletically to her feet he noticed a flash of naked buttock as her tight skirt rode up when she stood. He remembered she hadn't put her knickers or tights back on. Taking the flat box into the small kitchen she cut the pizzas into slices then popped them into the oven. It didn't take long to re-heat the food and soon she brought them back into the sitting room.

'Now. We came here to eat before you side tracked us in the hall so drink your wine and eat some pizza'. She sat down on the floor and held out a slice of the doughy product to him. He took her hand, pressed it against his cheek, kissed it tenderly then took a bite of the pizza which was tough and chewy having gone cold and been reheated. They gamely struggled through a couple of slices each before giving up and tipping the rest in the trash can. Sam made some coffee and they sat in the living room on the settee drinking and talking until Mark looked at his watch and said that he'd better be going.

'Where?' asked Sam.

'Back to my apartment?'

'No you're not. You're sleeping here tonight so give me a cuddle now'. They curled up gently stroking and kissing each other then much later when they were in the bedroom and had slowly undressed each other Sam looked at him.

'You are going to make love to me properly now' and a little smile flickered across her face. 'Don't you dare come before I do as I had to work really fast to try and match you earlier and I only just made it'. Soon they were entwined and he made love to her slowly, taking time for her and himself. He didn't come first she did, extremely noisily. As they were drifting off to sleep she stroked his chest and said quietly 'Thank you. That was good wasn't it?' and he agreed it was.

'There then, see' was all she said.

In the morning they were awake early and she happily succumbed to his advances and found herself impaled deeply as he placed her legs over his shoulders and thrust strongly into her.

He left her place just after seven and got a cab to his own apartment where he stripped off, had a shower, shaved, changed into a fresh set of clothes and caught another cab to the office. He was ready to face a new business day and whatever challenges came his way.

Sam arrived just after eight thirty and a normal day's hectic round of meetings, arguments, negotiations, discussions, planning sessions, competitive analyses, and being a Tuesday a full review of the previous week's trading results which were calculated by the finance department on Mondays ready for his perusal on Tuesdays. They always led to demands from him for reasons as to why things weren't as they should be, or if things had gone well, a round of congratulatory memos or phone calls saying well done.

Towards the end of the next month, Houghtons hit back with a fierce price cutting campaign. The Lovells camp were caught napping as they'd got lulled into a sense of false security as Houghtons had not reacted until then. When Raul briefed Mark he merely smiled frostily and said 'Well you know what to do we agreed that when I got here.....
so do it. Now we need those Far Eastern costs and new products. Where are they?'

He was gratified to learn that not only were they nearly in the US the first shipments having left Korea three weeks ago but that they were

265

much lower cost than had been expected, and that there were several new and innovative products to launch.

'Great. Now we'll fuck Houghtons good and proper. Raul get your people ready for a bloodbath which we'll win'.

'Caramba', grinned the half Spanish Head of the Electrical Division reverting to an old Spanish phrase in his mixture of excitement and worry. 'I hope you know what you're doing Mark as any further price reduction will blow big holes in our profitability'.

'Yes it will short term, but I told you I'd support you. Remember we can afford that as I'll cross subsidise margins and profits from the rest of the American Group. Houghtons can't. They'll have to fight alone like a lonely cowboy on the prairie with no-one to help him face up to the Indians so hit them on price again and get those new products out. Do that and we'll win. Trust me. It may take time but I know what I'm doing'.

Not only was his confidence catching but also very reassuring and although he only spent a small proportion of his time with the anti Houghton strategy he insisted that he was continually briefed on the progress of the campaign. Most of his time was devoted to the other two thirds of the Lovells US company. It had become sluggish and had not only lost its way strategically but lost confidence in itself.

That is a real problem in any business and Mark recognised it wherever he went. People's heads were down, they had been continually told that sales were bad, profits getting worse, no money for investment in advertising or marketing, and worse no replacement of people when they left. Thus as individuals departed their work got shared out among those that were left which was alright for a short while but as it had gone on for nearly a year and more people left, then the business was strangling itself.

Mark set himself a punishing schedule of travelling throughout the country. He made presentations to senior and junior management, spoke to groups of factory workers and made a video of himself and his philosophy of turning the company around which he insisted was shown to all people that worked for the business. The sales teams were special recipients of Mark's attentions as he knew that these were his front line troops who when motivated could tackle the world but if de-motivated or depressed could soon drop behind their sales targets.

Wherever he spoke, in canteens, break rooms, meeting rooms, his sincerity shone out for all to see. He gave a new vision for the future and asked them to back him as what he was offering was for everyone's good. Often he took Sam with him on these trips which was helpful as she could check on the reaction he was generating and make suggestions for improvement or different emphasis. He listened to her and generally acted on what she said.

Canteens were upgraded, offices repainted, replaced worn out manufacturing machinery in several factories and he personally took charge of three new advertising campaigns. He recruited key people to fill long empty gaps and thus reversed the stagnation that had set in.

He listened carefully to many people so that he could begin to understand the American way of life and insisted that not only was the execution of the marketing strategy fully compatible with that but also that it focussed more on the product benefits rather than simply knocking competitors which is what so much of American advertising did. His approach was bold and decisive, and it worked.

He flew to Brazil and was staggered at the sprawling city of San Paulo and especially at the contrasts in life style that were evident everywhere. Abject poverty, street urchins, dirt and despair, but on the other hand the complete opposite of the very rich with their wealthy luxurious living in enormous villas or apartments secure behind high walls topped with razor wire.

Their Brazilian factory was old, decrepit and frankly disgraceful and required huge sums of money to modernise it which together with the poor sales results and profitability helped him make his decision. Sell the business as soon as possible and get out of Brazil. There were better opportunities in America, Europe and possibly longer term the Far East. His mind made up he flew back to New York and told Chuck to find a buyer for the Brazilian business as soon as possible.

Back in America market shares that had been falling, stabilised and then grew as did sales. Profitability started to recover and Mark realised over and over again the basics of business were simple. Get the right strategy with a good product, support it properly, have the best people working on it and you win. He also knew that success bred success and so it was in this case. People started to believe that things could turn around, and surprise surprise, they did.

Increasingly there was whole hearted support for the new "Limey guy from England" who not only seemed to understand the American way of life and how it applied to business, but supported it and ensured the business strategy was compatible with that.

Houghtons relaunch failed. Try as they might they couldn't dislodge Lovells who had received terrific support from their customer base to their new products and lower prices. One morning five months after Mark's arrival Sam went into his office between meetings.

'Got time to take a call from Hugh Sperryman?'

'Who's he?'

'Well his secretary said that he was Senior Vice President for Saratoga and he thought it might be nice if you and he met for lunch. Hey are you alright?' she queried anxiously as he'd gone white and clenched his fists. He leaned back in his chair and swivelled to look out of his office window.

'Mark I said are you alright?'

'Yes I'm very alright thanks Sam. Ring them back and say no'.

She looked closely at him. 'No? You sure you don't want to meet him?'

'That's right I do not want to meet him'.

Later in the day she returned again to the subject of the lunch meeting with Hugh Sperryman. 'I told him no thanks and he said that was alright but would you prefer dinner one evening instead? I told him that was unlikely. Did I do right?'

You certainly did Sam, quite right' and smiling he turned back to some documents on his desk. 'Yes', he continued softly 'quite right. Now let's see what they do. My guess is the President of the company will call next'.

Sure enough a few days later there was a call for Mark from the Houghton's US President George Walters. Sam fielded the call and said that Mark was tied up all that day but she would be certain to let him know that Mr. Walters had called. Mark ignored that call and the next and the next.

Increasingly regularly he and Sam slept together. Their lovemaking was good, exciting, passionate and sometimes loving. She was clever at sensing his needs and could tell when his desires were urgent or demanding and he simply wanted sex. This was usually after he'd succeeded in a difficult negotiation or pulled off some major strategic move. Conversely she could tell when he wanted to make love slowly and lovingly, or to be pampered or seduced, or when he wanted to talk and maybe make love later. She was closely attuned to his needs, responded accordingly and their relationship become ever stronger. Sam the consummate lover and efficient secretary was a crucial part of his team at work, and in bed.

They were very discreet and were certain no-one knew of their relationship. Even when they travelled to different parts of America and had to stay away Sam would usually book them into separate hotels, she always into a slightly lower grade one than Mark's.

Often business meetings took place in his hotel suite and Sam was usually there to take notes of arrangements made. The meetings regularly finished quite late at night so as the participants left she did too usually sharing a taxi with another meeting attendee to be dropped off at her separate hotel where she was staying. Thus others saw her leave and stay somewhere different from Mark. What they didn't realise was that most times as soon as she'd walked into her hotel she'd order another cab to take her straight back to Mark's hotel where going directly up to his room she would spend the night returning early next morning to her own hotel.

Whilst generally happy with their relationship Sam was concerned that Mark was taking her willingness to sleep with him too much for granted. Matters came to a head one night when she'd had difficulty getting a cab back to his hotel and it was nearly an hour before she returned to knock softly on his room door. As he wrenched it open she saw that he was only wearing a bathrobe.

'About bloody time too whatever have you been doing? Come on I'm tired. Get undressed and into bed' he demanded as he walked back into the room with her following.

'Mark look I.......'

'Just get undressed will you. I don't want to talk I want to fuck'.

'That's just it' she replied raising her voice and stepping back. 'You want. Well what about me? Do you ever think what I want? Mr. Big Boss wants to fuck his secretary so alright lady, get your knickers off open your legs and let him into you. That's not what I want Mark. You used to be so tender so gentle, so loving. Now you're losing that. I'm becoming just a receptacle for your cock to pump out its juices'.

Her voice got louder 'I know how hard you work and the pressure you're under but I can help you not just in the office as your secretary but as your lover when we are alone. But don't take me for granted. Show me some respect and stop treating me like some sort of paid whore. I'm not a hooker here for you to screw whenever and however you want. I'm a woman who enjoys working for you and also happens to like and respect you as a man...... as a business man...... as my boss..... as my lover'. She glared at him. 'Now if you want me to stay and sleep with you ask............don't just take' she concluded angrily.

He said nothing for a moment but his eyes had flashed fiercely as she'd spoken. There was silence, tension then he relaxed, his eyes softened and he walked over to an easy chair.

'Come here.......please' and he held out his hands as he sat down. She walked hesitantly to him, paused for a moment and then sat on his lap.

'Sam I'm sorry. Of course I respect you. I think you are a wonderful woman both as a secretary where frankly I don't know what I'd do without you and as a lover where you are simply astonishing but you're right I have taken you for granted but it isn't lack of respect, simply thoughtlessness. Forgive me?'

Looking down at him she saw his worried expression and for a moment he no longer looked like the tough business man in control of everything but a small boy lost and asking for absolution and as she looked at him her anger melted away.

'Yes, of course I do and thank you for apologising. I know that's not an easy thing for you and so for that reason it's all the more important to me that you have said sorry. Right now we've got that sorted and I am here is there anything that I can help you with........this for example?' and getting off him she opened his robe dropped to her knees leant forward and slid her lips over his penis. He started to erect immediately and as she moved her head up and down on him he leaned back and relaxed until after a little while she let him slip out of her mouth. 'Shall I stay here doing this or do you want to go to bed?'

'Both. Stay there until......well you know........and then later, bed.......please'.

Her lips encased him again as she took him back deeply into her mouth. She slid up from the root to the knob end sucking hard until she got to the tip where her tongue flicked him rapidly before moving back down where she used her teeth to nip him in rapid succession all the way. The effect was startling and he couldn't remember any previous girl with such amazing technique. It was simply fantastic. Watching the movements of her head he stroked her blonde hair until suddenly arching his back he gripped her hair tightly as he groaned into his climax. She stayed on her knees after he'd finished.

'Nice darling?'

'Umm wonderful thank you'.

'Good, now get on the bed and you can watch me undress'.

This she did very slowly swaying slightly and playing with her breasts when they were freed from her bra before turning her back to him and bending forward as she removed her panties. She ran her hands up and down the back of her legs before straightening up, turning and walking slowly across the room, climbing onto the bed and standing astride him looked down from her full height. Swaying her hips she slowly bent her knees fully exposing herself to his gaze until she was crouching just above him.

As he reached up for her she laughed, laid down along side him and started to run her hands all over his body every now and then adding a few kisses. She refused to allow him to reciprocate on her and there wasn't much of his naked body that didn't receive the attention of her hands and lips. Eventually she stroked his part erection back into full hardness then smiling lay back holding out her arms to him. Quickly swivelling himself on top he felt her legs lock themselves tightly around his back as she pushed herself up towards him.

Later they cuddled closely together.

She felt happy and contented as he'd loved her wonderfully in bed tonight taking time for her and ensuring that she achieved satisfaction in her own right before he himself completed.

He reflected that she was amazingly good in bed but she was right he had been taking her for granted but her timely warning would correct that. However he also realised that he was starting to miss Abi and looked forward to the time when he was back in the UK to be able to see her again.

At work he continued identifying companies that they could buy. He was convinced that acquisitions together with a business strategy that took full account of the American way of life, plus upgrading the senior management around the various companies, then there would be no reason why the US company shouldn't become a real powerhouse of profit for the whole worldwide Lovells Group. A strong flow of American profits into Group Headquarters in the UK would transform the entire business.

He held a meeting with one of the takeover targets. It went well and they could see the logic of becoming part of the Lovells operation. The main attraction for him was that it gave Lovells a manufacturing base in Atlanta, down in the south of the enormous country and as a result they could lower their trucking costs dramatically as well as getting better access to their markets and customers in those vital and potentially profitable Southern States. There were many issues to sort out but the team that he assembled including some good American lawyers, his own finance team and Chuck were able to handle them confidently and comfortably under Mark's leadership.

What he didn't tell his team was that this was the first acquisition that he'd ever done. He simply let them think that he was an old hand at it. Finally there was a firm proposal that made financial sense to both sides and after a long telephone conversation with Dan back in the UK it was agreed that he would fly back to brief the Board on a formal acquisition recommendation.

What he didn't tell Dan was that he'd agreed in principle with the target company and signed a "Letter of intent to purchase" which was strictly outside his authority to do so but he was keen to show the potential acquiree that he was serious about buying their business and confident in his own ability to convince the main Board back in the UK of the sense in making this acquisition.

So he'd taken the risk and made the commitment. The question of what he would do if the Board turned down his recommendation only fleetingly crossed his mind. He knew that Dan's primary concern would be that Lovell's US business was only just starting to turn round and that it would be risky to be considering an acquisition at this early stage but he fundamentally disagreed and that was why he'd said he'd go back.

He was also missing Abi tremendously and although they spoke two or three times a week on the phone he really did want to see her again. After all it was virtually five months since they been together face to face.

There were no further phone calls from Saratoga but a couple of weeks after the first phone call from George Walters a letter arrived addressed personally to Mark.

From the Office of GEORGE WALTERS
President of the Company

Dear Mark,   16ᵗʰ September 2003

I have been trying to call you for a little while as I feel it might be a good idea for us to meet sometime to talk over a few areas of mutual interest.

It seems that you've been pretty darn busy lately but I hope you could find some time out in your hectic schedule for us to visit with each other. May I ask Mary Beth my secretary to call your secretary to find a time that might suit us both?

I hope so and look forward to meeting with you in the near future,

Yours truly,

George

GEORGE WATERS

Mark read it several times and realised that the other side were getting concerned. If they were that keen to meet, then his anti Saratoga strategy was working. Now the crucial question was how to phrase the response and he spent some time thinking about that. When he'd made up his mind he called Sam into his office and with a face that alternated between smiling and grimacing dictated a short reply.

Dear George,   September 20th 2000

Many thanks for your recent letter which I have read with
much interest but I am not sure that there is any value in a
meeting at this time. Please though do keep in touch.

Kind regards

Mark

MARK WATSON,
Chief Executive

'Let him put that in his pipe and smoke it' he laughed later as he
signed the short letter and tossed it back to Sam. 'Make sure Chuck
has a copy. Now I wonder what they'll do. If nothing else it'll unsettle
them. Good, time their cage was rattled. Now Sam my girl get me a
flight back to the UK will you. I want an overnight flight out of here on
Thursday which will get me back early morning Friday into England.
I don't know how many days I'll be staying yet so make it a single will
you and liaise with Dan's secretary to set up a meeting with him for
Friday morning and ask that the Board be convened for Monday. Oh
and if George Walters rings or writes tell him that I've gone back to the
UK for a few days and you don't know for how long'.

She bustled away to make the arrangements reflecting that it would
be strange without him for a few days.

Knowing he was leaving the American team breathed a collective
sigh of relief that he'd be gone for a while. He paid his executives very
well for exceptional performance. "Pay well, work hard, get results"
was his creed and its beneficial effects were seen in the improved results
coming though but the stress of working for Mark was high.

Most learned to cope and rose to the challenge. Those that didn't
got fired. It became well known that if you were good at your job and
could stand the frantic pace which he demanded then not only would
you get on well with him but you'd prosper financially.

He caught the overnight Virgin Atlantic flight to London and slept
off and on during the flight drinking only mineral water. Although it

departed three quarters of an hour late, it arrived in Gatwick ahead of time due to a strong tail wind.

CHAPTER 18

Walking into the terminal he was reasonably refreshed and ready for a day's work as he scanned the throng of people waiting for arriving passengers to emerge from the customs hall. Varied expressions showed, some anxious, some smiling, some worried, some expectant, some bored, some holding notice boards with a name or names on it and among the hundred or so people there that morning he spotted Graham who was among the smilers.

Good morning sir. Did you have a good flight?' asked Graham reaching for Mark's case.

'Yes thanks. What are you doing here?'

'Well I gather that someone from the States asked that you be collected so I volunteered. Straight to the office sir?'

'Yes please I've got a meeting with Dan Lewis'. Mark recognised Sam's touch in arranging the collection. He could have got a taxi for the short journey but knowing that he hated queuing and was possibly going to be tetchy after the long overnight flight she'd taken the hassle away.

'Listen I need to go to Northamptonshire tonight. Fancy taking me up there as I don't want to drive at the end of the day with all the time zone changes and not having a proper night's sleep?'

'Be a pleasure sir. What time do you want to leave?'

'Not exactly sure yet but around late afternoon. I'll let you know'.

It wasn't long until they arrived at the offices so thanking Graham and walking through reception he bounded up the stairs to Dan's office. Giving a quick knock he didn't wait for a reply before opening the door and striding across to the Chairman shook his hand firmly.

Once initial greetings were out of the way he briefed Dan in detail on what he thought about the US and Brazilian operations. Although he used some notes that he'd made on the plane he mainly spoke from memory.

Dan was amazed at Mark's grasp of the business and the depth of his thinking. His strategies were bold some even brazen in the audacity of thought but looking at what had been achieved already in the few months that he'd been over there Dan was filled with confidence in the new Chief Executive. He worried about the full Board though. Many of the members were opposed to taking risks and he was also concerned about the reaction from their Bankers and Fund Managers to an acquisition this early in the turn round and said so.

'It's got to be the right move Dan and I expect your backing for this on Monday at the full Board meeting.

'Well, it is a risk at this stage. Wouldn't you......we, be better to wait for a few more months before you start to acquire businesses and in the meantime devote your time to the core business? I'm not saying that it's wrong it's just the timing that is too early.

'Time is what we don't have Dan. If we don't buy Atlanta Trading someone else will and it's a perfect fit for our business. It would be foolish nay criminal to let it slip from our grasp because of dilly dallying over whether the time is right. Time is never right. Our task is to manage the time and the opportunity'.

'Well let's see how you get by on Monday with the Board. I'll remain neutral until then and make up my mind at the meeting'.

'You mean you want to see how others think before committing yourself. That's not good enough. I want your support and believe that I'm entitled to it. I've shown you already what I can do for Lovells and believe me making decisions that sometimes require courage to support them is what makes a good business into a great business. Don't hold me back Dan because I know that this is the right thing to do. What's more when we've got this one locked down I've got some more acquisitions lined up for us to make. So you'd better climb off the fence and get ready to back me. Just wait till I start on the UK and European businesses then you'll really see some sparks fly'.

Dan saw the passion in Mark's eyes and felt again the driving power flowing out of him. There was no doubt that Mark believed in what he was suggesting but could he risk supporting him. It could be a fight with the Board and although Dan had confidence in his new Chief Executive it was still only a few months that he'd been in the business and Dan wanted to be sure that the proposal really was the right thing for their US Company.

On the other hand he realised that Mark needed his support and he desperately wanted to give it to him but he had to be sure it was right for Lovells, and for his own position. He had built a personal reputation for shrewdness and clever business acumen, and didn't want to damage that by backing a hasty move from his Chief Executive especially now that his term as Chairman was coming to an end. He needed to think hard before Monday's Board meeting although he could see the argument from Mark's viewpoint.

Mark interrupted his thoughts. 'Dan I'm telling you that I expect you to back me on this. Now have you seen my initial thoughts for the restructure of the European Division?'

'Yes I have and they make a lot of sense. I'll certainly support you on that when the time comes. When do you plan to action that?'

'As soon as I can after I'm able to return to the UK at the end of my six month purdah which I remind you is only just over a month from now. I don't think there's much else to discuss today. As I see it regarding the American issue, you're happy with the overall approach and results and don't disagree with the principle of the acquisition but are concerned about the timing and our ability to absorb the new company without distraction from everything else that we're doing. And you're worried about the view of the Institutions. If I can convince you of those issues then I assume that I'll have your support on Monday. Right?'

'Yes, I guess that's about the size of it Mark'.

'Right see you at ten o'clock Monday morning'.

Mark left Dan's office and went to his own which was large but empty. Soon it would come alive when he moved back to the UK and operated out of here he thought. Sam would be in and out and meetings, arguments, discussions, decisions would fill his day but now it was just an empty desk, empty cabinets, empty tables, empty chairs and settee.

Drinking a cup of coffee he sat and thought carefully about how he could resolve the Chairman's concerns. He knew Dan would be an influential figure at the meeting and it was vital to have his support, but how could he strengthen his case for Dan?

Reaching for his diary he riffled through the pages then picked up the phone and dialled a number. He spoke at length to the person he'd rung. Finished with that call he looked up another number and made a second call.

Having completed the two phone calls he sat back and pondered for a few minutes before taking up his portable dictation machine which was always in his briefcase. He spoke rapidly into the machine for half an hour or so and then looking at his watch and realising that it was too early to call New York asked Martha to come in and handed her the tape.

'Quick as you can please'.

Martha dutifully went to her desk and typed up the memos and letters together with some further notes Mark had made on how he intended to present the case on Monday. These were to form an addendum to the presentation that he had prepared in New York which consisted of many graphs, explanations and appendices to some thick written documents.

By mid afternoon he'd finished reading and correcting the work Martha had completed and had rung Brazil and New York.

He also rang Abi and confirmed that he was back in England and was her offer of dinner this evening still available so around three thirty he asked Martha to let Graham know that he was nearly ready to leave and shortly afterwards he settled into the back of the big Jag.

They were away in time to avoid the worst of the traffic and shortly after six o'clock Graham called back to Mark who'd dropped off to sleep that they were on the outskirts of Northampton and where exactly did he live?

Then Mark sprung his surprise. 'Go to the station Graham. You can get a train back from there and I'll take the car on myself. Probably get you back quicker than having to drive back'.

Graham didn't comment but followed the signs to the centre of Northampton and the station. Getting out Mark peeled off fifty pounds in notes and gave them to Graham.

'Here. This'll more than cover your rail fares, and use the rest to buy yourself a nice meal somewhere. I'll see you on Monday and thanks a lot. Listen I've got various places to go next week. Will you drive me please?'

'Be delighted to sir'.

'Good but if you're going to be my driver for crying out loud stop calling me sir. All right?'

'Yes sir.......sorry, yes. But what should I call you?'

'Mark will do just fine when we're on our own. If there are others about, oh I don't know, you think of something'.

They grinned at each other and so started a long term partnership as Graham moved from security guard to become Mark's personal chauffeur.

Slipping behind the steering wheel Mark eased the car gingerly out of the station car park into the heavy rush hour traffic. He drove carefully getting familiar again with driving on the left. Although he hadn't actually driven himself much in America nevertheless his mind had become attuned to the American way of driving on the wrong side of the road.

Making his way to his apartment block he parked, went up to his flat and rummaged around for a while before running a very hot bath in which he soaked thinking of his long day. The flight, the meeting with Dan, the issues that needed resolving, how he'd tackle Monday's Board meeting and especially tonight's dinner with Abi.

Pulling out the plug he then stood under the shower nozzle feeling the bath water subside around his legs and feet while the warm shower water cascaded onto him. Slowly turning the temperature control to tepid and then taking a deep breath to cold he gasped as he stood it for several minutes, before stepping out to towel himself dry feeling quite refreshed.

Walking naked into the bedroom he picked up the phone and after again consulting his diary dialled a number. He was quickly put through to the person he wanted and continued the discussions that he'd had when he'd rung earlier in the day. The conversation lasted about five minutes and at the end Mark was pleased with the outcome.

He made a second call, but this one lasted longer and it took about ten minutes to gain the agreement that he wanted from this other person.

In the bathroom he shaved and then returning to his bedroom dressed carefully finishing by splashing on some aftershave as he heard his fax machine clattering. Abi had said come casual so he selected an open neck pale yellow shirt, dark blue slacks, a pair of black lightweight shoes and he slung a black sweater over his shoulders. Looking round he was glad that he'd arranged to have his cleaner continue to service the apartment weekly which meant that the rooms were fresh smelling, not covered in dust and that the clothes that he'd left there and not taken to The States didn't smell musty. Not being quite sure what the weekend would hold for him he threw some more clothes into a small grip put his remaining couple of suits into a suit carrier and dropped both bags in the hallway.

Collecting a bottle of champagne from the fridge, he walked back into the sitting room where in the corner his fax machine had some papers projecting from it. He pulled them out scanned them quickly and smiling put them into his briefcase. A quick look around then picking up the grip, suit carrier, briefcase and champagne he went to the car and set off for Abi's house.

As he drove he felt himself getting excited at seeing her again. Five months was a long time to have been apart even though they had spoken frequently on the phone and he wondered if there was any other man in her life. Much to his amazement he felt a shot of jealousy if there did turn out to be someone else and he pushed the accelerator down to get there as soon as he could.

When he turned off the lane and drove up the L shaped drive to her house his heart was thumping. Grabbing some large parcels that he'd brought back from America he almost ran to her front door which opened just as he reached it and there she stood, smiling broadly and holding her arms out to him.

They melted together hugging tightly for a few minutes before their lips found each other and they kissed deeply and intensely.

'I've missed you' they whispered to each other then Abi gently pulled him into the hallway and pushed the door shut behind them.

'Come in and let me look at you properly' she said softly leading him into her sitting room. He put his parcels down on a chair before submitting himself for her inspection.

'Oh you've no idea how much I've missed you. Come here' and pulling him towards her she kissed him again. Eventually they moved apart and sat on the settee where they held hands and talked of everything and nothing. She told him what she'd been doing, about the children and her writing while he spoke about America and how he was changing everything. Abi thrilled to hear him talk and was fascinated not only at what he said, but the passion in his eyes and voice as he made the

Lovell's American business come alive. He told her about his travels around the United States and his brief trips to Brazil.

'I've brought some presents for you and the girls. Would you like to see them? By the way where are the girls, are they out?'

'I've sent them to my parents......... for the weekend so we can be together......alone. I thought you might like that and not have to put up with the two of them chattering and battering at you about America all the time'.

'I wouldn't have minded, but being alone with you is going to be wonderful'.

'Are you hungry? I've got a casserole in the oven as it's quick and easy and saves me having to spend lots of time cooking. Let me go and have a peep at it and see how it's coming along. Don't go away will you?' she laughed as she left the room returning shortly announcing that it would be ready in a few minutes.

'Time for you to have these then. Would you like to open them? Err, I'm not very good at presents for ladies I'm afraid so I hope you'll like them'.

'Ooh pressies. How exciting. I'm sure they'll be lovely. What are they I wonder?' and taking the two parcels she sat down and opened the smaller of the two. 'Chanel perfume. Mark how clever of you as it's one of my favourites. Thank you', and opening the bottle she tipped a little onto her wrists and rubbed them together before leaning forward and holding one out for Mark to smell. He held it kissing it gently.

Laughing she moved back saying that she wanted to open her other present. She carefully untied the string and removing the outer paper revealed further wrapping which was rather pretty and showed stylised drawings of ladies in old fashioned underwear or old fashioned floating style gowns.

'Whatever's this? Have you bought me some naughty underwear?' she giggled.

'Not exactly. Go on open it. I hope you like it'.

She did and took out a pale green nightdress and negligee both trimmed with white lace. 'Oh Mark they're lovely' and standing up she held them to her throat and pressed them into her waist. 'Thank you. I'll keep them for a special occasion' she said quietly, and leaning towards him she kissed him again. 'I'll just go put them away then we'll eat as by now supper will be ready. Thank you for my presents, there are lovely'.

'Hang on I've got a bottle of bubbly in the car, I'll go and get it'. When he returned to the dining room Abi was waiting, so peeling off the foil and metal cage he carefully eased out the cork and slowly filled two glasses. 'Cheers'.

'Cheers' she smiled 'here's to the weekend. Now sit down and let's eat'.

On the table already waiting were plates of prawns, pickled herrings and smoked mackerel and again Abi was staggered at how quickly Mark managed to eat while holding conversation at the same time. She didn't know how he did it but in no time his plate was empty and he was refilling his glass while she, who'd hardly spoken still had more than half her food remaining.

'God, I've never known anyone eat like you. How do you do it?' she asked sipping her champagne and smiling at him.

'I think in a former life I must have been starved or unable to get food or maybe frightened that my plate would be taken away before I'd finished. I don't know but I always eat quickly. Sorry. Hope it doesn't offend you'.

'No it doesn't I'm glad to see you enjoy it'. Standing she leaned forward and kissed him gently on the forehead and then while gathering up their plates her hand stroked his neck. 'Stay there while I get the casserole'.

Watching her as she walked out of the room he wondered about tonight. She certainly seemed pleased enough to see him, was being very tactile and had sent the kids away so could he make a play tonight to get her into bed. Also if he was going to stay he could drink several glasses of wine but if not he'd have to be careful as he'd be driving back to Northampton. When she returned with a large pottery bowl from which delicious smells emerged he sat back while she served him inviting him to help himself to vegetables. Noticing her glass was empty he refilled it but left his own.

'Aren't you having any more?'

'No I've had a couple and have to be careful about drinking and driving back'.

She looked up and then staring straight at him spoke seriously but softly. 'You don't have to drive anywhere tonight. You can stay here........if you like'.

Instantly the atmosphere became highly charged and returning her look he said 'Thank you'. She smiled back saying nothing.

They ate, sometimes talking sometimes just being quiet and yet comfortable with each other in the silence. Again Mark devoured his main course quickly and Abi teased him about it and later on also about the way he gobbled his blackberry cream dessert.

Having cleared the dirty crockery and utensils into the kitchen and loaded the dishwasher Mark carried their coffees into the sitting room then plumped into one of the large armchairs. Abi came and sat on his lap. She stroked his hair and glancing down kissed him from time to time until she noticed that he had yawned for the second time in quick succession.

'Oh Mark you must be exhausted with all that travelling and meetings today. Sorry I shouldn't be keeping you up like this'.

'No I'm fine, just relaxed and happy'.

Getting off him she leaned down kissed his forehead then holding out her hands to him said very quietly 'Come to bed'.

Taking his hand she led him into the hall up the stairs and across the large upper landing to her bedroom. Following her he saw he'd entered a large pretty room furnished in pinks and soft peach colours. She flicked a switch to turn off the overhead lights and another to replace them with bedside lights and the room instantly became very soft, feminine and welcoming.

Releasing his hand she turned to him and giving him a quick peck on the lips said 'I just need to go to the bathroom. Why don't you get into bed and warm up the duvet for us' and looking at him from under her eyelashes she turned and walked into the en-suite bathroom.

Quickly undressing he slid under the covers noticing that he could faintly smell her perfume on the sheet under him. A little later the bathroom door opened and she stood there in the pale green nightdress and negligee that he'd bought her. The bright light from the bathroom behind showed that the outfit was almost see through and as she turned to close the door he could see the outline of her breasts and caught a glimpse of the dark triangle at the top of her legs.

Walking slowly across the room she took off the negligee and draped it on the foot of the bed, then smiling peeled back the duvet seeing Mark's naked chest as she slipped in alongside him. Leaning on one arm she bent her head to kiss him gently before speaking quietly.

'Mark listen. It's been a long time, over four years in fact since I made love. There's been no-one since Roger so please be patient with me. I do want to do this but you'll have to help me. Can you understand what I'm saying?'

'Yes darling. I feel very honoured tonight that we are together like this. I'll not hurt you I promise and I'll try and make it good for you...... for us both'.

He kissed her lips and her face and stroked her long dark hair and sensed that her initial tenseness was fading as she relaxed and started to respond to him. He slid his hand down to her breasts and gently played with them massaging and squeezing before letting his hand move further down her body as he searched for the hem of her nightie which he lifted and stroked her legs.

Slowly his hand worked upwards and he felt her tense again as he moved past her thighs and upwards to her bush which he stroked but gradually he felt her relaxing and she lifted her bottom so that he could pull the nightie up towards her neck. He lowered his face to her now naked breasts and slowly licked her nipples. Whispering to him that he should take the nightie right off he did so before again lowering his lips to her breasts. Her nipples had stiffened slightly. Letting his tongue circle and flick across one and then the other his fingers worked around her bush for a while before gently opening her pussy lips and massaging her until he moved to her clit which he rubbed slowly.

She moaned softly quietly calling out his name several times until raising his lips from her chest to her mouth he pressed his tongue deeply inside.

His fingers continued to massage her pussy which was now very wet and slippery and removing his hand from her lower regions he lifted himself above her. He felt her arms around his back as she whispered 'Yes Mark oh yes, please' and as he started to lower himself onto her she moved one hand to feel for his prick which she immediately realised was much larger than Roger's had been but guiding it to her pussy lips she gasped as he slid inside.

He was desperately keen to make their lovemaking last and for it to be a wonderful experience for her not just rushed sex so he moved himself slowly and purposefully concentrating on giving her the very best sensations from his penis, his fingers and his tongue that he could. Her breathing started to become more pronounced and she responded and moved with him as he gradually speeded up his movements. He alternated between kissing her lips, face and ears before making little forays with his tongue to her nipples which he licked and then let his tongue trail its way up her chest, neck and back to her lips. Her nails dug into his shoulders and she started to moan as her pelvic movements became more aggressive, moving in tune with his now much faster and stronger thrusting.

He slowed down almost to a standstill to ease himself almost right out of her before pushing in hard and speeding up again. He did this several times until eventually as he slowed she gasped 'No don't Mark, please, oh yes, yes, I'm ..... aah', and with a huge shudder and gripping him very tightly with her arms and her nails scraping down his back he felt her climax.

Instantly he thrust hard and fast and seconds later he too climaxed, pulsing several times and continuing to move although rather more slowly now until his penis had finished squirting. When he stopped moving he lifted his head away from her face and smiled saying so softly that it was almost inaudible 'Thank you darling. You were unbelievable'.

She just smiled back up at him and hugged him. 'Mark I don't know how or what to say but that was wonderful. Thank you, come here' and lifting himself off to lay by her side he cuddled her into himself, but after a few moments he saw that she was crying.

'Whatever's wrong? I didn't hurt you did I? You're not regretting it are you?'

'Not at all. I told you it was wonderful and I meant it. I'm crying because I'm happy. Isn't that silly. Was I alright for you? I mean was it really alright?'

'Yes darling it really was', and they lay together, his head on her shoulder and his arms around her.

She was happy with him lying next to her and his lovemaking had been fantastic. The only other man she'd ever slept with was Roger and inevitably as she lay there and much as she didn't want to make comparisons between Mark and Roger in any way, especially in their respective ways of making love, nevertheless she couldn't avoid the fact that Mark was not only considerably bigger but by far the better lover. Roger had been a good husband providing well for her and the girls, kind in every way as he was that sort of man, but in bed he'd been very much a "get on, get in, get done and get off type of lover" rarely worrying too much about her pleasure, whereas Mark had seemed to go out of his way to make it good for her. He was obviously very experienced in bed and she found herself looking forward to exploring his talents further.

'Mark darling' she said softly and when he didn't answer her she lifted her head and saw that he was fast asleep. 'Bloody typical' she muttered quietly then immediately felt remorse. The poor man had been awake for goodness knows how many hours since leaving America and must be absolutely exhausted. She wriggled around to get comfortable then snuggled into him giving him a soft kiss on his cheek before closing her eyes and drifting happily off to sleep.

In the morning she slipped out of bed being careful not to disturb him as he was still deeply asleep. It looked as though he hadn't moved a single inch in the night. Not taking her eyes off his face she pulled on her new green nightie and negligee then made her way downstairs.

Deciding to treat him to full breakfast in bed she quickly set up a tray, poured two glasses of orange juice, put the percolator on to make fresh coffee and dropped a couple of eggs into a saucepan. She found a comb and ran it through her hair and after hunting in her handbag found a lipstick. Breakfast all came ready together as the coffee boiled, the timer for the eggs pinged and just after that the toaster popped up the last two brown hot slices.

He was still asleep when she walked back into her bedroom so putting the tray on the end of the bed on the side away from him she knelt on the bed and leaned down to give him a kiss.

'Good morning' and his eyes slowly opened. 'You seem to have slept well' she added softly smiling at him.

He smiled back and said huskily 'Morning Abi. Oh I slept like a dead man' and then froze as he realised that here he was having slept in Roger and Abi's bed after making love to the dead man's widow.

'Oh Lord I didn't……..' but she put her finger on his lips and kissed his nose.

'I know you didn't. It's alright, really it is. Look I've brought you breakfast in bed. How's that for pampering?' and the moment of potential awkwardness passed.

Hefting himself up she tucked pillows behind his back and watched as he drank deeply from the large glass of juice and then cracked open the first egg. As usual he ate rapidly and was soon devouring the second egg and starting on a slice of toast. Abi buttered herself a slice of toast and munched on that never once taking her eyes off Mark's face.

He really was a very attractive man and she could feel herself starting to have extremely deep feelings for him. He drank half his cup of coffee and then stretching his arms above his head grinned and said 'Now I feel a new man and almost ready for anything. Any ideas on what should we do today eh?'

'Almost ready for anything?'

'Yes almost but I must go and have a pee before I do anything else' and handing her the tray he swung himself out of bed and strode across the room to the en-suite. She looked at his taut buttocks and naked back noticing several red scratch marks on his shoulders. Looking down at her hands she realised that they must have been caused by her fingernails last night.

When he walked back into the room he saw several things. Firstly the tray was now resting on the dressing table. Secondly her green nightie and negligee were on the floor by the side of the bed and thirdly she was lying on her side in the bed facing towards him with her head propped up on her hand smiling broadly.

'What's this?' he grinned.

'I've thought of the first thing we could do today' she grinned back and then screeched as he ran and launched himself onto the bed.

'Great. Now what's that I wonder?' and tugging the covers away he looked down at her naked body. Leaning forward he kissed her and then scooped her into his arms. They cuddled tightly and she could feel his erection growing as he pressed against her then sighed as he slid down towards her tummy and started to kiss her belly button before slowly trailing his tongue to her bush and onto her pussy. She felt a mixture of emotions. Embarrassment at being naked in the day light while being kissed there, something that Roger would never have done, however she also experienced mounting sexual desire as a result of the ministrations of Mark's tongue and fingers.

Holding his head and pressing him into her she groaned softly but continuously until a little cry emerged as she climaxed. To her amazement and delight he didn't stop but continued to love her there with his mouth as she stroked his head, his face and his back before sitting up and pushing him onto his back.

She held his penis and massaged it before lifting herself onto him to ride him slowly at first and then with increasing tempo.

Mark watched her she rode up and down with her eyes closed, her mouth part open, her breasts bouncing and her dark long hair swinging around wildly. After a while he twisted her over until she was beneath him again and he was pounding into her as they made love to each other passionately and deeply. Their climaxes were almost simultaneous and afterwards they lay together stroking and kissing each other.

'That was a great idea for something to do' he grinned. 'Got any other good ideas to follow?' A gentle punch in his chest was her reply.

She explained that usually at weekends she spent time helping the girls muck out their horse's stables but to ensure that they had time together she'd asked Sarah their girl groom who usually only came in Monday to Friday, to come in on Saturday and Sunday to relieve her of the task on this occasion and give them more time together.

'That's nice, now come here darling' and he pulled her to him.

The weekend passed in something of a happy haze for them, with visits to pubs for lunch or an early evening drink, a lovely French restaurant for dinner on Saturday evening, some walking in a nearby park where they watched a pair of grey squirrels running around chasing each other, and back in the house lots of lovemaking.

Abi drove them around in her eight year old Volvo. When she first got it out of the garage and Mark climbed into the passenger seat she apologised for all the assorted junk that cluttered up the car. He said that he hadn't really seen her as Volvo woman.

She smiled 'Well now you know. Remember I'm a mum with two teenage girls who for years have had ponies and now horses and needed to traipse around from one horse event to another towing a horse trailer with all the paraphernalia that was required, not to mention trips to ballet classes, gymnastics, swimming, birthday parties plus large suitcases and trunks to and from school. There's nothing else that really fits the bill except maybe a great big four wheel drive which is expensive to run, difficult to drive, cumbersome to park and not really at all practical. So you see that's why I'm Volvo mum'.

'And quite the sexiest one on the school run I've no doubt' he replied putting his hand on her knee in a protective sort of gesture. He left his hand there for a while and she liked the feel of his palm on her jean covered leg.

Abi realised on Sunday morning that she was close to falling in love with him but said nothing as she was terrified of being seen by him as a predatory widow trying to snare a man.

Mark knew his feelings for her were different from any he'd had for any woman before but didn't say anything in case she thought that he was trying to take advantage of a lonely widow.

He also felt quite differently about making love to her from when he made love to Sam. With Abi it was making love. With Samantha it was sex. Both women were good but both were different. Abi was warm, tender, gentle, loving and could be someone to live with. Sam was sexy, bright, efficient and a bloody good bonk but he wouldn't want to live with her. Would he?

He tried to analyse his feelings for Abi and asked himself if he wanted to settle down with her.

It wouldn't be an easy decision and he found himself unable to fully crystallize his thoughts. Certainly he loved to be with Abi, but did he love her? He'd missed her a lot when he was in America and now here with her he felt relaxed comfortable and at one with her, but he hadn't known her for very long. In fact he'd spent more time with Sam than her yet already he knew his feelings for Abi were quite different from those that he had for Sam.

He'd also slept with Sam many times yet this weekend was only the first time he'd slept with Abi. Concluding that he wasn't able to come to any decision about her or Sam he put the subject to the back of his mind on the basis that it would evolve and in time he would know.

When they eventually got up, showered and wandered downstairs Sunday turned into a lovely lazy day, sprawling around in the morning reading the papers and discussing various articles within them, at lunchtime munching on some cheese, biscuits, celery and slowly consuming a couple of glasses of red wine. In the afternoon they walked around the garden and then beyond into the land that went with Abi's house. There were just over three acres, of which two were fenced as paddocks for the horses, half an acre was woodland and the rest was taken up with a large garden of mainly lawn and shrubs.

The stable block was to the side of the house and Mark stroked the horse's necks and let them nuzzle his hand, as they leaned over their stable doors blowing softly down their nostrils. 'Do you ride' he queried.

'Not any more. I don't have time, but one day I'll take it up again. Maybe I could teach you to ride. How would you feel about that?' she queried.

'Oh I think I'll just look at them. When I was a kid on holiday I had a ride on a donkey on a beach. You know what? It chucked me off. I think that's on omen to stay away from horses'.

'But you said it was a donkey'.

'Horses, donkeys. They're all the same to me. I'll leave them to people like you and your girls' he chuckled as she took his arm and held him tightly.

'Talking of the girls they'll be back soon and then later I've got to drive them back to school. What shall we do? Do you want to come with us? I'll take about two hours there and back'.

'Won't you want time with them on your own? Surely you don't want me tagging along. No look if it's alright I'll stay until it's time for you to take them back and then I'll set off back to Crawley and you take them to school. Did you tell them that I was going to stay for the weekend?'

'Oh yes. I said that we had a lot to catch up on so that's why it was best for them to go to their gran and granddads'.

'Did they mind?'

'No but Charlotte gave me a bit of a funny look. As the elder of the two she'll probably guess we'll have slept together. It'll be interesting to see her reaction when she comes back and if she has any problems with that'.

Mark looked at his watch. 'If they are due back soon how about coming back inside for a while before they arrive?'

'Whatever for?' she giggled but continuing to hold hands they started to make their way back indoors only to hear the sound of a car turning into the driveway which being L shaped hid any vehicles until they were almost at the house. Letting go of his hand she turned and waited. 'That's probably them now. They're earlier than I thought they'd be'. It was and her father drove carefully up to the house and turned the car in the gravel that fronted the property.

As soon as it stopped the two girls jumped out and ran to their mother.

'Have you had a lovely time with Grandma and Grandpa?'

'Yes great. How's Smokey?' answered Emma the younger of the two immediately worrying about her horse.

'He's fine but I'm sure he's missed you this weekend' smiled her mother in reply. 'And how are you darling' she asked Charlotte her elder daughter who already bore a striking resemblance to Abi.

'OK. Have you had a good time Mum?' and she looked hard at Abi.

'Yes lovely'.

'That's alright then. I'll just go with Em and see Marcus. Is he alright too? Oh hi Mark. See you in a minute'.

'Yes he's fine too but go and see for yourself' and she ruffled her daughter's hair before she ran off after her younger sister as Abi's father brought a couple of overnight bags out of the car.

'I hope they've not been any trouble Dad'.

'Not at all. A pleasure to have them. You must be Mark then. Heard a lot about you from Abi….. and the girls' he added.

'Yes hello' and he shook hands with Abi's father.

'Dad are you going to stay for some tea?'

'No I'll get back. I think your mother has got a few jobs lined up for me. Not got a lot done this weekend you know. You're looking well Abi. You must suit her Mark' and he winked at her daughter's man before turning to Abi kissing her on the cheek and getting back into his car.

'Dad wait. The girls will want to say good bye. Hang on and I'll go get them' and she walked off round the corner of the house returning shortly with the two girls.

Emma ran to her grandfather and throwing her arms around his neck kissed him on his cheek. 'Thanks ever so much granddad for letting us come and stay. It would have been so boring at school over the weekend. Most people go home and it's really ghastly there on Saturday and Sunday nights'.

'Yes thanks a lot granddad' added Charlotte. 'Love to gran'.

'Bye girls. See you soon' and with that he started his Toyota car.

Abi went round to the driver's window leant in to kiss her father. 'Thanks a lot Dad'.

'Any time always pleased to have them, well bye love see you again before too long' and he drove off slowly. His wife Mary would want to know all about the new man in Abi's life. Seemed a nice enough chap but piercing eyes. Mind you Abi looked radiant so that was good as both he and Mary had worried about her since Roger had died so suddenly. Time she got a new man he thought.

The girls came indoors and wanted to know what was for tea and they started chatting to their mother and suddenly Mark felt a complete outsider. All through the weekend he'd been so close to Abi yet now in an instant it seemed that he wasn't part of her life as they clustered around her and she re-claimed her daughters like a mother hen gathering her flock. Abi caught his eyes and her glance melted the distance between them. 'Hey girls Mark brought you something back from America? Why don't you ask him what he's got you?'

Excited faces turned to him expectantly. 'Wait there girls' and he went to collect the girl's parcels remained from where he'd put them on Friday evening. What a long time ago that had seemed to be. Returning to the kitchen he held out the two large packages. 'I hope you like them and they're the right size'.

Wrapping paper was ripped away and exclamations of 'Oh wow' and 'Fantastic' were heard as the two children tried on their genuine American baseball jackets and hats.

'They're two of the top teams in America. New York Yankees and Chicago White Sox. A couple of times I've been to see the Yankees play'.

'Great it's really cool thanks' exclaimed Emma buttoning up her jacket and pulling the cap on back to front. She stretched on up tip toes to kiss his forehead as he leaned forward to make it easier for her to reach him.

'Yes thanks Mark. It's really kind of you' added Charlotte but she remained a few yards away and didn't approach him.

'Glad you like them girls. Hope they go down well at school'.

'Oh they will. Everyone will be mega jealous' bubbled Emma. 'They'll simply wee themselves with envy'.

'Emma really' scolded Abi.' Now then girls wasn't that kind of Mark? Tea will be in a few minutes so go and wash and take your weekend things to your rooms. They really do like them you know' she said quietly to Mark when the two girls had rushed out of the room.

Tea was a chatty affair with the girls filling Abi in on what they'd done over the last two days. Emma was the chirpier of the two but Charlotte gradually joined in the conversation although she kept looking at Mark and Abi.

'Did you two have a nice time?' she asked suddenly of her mother. 'What have you been doing?' On the surface it was an innocent question, but she was growing up fast.

'Oh well we talked a lot as we had masses to catch up on. And we've been out for walks and to pubs and on Saturday we went to a lovely French restaurant that my friend Monica recommended some time ago. It was really smashing. You know I think you two would like it so perhaps we'll go there soon'.

'Is that all you did?' asked Emma. Talking and pubs and a meal. Sounds boring to me'.

'Well it wasn't it was lovely. We had a really nice time together didn't we Mark?'

'Yes. It was such a change for me from my hectic life in The States that I enjoyed just spending time relaxing with Abi'.

'Did you buy Mum a baseball outfit?' queried Charlotte.

'No I didn't, I, umm bought her something else'.

'Some lovely perfume' Abi said quickly. 'Chanel one of my favourites. You can have a little when you go to a party if you want. Only special occasions though'.

'Can I have some too?'

'Yes Emma of course. You can both have some, but only when I say so. I'm not having you splash it all over you willy nilly whenever you feel like it. Now then it's time to get ready to go back to school so go and get your stuff and we'll be on our way'.

Charlotte looked carefully at Mark for a while until she asked 'Are you coming with us?'

'No. I'm going back to Crawley. I've booked into a hotel there ready for my meetings tomorrow, and then tomorrow night I'm flying back to the States'.

'Oh right. So you're not staying then?' and the elder girl went out of the room just as her younger sister returned lugging a suitcase and a sling bag over her shoulder.

'No, mores the pity' he called after Charlotte

'What's mores the pity?' asked Emma brightly.

'I'm going back to America'.

He saw the pained expression on Abi's face.

'Are you really returning tomorrow night?' she asked with apparent casualness but he sensed the tension behind the question and realised that they hadn't actually spoken about when he was going back. On the first night together he'd said he was going back next week, but hadn't specified when and it was a shock for her to realise that their time together was almost over. 'When will you be back again?'

'Oh about a month I guess, maybe a little longer it all depends on my visa. They're fussy about extending them'. He too felt the impending sense of loss coming up and promptly added 'but depending on how tomorrow's meeting goes I may stay another day and go back on Tuesday instead'.

'That'd be nice. Do you think you'll be able to?'

'I'll certainly try' and a smile flicked briefly across her face as he said it but she remained looking sad. Turning away quickly she asked Emma to go and start loading her things into the car.

'Mark you can't go like this' she started as soon as her daughter had left the room. 'We've not said goodbye and we've so much to talk about. Can't you stay here tonight? I'll be back in a couple of hours. Two and a half at most'.

'No I can't. I have to be in the office early tomorrow. Look I'll ring you when I get to the Hotel. I agree it's tragic that we're parting like this'.

'Oh if only Dad hadn't brought the girls back so early. No I don't mean that really as I miss them terribly when they are away from me.

Well I do I suppose. Oh hell I don't know what I mean. Mark.......' but her voice tailed off as Charlotte came back into the room.

'Em in the car already?'

'Yes go and get in too and I'll be right out'.

'Bye Charlotte. See you again I hope' called Mark.

'Yea, hope so and thanks for the baseball stuff' and for a moment it seemed that she might walk over to him but she turned round and picking up her collection of bags wandered out the door. 'Coming Mum?'

'Yes darling. I'll just wait while Mark packs his bag. Won't be a minute then we'll be on our way'.

When both girls were safely out of earshot she looked anguished as she asked 'Mark what are we going to do? You will ring won't you? Promise?'

'Yes I promise but I'd better go and pack hadn't I?' and he ran up the stairs to Abi's bedroom the scene of so much pleasure over the last forty eight hours. It took only a couple of minutes to throw his things into his bag and then he went downstairs to the hall where Abi was waiting car keys in hand.

'Drive safely' he said wondering whether to kiss her but she kept well apart and held the front door open for him. She ran to the old Volvo and shot off down the drive at high speed.

Getting into the Jaguar he was about to start the engine but something stopped him and he sat there thinking. She was right they couldn't part like this. He didn't know what would become of them and their relationship but after such a close and intimate two days they couldn't drive off in separate directions without saying a proper good bye. Sighing he reclined the seat and lay back. A couple of hours she'd said. Call it three. If he stayed the night he'd have to leave by five at the latest to be sure of missing the Monday morning traffic and getting to Crawley by eight. Ah well he mused closing his eyes some sleep now would make up for what would be a short night. "You're getting soft Mark my lad" he told himself. 'Falling for a woman' he muttered. Mind you she was some woman.

He'd dropped of to sleep but woke with a jolt when he heard a car crunching over the gravel its headlights illuminating his car. He sat up as the Volvo braked hard to a halt and Abi jumped out and ran towards him. He got out as well holding out his arms to fold her into him.

'Mark you stayed, you stayed thank you. I've been so miserable. I couldn't bear it to think that we weren't going to say goodbye properly. We've had such a lovely weekend and then it suddenly stopped. I've never known such an abrupt end to such happiness' and she hugged him very tightly.

'I know. I couldn't just leave either. Can we go in?'

'Yes of course. What on earth are we standing out here for? Come on' and taking his arm she led him to the front door and after a quick fumble with her keys opened it and pushed him inside. A quick backward shove of her foot and the door banged shut behind her. She flung her arms round his neck and pulling him to her kissed him for several minutes. Eventually she moved back and relaxed into his arms. Looking at her he saw tears trickling slowly down her cheeks.

'Hey' he whispered. 'Come on, it's only going to be a few weeks that I'll be away. You.....' but he couldn't continue as she really burst into floods of tears. He held her for a long while until the shuddering of her body subsided a little and then he suggested that they go and sit down and talk.

She nodded and with his arm round her they walked into the sitting room and sat on the settee turned towards each other holding hands.

'I just didn't think about it ending like that. What are we going to do? You do you feel something for me don't you? It wasn't.....isn't just sex is it? Is it as much of a wrench for you as it is for me? I don't know how I am going to bear to be apart from you. Mark?'

'Yes I feel very deeply for you and no it wasn't just sex. That was marvellous of course, quite wonderful but it was something much more but I don't know if I'm ready for a commitment. I'm not saying I'm not, I simply don't know. I need time to think. I've never really known what people meant before when they have talked about needing some space. Now I do. I need that space to think about you, me, my job, my life, and my feelings for you. You must let me think this out'.

'I will but what are you doing tonight? Staying here or did you just wait to say good bye?'

'Both. I'll stay the night but I've got to get up really very early so I won't want to be late to bed. I must get some sleep if I'm going to take on the Board tomorrow'.

'Abi sat up and wiped her eyes with the palms of her hands. She sniffed. 'Got a hanky? I must look a fright'.

'You look quite beautiful, as you always do' he smiled in reply.

After blowing her nose and wiping her eyes with the handkerchief she said more cheerfully, 'Stay there. I'm just going to wash my face' and she ran out of the room returning a few minutes later looking much better although her eyes were still red and puffy.

'I cried all the way home you know. Luckily when we were going the girls chattered on so I didn't have to talk much which was just as well but coming home I just cried and cried.

Charlie asked me if I liked you and when I said yes I did, she asked if I liked you a lot. I asked her why she wanted to know and do you know what she said? She said that you seemed nice and obviously made me happy. She also said she liked you too. Now that's quite something from her as she's very suspicious of men and me. Not that there's been anyone really. A few semi friends have taken me out for the odd drink or meal, nothing serious but she's not liked that. However she seems much more relaxed about you. Must be your delightful charm I suppose working on a young impressionable teenager as well as a thirty nine year old widow' she smiled.

'Must be' he grinned. She went to the cocktail cabinet and poured out a couple of large whiskeys. Carrying them over to Mark she grinned when he asked quietly, 'Why don't we take those upstairs? After all I really do need an early night and we could continue talking in bed'.

'Just talk? Oh I think we could do more than that on our last night together for some time don't you?' and holding out her other hand she led him upstairs to the bedroom but whereas the first evening she'd been nervous and shy now she was more brazen, almost sultry.

'I'm going to make this a time for you to remember when you're back in America so come on help me undress and she turned her back to him and lifted her hair so he could unclip her zip. He ran it down and eased the dress off her shoulders to slide down her body. Quickly she stepped out then laid it carefully over the arm of the chair. She undid her white bra, dropped that onto the chair before sitting on the bed to slip off her white panties.

Patting the bed she beckoned him towards her. She helped him undress then he took her in his arms and carefully and very sensuously made love to her.

Later lying facing each other she giggled kissing his nose 'I told you we could do something better than just talking'.

'You did and it was' he grinned in reply. 'Look we must talk'.

They did for ages about their feeling for each other, what could happen between them and how their lives might move more closely together. Abi was more open and forthright in expressing her feelings for him and said that she wasn't sure if she'd fallen in love with him but she thought that she might have done. If not then she was very close to doing so if that made sense.

He again said that although he was very fond of her he had to think before making any commitment to her but as he said that he thought about Sam and wondered about a relationship that was mainly with Abi but which somehow could include Sam.

'Penny for them' queried Abi.

Feeling guilty that she had challenged him just as his mind had moved onto thinking about another woman especially when he'd only just finished making love to her. Indeed his penis was still damp from her juices but he looked at her and smiled reassuringly. 'Look I'm sure we can work something out but give me time. This is so important don't hassle me for a decision. I'll come to it in my own time'.

Abi saw a cold look come into his eyes which seemed to bore right through her as he spoke and she shivered feeling a touch of apprehension. Was she rushing him? Was she rushing herself? Did he hold the same sort of feeling for her? Maybe not, but perhaps he would in time. Yes she'd let him have his time, his space and hopefully he'd come to the conclusion that they were right together.

'I understand darling really I do. I'll try not to pressure you but leave you to come to your own decision about us'. The cold expression faded from him. 'I just hope and pray that you decide that we are right together. There's so much to think about. Where we'd live, what we..........' She stopped as she saw the cold expression return to his eyes. 'Sorry. I'll shut up now. When will I see you again? Are you really going back tomorrow night? This time then in twenty four hours you'll be thirty thousand feet up in the air heading away from me'.

'Yes I will. Can we set an alarm for four thirty?' They kissed tenderly but without passion and soon he was asleep.

Abi however lay awake trying to rationalise her varying emotions. What were her real feelings for him? Did she love him? She thought that she did. Did he love her? Probably not. Was he fond of her? Yes. Was there a possibility of them living together? Could they do that if she loved him but he was only fond of her? What would the girls think about it? How would they react to her living and sleeping with another man? Charlotte had probably guessed that they'd slept together this weekend and hadn't seemed to mind but that was different from a more permanent arrangement. Where would they live? Mark wouldn't want to commute from Northamptonshire to Crawley every day so if she sold up and moved where would she buy or would they buy something together? Perhaps he'd buy something and she'd move in with him into his home. If that happened would she sell her house, or rent it out?

Her mind became more and more confused as question after question tumbled around. Turning first one way and then another she was concerned not to wake him but eventually she slipped quietly out of bed, tip-toed downstairs and made a cup of camomile tea which she sipped slowly. Its warm soothing effects relaxed her and returning upstairs she slipped into bed and soon dropped off waking with a jump when the alarm exploded into noisy sound.

Mark got straight out of bed and within a few minutes had showered, dressed, brought her up a cup of coffee and was sitting on the edge of the bed.

'Abi. I don't know what to say except thank you for a wonderful weekend. That sounds so inadequate but I don't know when I've been as happy before and I'm going to miss you like crazy. I'll ring you and write to you and I can't wait for the weeks to pass until I'm back and can take you in my arms again. There is nothing more I would like than to stay with you now but I can't. I have to go'. He paused. 'I'll ring you' and with that he held her hand, kissed her gently on the lips and walked away.

'Mark' she called but he just turned, smiled gave a little wave and went downstairs. She heard the front door open and close and his car start. She heard the tyres along the gravel. She heard it accelerating down the road until it faded into the distance.

The tears started and continued for a long time until she went to sleep again.

CHAPTER 19

He arrived at Lovells at seven thirty smiled at the security guard who raised the barrier as he approached the gatehouse then zoomed up to the office block and parked near the door.

Graham was standing in reception looking slightly apprehensive but relaxed when Mark grinned at him as he walked towards the stairs saying 'Hi there. Not on guard duty this morning?' and then seeing the worried expression on his new chauffeur's face added 'Relax. Look I meant what I said on Friday about you driving me. I don't know my movements yet but be on standby will you?'

'Right s.....err Mark. I'll let reception know where I am and then they can give me a shout when you're ready. Did you come from Northampton? You must have made an early start. Give me the car keys? I'll give it a bit of a clean for you'.

Mark had started up the stairs but leaning over he called 'Here you are. I stayed with a friend for the weekend left before five' and dropping the keys to Graham who deftly caught them.

In his empty office he started re-reading his papers running through in his mind the way he intended to make his presentation when Graham poked his head round the door. 'Here you are boss, breakfast' and gave Mark a slightly greasy paper pack which contained something hot. "Bacon roll. Got it from the canteen. Thought you might like it as you'd started early'.

'Hey that's really thoughtful thanks a lot. Now if you could find a coffee to go with it that'd be great'. Graham was back in a couple of minutes with the requested hot drink. 'Lovely, thanks. Now could you run me off ten photocopies of these' and he handed him the faxes he'd received at his apartment.

Slowly from about eight o'clock onwards the offices came to life as staff arrived for their start of a new week's working. Martha looked in and seemed horrified at the empty plastic coffee cup and greasy papers from his breakfast which she cleared carefully holding them in the tips of her fingers before dropping them into a waste bin, returning shortly afterwards with a china cup of coffee.

Dan looked in a little after nine and asked if he was ready for today's meeting and was surprised by Mark's confident assertion that he was looking forward to it. With a bemused expression on his face he left Mark alone who seeing that the time was now a quarter to ten picked up the phone and dialled America. After a few rings a sleepy female voice answered 'Hello who's this?'

'Wish me luck Sam'.

'Mark............do you know what the bloody time is? It's still the middle of the night here. I'm in bed and was fast asleep! Alright yea, good luck. Now let me get back to sleep. Good night'.

He felt remorseful for waking her but also a vision of her naked body flashed into his mind. Shaking his head and smiling he thought about his presentation. He'd got one shot to persuade the Board to back him and he wasn't going to balls it up.

Procedurally as Chairman then Dan was in charge and responsible for the Board and its meetings. However this one had been called expressly at Mark's request. He wanted to ensure that he maintained the initiative throughout so when he decided it was time he made his way to the Board Room having thought carefully about the psychology of when to arrive. Normally he liked to get to meetings almost last just before the scheduled start time and hence make an entrance. This time he'd decided to be first and command proceedings from the beginning. Steadily the other Board members arrived. The time was just ten o'clock.

Mark had positioned himself at the opposite end of the long table from where Dan would sit to ensure that when he was speaking the Board members would be turned towards him and hence facing wholly or partly away from the Chairman. He needed to engage with the people present to try and prevent them being influenced by Dan who he knew from Friday's discussions was not yet committed to the acquisition. Dan was a powerful force in the Board and several would be reluctant to go against his views even though their new Chief Executive was putting the proposal forward.

Dan called the meeting to order and announced that this was a special Board meeting convened to discuss a possible acquisition in the United States. He laid heavy emphasis on the word *possible* indicating clearly that it was by no means a formality and remained merely an option. Martha sat by his side pencil poised over her shorthand notebook waiting for the discussions to start.

Mark smiled and looked at each Board member in turn before beginning to speak deliberately softly, to ensure that they had to lean slightly towards him to be certain they could hear what he was saying.

'Companies can move upwards in sales and profitability, or backwards in both of these key parameters. Unfortunately our American business has been doing the latter for the last eighteen months or so. This has been caused partly through an outdated product range and lack of creativity in new product development, partly through poor objective and goal setting and partly through insufficient investment in modern plant, machinery and factories. That is also true in the UK and Europe but as you know my contract prohibits me from dealing with those areas for now. However I have been studying them carefully in the time that I've been in the USA whilst of course focussing the majority of my effort onto the American side of our operations. Soon I can return to tackle the challenges here and in Europe where major changes are required'.

He paused and saw that he certainly had their attention.

'But to return to the USA. You know it never ceases to amaze me how often the problems of a business are due primarily to one thing. Oftentimes' and he smiled using the American word alternative to sometimes 'it is not the strategy, the products or the factories that are wrong, although they are in our business, it is the management.

Management fails because it doesn't grasp issues, avoids dealing with problems, or is simply incompetent. We had all of those manifestations in America and I've dealt with them. We now have a changed management team that knows what its doing, is well rewarded and heavily incentivised to achieve the goals and results that are required. Just consider for a moment what has happened in the past few months.'

Mark raised his voice slightly and saw that he had the absolute attention of the Board as he handed out some documents which detailed the substantial improvements that had been made to the American business since his arrival there, and also outlined the key elements of the planned strategy that he and the US were now implementing.

'But in spite of those successes which our shareholders will be pleased to see, nevertheless there is a significant weakness in our strategy. We need a strategic base in the South as our operations are too stretched in that vast country. That opportunity presents itself in the guise of Atlanta Trading Corporation. Here are the details of their product portfolio, factory and warehouse locations, and crucially their distributor network in the south of the USA. That is what we need clout in the South'. He grinned. 'Sorry about that but it's true and Atlanta Trading Corporation gives it to us'.

He spent the next few minutes explaining where the two businesses were complimentary and where they were clashed but the complimentary areas far outweighed those where there was no synergy.

Next he passed out the latest set of accounts from the Atlanta based company together with a précis of what he had identified as their strengths and weaknesses.

'Mark these papers should have been made available to the Board before today so that members had time to consider them in detail' snapped Dan from his end of the table.

Martha scribbled furiously in her notebook then glared at Mark.

'No time Dan. I only received the details of the filed accounts just before I left America and without them the rest of the papers wouldn't make sense. Now gentlemen' and he quickly wrestled control of the meeting back to himself. 'What I particularly draw to your attention are the following points'.

He articulated several issues and ensured that the Board's attention was kept firmly onto the areas that he wanted. He spoke for another quarter of an hour before concluding. 'So to my mind the case is utterly compelling for us. Indeed it would be foolhardy and we would probably be failing in our duties to our major shareholders if we didn't proceed with this acquisition. However before I ask for your agreement to proceed there are two other points that I want to raise with you.

Firstly, Houghtons a major UK Company and one of our primary competitors also has an American subsidiary known as Saratoga Industries and they have been one of the major causes of our problems over there. To combat this we have attacked them very hard recently and I think that in another few months we will have caused them so much damage that they may approach us for some sort of merger or takeover. I would have no interest in a merger but a takeover would be beneficial to us as we could use their operations to strengthen our West

Coast American operations. So think about this fact as well when you consider Atlanta Trading.

Secondly, I propose that we dispose of our Brazilian business'.

He paused and looked carefully around the table seeing the shock on some of the other's faces. 'Our factory is old, inefficient and needs substantial sums of money spent on it to bring it up to modern standards. Its costs are horrific as its machinery is so clapped out that it frequently breaks down and we have to compensate by employing lots of people. It is in a slum area of San Paulo and suffers from high levels of theft and generally is run down and not for us. Have a look at these' and he handed round several sets of photographs which surprised or horrified the Board members when they saw the appalling state of their factory and its surroundings.

'It might surprise you to know that in spite of it not being what we want I have an offer for the entire operation from a Brazilian Company that has premises next door and wants to expand. They are in some sort of metal working business and so their requirements for factory conditions are different from ours where we are producing products for consumers. Here is the offer document which I've had précised and translated into English by our American Lawyers'. He handed out a further set of papers. 'If anyone wants the full original offer document in Portuguese they're welcome to it' he smiled as the people round the table started to look at the latest set of papers which Mark had handed out.

'Mark this is really extremely irregular. We convened this meeting to consider the possible acquisition of Atlanta Trading Corporation. Now you are presenting us with two other quite unexpected propositions which will need much study and I may say considerable discussion before we are in any sort of position to make any decision. You cannot and should not bounce these sorts of major issues onto the Board without prior notice'.

Martha nodded enthusiastically as her Chairman spoke while making extensive shorthand marks into her notebook, then looked daggers at Mark.

'Dan I believe that they are an integrated single proposition. Strengthen our position in the south with Atlanta Trading; take out Houghtons and gain a stronghold in the West, a double win; and finally dispose of a problem business using the money generated from that sale to part fund the acquisitions. Nothing irregular at all. Simply larger and more complex than you expected. It all makes perfect sense. Now let's look at the acquisition costs and method by which I propose to fund the exercise'.

Mark spoke slowly but quite loudly as he carefully explained the precise details of the acquisition financing details. It was cleverly thought out and in truth an excellent deal for Lovells.

'So gentlemen I have three elements of the master proposal for you to consider and support this morning. Firstly the acquisition of Atlanta Trading Corporation. Secondly the potential future acquisition of Saratoga Industries. Thirdly the disposal of our Brazilian Company'.

The Board had been riveted to what he had said. Now was the time to test that interest into support and backing for his plan. 'Are there any further questions or points that you would like me to answer?'

'Mark, you mentioned our major shareholders a few minutes ago'.

'Yes I did'.

'Well we need to consider their views on this, and also our bankers, especially as this will put us close to our banking covenants which as you know we cannot breech.

'I agree and I can tell you that they fully support the acquisition of Atlanta Trading and Saratoga if it comes our way and frankly they're delighted to learn we're getting out of that old Brazilian plant'.

'How do you know?'

'Because I have spoken at length with Martyn Simpson and Dominic Clegg. They are both fully behind my plan and they have in turn checked our intentions out with a couple of other shareholder institutions. Just to confirm that for you all here are copies of faxes that I received from each of them substantiating that'. He handed out photocopies of the faxes that had been sent to his apartment on Friday after his phone calls. He sat back and waited while his bombshell was digested by the Board members in general and Dan in particular.

'When did you have those discussions?' asked Dan.

'Oh I've been keeping them up to speed over the past few weeks and then on Friday I had a detailed telephone conversation with both of them. It was a confirmation of what I'd discussed with them before. The result is clear and you have it in your hands'. He leaned back.

'But you haven't discussed it with the Board'.

Mark leaned forward. 'I'm doing that now'. He placed his clenched fists gently onto the table raised one index finger and said vehemently, 'I told you when you took me on that I expected to be given the responsibilities of the job and allowed to get on with it. You can't pay me to do this job and then tie my hands together. I'm responsible for sorting out this company and so far I have made a damn good job in The States. Just look at the results. When I get back here I'll transform the UK and Europe. But for now we need this tactical and strategic change over there in order to implement the total American long term strategy and so I propose acceptance of my proposal'.

There was a long pause broken by the Chairman. 'Well gentlemen you have heard from our Chief Executive of how he plans to transform our business in America. I have to say it is more far reaching and fundamental than I had expected. Although I can see the logic of what is proposed it is in my view not without considerable risk'.

Had he done it wondered Mark? Had he got the Chairman to switch his views? Had he got the Board with him?

The Chairman continued. 'Whilst I could see the possible benefit of the acquisition of Atlanta Trading which I remind you all is what we were convening today to consider, to now ask in addition for a commitment to what amounts to an open ended cheque to acquire Houghtons American business is in my judgment unwise. As for disposing of our Brazilian business which may be in somewhat old premises in need of a little modernization, that is not what our strategy is about. We should be holding what we have and where necessary strengthening it by some careful acquisitions. I grant you that the funds generated from a Brazilian sale would ease the acquisition costs but I cannot support this total proposition as presented. It needs further thought and some more alternatives considered'.

'There are no alternatives. For Gods sake Dan, Brazil's a crap business, in a crap location, going nowhere and needing huge investment in new buildings, and machinery. Not good use of our money. What are you worried about? Where's the risk? We need to build and I am giving you the strategy to do that. Don't hold me up just because you lack the vision and courage to drive this business forward. It is precisely because of this lack of vision and then lack of assertive action that Lovells has got itself into the sort of mess that it has. I'll get you out of it but you have to work with me to do so. The bankers, who are known to be cautious people can see the logic. The major institutions either support or won't oppose it. Where's your risk? Now get off the fence and back me'.

He glared down the table at Dan. Martha's pencil which had been flying across the pages of her notebook stopped and she looked aghast at the Chairman who returned Mark's glare before dropping his eyes and looking at his papers on the table in front of him.

'What are the views of our colleagues around the table I wonder?' mused Dan aloud. 'Let's see. Gentlemen your views and thoughts please'.

There was silence for a few moments. The problem was that most of them agreed with both Dan, and Mark. From Dan's side they could see that the proposal was risky, possibly impetuous and taking them in a direction they hadn't expected. However looking at the argument from Mark's position they could understand his logic and many of them were excited by the opportunities presented in his plan.

The real problem was that they had to choose between Chairman and Chief Executive and that was the dilemma. Choose between the past and the future. Choose between staid and excitement. steady or risk.

'Well?' demanded Dan.

The response started slowly but gradually the debate became more interesting and at times heated as arguments were expressed and challenged. Mark answered the many questions and sensed that he was winning as gradually the Board members appeared satisfied with his answers. Even Dan looked less hostile although Martha continued to look frostily at Mark whenever she caught his eye.

Ugly miserable old spinster probably completely sexually frustrated and in need of a bloody good bonking to cheer her up he thought. Not from him though. He shuddered at the thought.

Suddenly there was silence. No more questions. No more argument. This was it. Mark would now find out if he'd swayed the Board or not. The Board rules said that he needed a three quarters majority for an acquisition, and a two thirds majority for a disposal. By bundling the three propositions of two acquisitions and one major disposal into one proposal he had made the task more difficult for himself as he now needed a three quarters majority for the whole bundle to be approved.

Dan looked round the table. 'We will take it the matter as one complete whole. The proposal therefore gentlemen is that we should acquire Atlanta Trading now, acquire Saratoga Industries if and when it becomes available, and dispose of the Brazilian business. All in favour of the total package?'

Mark felt the sweat on his back as he raised his own hand and waited for what seemed ages but was in reality only a few seconds before the first hand rose in support. Quickly others followed until six hands including his were elevated in support, from nine board members. Dan made the tenth member. Six out of ten he thought.

He needed one more to get to seventy percent arguably close enough to the required seventy five percent; two more to get to eighty percent and be home and dry. One more hand moved up giving him seventy percent.

'All those against'. Two hands were raised. Bastards thought Mark making a strong mental note to replace them in due course.

'There are no abstentions. Well now Mark we do not seem to have a clear seventy five percent majority for your proposition which my understanding of the rules governing these sorts of issues within this company sees as being required as it includes the intent to acquire two businesses. However with seventy percent you do have the required majority in excess of two thirds for the disposal. In view of the fact therefore that you effectively have one of the three propositions supported by the Board but not the other two I intend to cast my vote'.........he paused and looked round the table before settling his glance on Mark who didn't flinch but stared straight back at him. Dan again felt the penetrating power of the Chief Executive's eyes boring right into him. The room was utterly silent.

'My vote is....... to support the motion. The proposition to acquire Atlanta, Saratoga if it comes available, and get out of Brazil is passed. There being no other business I declare the meeting closed. Well done Mark'.

A mixture of emotions flooded through him. Elation that he'd won. Anger that it had taken the Chairman's casting vote to do it because of the men who'd voted against him, delight that he could now get on with implementing the American strategy that he'd worked so hard to develop, and if he was honest a slight touch of concern to be sure that he'd done the right thing. That only lasted seconds. Yes he had done the right thing and now he'd bloody well prove it to them. To the bankers, the institutions and the shareholders at large, as well as the Board and employees. Now though was the time for civility.

'Thank you. I am convinced that the Board has made the right decision' and with that he stood, smiled at the assembled Board members, winked at Martha who looked shocked, then made his way back to his office. It was all he could do not to run down the corridor. He shut the door and looked at his watch. Ten minutes past one. Just over three hours it had taken. Three hours in which he'd challenged their innate lack of risk taking, faced down the Chairman and forced his plan through. He picked up the phone and dialled America where it was a little after eight in the morning.

'Chuck the plan's approved. Yes the whole lot, all three parts. Now let's get it implemented. I'll be back tomorrow and we can go through the fine detail. Get a meeting set up with Atlanta's lawyers and ours. Get the planning team we spoke about ready to swing into action. We're going make this happen and pretty darn quick. Now can you switch me to Sam?'

A few moments of silence. 'How'd it go?' her soft voice queried down the phone.

'Great, approved. Now then' and he rattled off instructions and things he wanted done by her.

When he'd finished he settled back in his chair and reflected on this morning's work. He rang for Martha and asked her to get him on a flight as soon as possible to America.

Why had Dan changed sides he wondered? Had his oratory really convinced him or did he have some ulterior motive? Did he simply feel outmanoeuvred? Certainly he'd looked shocked when Mark produced the faxes and advised the Board that he'd got the Institutional and Bank's support. Maybe that's what did it. Deciding that he needed to know he walked down to Dan's office and entered after giving a cursory knock.

'Very competently done Mark. I can see that you are already a clever player at the corporate game. In time you'll be unbeatable. Sit down'.

'Thanks, but I really do think that it is the right thing for us to do'.

'I know you do. Initially I admit I was sceptical when you just proposed Atlanta but the plan you unfolded with, I must say great skill, makes perfect sense'.

'Thanks, but come on Dan what switched you over to my plan?'

'A number of things', and he started to outline where he thought Mark's plan was right, and where he thought were it's potential weaknesses. He explained that he'd thought about it very deeply over the weekend and then today as he'd listened and asked questions himself, and listened to the questions raised and the answers given to other Board members he could see for the first time the real benefits of a bold long term strategy for the American business.

'You took a chance though bouncing in those two other proposals. I could have ruled them out of order you know. Be careful if you do that again' he warned wagging his finger at Mark. Boards of Public Companies have rules you know and you have to play by them'.

'By them or with them?' laughed the younger man, 'or maybe both?'

They chatted about several other issues and then Mark took his leave and calling Martha in to his office rattled through a huge amount of work in no time at all leaving her with masses to do and sets of instructions that left her quite exhausted. As she walked out he asked about his flight and she told him that he could only get a British Airways flight out of Heathrow not Gatwick and it went into Newark should she book that? He nodded and asked her to let Sam know flight number and arrival time and to get Graham organized to drive him to the airport.

Sam called to say that Martha had faxed over his flight times and she'd see that he was met and also that George Waters from Houghtons had rung several times as he wanted an urgent meeting. Mark asked her to fix it for Friday.

He spent time reading documents and making phone calls until Graham looked in and said that they should leave for the airport. Mark nodded and said he'd be down in a few minutes, so when he walked out to the car Graham took his briefcase and held the rear door open for him. The journey took ages but eventually they arrived. He bade good bye to Graham, walked over to the BA desk where a pretty Chinese clerk smoothly but impersonally went through the check in procedure before wishing him a pleasant flight and pointing him in the direction of the business class lounge.

On the flight he read for a while, watched the film, ate his fairly tasteless meal and dozed on and off as the jet droned across the Atlantic. His mind went over what he'd achieved today and the business challenges back in America. He was several hours into the flight when he realized two things.

Firstly until that minute he hadn't thought of Abi all day and he'd forgotten to ring her before he left and secondly he was looking forward to seeing Sam.

Now he thought there I am again at my conundrum. Abi and Sam. Two women with different roles in his life. Abi, wife and mother. Sam, secretary and lover. Hell what had he just said to himself? Abi wife and mother? Mother yes, wife, heck that was a bit premature wasn't it? Whose wife? His? Not yet maybe not ever. His mind ranged around the subject without reaching any conclusions, and so he put it to the back of his thought process and started instead to consider again what needed to be done when he got back to America.

Fucking hell, there was simply masses to do. Ah well that's what he was paid his very large salary to do and if he was successful then he'd earn a large bonus. Very large indeed and with that happy thought he relaxed and thought about Sam.

After landing he walked through the airport arrivals area until he was in the queue, or as the Americans called it, "standing in line" where he waited about half an hour to shuffle slowly forward towards the notoriously unhelpful and often unnecessarily aggressive US Immigration Officials.

When his turn came he moved up to the booth, smiled and handed over his documents, answered the questions he was asked, had his passport stamped as was part of the visa form which was then clipped into his passport, then both were then handed back to him.

'Have a nice stay Sir', and he was dismissed as the official looked towards the waiting queues of people and called 'next'.

Collecting his cases off the carousel he walked to the customs line where a huge black woman official glanced at his passport, took the customs form and waved him on his way. As he walked out into the arrivals hall he spotted Chuck and giving each other a wave the two men shook hands and walked towards the exit. They were soon in Chuck's Oldsmobile car and on their way to the office.

Chuck turned to his boss. 'Right let me update you where we are' and it was soon clear that he'd organized everything that needed to be taken care.

The next few days were extremely hectic. Mark set a punishing rate of work activity and by Thursday mid-day they were ready for what might be a final meeting with Atlanta Trading Corporation to finalise the acquisition. During the days since his return there had been numerous telephone calls and exchange of faxes and so when Mark, Chuck and their lawyer flew down to Atlanta on Thursday afternoon they were hoping that it was to finally agree the deal.

They arrived at Atlanta's offices around five in the afternoon and were taken straight up to meet with the President of the company Hugh Goldbergman, a short chubby Jewish man who bustled around and spoke quickly punctuating many of his points by stabbing his hands in the air or directly towards Mark or Chuck.

Hugh had a couple of other members of his senior team with him and after coffee, pastries and greetings were out of the way he looked at Mark. 'We've gotta great business here and although we've agreed to sell to you you ain't gonna get it on the cheap. No siree'. You gonna have to pay top dollar for it. If you don't we'll sell to someone else. We got plenty of offers you know'.

'Hugh you know our offer price and it isn't going to move, not upwards at least. When we get to look in detail at the books if we find things we don't like we might make an adjustment downwards but there is no question at all of any increase on the price we've quoted you. That is a fair and reasonable offer bearing in mind that we have some considerable reorganisation costs to incur. Our offer is final. Now you accept that here and now or we'll leave right away and get the next flight back to New York. Your choice'.

Mark sat back and stared unblinkingly at Hugh who immediately felt uncomfortable under that piercing glare. Silence pervaded the room.

'You wanna leave Mark, you can leave I ain't stopping you, but you ain't buying this company on the cheap. We need a better price than you're offering for the business. Hell I've sweated my butt off building it up and it's now ready to grow and expand. You need to pay not just what it's worth now, but what it will be worth in the future'.

'Our offer is reasonable and will not be increased. As we say in England, take it or leave it, it's up to you but there is no more money going to be put on the table. None'. Throughout this little exchange Mark had not moved his eyes which continued to bore deep into Hugh.

The American looked away and looked around the room and across the assembled company of people. The discussion that followed ranged back and forth until after about an hour's talking there seemed nothing more to say. It was make up your mind time thought Mark staring intently at the tough talking, hard negotiating American.

'Well Hugh. What do you say?'

Taking a deep breath he looked back at Mark and grinned. 'OK fellas you gotta deal. Can't blame me for trying to get some more dollars for the business. I agree to your price. It's up to the attorneys now to get the agreements drawn up'.

'Sure is. Thanks Hugh. You won't regret it and you and your team will become part of Lovells if you want.

'Thanks Mark, but no. I've worked hard for many years to build this business now I'm tired and had enough. I'm gonna take my money, retire and relax. Buy a little cabin in the mountains and go there weekends and fish, maybe hunt a little. Some of my people will join you though. That's up to them'.

They discussed various final points and procedures until around seven the business was done. All that remained was several days work by both side's lawyers to finalise the arrangements. The two teams shook hands and then Mark and Chuck got a cab back to the airport. Their lawyer stayed and checked into a hotel for the night so he could get started first thing next morning on the legal matters. He was under strict instructions from Mark to get it done quickly and was on a bonus if he did so.

'Well done boss. He had me worried there for a while. I thought that he was really going to be difficult'.

'So did I Chuck, but you see once again the old maxim applies. Make a fair but slightly generous offer and then stick to it. That's what we did and it worked. Now hopefully those attorneys will get their act into gear and we'll have Atlanta Trading as part of Lovells sooner rather than later. Tomorrow we've got a meeting with Saratoga, and that's likely to be a different kettle of fish you know'.

Chuck noticed a different tone of voice and set of Mark's body when he spoke of Saratoga. If he could have seen Mark's eyes he'd have been even more concerned.

Their flight back was uneventful and arriving at La Guardia airport they took cabs to their respective homes. Chuck had a large ranch type house in one of the better suburban areas outside New York and Mark returned to his rented apartment.

After taking a shower he thought of calling Sam to come ask her to round but changed his mind and settled for an early night alone.

CHAPTER 20

He slept well as he usually did and woke early the next morning ready to come face to face with a Houghton's business. Ready to start to avenge his father. Ready to make them pay for what they'd done to his parents all those years ago. Yes he concluded while he shaved, today was very important and he was ready.

He was tense and irritable all day until Sam announced that the visitors were here.

'Let them wait for a while, I'll tell you when to bring them in'.

He sat and thought about what they were likely to raise and how he would respond. They would claim that he was trading at artificially low prices but he knew he was on safe ground there. They would probably threaten legal action and hope that the threat would make him give up. What he knew was that his strategy was working well and had in a few months brought the arrogant Houghton's US subsidiary if not to its knees at least made it stumble. How are the mighty falling he thought with grim satisfaction.

'Mark, they are getting quite restless. It's nearly ten minutes past the time of their appointment, and I don't think they are used to being kept waiting' Sam said quietly down the phone when she rang him again.

'Do 'em good. Look wait five more minutes then tell them I'm free and bring them through'.

The time passed then Sam knocked at the door before pushing it open and leading in four men. 'Mark, your visitors from Saratoga Industries'.

'Gentlemen welcome. Sorry to have kept you waiting but I was just finalizing another acquisition and matters were at a somewhat critical state. That phone call was vital in unblocking the process. Now it's a pleasure to see you. Let me introduce you to Chuck, who heads up our US businesses'.

There were handshakes all round. Sam asked the visitors how they would like their coffee and while they settled themselves around the conference table in Mark's office she bustled about pouring and serving before leaving the room quietly closing the door.

'It's a pleasure to meet with you Mark', opened George Walters for Saratoga. 'We think that it is important that we have this meeting and

I'd like to start by introducing the three other members of my team who are with me today. Hugh Sperryman, one of our senior Vice Presidents who has been trying to contact you for some time; Marshall Skelton who is our Vice President for Finance; and Dick Malton our corporate attorney. I'll come straight to the point'.

He took a sip of his coffee while fastening his eyes on Mark.

'We welcome competition from anyone whether that be on price, product innovation, new developments or whatever but we expect that it should be fair and reasonable competition and within the law of this country. However in our view the pricing tactics that you have been adopting are illegal and break several of our competition laws. Now we thought that if we discussed it like reasonable men we could come to an understanding that you would re-look at your prices and ensure that they were above cost, then we would be happy to fight it out in the market place and let the best man, or best company win. But you can't go on doing what you are doing'.

Dick Malton the lawyer leaned over and whispered in George's ear.

'Of course I want to make it clear at this point that this is a without prejudice discussion and we are in no way suggesting any form of collusion or agreement between us on price' George Walters added hurriedly. 'No Sir as I'm sure you know that is definitely against the laws of America. What I am suggesting is that the pricing strategy that you have adopted is obviously wrong, and possibly illegal and I am sure that if you look into it you will find that you need to raise your prices to ensure complicity with the law'.

'I'm sorry but I don't understand what it is that you think we are doing' Mark replied.

'Well it's obvious' blustered George Walters. 'You are selling below cost'.

'On the contrary we are selling above cost and making a reasonable margin'.

'Bullshit. You're selling below cost'.

'It may be below your cost, it isn't below mine. I have a very efficient production process, a streamlined supply chain, minimum cost operation and I can and do make money at my prices. In fact I'm thinking of offering a reduced price bonus offer to our customers for the next two months'.

Hugh Sperryman entered the argument. 'Mr. Watson we are not impressed with your statement. We all know that you are by virtue of your pricing tactics, for whatever reason, engaged in a campaign to damage Saratoga. Let me tell you that it won't work'.

Dick Malton the attorney now spoke. 'We'll use the full force of the law which I remind you is very powerful in this country to ensure that your trading tactics are fully investigated by the appropriate authorities and stopped, with severe financial penalties against your company and possibly you personally'.

'Well' replied Mark quietly, 'that is something that you would know all about isn't it, forcing other companies out of business? I tell you again that my selling price is not causing me to lose money and although it may be causing you problems it is in line with the strategy we have adopted to build market share in your part of the USA.'

He raised his voice. 'How dare you come in here and lecture me about selling below cost. That is a tactic that your business has adopted throughout time right from when your Charles Houghton's father established his company in the UK and destroyed many fine businesses then continued doing that during his expansion into America. You are the past masters at damaging selling prices and unfair trading practices to destroy competitors. I have no doubt that if the competition authorities here started to track back and investigate your company they would find some very interesting and undoubtedly illegal pricing, and probably other unsavoury activities as well to review'.

Mark stared at his opponents and watched carefully to see the reaction to his words. What cheered him was that there had been a flicker in George Walters's eyes and he'd glanced quickly across to Marshall Skelton the Finance man before looking back at Mark. Got you thought Mark. His salvo about Saratoga's past practices which had been pure guesswork on his part had obviously struck a point of vulnerability. How near the mark he'd been would show in the next few moments.

'The finance man Marshall Skelton was the one who responded. 'Our policies have always been in line with our company objectives and although in the past we may have.......'

He was interrupted by an urgent interjection from his lawyer.

'What Mr. Skelton is saying is that we ensure nowadays that our plans are in line with good corporate strategy and fully compatible with moral and legal requirements'.

'No doubt you do' replied Mark sarcastically. 'What you have done in the past is quite irrelevant to me now, provided that you don't indulge in any threatening legal activity over our policies which are, I again assure you entirely legal and don't infringe the laws of this country.

The fact that you cannot compete with us is your problem but don't try and change the rules of competition to simply protect your company which is less efficient, less focused, higher cost and losing to a better, leaner, more efficient competitor. A parallel with the American car industry and the way the Japanese tore it apart seems rather similar'.

Mark's voice had risen further and real venom had sounded in what he'd said.

There was silence for a while before George Walters snarled at Mark 'You'll regret this day boy. If you want a fight, then hells teeth you've got yourself a fight'.

He stood, glared at Mark then turning to his compatriots said loudly 'Come on we're leaving' and walked to the door. Wrenching it open he added 'Boy, you'll lose this fight and you'll be sorry you started it'.

Mark walked towards him and stopped when he stood only inches from the American. Pushing his face forward so that his nose was almost touching the other man, his eyes bored deeply into his opponent as he spoke softly.

'But I didn't start the fight. Your chairman did all those years ago back in England. But I tell you this George he may have started it........ but I'm going to finish it........and I'll win. When you need to find a buyer for what's left of your business call me'. His voice became almost a whisper but full of dripping menace. 'I'll be waiting.......... now get out'.

He opened the door and ushered the men from Saratoga into the outer office. 'Sam will see you out gentlemen............oh and .... have a nice day' and he walked quickly back into his own office shutting the door behind him and plumped down in his desk chair. He let out a long breath and then looked at Chuck.

'Well?

'Wow. I hope you know what you're doing boss because you sure sent them away real mad. Man they're fuming. Tell me what's all this about their chairman back in England?'

'Nothing for you to worry about. Now look Chuck, I want an up to the minute costing of our products that compete directly with Saratoga. Get finance to look carefully at every element of cost. My last examination of it showed that not only were we above cost, but we were making a small margin. I must be sure that that is still the case. However my review showed that since the adoption of our lower pricing tactics then the volume of our sales had increased significantly and the net benefit to us was substantial. If that is still the case and I'm sure it is we'll lower our price even further and drive volume even harder. As this is a commodity market there is a direct straight line relationship between price and sales volume. The lower the price the more we sell.

They obviously don't realise that our production from our new factory in Korea is far more cost effective than theirs from their old American factory.

This isn't a market for high prices and trying to create a segmented market sector. It's about supply and price, and in that we will win. We have to win. Now get on to finance and tell them to check, re-check and check again. No errors, no slip-ups, no mistakes. Got it?'

'Got it' grinned Chuck. 'I'll get after it now' and he left the room reflecting on the passion and animation that Mark had displayed towards the end of the discussions with Saratoga. He'd been almost hyperactive during the discussion and even now looked as though he was sitting on a cooking pot. What, he wondered drove him on this particular issue? He'd gotten used to Mark's drive, phenomenal work rate and cold ruthless streak but this was something different. This seemed to be almost a personal fight. No doubt he'd find out in due course but for now he'd better get this costing evaluation under way and soon he was carefully briefing their head of finance as to what was required.

'When does he want it?'

'Hey Stew, it's Mark who's asked for it so shall we say let's drop everything and do it now? I think so don't you?'

Stewart Fuller said that he'd put people onto it right away and get back to Chuck later in the day.

Meanwhile Sam had come into Mark's office after Chuck left. 'Did you send them away with a flea in their ear? They looked ………'

'What did they look like?' he interrupted.

'Oh sort of angry, worried, frustrated. I don't know. When they arrived they seemed a bit cocky mind you they were pretty pissed off at being kept waiting all that time. However when they left they were different. Sullen, exasperated, resentful, mad. I'm not sure exactly but they weren't happy bunnies I can tell you that for sure. Is that what you wanted?'

'Yes it was. We are going to……..' he paused as he'd nearly said that he was going to destroy Saratoga and force them to join Lovells as their only means of survival. He didn't though and merely continued ….. 'await what happens. They'll be back on the phone soon, you'll see'.

His eyes flashed, his face was flushed and he was breathing loudly so she realised that there was something really deep going on here. Something that she didn't understand, but she had seen that look on his face and in his eyes before and it was always to do with Houghtons. One day maybe he'd tell her what the issue was but as she looked at him he started to relax a little and she felt an overwhelming desire to go and cuddle him and tell him that whatever demons were driving him it would be alright. She wanted to tell him to confide in her and let her make it better whatever it was. But she didn't, just stood there watching his emotions churn.

He looked at her. 'This is ending up as a great week you know. Yesterday we got agreement from Atlanta to sell to us. Today we've fired the first torpedo into Saratoga and I think we've crippled them below the waterline. Our sales are in line with forecast, we've masses of cash in the bank and our operating profit is well in excess of budget. In short Sam my girl, we're doing great. Hey do you know that bastard George Walters called me boy. Boy? I'll boy him, arrogant sod'.

Sam could see how hyper Mark still was and she worried about him and wondered if maybe meeting and making love that evening would calm him down. While she pondered this question he seemed to snap out of it.

'Look get me Dan Lewis in the UK and then I want these people' and he quickly scribbled down a list of names and thrust the sheet of paper at her. She stood and looked at him still thinking about the evening until he snapped 'Well bloody get on with it. Dan first and then the others in any order you can get them. Come on Sam, chop chop'.

As she turned to flounce out of his office he reached for his briefcase and extracted something from it. Waiting until she reached the door he called 'Hey this is for you'. Carefully and as slowly as he could using an underarm movement he gently threw a small package across to her. She'd turned at the sound of his call and deftly caught the package.

'What is it?'

'Well open it and see. It's something I bought on the plane but in the meantime get me Dan'.

She dialled quickly and put the call through before opening the small parcel to reveal a spray bottle of eau de cologne of her favourite perfume of the present time "Ma Griffe". She gave herself a quick spray blew a quick kiss at his closed door, put the bottle in her handbag and realised how much she had missed him when he'd been away.

Stewart Fuller called late in the afternoon to say that he'd completed the check of costs and prices and although he was certain that their selling prices were above cost would Mark like to check the numbers for himself. Mark said yes he would and asked Stew to bring Chuck up with him and shortly the three men spent half an hour poring over the figures.

Eventually Mark grinned at Chuck. 'Right there it is clear as a pikestaff. We're not breaking the law so let's really turn the screw. Take our prices down another five percent which will keep us just above break even. Now let's see how Saratoga get on with that'. Chuck left to organize the brief to the sales management for Monday morning and Stew left to again double check his numbers. However he looked at it he knew that he was right. They were above cost and not breaking the law. He just hoped that he'd not made a mistake or missed something because it was based on his calculations that Mark and Chuck were going to squeeze Saratoga. He felt the sweat on his forehead as he made his way back to his office where he sat down and checked again.

Around seven when most of the others had left Chuck stuck his head into Mark's office wished him a pleasant weekend then Sam walked into his office to check whether there was anything else that he needed that night. When he said no she went back and finished closing things down, put on her coat and called 'good night' through the open door.

He replied 'good night' and after a short pause she shrugged and walked out of her office down the corridor to the elevator. Once on the street she hailed a cruising cab to take her to her apartment where she had a bath, got some eggs out of the refrigerator, made herself an omelette and curled up on the sofa to watch TV for the evening.

Mark stayed on at the office for a while running through some financial schedules and then looking at the time picked up the phone and dialled a UK number.

'Hello' said a soft woman's voice.

'Abi hi it's Mark. How are you?'

She said she was fine but missing him and the conversation developed from there. They talked for the best part of an hour and when they rang off she felt all warm and contented while Mark still felt somewhat unsure about his feelings for her. He thought about it for a while and then shut and locked his desk before taking the elevator to the ground floor where he walked a couple of blocks to a steak house that he frequented from time to time.

Entering the warmth of the restaurant, he was quickly shown to a small table in the corner where he ordered a sixteen ounce steak, fries and a salad, a glass of white wine, and a pot of coffee. It was served as was usual with American food service quickly and efficiently and he ate silently and thoughtfully considering the three major events of the week that had just ended.

Firstly he'd fought the Board and won.

Secondly he agreed a deal price to buy Atlanta Trading and faced down the aggressive owner of the business.

Lastly he'd fired a real salvo into Saratoga Trading and was increasing the pressure on them even more.

A picture of his father came into his mind, and he saw him from all those years ago when he'd come home that night a sad man to say that Anderson and Watson existed no more. He remembered the promise he'd made and now felt that he was truly on the way to starting to fulfil it. Yes he thought. First we'll choke the life out of Saratoga here in America and then when I'm back in the UK and Europe we'll start on their operations there. What made the plan particularly attractive was that the elimination of Houghtons as a competitor would actually be good for Lovells as well as achieving his long held ambition to destroy Sir Charles Houghton. A double win.

Finishing he asked the head waiter to call him a taxi and when it arrived he gave generous tips to the head waiter and the doorman before getting into the yellow cab and giving directions to his apartment where he had a whiskey and went to bed.

The weekend passed quickly and soon it was Monday morning when he was back at his desk around seven thirty with Sam arriving just before eight. She had hoped that he might have rung her over the weekend, perhaps to go out for a drink or a meal or to make love, but he hadn't and she didn't want to be seen as the clingy female chasing after him. She had missed him though especially when she was alone in bed and a couple of times she'd fantasized that he was next to her but he wasn't and so she'd passed a fairly lonely weekend.

The next week was very busy with meetings, visits to factories and customers, visits from suppliers and a further phone call from George Walters.

'Mark, we hear that you've lowered your prices again'.

'Nothing wrong with your intelligence information then George'.

'You can't expect to get away with it' he yelled.

'I'm not getting away with anything. My prices are clear and straight and my books are open to any inspection from any authority'.

'They'd better be boy because you're going to have to do that believe me'.

'Oh I believe you George but you really should start to get your mind around the fact that I'm pricing based on ultra efficiency throughout my organisation together with a super modern state of the art production facility in Korea. I'm using the latest robotics and modern manufacturing practices coupled with iron control of our costs. Your prices are based on inefficiency, an older generation factory and possibly a lack of clarity about your costs. Fight me and you'll lose George. Now I suggest you'd be better either cutting the costs in your business and trying to make money that way, or giving up and selling to us rather than wasting your time attempting to sue us or bringing in regulatory and enforcement authorities. By the way did you know that we've just bought Atlanta Trading?'

He paused and grinned as he heard the explosion down the phone. 'No you hadn't? The announcement is going out later today but I thought that you'd like to know in advance. I believe that you've stalked them in the past haven't you? Never mind best man wins and all that eh George. Remember call me when you want to sell up. Bye'.

He pressed the button for Sam. 'Get me our attorneys as soon as possible please'.

When the call came through he briefed the lawyers carefully and agreed to meet with them later that day so that he could take them through the numbers and his strategy which he knew was right but he would be grateful for a legal signoff. Maybe should have checked that earlier he thought ruefully but it was too late now and the battle was in full swing.

The lawyers arrived in force. Two senior partners and a couple of juniors. Mark explained the position without mentioning his long term intentions with Houghtons. They looked serious as he unfolded his plans and asked to examine the figures on which Mark was basing his strategy. Soon gathered round the table were the two senior lawyers, Chuck, Mark, Stewart Fuller a less senior accountant and the two junior legal people.

Stew explained the basis of his calculations and showed that their selling prices were legal and above cost. The lawyers questioned and probed at considerable length, asked for back up information and demanded to see past pricing schedules and product profitability analyses. They were extremely thorough and challenging but eventually expressed themselves satisfied that what Mark was doing was legal and above board but like all lawyers they hedged their opinion by saying that they were not accountants and that to be absolutely certain they'd like an independent firm of accountants to audit the figures. Nevertheless they felt that would confirm their view.

Everyone seemed quite relieved by their opinion, and even more so three days later when the independent accountancy firm also confirmed that Lovell's actions were legal but only just and they strongly advised against any further price reductions.

The American business overall continued to grow and Mark in fact spent far more time dealing with the rest of the US operations than with

Saratoga which remained a small part of their total North American company, but a part in which he had a very personal interest.

He flew to Brazil and confirmed to the management there that they would be closing the business and selling the factory to the metal bashers next door.

Two people accompanied him on this trip and he left them in Brazil to implement the closure as soon as possible. One was a senior operations manager who would deal with the actual factory closure and the other was a senior Personal Manager whose job was to handle the people issues.

Returning to San Paulo airport he took the Brazilian airline Varig's flight back to New York arriving around two am. He caught a cab to his apartment and quickly crashed out into bed.

When he woke on Saturday morning he realised that two weeks had now elapsed since his return to The States. Overall he was pleased with what he'd achieved. Having fought for and obtained the authority of the Board he was expanding his own authority and influence. He felt good in his decision making and enjoyed his authority but most of all he continued to get a real thrill out of doing deals and re-structuring the business. He also wanted to see Sam. No he thought that's not quite right. What I want is to sleep with her so he picked up the phone by the bed and dialled her number.

'Hi there. Fancy a meal tonight? You do? Great. I'll book somewhere smartish and pick you up around seven thirty, OK?'

She said that would be fine.

During the day he went to a gym, jogged a couple of miles around the city streets and felt better from the effects of the physical exercise. In the evening he called a cab and arriving at Sam's building told the driver to wait giving him a twenty dollar bill to be sure. He took the elevator to her floor.

His stomach fluttered while he waited for her to open the door after he rang the bell but then there she was, wearing an above the knee black cocktail dress, dark hosiery, black high heeled shoes with a fawn coat over her arm. She also had a surprisingly large handbag in her hand.

'Ready?' he queried.

'Yes. Where are we going?'

'Well there's a nice restaurant down by the river that's quiet so we can chat easily without having to shout at each other. I've been there before and the food's pretty good as well'.

'Is that where you take all your ladies then?' asked Sam with a cheeky expression and her tongue peeping out as she shut her apartment door.

'No. I've taken Chuck there a couple of times and some customers but no ladies, until now'.

'I'll believe you, thousands wouldn't' she grinned as the elevator whisked them down to the street level where slightly to his surprise the cab was still waiting. Mark had experienced New York cabbies before who when given some money to wait would agree to do so and then as soon as he was out of sight they'd gun the motor and drive off to find another fare. He gave the address and they were soon there.

He was right. It was quiet, the food was excellent and they had an enjoyable evening together but Sam noticed as the time wore on, more and more Mark turned the conversation to the buying of Atlanta, the selling of the Brazilian business and especially the possible acquisition of Saratoga. His eyes were alive and flashing and she could see that he was clearly very hyped up.

She imagined that he'd be getting sexually excited as well and a couple of times she deliberately rubbed her leg against his under the table. Making no other outward sign and careful not to be looking at him when their legs touched she wanted him to wonder if it was accidental or deliberate. As they finished the meal and were drinking coffee he asked if she'd like a nightcap.

'Yes that'd be nice but not here. Why don't we let our hair down and go to a club for a while and have some fun?'

'You serious?'

'Yes come on it'll be great'

'Do you know one or shall I ask the waiter?'

'No I know a couple. Let's just get a cab and go. Come on. Don't be all stuffy and boss like, it's after hours, you're out of school now, playtime. Do you good'.

In the cab Sam gave an address and shortly they pulled up outside an old building that had had the front remodelled and a garish neon sign proclaimed "Lee's".

With a little trepidation Mark hung back but Sam took his hand and led him confidently into the interior which got increasingly noisy as they passed the entrance booth and paid their ten dollars each entry price.

'One free drink with the entry ticket you'all know now' said the huge black bouncer who smiled and waved them through. 'Now you have a nice evening in there people' and he held the door open for them and gave Sam a ticket for her coat. She led the way into the smoky semi darkness turning to speak to him.

'Follow me' Sam said over her shoulder. 'Here's where we can drink and dance' and they fought their way to the bar and ordered drinks before plunging onto the dance floor. Shuffling and twisting themselves to the loud thumping disco music which played non-stop it was packed with lots of young people including some very pretty girls who having had several drinks were quite uninhibited on the dance floor. But it was far too noisy to talk and although Mark quite enjoyed jigging about on the floor especially when on several occasions Sam pressed against him, he soon got fed up with trying to shout and make himself heard.

'Look why don't we go somewhere less noisy where we can finish the evening off quietly together?'

'What did you say?'

'There you are. It's too bloody noisy here' yelled Mark. 'We're going'.

'Where to?'

'My apartment for a quiet drink. Come on let's get your coat and go. He took her hand and led the way out to the entry booth.

'Enjoy yourselves folks?' asked the bouncer. 'You didn't stay too long. Was everything alright Sir, Ma'am?'

'Yes it was fine, just a bit noisy'.

'Ah, well that's what some folks like. Here's your coat miss' and with that he very gently helped Sam shrug herself into it. 'Hope to see you folks again. You come back someday you hear. Have a good evening now' and with that he turned away and left Mark to lead Sam down the steps onto the street.

'Come on let's get a cab and go to my apartment'.

It wasn't long before he was putting the key into his door and stood back to allow her to enter. She took off her coat and sat in an easy chair legs crossed which allowed her skirt to ride up and show off a lot of thigh. He ignored the view while getting the drinks but when he plonked down in another easy chair facing her he did stare at her legs seeing an occasional flash of stocking top and suspender clip as she crossed and re-crossed her legs while they chatted about a range of things.

She asked what he thought of "Lee's".

'Too noisy, over expensive but quite fun I guess'.

'What about all the pretty girls there?' she smiled.

'Not my type'.

'Oh, why not?

'Too frivolous, too obvious, too putting it on a plate but not for real if you follow me. No, not my type at all'.

'And what is your type Mark?' she asked softly getting out of the chair and moving over to the side units on which stood his hi-fi system. Flipping through several tapes she selected one and put it on to play. The music started and was some rock band that Mark couldn't name but it was quite intense and flowing and Sam walked slowly back towards Mark and stopped a few feet away from him.

'So let's find out what is your type of girl. Am I your type?' and while she spoke she reached behind her neck to unclip the fastener at the top of her dress at the back. Looking directly at him her hand stretched round to the back zip which she slid slowly down. When it reached as far as it would go she stepped out of the dress and tossed it carelessly onto the chair in which she'd been sitting so recently. She was now just wearing black stockings attached to a black suspender belt over which was a pair of small black panties. A half cup black bra part encased and part pushed her breasts upwards and forwards. Black high heeled shoes completed the extremely sexy outfit.

'Well am I your type Mr. Watson?' She reached behind herself again to unclip her bra and leaned forward sliding it off her arms. Moving with the music she caressed her breasts before slipping her panties down to the top of her thighs exposing and waggling her buttocks as she turned around in a full circle slowly gyrating to the music. Facing him again she eased her panties down to her feet, stepped out and threw them at him who looking up from staring at her pussy hair deftly caught them. Moving right up to him she leaned down and he watched her breasts swing forward as she took hold of his tie. Pulling him to his feet she muttered huskily 'Come on get up. Well boss, am I your type?'

Putting her head on one side and letting her tongue expose itself and run along her lips she used her free hand to feel his crutch as he stood up and finding that his prick was already rock hard beneath his trousers she continued 'Oh I think that shows I'm your type of girl doesn't it? Come with me then and show me what you can do with your type of girl' and pulling him by the tie she walked backwards leading him into the bedroom.

Inside she let go of him and kicking off her shoes lay down on the bed raising one knee which she started to move slowly from side to side while running her hands up and down her stockings. 'Don't keep me waiting Mr. Watson. I want you and you need me. Come on Mark' she said softly as her hands moved up to the top of her legs and started to play with her bush before she started massaging the outer folds of her pussy.

Mark watched her erotic actions while undressing as quickly as he could then joined her on the bed. Climbing on top he entered her and started to make love slowly at first and then with her encouragement faster as her legs wrapped themselves round him and her heels pounded into the small of his back.

'Come on fuck me. Show me what you can do with your type of girl. Oh yes baby come on, fuck me hard…..now'. She held him tightly as he pounded into her quickly reaching his climax and spraying his seed inside her grunting fiercely as he came. She stroked his hair and the back of his neck and when he'd calmed down and slid off her she turned to him whispering 'I am your type of girl Mark, aren't I?' and hearing his soft reply of confirmation she cuddled him closely.

They lay quietly just holding each other and occasionally stroking or kissing until Mark suggested that they got in under the duvet rather than continuing to lie on top of it.

She said alright but first she had to take off her stockings so sitting up she undid the suspender clips and rolled down the hosiery, first one leg and then the other before unfastening the suspender belt itself. Holding that up with the four black straps dangling in his face she teased him asking if he liked her wearing underwear like that? When he nodded she smiled and said then in that case if he was a good boy she might wear them again for him sometime.

Just before dawn they woke on opposite sides of the large bed. Greeting each other with sleepy good mornings she felt his prick which was rock hard so she slithered down the bed and took him into her mouth taking him almost to the point of orgasm on two or three occasions before clambering on top and quickly riding him to another explosive climax.

God he thought. She was really something this woman. Pure sex and a brilliant secretary. What a combination.

'What do you want to do today?' he asked as they lay side by side calming down after their latest sexual encounter.

'Stay here and fuck each other senseless' she replied with a dirty laugh. 'I want to drain these completely dry' she added fondling his balls. 'How many times would it take to empty them do you think?'

'I've no idea. I guess the more I do it the faster they get replenished'.

'Really how fascinating. Marvellous little things aren't they' she grinned as she weighed them and squeezed them gently. For some time she played with his prick and his balls while giving him little soft kisses on his lips until taking each ball in turn she rolled them between thumb and forefinger. 'Nice darling?' she asked softly as she could see his erection growing again and shortly after he pushed her onto her back and was on top making love to her. This time it took him a long time to climax but Sam screamed as she hit an explosive orgasm long before he groaned loudly when he finally came.

They relaxed and held each other for a long time before getting out of bed and going into Mark's bathroom where Sam ran a bath and lay down to luxuriate in the hot foamy water while Mark went to the separate shower cubicle and enjoyed the stinging spray of the power shower.

When they went back to the bedroom the secret of Sam's large handbag was revealed as in addition to the usual collection of female necessities that inhabit handbags it was large enough to contain a pair of non crease lightweight slacks, a thin jumper, a clean pair of knickers and a pair of flat heeled loafer type shoes.

'Well I never' he grinned. 'You planned to stay then did you?'

'Ah well my Mother always told me to carry a spare pair of knickers for whatever eventuality might arise and it is advice that I took to heart. Mind you I'm not sure she had this in mind exactly. Now can we eat something I'm hungry' and with that she put on a little makeup and some lipstick before pulling a comb through her hair and pushing it through an elastic toggle to let it hang down the back of her neck in a ponytail.

Ham and eggs, orange juice, toast and coffee satisfied their hunger cravings and then they decided to go sightseeing around New York.

Their day was fun, light hearted and Mark hardly spoke about work at all as they acted like tourists and not people who'd been in the huge city for several months. They both realised though that having been so busy they'd hardly spent any time getting to know the city properly. In fact Sam had probably seen more of it than had Mark as most of his evenings and many weekends were spent working, whereas she'd had more free time.

In the evening he took her to a Mexican restaurant for dinner and then they returned to his apartment. He said that he didn't want to stay up late as he was tired but folding herself against him she whispered 'Oh I'll stop you feeling tired darling' and taking his hand she led him straight to bed where she sat and patted the duvet.

Sitting where she'd indicated he moved to kiss her lips but she pulled off his jacket and then pushed him gently onto his back. Leaning forward and reaching out to his shirt she undid it slowly button by button and as each button opened to show more of his chest she kissed the exposed flesh. Soon she reached his waist and leaving his shirt completely open she moved smoothly to his trousers. First the button at the top was popped open and then his zip was slid down.

Reaching forward she muttered 'up' and as he raised his buttocks she slid the trousers down to his ankles and off. His socks followed and then she started to run her hands over the outside of his boxer shorts which showed that he was already sporting an erection. 'Whatever have we got under here?' she queried and pulling back the waist band leaned forward and peeped inside.

'Oh dear it seems all trapped and stifled in there. We'd better let it get some fresh air hadn't we' and with that she pulled his boxers down and they were soon on the floor as well. He reached forward to try and kiss her but she smiled and slipped out of his clutch whispering 'No just lie there'.

Slowly her mouth encircled his erect manhood while one of her hands roved across his chest and the other gently played with his balls. She moved slowly up and down on him for a while before she lifted her head and started sliding up his body letting her tongue lick and trace its way across his belly, chest and nipples where she paused for sometime sucking and licking his little pink protuberances. He tried to push her head back down towards his penis but she wouldn't let him instead moving further up his body until finally she licked up his neck across his chin and teased her tongue over and around his lips. As he lifted his head up to respond to her lip teasing she just moved slightly away and quickly lifted her lightweight jumper over her head and unclipped and removed her bra. Putting her hands on his head again she pressed him back down before recommencing to lick and tease his lips while reaching down to the zip of her slacks which soon joined her other clothes on the floor.

Moving back down and leaning forward to allow her breasts to brush against his prick she pushed his erection between them then taking a breast in each hand she slowly rubbed them up and down the length of him for several minutes. Enjoying his sighs of satisfaction she continued for a while until she slithered back up his body and replaced her breasts with her panty covered crotch on his rock hard erection. Sensing from his noisier breathing that he was getting really ready to make love she lifted herself up pulled the gusset of her panties to one side and lowering herself guided him into her now extremely wet pussy while at the same time leaning forward she pushed her tongue deep into his mouth.

He folded his arms around her back and moved beneath her as their lovemaking started. They were entwined tightly together as their movements increased and their passion mounted together until rolling over they reversed positions. Mark now above her pounded into her and they both inexorably moved closer to their climaxes. He got there first whereupon Sam feeling him ejaculating inside her pressed hard against him until she too shortly reached her orgasm.

Afterwards they lay sated and happy and she gently played with his balls and now very limp prick while continuing to kiss his chest.

Later she got dressed and called a cab to go back to her own apartment. It was close on eleven o'clock when she let herself in so she ran a bath and laid there relaxing and reflecting on the two days that she'd spent with Mark. She shivered as she thought about their passionate lovemaking and smiled when she remembered them walking along Fifth Avenue hand in hand like love struck tourists. She giggled as she remembered her sexy striptease the previous evening and also how he'd obviously loved her seducing him tonight.

Ah well she shrugged the weekend with him is over and she wondered if there would be others like that. Was he changing his feelings for her or was she still just his secretary and bit of sex on the side? Surely there was more to it than that, wasn't there? Climbing out of the bath and towelling herself dry she brushed her teeth and hair and got into bed naked.

Lying there thinking of him she found her hands squeezing her breasts before moving down to her belly then into her bush. Remembering their weekend of lovemaking her fingers started to move slowly exploring herself but biting her lip she made herself put her hands to her side and tried to relax. Turning first onto one side and then the other she attempted to sleep but found her hands kept moving to her bush but with a great effort she tucked her hands under her pillow and eventually went to sleep, waking the next morning to the bell of her alarm.

Dressing quickly she caught a cab to the office and found Mark already busily at work with a room full of people engaged in some heated discussions. He merely looked at her as she brought in his coffee and asked her to bring coffees for the other people. No kindness, no compassion and certainly no reference to the weekend. Just another day at the office at the start of the week she sighed, and having dispensed the drinks got down to her own work realising that after all there probably wasn't anything deep in his thoughts about her. She was just his secretary and sex companion.

Mark's work pace quite exhausted most of those around him and secretly they were looking forward to when he'd return to the UK and leave them to get on with things here. Sure he'd totally changed the company and it was amazing what he'd achieved in the six months that he'd been there. Profitability had turned round. They'd disposed of their problem Brazilian business, acquired Atlanta trading, grown their market shares in virtually every category in which they operated, and hammered Saratoga cruelly. It was on this last point that many people remained puzzled. Why was it so important to do that?

Electrical components were only a small part of their business. Certainly Mark had devoted plenty of time and energy to the remainder of the business and his positive influence had been felt everywhere but this one area remained a key issue for him and he'd given special instructions that in the weekly updates and reports that he wanted sent to him when he returned to the UK there was to be a specific reference to Saratoga and their progress, actions, success or failures.

He instructed Sam to pack up and return a few days before he did so as to get his UK office set up. He also asked her to arrange the sale of his apartment in Northampton as he intended to buy something closer to Crawley.

So finally Mark's sabbatical in the USA came to an end. He called the management team together to thank them for their support, re-iterate what needed to be done and say how he was relying on them to achieve continually improving results, finishing by saying he intended to visit approximately every two months.

He called Abi to confirm that he was coming back and asked if he could stay with her for the weekend.

'Yes of course you can but the girls will be here and so you'll have to sleep in the spare room'. There was silence so she went on quickly 'Mark are you there?'

'Yes, I'm here. It's OK, I understand' but he couldn't keep the disappointment out of his voice.

'Darling I'm sorry. We'll get some time together, you know alone but it's too soon for you and I to be seen sleeping together by the girls when they're here. Of course in the future depending on what happens between us that will'.…… she paused, 'could change but for now you'll just have to be a good boy'. She could tell from his tone that he wasn't happy about it.

The conversation ended shortly after that and he said that he'd see her for dinner on Saturday night and rang off leaving her feeling vaguely uneasy and wondering if he only wanted her for sex after all.

CHAPTER 21

Mark flew back to England on the Friday evening Virgin flight landing at Gatwick in the early hours of Saturday morning where Graham met him and drove him to his Northampton apartment arriving around nine thirty. He told Graham to take the car back with him as he was going to be staying the night with a friend then he booked a taxi for later, had a bath and went to bed dropping off to sleep straight away and not waking until the radio alarm burst into loud music at six o'clock. He had a shower finishing with cold, dressed and was just about ready when the taxi driver rang the bell from downstairs.

It seemed to take forever to get to Abi's house but finally he was there as the taxi made its way up and round the bend in the drive. He paid the exorbitant fare, walked to her front door where it was flung open by Emma who was wearing the baseball outfit that he'd brought with him last time. She beamed at him and gushed that everyone at school had thought the outfit was super and were madly jealous and had he brought any presents or anything with him this time?

At that moment Abi appeared and blowing a kiss at him over Emma's head said brightly 'Mark how lovely to see you again. Emma really. It's not polite to ask if someone has brought you a present. Now Mark shut the door and come in'.

As the three of them walked into the large sitting room Mark noticed Charlotte sitting reading a book in the corner chair. 'Hi there Charlie. How are you?'

'OK I guess'.

'Now girls, go and check your horses for the night then wash and change and come down for supper'.

'I want to stay and talk to Mark. Do I have to go now? He's only just arrived' complained Emma.

'Yes now please'.

'Oh come on Em stop arguing. Can't you see they want to say hello without you around' added Charlotte walking over to her younger sister and pushing her gently out of the room. 'We'll be about ten minutes I should think' she added looking meaningfully firstly at her mother and then at Mark.

'Sensible girl' grinned Mark as he walked to Abi and hearing the back door shut pulled her to him. She relaxed into his arms and responded to his lips and her feelings for him were extremely intense.

'Are you really back now for good?'

'Pretty well. I'll have to make regular trips to America but only for a few days at a time and there'll be lots of trips to Europe, but yes, essentially I am back and based here. Now then stop talking and asking questions and kiss me again' and he pulled her towards him and she felt his strong arms around her.

Soon she pulled away and suggested they sat on the settee to wait for the girls to come back. They did, holding hands and looking at each other saying little. They were just happy to be with each other. A loud bang as the kitchen door was flung open announced that the girls had come bustling back into the house then clattered upstairs to wash and change for supper which when it started was a jolly occasion with Mark telling the girls lots of stories about America and Brazil.

Abi watched the easy rapport that he'd established with Emma and even Charlotte gradually became more relaxed in his company joining in the chat to tell him about the latest chart entries and her favourite boy bands.

After supper when Abi was in the kitchen getting coffee Charlotte looked at Mark and said 'You do like Mum don't you? She's been unbearable waiting for you, trying to pretend that you're just a friend but you're more than that aren't you?'

'What's more than a friend then?' asked Emma innocently.

'Oh a very close friend Em. That's what I meant. Mark knows what I mean don't you?'

'Yes'.

'Are you more than a close friend of Mums then?' queried Emma looking puzzled.

'Yes I am fond of your Mother but friends is all we are'.

Charlotte looked at him strangely then turned as Abi re-entered the room.

'Charlie thinks Mark is more than just a friend of yours. Is he Mum, is he more than a friend?' chirped Emma brightly.

'Oh well we'll have to wait and see. Mark and I are very good friends certainly. Now is there anything you two want to watch on TV this evening?' and the subject was turned neatly away from the delicate matter that had been causing Mark difficulty in answering.

'Yes, there's a film we want to watch don't we Charlie. Come on let's go and switch it on. Thanks for supper Mum' and leaving the table she led Charlie out of the room.

'Hey hang on you two. I didn't know what to bring you this time so there are some scarves, tee-shirts, records, other bits and pieces and some books about New York and America in general. Boring I guess compared with the baseball jackets but I'm not very good with presents for girls. You'll find them in the blue grip I left in the hall. Go and help yourselves'.

'Cor, thanks Mark' yelled Emma dashing into the hall. 'Come on Charlie let's see what's there'.

'OK coming' and turning to Mark she smiled. 'Thanks'.

Emma returned a couple of minutes later shouting 'Look Mum look what Mark's brought' and she was holding a real baseball which she tossed carefully from hand to hand some tee-shirts and assorted other items. 'Charlie's got one too haven't you' she yelled at her sister who was still in the hall. 'Mark this is fantastic. Magic. Thanks ever so much' and she ran across and kissed him on the cheek. 'Come on Charlie, let's go and watch that film' and with that she ran into the other room followed by her elder sister who also had an armful of things from Mark's bag.

She smiled broadly at Mark. 'Thanks again. It's very kind of you for the books and records and stuff. They're good' and although she didn't come over and kiss him as her impetuous younger sister had, nevertheless she did give him a warm friendly smile before moving through to join Emma in the other room watching television.

'Give her time. She does like you. It's just that she's protective of me, and herself I guess. She felt Roger's loss terribly. We all did but it took Charlie the longest to get over it. In fact I'm not sure that she's over it even now. Perhaps she'll never get over it. I imagine she's trying to understand what might happen with us and how that might affect her'.

Seeing him freeze a little, she smiled and went on, 'But that's long into the future isn't it. Now how about a brandy?'

'Abi I'm selling my apartment in Northampton and looking for somewhere nearer to Crawley. I might go towards the South Downs,

Brighton way. Or possibly more towards London, say Epsom, Reigate or somewhere like that'.

Abi was shocked. He'd said before that he was going to move to the south but that had been in the future but now he was saying that he was going to be moving a long way from her. She realised that he had no choice. He simply couldn't commute from her to Crawley so he had to go. But what should she do? Did he want her to come too?

She needed to ask, but was afraid to do so for fear of what answer he might give. Did he want her in his life or was this the start of the rejection?

'Of course' she replied making herself sound more light hearted about it than she felt. 'When will you start to look?'

'Sam will ring round the estate agents and get a short list of properties and then I'll have a quick whistle round myself of those and plump for something'.

'Sam, your secretary?'

'Yes, she'll be good at that I think. She's a very competent girl you know.

'Oh well that'll help a lot won't it? Save you a lot of time wasting. Do you have any particular type of house in mind?'

The talked for a while about what Mark might want but it soon became clear that he intended to make a statement about his life and position and wanted a large house with some grounds. They were still discussing various options when the two girls came in and said that they'd enjoyed their film on TV but thought that they go up and read some of the books that Mark had brought them back from America. They kissed their Mother goodnight and Emma again kissed Mark on his cheek. Charlotte came right up to Mark but didn't seem quite able to kiss him but she smiled and he was struck again by how much she resembled her mother at that moment. She said that she'd see him in the morning then turning blew Abi a kiss and said 'Sleep well Mum'. Then she was gone.

Abi looked at Mark. 'She's growing up you know but we mustn't rush things with them, her in particular' and so saying she changed places so as to sit next to him on the settee.

'No I guess not. Well can I kiss you again at least?'

'Yes, please' and she leant to him. Their lips softly blended together and time passed as they kissed and whispered to each other.

'Darling can't we sleep together tonight? I have been thinking of you for weeks now and I want you. All of you'.

'No we can't I'm afraid. Look Mark please let's not argue about it. I'll be in my room and you'll be in the guest room and that's the way it has to be'.

He sighed and deep down could understand her point of view but nevertheless he was feeling very much in need of her tonight.

They spent the rest of the evening talking and kissing gently. No deep passionate embraces, no undressing and no lovemaking. Around midnight Abi said it was time to go to bed and turning off the downstairs lights the two of them crept quietly upstairs. Whispering good night to each other they retired to their separate rooms.

Mark undressed and got into bed and lay there thinking about Abi, the girls, Sam, his work, the challenges ahead here in the UK and Europe, where he was going to live, what was to become of Abi and him. He had been putting off any decision something that was quite foreign to him, usually he assembled the facts of any situation well certainly business ones, weighed the options and alternatives, made his decision and stuck to it. This was different. He simply wasn't ready to settle down, or was he?

Would it be so bad if he and Abi moved in together? Maybe got married? What about the girls? Their weekly boarding school, St. Margaret the Divine, known by the all girl pupils as Maggies, was not too far from Crawley so it would be possible for them to continue there as now. Abi could sell up here and join with him. Maybe they could buy something together. Now that might be a possibility but then he cautioned himself. Was he getting swayed by the material things rather than the emotional issues? Could he devote himself to one woman properly and to his job? If so was that one woman Abi? Did he love her? Then there was Sam. How would she fit into his life?

The questions and various alternatives went round and round in his mind but gradually slowed as he became sleepy and sighing he relaxed and decided that he'd leave any further thoughts until morning. Having come to that conclusion he was almost asleep when he sensed rather than heard his door open.

'Are you still awake?' came a whispered question and he heard the rustle of clothing crossing the room.

'Yes. Abi is that you?'

'Who did you think it was silly? Of course it's me'. She leaned down and kissed him. 'Come on move over' she continued to whisper. 'Wait a minute and there was another rustle as she slipped off her nightie before he felt her naked body sliding into bed and then on top of him. 'Look we'll have to be very careful. No boisterous or noisy lovemaking darling. Just love me slowly, gently and very very quietly'.

'But I thought you didn't.....'

She interrupted him. 'I didn't but the thought of you here and me there separated by a few walls and about twelve feet of space was a few walls and twelve feet too much. I want you too Mark. I want you desperately but my girls are very important to me. You are too, but.....'

Now it was his turn to interrupt and putting his finger on her lips he whispered "shh" in her ear and kissed her pressing his tongue into her willingly open mouth. He started to erect so rubbing her belly up and down the length of his prick she reaching down lifted her hips and helped him slide deep inside her. It was all he could do not to groan with delight but he kept himself quiet. Very carefully they made love with her lying on top of him moving slowly and him gently thrusting up from below. Their climaxes were almost simultaneous and they remained together holding each other until their passions abated. He whispered that she had been wonderful and she said he had as well but it had been hell having to be so quiet.

It was completely dark and he couldn't see her at all as she carefully clambered off him and cuddled into his side. 'Hold me' she said quietly and he did while kissing her gently.

'Are you going to stay all night?' he whispered.

'No I can't it's too risky but we'll have some time tomorrow alone when the girls go out for a ride on their horses. An hour or so maybe a little more, but I'll stay for a little longer now if you'd like me to'.

They cuddled for a while until she said that she really ought to go back to her room. After she'd slipped out of the bed he heard her scrabbling around on the floor. 'What is it?'

'I'm trying to find my nightie which I took off' she whispered. 'It's the green one you bought me. Ah, here it is. Goodnight darling see you in the morning' and with that she was gone as quietly as she'd arrived.

He lay there and reflected on her and their lovemaking. There was something wonderful about her and sex. It was so soft, fulfilling and all embracing. Not as exciting as with Sam but somehow different. Better he wondered? No not necessarily but different. As he drifted off to sleep he felt happy and fulfilled. Not just sexually but mentally. Maybe it could work with Abi. Maybe he could settle down with her.

He slept and dreamed of a church wedding and there was Abi all dressed in white, Charlotte and Emma behind her, his parents, Abi's father, and at the altar stood the vicar in his long white robes with his back to the congregation. Suddenly he turned round and it wasn't a vicar but Sam with the robe held open wearing a black bra, panties, stockings and suspenders looking reproachfully at Mark and Abi. The organ struck up and as Mark turned to the sound he saw that the organist was Paul Feldman, covered in blood glaring at him before fading into the distance. He turned back to look at Abi. She was no longer by his side but sitting in the congregation looking horrified and instead Sam was holding his hand now dressed in a green nightdress. Emma and Charlotte were crying and ran out of the church. Emma stopped at the church door to throw something at him which bounced down the aisle. It was a baseball and it came to rest at his feet.

As he stooped to pick it up it disappeared so standing up and looking around he realised that everyone was gone and he was alone but no longer in the church. He was outside the old house that his parents had bought in Thornton Heath and his mother was looking at him through the downstairs window. Then she too faded.

Holy shit he thought as he woke with a start, what the hell was that all about? It was years since he'd thought of Paul Feldman or had him appear in a dream. Bloody hell what a strange thing the mind is he shrugged and turning over he went back to sleep for the rest of the night until there was a gentle knocking on his door and Charlotte poked her head round. 'Tea?'

'Hey thanks Charlie that'd be great. Come on in' and he sat up in bed as she walked across the room with a mug in her hand. He noticed that she blushed slightly as she looked at his hairy chest. 'Can I ask you something Mark?'

Here it is he thought. Here comes the question 'Did you fuck my mother last night?' although she would probably say sleep with rather than fuck.

'Sure fire away'.

'I want to ask you without Em around as she's a bit young for this sort of thing'.

Oh hell here it definitely comes.

'Are you fond of Mum? I mean are you and her going to become, you know, a couple?'

'Would you mind if we did?'

'No I don't think so, but are you?'

'I don't know Charlie. I haven't known Abi for long, only a few months but I am very fond of her and we have learnt a lot about each other from talking for hours on the phone when I was in America, and writing letters to each other. She quite likes me too I think'.

'Likes you? She's mad about you. She never stops talking about you. It's always Mark this and Mark that, Mark says or Mark thinks. Nice really in a sloppy sort of way but she's certainly much happier since she met you. All I wanted to say was that I like you too and so does Em so if you want to be Mum's boyfriend then that's OK by me, by us I mean. Alright? You won't tell mum we've had this little talk will you?'

'No Charlie I won't. It's just between you and me. Our secret'.

'That's all right then' and with that she did lean forward a little and for a moment looked as though she'd kiss him but she blushed again and walked out closing the door behind her.

He reflected for a while on this brief but important conversation while sipping his tea. Eventually he got up and tying a towel around him collected his wash bag from his grip, walked to the bathroom and carried out the four "S"'s. which he remembered from his time at school cadet camp as being shit, shampoo, shower and shave. Musing how it was funny that certain things remained in ones mind for ever he returned to his room, dressed and went downstairs to meet Abi and the girls.

'Hi you three and how is everyone this morning?'

'Fine. Did you sleep alright?' asked Abi with a cheeky sort of expression on her face.

'Took a little while to go off but then something seemed to relax me and after that I spelt like a log till Charlie brought me my tea this morning' he grinned in reply.

'I always sleep well' interjected Emma.

'Sleeps like a hog she does' added Charlie.

'I don't. I just sleep deeply don't I Mum?'

'Yes darling. The sleep of the righteous'.

'There see Charlie. I'm righteous'.

'Yea whatever' muttered Charlie. 'Did you sleep the sleep of the righteous Mark?' she asked looking intently at him.

'I'm sure he did. Now everyone sit down, breakfast is ready. Help Mark to cereals Charlie'.

So breakfast proceeded. Mark was sure that Charlie guessed that he and her mother had slept together during the night but she didn't say anything and remained friendly towards him and perhaps her little talk earlier in the morning was saying that it was OK by her if he and Abi did sleep together. After all fifteen year old girls were pretty worldly wise these days weren't they?

When they'd finished eating the girls helped clear away while Mark read the papers. He couldn't help looking at Abi, her girls and their domestic surroundings and wondering if he was ready for something similar. Maybe he was, as warmth, comfort and happiness flowed from the three of them and he felt he might like to be part of that.

Abi busied herself around the house before going outside to supervise the girls getting their horses ready until around eleven o'clock they were ready to set off.

'Have you decided which way to ride darlings?' she asked.

'Down past Dark Wood through the valley and then back along the ridge' called Charlie in reply.

'Oh that'll be a lovely ride on a bright morning like this. Have fun and take care' responded Abi as she made her way back into the house. 'Mark, come to the window and watch the girls ride down the drive' she called and soon he was by her side in the sitting room looking out as the two girls rode off confidently looking forward to their journey. She felt his hand roaming over her bottom as he stood beside her.

'How long will they be?' he asked quietly.

'Long enough for what you have in mind. The route they're taking is an hour and a half at least, two hours if they dawdle'.

'Come on then' he grinned and twisting her around dragged her to the bedroom where they spent the next hour making love deeply, passionately and in a totally fulfilling way.

Lying there he thought again about Abi and decided that he could live with her and enjoy a domestic scene provided she didn't interfere with his work and business pace of life. After all he reminded himself building his career and destroying Charles Houghton was what he wanted and nothing must deflect him from that course of action. They semi dozed and cuddled until Abi thought that they ought to get dressed and just as Mark was on pulling his trousers they heard the sound of hooves on the gravel drive.

He quickly finished dressing then went downstairs to meet the girls in the back yard that led from behind the kitchen to the stables.

'Good ride?' he asked thinking that while they'd been riding their horses he'd been riding their mother.

'Yes thanks. Great. Where's Mum?' replied Emma.

'Indoors somewhere I think. Shall I go and look for her for you? Is anything wrong?'

'No. just wondered that's all'.

Abi appeared at that moment and soon the conversation between the girls and their mother turned to horsy things at which point Mark walked back indoors and resumed his study of the papers. The rest of the day went by pleasurably enough and after supper the four of them played cards. Emma managed to win two games of "rummy" following which the girls wished the two adults goodnight and made their way up to bed.

Mark poured himself and Abi a whisky and they relaxed in the deep armchairs and started a serious conversation about their futures, their potential lives together, sharing a house, sharing their lives. Abi wanted to talk to the girls in the morning and then changed her mind and decided that she'd talk to them on their own when Mark wasn't around.

'OK. Look I'll go to Crawley tomorrow and that'll leave you the whole day for your chat to the girls before you take them back to school.

I do realise how important they are to you. We could make this work but you must realise that my career and my ambition are very important to me and will have to be managed alongside our relationship and my relationship with the girls'.

They talked for ages until eventually they went to bed in their separate rooms and although Mark waited hoping that Abi would slip in to see him as she had done the previous evening she didn't and he slept alone all night.

In the morning he dressed, rang and booked a taxi, carried out his ablutions and then joined the three of them downstairs for breakfast. When the taxi arrived he firstly gave Abi a quick peck on the forehead and Emma the same. Then he turned to Charlie. She looked at him and stretching up on tip toes kissed him on his cheek. 'Bye Mark. Come and see us again soon, especially Mum.........she'll miss you' and she smiled warmly at him.

'And I'll miss her, and you and Emma' he replied smiling 'but hopefully it won't be too long before we all meet up again'.

The taxi took him away and he settled down in the back seat and let his mind roam over his talk with Abi last night. After checking in at the hotel he spent a pretty miserable day on his own mainly taken up with studying papers and documents and went to bed early.

After he'd left Abi had sat the girls down and explained that she was thinking of moving and she had wanted to raise the subject when it was just the three of them. As expected it turned into a much broader discussion about them, the girl's hopes and fears for the future without Roger to look after them, and Mark's possible role in their lives. She said that she knew Mark could never replace Roger in their affections but she was very fond of him and was thinking of setting up home with him and how would they feel about it. To her surprise and delight they both seemed to be pleased with the idea and when reassured that they wouldn't have to change schools the matter seemed settled.

That night after her two children had gone to bed she went into each of their rooms to talk to them separately to satisfy herself that they really were happy about her and Mark living together. Emma thought Mark was fun and the conversation was quick and easy. Charlotte was more thoughtful and although fully supporting her mother's idea did ask a couple of times if Abi was sure about Mark as they'd only known each other for months rather than years but was comforted by Abi saying that she was absolutely certain with no doubts at all.

She then asked whether they were going to get married and her mother said that Mark hadn't asked her but she thought that at some time in the future they might and was that alright? Charlie said yes. So it was settled and Abi spent the rest of the evening wandering around the house thinking of the enormous task of packing and moving that would have to take place in the future.

Mark rose early the next morning and getting a taxi to the office was in by six thirty.

Sam arrived about an hour later, looking pretty if slightly vampishly dressed with a particularly short skirt and tight jumper. She enquired how his first weekend back had been.

What was he to say? He had to find time somehow to tell her about Abi but not now. 'I stayed with some friends on Saturday and came down here early on Sunday and spent the day on my own in an hotel'.

'You should have called me. I've rented a flat in town. I'd have stopped you being lonely and all on your own'.

'Sam I'm sure you would but look we need to talk to understand what our relationship is all about. Life's getting complicated and we have to establish where we both fit into each other's lives but for now can we concentrate on work? I need to see the following people and I want you to set up meetings with these groups'. They clicked into action as a business team all thoughts of relationships put aside as they concentrated on their work. He handed her three tapes which he'd dictated yesterday and soon the rest of the office people arrived and the week's work started to hum.

The powerhouse that was Mark went into overdrive over the following weeks as he set about the remainder of Lovell's business that was outside the USA.

Directors and Managers some from overseas were summoned, challenged, applauded or castigated. A few were fired. Mark sat in on many different meetings and offered advice, queried policies and wasn't afraid to throw established ideas out of the window insisting on new ways of doing things. Challenging and questioning everything he amazed everyone with his quick grasp of the main issues and his understanding of the tactics and strategies that were required.

He could see where they were failing and snapped out alternatives which he insisted were put into operation. His demands to see their files on competitors exposed the lack of their information and he was often heard to say 'But how the flying fuck can you beat your competitor if you don't know much about him. Find out and now'. Quickly he stamped not only his authority on the business but also his way of working. Everyone could see that things were going to change. Some liked it, some didn't.

Within three months Lovells had become noticeably sharper and faster responding.

Often he went to Sam's flat after work where they made love but he never stayed the night. Also occasionally when they stayed away at an hotel Sam slipped up to his suite after the business dinner was finished.

Chuck phoned one day to say that Saratoga were asking for another meeting and would he fly across for the discussions. Thinking quickly Mark said no and suggested that Chuck saw them. 'Make sure you've got at least one witness with you, preferably an attorney' he warned the head of their American business. The American laughed and said not to worry. Mark wondered about the purpose of the meeting. Chuck said that they'd been vague and unspecific except that they wanted to follow on from earlier discussions. This could mean one of two things. Either they were going to take legal action against Lovells, which would be costly for the company and possibly bad from an image and publicity point of view, or maybe on the other hand they wanted to explore the possibility of selling to Lovells. Well no good speculating, the reason would become clear in due course.

It did. Chuck rang the next week to say that Saratoga wanted to explore the possibility of a merger. They'd brought a plan with them which effectively merged the two electrical divisions together but left them with a controlling interest. Mark told Chuck to tell them to stuff their plan. If they wanted to merge that was fine but it would be on Lovells terms and the resulting structure would be of Lovells making, in which Saratoga would become a fully integrated subsidiary of Lovell's electrical division.

A further month went by until one evening at just after two am the phone rang in the flat that Mark was renting near Crawley until he found somewhere to buy and set up home with Abi. Instantly awake he grabbed the bedside phone and snapped 'Yes'.

'Mark hi this is Chuck. Sorry to call you at this time. I guess you were asleep but you asked to be kept informed day and night about Saratoga and we've done it buddy. They've agreed to all our terms and thrown in the towel. In fact looking at their books they couldn't have gone on for much longer before they'd have had to have gone for Chapter Eleven'.

This was a strange American legal option for a company in financial trouble, where it could take an action known as filing for Chapter Eleven protection from its creditors and hence stave off bankruptcy. Such a law was not operational in the UK but was widely used in America.

Sitting bolt upright in bed and switching on the bedside light he said loudly 'Hey Chuck that's great news. Well done to you and the team. Fan-bloody-tastic. We get the whole shooting match eh? Trade, goodwill, customers and those of their people that we want? Right now get on with integrating it into our operation over there. Remember we need to shut as many of their distribution depots as we can and that factory.......'

'Boss I know what needs to be done. We've discussed it before you left and when we last spoke. We have a plan and I'll deliver it for you'.

'Yea sorry but this is such good news Chuck. You don't know what this means to me. Well done' he repeated. 'Good night'.

'What's happened?' asked a sleepy Abi who occasionally came down to Sussex and stayed overnight in Mark's rented flat.

'We've got Saratoga. We've been after them for a while in fact ever since I came across them when I first went to The States and now they're ours. First step on the path to' he paused, 'oh never mind but it's something that's important to me........ to Lovells' he added.

Abi saw the passion that was in his eyes as he spoke. The conviction and importance of this action in America shone out and she recalled that she'd seen that look in his eyes before when he spoke about certain aspects of business. Now, in the middle of the night here it was again and although he'd never told her what drove him in this strange way she knew that it was something deep seated and terribly important to him. 'I'm so glad for you darling. Let's talk about it more in the morning shall we?' and she gave him a quick peck on the cheek and turned over facing away from him to go back to sleep.

He reached out to her and sliding his hands under her nightie pulled it up exposing her buttocks and lower back. 'Abi I want you......now' and in the absence of any positive response he slithered on top of her back and pressed his erect penis against her pussy lips which were not ready for him. Nevertheless he didn't wait but lifting her hips slightly he pushed himself inside and made love to her quickly and furiously, climaxing after a very short time. Not saying anything further and kissing her perfunctorily he climbed off and turned over to go to sleep leaving her to re-arrange her nightdress, turn onto her side and settle herself down to resume an interrupted night. But as she drifted off to sleep she reflected that he'd shown no interest in her wants or desires simply his own obviously surprisingly urgent yet selfish need for sex. Strange she mused how sexually excited he'd suddenly become. Was it simply as a result of acquiring that business in America? Did doing a deal turn him on like that she wondered or was there something deeper?

In the morning he was his usual kind loving self and they cuddled and talked quietly for a little while after the alarm woke them at six thirty, before he got up, showered, dressed and left for the office at seven o'clock arriving just before seven fifteen. He rang Dan Lewis who sounded pleased with their acquisition of Saratoga but also wanted to know about progress with some of the other acquisition targets that they had in mind in the USA, UK and Europe. Rattling off a quick update in reply once again Dan was struck by the Chief Executive's detailed grasp of so many issues.

Within six months, Mark had changed most of the senior management team in the UK and Europe and had enhanced his reputation as a fierce hatchet man.

Abi suggested that it might be best if she did the house hunting instead of Sam and after much looking and numerous visits to houses old, new, ruins and those under construction, he'd eventually bought an enormous house near Reigate. It was on its own in sixty aces of land and was being built on the site of an old manor which had burned down three years earlier leaving established gardens, grounds, paddocks and woodlands. The family that had owned it now lived abroad and had sold the site to a local builder.

Mark bought it with a huge mortgage whilst it was still under the final stage of construction. The grounds were badly neglected and overgrown but a specialist landscape gardening firm was engaged and within a month they had re-established order into the gardens and carried out the necessary pruning and thinning of the woods, re-fencing the paddocks and generally restored the outside areas back to show how they had been in their former glory. A swimming pool was also installed.

A couple of months later Abi, Charlie, Emma and Mark moved in and they became a family. When they'd told the girls that they were going to be in all senses a family Charlie asked if that meant Abi and Mark would be living together as a proper couple. They said yes.

'Good' she grinned 'because that will save Mum having to creep along the corridor at night'.

Emma's eyes widened at that revelation but she'd said nothing while Abi couldn't stop herself blushing as she realised how grown up her elder daughter had become.

They all settled in well together. Mark found that he enjoyed having a ready made family and Abi was happy that the transition from a threesome to a foursome family had gone so smoothly. She didn't think Roger would have minded.

For Mark there was a lot of comfort in having the ready made family and he worked hard to be a father to the girls and partner to Abi. He realised that he had fallen in love with her which he was happy about even if his relationship with Sam continually troubled his conscience.

He stopped working seven days a week, and tried to devote most of Saturday and all of Sunday to Abi and the girls including going to watch them play their various sports when they were in school teams playing against other schools. Somewhat to his surprise he found he thoroughly enjoyed standing on cold windy fields cheering on "Maggies" teams at hockey, or in draughty sports halls watching netball which was Charlie's favourite sport, or gymnastics at which Emma was particularly good. The more time they spent together the more Abi was certain that she'd made the right decision about Mark and the happier she became. They often went out to friends for dinner and people commented on how good they were together as a couple.

Mark had taken Sam out to dinner one night shortly after he'd arrived back in the UK and he'd told her about Abi and their plans to buy a home and live together as a family. To his amazement she'd taken it calmly and without any histrionics saying that she knew there was someone else in his life and when asked how she'd smiled wistfully and said it was her woman's intuition.

She asked if he still wanted her to work as his secretary and seemed pleased when he said that he did. That night when he dropped her back at her flat she got out of the car and then leaning in said 'Remember Mark I'm always here when you need me.......and you will need me you know'. Smiling sadly she went indoors while he thought about the implication of her last remark.

Within twelve months of coming back he'd completely stopped the decline in Lovells and the business was not only growing in both sales and profits but crucially its share price had started to climb on the stock market. Its progress wasn't straight up and like all stocks it wobbled around in line with the general market movements together with seasonal and market sector fluctuations, but its overall direction was steadfastly upwards and the price was now standing at £2.89 a share compared with £1.27 when he'd joined.

He'd sold several parts of the operation that were loss making and used some of the generated money to help fund some small acquisitions, raising the rest of the money from the City who if not exactly falling over themselves to lend him money were at least very approachable and certainly amenable to his bold and challenging ideas for the company.

Although fundamentally conservative by nature the City would back particular individuals if they felt that they were capable and had vision and the skill to drive their company's performance in the right direction. Mark had to spend considerable time meeting with the various Stock Holders, Banks, Institutions, and influencers of a company's share price and investment capital. All of them were impressed with him and his ideas and plans for the business and most decided to provide limited financial support when he asked for it but before committing really large sums of money they wanted to see how he got on.

But get on he did and gradually those largely faceless people who affected share prices started to believe that Lovells was definitely well on the road to success. As a result they started to mark up the share price and include it in their client's portfolios as a "buy" stock. It is often said that success breeds success and so it was with Lovells.

Mark himself also started to become featured not only in the city pages of newspapers but also in the gossip columns and he found that he was frequently shown in photo shots in which they often caught him unawares. His wining, dining and clubbing with clients, city institutions, stock brokers and suppliers inevitably meant that he moved in circles frequented by the paparazzi.

Generally he was not one who had gone in for long holidays. A few days break had sufficed for him in the past but now he realised that with Abi and the girls he'd need to devote proper holiday time to them so they went skiing in the winter and to the Caribbean in the summer.

Surprisingly he found he loved the relaxation and being away from work and having time to do things with Charlotte and Emma and realised that his life was fundamentally changing. He was a family man with a ready made family of two grown up children and a wonderful woman who one day might become his wife, but was for now his partner and lover.

Everything was all fine he thought, except that he was really missing sleeping with Sam.

CHAPTER 22

Mark was now in full swing of running the business and he loved it. His staff varied between being highly stimulated by working with him and terrified of him. He was known by all as a very hard task master with a golden touch. He also had a prodigious memory for all things except people's names.

He knew and remembered those with whom he came into regular contact but for those that he didn't then Sam had evolved a system where she would give him a reminder about the individuals he was either meeting or going to talk to on the phone so that he was seen as having the personal touch. She'd include simple points like when he'd last met the person, or a significant fact such as a marriage or birth of a child. It impressed those with whom he came into contact and started to enhance the myth of the superman running Lovells. Often if he was away he'd ring her for a quick telephone briefing but when she travelled with him on business then of course she had the information with her.

Within two years of his return the share price had risen to £3.40 and it was a stock and a company that the papers were always talking about and especially its exciting Chief Executive Mark Watson and his attractive partner Abi Stevens.

However he was starting to have some worries about Lovells. He'd done the easy part by disposing of the poor performing businesses and cutting costs. He'd shaken the business to its core, replaced unsatisfactory individuals, focussed people onto their challenging objectives and generated a new sense of purpose. The various Divisions and businesses within the overall Corporation were successfully chasing growth, new product development and cost cutting activities.

The share price was climbing but he knew that there was a limit to how far he could drive the existing business. What he needed to do was define a way in which he could transform Lovells from the medium sized international company that it was, into a truly large global player that he knew it could become. That would take planning, vision, skill and courage together with a not insignificant amount of money. He'd also not forgotten his ambition to avenge his father. He'd made a start by acquiring Saratoga in The States and now he had started to assemble a full breakdown of Houghton's operations around the world but he needed to know a lot more detail especially about their UK and European businesses.

Some was readily available from Companies House such as their published accounts, but being a private company and so not quoted on the Stock Exchange, Houghton's didn't have to produce glossy annual reports for shareholders which inevitably gave considerable detail about their business for outsiders such as a predator like Mark to read.

Realising that although bent on the destruction of Houghtons nevertheless he had a duty and responsibility to his own shareholders and employees to run the Lovells business in a proper and fair manner, he could not suborn the best intention for the company just to satisfy his own private ambitions. Indeed he was a Director and had legal as well as moral responsibilities to manage Lovells in the way that would provide the best results for its people and its shareholders. However if he could find a way of demonstrating that by acquiring Houghtons he would be able to enhance Lovells own competitive position then hopefully both his personal ambitions and the Company's needs would be served equally.

The important thing though was to find out much more about each and every one of Houghton's companies. The question was how?

There were a number of methods at his disposal. He could recruit some of Houghton's key people and once they'd joined Lovells pump them for information. That was alright but firstly he'd have to persuade them to leave Houghtons and secondly he'd only be able to do that if he had real and important jobs for them to come into and he couldn't just conjure jobs out of the air.

Another problem was that he needed people who knew about Houghton's operations in different countries.

Finally how could he justify all this recruitment from Houghtons without arousing suspicions within his own senior team?

Industrial espionage was another choice at his disposal. He knew this shadowy world was alive and thriving but what he didn't know was how to enter it. 'I'll have to think about that' he mused carefully as it was fraught with dangers of discovery. He could envisage the headlines in the Sunday papers screaming about dirty tricks, underhand dealing, and illegal activities. TV news bulletins would pick it up and relish the opportunity to go to town on such a story no doubt drawing parallels between the glamorous world of James Bond fictional spying and the entirely different world of industrial espionage which they would probably make look seedy and unpleasant. Nevertheless it remained a potentially powerful weapon in Mark's armoury.

His next option could be to embark on a round of discussions with his company's bankers, financial advisers, advertising agencies, public relations agencies, head hunters, city editors, other journalists, suppliers and simply any person or company that could give him information which could be built up into a complete picture on Houghtons.

All in all the whole Houghton's project was a huge task and Mark realised that he simply wouldn't have the time to do much of it himself as he had the Lovells business to run. No he'd need someone that he could trust to do a lot of the investigation and information gathering for him. Although he wouldn't disclose his own personal agenda to whoever he selected he would brief them in confidence on Lovell's long term plans to acquire Houghtons and that was all they'd need to know.

Yes that might be the way forward he decided. Now he needed the person for the job but where was he to find someone able to do that with the very specialist set of skills needed? He could hardly advertise on the Company's internal notice board nor could he ring one of the Head Hunting firms. He grinned as he envisaged himself making a phone call to Nigel who'd recruited him out of Thompson and Smith and saying 'Morning Nigel. I need you to find me someone to carry out industrial espionage and recruiting people from one of our competitors'. No, that wasn't the way to do it. But what was?

He pondered while carrying out his other duties and tasks. His team noted that he'd become a bit snappy and they were more careful than usual when arguing a point with him. Sam knew him well enough to know that he had something on his mind that was troubling him but she didn't feel able to question him properly about it. A couple of times she'd asked if everything was alright and he snapped back at her that all was fine, so she left it. If he wanted to share it with her he would but only when he was ready to do so.

However every time he had lunch or dinner with bankers, journalists or public relations agencies he'd drop the subject of industrial espionage into the conversation in a very gentle way. Usually it was when they'd been together for some time so it was neither an early or late subject of the conversation but buried in the middle and in this way he hoped to avoid it being remembered as a major item but simply a small point somewhere in wide ranging general discussion.

The months went by, nothing happened and he secured no leads at all until having dinner one evening with Colin Ringwood the head of a Public Relations company that was trying to gain some or all of Lovell's business Mark's ears pricked up when after dropping in his usual question "as to whether there was much Industrial Espionage about nowadays" instead of the usual bland response and short discussion which tended to be very general in nature the response was 'Yes there was. Why was Mark interested?'

Being careful to keep his voice level and avoid showing real interest Lovell's Chief Executive nodded seemingly absentmindedly and said that recently he was talking with a business friend of his who was enquiring about it for some issue to do with his company.

Colin looked at him carefully and then said that if Mark's friend wanted to take matters further this was a number to call and after checking in a small pocket diary scribbled a telephone number on his business card which he passed over to Mark.

'They are very good and extremely discrete you know. We've recommended them to other clients who have always been wholly satisfied with their service. If you wanted, we could help you with the introductions'...... he paused and looked at Mark 'for your friend's company'.

'Oh don't bother' replied Mark looking unconcernedly at his coffee cup. 'I'll pass the information on to my friend. He can take it further if he wants to. Now would you like a brandy to go with some more coffee?' and he deftly changed the subject.

His dinner companion shrugged, said that a brandy would be nice then turned again to the opportunities that he saw to improve Lovell's public relations which he thought were inadequate and lacklustre. A serious discussion developed in which his companion outlined the areas that he wanted to develop and build upon. He'd done his homework and was determined not to waste the opportunity to impress Mark as it was rare to be able to get to this important Chief Executive without him being surrounded, supported or blocked by some of his people, who usually tried hard to avoid new advertising or PR companies from getting a foothold. They had their own relationships with established agencies and contacts, and didn't want the equilibrium disturbed.

Mark listened carefully and promised to review with his team what Colin had said and agreed that he would get back to the PR man shortly.

'Had a good evening have you Mark?' queried Graham as he drove him home.

'Yes actually. Thought it was going to be boring as hell but he turned out to be an interesting chap with several good ideas and some useful information that I've been after for some time. Now just drive will you and let me think there's a good fella' and his mind started to work on the problem of how to approach the sleuth firm without disclosing his interest. Again he thought that what he needed was someone to handle this assignment for him but where the hell was he going to find that person.

He got home around mid-night and reminded Graham that he needed to be picked up at six the next morning as he had an early flight to Amsterdam. Creeping upstairs he saw that Abi was fast asleep so he went back downstairs to his study poured a large whisky and drank it slowly still trying to find an answer to his problem. He made a few notes on his computer about that evening's meeting, and then went quietly back upstairs, undressed and to avoid waking her slid carefully into bed beside the still sleeping Abi.

The alarm jerked him awake so leaning over to switch it off he gave Abi a quick peck on the cheek as he rolled out of bed before showering, dressing, and making her a cup of coffee. Kissing her softly he walked downstairs and out of the front door where Graham and the Jag were waiting for him.

Graham knew that Mark liked to be quiet in the morning and didn't like lots of chatter so he simply started the car and pulled out of the drive and drove quickly to Heathrow. Mark read the early papers that Graham bought for him every morning.

'What time you back tonight?'

'Not sure, I'll call Sam when I'm leaving the Dutch offices so check with her'.

He walked swiftly though the terminal building, checked in to the British Midland flight desk went through departures and waited a few minutes before the flight was called. There was the usual delay but shortly after eight o'clock the plane took off and about an hour later they landed at Amsterdam's Schiphol Airport where he was met by one of the young marketers from Lovell's Dutch business.

Travelling into the Dutch offices he fired question after question at the hapless young man who by the time they arrived felt that he'd been put through the wringer several times. Mark on the other hand had learnt quite a bit that he didn't know about the competitive situation in Holland including getting an update on Houghton's operations there. He'd often found in the past that more junior staff especially marketeers were very open and indiscrete as they wanted to impress, unlike their more experienced colleagues who knew the danger of giving away too much information to very senior people in the business and therefore tended to be more circumspect in what they said.

The morning was filled with meetings and discussions but after an early snack lunch they visited the two factories producing Lovell's products for the Dutch market. It was clear to Mark's keen and experienced eye that these were efficiently run plants so he was pleased with what he saw.

Returning to the Dutch offices the discussions then turned to the strategic development plan for Holland and as well as the Managing Director, Sales and Finance Directors being present he also met Hans Janssen for the first time who was the Head of Strategic Development for Holland and another of the Dutch senior team.

Hans was one of those people who impressed immediately. Thirty four years old tall and slim he was obviously fully in command of his subject and spoke earnestly, passionately and with great conviction about the future direction that they foresaw for the Dutch business. What particularly impressed Mark was his detailed understanding of the competitive situation and his fingertip knowledge of the various competitors in the Dutch market including Houghtons. What he recommended for the future direction of their Dutch business made eminent sense and Mark was happy to endorse the various proposals.

This completely surprised the Dutch team as he had a fearsome reputation for ripping Strategic Development plans apart and demanding complete re-thinks often in impossible timescales. On this occasion though he nodded intently during the presentation, asked few questions and was fulsome in his praise of the thinking and planning that had been outlined.

'Great. It has my full support, just get on and deliver it' was his parting comment. 'Now it's time I made my way back to the airport to get the seven o'clock flight. Hans would you be good enough to drive me so we can get to know each other a bit more and could someone ring Sam in the UK so she can organise my car for me.'

What the Dutch team didn't realise was that Mark saw Hans as a perfect choice for heading up his secret Houghton's project. All he had to do was persuade him that it was in his best career interest to take it on.

On the journey back to the airport he asked Hans more questions about strategy not only for Holland but more broadly for the rest of Continental Europe and found that he had several interesting ideas. He also probed his private life and was delighted to find out that he was single, had no special girlfriend, wasn't gay, enjoyed a good social life, and was clearly at ease talking with Mark. If he wasn't fazed by meeting Lovell's Chief Executive thought Mark then he probably wouldn't be unsettled by the challenge of the task that he wanted him to carry out. As they arrived at the airport he said that he'd be in touch shortly as there may be some interesting opportunities coming up within the Group.

Flying back he convinced himself that he'd found the right man for the job but now the question was how did he introduce him to it without disclosing the secret purpose behind the front reason? Letting his mind wander around the subject after take off he refused an alcoholic drink but asked for sparkling water from the pretty air hostess who felt herself go a bit wobbly at the knees when this attractive passenger looked her right in the eyes and made her feel sure that he could see deep into her thoughts which were saying "He was a definite bit of alright and if he made a pass she'd say yes".

By the time the captain announced that they were on final approach and would shortly be landing at Heathrow Mark's mind was made up. After landing along with all the other de-planeing passengers he shuffled along the aisle to the exit door. Sally the stewardess from whom he'd refused a drink was now standing at the front of the plane bidding goodbye to the leaving passengers. Mark looked directly at her, smiled, thanked her for a pleasant flight, wished her a good evening and walked off the plane into the terminal leaving her to fantasise about what a good evening she would probably have had if it had been with him. As it was she knew she'd have to fend off a randy first officer who'd offer to buy her a drink or two and then expect to get her into bed or her fellow stewardess a known prolific lesbian, who'd stroked her bottom a couple of times on the flight. She refused the offers from both and spent a sad evening alone watching television in her little flat in Feltham.

Mark though was elated. He had a plan. He had someone to action it assuming Hans agreed, and he was on his way to achieving both his personal and company goal. Graham met him in arrivals and as they drove out of the multi-storey car park Mark picked up the in car phone and dialled Abi at home.

'Hi how's you? Look I'm leaving the airport now and should be home in an hour or so. Book somewhere for dinner. I'll take you out to save you cooking tonight. Nothing fancy just somewhere we can have a relaxed meal and chat'.

Next he dialled Sam's office direct line but got her voice message saying that she'd left for the day and to leave a message. He broke the connection and dialled her home number. She answered after a few rings and seemed surprised to hear from him but while asking how the trip had been scrimmaged around for a piece of paper and a pen as she guessed that he wanted her do something.

'Hi Sam. Yea, good trip, good meetings. Wish all our businesses had teams like that. Now listen this is what I need you to do' and he rattled off a list of meetings that he wanted set up and also dictated a couple of quick memo's to her. She took it all down quickly and accurately and knew that she'd have to be in extra early in the morning to get all that done in addition to the pile of other work that she already had. She finished by reminding him that Graham had an envelope of papers for him.

He picked up the evening paper that Graham had provided glanced through it then tore open the large envelope that was full of papers, documents, planning schedules, memos from various members of his team and assorted notes from Sam. He started at the top as he knew that she would have put the most important items at the head of the pile. Engrossed in his reading and dictating replies or comments onto the little portable tape recorder that was in the car the journey soon passed. He liked to be able to record his thoughts as soon as they came into his head so he kept portable tape recorders in his home, his car, his briefcase, and of course his office.

His thoughts were interrupted when Graham's calm voice announced, 'About five minutes boss'.

'Thanks. Now I wonder where Abi has booked?'

'Do you want me to drive you there and bring you both back afterwards?'

'No you've had a long day. Drop me at home and either I or Abi will drive her car. You take the Jag home yourself. Pick me up in the morning, usual time. Oh by the way I brought you something back' and leaning over he put a package which was obviously a bottle onto the passenger seat.

'Thanks that's very kind'.

He knew that Mark was a real bastard to work for in the business but to him he'd never been any trouble at all, well except for that one time when he'd got lost taking Mark to a meeting. In buying him a bottle of something Mark again showed these occasional flashes of consideration. Like saying that he could take the Jag home as that saved him from having to drive back to the office, drop the Jag, pick up his own car and go home. By being able to go straight home in the Jag it would save him at least forty minutes.

When he arrived home Mark got out swung the car door shut, and waving Graham on his way walked quickly to the front door where he let himself in and called out for Abi. She was coming down the stairs fixing an ear ring into place and ran to meet him. Throwing her arms around his neck she kissed him softly. Breaking apart he asked where she'd booked and nodded approval when she said The Wheatsheaf, a pub with a restaurant attached not too far away but known to serve good food.

'Give me ten minutes to shower and change and then we'll go' he called as he ran up the stairs two at a time.

He was soon back downstairs and helping her into her coat he led the way to her car. 'Let's share the driving' he grinned. 'I'll drive there and you drive back' and so saying he got behind the wheel of her Volvo and leant across to push her door open. 'Time we got you something newer than this old bus' he muttered as Abi gracefully slid into the passenger seat.

'I like this old bus as you call it. I've always liked Volvos. When we first met I had this Volvo but if you want to spend some of that vast salary you earn buying me a new car then I certainly won't stop you' she replied mirroring his light hearted happy mood. He'd obviously had a good day as he was brimming with confidence and self satisfaction. Turning he smiled at her and she saw that his eyes were alive and sparkling. She felt something jolt through her. God he was so sexy, so demanding, so beautiful, so hers.

The meal was good and he was on stunning form chatting non stop and maintaining an amusing flow of conversation. He drank the best part of two bottles of wine with little apparent effect while she just had one glass as she was driving back. She could see that he was really hyped up and when she asked what was making him feel so good he merely said that something he'd been trying to make happen was starting to fall into place.

'We'll skip dessert and coffee and go home" he said waving the waiter over and asking for their bill after they'd finished their main courses without waiting for her agreement.

Leaving the restaurant he handed her the keys, held open the driving door for her then got in the passenger side.

She drove home somewhat distracted by Mark who started stroking her neck and left ear making her go all goose bumpy which became more pronounced when he started to run his hand up and down her thigh. She slapped his hand and pushed it away but he laughed and contented himself with leaving it lying in her lap.

'Come on darling drive more quickly. I want to get home as soon as we can'.

'You mean get to bed as soon as we can?'

'Yep'.

She took his hand and squeezed it as she pressed the accelerator harder and they were soon home and in bed. He made love to her intensely and quickly.

Next morning he left early as usual. After making her coffee he walked out of the house, slid into the back seat of the Jag greeted Graham and reached for the morning papers. The car swooshed away and in just under the hour Mark was sitting in his office.

Sam came in at a quarter to eight and picked up the tape he'd dictated last evening. She made him some coffee and then settled down to work in her outer office. When she returned later with the completed work they talked through the day and the many appointments and meetings that she'd arranged but as she was leaving he asked her to get Hans Janssen on the phone.

'Good morning Sir' came Hans's slightly stilted English which was more noticeable on the phone than when speaking face to face, or perhaps it was a touch of nerves as a result of an unexpected call from the Chief Executive so soon after meeting with him for the first time yesterday.

'Morning Hans how are you today?' Without waiting for an answer he went straight on. 'Look I've reflected on our meeting yesterday and there are some things that I want to talk to you about as soon as possible. Could you get over tomorrow to see me?'

Hans recognised the irony in Mark's question. Although he'd asked if Hans could come over tomorrow what he was actually saying, was "I want to see you tomorrow and whatever you've got organised you'll have to change to fit with me". He didn't mind. It was the prerogative of Chief Executives to turn their subordinate's plans upside down.

'Tomorrow will be fine. I've nothing that can't be changed. What time would suit you?'

Mark yelled for Sam and said that he needed an hour's slot tomorrow and could she move things round to find him one? She looked puzzled for a moment and then asked could he do it over a working lunch because he had nothing organised between one and two and that would save her from a major shuffling exercise?

'Come for a snack lunch. One o'clock alright?' Mark boomed down the phone. 'Right see you then' and he put the phone down and picked up a pile of papers and started to study them.

CHAPTER 23

Hans flew to England, took a taxi to Lovell's building and was directed to Sam's office who explained that Mark would be free shortly. Sitting in a spare chair he again racked his brains, as he had all last night, wondering what Mark wanted. Surely it wasn't anything to do with the strategic plan which he'd presented. No, he'd seemed happy with that and nothing that they'd discussed in the car had sounded any alarm bells except the comment as he was dropping Mark off that there might be opportunities coming up within the Group. Maybe that was it.

'Hans hi there. Thanks for popping over' Mark said briskly opening his door as if Hans had just walked across the street rather than flying in from Continental Europe. Shaking the Dutchman's hand Mark led him into his office. Hans looked around and was impressed with its size as it was huge compared to anything that he'd experienced before. A large mahogany desk with two chairs set in front of it for formal meetings, a coffee table and a couple of large settees were on the other side of the room. Along one wall was a matching mahogany sideboard and drinks cabinet and on the walls were various pictures which Abi had chosen. Thick deep pile carpet of an off white colour covered the room wall to wall. The whole office exuded power and control and Hans had to admit that he was a little intimidated by it.

'Come and sit over here and we can eat while we talk' said Mark as he led the way to the settees and coffee table. Sam brought in a tray of sandwiches and salad and two glasses of water. 'Coffee's ready whenever you are, just shout' she smiled as she left the two men alone.

'Right, now look Hans. I've had a look at your personal file this morning and you seem to have had a pretty good career with us so far. Prior to Lovells you were with Unilever weren't you? Excellent company and a good training ground. Your last appraisal says that you'll soon be ready for a bigger job and I've got one for you. How quickly can you get untangled from what you're presently doing?'

'Well that depends on who will take over from me and when Wiebe Werner my Managing Director can release me. I've got some major projects on at the moment and........' He stopped speaking as Mark waved his hand in a shaking movement.

'Leave Wiebe and your replacement to me. What I need you for is more important' and after reminding Hans about his undertakings of confidentiality that he'd signed when he joined the company Mark passed over a piece of paper which he asked Hans to read and sign. It was a special additional confidentiality document and he explained that he wanted Hans to work on a top secret project for him.

As soon as Hans had signed the paper and passed it back, Mark set out his thoughts about how he felt that Lovell's requirement to break through to become a truly global player could be best accomplished by the acquisition of Houghtons. He went into considerable detail and after speaking for nearly ten minutes took two large files from his desk from which he extracted certain papers and documents which he showed to Hans.

'What I want is a "Mr. Houghton" here working directly for me and finding out everything that he can about them. I want structures, organisation, details about their factories, their people, where they're strong, where they're weak, where we can attack and damage them, but remember the overall objective is to acquire them so we don't want to destroy them. I need to know about the Chairman, the Board and crucially about their financial position.

Remember they are a private Company, admittedly a big one but they are private and so it's much more difficult to get hold of information about their finances than from a public quoted company. I want to know about their new product development programme and their sales operations. If a member of their Board is having an affair I want to know. If half their senior people are queer or if one of them is up to his ears in debt I want to know. In short Hans I need to know every single damn thing about Houghtons.

You're to be my man to find that out. You will report directly to me on this and have access to me at any time. This is a very secret high priority project and you're the one I want to do it. You will discuss it with no-one. No-one do you understand. If you need anything typed that you can't do yourself only Sam is to do it. I trust her completely. Apart from that this is you and me only. Clear? It will be known as Project Ambition. Now any questions?'

Hans had been transfixed by the passion of the Chief Executive who had demonstrated such enormous conviction and determination and whose eyes had flashed and burned as he spoke so convincingly and motivationally about his secret project. He couldn't fail to be stirred and enthused by what Mark outlined and was sold hook line and sinker onto Project Ambition.

However being Dutch he liked to get everything properly organised in his mind and returned to the subject of who would replace him, what would Wiebe say, how long did Mark envisage the project would last and crucially what would happen to him afterwards?

'Here eat something' grinned Mark as he pushed the plate of sandwiches and salad towards Hans before getting up and walking over to his desk. 'No idea, as long as it takes but it's urgent and as you now realise high priority. Afterwards, also no idea but trust me. Do a good job on this and I'll see that you're rewarded. Not only will there be a big bonus for you at the end but we'll find you a new big job probably not in Holland though.'

Without waiting for an answer he went and pressed a button on his phone and as he walked back to the settee Sam came in.

'Coffee?'

'Yes and get Wiebe in Amsterdam for me please' and he picked up two sandwiches and took a huge bite out of one of them. He had finished the second one when the phone rang and Sam put the call through.

'Wiebe I need Hans for a special project reporting to me starting straight away. It's nothing terribly exciting just a lot of competitive analysis but I think he'd be good at it'. He winked at Hans who in spite of his Dutch reserve grinned while Mark listening to Wiebe's obvious sounds of protest down the phone devoured another sandwich and a stick of celery.

'Yes I know these things can be a bit inconvenient but needs must. I'm sure you can sort someone out to replace Hans. Talk to Group Personnel. That's what they are there for. Now can I have Hans from next Monday?'

There was more frantic protestation then when there was a break Mark cut in and said 'Alright Monday week then. Thanks Wiebe I knew I could reply on your help, much appreciated. Now I must go as I've got wall to wall meetings. Thanks again.

There we are Hans all fixed. Not sure that Wiebe is too happy, still the main thing is that we've got you released and you start here week after next. See Sam about an office, hotel and all the other details. Hey you're not eating. Something wrong with the sandwiches? Think we'll have to skip coffee as I've got to chair the planning group in the Board room in a few minutes. If you think of anything give me a call but in the meantime I'll see you on the sixteenth'.

Realising he was dismissed Hans stood and shook Mark's hand, assured him that he'd do a good job and confirmed that he'd start on the date requested. As he left the room he turned and said with great sincerity 'Thanks Mark. I won't let you down on this'.

'Better bloody not' and he stared hard at Hans who for a moment felt transfixed before his new boss turned away signalling that the meeting was over.

Hans returned to Sam's office. Muttering 'Hang on I'll get you a coffee' she went into Mark's office gave him a slim file which he took with him when he left for his planning meeting in the Board room. When he'd gone she invited Hans to sit down and poured him a coffee.

'So you're going to be working here then' she stated in a matter of fact way as if she knew all about the secret project. Maybe she did mused Hans. He didn't know how much the Chief Executive confided in his secretary.

'Yes from Monday week' but his Dutch sense of order required that he quiz Sam on the details of where his office would be, which hotel he'd be staying in, what would happen about a car as his in Holland was left hand drive, and several other relatively minor things that nevertheless were important to get straight if you possessed an orderly and enquiring mind which he did. Having satisfied himself that Sam would organise things satisfactorily he thanked her shook her hand and was about to make his way down to reception when Sam said quietly 'Look when you come here don't keep shaking hands like you do on the Continent. You'll drive Mark barmy if you keep doing that. Just shake his hand on the Monday when you first meet him again and then that's it. As for me we've shaken hands so no more, OK?'

Looking puzzled Hans nevertheless said 'right' and then left for reception where to his surprise when he asked for a taxi to the airport he was told that one was already waiting for him which Sam had ordered a little while ago. He realised that in Sam and Mark he was in the presence of a very efficient pair of operators and he decided that he was going to enjoy Project Ambition.

He spent the remaining days of that week and the rest of the next week closing down and handing over his current workload while also setting his mind to the new exciting task ahead.

His private life in Holland also needed pulling to a close, possibly temporarily possibly permanently and so deciding to rent out his flat he found a letting agency that would handle that for him.

Amongst his quite wide circle of friends he had two regular girlfriends with whom he slept from time to time and so he took Bridget out to dinner on the last Thursday evening and then back to his flat for a very satisfying bout of sex and saying good bye. On Friday he did the same with Annette who got a bit tearful as she'd always harboured hopes of a more permanent relationship with Hans and pleaded with him to change his mind and stay in Holland. Nevertheless in spite of his refusal she was her usual enthusiastic self in bed.

The following day his last Saturday he threw a party for as many of his friends as could make it and was delighted so many turned up including both Bridget and Annette. It was a good bash and he stumbled off to bed around four o'clock when everyone had finally left. He slept till nearly mid-day then got up feeling very jaded and with a thumping headache. Swallowing three aspirins and drinking a litre of water he set about tidying the flat finishing by mid afternoon after which he went back to bed.

Waking at six o'clock he felt refreshed and clear headed. He showered, dressed and then spent an hour or so packing two suitcases before locking his flat, took a taxi to Amsterdam Airport where he caught a KLM flight to Gatwick. The hotel airport bus took him to his hotel where he went to bed early.

It was a dull Monday morning when he took a taxi to Lovell's offices arriving just before eight. Enquiring if Mark was in yet he was surprised to be told that Mark had arrived before seven as usual.

Making his way to Sam's outer office and putting his hands behind his back he said 'Good morning. I am as instructed not shaking your hand'.

She smiled and he realised what a very attractive young woman she was.

'Go in he's expecting you'.

Knocking on the door he waited. A muffled 'Yes' came from the other side of the door.

'Good morning. I am reporting as ordered to start work on your project' and striding across the room he shook Mark's hand firmly who looking nonplussed retrieved his hand and motioned the Dutchman to sit down.

'Good morning Hans, welcome. Now have you thought about how you're going to tackle this project?'

'Yes I have given it much thought and here is what I propose as an approach'. He handed some sheets of typed paper to Mark who read them quickly.

'Looks fine to me but you are going to need some help getting the really confidential information. I have been given the name of a company that I think will be able to help you. How shall I put this........ they err....... assist with gaining information about other companies that is not easy to get hold of, not normally available if you follow my meaning?'

'Ah, you mean like spying?'

'Well that's putting a rather extreme label on it but yes I suppose that is what you'd call it. Does that cause you a problem?'

'No. I know it goes on but it is of course most important not to get caught. Can be embarrassing and could be illegal so we must be most careful'.

'Absolutely so it is important to establish precise rules of engagement and specify clearly that they must not undertake any illegal activity while gaining information for us. They'll probably ignore it but the important thing is that we can claim if ever we are hauled into court that we specifically instructed them not to do any illegal'.

Hans looked serious. 'Who are these people? Have you met them?'

'Yes. I met the head of the business Andrew Spicer'.

Mark's mind went back to the meeting. Shortly after his dinner with Colin Ringwood he'd rung the number he'd been given and an extremely professional sounding female had answered the phone. 'B I, can I help you?'

He'd said that he wanted to speak to Andrew Spicer and that he'd been given the number by Colin Ringwood. She'd immediately replied 'Fine, yes Colin was known to them but unfortunately Mr. Spicer was out at present but he'd call Mark back'.

He did later that same day and Mark liked the sound of his voice. Calm, deep, reassuring and measured. The B I man said that the best thing would be for the two of them to meet and suggested the Intercontinental Hotel at Hyde Park corner. They fenced around for a time that suited them both and finally sorted out Thursday evening at nine o'clock. Andrew said that he'd be wearing dark grey slacks and a blue blazer with a red tie. Mark jokingly asked if he would be carrying a copy of that day's Times newspaper under his left arm at which Andrew laughed and said no unless it would make Mark feel happier if he did.

On the Thursday he left the office at six o'clock and Graham drove him into London. They stopped in Chelsea and he ate in an Italian restaurant that he used quite often and was well known. He got efficient service from Luigi the owner who tonight served his house speciality of lightly grilled calves' liver with spinach, green beans and mashed potato containing grated garlic and horseradish. He washed it down with sparkling water. Getting back in the car they soon arrived at the Intercontinental and telling Graham to wait he walked in to the lobby just after nine.

Looking around he couldn't see anyone in a blazer and grey slacks so he settled down in an easy chair opened his evening paper and prepared to wait but hardly had he read the headlines than the voice he recognised from the telephone conversation asked 'Mark Watson?'

Standing up Mark nodded and looked carefully at the stranger who'd approached him.

'Hello I'm Andrew Spicer from Business Intelligence. How are you? I saw you come in and look around'.

Mark wondered how it was that he'd not seen Andrew but he'd seen him. Still he was a business man and Andrew was probably used to being invisible on assignments as he was a….. well what was he? A spy? An intelligence man? A detective? A researcher? A spook? He was all of those but spook sounded seedy and first impressions of this man were definitely not seedy, quite the contrary.

Andrew Spicer was not some grubby back street private detective slinking around after dirty stories and mucky bits of information. He was cultured, spoke well, undoubtedly well educated, nicely groomed and could easily pass for an army officer in civilian clothes, a senior businessman, a high ranking civil servant, or possibly a member of the diplomatic corps.

'Shall we go to a bar and talk over a drink? The nearest one is this way, oh and by the way would you like today's Times?' and he held out the paper that they'd joked about on the phone. Mark roared with laughter and decided that he liked this tall well dressed man.

'So Colin gave you our name did he? We have secured several assignments through him. Let's get a drink and I'll tell you about us and how we work?' He ordered a whisky for Mark and a gin and tonic for himself.

'Let me say at the start that our services do not come cheap but I can assure you that price is of relative importance. What matters is confidentiality and we do give excellent value and are totally discrete and confidential. You pay highly for our skills and you get the best. You could find people who are cheaper but the results they deliver will be poor in comparison to what we provide and may lack something in discretion. We deliver discrete value.

I've had a quick look at Lovells. You have been busy. Divesting your Brazilian business and making acquisitions in the USA. I also assume from the business disposals that you've made here you intend to continue that process in the UK and Europe? By the way how has the integration of Baylon Industrie gone? Must have been difficult that one with all the union problems at their French plant. Still I believe that you personally got involved in sorting it out didn't you? Nasty piece of work that froggie regional union boss Marcel isn't he? Tough bastard. Mind you I gather there are ways to appeal to his more co-operative nature. Still you got the deal through and that's what matters isn't it?' He paused. 'Tell me did your chauffeur Graham drive you up direct from your offices in Crawley this evening in your Jaguar or did you go home first to that lovely house of yours, built on the site of a burn out I believe wasn't it?'

He sat back and looked straight at Mark who was very impressed. What Andrew had done in just a few minutes was demonstrate to his potential new client an ability to gather information speedily and accurately. He was also intrigued by Andrew's reference to the French union leader's more co-operative nature and asked what he meant.

'Ah well now. Marcel's in his late fifties, married with a clutch of grown up kids and grandkids, a stalwart pillar of his local church and community. But he's also rather partial to pretty young men especially if he's put up in a nice discrete hotel and the young men are provided free of charge. I gather he can be much more helpful in the morning providing of course his companion for the night has done what he wants'. He laughed gently ' But get the right one and that isn't a problem is it?'

'I guess not' smiled Mark noting the point for future reference.

'If you need that sort service any time, men or women, old or young, here or overseas I'm afraid we don't provide it but I can put you in touch with someone that can. Mind you like us it's discrete and expensive. Now let me tell you what we actually do'.

Andrew spoke quietly for the next few minutes outlining the services that B I could provide. This was essentially obtaining any information that a client wanted to find out about other businesses. He explained that there was probably nothing that they couldn't discover and that they used all available methods of intelligence gathering that were available which included listening and talking to people, reading documents and papers, examining computers, watching what people did and where they went, filming and photographing, following individuals and noting their habits likes and dislikes, covert surveillance, infiltration including getting their own people employed to obtain inside views and information.

They could find out about production efficiencies or factory problems, strategic plans, business growth programmes, new product development plans, marketing spend, advertising budgets, intentions for new advertising, salary and wage rates. Management, staff and factory worker morale, union deals, recruitment intentions and personal information on individuals all the way from their bank account details to whether they were cheating on their wives, any sexual deviancies that they might have or secret addictions such as drink, drugs, gambling or pornography.

Some of the equipment they used was more sophisticated than that used by the police who were constrained by budgets and financial cutbacks, but B I scanned the international markets for the best in use by whatever force had it including intelligence agencies, police forces and the military.

'Almost without limit there is probably nothing we can't do or find out given sufficient time and money. That is what our business is about. Now if that is of interest, what can we do for you?'

Mark outlined his need to find out all about a particular competitor although he didn't name it nor did he indicate the personal nature of his desire to destroy Charles Houghton. He spoke quickly and quietly and Andrew made a few notes in a small pocket notebook. When he stopped speaking Andrew confirmed that this was very much the sort of assignment that they handled and he'd be glad to take it on but as there was a considerable overseas element to the unknown target company then costs would be high but as soon as he was told the exact company and precisely what information was required he could work out a price for the project.

'Right I'll be in touch. I have a particular person handling this for me. He's a Dutchman called Hans. You can expect a call from him in the next week or so'.

'Do you have any code name or project reference for what you want done? It helps sometimes'.

'Yes I've called it Project Ambition' admitted Mark a little sheepishly.

'Interesting choice of name. Alright I'll expect a call from Hans. By the way let me have his date of birth and his mother's maiden name will you? For security reasons when he calls. Now do we report progress to him or to you?'

'To him but he'll be working closely with me. In fact I've detached him from his other duties to work solely on this issue but if you can't get him any time, contact me. There's just one other thing. The range of activities you've described is extensive and some I imagine border on, or are in fact illegal. We could not countenance anything illegal'.

'Of course. All I've done tonight is outline the range of some of the things we can do. What you do when you engage us is to specify what you want, not how you want it done. That's up to us. We will not discuss how we go about your project or what techniques or methods we will use in getting you the information you want but your privacy will be totally protected. We would never disclose to anyone, whether private or official for which client we were working in the unlikely event of a breech or exposure of any sort. On that you have my word and you can reply on us totally in that respect. Its part of what our high fees guarantee'.

The meeting had finished shortly after that and Mark had shaken Andrew's hand before walking out of the hotel to the covered area outside where Graham was waiting in the Jag.

Mark's thoughts came back to the present and Hans.

'They come highly recommended and he impressed me when I met him. I've outlined what we want but not that it's Houghtons. I've said that you will be handling the project and that you'll be in touch when you're ready. By the way let Sam have your mother's maiden name and date of birth will you. B I want it for security reasons'.

Opening a desk drawer he extracted the business card that Andrew Spicer had given to him when they met 'This is the outfit. They're known as Business Intelligence and I liked Spicer when I met him. Impressive sort of chap. Right over to you. Keep me in touch and good luck'.

As he showed Hans out into Sam's outer office he told her that the Dutchman would give her his mother's maiden name and date of birth and could she phone that through to BI.

She made a note of the required information then showed Hans to the office that he would be using on the floor below.

Sitting down behind the desk he spread out his papers, took out a note pad and started to write. He listed several headings and against each elaborated and expanded on his original thoughts. He worked diligently and by lunch time had filled many pages with his neat somewhat formal writing style but as he was disturbed by the ringing phone he was pleased with what he'd achieved so far.

'Would you like me to organise some lunch for you or will you go to the restaurant in this building?' asked Sam. He decided on a snack in his office and soon a waitress from the restaurant knocked on his door and brought in a tray of cold meats, salad, some warm fresh rolls, a glass of orange juice and a bottle of sparkling water. Leaning back in his chair he ate slowly and thought about his project. This could be the making of him corporately he thought. If he did good job on this working directly for Mark then the career world could be his oyster. Yes he nodded this was the doorway of something big for him and he was going to make sure that he stepped over the threshold.

For the next three weeks he studied market reports, competitive analyses, documents and schedules. He read the many trade magazines in head office, and ordered trade magazines from their European offices to be sent to him.

He wrote to Lovell's overseas operations and asked for them to forward him any information that they had on an enclosed list of companies. His letter pointed out in the opening paragraph that he was working on a project for Mark and that he hoped that they would help him. What he was implicitly saying was that if they didn't he'd get Mark to force their support.

The list of companies was short, in most cases not more than three and they were different for each country to which he wrote, except that one company was on all the lists. Houghtons. Conscious of the need for security he felt that by ensuring the lists were different from one country to another the real interest in Houghtons would not be easily spotted. After all he reasoned it was unlikely that the country managers would compare lists with each other even if they discussed it at all.

He wondered when it would be best for him to meet with Business Intelligence and reflected that a chat with Mark might be worthwhile to get his view. He'd had a few brief "how's it going?" type conversations with him but now he wanted the benefit of Mark's incisive brain.

The problem was that Mark was incredibly busy and right now he was in the USA reviewing operations over there and wouldn't be back until Saturday, when he was at home for the weekend and then the following week he was off travelling throughout Europe on one of his whistle stop tours of their European businesses.

Mark called them his "quick look and see" visits. The businesses called them "search and destroy missions".

He asked Sam for her help in finding him a couple of hours with her boss.

'Well that's going to be a problem. I really don't want to interfere with his weekend and next week we're wall to wall all over Europe'.

'We are?' queried Hans. 'You are going with him then?'

'Yes There will be so much to catch up on after his week in The States and with him not being in the office here I'm taking the office to him. I meet him on Monday in Paris at the French offices and then I'll either stay there for a few days, or I might travel to the other European offices with him. We'll see. It's up to him what he wants'.

Secretly she hoped that he'd want her to travel with him. It had been so long since they'd slept together and she was desperate to get him into bed again. They'd had such great times before but now that he was living with Abi he was acting almost as if he was married to her and needed to be faithful. Well that was fine for him and Abi, but she needed Mark and was determined to get him again if not in any permanent sense at least from time to time and she was sure that the way that he'd looked at her recently indicated that he'd been thinking the same thing.

'Tell you what why don't you come over to Europe and meet him there? I'll fit you in early next week. What about an early breakfast meeting in his hotel room on Tuesday morning? I'll mention it when I phone him in Atlanta later today. I know it's important what you're doing and I'm sure he'll find you some time'.

Later she rang him to say that Mark would see him on Tuesday morning at six thirty in his hotel room in Paris. He'd be staying at the George V Hotel just off the Champs Elise.

Hans worked on for the rest of the week and being on his own at the weekend decided to explore London and work on the project.

On Saturday he enjoyed the late autumn weather as he wandered around Hyde Park, down Oxford Street and into Bond Street. He loved the hustle and bustle and although he'd been to London several times before it had always been for meetings or conferences and so he'd not explored the capital. He found a nice little restaurant for an early supper and then went to see Les Miserables at the Shaftsbury Theatre which he thoroughly enjoyed. Afterwards he walked back to his hotel in Kensington and after sinking a couple of brandies retired to bed.

Next morning he drove back to Lovell's Crawley offices which being Sunday were empty and quiet and he spent the day alone working hard on Project Ambition. Now there were several files of information about Houghtons and in reviewing what he'd achieved so far he was pleased with the progress that he'd made. He could also see the many areas on which he needed B I to work.

Sam rang him on Monday from France to confirm his meeting on Tuesday and said that she'd made the travel arrangements for him and that his tickets were with one of the other secretaries called Pat. He was booked into the Hilton in Paris for the Monday night. 'In case you can't get a taxi that early in the morning I'm told it's only about a ten minute walk from your hotel to Marks' she finished.

Hans reflecting on the efficiency of Mark's secretary finished putting his update presentation together then caught a late flight to Paris and deciding that he needed to be fresh the next morning had an early night at the Hilton.

Not far away Mark finished work for the day. He'd caught the early flight to Paris and been picked up by the Head of the French business. With him and the senior French team they spent most of the day closeted together with Mark demanding to know why sales, and crucially profits, were falling further and further behind target. Each of the departmental heads were strongly challenged and forced to explain to him in considerable detail what was going wrong and why. During the day he became more angry but when in the afternoon he sat down alone with Jacques Jolivet who ran the French business he was really boiling. Jacques knew he was in for a rough grilling from Mark who simply didn't tolerate failure or poor performance and he wriggled and made excuse after excuse.

When he blamed the economy Mark pointed out that the French economy was doing well. When he blamed poor new product development Mark said that since Jacques was responsible for product development within his own business the answer to that was in his own hands. When Jacques tried to shift the problem onto some of his key subordinates Mark simply retorted that if they weren't up to it replace them.

Finally Mark snapped 'Look Jacques. I pay you a lot of money to run this business, and frankly I'm totally dissatisfied with the results that you are producing. It's simply not acceptable. Sort it and sort it quickly........ or I'll sort you. Do I make myself clear? I'll be back in four weeks and I expect to see a substantial improvement in short term results and also a plan for a longer term recovery. This was a good business and we've added some acquisitions to it which should have made it an even better business. It may be that it's simply become too big for you to handle in which case you'd better let me know. I don't have time for poor performance and if you can't produce the results I can't have time for you'.

Staring hard at Jacques who felt like a wet rag Mark folded his papers and strode out of Jacques's office and into the office where Sam had set up her work base for the day. Instantly seeing that he was in a bad mood she knew that fireworks would be flying in all directions including hers if she wasn't careful.

'It's a fucking mess over here Sam. How could one man and his team balls up a good business so quickly? Now give me that file on German supply contracts'.

She fumbled around amongst her pile of papers to find what he wanted.

'Come on I haven't got all sodding day. I've got masses to do and I want it now'.

'You're not the only one that's busy Mark and this isn't my office you know. It's not easy decamping and setting up in a strange location just for a day or so but hang on it's here somewhere' and while he tutted, sighed loudly and walked round the small room clicking his fingers she finally found what he wanted and held it out.

'About time. If I was you I'd get that lot sorted into some sort of proper order' and snatching it from her hand he walked out to the boardroom where he studied the file. As he left she stuck her tongue out at his back.

Damn he thought that was wrong of him but Jacques had got him so riled up. However he was soon engrossed in the detail of a complicated potential new supply arrangement for some of their major customers in Germany that required substantial short term investment but which would over the course of the next few years save them millions of deutschmarks. An hour or so later Sam came in, put two folders down on the table and walked out without saying a word.

Opening the first he saw that it was the work he'd given her earlier in the day. Some had been face to face dictation when she'd arrived this morning but she'd also typed up the contents of several tapes which he'd given to her as well as having amended various reports on which he'd written comments. At the back she'd produced a typed schedule of his appointments for the rest of the week together with a summary of his travel plans. The second folder contained correspondence that he'd not yet had time to read which she'd classified into various groups; "important/urgent", "financial", "reading", and her final category "rubbish for chucking out – I think!".

As he went through the file of papers he realised yet again how much he relied on her and felt guilty about the way he'd snapped at her earlier on. He knew she'd be back in soon to take the letters and memos that he'd signed and he determined to say sorry to her then but when she did walk in he was on the phone. Flipping open the dictation folder and seeing that it had received his attention she took it, turned round and walked out without a word. She was mighty pissed off he thought.

Unfortunately he also didn't get the time later on to smooth things out as he had some visitors come to see him for a pre arranged meeting at five thirty which was likely to go on until nearly seven at the earliest to discuss how they might change banks in France to gain the benefits of some lower interest rates because Mark wanted to raise capital in France for the future French expansion plans that he had in mind. That is why it was so crucial to get the French business back on a growth track as if the banks saw the business falter it could affect their decision to invest or support the Company.

Still either Jacques would sort it or he'd get someone else in. Maybe fly Chuck over from America. His brand of "go-go" would shake Lovell's French management. Review next month he noted in his diary. For now though his mind focussed on the bank discussions.

Around six thirty Sam knocked on the board room door apologised for interrupting said that she was finished for the night and if there was nothing else he required that evening she would see him in the morning. Smiling with icy politeness before he could say anything she quietly closed the door and left the men to their discussions.

When Mark returned to his hotel later that evening the first thing he did after checking into his suite was pick up the phone and call her room.

'Hello?'

'Sam its Mark'.

'Yes?'

'Look could we meet for a drink or if you've not eaten then for dinner maybe?'

'No. I don't want a drink thank you and I've already eaten. I'm tired so I'm going to have an early night unless there's something that you want me to do business wise?

'No'.

Right. Don't forget your meeting with Hans at six thirty tomorrow. Breakfast is organised to be served in your room.'

'Thanks that'll be fine, oh and Sam......... sorry'.

'Yea whatever'.

He heard the click as she broke the connection. Damn. He thought of going to her room but she really did sound cross and fed up with him and he thought that it would be better to leave her alone until the morning as a good night's sleep would make her feel better. Probably the wrong time of the month for her or something he mused.

With that thought in mind he picked up the phone and rang Abi but for some reason it was a stilted conversation and he rang off after quite a short call. He then rang America and spoke to Chuck who never failed to cheer him up with his typical "up and at 'em" American approach to life and business.

Realising he was hungry he rang down for room service and ordered a well done steak, salad, a bottle of Chablis, and a pot of coffee. Wandering round the large sitting room that led off his bedroom he switched on the television and channel flipped for a while until he found an old movie in English. His dinner arrived and he ate while watching the film. After he'd finished eating he sat and finished the wine before going to bed where he thought about Abi and Sam until he dropped off to sleep.

Sam wearing dark maroon silk pyjamas lay on the bed in her room also watching television but anxiously hoping that Mark would come and say sorry in person and then make love to her. It was so long time since they'd slept together and she desperately wanted him. Wondering if she ought to go and see him she decided no. After all he'd been the one who'd been nasty so it was up to him to come to her.

Eventually realising though that he wasn't coming she whispered 'Mark you are a bastard' and a tear ran down her cheek. Turning off the lights she pulled up the covers and thought about him visualising his face and especially his naked body.

Her hands lightly squeezed her breasts before sliding down inside her pyjama trousers and into her bush. Softly calling out his name she bit her lip as her fingers moved further down to gently massage herself.

After a while she moaned softly then curling into a ball went to sleep.

CHAPTER 24

Hans left the Hilton at six o'clock for the short walk to the George V. Arriving early he killed a little time in the opulent ground floor public rooms until almost six thirty when he took the lift to the third floor and found his way to Mark's room. He rang the bell situated to the side of the door and shortly afterwards Mark opened the door with some gusto.

'Now then Hans how have you been getting on?' he started breezily. 'Come in and tell me where you've got to. Breakfast should be here soon'.

The Dutchman took his report out of his case and handed it to Mark. 'How do you want me to handle this briefing? Key points only, or page by page. I have made some progress I think but I have some questions and I would like your advice on certain points'.

At that moment the door bell rang again and getting up Mark strode over and opened it to reveal two room service waitresses dressed in traditional black and white maids uniform complete with starched aprons standing beside a trolley laden with trays and dishes.

'Le petit dejeuner monsieur?' *(Breakfast Sir?)*

He stood aside as they wheeled in the trolley, raised the side flaps, removed the covers from the dishes and while one of the girls correctly positioned the cutlery the other asked 'Du café monsieur?' *(some coffee Sir?)*

'Pour deux merci', *(For two please)* and then looking over his shoulder to Hans 'I'll have a quick look through your report first and then we'll cover the key points and your questions. Go on help yourself'. Turning to the two waitresses he smiled at each of them and dropped some small change into the hand of the nearest.

They each dropped a little curtsy and saying 'merci beaucoup monsieur' *(thank you very much Sir)* left wondering to each other when they were back in the corridor whether the two men had slept together the previous night and if they had it was shocking waste to womankind especially the tall Englishman who had opened the door to them.

Mark oblivious to the women's thoughts sat drinking his coffee reading Hans's document. After a little while he put it down and served himself some scrambled eggs and bacon and buttered a couple of slices of toast and then resumed reading while eating.

Hans felt it best to remain quiet and helped himself to bacon and eggs watching as Mark continued to read while shovelling food into his mouth which he hardly chewed before swallowing and then forking up another mouthful before he'd emptied his mouth.

In no time Mark had finished eating and pushing his chair away from the trolley continued to read quickly but now taking a pen out of his pocket he made some notes in the margin. Soon he'd got to the end of the file and pouring himself another cup of coffee looked at Hans. Much to the Dutchman's relief he smiled.

'Well you've made a great start. Now then can you elaborate on the points related to their laboratories in Spain doing all the European development work and also the comments you've made concerning their German financial issues.'

Hans leant forward to respond to Mark's questions. The discussions ranged widely over a large number of other subjects and he outlined the next areas he intended to tackle with which Mark generally agreed before adding 'However I think it's time we started to get inside Houghtons and see what we can really find out. Time to involve B I'.

Hans agreed that as he now had a good overall understanding of Houghton's organisation he needed much more detail which he guessed could be best obtained by Business Intelligence. He felt this would be a significant step change in the project. Soon their discussions finished so Mark rang for a taxi and put on his tie and suit jacket. 'Come on they'll have one by the time we get down' and the two men took the lift to the ground floor.

The doorman beamed at Mark and indicated that they should follow him outside where Mark pushed Hans towards the taxi. 'Get in. I'll drop you off. A le Hilton merci' *(to the Hilton please)* he commanded and the taxi pulled slowly out of the little roadway in front of the hotel and then shot off as it entered the mainstream traffic arriving shortly at Hans's hotel. As the Dutchman got out Mark wagged his finger at him. 'Two things Hans. First make sure you tell them to do nothing illegal. Second keep me briefed' and then turning back to the driver he gave his destination and sat back.

Hans went up to his room where he was amazed to see that it was only a little after eight o'clock. So much had been covered in the hour and a half that he'd been with Mark. Feeling excited but with a little trepidation he took out Andrew Spicer's card, put it by the phone then realised that it was only just after seven in England. He moved to the dressing table and wrote up meticulous notes of his meeting with Mark.

When he finished it was after eight so he picked up the phone and dialled B I in England. He explained who he was and that he wanted to speak to Andrew Spicer and was told that he would be called back shortly. He was, and was asked for his surname, the project name, his nationality and the name of Lovell's Chief Executive's secretary.

'Janssen. Ambition. Dutch and Samantha, err known as Sam'.

'Thank you. Now your date of birth please and your mother's maiden name'. The Dutchman gave both pieces of information. 'Good morning Hans. How can we help you?'

'I should like to meet you to discuss details of an assignment of which I think you already have some outline information'.

'I do. Would you like to meet today?'

'Yes but I am in Paris and don't arrive back in the UK until around lunchtime'.

'I guess you're booked back to Gatwick because of where you're offices are. I can't get down there today but if you could switch flights to Heathrow I could meet you at the Sheraton Hotel for lunch. If you can do that call me back on this number'.

Hans made the change of flight and at lunch time was standing in the wide foyer of the Sheraton wondering what Andrew Spicer looked like and trying to remember how Mark had described him. Tall smart well spoken. Well there were several people fitting that description but one man walked towards him extending his hand. 'Are you Hans?'

They went into the pseudo tropical pool area which was quiet, ordered drinks and a sandwich, and started their discussion. Hans briefed Andrew clearly and well, nevertheless the investigator asked many questions and sometimes queried a point several times to be sure that he had the briefing exactly right.

'Right that's clear enough. We'll get onto it straight away. I'll call you in about a week after we've had a preliminary scout around and give you some initial information, a quotation and timescale to complete the matter. The costs will be an estimate of course as these things don't always run smoothly but we are rarely far out. Anything else we need to know?'

'No, but I must stress that we would not want you to carry out any activities that are' Hans paused and looked around. 'Illegal' he whispered.

'Of course. Our written quotation will reassure you on that point. We understand the sensitivity for companies like yours'.

There being nothing else the two men shook hands and parted company, Andrew to his new seven series BMW parked in the hotel car park and Hans for a hotel bus back to the terminal buildings and then the shuttle bus that runs between Heathrow and Gatwick arriving eventually back at Lovells around four o'clock.

Sitting in his office he added notes of the meeting with Andrew Spicer to his file. He felt that a very significant step had been taken and that he'd given the key to Pandora's Box to this man Spicer from which only time would tell what would emerge. If B I were as good as Mark said they were then they could expect lots of information. If not then Lovells would have wasted a great deal of money but he was acting under Mark's direction and had faith and confidence in him.

With that thought he took out some folders and started a study of Houghton's Scandinavian operations which was an area of their business that he'd not looked at in detail before. This absorbed him until after nine o'clock whereupon he leaned back, stretched and getting wearily up from his chair packed up for the night. Returning to the hotel he had a snack then went to the bar where he drank several whiskeys eventually going to bed quite late.

The rest of the week passed quickly. He enjoyed detail and detail was what this project was about. Assemble the information. File it, cross file, match and compare. And think. Especially think. What was it telling him? What was it not telling him? Gradually patterns started to emerge and he thought he could begin to see where Houghtons were doing well and where they were not. It was by looking at what he was not being told as much as what he was that he deduced information which helped him form his theories.

By the end of the week he realised that to make much further progress he really did need the inside information which is what he hoped B I would bring him so he was pleased when the phone rang on Friday and Andrew Spicer suggested they meet on Monday morning as he had scoped out the project and had an initial cost estimate. He continued 'We've also got some quite interesting information to wet your appetite'. Hans felt a prickle of excitement.

Mark had spent the rest of the week travelling on his tour to other European businesses and was broadly pleased with Germany and Italy but less happy with Spain, deciding to return to that country for a more detailed review the following week. He'd sent Sam back to the UK on the Wednesday morning. Relationships were still frosty between them.

He spent the weekend with Abi and the girls and for once didn't bring any work home. He received and made a few telephone calls but overall it was a relaxing family weekend. Maybe we ought to think about getting married he thought.

Sam still miffed at Mark rang her parents who now lived in Weymouth to invite herself for the weekend. She arrived late on Friday evening. and over the next two days was fussed over and pampered by them while her mother made several pointed remarks about how it was time she found herself a nice man, got married and settled down. Her mother might be right she thought wondering if it was worth going on wanting Mark, or was he gone from her now?

Hans couldn't settle to anything over the weekend. He went to Brighton and did some site seeing, wandered along the beach, enjoyed an ice cream as he walked in the autumn sunshine and generally filled his time but his mind kept returning to Andrew Spicer and what he might be able to tell him.

Monday morning arrived wet and windy but Hans hardly noticed as his mind was buzzing with the coming meeting. Andrew arrived just before nine o'clock. Hans got him a machine coffee then asked him where he'd got to?

'Well firstly let me say that we can handle this project for you and we have put the resources in place to do it. The costs will be high….. here is our provisional estimate. It comprises a fixed element of cost and then some sliding scales depending on the complexity and problems that we encounter. Additional items will be charged as incurred but anything that is likely to be substantial we will agree with you before commitment. However bear in mind that sometimes we'll need a quick decision to take advantage of a particular opportunity that might arise. It is an interesting project and I am certain that we can deliver the information you need. So may I have your authority to proceed?'

Hans stared at the papers contained within a neat file that Andrew had handed him. He read the project scope, noted the comment that all methods employed would be in line with good normal commercial practice and that Lovells would not be exposed to any activities that would cause embarrassment or would be deemed to be illegal. All seemed fine until he reached the third and last page where it boldly summarised the costs.

Estimated project cost:£ 150,000 - £ 175,000 plus expenses.

Hans was staggered. He hadn't really considered what the project might cost but never dreamed that it might be of that sort of size. His heart started to thump and he felt a thin film of sweat come onto his forehead.

'Excuse me a minute' he muttered and leaving his office he practically ran down the corridor to the lift and up to Mark's floor. Bursting into Sam's office he said that he had to see Mark straight away.

'He's just starting a meeting' but then seeing the look of concern indeed almost anguish on the Dutchman's face she smiled and added 'Hang on I'll see if I can get you a couple of minutes'.

Knocking on Mark's door she said she was sorry to interrupt him but if he hadn't started Hans needed to see him immediately on a really urgent matter. Much to Hans's relief Mark came out straight away.

'What's up?'

'I have Andrew Spicer in my office'. Hans looked around Sam's office and then said very quietly 'Do you have any idea of what the B I project cost is likely to be? Look at this' and he held out the quotation.

Mark noted that Han's hand was shaking slightly as he handed over the file. Flipping to the back page he smiled reassuringly and said 'I guess that's about what I thought. I haven't time right now to read the rest, is it alright?'

'Yes it seems satisfactory based on a quick read. I will of course study it carefully before committing but it was the cost issue that I needed to show you'.

'Go ahead then. I guess we could get up to a quarter of a million before this is over'.

'You are approving this expenditure?'

'Yes, I said go ahead. Up to the one seventy five level it's yours to commit. Above that come and discuss before committing. Now I must get back to my meeting'.

'Mark will you confirm that decision in writing to me?' Hans's tidy Dutch mind was working fast. It wasn't that he didn't trust Mark who was after all the Chief Executive of the Lovells Group and whose word was obviously to be relied upon, nevertheless it would be better if in his file he had a memo from Mark approving the matter.

'Dictate what you want to Sam and I'll sign it later today. Now I must get back to my meeting'.

With that Mark returned into his office, shut the door and thinking this was going to be a fucking expensive project said 'Now guys I want two hundred and fifty thousand saved off the marketing budget this year. Should be easy out of the millions that you fellows have in your budgets' and he beamed at the three senior marketers who were in his office to discuss the latest advertising campaign. They saw his "this isn't a matter for discussion, just do it" expression on his face.

Hans told Sam that he would return to dictate a memo later that morning then made his way back to his own office where Andrew was calmly reading The Times.

'Err I just wanted Mark to be aware of the cost issue here but we have decided together that we should proceed. I will write to you to confirm that'.

'Thanks. Now who do I discuss issues with as they arise?'

'With me of course. I am in control of the budget and the project owner'.

'Fair enough but bear in mind if we need to move quickly on some issues we won't be able to pussy foot around waiting for authority to spend'.

'That will not be a problem' replied Hans stiffly watching the other man take a file out of his briefcase.

'Good. Now here are a few things we've established so far. They are somewhat random but did you know that their Finance Director at their Head Office is in debt up to his armpits and basically unable to make ends meet in his personal life. That's always dangerous in an accountant. Their Italian business appears to be doing some quite dodgy dealing with underhand and almost certainly illegal payments going on to obtain contracts from customers. Needs careful checking but we're pretty sure the information is right. In Spain the factory manager is a raving homosexual and seems to have inserted a couple of queers into his team, if you'll pardon the expression, and his control of technical specifications of their products appears inadequate to say the least'.

'There are several other pieces of information' and he handed the folder to Hans. 'We'll send detailed weekly reports and contact you as and when we need your response or approval for anything. Apart from that leave it to us. Now anything else you want to know at this stage?'

'No, but how on earth did you find these things out so quickly?'

'Hans do I ask you how you do your job? No, then leave us to do ours. It's what the modest fee that you are paying is for' he smiled. 'Now if there's nothing else I'll leave and get back to the task in hand'.

When he'd gone, Hans firstly went to Sam and dictated the authorisation that he wanted from Mark asking her to be sure that Mark signed it then returned to his office to reflect on the meeting with Andrew. He diligently studied the B I file adding the information to that he'd already gleaned himself. Making copious notes in his own files he knew this was going to be a very interesting few weeks or months.

So it proved to be. Hans worked closely with Andrew and each week received increasingly detailed written reports which gradually revealed the most amazingly comprehensive information about the Houghtons Company.

It provided for all countries in which they operated details about their factories, the number of production lines they had and the efficiency with which they were operating. Full organisation structures of all the Houghton's businesses were obtained. Detailed accounting information including profit and loss and balance sheet data, scores of photographs of factories and distribution depots both inside and out, product ranges, laboratories, brochures about the business, copies of internal memos, written reports on a whole range of subjects, financial analyses, market research data and information on the progress of new products.

It gave detailed information about the senior people in the company including whether they were married, where they lived, what type of houses they owned, their financial situation, personal habits and weaknesses, affairs they were having or had had, any known sexual habits or deviations. Photos, some long range obviously covert photography of people going about their daily business and private lives including some taken when the individuals were off guard such as in a night club, on a beach, the golf course, or cavorting in ways that they would rather not be known about. Copies of hotel bills, restaurant receipts, credit card slips and nightclub entrance charges.

Press cuttings were included from time to time when items of relevance either to the business or its people were reported. Snippets of gossip and hearsay were included clearly identified as uncorroborated but additional general background. One particular week, a complete copy of Houghton's overall three year Strategic Plan arrived together with copies of notes from meetings referring to that Plan and other major issues including the increasing difficulties that the business was facing in generating sufficient profitability.

What was remarkable was not only the speed and thoroughness by which the information had been gathered but the fact that it was coming from all parts of the Houghtons operation including overseas. What sort and size of organisation must Andrew Spicer have wondered Hans? They must have deployed dozens of people onto the project. No wonder it was costing so much.

In fact, whilst B I did have several of their own permanent experts on their payroll they also recruited people on short term contracts to gain information.

Additionally they made use of liberal quantities of bribery to obtain data. It wasn't always money. Often buying a few beers and getting into conversation with Houghton's employees in a bar close to a factory or office after they'd finished work, brought lots of information. Sometimes it was sex that was used as the lure as pillow talk gave a lot away or a night in an expensive hotel.

Other times in response to advertised positions they inserted people into the businesses as temporary office workers, or temporary factory operatives as most factories were continually recruiting labour. Jobs as security guards, especially night guards were also a good way of finding out what went on.

Computer specialists were used to gain access to the innermost secrets of a target's business and B I had several on their payroll. Most major companies usually have a few contract computer experts working alongside their own computer staff sometimes as a result of a particular surge of activity, the installation of new computer systems or upgrading old ones. Whatever the reason this was one of the easiest and most rewarding methods of gleaning important. Often staff, sometimes quite senior managers left their computers switched on when they finished for the night and so the B I expert rummaging around after hours didn't even need to struggle to find passwords to get into the company's system as it was left wide open.

Additionally B.I could and did hack remotely into a target company's computer systems from afar to delve around in their computer innards for sensitive information.

Miniature cameras could record lots of information and goings on. Jobs as office cleaners were another excellent source of information as when everyone had gone home for the night, documents left on desks could be studied and photographed. The contents of rubbish bins were examined.

It never ceased to amaze Andrew Spicer how careless companies were in allowing their employees to leave papers, files and documents, often dealing with highly confidential matters on desks, unlocked cabinets or only partly torn up in waste paper baskets. Shredders made B I's life much more difficult and they had on previous projects spent literally hours piecing and then sticking papers back together after they'd been through a shredder.

Microphones were hidden in offices, conference rooms and board rooms and long range directional microphones were used to listen into conversations in restaurants, the street or parks. Cars were covertly fitted with tracking bugs to monitor where they went.

In short B I used any and every means possible to gain information and their commitment to do nothing illegal was totally ignored. They were extremely discrete though and were remarkably successful in securing information without being discovered.

Hans's files grew thicker week by week and he realised that his task now was not getting the information as it was coming to him in barrel loads but to assimilate it, distill it into useable facts, then turn the whole thing into a set of information that would be useful for Mark in his goal to acquire them.

Andrew Spicer rang him at least twice a week to check that Hans was happy with the information and Hans in turn talked to Mark two or three times a week on Project Ambition usually face to face in the Crawley Head Office but if Mark was away then they had long telephone conversations.

He found Mark's incisive mind not only stimulating and challenging but also helpful in clarifying points or putting disconnected issues together. He was almost in awe of the Chief Executive's ability to remember disconnected facts, and refer back to a point from weeks ago which had seemed insignificant at the time but now connected with something else and hence made sense of another seemingly unrelated point.

One night when he'd asked Sam if she thought Mark was happy about the way that he was handling the project she smiled wearily and told him that if he wasn't then Hans would have known. 'You can be sure of that' she'd said slowly looking straight at him. 'One thing about Mark is that there's never any question as to where you stand with him' but even as she said that she felt some insecurity herself.

Mark, although seemingly his usual self of late had become more distant with her than before. She didn't know if it was her, or whether he was having problems with Abi, or perhaps it was sheer pressure of work. Working as closely with him as she did and seeing virtually all the documents that went across his desk she knew that he was worried about the continuing poor performance of the French business and thus the concern over the interest rates at which he'd borrowed money there to fund some factory expansion. Also she'd seen letters from the Company's own UK bankers expressing concern that the rate of profit growth seemed to be slowing and demanding to know what he intended to do about it.

The share price had been slipping a bit and that seemed to worry everyone.

He'd been travelling like a demon to see the businesses, customers, suppliers, bankers, agencies and the many hangers-on from whom Chief Executives couldn't always get away. He spent about half his time in the UK and the rest abroad.

This Project Ambition also seemed to be taking a lot of his time and it continually surprised her how he'd always find time to fit in meetings with Hans. Others often had to wait several days to get an appointment with him but not Hans. She had thought that she'd be typing up reports and notes regarding the project but Hans seemed to do all his own typing on his computer.

Dan, the old Chairman who'd been part of recruiting Mark had recently retired and the new Chairman Richard "call me Dick" Butler, who was ex Eton, Oxford, The Guards Regiment and former banker was less malleable and less prepared to give Mark a free rein than Dan had been. She knew that there had been some furious arguments between them, with Mark telling him to keep his nose out of the business and Dick refusing to do so.

One night just as she was thinking of packing up Mark who had been in a meeting with Dick stormed in, yelled 'Coffee' at her and swept through her outer office into his own inner office. When she'd taken him in a fresh cup he'd opened his cabinet and had poured himself a very large whisky. Slumping onto the settee he said 'Thanks' and smiled weakly at her as she handed him the cup. He looked exhausted.

Looking at him she longed to put her arms around him and comfort him, cuddle him, remind him that she was there for him or take him somewhere and make love to him so he knew how much she wanted him, how much she needed him, how much she could give him.

But she didn't simply saying 'You're welcome. Is there anything I can do to help?'

'Dick by name, dick by nature, that's our new Chairman. Chairman Dickhead. Fucking pompous idiot. Knows sod all about a business like this and trying to tell me how to do my job. How dare he? Look what I've done in the time that I've been here. Look where Lovells was when I came and look where it is now. Well I'll show him. I'm not having him piss me about. He's got to go'.

Mimicking the Chairman's slightly nasal whining tone of voice he went on. 'Do I think we're getting the best out of our people by continually adopting such a command driven, authoritarian management style and wouldn't we be better to take a more collaborative approach?'

Reverting to his own natural voice he continued angrily 'Collaborative approach I ask you. Bollocks to that. Tell people what you want, pay them well, incentivise them for outstanding performance and let them to get on with it. Check and follow up and if they can't hack it, get rid and replace. That's my management philosophy and it bloody well works'.

He paused, blew out his cheeks and took a deep pull at his whisky, a sip of his coffee and looking a bit helpless with a glass in one hand and a cup in the other Sam collected a small table from the other side of the room and put it down next to him. He rested the two drinking containers on it then immediately got up and paced round the room hands deep in his pockets head down muttering before he came back to the settee plonking down again. Finishing the rest of the whisky he slowly sipped the coffee before looking up at her still standing in front of him.

He looked straight at her and those eyes of his did what she'd seen so many times before. They turned cold and bored straight into her. Unable to help herself she shivered and looked away for a moment but when she looked back and returned his gaze his eyes were still boring deeply into her but as quickly as they'd changed to penetrating ice they seemed to warm again and lose their intensity as he smiled.

'You know Sam my girl I think we've got a bit of a fight on here and he's going to lose. I don't think we need a twit of a Chairman like Dickhead with his fucking crackpot ideas trying to interfere with what I'm doing. What we want is either a benign old codger like Dan was or a sharp modern thinking guy with whom I can work. One or the other but definitely not Mr. Dickhead'.

He grinned at her. 'Could be a bit of blood on the carpet. Better make sure it's not mine.......ours eh?' Pausing he continued. 'You busy tonight? We don't seem to have had much time together recently do we? How about a meal and a few drinks. I feel like getting pissed and letting my hair down. Abi's away in Spain for a few days with the girls so there's no rush for me to get home tonight. What do you say?'

Her heart jumped. She wanted to throw her arms round him but instead she looked puzzled and putting her head on one side and letting her tongue show slightly between her lovely white teeth gave the impression of thinking whether she had anything else on before letting her face clear and smiling.

'That would be lovely. As it happens I'm free as well but don't get pissed. If there's one thing I can't stand its men that I'm out with getting drunk. Any rate you don't get pissed do you? You seem to be able to drink without it affecting you'.......she paused from looking at his face and let her gaze move down at his crotch and then back up to his face. Smiling she asked 'Are you ready now?'

'Yes to hell with this lot. Let it wait till tomorrow' and picking up all his papers and files he shoved them in his two top desk drawers, locked the desk, switched off the desk lamp, picked up his briefcase, put it in the wall safe then after a quick look around the office walked towards her. 'Come on Sam time to go eat, drink and........' he smacked her bottom.

'And Mark?' she replied softly reaching for his hand and squeezing it.

'Have some fun' he laughed.

Taking her cue from him she quickly tidied and locked her own desk, switched off the computer screen but noticed that his eyes followed her every move. 'I need to go and freshen up before we leave. I'll only be a few minutes' and picking up her bag she walked down the corridor to the ladies where she went to the loo, washed her hands and face, combed her hair and re-did her makeup. She dabbed some perfume behind her ears, on her wrists, down her cleavage and on an impulse lifted her skirt to give a quick squirt at the top of each leg. A couple of tugs to ensure that her hold up stockings were taut and not wrinkled and with a final application of lipstick she was ready for whatever the night held for her. Hopefully Mark she thought.

He was loitering in the corridor between the ladies and the lift and looked really pleased with himself.

'You look...... and smell nice' he smiled as he pressed for the lift which opened straight away.

She gave a quick curtsy. 'Thank you Master. It's amazing what a touch of war paint and a few drops of perfume will do. Now where are we going?'

'Brighton'.

Graham was waiting in reception and if he was surprised to see his boss and secretary appear together and seemingly in happy moods he didn't show it.

'We've had a busy day and it's not ended yet so we're going to finish over a meal. You go home. I'll drive myself tonight. See you in the morning' stated Mark in a voice that brooked no argument. Walking out he led the way to his car where holding the door open he watched as her skirt rode up exposing her legs and stocking tops when she got in, an action not entirely accidental on her part as she twisted herself into the passenger seat.

Grinning he walked round, slid behind the wheel and set off for the coast. As usual he drove fast and they didn't say much to each other as he seemed pre-occupied but the time quickly passed and soon they were cruising along the sea front by which time he'd relaxed.

'It's always a bit of a bugger to park in the old town at this time of night so we'll go in here' he said as he headed into the car park of the Imperial Hotel clearly marked

HOTEL GUESTS PARKING ONLY.

Getting out after he'd squeezed the big car into a corner space he took her hand and led the way to the hotel entrance located in the corner of the car park. They entered the traditional old hotel and walked through to the front reception.

'Go and sort out a taxi with the doorman will you while I have a quick pee' he asked but as she left and went through the swing doors he darted over to the large reception desk and smiling broadly at the receptionist said that he'd rung half an hour ago and booked a suite and could he sign in now. The formalities were completed in no time at all and pocketing the key he walked innocently towards the front doors just as Sam came back in.

They went to a little Italian restaurant, had a pleasant relaxed meal and Mark although looking tired was on sparkling form and appeared to have forgotten his problems with the Chairman.

Sam was worried though as he'd had a couple of gin and tonics before the meal and drunk a bottle and a half of Sauvignon Blanc wine, she having consumed the rest. A couple of times she queried him about his drinking and driving as she knew he was always very strict about not doing that. He didn't mind speeding which was a good thing as he was a very fast aggressive though extremely competent driver, but she'd never known him drink and drive. In fact it was very unusual that he'd driven down tonight after having had that large whisky in the office.

Although as usual a considerable amount to drink had little apparent effect on him he would now be way over the drink drive limit but not wanting to spoil the evening and damage his good mood she didn't press the point for the present but nevertheless worried about the drive back.

Over coffee he suggested they have a nightcap at the Imperial and feeling warm and happy she agreed but in the taxi back to the hotel she still worried about him driving.

'Do you know the way to the bar?' Sam asked as they wiggled through the swing doors.

'Oh that'll be crowded. I thought we might have a drink somewhere quieter' he grinned dangling the room key in front of her.

'Mark Watson you wicked old devil. When did you book that?'

'While you were tarting yourself up at the office then collected the key when you were organising the cab. Did you enjoy the meal by the way?'

'Yes but I think I'm going to enjoy the nightcap even more' and as she looked at him he saw her eyes were sparkling and alive. She was excited, happy and relieved that not only was he not going to drive but that after all this time she'd got him to herself again and they were going to bed.

Getting out of the lift they walked down the corridor holding hands until they reached the double doors of his suite which he quickly unlocked and stepped aside for her to enter. Pushing the door closed behind them he led her to the large sofa and pulled her down by his side as he flopped into its deep cushions.

'Sam' he said softly as he kissed her gently then eased himself away. 'There should be some champagne somewhere. Like a glass?' and without waiting for an answer he stood up and walked over to the far side of the room where an ice bucket held a chilled bottle. Carefully filling two glasses he carried them back to the sofa where she had kicked off her shoes and sprawled out.

'Umm lovely' she sighed taking a deep swallow and patting the sofa. 'Come here and kiss me again' and soon the two of them were deeply entwined. His hand travelled down from stroking her neck pausing briefly on her breast before finding its way under the hem of her skirt.

'I'd like to have a bath' she whispered putting her hand on his. 'Why don't you come and wash my back for me?'

'Just your back?'

'As a poor helpless naked woman I'm sure I won't be able to stop you washing other parts of me if that's what you want to do'.

Disentangling herself she kissed his nose. 'Give me a few minutes and then come in. Bring the bottle with you' and leaving him on the sofa she walked into the huge bedroom off which she found the bathroom.

Soon the sounds of running water could be heard then when it stopped he guessed she was in the bath. Grinning broadly he undressed draping his clothes on the settee. Picking up glasses and bottle he followed her into the now very steamy bathroom where she was lying in the huge corner bath covered with masses of bath foam.

'Oh you are looking pleased with yourself aren't you?' she said holding out her hand to his rapidly erecting penis. 'I think we'd better get that under this nice hot water don't you? After all we don't want it getting cold do we?' Lowering himself into the bath the water rose almost level with the rim. Carefully filling two glasses he gave her one keeping the other for himself then reached over to put the bottle on the floor.

'Cheers, now where's the flannel so I can wash your back?' and as she turned round so her back was towards him he slowly massaged her neck and spine before reaching around to play with her breasts.

Twisting round again to face him she slid her legs past his on either side before sliding onto his lap where with a little wriggle he was inside her. Slowly at first then gradually speeding up he thrust upwards while she bounced up and down on him causing large cascades of water to slop over the side of the bath onto the floor. Reaching behind her she found then tugged out the plug chain so as their movements became more animated the quickly subsiding water stopped slopping outside the bath.

When it had emptied and they were slithering about on the wet, slippery, warm porcelain he suddenly gasped 'I can't hold on much longer' and in response he felt her pussy squeeze him several times until he spurted deep inside her. Leaning forward she held him as he relaxed until she felt him deflating and slipping out of her.

'Sam I'm sorry but…..'

'It doesn't matter darling as long as it was good for you? We've got lots of time yet and that great big bed to play in. Now that you've……. shall we say released some tension you'll be able to relax and make love to me for hours won't you? She gave him a deep kiss. 'Come on let's explore the lovely room that you've booked' and getting out she wrapped a bath robe around herself and held one out for him. Shrugging himself into it and tying the belt into a knot they wandered hand in hand from the steaming bathroom through the bedroom and back into the sitting room where opening the curtains he led them outside onto a balcony.

'Brrr it's freezing' shivered Sam.

'Yes, bit bracing isn't it. Mind you the cold will make your nipples stand out' he laughed putting his arm around her neck and sliding his hand down inside the top of her robe to roll a nipple between thumb and forefinger. 'Listen to the sound of the sea' he went on while continuing to rub her as she relaxed and leaned against him.

'Yes it is lovely but its December and bloody cold. Come on let's go in and go to bed' she said stepping back inside. Following he saw that she had taken off her robe and was walking into the bedroom where pulling back the sheets and blankets she leant back against the head board playing with her nipples.

'You're right they are getting hard but I don't know if it was the cold or thinking of you that's done it' she grinned.

Mark felt himself erecting again so slipping off his robe he lifted her hands away replacing them with his lips noting that both nipples were now standing proud. Sam slid down the bed until she was lying flat and he followed her movements sliding on top of her. They made love very slowly taking lots of time and on this occasion Sam produced one of her noisy climaxes before he erupted inside her.

Lying together they dozed until sometime during the night realising that they were both awake she climbed on top of him and rubbed her crotch with its quite dense pubic hair up and down his flaccid prick which soon had the desired effect so pushing him inside herself she rode him to a robust and satisfying climax managing her timing so that her own orgasm arrived at the same time as Mark was groaning with his third ejaculation of the night.

They slept well waking early and deciding they wouldn't bother with breakfast after a quick shower and putting on the same clothes as they'd been wearing yesterday they went downstairs, checked out, ignoring the somewhat haughty looks from the prim and snooty little receptionist. Getting in the car Mark drove fast to Sam's flat where he pulled up and smiled at her.

'See you later and Sam it was a great night. Thanks. I.......'

She stopped him. 'I know Mark but do you know how long it is since we made love? No? Well it's a very long time, too long. Does it really have to be like that? Surely there could be a place for us as well as you and Abi? We're good together you and I, in bed, in the office, everywhere. Think about it, about us'.

Looking serious she continued 'I do need you Mark and you need me too' then blowing him a kiss she swung the door shut and ran into her apartment block.

Mark gunned the engine and swung off towards the office thinking about what she'd said. She was right they were good together and he had missed sleeping with her but there was Abi to think about. He kept some spare shirts, ties, underclothes, razor, wash kit and hairbrush at the office so arriving just before eight he went straight into the little shower room that led off his office and soon was groomed and ready to face the day.

Graham had noticed his later than usual arrival and saw before he changed that he still had the same shirt and tie as yesterday but he said nothing and waited in reception for his orders for the day. Mind you he thought funny that Samantha wasn't in yet. Oh well nothing to do with him what his boss got up to.

Sam took a taxi to the office arriving around nine o'clock looking pretty, fresh and wearing a different outfit from yesterday.

'Morning boss' she called through his open door and Mark who was just finishing a meeting with the Finance Director returned her greeting.

'Hi Sam, bit late this morning aren't we? Out gallivanting were you last night?

'Yea I had this real heavy date' she countered sensing he was in a very good mood.

'Have a good time then did you?' asked the finance director smiling at her as he walked out of Mark's office.

'Not bad'.

When she took in his cup of coffee he was alone and looked at her, 'Not bad? You seemed happy enough as I seem to remember it my girl' and as he smiled she could see that he looked less tired this morning and perhaps even a few of the lines around his eyes that she'd noticed when she'd had been lying awake holding him and looking at his sleeping face had gone.

'As I said not bad' then lowering her voice 'in fact good, fucking good but please don't ignore me again for so long. I told you earlier this morning that you need me and if you're honest with yourself you'll acknowledge that. After all I willingly admit that I need you so let's be grown up about it and find a way'. She paused and looked hard at him. 'Right now then what are the plans for today?' and the moment of fun and intimacy passed and the business team of Mark and Sam swung into action running Lovells.

Later that morning his phone rang. 'Mark I've got Hans on the line and he's in Italy. Can I put him through?'

'Yes' and when the call was connected he greeted his Dutchman enthusiastically something that cheered Hans as Mark was somewhat unpredictable when he answered the phone.

He explained that he was in Italy to learn more from a Houghton's employee that Andrew Spicer's people had found who was willing to talk about the bribery techniques that Houghton's were using to gain new contracts. The employee wanted to leave Houghtons and would be happy to come to Lovells but he wanted some reassurance as to what his role in Lovells would be before he opened up and spilled the information.

'Tell him what you like, but be very careful about offering him a job. Lead him along as far as you want in order to get the information but commit to nothing Hans'.

'Is it not rather unfair to lead him along into thinking that there may be a job with us and then dropping him?'

'Unfair be fucked. Your job is to get the information and if you have to shall we say slightly open a door and then later close it, so be it. Clear?'

'Yes, quite clear' Hans replied grumpily still unhappy but guessing that it was that sort of ruthlessness that made Chief Executives good at their jobs.

He then went into considerable detail on the discussions that he'd had so far with Signor Giordano who'd admitted that Houghtons were using bribery to secure Government supply contracts.

The Dutchman finished briefing Mark. 'That's about it but it is I think most useful information do you not agree?'

'Certainly but we need the proof. Get your Italian turncoat to provide the proof as without it then its all just hearsay. What are your plans now?'

'I return to England later this morning and start to pull things together. After all I have been working exclusively on this project for nearly four months and it is starting to come to a conclusion. There is little further information that I need. Now comes the task of making sense of it all and producing the report for you and the Board'.

'Well for me certainly. I'll decide how much of this we present to the Board. Remember this is a specific project which I have commissioned and we don't want to get the Board all flappy, especially Dickhead.......... erm sorry I mean especially The Chairman. You and I will determine how we eventually put the information to him and the Board. Now then anything else?'

There wasn't. Hans rang off and later in the day made his way back via Gatwick to the office where he started wondering how he could put the piles of information, sheaves of documents, plans, reports, computer data and the rest of the extensive database that he'd assembled into a report that would be readable, understandable and above all compelling, leading to the conclusion that Lovells should start to plan a strategy to acquire Houghtons.

CHAPTER 25

Mark had four problems on his mind.

Firstly how was he going to deal with Chairman Dick Butler.

Secondly Abi had been raising the question of their relationship and whether they were just going to continue to live together or whether they might marry?

Thirdly the company share price at £4.02 was not rising as it should in view of their improving performance. It ought to be £5 or higher.

Lastly Project Ambition was nearly complete. Hans had done a stunningly good job on it but now Mark had to find a way of presenting it to the Board to obtain their approval to a strategy which could best be described as "get Houghtons" without disclosing precisely how the information had been obtained or why he was so keen to acquire and close down that particular business competitor.

'Life's tough you know' he'd said to Graham one morning as he was being driven in to work. 'All bloody problems and no easy solutions'.

Graham knew that on the rare occasions when Mark spoke to him about work his role was to listen and make encouraging, soothing or brief questioning remarks but not to try and join in the conversation in any meaningful way.

'Always was and always will be but that's what you're there for isn't it boss'.

'Yea I guess so. Still sodding tough though' and he relapsed into silence as he sat brooding over his four issues of which the most pressing one to sort out was Chairman Dick.

It's a question of him or me thought Mark. I can't go on with him interfering in the business the way that he is and what compounded the problem was that Richard Butler was hopeless. He was old school style, out of touch with modern business thinking, timid and a blockage. Mark knew that the Institutions had been concerned that he had been able to manage the former Chairman so easily but nevertheless the two of them had made quite a good team and Mark had valued Dan's advice and help.

Now this new guy who'd been plaguing Mark for the many months since he'd arrived, had nothing constructive to offer, was wholly risk averse, and couldn't see the bigger picture. He was opposed to any further acquisitions on principle and felt that they should spend a few years "running the existing ship smoothly into calm clear waters before considering stretching themselves with the challenges of any more acquisitions".

Mark fundamentally disagreed.

To start with Lovells needed to continue to expand. He had to ensure that while controlling costs the sales revenue continued to increase in order to fund the growth and expansion plans that he had for the business. Growth in sales coupled with tightly controlled or if possible reduced costs would result in an increasing flow of profitability which would enable them to invest in research and development, in advertising, in building new factories, in expanding some existing factories, in being able to lower prices where necessary to fight off competition and crucially in being able to afford to pay above the industry norms so that they could attract, reward and keep the best possible people.

All those factors meant that the business simply had to keep growing. The problem was that many of their markets were static and so what was known as internal growth was getting harder to achieve. Whereas in the past acquisitions had merely helped the growth now they were essential.

Also he specifically wanted to get hold of Houghtons so he could keep his promise to his father. Mark still visited his parents from time to time and every time he saw his father it reminded him that it was the Houghtons that had destroyed Christopher's business and Charles Houghton would pay for that.

But it would be tricky getting rid of the Chairman. If rumours of a bust up between Chairman and Chief Executive leaked into the press then Lovells share price would drop. That would affect the financial stability of the business and all Mark's plans were built on the premise that the business was financially sound. A strong share price gave him the strength to work with or challenge the Institutions who were made up of faceless Pension and Insurance Companies, Fund Managers, Banks and other Money Organisations that invested in companies. With their on-going financial support the share price would hold. Without their support it wouldn't. It was as simple as that.

Considering the members of his Board and their position was important. Mark knew he could count on the majority of them to support him if it came to a show down. He remembered the punch up he'd had not long after joining Lovells when he'd defeated the old Chairman on a point of strategy. Funnily enough he remembered that was also over whether they should make an acquisition, on that occasion in the USA. He'd won that time and what a success the acquired businesses had become in Lovell's hands re-paying the purchase price time and again.

What Mark needed now was a way into the Institutions and some informal exploratory discussions at senior level with them to determine whether they would countenance a change of Chairman and that was going to be extremely delicate. He had to position his discussions as to what was best for Lovells and hence the shareholders in general and the Institutions in particular, not as a row between him and Richard Butler.

Although he met with people from the Institutions occasionally to keep them abreast of the company's performance what he needed was a real entry into the most senior Institution people, those who were at the very top whose views and attitude would be essential to know and mould to his way of thinking. How the hell was he going to do that he pondered? Flicking though his list of contacts he thought of Colin Ringwood, the head of the PR firm that had put him in touch with Business Intelligence. Colin had claimed to have excellent contacts in the Institutions. Now was the time to find out and as soon as he got the office that morning he asked Sam to get hold of Colin.

She squeezed his diary appointments around to create a fifteen minute slot and getting Colin Ringwood on the phone put him through. Quickly dispensing with the introductory niceties Mark got straight to the point.

'Colin. When we first met told me that you had high level contacts in most of the major Institutions. If that's correct I have a vital public relations role for you. If not, tell me and we'll avoid wasting each other's time'.

'That's right Mark. We do. My firm has specialised in Institutional work and contacts for some years and I can say with confidence that I am sure we could help you. What exactly is it you want?'

Mark explained broadly what he needed but didn't disclose the reason. He was relieved when Colin said he was certain that he could get meetings with the top people in the Institutions and suggested that the two of them meet to discuss which Institutions he wanted to talk to and plan the tactics. Telling Colin to hold on Mark buzzed on his other line for Sam to bring in his diary and taking it from her searched for a suitable time and date that suited them both. That wasn't easy as Mark's diary was crammed full including most evenings, but it was one of the evening arrangements that Mark thought would be the easiest to change and so the two men agreed to meet over dinner at an expensive restaurant in London's West End the following evening.

'But Mark' sighed Sam as she watched him cross out the previous arrangement. 'I've spent ages trying to fit that guy in for dinner with you tomorrow. It's been in the diary for weeks and I've had to re-arrange it once already'.

'Well do it again. He's a boring old fart in any case. Seeing Colin is more important'.

Sam rang Mark's dumped dinner guest who was the head of one of Lovell's biggest packaging suppliers and putting on her softest sweetest voice said that she was so sorry but Mark had been called to an important meeting tomorrow evening and could she find another slot to replace the cancelled arrangement. The supplier was most unhappy but Sam wheedled and sweet talked him explaining that if she'd had her way she wouldn't have changed the meeting for absolutely anything but Mark was being so totally unreasonable with her that she desperately needed help to find another date. She had crossed her fingers as she told the lie something she'd done since a little girl which she thought made it not a real lie.

It worked and the supplier immediately felt sorry for Sam as the poor secretary had been put in an impossible position and yes of course he'd change the date and when did she now suggest? They found another date three weeks on.

The first thing Mark did when he and Colin Ringwood met was to thrust a confidentiality agreement in the PR man's hand. 'Read and sign that' he demanded brusquely and sat watching while his companion did as instructed.

'Right now look this is what I want and why I want it' and taking Colin fully into his confidence he explained his problems with the Chairman and why he needed to remove him. He also explained the reasons Lovells needed to acquire a major business ideally Houghtons and the Chairman's objections.

Colin produced from his briefcase lists of his company's contacts in the Institutional field and it read like a who's who of that industry. They agreed terms for the engagement of Ringwood PR and Colin agreed to set up a series of meetings.

He suggested that he should also be present at the first few indeed maybe all of them in order to gauge how they were going and if any change in approach would be desirable and after a few moments thought Mark agreed.

Colin also proposed that while some of the meetings would be formal and in the offices of the particular Institution, some could be in Ringwood PR's London office while others might take place in restaurants or at sporting functions such as a private box at Ascot Races, Lords Cricket Ground or other upmarket sporting venues. One highly influential individual Colin thought would be best tackled at a nightclub where the champagne was expensive as were the hostesses but it was known to be favourite haunt of his.

The next morning Mark told Sam to give priority to any meetings fixed up for him by Colin Ringwood.

So he had a plan to start the process of dealing with his troublesome Chairman.

Now he had to decide what to do about Abi as he was very fond of her and the two girls. In fact when he thought about it rationally he could believe that he loved her. The problem was Sam whom he didn't love but he was incredibly attracted to her. She was uninhibited, fun, adventurous, sexily very attractive without being tarty, wild, a hopeless cook, funny, completely understood him and his moods, but most of all she was absolutely fantastic in bed.

Abi was charming, intelligent, witty, mentally stimulating, comfortable, thoughtful, older, attractive, amusing, safe, a brilliant cook, enjoyable in bed and would make a great wife.

In many ways he could wish for nothing more but he also knew that he wouldn't be able to give up on Sam. Their recent night in Brighton had proved that to him. He needed her in the business but he especially needed her in bed. She was like a drug and provided a sexual release valve for him quite different from Abi and he wouldn't know how to turn it off without her. He'd challenged himself before on whether he could love two people and come to the conclusion that he couldn't. But he didn't love two people. He thought that he loved one but needed the other.

Realising that it was unfair on Abi to simply carry on living together as they were he concluded that he owed it to her to make it a permanent arrangement and in so doing perhaps he could give up on Sam, at least in bed. Wondering if he was kidding himself nevertheless he decided that he would ask Abi to marry him. After all he thought if Abi and I got married perhaps somehow I'll feel differently about Sam and more importantly she'd probably feel differently about me.

On the evening after his dinner with Colin Ringwood he left the office earlier than usual with Graham dropping him home around seven. Abi was surprised and delighted to see him back so early and when he'd come downstairs after taking a shower they sat in the conservatory, an enormous room but as it was centrally heated and all the glass was triple glazed it was a favourite of theirs to sit in the dark cuddled together on one of the wicker settees and watch the stars through the glass roof.

Usually they drank some wine, but tonight Mark opened a bottle of champagne and when Abi asked what they were celebrating he'd smiled as he replied.

'Nothing yet but I hope that very soon we will. Look darling I know that we get on well together and the girls like me, at least I think they do, and my feelings for you are very deep and sincere. I also know I'm not an easy person to live with. I get moody, and forget things like birthdays but well I think I'm..........' he stopped. Damn this was hard and he tried again. 'What I mean is we are a great couple and we live together, have fun and...........'.

Stopping again he realised that this wasn't going the way he wanted at all. Why? Words were part of his natural skill set. Persuasion, logical argument, convincing people was what he was good at. What was making this so difficult? He looked at Abi and although the room was dark there was enough light from the stars and the moon to bring a pale glow into the room so that he could see her lovely face quite clearly. She smiled with a quizzical expression while leaning forward towards him.

'And Mark?'

'Abi I think we should get married. I mean I would like to get married to you. That is to say I love you, so will you marry me……..
please?'

'Is that what the champagne is for?'

'Yes'

'But I might say no'.

'You won't though will you?'

'No'.

'What? What do you mean no?' he asked anxiously and quite loudly.

She laughed. 'No, I won't say no. Yes I'd love to marry you. Thank you and I promise not to turn into a nagging old crone who tries to tie you down. We have a great relationship and it might surprise you to know that I love you very deeply and have done for a long time but I didn't want to crowd you or rush you into marrying me. You had to come to want it in your own time and your own way. Now that you have I can't tell you how happy I am and so will the girls be. They've been nagging me for ages as to whether we're going to get married and in answer to your question about them a few moments ago, yes they are very fond of you. You treat them just as though you are their father and that can't be easy for you and they love you for it, and so do I'.

She kissed him softly and then said quietly 'Be in no doubt about my answer. It's yes, yes, yes. Yes I will marry you'.

'Abi, I'll make you so happy I promise you I will. Thank you'.

'I know. Now what about some of that champagne' and she watched as he carefully poured the fizzing liquid into their glasses and then they resumed their closeness together on the settee and excitedly discussed arrangements, timings, locations, guests and all the many things that a happy couple that have just agreed to share their lives together as man and wife need to discuss. Later they walked hand in hand through the house and up to bed where they made love tenderly and happily.

Afterwards they lay together not speaking just happy to be holding each other in the relaxed calm and happiness that comes from successful lovemaking. Mark thought that he'd made the right decision but worried what Sam would say when he told her and he couldn't help being concerned as to how it might affect their work together.

Abi's head was spinning with thoughts of becoming Mrs. Watson, of whether their marriage would last for ever, momentarily she worried what her dead husband would say if he could but she thought that he'd probably be happy for her. The girls would be alright about it as they really were very fond of Mark.

She wondered about the wedding itself and which registry office they'd use and where to hold the reception. It would be nice to have it here at their home she thought with all their own surroundings filled with friends. The girls would be bridesmaids and they'd love that. It had taken a long time but she was sure that not having pushed Mark into marriage and letting him decide in his own time had been the right thing to do so she snuggled down to sleep enjoying the sound of his breathing.

In the morning after the alarm had gone at its customary early hour when she'd asked Mark about timing for their marriage she been so delighted when he'd said 'As soon as possible. Why wait? We want to do it so let's do it. Can you sort out dates and let me know then I'll clear my diary. I'll call you this morning with some no-go dates, board meetings and suchlike but there won't be many then you can get on with it. I thought about the Caribbean or maybe Bermuda for the honeymoon. What do you say?'

She said she'd be happy to go anywhere with him but did he have to get up at this moment as she thought that it might be nice if they made love before he left for work as it wasn't every day that a woman woke up next to her future husband. Caught up in the happiness of the occasion Mark smiled and pulled her towards him.

Usually when Graham pulled up outside the house Mark came out straight away but this morning he had to wait for nearly half an hour before his boss appeared. Expecting him to be flustered and grumpy for being late or having overslept Graham was amazed at the cheerful greeting he got including being told that it was a lovely morning even though it was still dark, cold, cloudy and looked about to rain. Getting in the back of the car Mark picked up the morning papers and skimmed them before asking Graham if he'd ever been to Bermuda.

'No boss, never have. Bit far for me and the missus. We like Spain or Portugal why you thinking of going there?'

'Yep. Good place for a honeymoon I believe'.

'Whose honeymoon?'

'Mine. Abi and I are getting married, don't know when exactly but soon but keep it to yourself please'.

'Congratulations. She's a really nice lady and I reckon you'll make a great couple. Let me know when I can talk about it won't you boss'.

Arriving at the office, Mark wondered about how to tell Sam and crucially how she would react. In the event he thought that it went alright. At lunch time when he had no meetings he asked Sam to get him a salad some French bread and some sparkling water and when she brought it in he asked her to sit down as he had something to tell her.

She listened apparently unemotionally and when he'd finished speaking and assuring her that their work would continue together unchanged, but their personal relationship did have to change, she smiled said she understood, got up, kissed him on the forehead, said that she was very happy for him and she was sure that Abi and he would make a great couple and congratulations to them both. She made no mention of their own past sexual relationship and to Mark she seemed quite alright if a little quiet for the rest of the day. He was surprised and pleased.

But what he couldn't know was that she was absolutely devastated by his announcement. She loved him desperately although she'd never told him and now that he was going to get married she thought that their relationship must end. But could it? Could she give him up? Equally could give her up? He must feel something for her. All the times they'd slept together where the sex was always good and sometimes mind blowing. Was all that to end?

Could she just be the loyal and efficient secretary and not the discrete lover? She simply didn't know. She thought about whether she ought to leave and go and work somewhere else. Of course she knew it was morally wrong being his lover while he was living with Abi, but it seemed different and less bad than if he was married. Now he was going to be married and he'd already said that he still wanted her as a secretary but not as a lover. How could he do that? Did she mean nothing to him as a person, as a woman, as a lover? Is that all she was to be, his secretary?

However she determined not to show him how much he'd hurt her by his announcement. She didn't blame Abi or even resent her in fact on the few occasions that she'd met her she'd quite liked her. Still Abi was the lucky one who'd got Mark, and she had lost him.

That night sitting alone in her flat thinking about Mark she started to cry. The tears poured from her and her body was racked with deep sobs and tearing sadness. Eventually she went to bed and cried herself to sleep thinking of the times they'd made love right there in her bed. Several times in the night she woke and thought of him and that brought on more tears but when morning came she was all cried out. She felt empty, depressed, miserable and lonely and didn't know how she was going to face him at work that day. Perhaps she should take a couple of days off but then she realised it wouldn't make any difference. He'd still be there when she got back. She'd be his secretary and Abi was going to be his wife. That's all there was to it.

She showered, got dressed and drove to work her mind still numb. When she arrived Mark greeted her cheerfully.

'Morning Sam. Crikey you look at bit rough this morning' and with that confidence damaging comment he plunged into his day's work.

'Well whose bloody fault is that' she said quietly to herself but shrugging her shoulders and giving a quiet sigh she got on with the myriad of tasks that made hers such an interesting and demanding job, although now there was a huge void in it.

Mark's day was mainly devoted to internal meetings and phone conversations with Colin Ringwood regarding meeting the key people at the top of the Institutions and he was impressed with the speed by which Colin had started to make the appointments with the various people.

Feeling good that day he was certain that it was the right thing to be marrying Abi and with Colin working on the plans for the Institutional meetings he was well on his way to sorting out Chairman Dick. In Mark's mind, the problem was resolved. He'd think carefully about a problem and then once he'd decided on a particular course of action as far as he was concerned the problem was all but solved.

So two of his four problems were dealt with. Now he needed to address the nagging problem of the share price but he simply couldn't do that on his own. It was all about the perception that the Company was held in by the Institutions that affected the share price, and their opinions were often fickle and easily influenced, positively or negatively.

The senior people he'd be meeting from the Institutions were the very people that could help or damage him, and the share price. They would be well briefed by their own staff but the impression that Mark personally made on them would have a major impact. It could help him get the share price off its current plateau and start climbing again, or it could knock it off and result in a plunging price.

On the positive side the overall business was doing well. Its market strength was continuing to increase, and its new product launches over the past couple of years had generally been successful as had the new factories that had been built. Mark was known to be a "hands on" executive of the company who drove hard for outstanding results. He had plenty of personal charisma and was seen as lucky. Many years ago Napoleon had said that he wanted lucky generals. Equally business needed lucky managers and directors and if the head of a business was thought to be lucky then that held him in good stead.

On the negative side the French business was still languishing and the borrowing that Mark had personally authorised from the French bank to expand in France was costing them dear as the interest rates had penalties related to performance and currently the French business was still underperforming.

Furthermore he knew that the next big step for Lovells had to be a major acquisition and Houghtons fitted the bill exactly but if Chairman Dick had been spreading the word around the City that Lovells wasn't ready yet for another major acquisition then he'd have to work hard to change that perception. His final intricacy was that being seen to be disloyal to his Chairman could be seen by the City as an extremely negative matter. They liked harmony not disloyalty in Boards of Directors, especially between Chief Executives and their Chairmen.

Yes, all in all Mark realised he was going to have to handle matters with kid gloves. One badly played card, one poorly executed discussion could be disastrous. Shit he thought, this was going to be bloody tough. Then he grinned as he thought that if he pulled it off nothing could stop him. He'd get rid of the Chairman, the share price would start to rise, he'd get a green light for a major acquisition and he'd be in the strongest position he could possibly be to pounce on Houghtons. But that was his forth problem. Was he ready for Houghtons?

Hans had done a brilliant job unravelling them admittedly with help from B I but Mark knew that his Dutchman had pulled together the amazingly complex set of information about Houghtons operations around the world into a document about an inch thick. To have reduced the files, papers, photographs, data and information that filled a couple of filing cabinets with all the back up information to create this single document was nothing short of amazing but Mark had one final task for him as he called him into his office.

'Hans I need a four page summary of this which covers all the key points, strengths and weaknesses' he said pointing to the file. 'Can do? Good. I'd like it by tomorrow evening please'.

Hans looked at him and blinked several times. Mark thought for a moment that the Dutchman was going to cry.

'Four pages? Mark do you know what you are asking? This is probably the most comprehensive competitive analysis ever undertaken. Certainly the most thorough and detailed as far as our sort of business is concerned. I have drawers full of information, documents, folders, files, computer schedules, tapes, videos, photographs and I worked desperately hard to produce what you have on your desk to make it a document of which I can be proud and which would be invaluable for you and our company.

It gives you a meticulously constructed summary at the front and is then carefully separated into various sections that make thorough and detailed reading of the complexity of Houghtons'. His voice grew louder. 'It has cross references and an easy look up index system and now you want the salient points in four pages? What are you thinking of?'

Lapsing into Dutch he finished loudly 'Onmogelijk kan het worden gedaan niet. Totaal gek' *(Impossible it simply can't be done. Totally mad)* and he stared at his Chief Executive.

Mark sat quite still thinking rapidly. His instinctive reaction was to tell Hans to 'Get on with it and don't waste my fucking time telling me it can't be done' but he sensed that on this occasion a better approach might be to appeal to Han's vanity and professional pride.

Speaking quietly he started. 'Hey calm down Hans. You know that I think you've done an amazing job on this project and quite frankly I don't know anyone who could have assembled that amount of information then distilled it in such a clear comprehensive way to produce a document of competitive appraisal in the way that you have. A remarkable achievement. In fact whatever you ever do in your future career nothing will match the exemplary achievement that you've created here with this.

By the same token no-one but you would have the skill or ability to be able to extract the key points into a short summary. Let me explain why I need it.

You see I am going to be talking to the Banks and other Institutions abut our acquisition plans as I need their support and help. They are crucial to drive up our share price and back our plans to create a global player that Lovells and Houghtons together will become. When we are fully ready obviously we'll brief them in detail but for now I need to be able to give them a flavour of what we have in mind. To do that I need your help to create the short summary which gives their very senior people the big picture about Houghtons without all the detail. I know you can do it for me. I'm really relying on you for this. Obviously it's difficult and the timescale impossibly short but sometimes we can't choose our time as the choice and demands are made for us. Now then my clever and reliable Dutchman, can do?'

Marks eyes had bored into Hans all the time that he'd been speaking and the Dutchman felt himself cornered, calmed down, flattered, challenged, motivated but above all persuaded, that he could actually do the impossible that was being asked of him.

'I can try Mark', he replied quietly wondering how the hell he was ever going to do what was asked.

'Thanks. I knew I could reply on you. It's really great knowing that I have such a competent guy working on this project. Now let me have it by tomorrow evening won't you' and with that Mark stood and putting his arm around Han's shoulder gently led him to the door patting him on the arm as he did so.

Han left the office and went for a walk enjoying the sunshine and deliberately letting his mind go blank. If he thought about what he'd been asked to do he knew it was impossible. Somehow though he had to do it. The secret was to let his mind roam freely in an uncoordinated way so that eventually it would find its own method of selecting the information that was required. He walked for nearly two hours before returning to his office feeling calm.

Entering his own office he put a "do not disturb" notice on the door handle, sat down and leaned back in his chair allowing his mind to continue to wander over the problem. He closed his eyes and thought carefully. For perhaps an hour maybe a little more he didn't move and anyone looking in would have thought that he was asleep but suddenly he flipped his chair upright, grabbed a pad of paper and started to write furiously. He remained in his office all day only leaving a couple of times to pee and get coffee but by the end of the normal working day he'd got a summary of sorts typed onto his computer. The only problem was that it was twelve pages and Mark had been insistent on four pages. Hans could understand why but it didn't help him to achieve it.

By eight o'clock he got it down to ten pages but couldn't see how to shorten it any more without leaving out whole sections of information that even a summary required. By nine o'clock it was down to eight pages and just before midnight it had been trimmed to seven. Yawning he stood, stretched and decided to give up for the day and return to the matter in the morning.

Mark forgot about the titanic struggle he'd set Hans as soon as the Dutchman had been ushered out of his office as he'd been busy with meetings, and in between had phoned Abi with "no can do" dates to fit the wedding and honeymoon around.

They'd decided that it would be best if Abi made the arrangements for the wedding and reception and later that day she rang to confirm the date which she'd fixed with the registry office in Crawley. Mark was to sort out the honeymoon. Usually Sam made all his travel arrangements but he didn't think that he could very well ask her to fix up the honeymoon so he rang the travel agent that Lovells used and asked for someone to come in to see him with brochures about Bermuda. Later when the nervous manager of the travel agent had been shown into Mark's presence he'd outlined quickly and clearly what he wanted.

'First class air travel on British Airways, a limousine to collect us on arrival and the best Hotel in Bermuda with a large suite facing the sea. Clear? Right off you go and fix it up. The best mind you'.

That night all he would tell Abi was that their honeymoon destination was somewhere exotic, warm with clear blue sea and white sand and they'd be happy there. She said that she'd be happy anywhere with him but that it sounded lovely. She also said that they needed to tell the girls this coming weekend of their plans to get married.

'Of course, we'll do it together. Now I'm going for a swim, want to join me?'

He often swam at night in their pool and usually Abi let him do so as she knew that he enjoyed being alone in the water and used the time to think as he swam up and down. Tonight though she said that she would join him and went upstairs to find a costume coming back shortly afterwards in a bright red bikini. Walking across the grass to the floodlit pool she watched her future husband pounding through the water. As he approached an end she sat down on the edge coping stones to wait for him to reach the wall. Although the night was cold she sat dangling her feet in the warm water until he stopped slightly out of breath, looked up, smiled and then splashed her.

'Rotter' she giggled and as he pushed off she slipped off her robe, dived in and swam after him. She was a good swimmer but nothing like as strong as him and couldn't catch him so after a few strokes she turned and swam slowly back to the shallow end waiting for him to return. He glided up to her and then standing took her in his arms and kissed her.

'Why Mr. Watson' she smiled 'I do believe that you've forgotten to get dressed for your swim' as she let her hands wander down to his genital area.

'Well Mrs. Watson to be, don't you think it might be a good idea for you to join me free and unencumbered' and so saying he reached around to unclip her bikini bra top which he threw onto the pool side. Giving her breasts a quick squeeze and her lips a kiss he ducked down below the water and she felt her bikini pants being slid quickly down her legs. Stepping out she let them float off underwater while Mark surfacing again took each breast in turn to kiss her nipples before pulling her face to his. Kissing her passionately she could feel his erection pressing against her thigh.

To make love to his future wife he pushed her against the pool wall thrusting deeply and purposefully into her and soon they were gasping and panting with excitement and passion before exploding together on the crest of a climax that ripped through them together. Holding his buttocks Abi pulled him to her for some time still kissing him until he slid out from her. Letting go of each other he floated off on his back a little way down the pool while she swam to the side of the pool and conscious that he was probably watching climbed slowly up the steps. Turning she saw that he had indeed watched every movement and was glad that she still had a taught figure with firm breasts and a flat tummy even after having had two children.

Picking up her towelling robe she wrapped it round herself and flopped down into one of the colonial style chairs that was on the veranda of the summerhouse to the side of the pool area and taking a towel she gently rubbed her hair dry while watching him swim lazily this time up and down a few more times before he too got out and walked naked towards her.

Unlike her he didn't cover himself but he did pick up another towel and dry his hair before he too dropped into a chair. They chatted for a while until Mark leaned over, whispered 'bed darling' and taking her hand walked still naked across the lawn into the house and upstairs to their bedroom where he carefully undid her robe and gently pressing her onto their bed made love to her again.

Hans rose early the next morning and was in the office by six o'clock where he found the inspiration to reduce his summary to six and a half pages. By lunch time he'd re-written it several times again and it was now six pages however by reducing the type font size he got it to five and decided that it was simply not possible to do better than that so he printed it off.

Walking into Sam's office he asked her to let Mark know that he'd completed the summary. Handing it to her he said sadly 'It is five pages not four like he asked but I simply cannot do what he wants in four. I'll be in my office when he's ready to discuss it' and returning to his office he suddenly realised that his project work of these last months was now complete. His task was done. What was to become of him now he wondered? Life would seem quite boring he imagined. No more meetings with B I. No more clandestine discussions, reading secret reports or looking at photos taken unknowingly. No more complex documents to unravel, and no more reams and reams of computer prints looking into the entrails of a competitor. He felt both elated and sad. Elated that he'd completed the task satisfactorily and sad that it was all over. His reverie was broken by his phone ringing.

'Hello this is Hans speaking'.

'My office now' snapped Mark's voice and the line went dead.

Practically running down the corridor he went into Sam's outer office and she motioned him to go straight into Mark. Pausing to take a breath he ran his hand nervously over his hair, straightened his tie, knocked and entered.

Mark was sitting at his desk looking stern with the five page summary in his hand. 'What did I ask for Hans? Four pages and what have you given me? Five'. There was silence and Hans was about to explain why he simply hadn't been able to achieve what he'd been asked but Mark raised his hand to silence him. 'Five pages................ of the most brilliant summary I could have possibly hoped for. Hans it's fantastic. Someone could pick this up and get the key salient points about Houghtons which is just what I wanted. Well done. A fantastic job' and he smiled broadly at the Dutchman.

'It's what you wanted?'

'Yes all and more than I could have hoped for. I really didn't think it could be done but you've done it. Tonight I'm going to take you out to dinner to say thank you for the effective way you've handled this whole project. Oh and sorry about my little joke there by the way about pretending to be cross that it was five pages not four'.

Out load Hans said 'Oh no problem Mark', but inwardly he thought "sadistic bastard".

Over dinner that night Mark fascinated and somewhat frightened Hans with his grasp of the business, his wide knowledge of their industry all over the world and his ideas for future expansion of Lovells. He suggested that the Dutchman took an extra month's holiday as a thank you. He also confirmed that he would receive a large rise in salary effective immediately and a bonus equal to six months of his new salary. Finally he said that while Hans was away he'd put his mind to a suitable new role for him as he didn't think he should go back to Strategic development in their Dutch business. That was far too mundane for him now and he needed a bigger and more important challenge.

Hans went to bed that night quite drunk, happy with his salary increase, bonus and holiday rewards, and well satisfied with the end of the project.

Mark went to bed thinking about the forthcoming meetings with the Institutions and the future acquisition of Houghtons.

Sam went to bed alone crying still distraught over the change in her relationship with Mark.

Abi went to bed and laid awake thinking about the wedding, wondering what to wear to the registry office and for her going away outfit, about telling the girls tomorrow when they came home and how they'd react, and whether to wake Mark and make love to him.

She didn't but let him sleep.

CHAPTER 26

The day of the wedding dawned warm and sunny. Abi had slept alone last night as Mark had stayed with his parents so as to preserve the tradition of not seeing the bride on her wedding day before the actual wedding.

The girls brought her a cup of coffee and sat on the bed chattering excitedly. Abi asked them if they really were happy that she was marrying Mark and they both said that they were so Abi's last worries disappeared, replaced with a touch of nerves about the day ahead.

When she'd finished her coffee she slipped on a loose sweater and a pair of jeans and wandered downstairs where her friend Maggie who'd come over the previous day had already made a light breakfast. Abi had thought it fitting that she be Maid of Honour as it was at Maggie and Brian's dinner party all that time ago she'd met Mark.

The hairdresser arrived and set to work on her lovely dark flowing tresses and when he'd finished her hair really did look wonderful.

The girls went through stages of flapping, calmness, eruptions of panic as something didn't fit but eventually everything was dealt with and time marched on to when they would have to leave for the registry office.

Charlie came in at one point holding the phone and saying there was some bloke wanting to talk to her.

'Who is it darling?'

'Dunno you'd better see what he wants and get rid of him' she grinned.

'Hello?'

'Abi I love you and can't wait to marry you my darling. You are going to make me the happiest man alive today'.

'Oh Mark, I love you too and I am just longing to become Mrs. Watson. Not long now darling before we are together, for ever', and wishing each other fond farewells and blowing kisses they put down their respective phones.

'Sweet' intoned Charlie. Abi stuck her tongue out at her daughter.

'What's sweet' enquired her younger sister entering the room.

'Mum and Mark playing kissey kissey and getting all lovey dovey on the phone'.

'Thought they save that for later and their wedding night bonk'.

'Emma really' rebuked Abi feeling herself going a little pink.

Both daughters grinned and then Charlie speaking for them both told Abi that they were happy for her and Mark. Emma nodded her agreement too.

Just before twelve Mark accompanied by Bob an old friend of his arrived at the registry office which was already filled to overflowing with the congregation sitting chatting quietly. He saw Sam near the front in a short white dress that showed off her excellent legs to perfection. She smiled and mouthed "Good luck". A little after mid-day there was a rustling from behind and Abi, Maggie, Charlie, Emma and Abi's father were all assembled at the back of the room.

Mark turned and the vision of Abi simply took his breath away. She looked exquisite in a long white wedding dress that fitted her tightly and thus showed off her figure perfectly. It had touches of pale pink on the short sleeves and around the waist and the bridesmaids and Maid of Honour's dresses were made of this same pink. The whole effect was soft, pretty and one of gentle beauty.

Taking her arm Abi's father led her slowly down the aisle and she simply glowed with happiness. Maggie, Charlie and Emma followed and soon the procession halted at the front before the somewhat austere registrar who nevertheless gave all assembled a welcoming smile and started the brief ceremony which was over in a matter of minutes when he finished with the words that Abi and Mark were husband and wife and thus entitled to kiss each other. They did for quite a long time, to the delight of all the assembled company.

Afterwards everyone milled around chatting for a while until the newly married couple climbed into a vintage Rolls with Graham at the wheel who'd been surprised that the owner of this veteran machine was sitting in the front passenger seat and allowing it be driven by a stranger. What he didn't know was that in making the arrangements Mark had added a substantial additional amount of money to the usual charge so that Graham could drive. He'd done this for two reasons. Firstly he'd wanted good reliable Graham to be part of the day's happy events, and secondly he'd thought that his driver would love the opportunity to drive such a splendid old machine.

As they set off the usual flurry of confetti descended on them from all directions and Mark noticed that Sam had pushed herself to the front and laughingly tipped the content of her box a little over Abi, but a lot over Mark. Her eyes met his and he saw deep sadness there in spite of her smiles and for a fleeting moment he remembered some of their past times together. As the car pulled away he couldn't stop himself from turning round and there stood Sam a little away from everyone else just staring sadly at the departing vehicle.

Shrugging he told Graham to drive slowly and take a longish route so that they could sit and watch the world go slowly by from the old open car. Finally they turned into their driveway and drove up to the front of their house where crowds of people were waiting. Nearly one hundred people had been invited far more than had been at the registry office and it seemed that most of them were on the front lawn and drive as the newly weds arrived. Cheers rang out then everyone made their way into the huge marquee that had been set up on the lawns at the rear of the house.

The reception which went smoothly was enjoyed by everyone who dutifully laughed at the appropriate points in the speeches and had particularly clapped Abi, when unexpectedly she had stood and said that although it was unusual for a bride to make a speech, she just wanted to thank her two daughters for being so understanding and sharing her happiness today then she thanked Mark for having asked her to marry him.

Mark made sure that his parents Betty and Christopher found people with whom they were comfortable talking and several times during the day went over and spoke to them. His mother somewhat overwhelmed by the scale of the wedding nevertheless enjoyed it and Christopher established contact with a couple of fellow masons with whom he shared knowledge and experiences of the strange rituals and world of the Masonic fellowship.

Later a dance band struck up and Mark whispered to Abi that it might be a good time for them to slip away. She squeezed his hand and went indoors to change returning half an hour later looking quite stunning in a deep plum skirt and jacket outfit with matching shoes, handbag and pill box hat set at a jaunty angle on her head.

'Alright?' she asked quietly of Mark who'd also changed out of his morning suit and was now wearing a dark grey suit.

'Fantastic. You'd better be careful as dressed like that someone might want to marry you'.

'No chance. I've got my man thank you'.

'Come on then. Let's make a run for it' but they had no chance of getting away unnoticed and crowds of people gathered to wish them well. Maggie thrust Abi's bouquet of pink and white carnations into her hands and told her to close her eyes and throw it to the crowd. Laughingly she did hoping that Charlie or Emma would catch it but when she opened her eyes it was Sam holding the flowers.

'Have a lovely holiday you two. You never know I might be next now I've got these' called Sam smiling broadly but Mark saw that the smile was on her face only and her eyes looked sad.

'Thanks Sam. Goodbye everyone' and with "goodbyes" and "good lucks" echoing around the grounds finally Mark and Abi slid into Marks Jag and Graham roared off tooting his horn and flashing his lights. As they reached the road he stopped the car, jumped out and ran round the back to quickly untie the cans and bottles that had been affixed to the rear before jumping in and asking 'Where to boss?'

Mark gave the name of the hotel he'd booked for the night several miles away from Gatwick from where they were flying tomorrow and when they arrived at the large country hotel he slipped two twenty pound notes into his driver's hand, thanked him for driving them today, said that he hoped he'd enjoyed the old Rolls and that if anyone found out where he and Abi were staying tonight he'd cut off Graham's balls very slowly with a rusty knife.

Graham grinned as he carried their bags into the hotel for them staying just long enough to check that everything was alright before agreeing what time he'd pick them up next morning.

'I hope you'll both be very happy' he said slightly stiffly then he left the newly marrieds alone.

'Drink down here or shall we go up?'

'Let's go up darling. I just want to be alone with you'.

The porter carried their luggage upstairs and wished them a good night as he closed the doors to the suite which was a large room with several vases of beautiful pink roses and on the table an ice bucket with a cold bottle of pink champagne. In moments Mark had opened the bottle and poured then they clinked glasses before toasting their future lives together.

They sat and talked quietly and both seemed reluctant to break the peace and quiet of the sitting room by going to bed. When the bottle was empty Mark asked if he should have another sent up but Abi thought that it might be time for Mark to carry her over the threshold to their nuptial bed where he was welcome to exercise his marital conjugal rights.

Smiling he duly picked her up and carried her round the room before pushing open the door to the bedroom. Carrying her over to the enormous four poster bed he laid her down carefully and said quietly that he loved her.

'I know you do darling. Now come and make love to your new wife' and reaching up she pulled him down to her. He kissed her and then taking his time undressed her revealing a very pretty pale yellow and white camisole and matching pair of French knickers. He sat gently massaging her breasts before slipping off the delicate underwear. Rolling her hold up stockings down her legs and off her feet he then started to undress himself while continuing to gently kiss her face, neck and naked breasts and although he struggled a bit he managed to rid himself of all of his clothes without really stopping loving her body and lips. He slid down the bed and kissed her bush before probing her pussy lips with his tongue until sensing her arousal he moved above her and pressing himself inside made love to her with all the skill and tenderness that he could.

They woke next morning happy and naked when the knock sounded at the door of the room. 'Hang on a minute' Mark shouted as he leapt out of bed and grabbing a robe that was hanging in the bathroom walked through the sitting room and opened the door onto the corridor where a patient waiter pushed a trolley into the room and wished them a good morning.

The newly married couple giggled their way through breakfast then went back to bed to made love again. Abi bathed while Mark showered then after dressing for their flight they made their way downstairs to where Graham was dutifully waiting. Having settled the bill they got in the car and were driven to Gatwick where checking in they waited in the lounge reserved for first class passengers before being invited to board the plane for their seven hour flight to Bermuda which passed smoothly if somewhat boringly.

Their hotel was lovely, set right by the beach and they had a large suite overlooking the sea with an enormous balcony which was more like a patio than balcony.

They spent the next three weeks doing all the things newly married lovers do.

Walking hand in hand on the lovely deserted unspoilt beaches. Finding little restaurants where they sat in dim corners eating simple food or enjoying exemplary service and outstanding quality meals in swish five star establishments. Exploring and being fascinated by the water buses which take people to every part of the island. Being together and very much in love.

Their love for each other deepened and whether making love, talking, walking or just being together they were at peace and harmony with each other and the world.

Mark had agreed this would be a real holiday and that he wouldn't continually ring the office or have documents sent to him to deal with provided he could ring in a couple of times a week, just to keep in touch. He did this on Tuesday and Friday Bermuda lunchtimes, morning time back in the UK.

Sam politely asked him if they were having a good time, how Abi was, if the hotel was alright, had they done much swimming and what the weather was like? She then reeled off for him the key information that he wanted to know, that day's share price (down slightly), latest sales and profit figures (above budget), responses to certain matters he'd put in hand before he left or had asked her to deal with on an earlier phone call, raised particular queries and ran through the appointments that she'd fixed.

Then she passed him on to different people who wanted to speak to him, usually the Finance Director and Marketing Director but sometimes others. She always arranged for whoever was the last to speak to him to route the call back to her so she could check whether he needed anything else.

Each of these holiday calls took about an hour and then he went to the hotel bar for a beer and to meet up with Abi who didn't resent the time he'd been on the phone as she knew that important though she was to him, his work was of almost equal importance and that he was in many ways a driven man always pushing himself to achieve greater results. She also knew that his was a very demanding job and that he simply wouldn't be able to not contact his Company for three whole weeks. Hell most weekends he made or received several phone calls and she'd had a secret fear that he'd work every day but he stuck to his promise of two calls a week and devoted all the rest of the time to her.

But after his first call back to the UK he was all tensed up so she persuaded him to go to their room, get undressed then she gave him a relaxing back, neck and shoulder massage. Before long he turned over pulled her head down towards his erection and slipped himself between her lips. She soon sensed that his climax was imminent so lifting her head aside and replacing her lips with her hand she rubbed quickly until he squirted his semen over her hand, wrist and his belly.

'There now, better?

'Need you ask? Can I get this treatment after every call back to the office?'

'I guess something might be arranged' she smiled. 'Come on time for lunch' and running into the bathroom she quickly washed off his emissions and leaning back into the bedroom threw him a towel to wipe himself. As he did he couldn't help reflecting that if Sam's lips had been around him a towel wouldn't have been necessary.

Thus a pattern was established and for the other calls during their holiday as soon as Mark left the pool area to go up to their room to phone back to the office Abi went with him and waited in the bedroom for him. When he'd finished some form of sexual enjoyment followed.

All too soon though the three weeks came to an end and they were met by the faithful Graham at Gatwick in the early hours as it was an overnight flight. He drove them home and they spent the weekend catching up with Charlotte and Emma who marvelled at how brown they both were.

On his first Monday morning after the honeymoon sitting in the car on the way to the office Mark wondered how Sam would react to him. He wasn't exactly worried just concerned. He also thought about the coming series of meetings with the Institutions.

'So you had a good time then boss over in Bermuda?' queried Graham. 'Didn't fall into that famous Triangle then? What do they think about it over there? Is there anything in those stories do you think?'

'Great time thanks. Lovely weather and hotel. Super food and I think that stuff about the Bermuda Triangle is a load of old bollocks. Any rate didn't worry us'.

'Well my missus wouldn't go. Quite concerned she was when she heard where you and Mrs. Watson had gone. She's read this article see, some time ago it was in the Readers Digest I think, about all them planes and ships that have gone missing in that triangle. Now she thinks...........'

'Graham, shut the fuck up will you. I'm trying to think and if you keep rabbiting on I can't. I need to get my mind back in gear after three weeks away. We're going to be busy this week chum so lots of late nights I'm afraid'.

'No problem. I'll tell you my missus's theory some other time shall I?'

'Yes do that' and he slumped back and flicked through the newspapers but he didn't really read them as his mind was whirling around the Lovells empire. He knew from his calls back while they'd been away that broadly things were ok and under control, except France which continued to produce disappointing results. The share price though seemed to have rallied a little and now stood at £5.42 but the coming meetings would really start the process of either pushing it up or totally wrecking it. Not much in between the two options. A fairly stark set of choices.

Whilst he'd been away he'd thought about how he was going to handle the meetings. He was clear on what his approach and tactics would be but if he called it wrong not only would he fail to drive up the share price but quite the reverse as it would certainly go down, but more importantly wouldn't get rid of Chairman Richard Butler. If he failed then he'd probably be for the chop himself as in these sorts of high stakes business manoeuvres there couldn't be two winners. No, either he'd win and start to clear the path to acquire Houghtons, or he would out on his ear and known as the man who fucked up big style.

Looking up with surprise he saw that they were pulling into the office car park. Calling 'Thanks see you later' to Graham he got out and walked briskly into the main building, smiled at the receptionist, bounded up the stairs and pausing for a moment opened the door to his office suite and walked into Sam's office.

Whatever he thought might happen, didn't. It was just like old times as she smiled warmly, said he looked brilliantly well, what a lovely tan he'd got and that she was glad to see him back. Thanking her he moved through into his own huge office and sitting down at his desk saw the neat piles of files, papers and notes that Sam had already laid out ready for his return.

'There's an absolute mountain in addition to those', she said following him in with his coffee. 'You get on with that lot and when you've cleared yourself some space I'll bring you the next batch. All the urgent stuff is there though. I've left your diary clear for this morning but then you're booked solid minute by minute. Couldn't squeeze a gnat's whisker between appointments. Before you start though Colin Ringwood wants you urgently about three meetings he's set up for this week; finance need you to clear some capital expenditure authorisations which they say are holding things up until you've signed them; Hans says he had a lovely holiday thanks and he's ready to talk about his career with you; and The Chairman would like to discuss a number of matters with you as soon as possible.

'Right get finance up here then get Colin on the phone, find a slot for Hans later this morning and tell the Chairman to fuck off. I'm too busy to waste time with him today'.

'He said it was urgent'.

'Tough'.

She turned and walked out of the office wondering if Mark's eyes were following her. In fact after a quick glance at her as she turned away from him he looked down at his desk and picked up the folder marked "PRIORITY". He called after her 'If Dickhead hassles you fix an early breakfast meeting with him tomorrow'.

Sam sat at her desk and felt a wave of sadness engulf her. She'd steeled herself for this morning and had been determined to act and project the cool efficient secretary and not some love struck female desperately in love with her boss. It had nearly worked but the sheer impact of him walking through her door a few minutes ago had been like a physical blow into the pit of her stomach. This morning she had styled her hair a little differently worn a short skirt, a tight fitting skinny rib jumper, a bra that enhanced and accentuated her breasts and used one of his favourite perfumes. She knew she looked good and normally he'd have made some complimentary comment. Today he'd said nothing.

Her last three weeks had been horrendous knowing that he was with Abi, alone, just the two of them. She'd kept imagining them together. Swimming, holding hands, eating, drinking and making love. Especially making love. After all that's what honeymoons were about weren't they? She wondered how she and Abi compared in bed. Was Abi better than she was? Did she do all those things that Mark liked? How did Abi's body compare to hers? Abi was around ten years older, but she was attractive, dressed well, spoke perfectly, clearly a capable mother and sorry to say, a really nice person. But was she sexy and did she satisfy Mark?

Sam knew that her own abilities in bed were very good. Several past lovers had told her that and although she hadn't slept with anyone since Mark had first made love to her she knew that when she and Mark made love it was stunningly good. He was a good lover with a lovely body and most of the time he could be really considerate to a woman's needs. Other times though he just needed sex. She provided a solution to whatever need he had whether that was long slow wonderful lovemaking, a quick fuck or just a blow job. Did Abi do all that?

Sniffing back a tear and blowing her nose hard she picked up the phone and asked the man from Finance to come up and see Mark to get whatever papers needed signing dealt with. When he left she got Colin Ringwood on the line and put him through then the Chairman rang and asked what time Mark would be free to see him.

'Erm he's terribly tied down already Mr. Butler but he did say that early tomorrow morning would be good as he'd have caught up by then and fully up to speed to discuss whatever you need at that time. Could you give me a list of items you'd like to cover and I'll see that Mark has it before your meeting'.

She waited and after a short silence The Chairman said grumpily 'What time tomorrow morning?'

'Mark suggested a breakfast meeting at around seven tomorrow. Would that suit you?'

More silence and then a grudging 'Very well make the arrangements?'

'Yes Mr. Butler and I know Mark will be pleased to be able to have time with you' was the way she concluded the conversation. He really was an obnoxious man, no wonder Mark couldn't stand him.

So the day passed and although every time Mark spoke to her or she went into his office she felt wretched, she managed to keep up a cheerful appearance and between them they got through masses of work. Around seven o'clock he rang and asked her to get Graham ready to take him into London and then to come into his office.

'Thanks Sam, it's great to have the team in action again eh? Look I brought you back a little something from Bermuda. Hope you like it' and he held out a small package about twelve inches square. 'Can you tidy this lot away as I'm running a bit tight for time? See you in the morning' and with that he smiled and walked out to find Graham waiting downstairs in reception.

She tidied his papers away, locked his desk then taking her package went into her outer office to put her own things away. Picking up her handbag and present she went home, changed into jeans and a tee shirt, made herself a mug of soup and flopping onto her settee slowly sipped the hot liquid.

She'd known that it was going to be difficult seeing Mark again. No, not difficult plain awful. She ached for him and wanted him but especially wanted Abi not to have him. Had Mark given her up for Abi for ever? She doubted it. No he'd want her again, she'd just have to be patient. Feeling a little better with that thought she tore off the wrapping paper to reveal a painting of several of the colour washed houses for which Bermuda was famous, grouped around a little cove. The whole scene looked idyllic and very romantic.

Imagining Mark and Abi holding hands in the cove, the tears came until she could only see the picture through a blur. She stayed like that for ages until the tears stopped although she still could see in her minds eye Mark and Abi on that little cove walking, swimming, making love.

Oh God why Abi and not her? The tears came again and this time she rolled onto her side and cradled the painting to herself. She didn't know how long she stayed there but eventually still sniffling she got up and walked round her apartment to find a place to hang the picture. She could of course chuck it away but if he ever came here again he'd be upset if it wasn't there. She couldn't ignore the fact that she'd see him every day at the office and she couldn't pretend that he and Abi hadn't been to Bermuda on their honeymoon so she was damned if she was going to let a bloody picture crease her up every time she looked at it. Getting a hammer and some nails from the kitchen drawer after several attempts she eventually succeeded in getting a nail to stay in the wall. The painting was duly hung above her settee.

Opening a bottle of wine she poured a glass then forcing herself to stand back and look at the painting she saw the beauty that had been captured in the scene and this time although she had to gulp hard no tears came, well almost none. Looking at the painting was going to be part of her therapy in getting into the new relationship she'd have with Mark, for now at least.

One day he'll want me again he said to herself as lifting her glass she toasted the picture. 'To us my darling' she whispered.

CHAPTER 27

The object of her toast blissfully unaware of the effect that the picture had created for his secretary was being driven speedily towards London. He read some briefing notes in the back of the car that Colin had prepared for their meeting with the first Institution. They stopped in Piccadilly to collect Colin from his office in St. James Street and Mark used the remaining time to ask a few final questions.

The Deputy Chairman of National Bank was to be his first Institutional high level contact. Colin had cautioned against a formal presentation or being too pushy and had recommended a more relaxed approach and to allow the Bank man to made the running.

'Look he knows broadly what you want to discuss as if I hadn't given him some indication he wouldn't have agreed to meet you. He'll probably be on his own but might have a lackey with him to make notes. They're giving us dinner at the Bank. You'll have plenty of time so don't try and rush things' Colin counselled during the final stages of the car journey.

Graham pulled up outside the imposing old building in the middle of the City just round the corner from the Bank of England. A liveried flunkey held open the large doors of the building as Mark and Colin hurried up the steps then ushered them to the reception desk manned by a uniformed security guard who having checked their names picked up a phone and told someone that 'Sir Steven's guests have arrived'. Acting on unheard instructions he invited them to take the lift to the eighth floor.

As the lift doors opened a pasty faced young man of around thirty was waiting and introduced himself as Daniel, Sir Steven's personal assistant. He invited them to follow him and led them to a small wood panelled room where a middle aged waitress in formal waitress outfit smiled and asked what they would like to drink. Colin settled for a gin and tonic while Mark asked for sparkling water. Pasty Face thought that he would enjoy a glass of grapefruit juice. The three men stood around making small talk with Pasty Face explaining that the various paintings and photographs lining the wall were mainly former chairmen or senior directors of the Bank.

Pasty Face stiffened slightly as the door opened and a tall impressive looking man of around sixty with white hair walked in. 'Gentlemen good evening and welcome to National Bank. Daniel has been looking after you I hope. My usual please Margaret' and shaking hands with both Lovells men he collected his whisky and soda from the waitress and raising his glass said 'Cheers, here's to an enjoyable evening. So how are things in the world of commerce and consumer goods?' and a general conversation developed which helped break the ice. After a little while the waitress who had slipped out of the room a couple of times approached Daniel and whispered something to him. He waited until there was a pause in the conversation then advised Sir Steven that dinner was ready who promptly suggested that they adjourn to the next room to eat.

He led the way into a similar but slightly larger room where the table was laid for four. The Banker sat at the head and gestured for Mark and Colin to sit on one side while Daniel took his place without being bidden on the other side opposite the two Lovell's men and to the right of Sir Steven. A selection of various smoked fish was served straight away and conversation flowed easily during which Sir Steven asked several questions of increasing detail and probed hard about Lovell's business.

After the second course of wild mushroom soup Daniel slipped a small note pad about the size of a postcard onto the table near to the right hand of Sir Steven's who ignored it as he concentrated on Mark's reply to his last question.

Mark was starting to enjoy the evening. Although not nervous at the start he had been apprehensive as he was aware of the risks he was running in going against his Chairman but now that he was starting to understand the direction of the banker's questions he could use his tremendous ability to think quickly on his feet and was able to steer the nature of the discussions broadly in the way that he wanted them to go. While he was answering another complicated question at some length and admiring the thoroughness with which the banker had obviously prepared he saw that Sir Steven had opened the little note pad and made a couple of notes in a small precise handwriting style.

As the main course of citrus spiced rack of Welsh lamb cooked slightly pink accompanied by french beans, baby new potatoes, and carrot batons was served, the discussion moved onto the subject of Lovell's need to continue to expand through acquisition.

Mark declining any wine was now fully in his element and launched into his reasoning as to why the company needed to grow in this way. His passion and belief stood out clearly and the Banker who'd seen many business leaders explain their strategies to him had become cynical as they always offered "jam tomorrow". However what impressed him tonight was the clarity of strategy that Mark displayed and the carefully thought through arguments in favour of his plan.

Sir Steven was also captivated by Mark's eyes which were penetrating his with an intensity that he had never seen. This was a man so convinced by his own plans which were demonstrably sensible yet carrying an element of risk that he was persuaded that the Company should be backed and that Mark should be supported in his ambitions.

An excellent and varied selection of cheeses was offered after the main course had been cleared away, followed by a large bowl of fresh fruits during the consumption of which Mark again pressed his belief in the acquisition part of his strategy.

The Banker could also see that Lovell's current share price was undervaluing the business and he made another note in his little book to ask his dealing rooms tomorrow to buy a large chunk of their stock. After all if this chap pulled off the expansion plans to turn Lovells into a real Global player then the bank would make a lot of money by buying now before the share price started to rise considerably higher.

'Let's have some coffee shall we?' stated Sir Steven as he pushed his chair back looking at his little note book. 'Now the fifty million dollar question is who are you going to buy? I guess there are several candidates and I'd like to hear your thoughts on this point. I can see and accept your argument for wanting to acquire, what I need to be happy about is who? Buy a duff one and you'll screw everything up won't you and then where will we be?'

Mark, noting the use by Sir Steven of the words "where will we be" rather than "where will you be" indicating some possible joint commitment paused while Margaret served coffee and Daniel fussed around offering brandies or other liqueurs. Mark just took coffee, Colin asked for coffee and a malt whisky while Sir Steven declined coffee but accepted a brandy and lit up a large cigar. Mark started to speak quietly forcing the Banker now enwreathed in a cloud of cigar smoke to lean forward to hear more clearly.

'Well if we start with America there are a couple of potential targets, whilst in continental Europe I think there are only really three major opportunities, one of them in Italy and two in France. I'm ruling out the Far East at present although as I explained earlier in the longer term we have to build a bigger presence in that region, possibly even into China. No I think the key is nearer to home. In fact my preferred and lead candidate is Houghtons who although a UK company has many overseas operations and in lots of ways compliment us in that where they are strong we are less so, and where we dominate then they are weak. So there won't be too much overlap and the benefits should be realisable quickly. They are badly run and the opportunities to take out cost and improve efficiencies are enormous'.

'I'm glad to hear that you're not planning to acquire anything in France. You've still got problems there haven't you?'

'Yes but I am about to change the Head of that business for an excellent man from our Dutch business who has worked on a special project for me recently. I believe that he will turn that business around for us. No it's Houghtons that we want. In fact I have a short summary of their few business strengths and very many weaknesses here which you might like to glance through' and handing over Han's five page summary he sat back to watch Sir Steven carefully and slowly read the paper.

Colin caught Mark's eye and winked.

When the Banker looked up Mark continued 'We've conducted a major competitive research project on Houghtons and there isn't much we don't know about them. In fact I'd venture to say that we probably know more about them than they do themselves and the more we know the more it makes sense for us to acquire them.

'Hmmm' grunted the Banker. 'Are your own Board fully with you on this matter?'

Here it was. This was the point where he had to explain the difference of view between himself and his Chairman.

'My own executive Board yes absolutely' lied Mark without blinking. He hadn't even discussed Houghtons with them. Sure they knew of and supported in general terms his wish to continue to acquire businesses to maintain the growth of Lovells but they didn't know about his secret plan for Houghtons nor did they know what Hans had been doing except the vague comment from Mark that he was researching competitive threats and opportunities.

'They are fully with me on this but I am afraid that Richard Butler has a different view and there is no point in me saying that he doesn't. He believes that we should consolidate what we have, batten down the hatches for a while and then think about modest expansion in two or three years. In my view he is wrong, utterly wrong. Frankly I can see it becoming a problem if he is going to block, or try and block what I want to do which I'm convinced is entirely the right way forward. I hope after tonight you'll share my view'.

The Banker said nothing but returned Mark's stare for a while.

'So what do you propose to do about that? Bit tricky isn't it if the Chairman and Chief Executive don't see eye to eye on such a major element of business strategy? Can be unsettling in the City too you know. Can't both be right can you?'

Well here goes thought Mark. 'No I'm afraid he's wrong and I'm right but I need help to deal with that roadblock'.

'You certainly do if, and I say if, yours is the right course of action. That is the crux of the matter. I have to remind you that Dickie Butler is a man of experience and knowledge and usually his views would be seen as sensible'.

There was silence for a while and Mark wondered if he'd blown it. He looked at Colin who smiled reassuringly then he looked back at the Banker.

'Look Mark I'd like to thank you for coming here this evening and explaining so clearly and openly to me what your business strategy is about and where you see your company going. I understand your problem with Dickie and I need to think about the whole thing. I'd like to consult a couple of other members of the Bank. I have to say though'...........he paused. 'I'm inclined towards your view that to stop and consolidate now may not be the wisest course of action as it could allow competitors to catch you, or worse still maybe even buy some of those businesses that you may be after in due course. Houghtons will be a bigee for you. Sure you can cope with it?'

'Yes absolutely'.

'All right well thank you again for coming. Daniel will show you down' and with handshakes all round the meeting was at an end. Daniel led them along the deeply carpeted corridor to the lift and travelled down with the two visitors shaking their hands when they reached the large marble entrance hall where Graham was sitting reading the Evening Standard.

When they were back in the car Mark who could contain himself no longer looked at Colin and asked 'How did we do or rather how did I do? Will he support me do you think?'

'Yes'.

'Are you sure?'

'No. No-one can be sure of the outcome of those sorts of meetings but I'd say from his final comment that "he was inclined towards your view" was as near as we could have got tonight to a yes. Time will tell but I'll lay you a bet that you've got your first Institution in the bag. By the way I think you handled it fine. You let him talk and ask you questions. That was important. Now I'll buy you a drink, in fact I'll buy you a couple or three' and leaning forward he directed Graham to a club near Bond Street. They stayed for a while talking over the evening's meeting, then later Graham took them home dropping Colin off first before whisking Mark south towards his large house.

Remembering that he had an early start tomorrow with the breakfast meeting with Dickie, as Sir Steven had called him he closed his eyes and allowed himself to drift off to sleep waking when they got home. Reminding Graham that he needed to leave half an hour earlier than usual he crept quietly upstairs, undressed without waking Abi and slipping into bed lay there quietly thinking again of the evening.

'I'm not asleep darling' Abi said quietly. 'Have you had a good evening?'

'Yes' and he pulled her towards him 'but it isn't finished yet' and she sighed happily as he ran his hand under the hem of her nightie and after stroking her bush moved up to fondle her breasts before making love to her.

Next morning Mark was in the office by six forty five and grinned when seven o'clock came and went and The Chairman wasn't to be seen. He knew that it would be difficult for Richard Butler to get here at that early time as normally he didn't arrive until around nine thirty.

Part of the reason why Mark had suggested such an early time was to irritate his Chairman and make it difficult for him, as by being late then he would be at a disadvantage in that he'd have to start the meeting by apologising.

A little after seven twenty five Mark's door opened and The Chairman walked in. He was obviously not in a good mood and clearly disliked having been set up in this way. Mark rubbed salt in when after Richard Butler had said sorry he was a bit late Mark replied breezily 'No problem I've been here for ages as I usually am. Now what do you want to see me about. I didn't know what you wanted for breakfast so I've had some scrambled eggs toast fruit and coffee brought up. Alright?'

They served themselves from the covered dishes that had been sent up from the restaurant and while they started to eat Chairman Butler ran through a list of things he wanted to discuss none of which seemed to Mark to be very important and he said so.

Butler stiffened. 'Mark I had hoped that the three weeks away that you and your new wife have just enjoyed might have brought you to a more conciliatory tone in our relations but unfortunately it does not seem to be so. Now, there are matters that we need to discuss and I want to do that now'.

Sighing deeply Mark listened as more minor issues were raised responding to which he managed to keep his temper but he was a bit shaken when Dickie said that he'd been thinking again about Mark's plans to grow Lovells into a global player through major acquisition and having considered it more and consulted widely in the City, he had to tell Mark that he remained opposed to that strategy and he was sure that the City would be as well.

'Forget it Mark. Consolidate and review in a couple of years that's what we are going to do'.

'No we're bloody well not' yelled Mark. 'We're going to grow big now whether you like it or not so get used to it. I will not be held up by you or anyone else that gets in my way. I know what's right for this Company and I'm going to implement the correct strategy with you or without you, understand?'

'I shall oppose you at every step of the way. I have strong support. Even your own Board are not wholly convinced that you're right'.

'They'll do what I want them to when I have set out the detail and they understand what I am saying is the right way forward. Don't you worry about them. They'll support me. If you won't then that's a pity but let me tell you Richard if you take me on and fight me over this you'll lose. You'd better get used to that fact. I also have contacts and friends in the City you know. I….. will….. win'.

There was silence as the two men glared at each other and Mark's words hung in the air. Getting up Richard Butler stood and stared at Mark. 'I doubt it Mark, I very much doubt it' and he walked slowly to the door and left without speaking further.

Sam put her head round the door. 'Morning' she said brightly. 'Are you having a good day?' and watched as Mark's face relaxed from frozen fury into one of his lovely grins which made her stomach jump.

'Yes brilliant. Bound to be with that tosser in here to start things off eh? How anyone who is supposed to have such experience can believe that we should consolidate and not expand defeats me. Still I am in the process of sorting him out and when it comes to the crunch it'll be him that loses. Believe me Sam I'm going to win'.

She wanted to fling her arms around him and say that of course he would win but she merely smiled.

In the evening Mark and Colin had a meeting with the second Institution on Colin's schedule. This time it was one of the largest Pension Companies and there were two members of the top level Board at the meeting. Like the previous evening the discussions seemed to go well and Mark and Colin left feeling pleased with themselves and thinking that they might now have two Institutions on their side as their hosts hadn't seemed too put out at the knowledge that Mark and his Chairman didn't see eye to eye on strategy.

Mark started to feel more confident that he was going to be able to outmanoeuvre Richard Butler because in spite of his bravado that morning he knew that his Chairman was well connected and to overcome him he was going to have to go right to the top of the major City influencers which was exactly what he and Colin were doing.

Over the next two weeks they met with several other key influencers in the City. One meeting took place in Colin's offices, one was at Ascot Race course where the major Insurance company that they were meeting had a private marquee, one was at Covent Garden Opera House where they took a box and were able to talk confidentially during the intervals, but the others were held at the particular Institution's own premises except for the last one which was with the Deputy Chairman of one of the major Financial Fund Managers a corpulent but short man in his late fifties, and that took place at a smart West End restaurant followed by a nightclub which Colin thought their guest would enjoy.

Arriving at the club Colin led the way pausing at the small desk where a pretty blonde girl said hello to him and smiled at the other two men. After they signed in Colin led the way downstairs from where loud music could be heard. On a small stage at the opposite end of the club a succession of girls came on to writhe and strip to overloud music while in the main floor part of the club there were several tables at which various men sat watching the strippers. Some were alone, some in groups of two or three. Various girls wandered around the floor and approached the men at the tables asking if they'd like some company which they explained would cost £ 150 for them to sit and chat.

The girls were pretty and of different nationalities. If a man said no they moved away without argument and tried another table. Their role was to listen to the men's grumbles about their jobs, their bosses, their wives, their kids, their mortgages, their lives, to laugh at the jokes they were told but primarily to persuade the men to order champagne at ludicrously inflated prices. Once they'd got the first bottle ordered they were adept at continually filling their punter's glass while only wetting their own lips and it wasn't long before a second bottle was ordered.

Later in the early hours of the morning when the club closed around three am then some of the girls could be persuaded for a further fee to go off somewhere with their man for sex.

Settling themselves at a table on the floor of the club they had soon been approached by a selection of girls all of whom they waved away but when one particularly erotic strip act finished Sir Raymond Booth turned to Mark.

'Now then I know you're itching to tell me all about your plans and the problems you are having with Richard Butler. Not surprised that you two don't get on. Chalk and cheese I'd say. He came to see me a couple of weeks ago you know' he paused and seeing Mark's expression went on 'you didn't know did you? No matter he told me all about how he thought Lovells needed to consolidate their position whereas you wanted to expand and make acquisitions. Seemed obvious to me that he was wrong but I didn't enlighten him. Seemed a pity to upset the chap but when Colin here said that you wanted to meet up and chat about Lovell's future strategy then I put two and two together and well, here we are aren't we? I've been talking to a few chums in the City and I gather that you've been doing the rounds to drum up support for your plans. Got to me at last eh?'

'Sorry, I didn't see anyone in any particular order it was all to do with when we could get appointments' replied Mark worried that the financier was miffed that he was the last that they'd seen but reassured that he seemed to have understood the strength of Mark's case without even hearing it directly from him.

'I know' twinkled the older man. 'Can you handle the integration of Houghtons as I gather that's who you're after? Any particular reason why it's them?'

He was well informed thought Mark who would have liked to have told the old financier what Charles Houghton had done to his father's business all those years ago but didn't as then the old man might think the motive was solely personal revenge in which case he'd be unlikely to support it rather than soundly based on business logic which should justify his support. Instead he simply replied that he felt Houghtons was a business in trouble and would make a good strategic fit with Lovells.

'You're right on both counts. I've had my people do a thorough evaluation of yours and Houghton's businesses and I can see the logic and synergy of an amalgamation of the two enterprises. They are in trouble all right and they will make an excellent fit with you but Sir Charles has a reputation as a difficult bugger and being a private company he calls the shots. You'll have to find a way to get him on your side you know'.

'I know. So do I take it that we would have your support Sir Raymond?'

'Good grief yes. Can't say I ever liked Richard Butler. Pompous idiot and I have to tell you I was surprised when he got the job of Chairman. Seems to be pretty useless at it if you ask me. Time for a change of Chairman at Lovells maybe? We'll have to think about that but you need to get on with making your acquisitions as I imagine there will be others after Houghtons won't there? Right. Glad we've had this little chat and that we see things from the same perspective. Nothing else we need to talk about is there as I'd like to get that little darkie over and chat to her' and so saying he beckoned a short slim black girl who switched on a smile, sashayed over to their table and said her name was Marcia.

The old financier from then on ignored Mark and Colin and leaning close to the girl was soon stroking her leg and whispering in her ear. It was later in the evening after another bottle of champagne that he suggested the two of them left the club and went somewhere quieter such as his flat in Kensington. When she pointed out that she wasn't allowed to leave until at least two thirty in the morning he lumbered to his feet and wandered over to the lady who was in charge at the club. After a brief chat he returned and told Marcia that Ruby would be happy for her to leave now.

'How did you do that?'

'Well you see my dear the reason they don't want you or others to leave too early is so that you can persuade blokes like us to buy the very expensive champagne, drinks, cigarettes, meals and so on. As I've paid her for the equivalent of another four bottles of bubbly she's quite happy for you to go'.

'Fantastic you dirty old devil' grinned the black hostess 'but we must leave separately'.

'I know' smiled Sir Raymond. He shook hands with Colin and Mark, wished them luck with their plans, thanked them for a pleasant evening and walked out of the club to meet up with what he described as "his dirty little bit of midnight". How their evening went on and whether he got what he wanted Mark and Colin never knew but what they did know was that they had another Institution on side.

Overall therefore at the end of their charm offensive on the City Institutions they thought that they had six definite yeses, one maybe, one definite no and two undecided. Not bad Colin said.

Now Mark's problem was to decide how to make the approach to Houghtons. He also had to sort out their French business which was still showing no sign of improvement but most of all he had to find a way of actually getting rid of his Chairman hopefully now with the City's support.

In the event he didn't need to worry about Chairman Dickie as The City has its own way of dealing with these things and given the opportunity it can be very influential and effective at creating change in the top management of companies. What it didn't like was being bounced with things that surprised it or that it didn't understand. In this case though the need for change was clearly understood by virtually all the major Institutions and even those that didn't wholly support the change idea wouldn't stand in the way. It took some time but after several months of meetings, discrete phone calls and the odd discussion over a lunch or dinner, a plan was created.

Therefore it was nearly five months after Mark had embarked on his charm offensive with the Institutions that Richard Butler responded with alacrity to the phone call to meet for lunch with two senior City people to discuss Lovells. He was flattered and saw it as an opportunity to present his thoughts and slap down that upstart Mark with his grand ideas for acquisitions and fast growth.

The distinguished gentleman's club where they met had been in existence since the early eighteen hundreds and was quite busy for Wednesday lunchtime. They made small talk over drinks before moving through to the dining room where a table had been reserved in a quiet corner.

Having enjoyed their consommé soup Richard Butler was just starting to outline his ideas for the business while cutting into his rare roast beef, when the bombshell that perhaps he ought to consider moving on was dropped on him. He paused with fork half way to his mouth.

'I beg your pardon? Are you suggesting I give up as Chairman of Lovells?

The fork stayed there hovering between plate and mouth as he took on board the confirmation that this was exactly what was being suggested.

'Richard there's a nice little engineering business in the Midlands that really could do with your sort of skills and ideas for containing growth and concentrating on getting things right' smiled the first Institutional man. 'They need you or someone like you. Look on Lovells as moving on to a new phase'.

'But am I to take it that you disagree with my thoughts on Lovells' queried the beleaguered Chairman rather pompously.

'I wouldn't put it quite like that but we do think that Mark's ideas for growth, whilst definitely having some risks attached to them, are nevertheless extremely well thought out. Bold yes, tough yes, but frankly we'd like to see him succeed. We've listened to what he has to say and we like it'.

'Basically Dickie old man the City wants to back him' added the second Institutional man.

'But I have my reputation to think about. It's not as though I've been there for years and won't it be seen as somewhat strange for me to be going? What about the effect on the share price?'

'Not a problem old boy. You can announce that you feel you've completed what you wanted to do when you took on the Chairmanship and now the business is in fine shape for further advancement. You feel that a new Chairman together with Mark Watson can take the business forward to even greater heights'.

'Completed what I wanted to do eh? Even greater heights' repeated Richard Butler quietly. 'Yes that might sound alright I suppose. When did you have in mind?'

'Well Dickie these things are best done quickly. Now Lovell's AGM is in five week's time so if we all get our skates on we could get an announcement out in time to give the statuary four week's notice of such a change'. What do you say? Come on eat your lunch. This roast beef is really splendid be a shame to waste it and how about some more of this rather nice claret to wash it down?'

Richard Butler thought quickly. He had no option. If the City had made up its mind that it wanted a change of Chairman it would happen whether he liked it or not. He could fight but he'd lose and in the process he'd alienate any support that he might have. Alternatively he could willingly go along with the plan and still be a respected person with the City's support.

'The Midlands you say? Needs my sort of skills? Whereabouts in the Midlands?'

'Coventry'.

God Coventry somewhere near Birmingham. Awful sort of place, dirty, full of factories, relic of the industrial revolution, no culture, spoke with funny accents and rained a lot, still he could go up and down by train and wouldn't have to stay up there so perhaps it wouldn't be too bad he supposed.

'As a matter of fact I had been thinking that it might be time to seek pastures new you know. Lovells has achieved a lot during my time short though its been and I can look back on the fact that it is an infinitely better business now than when I joined. Oh yes, no doubt about that, no doubt at all'.

'Quite. Now how about some dessert Richard?'

'Yes thanks. Do you have anyone in mind as my replacement, umm I mean my successor?'

'Yes. We've sounded out Tim Nelson. Good chap. Keen to take it on. Glad you can see the way forward Dickie old man. Resign this week will you? Good. Now let's get some brandies organised for the coffee shall we?'

So it was done. Ruthlessly, silently, swiftly, effectively. One Chairman removed and another already primed and waiting in the wings ready to be installed.

Richard Butler had another large brandy in a bar on Victoria station while waiting for his train. Arriving at Crawley he caught a taxi from the station to Lovell's offices and having taken the lift to the executive floor wandered into Sam's outer office reeking of brandy fumes and swaying slightly.

'Is he free?' he asked a little too loudly making his way towards Mark's closed door.

'I don't think there's anyone with him at the moment. Let me check' and she ran to get in front of the Chairman, knocked and opened Mark's door.

'Mark, the Chairman is here. He'd like to see you'.

'Now if you please as it is a matter of some importance' and he pushed past her and strode in. Mark looked up in surprise and noticed Sam now behind the Chairman was making movements close to her mouth with her hand as if holding an imaginary glass to indicate that he'd been drinking.

'Richard what a pleasant surprise. Would you like some coffee?' and he rose from his desk and led the way over to the easy chairs on the far side of his office.

'No. Mark I've been thinking. We don't always see eye to eye I admit but looking back over the time that we've worked together then we've achieved a great deal. Look at where Lovells is now compared with where it was before I......we came onto the scene'. He held up his hand to stop Mark commenting. 'No don't interrupt. I have been considering my role and what I want to do now and frankly I think that I've achieved most of what I set out to do when I accepted the position here. Look at the share price and where it now stands. Look at how we've improved profitability, cut costs, reduced waste and streamlined our factory operations. Yes we've done a lot and I'm proud of the, I might say, not inconsiderable part that I've played in that process'.

Mark was getting angry listening to the other man pontificating and was about to say that frankly Richard Butler had done none of those things and that any improvements were entirely down to him when the Chairman staggered him by his next statement.

'So taking all things into consideration including the fact that I've been approached by some rather important people in the City where as you know I am pretty well known and asked to take on the Chairmanship of a major well known engineering business in the Midlands....... I have decided to resign as Chairman of Lovells'.

He sat back and watched Mark's face. Yes, he thought that he'd put that over rather well. Careful application of the reason for the change made it sound as though he was needed more in the engineering business than at Lovells. Frankly he had no idea of the size of his new business but didn't do any harm to chuck in the description "major well known". That added a certain understated importance he thought and seemed to flow off the tongue nicely. He'd practiced his little speech on the train and reflecting on it now could see where he could improve it a little more for when he had to give it next time. The Board tomorrow he imagined and then at the golf club on Sunday probably. Yes at the golf club he'd increase the effect of the influence that he'd had on Lovell's results.

'Now as you know technically it is the Board of Lovells that appoints me and so it is to them that I need to tender my resignation. Would tomorrow be satisfactory? That will give time to get the notification out to shareholders in time for the AGM'.

Mark was dumfounded and delighted. It was almost as much as he could do not to leap up and shout hooray but composing his face into a placid look he replied solemnly 'Yes I imagine it will. You've really thought about this haven't you? Well I'm sure you've taken the right step. I'll call an extraordinary Board meeting for tomorrow. Ten o'clock suit you? Anything else we need to discuss Richard?'

'No. I'll toddle along now and write out my resignation letter. Sam type it for me will she?'

'Of course. I'll ask her to come to see you. Can you ask her to pop in as you go out please?' and he sat back totally bemused.

'What was that all about? He stank like a brewery? Hey put me down' Sam squealed as when she came into his office he picked her up and swung her round two or three times.

'Halleluiah. Halle-fucking-luiah. The stupid old coot's resigning. I told you I'd get him out didn't I Sam. All the talking in the City that Colin and I did has paid off. He's going. So much for his much vaunted connections. We've got him. Now nothing can stop me. Now I'll get Hou.......erm I mean now I'll get what I want. You've no idea what it means to me. Go and see him in a little while as he's writing his resignation letter. Type it up and get him to sign it. Take a copy and let me have that and lock the original in the safe. Next tell everyone that there is an extraordinary Board meeting at ten o'clock tomorrow. Must attend. No excuses or absences. I want everyone there and get me Colin on the phone'.

She hadn't seen him so happy for a long time. 'So who's going to replace him?'

Mark almost dropped her. The smile vanished from his face. 'Shit I've no idea. Oh fuck it could be someone worse. No, they wouldn't do that to me would they? Would they Sam?'

'I'm sure they, whoever they are wouldn't. Why don't you go and ask him?'

The words were barely out of her mouth before Mark shot out of his office through hers and into the corridor, nearly knocking a couple of people flying as he rushed down to Richard Butler's office.

'Did your City contacts say anything about your successor?' he asked as he burst in.

'What, oh yes. Chap called Tim Nelson, quite well known I believe. They think you and he will get on like a house on fire. Now I must get on with this letter. I'll be ready for Sam to collect the draft in about half an hour'.

Tim Nelson mused Mark. He'd heard the name and as he walked back to his office he determined to find out something about this person who could be his next Chairman. Richard Butler was right in stating that it was the Board that appointed the Chairman but he had to be sure that it was someone with whom he could work. Back in his office he spoke with Colin and asked if he knew a Tim Nelson. He did and Mark liked the sound of what he heard.

Later in the afternoon, Richard Butler strolled into Mark's office and announced that he'd given the letter to Sam to type and that he'd be in the next day to attend the Board meeting and formally tender his resignation. It wasn't long after he'd left when Sam rang though and said she had a Tim Nelson on the phone who'd said that he thought Mark might want to talk with him.

'You bet I do. Put him through'. He waited till the call connected. 'Hello Mark Watson speaking'.

'Mark. This is Tim Nelson. I imagine you know why I'm ringing you?' The unseen caller had a strong, pleasant, cultured voice.

'Yes'.

'Might be a good idea if we could meet. As I gather time is rather critical in relation to notification to shareholders and the AGM I guess sooner rather than later would be good. Are you free this evening by any chance? If it helps I could come down to you in Crawley to make things easier for you'.

'That would help yes. What time will you get here?'

Tim explained that he had to finish off an existing meeting in London then he'd get to Victoria and catch a train as soon as he could but that he hoped to arrive around seven. Mark liked the sound of the man but reserving judgment until they'd met said he'd have Graham waiting at the station exit with a name board to collect him.

Sam consumed with curiosity decided to work late as she wanted to meet the potential new Chairman and also see how Mark took to him. She'd hated seeing Mark got angry or depressed as a result of his disagreements with Richard Butler and she hoped for his sake that he liked the new appointee better. It was nearly seven thirty when she knocked on Mark's door and introduced the new man.

'Hello I'm Tim Nelson. Delighted to meet you'. Shaking hands Mark invited him to sit down. Tim was well dressed in an obviously expensive dark grey suit with faint white stripes, a pale blue shirt, red spotted tie with matching handkerchief in his top pocket, which in some people looked an affectation but seemed somehow just right with Tim and highly polished black shoes. A short man in his late fifties, around five foot five, slim with fair hair, cultured with a surprisingly deep voice, he created an immediate impression of great confidence and competence.

Sam hovered, sorted out coffees then checking that she wasn't needed any more bade the two men goodnight.

Mark always felt that first impressions of people counted for a great deal. Often he'd backed his judgement of people based on an initial meeting and he'd rarely been wrong. He sensed that Tim might be a man with whom he would work well. The next two hours confirmed that.

Tim asked him to explain how he saw the business and like so many others was captivated by Mark's grasp of the business, the ease with which he explained complicated elements of strategy and most of all the evident passion and commitment that he had for Lovells. His eyes pierced with an intensity that Tim had never seen before and he realised he was in the presence of a man totally committed to his ideals and goals.

The potential new Chairman asked probing but sensible questions and although he had an easy manner he was obviously tough. The more Mark talked with him and responded to the questions the more he liked Tim. They worked late before Graham drove them to a local restaurant where they continued talking over a meal before Tim caught a late train back to London.

The two men parted each secure in the knowledge that they were going to be a good team together. Graham drove Mark home and Abi saw a very excited husband when he walked in that night. He talked non stop until Abi said that although she loved to hear him talk abut the business she was tired and had to go to bed and was he coming. He said no, as he was too hyped up at the moment and needed to sit and think so going to his study he did with the help of a couple of large whiskeys.

The next day the two crucial Board meetings took place.

Opening the first at ten o'clock Mark explained to a slightly puzzled Board that he'd called this extraordinary board meeting as the Chairman had a statement to make and then sitting back he handed over to Richard Butler who solemnly and slowly read it his letter of resignation. Concluding he handed each member a copy before elaborating on his achievements at Lovells and the need that the City now had for him to go elsewhere.

There was a certain amount of embarrassed looking around the table by members of the Board who all knew that he and Mark simply hadn't got on and that the achievements which Richard Butler attributed to himself were in reality Mark's work. They were also deeply impressed that somehow their Chief Executive had succeeded in the difficult task of getting The Chairman ousted by the City. Whilst recognising his skill in doing this, for some it gave them a slight shiver of fear as they understood the completeness of Mark's power and influence which now not only extended throughout the Company but also into the inner workings of the mighty City.

Mark said that the Board would accept his resignation from the date of the coming AGM and then drew the meeting to an end. Richard Butler left and after he'd gone Mark advised that there would be a second meeting that afternoon so that the candidate to be the new Chairman could meet the team. He added that he'd met him last night, liked him a great deal and thought that he was exactly the sort of Chairman they needed. Later when the Board had also met him they agreed and so the Lovell's Board formerly asked Tim Nelson to become their next Chairman effective from the coming AGM.

The Lovells share price was now over £6. Over the past two weeks it had popped above for a day to £6.02 and then dropped back to £5.89 where it stayed unmoving for two days before climbing to £5.92, £5.96 and then finally over the major barrier to £6.04, up again to £6.11 before settling back at £6.08. This was important as it showed that Lovells was a stock in demand and that the Institutions were now buyers of the shares. Cautious buyers certainly but buyers nevertheless. It also meant that the City were happy about the change of Chairman.

The AGM went smoothly. Richard made a short speech explaining his reasons for resigning. The various obligatory pieces of business were run through quickly and after the formal votes to accept the report and accounts, re-appoint the non-executive directors, the auditors and solicitors, together with a few minor technical points to do with issued share capital Richard proposed the confirmation of Tim Nelson's appointment as Chairman. It was passed unanimously.

Tim spoke briefly and was fulsome in his compliments about Mark being the driving force of the business and how much he was looking forward to working with him. He then declared the meeting closed and all adjourned to an anti-room for sandwiches, snacks and a glass of wine. By about three o'clock most people had drifted away so Mark offered a lift back to the office to Sam, Tom Gibson their recently appointed new Finance Director and Roy Bennett the Purchasing Director.

Graham zipped them through the traffic and they were soon back in Crawley.

The following day the financial pages of most newspapers reported on the change of Chairman at Lovells giving it varying amounts of coverage. In the two main tabloids it was covered somewhat emotionally.

The Express blazoned **"BUTLER BUNDLED OUT"** while The Daily Mail's **"BUTLER BOUNCED"** was their approach. Both papers then gave a little more detail about Lovells and how it had grown under Mark's leadership with little help from the pompous Richard Butler. The Independent went with the intriguing headline **"WHAT THE BUTLER DIDN'T SEE"** and hinted darkly of a plot by Mark and The City. The Times **"CHANGE OF CHAIRMAN AT LOVELLS"** was more circumspect, whilst The Daily Telegraph led with the phrase **"NELSONS VICTORY"** and devoted several favourable column inches to Lovells and Mark in which although not saying that Richard Butler had been kicked out left its readers in no doubt that the City had worked behind the scenes to effect the change to support the dynamic Chief Executive of Lovells in his ambitions plans.

Mark read them all smiling with grim satisfaction.

CHAPTER 28

Gatwick airport at six o'clock in the morning was just coming to life. Some kiosks were already open others were in the process of opening. People were milling around with long queues for charter flights to holiday destinations while business people made their way purposefully to their requisite check in desks.

Sam wearing a mustard coloured jacket, white jumper and black trousers met Mark at the airport. He took her small overnight case, added it to his own for check in which was quick and soon they were on the flight to Rome.

After landing they walked into the arrivals hall to be met by one of Lovells senior Italian managers who led them to his car which was parked illegally just round the corner from the terminal building. Smiling his thanks to a nearby police officer with whom he shook hands in the process slipping the official a large denomination bank note, he drove off with some panache and shortly they were on the motorway leading to Lovells offices. The purpose of the meeting was to finalise acquisition discussions with a local competitor one of the three targets that Mark had spoken to the bankers about.

Lovell's Italian business was a good one, growing fast, profitable and staffed by a senior team who continually demonstrated a "can do" attitude much liked by Mark.

It was a long day starting with meetings all morning in Lovell's offices dealing with the current trading position and future strategy which Mark happily endorsed. After lunch they discussed Houghtons and then later in the day they prepared for the six o'clock meeting with the Italian competitor ItalaChem which was a small business that needed either to be bought out and integrated into a larger company like Lovells, or given a massive injection of capital to enable it to pay off its mounting debts and re-invest in itself.

Lovells had no intention of just putting money into them they wanted to buy them and gain the benefit of their trade, sales contracts and connections by converting the product range to their own. Mark was there to finalise the deal.

The talks went on until about eight o'clock when they broke for some food brought in by a nearby catering firm, then they continued

455

talking over spaghetti, chicken, salads and wine. Mark didn't drink alcohol and stuck to mineral water.

By ten thirty the deal was done. ItalaChem would sell to Lovells and the two teams shook hands on a "sale in principle agreement" with most of the terms and details agreed and only a few minor issues to sort out. After they had left Mark stretched and walked round the room. 'A good day's work I think' he smiled. 'Great job Louigi. Wouldn't have happened without your recent efforts. Talk to Legal and get an Italian lawyer to draw up the sale agreement and let's try and wrap it up by the end of the month. Right if there's nothing else I'm off to bed. I've an early start again tomorrow to Paris. Can you get a taxi for Sam and I please?'

It was all a bit of an anticlimax as they stood around chatting until the taxi arrived but soon Mark and Sam were on their way to the airport hotel where they were both staying for the night.

'Nightcap?' she queried after they checked in.

'No but can we just sit down and run through a few things for the rest of this week. I'd had enough of those offices or we could have done it there but frankly it was a bit stuffy and I needed a break. Now where's the itinerary for tomorrow?'

Sam reached into her briefcase for tomorrow's programme in France. The discussions didn't take long then Mark yawned and stood up. 'Goodnight I'm off to bed'.

There was no invitation for her to join him. It was a simple statement of fact and much as she yearned for him he hadn't made any offer, not even a hint. They travelled up in the lift together. He got out at the fourth floor. 'Thanks for your help today' he muttered while she continued up to the sixth.

In her room she sat on the bed for a while deep in thought. She wanted Mark back it was as simple as that. Since he'd got married he'd ignored her sexually and clearly now saw her just as a secretary but that wasn't what she wanted. Frankly it was more than just wanting him she was desperate to get him back. Sharing him with Abi meant having an affair with a married man which she knew was morally wrong but she simply didn't care. She wanted him so much it hurt.

It didn't take her long to decide what she was going to do and having changed she made her way back down two floors. Opening his door to her knock he looked surprised to see her as he said 'Hi did we forget something?'

'No Mark. We didn't, you did. You forgot us. You and me' and she pushed him backwards.

'Ah look Sam' he said as he walked across the room and stopped by the desk unit on the far side of the room turning to face her. 'We can't. There's Abi to consider. What we had is over. It's strictly business between us now'.

She stepped into the room and pushed the door closed. 'If you truly think that then I'll leave. If you want me to go I will....... but I don't think you want that do you?'

She took a step towards him. He neither moved nor spoke just looked at her.

'Do you want me to go?' Her voice had become quieter as she took a further step.

Yet another step meant half the distance between them had now been crossed. Her tongue peeped out between her lips as still looking at his face she undid the top button which was one of several that ran up the front of her pale blue dress. Undoing a couple more and giving a shrug of her shoulders and a wriggle of her hips the dress slid down to her ankles revealing that she was only wearing a pair of dark blue lace top stockings, a dark blue suspender belt and high heeled dark blue shoes. Apart from that she was naked.

Her next step left the dress on the floor. 'Shall I leave' she asked softly watching the way his eyes roved over her body. 'Yes go on look. Look as much as you like as it's all for you no-one else. You like me like this don't you?' she continued softly, hooking thumbs and forefingers into her front suspender straps. Stretching them away from her legs she let them go so they snapped back against her thighs with a crack. Taking a new step she was almost near enough to touch him.

A final step and still he hadn't moved or said anything just stared into her eyes as her hands reached out and undid his shirt buttons before spreading it wide open.

'Do you really want me to go?' she whispered watching his face as she crouched down face upturned, her eyes never leaving his. Quickly her hands felt for then undid his two trouser band buttons and zip. The trousers fell to his feet and his boxer shorts quickly followed. His penis reared up at her but holding it up against his belly with one hand she leaned forward to cup his balls in the other. Now her eyes left his as she kissed his balls before gently sucking each in turn. As he sighed loudly her tongue travelled slowly up the underside of his penis to the very tip where her lips encircled and then released him replaced by her hand which slowly rubbed him as she looked at his face and in an almost inaudible voice asked the question again.

'Shall I go Mark?'

When he remained silent her lips enclosed him again. Moving her head slowly up and down the length of him she felt his hands stroke her hair. While she squeezed in her cheeks and applied as much suction as possible he started to slowly move back and forth in time with her and before long he gripped her hair tightly starting to hurt her as he moved more quickly. She continued moving her lips back and forth on him while at the same time her hands gripped his balls and massaged them hard. Her teeth nipped him from time to time.

Feeling him grip her hair so tightly that it really did hurt suddenly she tasted his warm eruptions which coincided with a loud exhalation from him as he pressed himself against her face.

She continued to move until he'd finished then leaning back onto her haunches she let him slide out of her lips and making a circle with the thumb and forefinger of her left hand she firmly gripped the base of his still erect penis and slid the tight ring up to the tip. As she expected a small emision appeared but with a quick flick of her tongue it was gone. Repeating the process with the thumb and forefinger of her other hand this time nothing appeared. She'd emptied him, for now.

Smiling she took his penis in her hand and led the way to the bed saying 'Come here'.

As he lay down she leaned over him to kiss him letting her tongue explore the inside of his mouth as she knew this excited him after she given oral love to him. While she was kissing him she wondered if Abi did what she'd just done for him but putting thoughts of Mark's wife out of her mind she kissed him all over his face, his eyes, his chest, his nipples, his belly and finally back to his lips and while she kissed him her hands continually played with his cock and balls.

Determined to show him what he was missing she did everything that she knew to show him how much she loved and wanted him.

Climbing on top of him she whispered 'Now I'm going to fuck the brains out of your skull darling' and rode him slowly at first but then with increasing vigour to another shattering climax.

'Sam' he said softly when they'd both calmed down. It was the first word that he'd spoken since she'd started to seduce him. 'Sam' he repeated and hugged her into him.

'Darling just lie there. I'm here for you now and everything will be alright as I can make you so happy. Hold me tightly darling, hold me all night' and with those comments they cuddled quietly together.

Mark was experiencing mixed emotions. Regret and concern that he'd betrayed Abi but worryingly arousing thoughts about Sam who for her part was just happy that she'd got her Mark back again. For how long she didn't know but she'd got him for now and sighing happily she too slept.

The alarm jerked them both awake. It was six o'clock. They were cuddled together with him lying behind her.

'Do we have to leave so early Mark? Couldn't we get a later flight..... please? I'll make it worth your while I promise,' she said softly looking over her shoulder.

He looked at her. 'There's masses to do in Paris you know and Hans is coming over just after lunch but ok hang on I'll ask the hotel to see if there's a later flight'.

Picking up the phone he dialled the concierge and explained that they were booked onto the Alitalia eight o'clock flight to Paris. Could he see if there were any later flights this morning?

'Si il signore, un momento per favore'. *(Yes Sir. A moment please)*

Mark held the phone and ran his fingers up and down Sam's spine while he waited.

'Si ci e un Alitalia a quindici undici un altro, Air France, a quindici quaranta' *(Yes there is an Alitalia at eleven fifteen or another, Air France, at eleven forty)*.

'Sorry can you speak English please'. He listened to the translation and then replied 'Ok switch our bookings to that later Alitalia will you'.

The concierge who was used to making flight changes for guests at short notice confirmed that it was no problem and that Mark should go to customer services at the airport to have the ticket change endorsed.

'Right my girl now we have a little longer in bed' and as he spoke Sam felt him rubbing his erect prick along her bum crack. She waited for a few moments but he continued to do it.

'Mark if you really want to do that I don't mind trying .... but you'll have to be gentle with me'.

'No here's fine but thanks for the offer' he chuckled reaching round to play with her pussy but filing what she'd said into his memory before pushing himself into to her from behind realising that during the night she'd taken off her sexy underwear.

She for her part was glad that he turned down her offer of anal sex. A former boyfriend used to like to do it so she'd obliged him a couple of times but she hadn't enjoyed it and found it extremely uncomfortable. With Mark who was so much bigger in the cock department she wasn't sure that she could have taken him inside her, still as she would do anything for him she'd offered and that was what mattered. Something else that mistresses did and wives probably didn't she grinned to herself and then forgot all about it as Mark pulled her into a kneeling position and started to pound in and out of her.

Leaning on her elbows and pressing her face down onto the bed sheet she pushed her herself back into him in time with his rapid rhythm. He reached around her cupping her breasts gently pinching her nipples. She grunted as sliding himself out of her very wet pussy he flipped her onto her back before re-entering her.

He moved slowly in her while kissing her lips and breasts. 'Come on this is for us both' he whispered as he leaned forward. Encouraged she gritted her teeth and concentrated on the feelings that were starting inside her which soon together with Mark's careful attention to her needs using his cock, his lips and his hands started the waves of passion rising in her culminating in an orgasm so intense that as well as screaming as it happened made her cry tears of happiness before her lover climaxed as well.

Clinging to him she relaxed and slowly let herself down from the peak to which he'd just taken her. 'Mark my darling, my own dear darling Mark thank you. That was so wonderful. You're so........' but her voice tailed off. 'I........' she paused as she'd nearly said that she loved him. She did desperately but telling him would be a huge risk as it might frighten him off.

'What?'

'Nothing. I just wanted you to know that you're wonderful' and she took him in her arms and said quietly 'Just hold me again'.

They lay entwined together for nearly an hour until with the clock showing seven thirty Mark commented 'Come on it really is time we got up now. I'll go shower and you should go back to your own room to get dressed'. Throwing back the covers he got out of bed.

'Time for a quickie?' Sam pouted as she twisted herself around to point her naked bum at him.

'Out you little minx' he roared lunging at her aiming a smack at her pert bottom. She tried to swing herself forward but her arm gave way and she flopped onto her tummy just as his hand landed with a mighty crack on her right buttock.

'Yow. That hurt'.

'Sorry didn't mean it to be that hard. Any rate come on Sam fun's over, time to get dressed and go to work' and she realised he meant it. His mind was now clicking into work mode and away from her so getting out of bed she picked up the dress from the floor and quickly buttoned it up, slipped on her shoes, rolled the stockings and suspender belt into a little bundle in her hand and blowing him a kiss opened the door.

'Give me half an hour to get decent and I'll come back here shall I?'

'Yes I'll get some breakfast ordered up for us and Sam......thanks. Seems such an inadequate thing to say but you know what I mean'.

'Yes darling I know what you mean'. Smiling she left his room and wandered happily down the corridor to the lifts, up two floors and into her own room where she slipped off the dress and turned on the shower.

Peering in the mirror she could clearly see a vivid red mark on her buttock. After staring at it for a few moments and without quite knowing why she raised her fingers to her lips kissed them and transferred the kiss to the red mark.

'I'm all yours darling Mark to do with whatever you wish' she whispered as she stepped into the hot shower.

They met up again around half past eight. Mark had ordered scrambled eggs and cold Italian meats for himself and some fruit and cereals for her. He was doing his usual trick of eating one handed, writing notes with the other and talking on the phone at the same time. Pointing he invited her to help herself to food and coffee and while she ate and waited for him to finish talking she looked around the room and stared for a while at the bed where she had been able to love him and hopefully bring him back to her. Wondering if he would ever leave Abi and live with her she was dreaming quietly of such a potentially blissful scene when she realised that he'd put the phone down and was looking at her.

'Sorry what did you say?'

'I said we need to get going soon. Can you settle the bills while I just make a quick call to Tim Nelson?'.

The flight was late leaving and Mark got tetchy waiting in the airport but cheered up a little as on the flight the pilot managed to make up about ten minutes time even on that short journey. A car met them and whisked them to their Paris offices where Mark marched straight into Jacques office.

'Bonjour Mark. How are you? Now what can I do for you. As you set up this visit at short notice I've not prepared anything for you'.

'I'm fine thank you', but you won't be in a minute he thought.

'Jacques I'll come straight to the point. At previous meetings I've told you that I wanted the French business sorted out and turned round. You have clearly failed to do that. I've spoken to you about the situation here several times and all I get is excuses. Time has run out. I want you to leave the business now. Co-operate and go quietly and we'll sort out a decent severance deal for you. Fight me or argue and you'll get not a brass euro as I'll fire you for incompetence. You can sue me if you want but we'll fight you all the way. The choice is yours'.

'Mark you don't understand. Things here are difficult'.

'That's why I pay you a large salary to deal with the difficult things. I'm not going to argue with you. Clear your desk and go. Shall we say one hour? I have your replacement on the way here now. It's Hans Janssen from our Dutch business although recently he's been working for me on a special project. I'll introduce him to your team and settle him in. Will you brief your team about your departure or shall I?'

'Does it make any difference what I want or say?'

'Depends on whether you want a good severance package. By the way here is what I will pay you if you go quietly and quickly. Read it, sign it and it's all over. Argue about it, refuse to sign and you get nothing'.

Jacques carefully studied the closely typed sheets of paper that Mark laid in front of him. The terms were generous providing he left immediately without any fuss. He'd have to agree as he needed the money to tide him over until he could find another job. He knew Mark wouldn't negotiate or give in. No, there was no realistic option but to agree to sign. He found his pen, signed with a flourish and handed the paper back to Mark.

'All right Mark. I know it's no good arguing with you. Your mind is obviously made up. I shall leave with dignity. I will call my team together, those that are here today that is and tell them I am leaving. I'll leave it to you to introduce Hans to them after I've gone. It's sad you know as given more time I am sure I could have turned this business around. Still time is not with me. Alors. C'est la vie. Au revoir Mark'.

'Good bye Jacques' and he walked out leaving the Frenchman to sort out his personal effects and call his team together. He walked along the corridor until he found the office in which Sam had installed herself and he nodded confirmation to her question as to whether Jacques had gone quietly.

'Let me know when Hans arrives will you'.

The rest of the day passed quickly. He introduced Hans to the now sullen and surly French team. He told them that he expected them to support Hans and reminded them that the reason that there had been a change was because the business simply wasn't performing. He made it clear that he had every confidence in Hans and looked forward to rapidly improving results.

'Keep me posted Hans and if you need any help shout, OK?' were his final words to the new head of the French business.

More phone calls to the UK and America, and a quick couple of calls to other European businesses and then he and Sam left for Charles De Gaulle airport and a flight back to Gatwick where Graham picked them up. First they dropped Sam off at her flat then as he was driven home Mark thought about Sam and the night they'd had together and realised that much as he loved Abi and he did, he simply couldn't give up Sam.

Abi felt that he was thoughtful and distant during the evening shrugging it off as work pressure but she was surprised when they went to bed that he didn't try and make love to her even when she ran her hand over his chest and down to his penis. Usually he was raring to go when he'd been away.

'Darling do you mind if we don't I'm totally knackered' he muttered turning over and lay thinking about Sam before going to sleep. Disappointed but not concerned Abi lay awake for a while listening to his rhythmic breathing before sleep also overcome her.

He left early the next morning his mind still in turmoil over his betrayal of Abi but his feelings for Sam. Graham driving him straight into London for a meeting noticed that his boss was grumpy and so took care to keep quiet but while Mark was in his meeting he rang back to warn Sam that their boss was in a bad mood.

Coming out of the meeting Graham caught another grump as he asked Mark if it had gone well. He got a 'No fucking awful if you must know' reply and so keeping quiet he drove his boss back to Crawley as quickly as he could while Mark reflected on the unsatisfactory discussions with lawyers which he'd just had.

He'd wanted a review of how best to approach Houghtons for a takeover. They had warned that it would be a very difficult target to capture as not only was it a private company but it was run with a rod of iron by Sir Charles Houghton himself who would be the key to get agreement to sell. Their view of achieving this was close to zero but they did advise starting some approaches to other directors in the business to try and win over some of them.

One good thing though was that a lawyer called Caroline Burton had been on fine form in the meeting. She seemed to understand why Houghton's was such an important acquisition and had helped Mark to think creatively around the problem. They'd needed someone like her to sharpen up their legal department he thought but the problem remained of how to actually get hold of Houghtons and he brooded on it as he was driven back to his office.

Sam spotted his bad mood immediately he walked into her office. Even if Graham hadn't tipped her off she'd have known that this was going to be a day when fireworks would go off anytime. So it was. Every meeting resulted in rows or rebukes from him to the participants. His telephone calls were bad tempered and the message quickly went round the business to be very careful what was said to him that day.

When she went in to his office at the end of the day to check whether he wanted anything else done that evening she decided to try and find out what was the cause of his bad mood. After all only twenty four hours earlier they had been so intimate and he'd been his wonderful loving sexy self.

'Well you've managed to hack off most people today. What's up?'

He looked up at her and his eyes lanced into her making her shiver as she felt she'd been pierced. He stared for some time and then said softly 'Nothing. You going now?' and looked down at his papers. She felt dismissed. Should she stay and probe further? It was difficult with him in this sort of mood. He might relax and invite her to sit down and unburden himself or he could fly into one of his real tempers.

Not willing to risk the latter reaction she simply said 'Goodnight' then turning at the door added 'I'm here anytime, anywhere, anyhow, for anything you want. Don't work too late'.

When she'd gone he stared at the door that had closed behind her. Damn he thought and getting up walked to her office but she'd left. All that remained was the smell of her perfume and the papers, files and other paraphernalia that was neatly stacked or stored in her office. He wandered around touching her chair, her word processor screen and her desk before walking slowly back into his own office where he poured himself yet another cup of coffee and sitting in his big swivel chair contemplated life with Abi and Sam.

He knew that what he and Sam had done was wrong but somehow he knew they'd do it again of that there was no doubt. Finishing his coffee he rang down for Graham to get the car ready and locking his desk and office he was driven home.

Graham carefully kept his greeting to a simple 'Evening. Straight home is it?'

'Yes please. Have you had a good day because I've had a lousy one but you probably know that already?'

'I did hear you were a bit touchy boss. Still that's life ain't it?' and he lapsed into silence waiting to see if Mark responded in which case

465

they could have a chat as they sometimes did or whether there would be a silence all the way. It was quiet for a while until Mark asked about Graham's wife who'd been unwell and had been to the doctors for an examination.

'Well she needs an operation on her back but it'll be about two years on the waiting list. Terrible ain't it what the NHS is like nowadays and her in such pain. Shocking it is to see her like that. Still nothing to be done about it just got to put up with it and wait'.

'Maybe' and then silence returned as Mark read some documents, scanned through the Evening Standard newspaper and wrote something using the top of his briefcase as a table. When the car stopped outside Mark's house he leaned forward and handed Graham a cheque which the driver saw was made out on Mark's own personal account, not a company cheque.

'Four thousand quid. What's that for boss?'

'For your wife's operation. Get it done privately. Should be all over in weeks rather than waiting a couple of years'.

'Here I can't accept that Mark'.

'You can and will. Goodnight. Usual time tomorrow please and don't mention this again' he said tapping the cheque in Graham's hand.

Now you see thought Graham as he drove away that was what was so amazing about Mark. A bastard to work for but blessed occasionally with great generosity.

Many weeks passed in the usual whirlwind of meetings, discussions, negotiations, frequent trips abroad including a quick two day visit to America and the other myriad of things that were involved in running an international business. Mark had also been keeping in close touch with Hans now firmly established as head of the French business and was pleased with the progress that was being made. It was already obvious that improvements were coming through and the predicted results showed that the profit decline would soon stop and start to turn into profit growth.

Lovells had put out several press releases confirming the expected improved results from France and this was noticed by the City who reflected their general approval by pushing up the Lovells share price on the London Stock Exchange so that it now stood at £ 6.54.

The French bank from which Mark had borrowed money to fund the French expansion was reminded that its interest rates on the loan would have to be reduced as the situation in Lovells French business was improving and after some grudging negotiations they agreed to reduce the interest rate by half of one percent.

One afternoon Hans rang.

'Mark we have a problem with the Union. We need to close the old factory near Marseilles and integrate it with the new one in Toulouse. They are utterly opposed to it and we have come to the end of weeks of negotiations with no solution. We now face the prospect of a long and damaging strike which we might not even win. I must shut that old factory as I can save millions of euros but if we have a strike I'll lose millions'.

'Whatever happens we have to have those integration benefits Hans. Who is the union leader causing the problem?'

'Some guy called Marcel something or other. Not sure of his surname. I think you've met him in the past'.

'And he's the sticking point?' Mark's mind was flashing back to a dinner so long ago with Andrew Spicer when the spook had said that Marcel could be bought off by providing young men for sex. 'OK Hans thanks for telling me. Let me think about the problem for a while'.

Ringing off he asked Sam to get him Andrew Spicer. After the initial pleasantries Mark came to the point. 'A long time ago we spoke about a French Union leader in the south of France. We have a problem with him and you said that there were ways to help gain his co-operation. We need to activate that co-operation. How do I go about it?'

'Hold on' and down the phone line he could hear the sounds of a computer keyboard being tapped. 'Ah ha yes Marcel Devreux. Likes young men. Right what do you want to do? Shall I make the arrangements for you?'

'Tell me what has to be done and we'll organise it'.

'I'll call you back either later this evening but you organise nothing, we'll do all that for you' and the call ended.

A sequence of phone calls followed starting with the first from Andrew Spicer to a contact in Paris who listened carefully and then rang someone in Marseilles who in turn asked a few questions for clarification and then agreed to "look into matters and ring back". He did. The Paris man rang Andrew, who rang Mark at home later that same evening just as he was going to follow Abi up to bed.

'Right all fixed. Invite the French union team to your factory in Toulouse next Tuesday to meet with your guys to further discuss the factory closure. We've checked that he's available so we've made arrangements to put Marcel up in an hotel in Toulouse for the Monday night. The necessary friendly company will be provided. Naturally no mention of this to your people but let's just see where things go the next morning. No guarantees of course. Good luck' and he rang off.

Mark felt excited at the prospect of resolving the French problem and Abi saw when he'd undressed that he was fully erect so smiling happily she held out her arms to welcome him to bed and to her body.

Ringing Hans the next morning Mark suggested that they set up a make or break meeting with the union next Tuesday. I could pop over on Wednesday to see how you've got on. I have a feeling you might make some progress'.

'Why do you think that?'

'Oh just a hunch, premonition perhaps. Keep in touch'.

What Hans of course didn't know was that the following Monday evening Marcel checked into the small discrete hotel in the southern part of Toulouse and went first to the restaurant where he feasted on pate de fois gras, wild duck cooked very rare, salad, some very smelly soft French cheese all washed down with a good bottle of burgundy and finished off with a large brandy.

Retiring to his room he read the paper for a while until there was a quiet knock on the door which he opened with some excitement. A middle aged woman stood there and behind her he could see two young men.

'Monsieur je pense que vous prevoyez que quelques jeunes homes vous joignent per compagne ce soir? *(Sir I think that you are expecting some young men to join you for company this evening?)*

'Oui tres bien. Entrez mes petit personnes'. *(Yes very good. Come in my little people.)*

The lady outside his door nodded and ushered two young men, one short, dark and around seventeen the other taller with long fair hair perhaps a year older, dressed in jeans, tee shirts and trainers into the room reminding them that she'd collect them tomorrow morning around seven o'clock. Marcel beamed as licking his thick fleshy lips in anticipation of an enjoyable evening of debauchery he shut and locked the door.

Next morning the Lovells team were assembled in the Toulouse office waiting for the French union team to arrive. They did just before ten o'clock and when everyone was seated Marcel in opening the discussions stunned the meeting by announcing that the negotiations had gone on for too long. The Union had never stood in the way of progress and provided that those workers who would lose their jobs were treated generously then he could see no reason for further delays. After all he added, management and union should work together for the greater glory of the company, and of La France.

If his own team were surprised they didn't show it as they realised that he'd been nobbled by the Company although they didn't know how. The Company team however were simply staggered.

The morning was spent discussing the finer points of the proposal for the closure of the Marseilles factory and by two o'clock the deal was done. There was much shaking of hands and slapping of backs by all concerned.

Later that night after a light supper some wine and chat with his wife, Marcel suggested they go to bed. He enjoyed the sex with her although as he drifted off to sleep he smiled remembering the things he'd done last night, especially with the tall fair haired boy who'd been very inventive. He decided he'd like to meet him again.

Hans rang Mark and gave him the good news that the deal was done and queried how on earth Mark had persuaded Marcel to drop his opposition to the deal.

'Me Hans? I did nothing. Something must have helped him see the light. All sensible men do eventually you know' and with that somewhat enigmatic comment he broke off the conversation by telling Hans that he wouldn't after all be coming over tomorrow. There was no need he explained as the deal was finalised and now it was up to Hans and his team to get on with the closure and integration process, which they did extremely competently.

CHAPTER 29

Caroline Burton the high flying corporate lawyer next came to Mark's notice as a result of a law suit that Lovells filed against a competitor. It concerned a product which Lovells had been selling and marketing for many years that had a patented opening device and a very distinctive label design that was unique and distinctive.

Suddenly a Danish company launched a similarly shaped cheaper product with a label design and shape virtually identical to the Lovells product and with an almost identical opening device to that which Lovells had patented.

Lovells sued in the High Court under legislation known as "passing off" in which it is illegal for a product to make itself "confusingly similar" to use the correct legal phrase, to another already existing product. The complex case lasted for a week.

Although the actual arguments in court are put forward by bewigged barristers it is the solicitors like Caroline that do all the preparation work, research the issues and generally provide the information which the barristers can then use to argue the case in court. The fact that Lovells won was due in no small part to her exacting attention to detail and painstaking research involving trips to Denmark, America, Austria and several locations in the UK to interview people, obtain statements and prepare their case.

Mark was delighted with the outcome and decided to take her out to dinner. He had two purposes in mind. Firstly he wanted to thank her for all her hard work on their case and secondly he wanted to offer her a job.

He'd considered for some time that they should have a lawyer on the top management team as he thought it would improve the quality of their decision making and save considerable lawyer's fees to solicitor firms like Cracknall Black and Foster for whom Caroline worked. Asking Sam to get her on the phone he waited for the call to come through.

When the connection was made he thanked her for the effective way she'd handled the recent case and then after some general conversation about various subsidiary issues he turned the conversation to her work and where she saw herself going in future.

'Do you intend to stay in the profession or had you thought of branching out into industry?'

She replied that she'd thought about it but the right opportunity hadn't arisen and in any case her work in the firm was exciting and fulfilling and she saw no real reason to move out of the profession and into industry. They spoke for some time concluding with him inviting her to have dinner one evening.

'I'd love to. Thank you'.

'Great. I'll get Sam to fix a date'.

It was organised about a week ahead and as he was leaving for Graham to drive him to London she gave him several files of papers to read and said softly 'Behave yourself with the lawyer lady Mark. They can be quite a handful you know. Don't forget that I'm always here for you'.

'I know' and he grinned reassuringly at her as he left. Cupping her chin in her hand she wondered if there was an ulterior motive in taking this Caroline Burton out to dinner.

By co-incidence they arrived almost simultaneously. He waited while she handed her coat to the head waiter who greeted Mark deferentially and said how nice it was to see him again. Flattered that he'd been remembered as it was several months since he'd used this particular restaurant, what he didn't know was that Sam when making the booking had personally spoken to the head waiter to explain that Mark was head of a very large business and might want to use the restaurant again regularly, but that depended on the service and food quality tonight. It was a device she often used when booking restaurants for him and it always guaranteed him excellent service.

Now that she was close to him in a relaxed environment Caroline realised how attractive Mark was and she enjoyed her evening talking with him. She even found herself slightly but subtly over doing her attentiveness by looking at him from under her long eyelashes while trying and failing to hold his gaze which was piercing, riveting and possibly slightly cruel she reflected. No not cruel but demanding, yes that was it. God she thought I bet you're dynamite in bed and for a moment she imagined them naked in a passionate embrace then realising that she'd missed something that he'd asked she blushed and apologised. 'Sorry say that again'.

'I said that we've been thinking of taking a lawyer into our company as a member of my top team as legal director'.

'Good idea. More large companies are doing that nowadays and although there are some downsides generally it seems to work out well for them. It's all about fit. Get the right person and make sure they've got a proper role and it can be very beneficial'.

'Exactly. Now you and I don't know each other very well so tell me about yourself.

She did and in a few minutes gave him her career history starting from University where she gained a first class degree, through her first job in the law with a firm of solicitors in Nottingham, her marriage and subsequent divorce, her move to London and her work with her London firm.

He listened carefully, asked a number of questions then smiled. 'Look I'm a person who makes up my mind quickly and usually I'm right on people things. I'd like you to come and join us and be our legal eagle. I don't know what you earn at the moment but I'll better it with a great salary, pension, health insurance, life insurance, expensive car, bonus on performance. Interested?'

'I could be. I've been at my firm now for some time and if I'm going to move on then it's either within the profession for a junior partnership or possibly into industry. Tell me what you'd see my role being then make me an offer I can't refuse'.

She looked straight at him and thought that if he hinted the offer involved going to bed she'd jump at it but he didn't and in reality she supposed that she was glad as it would be impossible to work together following something like that but she did briefly hanker after the thought of having sex with him.

Telling herself to stop being silly she smiled and listened carefully to his reply. It was certainly an offer to make her eyes water and she'd be a fool to turn it down. If it didn't work out she could always go back into the profession but if it did then the commercial world was hers. She raised various questions, clarified other issues then sat back thinking rapidly while drinking her cup of coffee.

'You say you're a person who makes up his mind quickly. Well so am I. The answer's yes. I'd love to come and work for you. Thank you'. They shook hands. He said that he'd get something in writing to her the following day. She said when she'd got it provided there weren't any queries she'd sign to accept and then resign.

Six months later Caroline became Legal Director at Lovells and one of Mark's key team members. She soon came to admire him and wasn't afraid to stand up to him and argue her point if she thought he was incorrect. This led to some very robust exchanges between them but he respected her views and judgment and found her to be a very valuable member of his team.

She settled in well enjoying the transition from profession to commerce and particularly enjoyed the additional financial benefits of her huge salary and having a company car. She chose a silver Porsche and also decided to move home and give up renting a flat in Islington, so with the help of a substantial mortgage backed by her huge salary she bought a large two bedroom apartment in one of the new tower blocks in Docklands with a big balcony overlooking the river.

Sitting there surrounded by boxes of unpacked furniture and personal effects on the night she'd moved in, she gazed around before moving to her balcony and looked over London, the Thames and the lights. Excited she felt that if she hadn't quite arrived in life yet at least she was well on the way. Yes, to her that night it all looked good.

Andrew Spicer came to Lovell's offices to help Mark decide how to proceed. On the desk was the Houghtons dossier that Hans had created. Opening it the two of them particularly focussed on the directors of the business who were all based in the UK although they noted that one, apparently a keen salmon fisherman, had a small second house in Scotland. Another had a holiday home in Spain.

Re-reading the papers it was clear that one area about which they needed more in-depth detail related to those Houghtons directors. They had considerable information, but they needed to extend that knowledge to find out in more depth about the directors. Their strengths, weaknesses, foibles, personal financial positions, whether they had a mistress or were a secret gay, or possibly a drug habit to support in short they needed to know everything about them. If they could do that then there might be some opportunity to apply some more leverage.

The share position also was interesting because as a private company then the shares were not quoted on the stock exchange and so individuals holding shares might be wealthy on paper but with no real opportunity to sell and realise that value they were effectively worthless. Their only real chance to turn paper into cash was if the company would buy them back, but why would it or indeed could it afford to do that?

But depending on the terms of any acquisition if a Houghton's director was offered a large cash payment considerably above the nominal share value to persuade him to sell his shares in the event of a takeover, he might be persuaded to support Lovells takeover approach.

'You need to find a key for each of them with which you can unlock them from Houghtons and get them on your side. Then that'll just leave old Sir Charles himself' advised Andrew. I'd talk with Colin Ringwood if I was you. After all he helped you with the City didn't he?' His eyes twinkled as he subtly let Mark know they he'd been keeping an eye on what was going on. 'By the way it might be advisable to let us get an update of Houghton's latest financial position for you. I think you'll find it's got worse'…..he paused and looked hard at Mark……'considerably worse. They've lost a big contract from a long established customer. Now that wouldn't be anything to do with you would it?' He smiled as he asked the question.

'Oh I think I did hear something about that but I don't keep too close to the day to day details you know' replied Mark lying furiously as he knew all about the issue. In fact it was one of those instances where he had secretly instigated the use of a paid young lady to keep a certain buying director from one of their major industrial chemical customers company for the night. A couple of days later when the Lovell's team had presented a big and complex deal to that same customer executive, after some discussion and hard negotiating it had been agreed that the Houghton's product range would be completely discontinued for the next two years and replaced by Lovells range. It was a major coup for Lovells and a serious blow for Houghtons.

This technique of supplying "company" was something that Mark organised quietly and discretely when he saw that in a particular case it could help his business. It didn't happen often and he never discussed it with any of his people as he arranged it without anyone knowing through a lady called Eve whom he'd never met but not long after his first meeting with B I, Andrew had given him the contact in case of need.

Eventually the discussion ended. It was agreed that they would try and get a meeting set up between Sir Charles Houghton and a firm of Merger and Acquisition advisers that both Colin and Mark knew. Leaving Mark out of the direct discussions with Houghtons at this stage would enable a second approach to be made directly between the two principle protagonists if this first approach failed.

Now that there was a plan to get on with things Mark was more relaxed as he hated waiting and indecision.

The share price continued to climb steadily. Up a little one day, then down a little, then up again, then perhaps several days of going down before a significant jump up again. It was now close to £7 and City expectations were that it would sail through that barrier before settling for a while.

In the meantime he was frantically busy, visiting America every eight weeks and regularly blitzing into European businesses causing consternation and occasionally havoc with his visits. Sometimes Sam accompanied him sometimes he went alone.

One morning Phil Church the man in charge of the Mergers and Acquisitions firm that they'd recruited to sound Houghtons out on the possibility of a merger or takeover came to Marks office and Caroline joined the meeting.

'We tried for a meeting with Sir Charles but to no avail however we had an hour or so with two of their senior people, both directors. One looks after marketing and the other covers finance. Whilst denying that they had any difficulties they were not wholly convincing when they said it. I'd say they're either in, or are running into very serious problems but the business is as you know run like a rod of iron by Sir Charles and being private we can't utilise any City leverage to put pressure on them to talk or consider selling to you.

There's no point in approaching their bank at this time. We've made a few discreet enquiries through some banking connections and although it's generally recognised that Houghtons are in choppy water it's not thought at the moment that they're about to sink. Until they get nearer to that point of disaster their bank will remain tight lipped and unhelpful. We'll need to keep close though so that if they do look as though they're going to hit the rocks their bank will be the first to look for a lifeboat to resolve the problem quickly and avoid them, the bank

I mean, from losing a load of money. It could happen very suddenly. I think the next step if you want to buy Houghtons will be for you to meet with the old man himself. Face to face'.

Both Phil and Caroline were shocked at the sudden change that came over Mark's face into a look that combined shock, hatred and horror somehow all in one.

'Hey Mark are you alright?' they asked simultaneously.

'Meet Sir Charles' he said menacingly quietly. 'Me, meet him face to face?'

'Look I'll come with you make sure you keep to the straight and narrow as it were' interjected Caroline.

'Meet him, after all this time. I've read articles about him in the press, seen him on the TV news a couple of times but now you want me to meet him?'

'Look if you don't think it's a good idea we'll think of something else' added Phil worried about the apparent effect that his suggestion had had on Mark. Surely he wasn't afraid of the old industrialist? No from what he knew this guy Mark Watson wasn't afraid of anything. It must be something else. Perhaps they'd had a falling out in the past. Any rate whatever it was it had certainly rocked him.

Caroline looked at Mark and she experienced that terrible piercing stare of his. She tried but couldn't hold his eyes, so looked down at her papers and waited for him to say something. Like Phil she was amazed at the effect that such a simple request had caused. Looking back at him she saw he was still staring at her but less intently. He turned to Phil. 'All right see if you can set it up. Now leave me and let me know when the meeting is to take place. Oh and thanks Phil. Useful meeting'.

They both left him sitting in his office staring into space but as they closed his door Caroline stopped by Sam's desk.

'Is he alright today?'

'Yes he's his usual grumpy self' and then feeling remorse flood over her for criticising her beloved Mark she added quickly 'but he's so terribly busy and has so much on his mind with such a huge job it's not surprising really is it? Why?'

'It's just that he seemed to take a bit of a funny turn when we mentioned Sir Charles Houghton to him' Caroline replied looking hard at Sam intrigued by the way she leapt to Mark's defence. More than just a secretary backing her boss? Something going on between those two she wondered? Maybe, but nothing to do with her if it was.

'A funny turn? I'd better go and see he's alright then'. Sam rushed to Mark's door going in without knocking. Caroline not only noticed the speed with which she went but realised that no-one else would dream of entering without knocking.

'Hi there' Sam said as brightly as she could, but he ignored her and stayed staring into space. 'You OK?' No reply. 'Mark are you alright?'

He seemed to suddenly become aware of her. 'What?'

'I asked if you were alright? Caroline and Phil thought that you'd had a bit of a funny turn. You really shouldn't work so hard you know. Why don't you take the rest of the day off? I'll re-sort your diary'.

What she wanted him to say was "Yes and you take the rest of the day as well and let's go somewhere and make love" but he didn't. He just slowly looked at her and she saw the anguished look fade from his face to be replaced with one of grim determination.

'I'm fine Sam. Really I am. I've not had what you interestingly call a funny turn it's just that I think I'm getting near to something that I've been after for years and now it might be coming to me. It's a bit of a shock that's all'.

He smiled warmly at her. Her heart thumped. God she wanted him.

'Mark. I don't understand what that means except that I can see it's important to you. I hope whatever you want to happen, does'.

'It will, oh yes it definitely will'.

When she was back in her own office she rang Caroline and said that Mark was fine it was something to do with completing an old task. 'I've noticed before that he's touchy about Sir Charles Houghton' she finished.

'Oh well as long as the boss man's OK. That's what matters isn't it? I'm just talking it over with Phil here as Mark was fine till we mentioned Sir Charles. That's what seemed to trigger him off but if you've noticed that before then there's the mystery solved. Well it isn't of course as the real puzzle is why he gets so upset at the mention of his name. They must have had a scrap or problem before I suppose. Maybe we'll find out one day'. Caroline paused before adding 'Look after him Sam' and listened very carefully for the reply.

'I always do. We're a team you know. Him and me. We need each other'.

'I imagine you do' Caroline replied softly as she put down the phone. Yes there was definitely something there between them. Well well.

Business continued as usual. Phil Church and Colin Ringwood met to draw up a plan to get a meeting set up between Mark and Sir Charles. They knew that it wouldn't be easy but it had to be done.

First they approached Houghton's PR firm to see if they could help with contacts at the top of the firm. They couldn't. Next they contacted Houghton's lawyers to see if they could open an avenue through them. Again no. Houghton's advertising agency couldn't help and several dinners or lunches that Colin endured with various journalists all led nowhere. In fact whatever they tried led only to dead ends.

Sir Charles Houghton was not only very difficult to get at from outside but almost a recluse. He kept himself very private apart from membership of one of the oldest and very traditional gentlemen's clubs in London. Colin knew some other people who were members and managed to get himself invited in as a guest one evening, where following a discreet changing hands of fifty pounds the head porter quietly told him that more often than not Sir Charles tended to drop in on a Thursday evening. This was their one piece of success. The problem was what to do with it. How could they turn that seemingly minor piece of information to their advantage?

Colin and Phil met with Caroline and as the Board Room was free they ensconced themselves in there to chew the problem around.

'If his club is one of the few maybe only places we've found where he's off guard so to speak then we need to find a way of getting at him there as that might be as good a place as any to propose a meeting between him and Mark' suggested Phil by way of opening the conversation.

'Now there's a statement of the obvious if you like' grinned Colin. 'There's no point in just going up and saying oh hello Sir Charles, I think a meeting between you and Mark Watson the Chief Executive of Lovells would be a good idea. He'd run a mile. After all the two companies compete like cat and dog. Probably the last bloke he'd want to meet'.

'We need someone to act as a go between'.

'Doesn't Tim Nelson our Chairman belong to that club?' asked Caroline. Let's ask him. He's here in the office today'.

They rang and explained their need to Tim who joining them readily agreed to help.

'I don't know him well, but I do know him well enough to buy him a drink and have a general chat if that's any help?'

'Any help? It's exactly what we need' exclaimed Caroline. 'Tim that's fantastic' and she blew him a kiss. 'Come on let's go talk to Mark'. Bustling into Sam's office they asked to see him straight away and being waved on they confronted a surprised looking Mark.

'Hey a deputation what's up? You look as though you lost a penny and found a pound.

'Mark I gather you want to meet Sir Charles Houghton face to face as part of our plan to acquire them. Well I know him slightly and we belong to the same club. I might be able to facilitate that meeting. Like me to try?' queried Tim.

Keeping his external expression neutral he nodded. 'Yes that would be very helpful. He's so bloody secretive we can't find a way to get to him and as you well know he is the absolute key to this'. The four men and Caroline talked for some time and then it was left to Tim to get the meeting organised.

Outside work though Mark was becoming increasingly tormented by his feelings about Abi and Sam.

He loved Abi deeply together with the girls, and the four of them got on fantastically well as a family. Emma even occasionally called him "Dad" by mistake. However he also had deep feelings for Sam and although he didn't think that he loved her he was incredibly fond of her. Was it really that he was fond of her he asked himself over and over again, or was it simply that he loved having sex with her? No he was sure it was more than that but how could he rationalise in his own mind the two women in his life?

Abi was his wife, confident and lover. He liked to talk to her and often shared business problems with her as he found that her incisive and enquiring mind helped him think things through. They adored each other and he knew that he meant a great deal to her as she certainly did to him. He wanted to live with her for the rest of his life and not only did he not want to do anything to hurt her or the girls but he couldn't ever envisage wanting to live with anyone else. She provided a perfect home life for him. A sanctuary, a haven of peace, calm, safety and love.

Sam though was like an addiction. He'd tried to give her up but every now and then he simply couldn't help himself and they went to bed. Each time he treasured it while it happened but afterwards was filled with remorse. Classic symptom of an addict he realised. Keep telling yourself that this is the last time, and so it is. Until next time. The next time though would be the last time, definitely. And the next time. Then that was going to be the last time. Perhaps the next time would be? Or the time after that. Maybe the time after that. And so on.

He'd argue to himself that he needed her for his work. Well he did but he would always be able to find someone else for that. No, it wasn't work but her innate understanding of him, his moods, his needs, his desires that hooked him into her. But even that wasn't the whole reason he corrected himself. In addition to all those things she was simply fantastic in bed. Innovative, exciting, fun, completely uninhibited she was every man's dream and was his whenever he wanted. Never complaining always there. Just for him. Oh god what was he to do? He couldn't give her up but he'd never want to replace Abi with her. Why was life so complicated?

It soon got even more complicated.

Abi wanted to talk to him about a serious matter but the problem was finding time to do that. During the week in the evenings if he wasn't away, he was usually tired and on Friday nights he either just liked to relax, flopping in front of the television and letting his mind wind down from the week or frequently they went out to dinner with friends or entertained at home.

Saturdays, during the day they did things together but not of a nature for serious talking and in the evenings like Fridays they entertained or went to friends for dinner. Sundays just seemed to wander past as sometimes they went out for a walk in the country or drove to the coast, or if the weather was right they'd spend time sunning themselves and swimming in their pool. In the evening he would start to wind himself up for the coming week.

All in all she thought that a Friday evening might be the best time especially if she could persuade him to get home early for once and they had nothing organised. Deciding to enlist Sam's help she rang and said she wanted to arrange a special dinner so could Sam sort out Mark's arrangements so that he could get away early one Friday in the not too distant future.

'Nothing wrong is there?' queried Sam wandering why Abi had called her.

'No, it's just that frankly he's whacked out when he gets back on Fridays and I need a bit of time to talk about something over dinner at a reasonable time for once' she laughed.

'OK. Look this Friday he's actually got quite a light afternoon. I'll try and keep it clear and pack him off early. How's that?'

'Great if you can do it. Thanks Sam'.

After the call Sam pondered what Abi wanted. Perhaps she wasn't getting enough sex and wanted to get him home early for a wild night in bed. It was bad enough knowing that she had to share him with Abi but being asked to get him home early so that his wife could screw him was too much. No it wouldn't be that she thought as knowing how quickly Mark could get aroused she was sure that Abi wouldn't have any problems in that respect so it must be something else. She shrugged. Maybe the best thing would be to get him off early on Friday and hope to find out soon after that.

He was away in Belgium for two nights that week, so when he arrived in the office in Friday morning and started as he usually did by spending a little time with Sam checking on his arrangements for the day he was surprised when she said that his diary was clear from four o'clock onwards.

'Why don't you get off early for once? Go home, spend time with Abi. Have a nice evening together. You're looking tired and you've had a very hard couple of weeks. Go on, do you good'.

If only she could persuade him to stop work early and go home with her. She'd take his mind off his hard couple of weeks all right but that wasn't possible. This time she had to help him get home to Abi.

'I'll ring Abi and tell her to expect you home early. Now this morning you've got Caroline lined up for nine o'clock and then your Strategy Review Group meeting at ten through till twelve. Finance twelve till one. Working lunch with Colin. Tim Nelson at two. Marketing update at three and then free. You could clear up, and go home around four.

Can you sign these letters and check through this post before Caroline comes. I'll warn Graham you're going early' and she left his office.

Yes, it would be nice to spend extra quality time with Abi he thought as he read the first letter that he needed to sign. While he was doing that Sam dialled Abi.

'Hi it's Sam. All fixed. The great man will be leaving soon after four, so home around five to five thirty I guess. Have a nice evening. Bye' and she rang off before her voice choked a little in the back of her throat and gave away her true feelings.

Sure enough the day tightly controlled by Sam went as planned and when Graham drove him home he realised that his boss was in a chatty mood.

'The missus is walking real well now after her operation. Amazing it was going private. They was so kind and helpful. Not like the NHS. She was done and up and walking within a couple of days. She ain't got no pain at all now. Don't know how I can thank you Mark. Ever so kind it was. If there's ever anything I can do to help you you've only got to say. I don't mean money as I haven't got much of that. Don't know what I mean really but thanks so much'.

'Pleasure. Glad to have been able to help. I say it seems bloody odd going home at this time doesn't it. Feels like I'm skiving off'.

'Why not? No one else works as hard as you do. Well except Caroline Burton. She's a worker and no mistake and a real nice lady. Posh and clever. Surprised she isn't married. Still up to her I suppose. Your Sam's a worker too you know. When you're away she's often at the office till gone nine o'clock at night sometimes even later. Now me and the missus is thinking of going to Tunisia for an holiday. Have you been there? Is it aright? We aren't too keen on foreign food and they're Arabs aren't they. Well I don't think I'd mind it but the missus is a bit worried about hygiene. Do you think we'd be alright?'

Mark reassured his driver that nothing disastrous would happen to them if they went to Tunisia and then chatted off and on while reading the evening paper until they pulled into home where Graham confirmed that he'd pick him up at six thirty on Monday morning.

'Hello darling you're early how lovely' cooed Abi as she enfolded herself around him wafting subtle perfume smells while kissing him gently but possessively.

'Umm that's nice. I must do this more often'.

'I wish you would. Go have a swim, relax and then let's have an early dinner' she smiled and nodding his agreement he did as suggested. Pounding up and down the pool he soon worked off his aggression from the week and felt relaxed with slightly aching muscles when he walked indoors for a hot shower. He came back down in slacks and a loose sweater and getting a bottle of wine from the fridge poured them both a glass.

They asked each other how their week had been and talked over a wide range of subjects until glancing at the clock Abi said that dinner would be ready and that he should go into the dining room. That was strange as when they were on their own they usually ate in the large kitchen but raising his eyebrows he did as requested.

Entering he saw the table laid with their best cutlery and china with several candles already alight, some scented and some purely for decoration. As it was getting dark outside the effect was exactly as Abi had wanted. Warm, calm, romantic and intimate.

A quick mental check relieved Mark that he hadn't forgotten her birthday or their wedding anniversary and after a moment's panic that she might have found out about him and Sam he put that thought aside as he was sure that if she had she would have said something to him more directly. No it wasn't Sam and so he was intrigued by the unusual setting and waited with considerable anticipation to discover the reason for which Abi had gone to this trouble.

The meal was simple but that added to its charm and delight. A home made pate and wafer thin toast to start, followed by grilled sea bass, salad and new potatoes. Dessert was a raspberry roulade and cream and they talked continuously while they ate. It was when they had finished and she had served the coffee and poured Mark a brandy that she took a deep breath and raised the question that had been troubling her so much.

'Mark darling there is something that I want to ask you. Come into the sitting room. We'll clear the table later'.

He was really curious now although there was still a tinge of concern in case she was going to raise Sam. Perhaps she'd put on the romantic dinner to soften him up then make love to him before asking if there was anyone else.

As he sat on the sofa she did too. Taking his hand she looked at him and spoke softly.

'Darling we are happy as a family aren't we, the four of us. You, me, Charlie and Emma? Especially you and me?'

Oh shit here it comes he thought, subtly bracing himself for the dreaded question. 'Are you having an affair?'

'Yes I couldn't be happier. I love you and the girls. Different sort of love for you from the girls but yes darling I am very lucky incredibly happy and love you all. Why what's brought this on? That lovely romantic dinner, sitting closely together now? There's something on your mind isn't there? Come on Mrs. Watson, out with it'.

'Charlie and Emma are very fond of you and you know I adore you'.

She paused but Mark still couldn't relax. Was she going to ask him about Sam? Was she leading to the big question and if so how would he answer it?

'Oh sweetheart relax. You're looking all tense...... guilty almost'. She laughed and kissed him lightly on the nose. 'Charlie and Emma are the children of Roger and me, not you and me. Roger isn't here now and I don't regret for one minute marrying you. Everyday I'm so glad that I went to that dinner party where we met. I wouldn't wish to change anything about our lives together........except perhaps one thing. Do you regret us not having children of our own? You and me. Us together. What I'm asking you my darling is would you like us to have a child......or children together?'

The sense of relief that the issue wasn't Sam was immediate but replaced instantly with a violent swirl of emotion. A child of their own. He'd thought about it from time to time, and they'd talked vaguely about it in the past but he'd tended to put it to the back of his mind. Now Abi was offering him something precious and unique. A child of their own.

'Say something darling' she smiled softly. 'Even if it's no'.

'Abi are you sure you know what you are saying. You're not......I mean.....it's a long time since you had kids. Are you sure you're ready to go through it again? You know childbirth and all that'.

'You mean I'm not as young as I was' she laughed. 'I'm only just over forty. I'm healthy and I had both girls quite easily......well morning sickness was a real pain but their actual births were quite straightforward. Painful but straightforward and neither took too long. Yes my love I'm very sure. If you want a child I'd be happy to try for you.......with you. It's your choice darling. No, I suppose it's our choice but you have to really want it. We can think about it, we can talk about it, we can forget it if you prefer. We don't have to rush to a decision.

I know I've surprised you, shocked you maybe but I've had time to think about it. In fact I've been thinking about it for ages. I think about you all the time as a father of our child, children perhaps' another smile. 'When I look at you at dinner, in the garden, when you're with Charlie and Emma, when you're asleep in our bed especially after we've made love then I think how wonderful it would be if the seeds you'd planted in me could grow into our child. I love you so desperately and I want to do this thing for you, with you. For us. Darling let's make our child'.

'Abi' he replied so softly she could hardly hear him. 'I don't know what to say. Yes it would be wonderful to have our child but what about Charlie and Emma? What will they think?'

'I don't know but I think they'll understand. We'll have to talk to them in time when, if, we know we're going to have a baby. Do you really mean yes? Do you want to think about it? It's a big step from which there's no going back. This isn't one of your business decisions where if it is wrong you can change your mind. This is about creating a human being, about starting a life. A life that only we can make'.

'Yes darling I'm sure'. He kissed her gently and for a long time. 'Yes darling, please. It would be wonderful as long as you are sure quite sure that it isn't going to cause problems with Charlie and Emma. OK they're yours and Roger's children but I think of them as my own and I try and treat them as if they were my own. I'd hate anything to spoil that'.

'We won't let it now cuddle me'.

'I can't I'm too excited. Let's walk round the garden' and leading her to the French doors they went outside.

The evening was getting chilly but with a clear sky and by the light of the moon they could clearly see their long lawn so walking hand in hand they wandered together happy, not speaking, each deep in their own thoughts. Soon they came upon the summer house by the little lake that lay at the end of their garden. Abi shivered as Mark led her inside and fumbled around for some cushions which he carefully arranged on the floor. Looking quizzically at him she said nothing as he gently pulled her down and pressed her into the soft comfort of the various cushions and covers.

'We could always start the baby making process right now' he said softly and for answer she wrapped her arms around him and pulled him down onto her. Their lovemaking was slow, gentle, and wonderful and for them both it exemplified their total love for each other. Later they walked hand in hand back to the house and up to their bedroom where they quickly undressed.

'Just hold me darling' she asked and he did as they slowly went to sleep.

Next morning Mark was particularly cheerful and reminded Abi that Emma would be coming home later that day from boarding school while Charlie would be back tomorrow from University for a week's break.

'I think we should have another go at this baby making lark' he chuckled after he'd brought up her morning cup of coffee and taking off his bathrobe jumped into bed, rolled her on her back and vigorously made love to her.

For them both but Mark particularly the weekend went past in a flash. The girls came home but they said nothing to them and when he and Abi were in bed the love making was very special.

It wasn't until he was in the car being driven to work on Monday morning that he thought of Sam. God a whole weekend and she hadn't entered his thoughts. He couldn't remember a time when he'd blanked her out of his mind for such a long period but as he walked through her outer office and smelt the lingering scent of her perfume that always slightly pervaded her room he realised that his life was going to become much more difficult.

'Morning. Have a good weekend?' she asked when she brought him in his coffee. 'Do anything special on your early home day on Friday?'

'No not really. Just had a nice quiet dinner with Abi, chatting and so on. You know the sort of thing. Now what's on for today?' and he clicked into business mode and she responded by briefing him on his diary commitments and series of meetings that were lined up for him but as she left him she wondered about his answer.

She thought he'd answered her question about the weekend just a bit too quickly. Bet Abi got him in bed as soon as she could and screwed him all night or maybe all weekend if the girls weren't home. Bitch. Oh Mark why her and not me?

So life went on for a few days until Tim popped in to tell Mark that he thought next week they should try and meet with Sir Charles at the club.

Although Mark was his usual frantic self, for him everything was focussed on the coming meeting with Charles Houghton. He was frequently bad tempered and often his staff thought that he didn't seem to be listening to them properly.

On Thursday evening Graham drove Tim and Mark up to London and dropped them off outside the club. 'Go and park somewhere nearby and we'll call you when we're ready to leave' commanded Mark as the two men got out of the car. Graham thought Mark was looking tense.

Inside Mark could sense decades of discussion, talking, intrigue and plotting that seemed to exude from this old building. Dark oak panelling, elaborate chandeliers hanging from high ceilings, whispered conversations and discrete service from the club servants as the waiters and bar men were known. Although forced some years ago to open its doors to women nevertheless very few females ever entered the building. It was a male environment and Establishment male at that. This was the preserve of very senior civil servants, Members of Parliament, long established businessmen, wealthy individuals, Bankers and other Institutional people.

Tim bought Mark a gin and tonic refusing to get him a mineral water. 'For heavens sake relax and drink this'.

But Mark was anything but relaxed and sat like a coiled spring hardly able to make small talk with Tim who sensed that for Mark there was a lot more to this meeting than appeared on the surface. Time went by slowly and it was nearly eight o'clock when Tim gently tapped Mark on the knee. 'Here he is'.

The tall florid faced heavily overweight man walked slowly to a deep wing armchair in the corner and dropped forcefully into it's leather embrace. The club steward approached and smiled. 'Your usual Sir Charles?' then hurried away to get the drink returning shortly carrying a silver tray with a large whisky with ice tinkling in the cut glass tumbler and a soda siphon . A small squirt then the glass was set on a small linen drip mat on a table to the side of the chair. The Evening Standard newspaper was handed over as well.

Sir Charles nodded acknowledging his drink and paper. Taking a large pull of his whisky he let out a long sigh before putting the drink down and opening the paper.

Making "go and talk to him" motions Mark was frustrated that Tim just sat and watched their target but he smiled and made "don't be impatient" signs.

A clock ticked loudly in the corner. There were several people in the large room. Three other men were alone like Sir Charles. There were another four groups of two men, each talking quietly with their heads close together and one group of three in animated yet quiet conversation in the far corner. Still Tim waited and watched. Eventually Sir Charles raised his hand and beckoned the club steward who approached, listened and then returned to the bar. Immediately Tim rose intercepting the Steward. A short conversation then Tim walked towards Sir Charles with two glasses in hand.

'Charles, how are you. Thought I spotted you over here. I've taken the liberty of getting you the other half. Mind if I join you?'

He sat down and although Mark couldn't hear what was being said he watched the body language of the two men which seemed quite relaxed and friendly. They talked for several minutes and there was even the sound of quiet laughter at one point. Suddenly Tim turned and beckoned Mark to join them.

His heart thumped as he walked over. His legs felt like jelly and he wondered for a moment if he was going to faint. He'd never felt like this before in any business situation. In his mind he heard his childish voice from all those years ago saying 'Don't worry Dad I'll get Houghton for you one day'. The sweat ran down his back as Tim smiled and introduced him. Finally Mark was standing directly in front of his enemy. Holding out his hand he calmed his breathing and forced a smile.

'Sir Charles I've heard so much about you. I'm glad to meet you at last'.

The old industrialist rose slightly and shook hands. 'Likewise, sit down' and he motioned to Mark to find a chair and pull it up to join them but as he turned to do this the ever attentive club steward appeared as if by magic with another chair.

'Mark and I were having a drink here this evening chatting over a few things and when I realised that you'd come in I thought it might be a good idea if you two met. You never know there might be things that you have in common to chat about. So how's business then Charles?'

'Be better if this Chief Executive of yours didn't keep pinching our best people together with our contracts in the UK and bashing us about all round the world. You are a tough competitor Mark Watson and no mistake. I don't like what you're doing to us and I think you'd better stop before we react and teach you a lesson'.

He glared at Mark breathing heavily though his wide flared fleshy nostrils. Although in keeping with the club's rules that conversation should be quiet, nevertheless he'd somehow managed to convey a dominating demand.

Mark didn't flinch but stared straight into the older man's eyes. Neither wavering nor moving he said quietly but menacingly 'Alls fair in love, war and business Sir Charles. I think we have the better business which is why we are succeeding. In fact I would like to find a way of discussing with you at some early date an opportunity for our two businesses to stop fighting each other'.

Sir Charles's eyes flickered away from Mark's gaze to Tim and then returned.

'How?'

'Perhaps we could discuss putting the two businesses together'.

'What some sort of joint venture?'

'Not exactly. I think your interests would be best served by merging into us. For Houghtons to become part of Lovells'.

'Take us over? You are stark staring barmy. If you think we're going to sell to you then you are very much mistaken. Let me tell you that we have no need to sell. I run a fine business which is financially strong and growing. It is us that is on the takeover trail and we're not contemplating selling up. Definitely not young man. Tim I thought that you had a good Chief Executive. Seems to me that he's just a hot head with some potty ideas. No you can forget that idea. Understand? Now it's time I went'.

Heaving himself out of the chair he slurped down last of his drink. Shaking Tim's hand he said 'Thanks for the drink' but looking at Mark he snorted 'Take us over, nonsense' and walked off without shaking hands.

'Well you've rattled him' grinned Tim as he turned to Mark. 'First shot to us I think'.

'Think so? I thought I'd just pissed him off. He dismissed the idea out of hand. Mind you I didn't handle it well. Came onto what I......we wanted a bit too quickly. Should have chatted around it a bit more first I suppose but it just sort of seemed right to bang it at him up front like that especially when he made that crack about teaching us a lesson, arrogant bastard'.

'Yes you're right you did go in a bit hard and fast and he is somewhat put out' laughed the Chairman. 'Still no harm done. Now let's meet in the office tomorrow with Caroline and a few others and plan the next steps. We've started so now we've got to finish it. One day you must tell me what it is about him and you'. He looked hard at Mark. 'Never let personal issues cloud your business judgment'.

Getting in the car Graham drove them to Montpelier Square where they dropped Tim off at his London flat, before heading out west on the A4 and eventually via the M4, M25 and M23 they whizzed down towards Sussex and Mark's home. Graham sensed that Mark wanted to be quiet so he didn't talk.

Walking quickly upstairs Mark saw that Abi was deeply asleep. Going back down he went into his study and sitting down in the armchair picked up a dictation machine rattled off some notes on his meeting tonight before pouring himself a whisky. He sat and thought about why tonight's meeting had not gone well.

The answer was simple. He'd ballsed it up because he'd allowed himself to become angered by Sir Charles's needling of him. Instead of gradually bringing the subject round to a takeover he'd gone straight in with a frontal assault and been repelled. Damn. How could he have allowed himself experienced as he was, to be triggered off like that? Stupid. Mind you he'd met Charles Houghton and although the old man may have knocked him off course tonight, next time he'd prepare more carefully.

He'd finally come face to face with his long time adversary. The surprising thing was that he now felt calm having met the enemy face to face as he realised that he was now wholly confident that he could defeat the old man. He was going to win.

'Darling why are you sitting down here? Come to bed' Abi said as she came sleepily into the small room.

'No let me stay here and think for a while. I've got a lot on my mind at the moment'.

Moving to stand behind him she massaged his neck then leaning over him she ran her hands up and down his chest before manoeuvring herself in front of him pulling his head towards her breasts. 'Let me put something else on your mind' she giggled climbing onto his lap and kissing him sensuously. 'Now why stay down here alone when you could come to bed and make babies with me'.

Obediently he followed her upstairs where taking off her nightie she watched as he quickly undressed.

CHAPTER 30

Meanwhile the complex planning necessary in order to acquire Houghtons was underway. Over the next few weeks a great deal of work was put in hand at Lovells mainly involving Mark, his Finance Director, Caroline, some trusted external advisers, and their bank. Mark brought Hans back for a few days to help sort out the priorities for their attack on Houghton.

Deciding that he needed to explain the acquisition strategy to the very senior people in the business from every country in which Lovells operated Mark called the heads of all the Lovells businesses together for a conference.

Sam booked a conference suite at the Heathrow Sheraton Hotel and most of the overseas delegates flew in that morning in good time for the start of the meeting at eleven am. Chuck had arrived the previous day in order to get over the jet lag of a trip across the Atlantic.

The meeting started with an explanation by the Finance Director of the current trading position of Lovells which clearly showed the enormous progress that had been made over the past few years. Although he didn't say so no-one was left in any doubt about the improved business performance since Mark had taken over. Details were given of performance by product, brand and country demonstrating their strengths and weaknesses.

After a short break for a buffet lunch the proceedings resumed with Mark taking the stage and outlining a new share option and bonus scheme for all of the very senior managers and heads of business represented in the room dependant not only the performance of their own particular areas of responsibility but crucially on the Company share price moving ever higher. In ringing tones he reminded them that the higher it went the greater the financial rewards to them when they came to sell their optioned shares.

He continued by underlining the need for further acquisitions in order to build their business to be stronger and more proof against competitive threats, to be able to fight more strongly with their major customers and withstand the pressure for improved prices that they continually received from their suppliers, but also importantly to provide an even greater return to their shareholders which drove a higher share price.

Returning to their need to acquire other companies he stated 'We have a number of potential candidates' then listed several companies including Houghtons. The screen was filled with chart after chart of information about the various companies and the delegates could clearly see the benefits of each of the potential targets but of them all Houghtons made the most sense.

A useful open question session then followed with Mark being very open about his hopes and desires for the business but he carefully kept the fact that it was really only Houghtons in which he was interested, carefully hidden.

The meeting finished a little after four o'clock in time for the European delegates to fly back to their respective countries that evening. Chuck, who was on a late evening flight back to The States joined Mark some of the UK people and Sam for a drink before catching the airport bus to terminal four to catch the British Airways late evening flight home. The last few people drifted away leaving only Mark and Sam sitting in the bar.

'How do you think it went?'

'Fine. I know from the comments I picked up that they really appreciated you being so open with them. I'll tell you one thing though boss you're a great public speaker. If ever you give up business you should become a politician. You'd have no problem getting elected'.

'Yea maybe' he laughed 'but the trouble is I couldn't stand all the politics. If I could just get the country organised like a business and have things done my way it'd be alright'

'Well I'd definitely vote for you' she said looking straight at him. 'Anytime'.

'Thanks, now time we went home'.

'Yes if that's what you want. They've got some rooms available here if you'd like to stay....... us to stay that is?' She smiled at him her tongue peeping out.

'Sam no. I'm going home. Graham's waiting'.

'No he's not'.

'What do you mean he's not waiting? I specifically told him to wait until I was ready to go home'.

'And I told him that he wasn't needed tonight as it was likely that you would be staying. I've brought your spare clean shirt and shaving kit from the office if that helps' she said softly.

For a moment he nearly exploded and told her not to bloody well interfere with his arrangements without checking with him first but he stopped himself realising that often that was exactly what he needed her to do. He looked at her.

Sam could see the turmoil going on in his mind so watching him very carefully she waited and said nothing as it was he who had to decide whether to take up her offer. She had to be very careful now as a wrong word, a wrong gesture, a touch of pressure in fact anything could trigger a rejection.

Time stood still. He was going to say no. Perhaps what they'd had was over. Still he said nothing just stared at her. Eventually not able to accept the suspense any longer she uncrossed her legs and sat forward with an enquiring look on her face as she couldn't stand this void and had to force a decision even if it was the end for them.

'Mark don't make me beg. I've always been here for you when you needed me. I've never turned you down. Now I want you. Tonight'.

Still he said nothing.

'All right then.........I'll beg you. Please stay here with me tonight. Do I have to get down on my knees? I will if that's what it takes. Mark.........please'.

The pause was prolonged before he squeezed her hand. 'No Sam. Sorry. I'll get a taxi home. You've got your car haven't you?'

Not trusting herself to speak she nodded and then getting up walked quickly to reception, asked for a token to exit the car park and left the hotel.

Running across the car park the tears started before she reached her car but when she was inside and had closed and locked the door her head fell forward onto the steering wheel and great sobs wracked her whole body. She stayed there for a long time until eventually they subsided sufficiently for her to drive home. Anger and frustration made her drive fast almost recklessly but the hurt was pounding through her as tears streamed down her face.

It was devastating to have been rejected like that. She loved him and he didn't love her. That wasn't new but she'd held on to her hopes that one day he would fall in love with her even if only a little bit, but it was obvious now that it simply wasn't going to happen. She wanted love and to be loved not just sex, although tonight she had wanted him sexually. Whereas once he'd have jumped at the chance to take her to bed, indeed would have probably initiated it, now he was holding her away at arm's length. That was new and she didn't like it. Not one little bit. Abi had got him completely.

When she got home she saw the painting of Bermuda, the symbol of Abi and Mark's love, marriage and honeymoon. Wrenching it off its hook she hurled it across the room smashing the frame when it hit the wall. Running into her bedroom she flung herself onto the bed and started to cry again. It was a long time before she finally calmed down but still weeping she fell asleep where she lay not waking until much later.

Getting up and feeling terrible she undressed, pulled on some pyjamas and having peed, washed and brushed her teeth was about to climb into bed properly when she suddenly realised that in the morning Graham would turn up at the Sheraton to collect Mark whilst he would be at home. Instantly she went into her lounge, found her pocket book and apologising for ringing so late told Graham to collect Mark from home in the morning.

'Right ho' he replied cheerfully. He didn't tell her that Mark himself had rung about half an hour earlier to tell him exactly the same thing. 'That's odd' he thought that they'd both rung him but shrugging his shoulders he went back to watching a repeat episode of Inspector Morse on TV.

On the long slow journey back home in the black cab Mark reflected how he'd been terribly tempted by her. Why had he said no he wondered? He'd been unfaithful to Abi with her so many times before why would one more time make any difference? He didn't know except that at the back of his mind was their intention to try and start a family. While he'd been sitting with Sam desperately wanting to say yes he'd kept remembering the decision that he and Abi had made. It had worked to keep him faithful tonight, perhaps it always would, but even as he thought that he knew it wouldn't.

That evening in bed he and Abi made love but as they cuddled together afterwards he couldn't help thinking that he could so easily have been lying with Sam in his arms at The Sheraton. He lay afterwards thinking that their lovemaking this evening had seemed somewhat lacklustre but it would have been very different if he'd been with Sam.

In the office next morning Sam took in his coffee and left without saying a word. All day she was polite when others were around but when the two of them were alone together she was surly, monosyllabic and generally miserable. She left at five not even saying good night to him. He couldn't ever remember her leaving so early before and never without saying goodnight.

He tried ringing her flat before he left for home but it just clicked into her answer phone. On the way home he used the in-car phone a couple of times to contact her but again there was no answer just her answering machine. He didn't leave a message.

The following day he went straight from home to London for a meeting with Lovell's bank and didn't arrive at his office until just after lunch. Whereas normally she'd have rung him in the car and asked what he'd like for lunch this time there had been no call and there was no lunch waiting.

Deciding not to make an issue of it he simply walked to her outer office and asked her to get him a sandwich from the restaurant.

By five o'clock he'd had enough. All right he'd turned down her offer of sex. So? Was it such a big deal? She must realise that it couldn't go on like it had before although to be fair she didn't know that he and Abi were baby making. 'Time she bloody well grew up' he muttered to himself adding 'moody bitch' a trait he'd not noticed before.

As she dropped off the last of his typing for signing he said somewhat over loudly 'Sam for fuck's sake snap out of it will you. OK so you are pissed off with me. Sorry, but don't go around making everyone's life a misery'.

'Making life a misery? You're a fine one to talk. Do you know what you've done to me? Chucked me aside like a piece of waste paper. A scrap that you've done with after everything that we've shared together. The work, the pressure, the problems, the confidentiality, the fun...... and the lovemaking. Especially the lovemaking Mark. I've never refused you. When I was tired or didn't feel like it or had a headache I never turned you away. I was always there for you. Sometimes you were kind and loving and it was wonderful. Other times you just screwed me purely for your own pleasure when I was nothing but somewhere for you to put your cock. But I didn't complain. Did I ever protest? Did I say no? Have I refused to do things with you......for you?

Now for some reason it's all over. Just like that. Thanks mam. Sod off mam. Why? What have I done? What's suddenly changed? You've been different ever since you went home early that Friday afternoon. What happened? Did Abi give you the shag of your life? Did she do things for you in bed that she didn't before but that I do for you? She paused. 'Sorry that was cheap but something's changed and I don't like it'.

The tears welled up in her eyes and started to run down her cheeks. 'Damn. I'm sorry I didn't mean to cry but I don't know what to do. Is it over between us? Are we finished? What can I do to bring you back? You mean so much to me. Mark please' and her voice tailed off as she looked miserably at him sniffing and crying and wondering whether to tell him she loved him.

'Here' he said softly handing her his handkerchief which she took and wiped her eyes before blowing her nose on the linen which smelled of his aftershave.

'Sam I don't know what to say. Yes things are different now and yes it was to do with that Friday and although I can't tell you why it isn't because of what you so crudely suggested just now'.

'I said I was sorry for that crack'.

'Look go home now. Let's see how things look in the morning eh?' Maybe talk again then'.

'Couldn't we talk about it now? If you don't want to talk here in the office lets go for a drink somewhere. I won't make a scene, promise. Please I must find out what's suddenly changed and why'.

'No Sam tonight's not the time. We will talk but not now. Go home'.

She left his office still crying and soon there was silence from her outer office. Of course she was right. She'd never refused him and a series of images came into his mind of the many times they'd made love. She was so exciting and inventive in lovemaking he would miss her. But there was Abi and the baby they were trying to create. Surely that was more important. Wasn't it?

Trying to put the problem out of his mind he rang America and spoke to Chuck and then made a series of other calls. The end of the day was one of his favourite times to ring people and he was on the phone for at least an hour and a half including a quick chat with Hans who was really making France fire on all four cylinders.

Leaning back his hands behind his head he closed his eyes and thought deeply about what he ought to do. What he had to do. What he wanted to do. The answer seemed clear but was it right? Yes, it was for him. Swinging the chair forward he picked up the phone.

'Graham. Sorry for the short notice but I'll drive myself tonight. See you tomorrow'.

He broke the connection, dialled another number and spoke briefly.

When he'd finished he locked his office and walked along the corridor, down in the lift, through the empty reception and across the car park. Getting in the Jaguar he started the engine and drove slowly towards the exit barrier nodding his thanks to the gatehouse guard. His journey took about twenty minutes. He pulled up, parked, got out, locked the car and went into the modern block of flats.

Exiting the lift it wasn't long before he had reached the right front door. Staring at it for several minutes he took a deep breath and pressed the bell. Hearing footsteps he stood back and waited. The door opened slowly and Sam looked at him.

'Yes?'

'Can I come in?'

'Why?'

'I want to talk'.

'What do you want to talk about? I thought you said it all in the office'.

'No I didn't. You're right, we need to talk'.

'Oh well you're too late for talking. I'm going to go out with some friends to a club to try and cheer myself up'.

'Oh were you. Well you're not any more. There's been a change of plan' he said pushing his way inside and shoving the door shut.

'Piss off Mark' she replied angrily. 'I don't want a change of plan as you put it. I've got my own plan and my own life to lead outside work. Inside I work for you. Outside now that you don't want me then it's my life. I can do what I want, when I want, with whom I want, as I want........'

What more she was going to say was unclear as pulling her towards him and lifting her chin upwards he kissed her lips gently. She remained motionless neither responding nor resisting until unable to help herself she relaxed into his body returning his kisses for a while. Moving apart she looked up at him.

'This isn't fair' she whispered as the tears started again. 'It's not fair at all and you know it. Not two hours ago you said that you didn't want me. Now you come here and kiss me. What is it with you? You can't just bounce me around on a string. Pull me up then drop me down'.

'I know'.

'Well what is it then? What have I done wrong? Why are you shutting me out? Just tell me how I've upset you and I'll put it right. I'll do anything Mark, absolutely anything.. Just let things get back the way they were. I know you're married to Abi and I know I can't replace her but let me share you. I'll never embarrass you or hurt you or her or your girls. I'll be discrete as I've always been. Remember when we were in The States and I used to sneak back to your hotel when no-one was around? Nobody found out. We had fun and there was no harm. All the time we've slept together here in England or in Europe no one knows, no one's ever found out and its been wonderful. What's changed?'

'Sam you are right we did have fun but something has changed but it's nothing that you've done. It's a decision that Abi and I have made about ourselves, our lives and we've..........' he paused as he couldn't bring himself to tell her about the baby. 'It's just something we've decided. I know that doesn't make sense to you'.

'You're damn right. It doesn't. What's this great decision you and Abi have made? Why must it affect us?'

'Look leave it Sam. I'm sorry I shouldn't have come here tonight. I'll go. See you in the office in the morning'.

'No don't go. Stay and talk to me. Tell me how it can get back like it was'.

'It can't......good night'.

With a sound that was a cross between a wail and a sob she leaned back against the wall and then slowly slid down onto the floor tears pouring down her face as she watched him walk to the door. He turned the handle and glancing round was shocked to see her as a crumpled heap on the floor. His heart went out to her so he strode back and knelt down.

'Sam please I can't bear to see you like this'.

'Well go then you won't have to' she snapped through her tears.

He tried to get up. He should go. He ought to leave her there but in that moment his deep feelings for her overcame him so he kissed the top of her head and then as he put his arms around her the tears came more strongly. He held her, and made soothing sounds while stroking her until eventually her body stopped juddering but she still couldn't speak as she was gasping and sobbing, her head in her hands her hair fallen around her face.

Looking up at him her tear streaked face was a picture of utter misery. No longer the tough efficient high powered secretary, simply a woman devastated at losing the man she loved.

Handing her his handkerchief again he sat cuddling her saying softly 'Sam I'm still very fond of you'.

'Not fond enough to tell me what's changed though'.

'I can't so please don't go on asking about it. Look I ought to go but I don't want to leave you in this state'.

'Forget it. Forget me. I'll be alright. Maybe I'll get another job. Go home to Abi and your great decision. Did you tell her about us is that it?' She raised her voice. 'Did you say that you've been fucking your secretary for the last few years but you're sorry and it won't happen again?'

'No I didn't tell her about us. Look Sam leave it please'.

'Leave it?' she yelled. 'We've been lovers for years ever since that first time at your flat in Northampton. We're good with each other whether it's at work, in the office or at meetings and we're bloody good in bed. Lovemaking with you is wonderful for me and I know it is for you as well. You can't throw all that away'.

He looked at her then for the first time that she could ever remember he dropped his eyes and looked away. Mark, the man who always held other peoples stare. The man who never backed down but here he had just given in to her. It was disconcerting and unnerving.

Silence reigned for a long time as they sat side by side each lost in their own thoughts.

'Not much point in sitting here all night is there?' she said more calmly. 'Go home. You haven't helped by coming here and I still don't know why we have to stop being lovers'.

He knelt up. 'We're trying to have a baby' he said softly 'Abi and me I mean'.

She stared up at him dumbstruck.

'A baby? You and Abi? You want a baby?'

He nodded continuing to look down at her.

Oh God now she could understand. If they were trying for a baby no wonder he wanted to be the faithful husband.

'You should have told me'.

'I know. Sorry. I'd better leave now'.

'Yes you should. No.........wait........please. Stay for a while. Let's talk. I won't get all histrionic on you and no more crying, promise' she said sniffing and wiping her eyes again with his handkerchief. 'Look we've got to talk. We can't just leave it like this. Stay for a while and I'll make us some coffee or what about a drink? Yes go on I'll pour you a drink. I've got some whisky. I'll have one too. Please Mark don't go now. We can work something out I know we can. Stay at least for a while and talk with me about us'.

Her words tumbled out as she desperately tried to prolong the time he was there with her. Moving to the cabinet where she kept her drinks she poured him a large whisky and a small one for herself.

'Here you are. Look whisky is that alright? You like whisky don't you? Mark talk to me'.

So they talked. She said that she didn't see why things had to change, after all their relationship hadn't come between Abi and her girls before so why should it now?

He said this was different.

She asked why?

He said because it was. The baby made it different.

Their talking went on for ages and Mark had another couple of large whiskeys. She noticed but didn't say anything as Graham would drive him home. Glancing at the clock she saw that he'd been there for nearly two hours but they'd still not resolved how their relationship could continue in these new circumstances.

'Won't Graham be wondering why you've been here so long?'

'I'm driving myself tonight'.

'Oh'. Silence descended and they looked at each other.

Looking at his empty glass he said 'I'll get a taxi' but it coincided with her saying 'You'd better stay here tonight as you've been drinking'.

They smiled at each other and made "after you" gestures.

'I'll kip down on the sofa if that's alright'.

'OK'.

They chatted for a while longer then without the usual familiarity of going to bed together he said it was getting late. She went to the bathroom first then going into her bedroom called 'Goodnight' from the doorway before shutting it firmly, undressed, found a clean nightie and got into bed.

He poured himself another whisky which he drank thoughtfully before removing his tie and shoes turning off the light and curling up on the sofa. After a few minutes her bedroom door opened and she appeared with a blanket.

'You might get cold. Have this' and dropping it on him she went back to her bedroom.

He would have loved to follow her into her bed but he just lay there struggling with his conscience.

Sam lay with her mind in turmoil thinking through the implications of what he'd said. A baby. No wonder he'd gone all protective and righteous on her. How the hell could she fight that? It wasn't another woman at least not in the classic sense but could she share him with a baby? What happened if he got all paternal and started to talk to her about dirty nappies, breast feeding, teething, baby's first tooth, first steps, showing her pictures of the growing child? She couldn't stand that.

Wide awake she turned first one side and then the other as her mind went over the question a baby. Perhaps it wouldn't happen but what if it did? Her mind churned incessantly.

It was sometime in the night when he heard her creeping through the living room into the kitchen and then the rattle of glasses and the sound of a tap running. Not knowing quite why he did it he rolled quietly out from under the blanket and tiptoed into her room quickly taking off his shirt, trousers and socks. For some reason he left his boxer shorts on. She hadn't put on her light but soon he heard her returning.

Pausing by the sofa she saw he wasn't there and assuming that he'd gone to the bathroom walked on into the bedroom. He sensed her feeling for the edge of the bed and then she lifted the duvet and slid inside.

'Sam' he whispered as he reached for her.

Her shriek was deafening. 'Mark what the bloody hell are you playing at. You frightened me half to death?'

'Sorry. That's all I seem to say tonight isn't it. Sorry. Look its bloody stupid us rowing like this. I've been lying there and thinking as to how we could try and find a way through this and get things back the way they were. I mean that is if you'd like to try?'

'Of course I would but what's changed your mind so suddenly? I know you're unpredictable at times which is part of your charm but this is weird. You go all cold on me at The Sheraton and turn me down and then here tonight you tell me you can't sleep with me any more because you and Abi are trying for a baby. Now you're in my bed. What's up? Did you wake up and feel randy or perhaps you couldn't get to sleep and have been lying there with a hard on? Is that it and with me just a few feet away you decided to slip into my bed and screw me? Good old Sam always horny and up for it so I'll just nip in there and give her one? Is that it?' she asked loudly near to tears again.

'No. I've been lying there on that sofa thinking things through and you're right. We are good together and we need each other. I'm sorry that I was so selfish thinking of Abi and the baby but I can't and don't want to shut you out. There's too much of us together that's gone before and we've so much ahead of us. I really don't know how I'm going to cope but I'll find a way forward for the future. Now is now. Does that make any sense?'

'Oh my darling come here' and pulling him to her she kissed him in the darkness the tears running down her cheeks. 'Just hold me will you don't rush into .... I mean just let's get....... oh I don't know what I mean. Let me enjoy you here in my bed before we make love. Let me have the pleasure of you just being here' she said crying properly now.

'There's no rush' he said softly. Kissing her again he held her tightly until she stopped crying.

Wiping her eyes on the duvet cover she could feel him against her but he wasn't erect. That was unusual as usually he was as stiff as a pole and raring to go the moment his arms were around her in bed. Still she had asked him to just hold her and she'd been crying so she lay next to him savouring his closeness. She loved the feel of his body, his smell, his way of lying next to her when he was asleep but especially the way he made love to her. Her hand slid down his body as she massaged his chest and then his abdomen above the waist band of his boxers for a while before letting her finger tips slip under the elastic and entwine themselves in his dense pubic hair. She felt further down and reaching hold of his flaccid penis started to run her hands around it but nothing happened. No stiffening no enlarging, no erection. Absolutely nothing. It just lay there unmoving, limp, floppy and soft.

'What's up darling? Are you too tired? Don't you want to make love to me?'

'Yes of course I want to love you'.

Sliding down the bed she pulled his boxers off and rubbed his limp penis for a while before moving further down to lick and chew his balls something that normally made him burst into a throbbing erection but tonight he remained utterly flaccid.

God didn't he fancy her any more? He must. After all he was the one who'd initiated things and got into her bed. This had never happened to her before with any man. Hell what was she to do?

She knew that it happened to all men at sometime or other often if they were drunk or unwilling to make love for some reason. He wasn't drunk. Sure he'd had a few whiskeys but she'd seen him drink oodles of booze many times before then fuck her into orbit. No it wasn't drink. He must be willing or he wouldn't be here now. What else?

Taking him into her mouth she sucked hard. Nothing. Letting him slip out of her lips she licked up down and around him while gently massaging his balls thinking furiously. He just flopped around lifeless in her hands and mouth.

Racking her brains as to why men sometimes couldn't get hard she remembered reading that high blood pressure caused erection problems but she was sure that Mark didn't suffer from that. She also remembered that it could happen if the man was suffering a guilt complex from committing some awful crime or being with a mistress instead of his wife. Was that it? Was he now feeling guilty because he and Abi were trying for a baby and he was here sleeping with her?

In spite of all her efforts nothing happened. He remained as limp as a flag on a pole with no breeze. Sliding up the bed remembering that she'd also read that in these circumstances it was absolutely essential not to make a big issue out of it she hugged him and whispered that he was probably overtired and why didn't they just hold each other.

'Sorry' he said quietly. 'That has never happened to me before'.

Nor me she again thought but said 'Darling forget it. Just lie there and relax. It doesn't matter, really it doesn't. What matters is that you are here with me in my bed, in my flat' and so they lay still and snuggled closely to each other but although she was soon asleep he lay awake for a long time worrying about his inability to gain an erection.

Waking early in the morning and with first light just peeping through her curtains and conscious that she was still asleep he wriggled himself free from her realising with enormous relief that he was sporting a very decent erection as he usually did when he woke up. Pushing her hair out of her eyes he gently kissed her lips.

'Good morning. I'm sorry about last night but things seem to be back to normal' he said quietly.

'Umm' she muttered sleepily and kissed him back before reaching down for him. 'So they are. Well you'd better put it to good use then hadn't you' and she pulled him on top of her and smiled in the semi darkness as he started to make love to her. To her delight he took his time and she felt her own climax building until they gasped to each other that they couldn't hold back any longer and exploded almost simultaneously. Calming down and separating their bodies they both thanked each other and said how silly the last few days had been. For a while they laid together quietly until he looked at the clock and noting that there was still at least half an hour before they needed to get up, leaned over to her.

'I'd just like you to check that the equipment is still working alright' he chuckled as he stroked her breasts.

'Oh well in that case I'd better go down and have a good look' she giggled diving under the duvet and finding his prick which was starting to stiffen. Sliding her lips over him she slid her head up and down a few times before moving back up. 'Everything seems fine to me sir' she smiled. 'Would you like me to go back down there?'

'No, I want you up here' he chuckled and lifting her so she straddled him he pushed himself up into her warm moist body. Leaning forward she raised her nightie and lowered her breasts into his face. Moving more quickly she then leant backwards to grasp his legs so giving herself some extra leverage as she rode him to a gigantic climax. She didn't orgasm herself but wasn't important. What mattered was that he didn't have an erection problem and had made love to her. Flopping forward she gasped 'Thank you darling'.

They lay together for a while before getting up, showering and getting dressed. Looking with distaste at his crumpled shirt he suddenly had a vision of Debbie ironing his shirt all those years ago.

'Here wear this' called Sam dragging him back into the present and seemingly able to read his thoughts handed him an unopened shirt box. I bought you a couple of shirts some time ago for your next birthday. I keep meaning to take them into the office but somehow never remembered. You might as well use one now'.

'Haven't got any clean underwear have you as well?'

'Not men's but you can have a pair of my knickers if you want. Any preference for colour or style?' Laughing she opened a drawer in her dressing table and pulling out some underwear held various garments towards him. 'Now what about some pretty pink panties? No, well how about these white lacy French knickers? Or maybe a little black thong? No you're too big to fit into one of those' she giggled.

Declining her offers he pulled on yesterday's boxers as she made a mental note to buy some men's underwear in case of a future similar need.

They dressed, had coffee, cereal and toast and then drove to the office in their own cars.

As she drove, although happy that she'd got Mark back at least for now she knew she was going to have to be very careful about the baby and its effect on their relationship.

Abi had been disappointed the previous evening when Mark had called to say he had a meeting that would go on late and so he'd stay in an hotel and wouldn't be home that night. It had been a very brief conversation.

She wanted to tell him she was pregnant. She was never late with her periods and in fact the only two previous occasions she could remember when she'd been late was both times when she had become pregnant, and she felt pregnant again.

It was something she could instinctively feel. All those years ago she'd had the same sensation even before confirmation and this time somehow she also knew but before going to see the doctor she went into Boots and bought a self pregnancy test kit. Sitting on the loo at home she waited for the coloured indicator to go blue. It did. She and Mark were going to be parents.

Immediately some elements of worry leapt into her mind. After all she was over forty and there were risks having a baby at that age both for her and the unborn child. What would Emma and Charlotte say? Would Mark be pleased? What would he think of her as she got fatter and fatter? Would he still fancy her? Then she smiled with the calm delight of someone for whom a pregnancy was a wanted event. Yes they had both wanted this baby and it would be a much loved child born into a privileged lifestyle.

The next day dragged as she waited for him to come home so she could tell him but he was late that evening with Graham not pulling onto their drive until nearly nine o'clock. As he came in the front door she waited for him at the far end of the hall.

'Darling. You're late you must be tired, come and relax' and pouring him a glass of white wine and a glass of water for herself she settled him into the kitchen to serve supper of cold home cooked gammon, new potatoes, salad, followed by cheese.

When he'd finished she squeezed between him and the table so he pushed his chair back as she sat on his lap.

'Are you ready for some news?' she paused smiling at him. Seeing her looking radiant and before she spoke her next words he knew what she was going to say. 'We're going to have a baby darling. I'm pregnant'. There was a pause before she added anxiously 'You are pleased aren't you?'

He didn't know what to say. His heart leapt and he pulled her towards him. 'I couldn't be more delighted. It's fantastic news. Are you sure? I mean when did you know?'

'I thought I've known for a couple of weeks but yesterday I bought a self test kit and it went blue. That's positive and means I'm pregnant. I was going to tell you last night but with your late meeting and you being away I didn't want to blurt it out on the phone so I've waited until you came home tonight. Kiss me?'

He did tenderly while feeling a flicker of shame that he'd been in bed with Sam when Abi had been waiting to tell him that she was pregnant with their child. He realised that there was nothing that he could do about it now but it underlined for him just how inter-twined the two women and his life were and how complicated things were going to become.

They went into the sitting room and sat next to each other on the deep settee and talked of their future, their baby's future and how their life would change. They discussed telling Charlie and Emma speculating how they might react. Presently they went to bed and after Abi assured him that they were quite safe to make love as usual they did, very tenderly.

At Lovells the work went on. Their bank had made tentative contact with Houghtons bank and in the discrete and cautious way that these things were done it was made known to Houghton's bank that there was a white knight standing by if the rumoured financial problems became real.

Houghtons suddenly cancelled several advertising campaigns. The first to be dropped was in France followed quickly by Germany and Italy. In the UK they didn't completely cancel any advertising but they did reduce the frequency. No reasons were given but industry gossip was that they couldn't afford to spend the money.

A good set of half year results pushed Lovell's share price close to £8 and it was again being quoted as one of the boom shares and not only becoming a darling of the stock market but Mark's picture was rarely out of the newspapers now. If he wasn't being featured on the financial pages then he was in the general interest or lifestyle sections.

One of the main selling women's weekly magazines asked if they could do a feature about the wife of a successful businessman and after some thought Mark and Abi agreed. When it came out it was heavily slanted in favour of Abi and what a beautiful home she had created for herself and the children while her husband was rarely there being so busy dashing about all over the world running Lovells business. It made him out to be somewhat selfish and self centred.

'Balls to them' grunted Mark but she knew the printed comments hurt him and she vowed to be much more careful with any comments she made to journalists in the future. It wasn't that she'd set out to paint Mark like that. It was just that she'd answered honestly and said that yes he did sometimes forget things like birthdays and wedding anniversaries. This had been printed as

> "While Mark Watson hasn't time to send a card to his wife on her birthday, he never forgets a business meeting".

Abi hadn't mentioned her pregnancy to the magazine as they hadn't told the girls yet and the last thing they wanted was for the press to blurt it out before they spoken to Charlotte and Emma. They'd decided to tell them when they came home for their next vacation in a couple of weeks.

Mark's life remained as hectic as ever although for a while on several evenings he did try and get home to Abi earlier than was normal but this only lasted for just over a week before he was back to returning around ten o'clock or later.

Assembling his team of advisers in the office on Tuesday morning he asked for their views on the next best way to approach Houghtons. He was told that their Bank was on standby and had been in dialogue again with Houghton's Bank to confirm the real interest that Lovells had in the acquisition. They debated whether another direct approach from Mark or Tim might be the best way forward, and it was agreed that they would try again. Tim favoured a subtle approach through his club in London the scene of the first unsuccessful meeting. Mark preferred a more direct approach such as picking up the phone. The concluded that they'd try both, Mark first and then a follow up by Tim.

As the meeting was breaking up Caroline stayed behind asking to have a word with Mark. 'You know it's going to be really tough to get Sir Charles Houghton to sell out to us. He'll hang on for grim death as with guys like him it's a matter of pride. His father's business and all that. He'll never give up you know. You'll have to catch him with his fingers in the till which will be difficult as it's his till, or his dick somewhere it shouldn't be and with that ugly old dragon of a wife of his I doubt if he'd dare'....... she paused then grinned. 'Mind you with her as his wife maybe he would. Anyhow it looks like a long hard slog and we just have to keep at him, hammering his business and waiting to pounce when it all goes arse over tit up shit creek'.

He smiled at her use of colourful descriptions which from her didn't sound smutty, just graphic.

He rang Sir Charles who clearly didn't want to waste time on pleasantries but got straight to the action.

'What do you want? Haven't rung me again with a damn fool idea of buying Houghtons have you? If so we've nothing to say'.

'No. The offer is still there Sir Charles but what I wondered was whether we could meet up for an informal chat. Nothing specific just exchange thoughts and views about the latest Government policies, our Industry and so on. What do you say?'

There was a long pause. 'Yes maybe we should meet. Maybe we shouldn't. Let me think about it for a few days. But don't bother to ask us to sell to you. My business is fine and is not, repeat not, for sale. Is that clear? Goodbye'.

CHAPTER 31

It was the next weekend when they told the girls about the baby.

On the Saturday morning after they'd all finished breakfast Abi cleared the plates and asked the girls to stay sitting as she and Mark had something to tell them. Pouring more coffee all round and moving to stand next to Mark who was sitting in the chair at the head of the table she took a deep breath while reaching for his hand.

'Mark and I have got something to tell you both'. Her daughters looked up interestedly.

'We're going to have a baby. Mark and I. You two are going to have a little brother or sister'.

'Bloody hell. You randy old pair. That's a surprise and no mistake' exclaimed Charlie. 'A baby, well I never. Wait till I tell my friends that my parents are having a baby. They won't believe it'.

Emma said nothing, just looked totally shocked and stared first at her mother and then at Mark before speaking slowly and quietly. 'A baby. Crikey'.

Charlie got up from the table said 'Congratulations', kissed her mother then kissed Mark and sat back down. Emma stayed for a moment at the table and then following her sister's lead also kissed Abi and Mark before walking slowly from the room. Abi looked after her with concern on her face.

'Charlie go and see she's alright darling will you please. How do you feel about the fact that you're going to have a baby brother or sister?

'Don't know really. Hasn't sunk in. Not surprised though the way you're always holding hands, being tactile with each other and I imagine probably bonking each other senseless in bed, even at your ages'.

'Charlie really!'

Grinning broadly at her mother she slipped out of the kitchen and went in search of her younger sister.

Turning to Mark, Abi said softly 'Charlie seems OK about it but did you see Emma's face? I think I'll go and find her and see that she's alright'.

She too left the kitchen leaving Mark alone with his thoughts which ranged over the coming baby, Abi, Emma and Charlie, and the latter's suggestion that they bonked each other's brains out. He thought that although they had a good sex life he wouldn't describe it quite like that, whereas with Sam sex was exactly like that. He worried for a moment about his failure to gain an erection the other evening but hopefully it was just a one off event. 'Bloody hope so' he muttered as he got up and wandered off to his study.

Sitting at his desk he thought of Sir Charles noting that he could do that now without getting into an internal turmoil. He considered that their plan to seize Houghton's was going well if slowly and he set his mind to trying to find a way to get closer to the old man and speed up the process.

'She's alright I think just a bit shocked but we'll just have to keep an eye on her as she always was the sensitive one of the two of them but Charlie's absolutely fine about it. In fact I think she's rather proud of us' Abi announced as she rejoined Mark in his study. As he looked round at her she kissed him softly. 'Thank you darling' she breathed almost inaudibly.

'What for?'

'Just being you. Being the father of our coming baby. For loving me and the girls. For everything. I'll leave you now as I imagine you've got lots to do'.

He was still working in his study later in the morning when Emma came in. 'Are you very busy or can I ask you something?'

'Yes of course. What's up?'

'Well when the baby arrives, your and Abi's baby, you will still like me won't you? I mean I know that you're not my real dad but I sort of look on you as my dad and feel that you love me and I........well I wouldn't want.......oh I don't know.....'. Her voiced tailed off and she looked lost.

'Hey come and sit down' he said kindly. 'You're right I'm not your father and I never can be but I've always tried to treat you as if I was and to hear you say that you look on me as your dad is a great honour. But don't worry. I promise you that I won't let our new baby come between us, or between me and Charlie. It'll be kind of shared love. Love has an infinite capacity to expand you know so the love that I feel for you girls won't be diminished by the love I will feel for the baby'.

She looked at him but there was still a worried look on her face.

'Sometimes Em things change suddenly and it seems to throw everything out of place and I can see that from your viewpoint this is one of those situations. But there will always be a special place for you in my heart and my life. You and Charlie are very special people to me and will always be so'.

He smiled as reassuringly as he could and was pleased to see her face relax and a smile appear.

'Thanks Mark. You didn't mind me asking you did you?'

'No, I'm glad you did. Now anything else on your mind?'

She shook her head and then leaned forward to give him a kiss on the cheek after which she again said 'Thanks' and was gone.

He turned back to his desk and restarted working until Abi called lunch was ready.

The girls seemed cheerful during the rest of the day and that evening they all had a happy family supper. When her daughters had gone to bed Abi smiled at Mark and looking somewhat coquettishly at him asked 'I know it's quite early but shall we go to bed.........so you can bonk me senseless?' Grinning he switched off the television and they went upstairs together.

Sunday passed with their normal Sunday type activities. The girls rode in the morning while Mark and Abi read the papers. In the afternoon they all went for a walk and some friends of Charlie's came to the house for the evening, so the girls and Charlie's friends nattered in the kitchen while Abi and Mark went into the sitting room and listened to music before going to bed.

Graham picked him up as usual on Monday morning and another hard working week started. On Wednesday morning Sam rang through and said that she had Sir Charles Houghton's secretary on the line and would he take the call? He said yes.

'Mr. Watson? I have Sir Charles for you. One moment please'.

A pause, a few clicks and then the old man's voice boomed down the line.

'Morning Mark. Now about this meeting you suggested. How about the fifteenth of this month?'

Mark looked at his diary and noting that he could shift things around to accommodate the old man agreed. 'What time and whereabouts? Do you want to come here, or shall I come to you, or perhaps it would be better somewhere neutral'.

'My club again? Lunch time say around twelve thirty suit you?'

So it was settled. After the call was finished Mark puzzled as to what had triggered the old man into ringing him.

What he didn't know was that the previous day there had been a very fraught meeting at Houghton's offices. His bankers, his lawyers and his own Finance Director had all warned Sir Charles that the business was running deeper and deeper into trouble. It was dangerously close to breeching its banking covenants in that it was likely to exceed the agreed maximum borrowing limits and overdraft facilities, something the bank would not tolerate.

His Bankers had been adamant. 'Sir Charles, you have to do something to cut your costs, or increase your sales...... preferably both, and quickly. Whilst we are not saying the overdraft might not be reviewed it will be costly very costly indeed as we would require a substantially higher interest rate because your business is now classified by us as extremely high risk. Also we would need some of the debt burden paid off before we could consider renewing your borrowing facilities, irrespective of the rate of interest. I do urge you to implement change very rapidly. You could of course consider selling off part of the company in order to reduce your borrowings'.

'Never. We'll fight our way out of our present difficulties and emerge intact and stronger. If there is nothing else gentlemen I wish you good day'.

The meeting over, the various people present had trooped out leaving the old man alone and considering the problems. However confident he might have sounded in the meeting in reality he knew the problems were substantial and that his business was in real trouble. The banker was right. He either had to increase sales, cut his costs, or preferably both to improve profitability. His problem was that he didn't know how to do either. All of their recent sales strategies had failed and his costs were escalating too fast.

This was all in contrast with his main competitor Lovells who seemed to have a magic touch. Their new products appeared to sell well right from point of launch. He knew from reading the market research reports that Lovells share of the market was continuing to increase and due to their heavy past investment in new plant and machinery they had modern efficient factories all over the world that produced products extremely cost effectively, especially in Europe. They were formidable competitors and Houghtons were losing out to them everywhere. He sighed as he reflected on his problems and turned potential solutions over in his mind. The trouble was he couldn't see any except to sell some of the business. Maybe a chat with that young Head of Lovells might not be such a bad idea and he'd concluded that he would ring Mark.

Following the call Mark held a council of war. First to arrive was Caroline wearing a tight fitting pale cream short skirt which displayed her excellent legs and matching jacket which subtly accentuated her bust perfectly. Mark watched carefully as she made her way around the room to her place at the table and not for the first time admired her neat bum. The Finance Director was next along with his number two together with Colin Ringwood from the PR company, Andrew Spicer from B I, a senior manager from one of the major financial institutions, Martyn Simpson from Scottish National Bank who had interviewed Mark all that time ago to see if he was the man for Lovells, and Tim Nelson their Chairman made up the rest of the meeting attendees.

Mark opened the meeting by explaining that to his surprise Sir Charles had called and suggested a meeting and that this was fixed for the fifteenth, just over a week away.

'My question to you all is simply this. Why? In the past he's been reluctant to meet with me and vehemently against any co-operation, merger or takeover so why would he call and ask for a meeting? Has his business deteriorated so much that he now feels that an approach from us is worthwhile? Are other potential predators closing in on him? What exactly is the state of their business? Is their bank putting demands onto them that they can't sustain? In short gentlemen and Caroline, I need to know why and so I want an up to date status report on Houghtons and I want it now'.

The discussions took most of the morning and every conceivable avenue that they could think of was debated, challenged, argued and discussed. At the end it was agreed that Houghtons were almost certainly in deep trouble so all members of the meeting would spend the next few days trying to discover as much up to date information as possible and then reconvene together the day before Mark's meeting with Sir Charles.

The days flew by with Mark making two trips to Europe one to their French business which was now in good shape and performing well following Hans's appointment there. His other visit was to Holland where all was also well.

The weekend though was somewhat unsatisfactory as on Saturday morning Abi felt quite unwell and was sick on several occasions. Although Mark was worried she assured him that it was a normal progression of her pregnancy and that it wouldn't last too long and she'd soon be feeling fine again. She spent most of the day in bed and Mark took her cups of tea which she sipped slowly, and light meals which she left untouched because as soon as she tried to eat she had to rush to the bathroom to be sick again.

On Sunday morning Mark got up very early while Abi was still in bed and went into his study. After writing several pages of notes and dictating rapidly into his little machine, he saw that it was nearly seven o'clock so picking up the phone he dialled a London number.

'Hello Caroline Burton'.

'Caroline hi there. Sorry to disturb you. I hope I haven't woken you'.

'No I was just thinking about getting up. What can I do for you Mark?'

'Look I've got a whole pile of issues I want to discuss about Houghtons. We could cover some of them now and the rest we'll tackle tomorrow morning. Can you come in early?'

'Yes of course now what are these issues?'

'Well I've been thinking about Houghtons and why the old man might have agreed to see me. It's out of character and so different from our last meeting. Indeed the final comment he made to me was that their business was not for sale, so why would he want to meet? Looking at the latest intelligence reports I've received it seems that several of their European businesses are in real trouble. Spain has virtually had it, losing money, lost lots more market share and in trouble with the banks there. It's believed that they've had to transfer funds from the UK to bail out that business, funds they can ill afford to move. Germany not much better. Crappy old factory, serious industrial disputes with the German trades union, output at an all time low and morale through the floor. Italy's been a mess for years and now it's totally knackered. We've just recruited one of their senior production people and he can't stop telling us what a mess Houghtons is in".

'How did you get all that stuff?'

'Competitive intelligence. I've got masses of data on Houghtons and this just updates it'.

'That doesn't answer the question. That is sensitive information. I hope you've not been doing anything underhand, or worse still illegal'.

'Of course not. We have simply refined and improved our intelligence gathering procedures with the help of a specialist outside agency called B I. Most of the stuff comes through them'.

'All right so their European businesses are in trouble but that's not really new information is it?'

'Well the extent of their problems is new. Now two things we need to consider both of them complicated. Firstly if I look at the way they've got their business set up now, they seem to have re-organised their financial and reporting structures. These press reports speak of Europe now being a separate trading entity. It looks to me as if effectively they've hived Europe off from the rest of the business which is as you know predominantly in the UK. The information from our Italian production man seems to confirm that. Now if that's so then maybe they're parcelling Europe up for a sale. But who would buy it in the state that it's in?

Secondly I have a report from our bank. Their belief and when a bank says that something is their belief you can be pretty darned sure that they know, is that Houghton's bank have done two things. One, they've syndicated part of the loan to another bank. That indicates that they are doubtful of getting all their money back and are trying to hedge their bets or at least reduce their risk capital by sharing the debt with another.

Two they've apparently given Charles Houghton an ultimatum to pay down some of the debt immediately until he can start to drive up profitability. Both of those are difficult for him to do. He can't pay down the debt as he simply doesn't have the free cash to do it and he can't drive up profitability as he has falling sales, falling market share, he's losing customers and Europe which for years was a golden goose for him is now an albatross round his neck which like the Ancient Mariner he may well be trying to offload.

He's a man with serious problems.

Can you think about and then we can discuss tomorrow from what you know of their structure and particularly the tax implications, would the sale of a separate European trading organisation be practical for him and what would be the issues for us if he did offer it for sale, and if we bought it. Lots of "ifs" I know and here's another one. Some of their European factories supply product to their UK customers but very little happens the other way. In other words virtually nothing manufactured here goes to Europe. Now if we just bought the European business do you think we'd be committed to continuing to supply their UK business? I wouldn't want to do that as it means that I'd be supplying and perhaps keeping alive our main UK competitor.

But to return to the structure and if they've separated Europe. This isn't something that's suddenly happened. They seem to have been re-organising for the last couple of months but they've kept it pretty quiet. However these press reports appear to indicate that the process is complete. So what might he be able to do now in terms of allocating any UK losses and the resulting tax benefits from that to a separate European entity, or might he be able to do it the other way round and transfer the losses from Europe to the UK? Is that likely to be beneficial to us or not if we buy their European business? Or their UK business?'

While Caroline tried to digest these questions Mark threw several more at her and the discussion became more complex, highly involved and went on for over an hour with point and counter point being debated, argued and considered. She made extensive notes while he spoke and then used those to help her discussions. Finally they finished and she said that she'd think carefully about these matters and be ready to talk to him first thing in the morning. Thanking her he rang off and turned his attention to other business issues.

She sat thinking for a while then got up, showered, dressed, had a quick breakfast of muesli and toast before settling down to work on the questions that Mark had posed to her. Around eleven she rang a friend that she'd previously arranged to meet for lunch and said that she'd have to cry off but if he wasn't doing anything that evening he could come round and she'd cook a meal for them and, she added quietly, he was welcome to stay the night if he wanted. He did.

CHAPTER 32

Monday morning and the team assembled to discuss Mark's coming visit to Charles Houghton.

Caroline had worked hard all the previous day after Mark's phone call, only stopping when her door bell rang and Steve her dinner guest appeared grinning, clutching a bottle of wine in one hand and a toothbrush in the other.

Presenting her thoughts on the implications of the Houghtons re-organisation she considered that the corporation tax implications were probably beneficial but warned that she was waiting for a call back from a top European lawyer based in Brussels who specialised in this sort of thing.

'Presume we'll have to pay for his opinion. Thought I paid you to give me legal advice' grumbled Mark.

'You do' she replied frostily, 'but sometimes in legal matters it is better to have a second opinion especially where complex taxation issues arise. I considered this to be one of those occasions. Now if I may continue' and she did so noting the twinkle in Mark's eyes as he bowed his head slightly and gesturing for her to proceed. The meeting took most of the morning and helped Mark clarify his thoughts on Houghtons.

He remained frantically busy at work but at home he and Abi only made love infrequently now. She was much less enthusiastic than before her pregnancy and he guessed this was probably normal for pregnant women. While disappointed he was still thrilled about the baby so happy to accept this temporary change in their intimacy.

The meeting day arrived and all morning he was like a cat on hot bricks. Graham drove him into London and dropped him off outside Sir Charles's club where once inside the head club servant said that Sir Charles had arrived and was waiting for his guest in the members bar. Remembering the way he walked quickly though to the bar which was quite small and smelt of wood, furniture polish and expensive cigars. As he entered his elderly adversary rose and held out his hand.

'Mark nice to see you again. Now what will you have to drink?'

'Sparkling water please'.

'Bloody hell. Don't you want a proper drink?'

'No I'll be fine with that. Alcohol makes me sleepy at lunch time'.

The waiter was already hovering and took the order for water and a whisky for Sir Charles. The two men made small talk until the drinks arrived then wishing each other "cheers" they sat back and Mark waited for Sir Charles to make the first opening of real conversation.

'Well how are Lovells finding business these days? My chaps tell me you're doing pretty well'.

'Yes we're on budget for sales and above budget for profit' but seeing the older man frown he added quickly 'but it isn't easy and we have to work very hard indeed to achieve those results'.

'Umm. We work hard too but we're finding life pretty tough. Nothing we can't resolve of course, just need a bit of time and the odd spot of luck. Business needs luck you know. My father was a lucky man. First-rate at what he did and blessed with an innate natural luck. Stood him in good stead many times especially when he was building the business'.

If the other had been watching closely he would have seen the younger man's jaw set firmly and his eyes go ice cold. Lucky or destructive wondered Mark remembering again the night his own father had come home and said that it was all over but with a big effort he kept himself looking relaxed as he listened to the old man pontificate about his father's exploits.

They chose their lunch and although the head of Houghtons ordered a bottle of burgundy Mark again insisted on sticking to sparkling water. When they entered the dining room it was quite full but their table was reserved and after sitting down the waiter poured one glass of the rich red wine. Slowly as they ate the conversation turned to matters about their industry and they speculated how it might evolve in the future with the increasing power of the big supermarkets and whether the Government would ever intercede to take the pressure off their suppliers such as Lovells and Houghtons who were being squeezed and pressured more and more. The two men thought that much as it might be desirable it was unlikely to happen.

They bemoaned the continual decline of wholesalers which was where Houghton's and Mark's father's businesses had originally started. They talked about the difficulty of recruiting high quality staff especially in senior roles and it was at this point in the conversation that Sir

Charles emboldened by two whiskeys before lunch and the best part of the bottle of red wine during lunch, leaned forward, pointed his finger at Mark and muttered menacingly 'It's time you lot stopped poaching my people'.

Wondering whether to give an "all's fair in love, war and business" response, or to respond more directly and tell the old man to "piss off" Mark looked back at his enemy as that was how he now clearly saw him.

'Some approach us directly and others we headhunt if we think they can add value to our business but the total number that we've taken is limited and frankly I'm surprised that it is such a matter of obvious concern to you. However if it helps I'll ask our people to lay off for a while and not poach any of your team, at least for the time being'.

'Good. Now you've probably been wondering why I suggested that we meet. Well I've been thinking and I asked myself whether there was any value in us discussing some form of joint venture together in chemicals. If there was you could have access to our development and new product ideas, and we could have access to your sales and marketing operation. Might be a win win situation don't you think? Europe first as a trial and then depending on how that goes we could consider other geographic areas. What do you say?'

Of all the reasons for this meeting that had been considered by Mark and his team this was not one of them and the old man had caught him cold.

Thinking rapidly he could quickly see some advantages but also lots of problems. It was true that Houghtons were good at product development in their chemical businesses and had recently launched some excellent new garden pesticide products which were well ahead of the market. What Houghtons were not good at was sales and marketing, but Lovells were.

Mark could see the benefits from Houghton's view point but what were the benefits from Lovells? Access to Houghtons chemical developments yes, but success in selling and distributing them would mainly help Houghtons, not Lovells.

'That is a very interesting proposition I must say and not one that we had considered. I'd like to consult some of my team and think about it before getting back to you. I can see it might make sense for your business but I'm less sure about the benefits for us'.

They talked around the proposition for some while as the old man consumed a glass of vintage port. After coffee Mark said that he had to get back to the office and thanking Sir Charles for lunch he left his enemy sitting there at the table beckoning for another glass of port.

Smiling at the club porter he walked onto the street where Graham who was parked right outside immediately jumped out and opened the rear door to let him into the car. Asking 'Back to the office?' and seeing Mark's thoughtful nod he swung the car into the post lunchtime traffic and started to head out of town back to Crawley.

Leaning back he thought about the old man's proposition. It didn't make sense and the more he thought about it the less he liked it. All he could see was that the benefits would be Houghtons and little or none to Lovells. Also the "hands off my people" had been another odd thing to do. He rang Sam.

'How did it go?'

'Odd, very odd. I'd like to see Caroline and Tim when I get back'.

'Right. There are several messages for you and I've finished all your dictation it just needs signing'.

When he got back Sam summoned Tim and Caroline who listened as Mark explained what had occurred. All three of them considered Sir Charles's suggestion to be odd as it offered little benefit to Lovells but much benefit to Houghtons. Because it was so one sided in its benefits then surely the old man could see that it wouldn't appeal to Lovells and the meeting broke up with them all agreeing that they would go away and think about it carefully to see if they could find any merit in the proposal.

The next day Mark flew to The States and spent three days over there instead of his usual two as he examined their American business in detail and pushed Chuck to improve even further on the impressive results that he was achieving. After heated discussions Chuck agreed that perhaps he could squeeze a little more profit out of the American operations and he undertook to confirm within a week. That was good enough for Mark who knew that once Chuck had committed himself to finding profit improvements he would so he flew back to the UK satisfied with what he'd seen in America and happy that results were going to get even better.

The day after he returned he rang Sir Charles to say that he couldn't see any real benefit to Lovells from the proposed link up and wouldn't therefore be proceeding. Sir Charles said that he was making a mistake but if the decision was made then so be it.

Although he was sure he had been right to turn the joint venture down nevertheless he couldn't help wondering if somehow he'd allowed the old man to slip out of his grasp.

Weeks passed. Lovell's business continued satisfactorily with the share price now close to £ 9. Their banks were supporting their strategy and Mark felt on top of everything except that they were no nearer to acquiring Houghtons and so he was still a long way away from achieving his ambition to put the old man out of business.

Abi continued to get fatter and by seven months was enormous. She assured Mark that it was quite normal as some women carried their babies right in front which made them look bigger than other women.

He liked to lie next to her and feel her tummy and was amazed when he could feel the baby move within his wife. Their sex life had dwindled to almost nothing now. It wasn't possible to lie on top of her and although they made love in a few positions that Abi found comfortable he knew that she was really doing it for him rather than wanting to make love herself. As her pregnancy advanced further she used her hand to bring him to a climax because she'd made it clear that she would prefer that he didn't penetrate her any more until after the baby was born.

He didn't want to do anything to hurt the baby or put Abi to any physical or mental pressure so while he laid there and let her satisfy him he couldn't help thinking of Sam and how she would pleasure him. He hadn't slept with her for a long time and although ashamed of himself for thinking of her while Abi was doing what she was nevertheless he was desperately missing Sam's sexual skills.

By eight months Abi had ballooned out like the proverbial whale so when Mark asked her if she felt up to attending a major charity dinner for their industry at The Grosvenor House Hotel in Park Lane, London. she said she'd rather not.

'If you need a female partner invite Caroline' she suggested.

'Oh she's already going with one of her men friends. No problem I'm quite happy to go on my own'.

'That'll unbalance the table seating plan won't it? Why not take Sam. She's bright, attractive and unlikely to be overawed by the evening.

'Well that's an idea I suppose. I'll find out if she's free that night' he said trying to keep any excitement out of his voice.

The evening of the Charity dinner arrived and Lovells had taken two tables each of ten people and had booked a private room before the event started to entertain some of their major customers to drinks. It was a good way to renew or cement relationships, and the Sales and Marketing Directors were busy finding key people from their customers and introducing them to Mark.

He was good at this part of his job and managed to give each person to whom he was introduced the feeling that they were special and probably the company's most important customer. It also enabled him to ask questions and find out how Lovells were perceived by their customers. He had always found this sort of feedback important and usually identified something that they could improve.

Sam arrived during the drinks session and circulated dispensing good humoured chat and seeing that waitresses kept people's glasses filled. She looked dazzling and there wasn't a man, or woman, in the room that didn't notice her which wasn't surprising as she was wearing a bright red dress that was low cut and showed large amounts of cleavage. It also had a V shaped slit in the front of the skirt which narrowed to a point about half way between her knees and crotch. When she turned it could be seen that her back was bare to the waist. It was a striking gown which could have looked tarty, but on her and the panache with which she wore it looked simply stunning.

She was on the opposite side of the room from Mark who was conversing with someone she didn't know. His eyes flicked past the man to whom he was speaking and widened in delight as they traversed her body from head to toe and back again. He stopped when he reached her eyes and for a nanosecond they both felt a flash of sexual desire spark between them. Giving her the briefest nod he turned back to his guest saying that it had been very interesting to meet him and hoped he'd enjoy the rest of the evening. Taking his time he worked his way around the room until he was close to her and she was able to say 'Good evening' to him.

'Hello Sam' he said slightly over loudly. 'I'm so glad you could come this evening. You really do look quite delightful. New dress I'll be bound. Suits you …….what there is of it' he laughed. A couple of people near to them joined in the laughter.

'Thank you and yes I treated myself' then smiling she leaned towards him her tongue peeping out before saying very softly. 'If you think it's not a lot of dress you wouldn't believe how little there is underneath it………but you're welcome to investigate later'.

Moving away she said brightly 'Oh look your glass is empty let's find a waitress to put that right' to one of their guests standing on his own with an empty glass who felt a warm glow come over him as Sam stood in front on him and engaged him in conversation. Watching his eyes creep to her cleavage as he was a customer she let him enjoy the view. That's all he's going to get though unlike Mark who can have all of me any time she thought. It was so long since they'd slept together. She knew he'd tried to be faithful to Abi but from the look on his face when he looked at her he obviously needed her tonight.

Soon the Master of Ceremonies invited all guests and hosts to make their way to the Great Room where the dinner was being held. As the largest ballroom in London capable of holding nearly two thousand people it was popular for major events such as this charity dinner tonight.

One of the other great attributes of The Grosvenor House Hotel's huge banqueting room was the ability to serve so many people at the same time with hot food. There were armies of waiters and everything ran like clockwork. The food was good, the wines plentiful. Mark and the other Lovells senior management were good hosts and their guests enjoyed themselves. Fortunately the speeches were relatively short and the main after dinner speaker was a former judge who spoke amusingly about some of his courtroom experiences. The audience enjoyed it and then after coffee and liqueurs the band started to play for the dancing to start.

Sam and Mark had hardly spoken during the dinner as she had deliberately sat herself on the opposite side of the table from him but when the dancing started people got up and moved around either to the dance floor, or to find time for a chat with acquaintances, colleagues or friends among the throng of milling people. Sam stayed where she was and talked to those nearest to her while Mark circulated around the other table that Lovells had taken and talked to the various guests for a while again dispensing his special brand of making people feel important before making his way back to his table. Caroline who had been on the other Lovell's table appeared and taking his hand led him to the dance floor where they stayed for a little while jigging in time to the overloud pop music that the band was playing. When they'd had their second dance he led her back to her table.

He disappeared for a little while then re-appeared looking pleased with himself and started to chat to people again. The band started to play an early Elton John number and as soon as it started he walked over to Sam and interrupting the conversation that she was having with another of their guests asked if she'd like to dance.

Looking surprised she paused before saying yes that would be lovely then walked with him towards the dance floor. Not long after they arrived and started to dance the music came to an end.

'Oh shame. I love those old Elton songs, and it was a nice smoochy one too'.

'There's better coming shortly, ah here we are' he replied looking hard at her as the unmistakable introduction to "Lady in Red" started playing.

'That's a co-incidence seeing I'm wearing a red dress and we've just got to the dance floor'.

'Co-incidence, bollocks. I asked them to play it after an Elton number so I had time to get you on the dance floor'.

'Did you now, how clever. Come on then Mr. Chief Executive dance with your own red lady' and she melted into his arms moving her hips very slowly from side to side while pressing her pelvis against him as they danced close together. 'I thought that old female man eater on the other table with whom you were talking earlier was going to devour you. I felt quite jealous'.

'No chance. Just doing my corporate duty. There's only one person I'm going to have tonight'.

'Who's that?' she queried putting her head on one side and running her tongue over her lips.

'Well now' he grinned looking around. 'Where is she. Let me see. Ouch you trod on my foot young lady'.

'Serve you right. Tell me who or I'll do it again?'

'You know the answer to that'.

'Say it. Go on say who you want'.

'You. I want you. Look my room number is…….'.

'I know what it is silly. I made all the bookings. I'll come to you after you've gone up. Are you staying up late tonight?'

'Not down here but upstairs with you well you never know do you?'

'No you don't. We'll have to see won't we but thank you for organising this music' and as the dance floor was packed with people she took a chance and slid her hands over his buttocks, squeezed and pulled him into her.

They stayed for a couple more dances before returning to their table and as it was nearly midnight several people were leaving the huge room. Mark went around to their guests who were still left shaking hands and thanking them for coming. He said goodnight to the Lovell's people and that as he had a busy day tomorrow he thought an early night might be in order. 'If you call midnight early that is' he laughed as he left.

Manoeuvring his way through the crowds of happy attendees and walking up the curving staircase at the end of the huge room onto the balcony he paused briefly and looked down. Sam glanced up at him and then looked away. It didn't take long to get to the lifts and soon he was in his suite where he undressed, showered, wrapped himself in one of the fluffy white bathrobes that hung behind the bathroom door and went to the fridge to take out one of the two half bottles of champagne that nestled there. With a pop it opened and he poured himself a glass of bubbling liquid and sat on the settee.

It was nearly half past midnight when there was a soft tapping so walking quickly across the large room he carefully opened the door and stood aside to let her in.

'Hi. I was starting to wonder if maybe you'd changed your mind and weren't coming'.

'No it was just that I couldn't get away. I didn't want to leave too soon after you so I carried on chatting to various people but here I am sir all yours to do with as you wish. Can I have a glass of that bubbly please?'

Pouring it he turned towards her and smiled. Her heart jumped as she moved towards him, took the glass and drank deeply.

'Cheers. Here's to us....... tonight' she whispered as she put the glass on a side table.

'To us' he replied as he pulled her towards him lifting her chin to kiss her softly and lovingly.

Responding she pressed her body into him and relaxed completely. She felt his hands around the back of her neck groping for the catch on the thin halter neck hand. Knowing it was a tricky double clip which was then covered with a Velcro fastener to hold it securely in place as it was the only thing that stopped the whole outfit from sliding down to her feet, she eased herself away from him, raised her arms to reach behind her and in seconds the complicated fastening was undone. Reaching for the zip she quickly slid that down and as the red gown slid to the floor she stepped out, caught it, draped it over a chair and slipped off her shoes.

All she was now wearing was a tiny red G-string which barely covered her bush. She slowly turned her back enjoying hearing his intake of breath as he took in the fact that nothing covered her bottom except for a thin red string that led up between her buttocks to a slightly wider string band running round her waist.

Turning back to face him and pleased at the reaction on his face she whispered 'I told you there wasn't much under the dress' then putting her hands on his shoulders to press him downwards she added softly 'Now are you just going to look at it or are you going to take it off for me?'

His answer was to crouch in front of her and ease the flimsy scrap of material down her legs past her ankles and as it came free he put it into her outstretched hand. Smiling she took it from him tucked her index fingers into each side of the tiny undergarment and stretching it wide apart hooked it around the back of his neck pulling his head firmly towards her pussy as she leaned back against the large solid oak table that took up one corner of the room.

When he started to kiss her she wriggled up and sat on the edge of the table so he stretched up to reach the higher target that now presented itself. Her ankles went round the back of his neck and leaning her arms behind her she leant back spreading her knees apart completely exposing her most intimate self to his tongue, fingers, and eyes. As he worked on her she felt her passion waves starting and it wasn't long before her climax was approaching so reaching forward she held his head and ground herself hard against his face as she exploded wetly, satisfyingly and noisily.

While she recovered muttering softly 'Thank you darling' he stood and opening his bathrobe positioned his erect penis at the entrance to her now very wet pussy and with a sudden thrust was inside her. Lying back flat on the table her legs wrapped around his waist, her hands gripping the side she revelled in his enormously strong and powerful thrusts. She laid looking up at him as he pounded into her with his eyes closed and she sensed that he was trying to hold back for her. Gripping the table tightly she jerked herself against him.

'Oh baby that's it fuck me, fuck me hard. Come now. Come if you want don't wait for me' and squeezing her pussy on him she pushed her breasts together as she felt him ejaculating into her.

'Sam' he gasped as he continued to move in and out of her while his prick pulsed and squirted.

'Schh baby, don't stop. Come. Just keep coming darling until you've finished. It's alright I'm here and I'm all yours my darling'.

When he stopped moving he looked down to her lying flat back on the table her hands still clamped around her breasts, her legs still around his waist. Easing himself out of her he leaned forward, moved her hands away and kissed her breasts and nipples before moving to her lips which he treated to deep gentle loving kisses.

'That must have been so uncomfortable for you' he said kindly and taking her hand he helped her off the table and led her to the settee where he pulled her onto his lap and handed her a glass of champagne. They cuddled and kissed and told each other how much they'd missed making love. She said that she was always there for him and he said he knew that. Soon they'd finished the first half bottle so when he suggested that it might be a good idea to get the second bottle opened she jumped off his lap, went to the fridge, opened the bottle and brought it back.

Reaching the settee she handed him the bottle and then sinking to her knees opened his bathrobe and slid his now very slack prick between her lips and started to excite him by licking and chewing. Immediately she felt him stir and as she continued to work on him he erected to his full impressive size. Letting him slide out she asked 'Would you like me to bring you off like this now?'

'No let's go to bed'.

They did as he demanded and he made love to her slowly and for a long time before he pressed himself down groaning as he pumped his seed into her again.

Lying side by side he thanked her again and then quickly went off to sleep but she laid there for a long while so happy. She softly stroked his hair, his chest, his thighs and his belly. Briefly she took his limp prick in her hand and played with it for a few minutes while he slept, wondering if that would giving him an erotic dream. It flickered two or three times and enlarged a little but he didn't erect and soon she too was asleep.

They woke at six when the alarm shrilled and he looked at her, stroked her face, kissed her delicately and whispered how wonderful last night had been.

'I've got to go darling but let's not leave it so long next time' and giving her a peck on the lips he slid out of bed and went into the bathroom, where he showered, shaved, splashed on some aftershave, and walked back into the bedroom. Sam had turned over and was lying on her side.

Dressing quickly he moved to the bed, sat down and stroked her hip. 'Sam darling don't leave it too late to get back to your own room will you. You don't want any of our people to see you walking about this morning still in your evening dress'.

'No I'll get up when you've gone and don't worry I'll pop on a bathrobe to go back. Can you pack my dress in your bag? Oh and is it alright if I'm late in to the office this morning? It seems to have been a bit of a short night's sleep'.

'Really why was that?'

'Not sure but I think it had something to do with a lovely man making love to me'.

'Sure, come in when you're ready. Bye my darling' and he left the room.

Exiting the lift he walked over to reception, signed his bill and turned to Graham who was waiting for him.

'Anyone else sharing the car with us Mark? Sam coming?'

'No I don't think so. When I left the dinner last night she was busy chatting to people. Probably having a lie in. Come on off we go. She'll make her own way to the office'.

Sam laid thinking about their lovemaking but especially the fact that this morning he'd called her "darling". Three times. She'd got him back but for how long? Would he ever leave Abi and the girls and there was the baby to consider? Sighing she rolled onto his side of the bed and whispered 'Mark I adore you'.

Just before quarter to eight Mark walked into his office, sat down at his desk, picked up the phone and rang Abi.

They chatted for a while then he finished the call and picked up a file that he'd been working on the previous day.

It was a little after ten o'clock when Sam brought in his coffee, smiled, said thanks again for last night and left to catch up on her work, still dizzily happy he'd called her 'darling'. Three times. He'd never called her darling before.

CHAPTER 33

It was the next week when everything happened.

Abi phoned on the Tuesday afternoon and told Mark that her labour had started, that a friend was on the way to take her to the hospital and that he shouldn't worry but just wish her luck. Mark yelled for Sam to cancel his appointments for the rest of the week ran downstairs and drove himself to the hospital.

He was there waiting when Suzy a long time friend of Abi's pulled up to the maternity entrance and helped her out of the car. In spite of Mark snapping orders to anyone and everyone that he could see, the staff took charge and suggested that as they had coped with this situation many times before he should keep quiet and let them and his wife get on with things or else he'd have to leave. Scowling he did as requested and accompanied his wife to the delivery room where about five hours after she started her labour Chloe Sarah Watson arrived into the world.

As he held the little crying bundle of humanity he was overcome with such strong feelings of happiness, compassion, wonder and joy that he couldn't remember anything before that had ever made him so happy. He kissed Abi and when she asked if he minded that it was a little girl and not a boy, he said no and meant it, but he did hope if they had another child it would be a boy.

There were no complications for Mother or baby so on Friday morning Abi, baby Chloe and Mark left hospital and he drove them all home where Abi's mother was waiting for them.

After the obligatory cooing and ahha-ing, Abi carried Chloe up to the nursery, breast fed her, changed her nappy then settled her down into her cot, an old piece of baby furniture which she'd saved after Emma was born as she and Roger had talked of having more children but his untimely death had prevented that happening.

Mark felt fairly useless and helped where he could but like most new fathers he was less comfortable handling the tiny bundle of life than was Abi who found that all her previous maternal feelings and skills had returned.

It was during the morning after the homecoming day that Sam rang him.

'Hi boss. How's the baby, and Abi of course?'

'Both fine. I'll be back next week.'

'Right. Look I know you don't want to be disturbed but Andrew from B I rang and said he wanted to see you if possible or failing that then to speak to you urgently. I told him you'd just become a father and could it wait until next week and although he said it could if it had to, really he would prefer to talk to you before that as it's something personal about Sir Charles Houghton which you would find very interesting'.

'Alright I'll call him later today. Anything else that can't wait?'

'Yes masses but Abi and your baby are more important. See you Monday, oh and Mark'.

'Yes?'

She wanted to say that she loved him but didn't dare. Should she say that she missed him or that she was there for him if he needed her? Probably not when he was still reeling from becoming a father but she did love him desperately and thinking of him with Abi and baby Chloe was tearing into her like a knife.

'Oh nothing, see you Monday'.

When she'd rung off he mused as to what could be so important about Charles Houghton and after turning it over for a while in his mind he went into his study and dialled Andrew's number.

'Mark. Congratulations are in order I gather. Everything OK?' Receiving confirmation that it was he went on. 'Look sorry to trouble you at this happy time but I thought that you'd want to know this straight away.

Firstly, as you know Colin Ringwood and I have been getting close to several of the Houghton's Directors. It is very clear that many of them are extremely unhappy with Sir Charles and his handling of the Company and they feel that there is no longer any future for the business. A number of them have talked with Houghton's bank and they've even had a secret meeting with an insolvency practitioner. Now you only do that if things are pretty dire and you think the business is going bust and so need to protect yourself legally from any charges of insolvent trading.

We're sure that Sir Charles is unaware of these discussions but we are convinced that if a suitable offer was made to the dissenting Directors they would happily agree to sell their individual share allocations to you in a takeover. After all they are worth nothing to them as they stand now and if the business collapses the paper shares they hold in Houghtons as a private company are worthless. But at a stroke you could turn valueless pieces of paper into real money for them. Of course that wouldn't give you control as Sir Charles through his and his wife's personal holdings in the business, plus a family trust which he administers holds substantially more than half of Houghtons shares however to have his senior team wrapped up and in your pocket would give you a very strong bargaining position with the old sod'.

'Anything else?' Mark was puzzled as this was interesting but not so urgent that he had to interrupt his time with baby Chloe and Abi and he said so.

'Quite which is why I'll now move onto the second and more important point. You'll remember that you also asked my firm to keep a close eye on Sir Charles himself and find out everything possible about him. If I remember rightly you said somewhat graphically that you wanted to know if he farted, when, where, how often and how loudly.

Therefore I've had some of the best teams in B I watching and checking him out extremely carefully. Now I don't know about his farting habits but what we have discovered is that our reclusive, upright, pillar of the Church, very moral family orientated Sir Charles has a naughty secret.

He's very careful about where he goes and what he does and he covers his tracks well but there is one thing that we've discovered. He likes girls. Young pretty ones. I don't mean underage or anything pervy like that, just good lookers in their twenties. What's more he has a small London house in a little mews near Paddington Station which we don't think his wife knows about. As far as we can tell it's a Company asset which we believe is slid through the books as a West London office. We're checking that by the way but an office it's certainly not. It appears to be for his personal use and where he has his assignations'.

'Well well well. How did you find that out and are you sure?'

'Oh yes quite sure and as for how we found out, shall we just say that we got very suspicious one day recently when we followed him. Remember that their head office is in Leeds but they also have a London office near Euston Station. We've been covering both. Last Wednesday late afternoon he drove off from the London office in his Rolls and then parked it in a multi-storey car park not far away just off Baker Street. That seemed odd. I mean why drive for about ten minutes and then put an expensive car like that in a public car park rather than leaving it secure in the company car park? Then he walked back up Baker Street to the tube station. Fortunately I had two operatives on the case that evening and they followed follow him. He caught the tube to Green Park. From there he walked along Piccadilly until he picked up a cab which took him to High Street Kensington tube station. We were so lucky in getting a cab immediately so we could continue to follow him. Often these sorts of surveillance operations go wrong simply because there isn't a cab available. From Kensington he got another tube to Paddington and finally he finished his very strange journey by walking to his house.

No question in my mind he was being very careful indeed to shake off any possible followers. If you think of a map of London he went all over the place. Why for example didn't he just drive to the house where residents can park in the mews? Why leave his expensive car in a public car park off Baker Street? Why hop on and off tubes and taxis? The answer is because he was making bloody sure he wasn't followed and we soon found the reason why. Not long after he arrived a taxi pulled up and a girl in her twenties got out and rang the bell. Blonde bit tarty but quite pretty by all accounts. He let her in and she stayed the night'.

'Perhaps she was his daughter or a niece or the daughter of a friend, and how do you know she stayed the night?'

'Perhaps she was...... except she wasn't. While one of my guys kept watch the other went to get their car then they spent the night in the car keeping watch. The next morning when she came out the way she kissed him in the doorway showed quite clearly that she wasn't his daughter or niece. She was a professional. We've got some photos of her as she walked away to get a cab at Paddington Station which as you know is only a few minutes away. A bit later another cab pulled up and Sir Charles came out, locked up the house and went. My guys followed the cab which took him to the Baker Street car park where he'd left his Rolls the night before. From there he drove himself back to his London office.

He seems to spend two nights a week in London generally Wednesday and Thursday so as this occurred on Wednesday we decided to check him out again on the following night using a three man team. We had one watching the house, and two others ready to follow him. This time he left the office around six and drove to the same car park but caught a taxi to his club where he stayed for about an hour. When he left his club he took a cab to Victoria and then travelled by tube to Blackfriars, another cab this time to Oxford Circus and then finally another tube to Paddington from where he walked to his house. Nothing happened for nearly two hours but just before ten a taxi pulled up and a girl got out. Different one from the previous night as this second one was Asian, probably Indian, She also stayed the night.

Now what do you think of that eh? Our Sir Charles is not so morale or upright as he'd like everyone to believe. Quite a turn up for the book. Not sure what you want to do about it but thought that you should know as soon as possible'.

'Andrew you're right I don't know what we can do with the information but I'm glad we've got it. Thanks a lot. Now I really must go as I want to see my own very pretty young lady called Chloe. Bye'.

A thoughtful Mark sat for a few moments and then getting up went back into the sitting room where little Chloe was nuzzling into one of Abi's breasts slurping away happily while making contented little grunting sounds. He sat and watched and in a while Abi changed Chloe to her other breast.

'She seems to like that'.

'So she should. Best quality milk, warm, freshly made and available on demand. Plenty here if you want to try some too' smiled Abi engagingly but Mark felt strangely shy and declined her offer. 'Kiss me then while I'm feeding her and he did carefully and gently and then he kissed the baby's almost bald head.

All through the rest of Friday and the weekend he delighted in spending time with Abi and Chloe when she was awake. It was a great help having Abi's mother there to take care of things. Charlie and Emma both came home and were delighted with their little sister and willingly helped Abi with the many things that babies required to be done for them. Masses of presents, flowers, and cards arrived each day and several of their friends called "just to have a peek at the new arrival" but although he was very focussed on his wife and baby his mind kept nagging him about Sir Charles, the secret house, and the mysterious girls.

He wondered if Andrew's people had been mistaken about who the girls were but then why did Charles Houghton go through the elaborate deception routine with tubes and taxis? The girls must be secret girlfriends, mistresses, or hookers. The question was what to do about it and did it give him a way to get at the old man?

Eventually the germ of an idea came to him. It wasn't very nice but then he reminded himself that what old man Houghton had done to his father's business wasn't very nice either.

He let it roll around his mind for a few days and tried to work out how he could spring a trap that would ensnare the old man. Often before in his life he'd found that the first inkling of an idea if allowed to quietly grow and develop could turn into a plan of action for implementation. By the following weekend he'd decided what he was going to do but to actually implement his plan he had to meet with Charles Houghton again somewhere secret. Picking up the phone he asked Sam to get the old man. Before long the connection was made and the opening pleasantries completed.

'Charles it might be a good idea if we met again to see if we can find a way to achieve what we both want. You want some form of joint venture. We don't. We want to buy your Company. You don't want that. On the face of it we have an impasse but I've usually found that with a bit of good will and creative thinking sometimes, indeed often, a way through can be found. Now before you shout and tell me your business isn't for sale, keep an open mind and let's meet to discuss your ideas and mine.

I don't know what your movements are in the next couple of weeks. I'm in Europe most of next week so perhaps we could meet on our boat. We have a motor yacht in the Med. It's very private and conducive for discussion and happens to be free and available. What about meeting there, say next Wednesday? You could stay on for a few days afterwards in peace and quiet if you'd like to study the proposition that I'll bring with me. You could take Belinda with you or maybe you'd prefer to be alone and if so I could arrange for some friendly company to join the boat so you don't get too bored'.

He paused and waited. Would the old man take the bait?

'Maybe we should meet. Let me think about it Mark. I'll call you back this afternoon'.

The call finished and Mark sat staring into space. Would it be as simple as that? Would Sir Charles Houghton, Chairman of DGH, head of a large business in desperately serious trouble meet him on Lovell's boat, and if so would he stay on, and if he did would he accept some illicit company? So many imponderables he thought grimly and his mood remained guarded for the rest of the day until Sam said that she had Sir Charles on the phone. He snatched up the receiver.

'Mark. As you know I am wholly opposed to selling all or indeed any part of my business to you'. There was a long pause. 'However it is true to say that we are facing a few temporary trading challenges at the present. They are of a minor nature but it may be useful to renew the discussions that we had recently. Your offer of using the boat sounds ideal so we can talk confidentially'.

'Fine now have you given any thought to my offer for you to stay on for a day or so?'

'Yes I have. Sounds nice. Can I let you know tomorrow whether Belinda will be with me?'

'Sure whenever you like' replied Mark.

Damn this wasn't what he wanted. He needed Charles Houghton on his own not with his wife. Would he go on his own and not take Belinda? Was he hooked? If not he was certainly nibbling and Mark could visualise the hook poised outside his adversary's thick fleshy mouth but it wasn't until the next afternoon that the prey returned to the bait. Sam put the older man through to Mark.

'Afternoon Mark. Look Belinda's been thinking for some time of going to a health farm for a few days with a friend of hers and as she's not too good on boats, seasickness and so on it seemed that it might suit us both if she went off to enjoy her carrot juice and exercise routine while I stay for a day or so and work on whatever proposition you put forward. Alone although I imagine there will be other people on board, crew, staff, waitresses ….. err whatever if you get my drift. You mentioned company I think?'

'Quite. Yes we can organise that and I'm sure you'll be very comfortable on the boat' Mark almost yelled as he knew that the bait had been completely swallowed. Calming down he continued 'Next week then. If you fly to Nice we'll pick you up at the airport and if you think of anything else let me know otherwise I'll meet you on board next Wednesday'.

They rang off, both reflecting on the conversation.

Charles Houghton intended to make a fight of it. Everyone was telling him he had to sell and they might be right but he was dammed if he was just going to give in and sell Houghtons to that young upstart from Lovells who seemed to think that the only route was to sell to him. No he was going to give him a bloody nose. He'd see what the offer was, enjoy whatever entertainment Mark provided on the boat then he'd hawk the business around to other potential buyers.

In the past there had been interest from a number of companies wanting to buy Houghtons but that interest seemed to have dwindled away as his company's performance had deteriorated and their financial problems became more widely known. His bankers were telling him Lovells was the only game in town but he wasn't going to give up yet.

Mark couldn't believe how easy it had been in the end to get the old man into the spider's web, twisted into an inescapable bundle and soon to be destroyed. Well maybe that was a bit premature as all old man Houghton had done was agree to enter the spider's web, but when he does then I really will have him thought Mark happily.

When Sam next went in to him she could see how hyped up he was and knew that when he was in that mood he wanted sex. If things were different and there wasn't baby Chloe around to complicate things she'd suggest they went to her apartment and screwed. Maybe she should offer anyway?

'What time you leaving tonight? There are several reports here for you to read and you've still got to prepare for the quarterly meeting with the Bank next week. Do you want me to stay on and work late with you?' She was practically throwing herself at him. If he wanted her surely he'd take up her offer?

'Thanks Sam but no I'll take the stuff home as I want to be with Abi when she gives Chloe her ten o'clock feed. Do you know it's marvellous and quite humbling to see Chloe at Abi's breast.........'

'Sorry Mark' she interrupted, 'I think my phone's ringing' and she fled out of the room into her own outer office. It was bad enough to know about the baby but she certainly didn't want to hear all about the wretched kid sucking Abi's milk swollen tits she thought viciously. I want Mark loving my breasts in my bed she yearned quietly to herself. God she missed Mark and she knew he needed her, but not tonight it seemed. Tonight he'd be with his family but I bet he's still not yet getting any sex from Abi. Good that'll make him boil up even more for me she snarled quietly to herself.

He went home early again and after spending some time with Abi and the baby at their late evening feed occasion departed to his study to assemble his presentation for the Bank. Whilst expected to be routine it was never wise to take banker's visits too lightly as all companies needed the support of their banks in good times and especially in bad times. Although Lovells was very well placed financially and was seen as a star client by their bank Mark always worked diligently to ensure that he kept them fully briefed by telling them enough, but not too much. Their share price had now clambered through the £9 barrier and was moving strongly ahead.

The press was full of speculation that a major acquisition could be on the cards and advised people interested in buying into a growth company to buy into Lovells. Houghtons weakening position was also mentioned and most papers seemed to think that a merger or acquisition of the two businesses was an ideal solution.

He had meeting after meeting to finalise an offer for Houghtons that made sense to their various stock holders and not least old man Houghton himself who it was believed had mortgaged the enormous stately home in which he and Belinda lived and re-invested that money plus most of what was left of his own personal fortune back into the business to keep it afloat. In short not only was his business running out of cash but so was its owner.

Mark was convinced he could pull the noose tightly around the neck of his quarry thus bringing Houghtons into Lovells and destroying the old man. Most of Houghton's team were on side so all he had to do was get the old man alone for a few days on the yacht and he'd have him too.

He pressed the intercom to Sam and asked for no interruptions or calls for the next fifteen minutes then checking the back of his diary quickly found the number he wanted and dialled on his direct private line. The call was answered after just a few rings and a carefully modulated female voice asked if she could help.

'May I speak to Eve please, this is Mark'.

'One moment sir..............you're through now'.

'Hello?'

'Eve it's Mark, reference number two six five' he said giving his code.

'Hello there' she replied tapping the name and numbers into her computer and watching Mark's details come up on the screen. Mark Watson a big business tycoon who never booked for himself always for others. 'Can you give me your first password and date of birth please?' He gave both. 'Thanks and now the second and fifth numbers from your six digit number'. She listened and tapped it on the keyboard. 'Now your second password' and when the screen verified the information she asked 'So how can we help you today?'

'I need two of your girls to go to the South of France. They'll travel out on Thursday and entertain that day or Friday through to Sunday, possibly Monday or Tuesday. They need to be really nice and classy and very open minded if you understand what I mean'

'All my girls are nice and classy' Eve chided gently 'and open-minded as you so charmingly put it'.

'Sorry but this is important to me'

'It is important to me too. Do you have any particular type of girl in mind and are there any unusual requirements?'

Eve who ran a very high class call girl network was extremely careful to establish the specific requirements of her clients so that she could furnish a model to suit exactly what was requested.

She had dozens and dozens of girls on her books. Some were full time very high-class hookers. Others were well to do girls who were uninhibited, had no proper job and just wanted to earn money from time to time. Yet others were secretaries, estate agents, legal assistants, bank clerks, advertising or marketing girls even a supermarket checkout operator. They all worked for Eve when they weren't working at their normal jobs.

Most were in their twenties, some in their early thirties and she had a few older girls in their late thirties or very early forties. Whatever the age, colour or creed of her girls they all shared three things in common.

Firstly they wanted to earn lots of money. Secondly they were extremely attractive. Lastly they enjoyed uninhibited sex.

Eve's girls came from many different walks of life but they had all succumbed to an approach from one of Eve's talent scouts, two female and one male who frequented top class bars, restaurants, and clubs mainly in London as this was where they had the greatest success in persuading potential recruits to join Eve's operation.

There was never any compulsion or heavy persuasion as their experience was that if they could find the right girl who wasn't in a permanent or serious relationship, talk to her about international travel, entertaining, expensive clothes, top class hotels and restaurants around the world plus the opportunity to earn huge sums of money, they would express great interest and usually agree to a meeting in a private office just off Piccadilly in London's West End in order to find out more details.

Some of the girls after being quizzed about their past and current sex lives and their sexual likes and dislikes started to realise that they were being sounded out to become a call girl and simply strode away in high dudgeon. Some giggled nervously said that they would think about it but quickly ended the conversation and got away as soon as they could. However a surprising number asked for more information which Eve gave in an open and honest manner. She needed the girls to really want to do this work so she didn't try and compel or force them. They had to want to do it for themselves.

Once they passed the interview the next step was to meet one of the girls working for Eve. This was set up within the next couple of days. Nine times out of ten once they had met a working girl and found how much money they could earn through that lifestyle, most said they would like to try it out.

Eve had a long-term partner with whom she lived. He ran his own executive car hire business and it was as a result of her hiring a car one day that the two of them had met. They ensured that their financial affairs were separately constructed so that there was never any risk of him being accused of living off immoral earnings.

However as her clients came not just from Britain but Europe, the Middle and Far East, America and Africa and included judges, senior policemen, barristers, diplomats, accountants, politicians from all parties, a rear admiral, a couple of generals, an Air Vice Marshall, lots of businessmen and even an Australian media tycoon she felt reasonably secure that she knew enough people to ensure that she never got into trouble with the law.

For this reason she refused to have anything to do with drugs, child sex, smuggling, guns, people trafficking, illegal immigrants or anything else that she thought of as nasty or unlawful activities. She didn't consider what she did as illegal or immoral, merely putting people with particular needs and who could afford the high fees in touch with each other.

Eve managed the first appointment for new girls extremely carefully and always explained to the client that their date was new to the experience. This appealed to some clients especially as she promised a full refund of fees if the girl did not live up to expectations. She'd only had to pay out on very rare occasions.

Once the first date had gone all right the new girl usually contacted Eve the next day to ask for a further date as she'd now experienced a taste of the excitement, money and a possible new high life, so in order to hook them into her web Eve got them another booking as soon as she could if possible within the same week. She then deliberately left a gap of at least two and sometimes three weeks before arranging the third date. This time gap usually resulted in the girl ringing a couple of times to ask if there were any more dates available. The second call was the one that Eve wanted as it signalled that her new pussycat was hooked into the sex service lifestyle.

It was a formula that had been developed over the years and now she had a very extensive network of girls who would perform every conceivable sexual service for which any client, male or female could ask.

Coming from a broken home she'd been taken into care when she was seven years old. Her early life had been a succession of foster homes some of which had been alright but others had been dreadful. On several occasions she'd been sexually assaulted by one or other of her many foster fathers or uncles, or beaten by foster mothers or aunts, so when she was nearly fifteen she'd run away and never gone back. Social services made a perfunctory attempt to find her and then gave up simply listing her "missing – run away".

Originally christened Yvonne she'd found her name was often shortened and eventually changed it to Eve.

Attractive, resourceful and looking older than her fifteen years she'd hitched around the country doing odd jobs. Drifting south she'd worked as a waitress, served in shops, been a cleaner, valeted cars, got bored working in an office as a junior filing clerk and finally finished up in London a long way from her native Manchester. She slept with various young men usually in return for a meal but occasionally to satisfy her own sexual needs. With no academic qualifications she wafted in and out of various mundane jobs none of which paid very much and so finding the weekly rent for her miserable little one room bed sit south of the Thames was a real struggle.

One night virtually broke she wandered into a pub in Vauxhall which unknown to her was used by street prostitutes to find clients. Ordering a whisky and knowing that she couldn't afford to pay this week's rent she'd concluded that her only option if she wanted to keep her little room was to sleep with her landlord who'd pestered her many times. The whisky used nearly all her money. She had been there for about five minutes and was staring morosely into her glass contemplating the horror that was to come tomorrow with the landlord who always reeked of stale sweat and wore a filthy vest but no shirt most of the time, when a man sidled up to her and asked if she was looking for business. She soon realised what sort of business he hoped she was in when he whispered that he'd give her £20 for a quickie.

Broke, faced with the prospect of sleeping with the awful landlord here was an alternative. This man wasn't smelly or dirty and although she would describe him as a bit of a creep he seemed clean and harmless. If she slept with the landlord that was like doing it for money wasn't it she thought quickly to herself? Nodding she followed him outside round the corner to a run down street on which there was a derelict building site.

She hadn't any condoms with her and nor had he so she refused to let him penetrate her. Instead after unzipping him she rubbed his rather small prick briefly until it was erect before kneeling down to take him in her mouth. It was over very quickly as she'd only just begun sucking him when he ejaculated. Leaning away she spat out his emissions while he thanked her, zipped himself up and scuttled away. It was sordid and very demeaning but she was twenty pounds better off than when she went into the pub, could pay this week's rent, not have to have sex with her landlord, and it had taken less than ten minutes. She hadn't even had to undress.

That was the start of prostitution for her and soon she was earning a lot more from her night time activities than her daily wages so she gave up working at legitimate day jobs to work as a prostitute mainly at night but sometimes during the afternoon as well. When she didn't pull punters in pubs she took to standing on street corners and although she would get men that way she was always very frightened about the risk she was running getting into strange men's cars. She had several scary experiences and got beaten up a couple of times and once had to slam her fist into a punters balls as she was really frightened to stay in the car. He screamed but she got away.

She was arrested by a burly policeman for soliciting but he offered to drop the charges if she'd give him a freebie. She did in the back of the police car and good as his word he let her go.

Shortly after that there was a big police crackdown on prostitution in the south London area so she moved to Soho where she walked the streets and took punters to a grimy first floor flat which she rented in a dingy building just off Wardour Street.

She earned quite a lot of money until one night she was threatened by two thugs, one black and one white who offered her protection in return for half her takings and free sex whenever they wanted. Saying she'd think about it she promptly left Soho and moved out of London to Boreham Wood where she advertised in sex magazines and over the course of the next couple of years started to move herself upmarket.

Once she'd had a client who asked if she'd be interested in a threesome. It didn't take long to fix up and she netted over three times the fee she'd have got for a session on her own. This got her thinking that maybe there was more money and less risk, both to her health and from possible violence if she could get into the procurement side of prostitution.

Knowing several other girls in the business and with carefully worded advertisements in certain sex magazines her idea paid off.

Within twelve months she was largely an organiser rather than a doer although for certain former clients from time to time she'd still turn a trick herself but she no longer screwed men for money, at least not in the physical sense, only financially. Her contact list and bank balance increased steadily and she was careful to only take on girls that were attractive, broadminded and trustworthy.

From the girl's point of view it was easier and safer to respond to a booking arranged by Eve as they knew that all the clients were vetted rather than having to find their own clients with all the risks that would be entailed.

Her business expanded and over the years she became more selective about her girls continually refining her list adding girls with different nationalities and colours and increasing prices to meet the varied demands of her now extremely upmarket clientele. Mostly these were business men who wanted a girl or girls but sometimes she was asked to provide gay partners so she got her scouts to find few males to join her operation who would satisfy that need.

She also had a growing number of lady clients. Some were frustrated housewives looking for some sexual excitement during the day while their husband was at work but the majority were business women most of whom simply wanted a male stud to service them when they were in town overnight. Occasionally they asked for a girl or girls.

For example she had one high powered lady barrister from Sheffield who came to London from time to time to handle cases in the High Court and when she did she always rang and booked two of Eve's contacts for at least one of her nights in London. Sometimes she asked for two males or a male and a girl but her most frequent request was for two girls for a lesbian threesome.

Now some fifteen years after she first started she had bought herself a huge house near Epping Forest in Essex and worked on word of mouth or through the Internet. Her services were discreet, available if you knew how to find them and extremely expensive. The clients paid her and she paid the girls directly into their bank accounts the rates varying depending on the time booked, whether they were required just in the UK or overseas, what services the client wanted and the experience of the girls. She could even provide business receipts if required.

'No not really I'll leave it to you Eve but make 'em really nice, please' continued Mark.

She laughed. 'No problem. Where are they going to stay and what are they going to do in Cannes apart from the obvious that is'.

'They'll be on our yacht that we use from time to time. The guest that they'll entertain will already be there.

'Sounds lovely, I'll look through my files and send some suggestions round by motorbike courier. Ring me when you've decided and I'll make the arrangements. Usual terms?'

'Fine, I'll call you later'.

Mark put down the phone, picked up his diary and dialled another number. A male voice answered.

'Some time ago I was given your number by Andrew Spicer. There is a confidential job to be done, filming in the South of France. Leave tomorrow. You'll be away for a few days. Don't get seasick do you?'

'Not usually but I don't know if I'm free. I can't just drop everything you know'.

'I'm told you're the best and this is important. B I recommended you so now can you do it or do I cross you off my list and find someone else for this and future jobs?'

'Hold on'. There was a pause and then the voice said 'Well I think that by shuffling things around a bit I could do it'.

'Thanks, thought you would now listen carefully' and Mark explained exactly what he wanted. The film man had no idea exactly who'd rung him but he knew what he had to do and that he was to submit his bill to B I.

Mark had another call to make and asked Sam to get the skipper of the company yacht. After a few minutes she buzzed, said that Captain David Stevens was on the line, that his wife's name was Mary and that they had a one-year-old son called Peter.

After asking about his wife and baby son he said 'Now David listen carefully' and explained about Sir Charles and some girls coming on board. They discussed an itinerary then Mark finished the call.

'Billy and the Agency are here for their appointment with you' said Sam through the intercom once she saw that Mark was off the phone.

'OK send them in and I'm expecting a parcel. Call me when it arrives will you'.

The discussion didn't take long. Mark agreed the agency's proposals, showed them out and then settled down to study some documents soon becoming deeply engrossed in them.

He had the ability to read quickly and also to concentrate even if interrupted by incoming phone calls which was one of the keys to his phenomenal work rate.

Later in the afternoon Sam came in with a package about eighteen by twelve inches in size, nearly half an inch thick clearly marked for the attention of MARK WATSON ONLY. 'I think this is what you wanted. Shall I open it for you?'

'No just put it over there' he said waving vaguely to the other side of the office.

He stayed at his desk for a while then strolled over to one of the armchairs, poured another cup of coffee and picked up the package. It was well sealed. Inside was another sealed package also clearly marked only for his attention. Eve was very careful and thorough.

The inner package contained large three envelopes each of which was also carefully sealed. He selected the top one and opened it to reveal a blue file.

Inside there were several photographs and a one page written statement.

He looked at the photos first. There were half a dozen, each eight by six inches and showed her in various outfits and poses. She was certainly a stunning girl with shoulder length very pale blonde hair and a natural slightly quizzical look that promised all sorts of fun and excitement.

In the first she was wearing a low fronted white evening dress.

Other pictures were of her draped on a settee dressed in delicate red and black lace bra and pants with matching suspenders and black stockings. In another she was sprawled on her back across an unmade rumpled bed with a cigarette in hand, hair tousled and a blue negligee half on and half off looking as though she had just finished a wild bout of sex.

Yet another showed her completely naked walking out of the sea on a deserted sandy cove.

The final two demonstrated her ability to role play for her clients. In one she was dressed as a schoolgirl with a really cheeky facial expression, her hair in pigtails, white shirt partly open and a grey pleated very short skirt. In the other she was wearing a tight black leather jacket unzipped almost to the waist showing off most of her considerable bust, skin tight black leather trousers, black thigh length high heeled shiny boots, a black riding crop in her hands and a sneering expression on her face.

He looked at the pictures for a long time before selecting the single sheet of paper and read about this attractive girl.

PENELOPE

A charming very attractive well spoken and well educated young lady, 5 foot 7 inches tall, 24 years old with a lovely 36d-22-34 figure and long blonde hair, who went to school at Cheltenham Ladies College before spending a finishing year in Austria. At school she was good at sport and particularly shone at tennis, swimming and netball.

Returning from Austria, Penelope joined a major London Estate Agency where her ability to charm clients with her natural warmth and openness made her highly successful in her role selling expensive houses and apartments to wealthy clients.

Although not brilliant academically she does have a great aptitude for foreign languages and is completely fluent in French, and Spanish, competent in German and can converse reasonably - if somewhat slowly - in Russian. She also has a few but growing number of words and phrases of Arabic.

Among her many attributes she is a good conversationalist with a proven ability to listen as well as lead a conversation, and she possesses a pleasant sense of humour.

Fully experienced in all forms of sexual services, we are not aware of anything that is taboo for her. She enjoys girl/girl scenes and will take part in two/three/foursomes in any combination of male or female.

Penelope has been with us for two years now and is in great demand from regular clients.

He looked at the next file and read about Annabel. Good school where she gained lots of O and A levels and had then gone to University. Sailed through and left with a 2:1 degree in Social Science. Spent a year drifting around the world and returned to Mummy and Daddy who lived just outside Winchester in a large white house with a swimming pool, tennis court, four acres of gardens and an assortment of dogs, cats and an old pony which Annabel used to ride in local shows when she was a teenager. Quickly bored with doing nothing she moved to London and stayed with an old friend from school spending her allowance and doing most of the clubs which was where she met one of Annie's scouts. One week later she had done her first job and now after three years was another of Annie's top rated special girls with no sexual inhibitions or hang-ups at all.

She had a slightly different set of posed photographs except for the obligatory evening dress outfit but they all showed her to be equally attractive but quite different from Penelope. Shorter with dark hair, and although a nice figure not quite as fulsome as the blonde.

The third and final set of pictures showed a girl called Jackie. Mark scan read her details which included the fact that she was a qualified accountant, glanced at her pictures but for reasons he couldn't explain closed her file. Walking back to his desk he picked up his direct dial phone and called Eve.

'Penelope and Annabel will be fine' he said quietly.

'I thought you'd like them. Remember Jackie for a future occasion though as she's really very good at what she does and extremely bright. Now what are the arrangements for my girls?'

Those discussions agreeing the details and fees didn't take long and as he put the phone down he wondered about Eve. They'd never met but he had seen her picture which showed an attractive if slightly plump woman in her late forties.

He leaned back in his chair his hands behind his head. Was his plan hatched all those years ago finally coming to a successful conclusion? Could he spring the trap to catch DGH and Sir Charles Houghton and avenge his father?

He smiled but it wasn't a pleasant smile as his eyes were like ice and anyone who saw them would have shivered, and worried.

CHAPTER 34

The next few days saw a succession of people whose lives were drawn inexorably together making their way to Nice and Lovell's yacht.

Mark flew to Germany on Monday and spent the day questioning and challenging leaving the German management team exhausted by his continuing demands for improved performance then the next day he flew to Spain to repeat the process there.

Javier Alvarez who ran Lovells Spanish business was mighty glad at the end of the day to drive his Chief Executive to the airport in Madrid for the short fight to Nice. As Mark walked towards the check in desks the Spaniard crossed his fingers that there were no flight delays which might cause his Chief Executive to stay longer in Spain. He was lucky. The Iberia flight was on time and as Mark disappeared into the departure section of the terminal Javier heaved a sigh of relief and drove home where he unburdened himself to his wife Elena who suggested that her husband go and relax in a hot bath.

After he'd soaked for a long time she went in and propping herself on the edge of the bath gave him a relaxing shoulder and neck massage. When she thought that the tension had eased she suggested that they went to bed where he soon found that the problems caused by Mark's visit were quickly relegated into the far recesses of his mind while the things that Elena were doing to him were right at the front of his attention.

Landing a few minutes ahead of schedule Mark walked out of Nice airport and immediately spotted the car with David Stevens standing beside it. Smiling broadly he walked quickly towards the slightly nervous yacht captain.

'David how nice to see you again. Let's get going?' and without pausing he opened the car's rear door and slid inside. The sailor ran round to the front passenger door and getting in quickly muttered to the driver who nodded and gunned the large black Citroen car into action.

A furious fast drive from Nice airport to Cannes soon brought them to the marina where the driver stopped at the dock gates and spoke in fast unintelligible French to the dock police. Cleared to pass he zoomed to where the Company yacht lay moored stern on against the jetty, its gangplank guarded by two large uniformed private security guards.

By no means the largest vessel in the marina, indeed it was dwarfed by some of the huge ocean going yachts mainly belonging to rich Arabs, nevertheless at nearly a hundred feet in length it was of significant size and although an infrequent visitor Mark was always stirred when he walked up the gangplank of what he thought of as his yacht. He'd persuaded the Board to agree to lease a sixty percent share in it just over a year ago and it had been extensively used by various members of Lovell's businesses for customer or supplier entertaining. The other part share was owned by a German furniture making business that used it for similar purposes to Lovells.

Captain Stevens followed him up the gangplank. The first officer who was awaiting their arrival saluted smartly. 'Welcome aboard again sir'.

Nodding his thanks Lovells Chief Executive walked confidently forward from the rear deck towards the ship's superstructure. 'Where have you billeted me tonight then?' he asked over his shoulder.

'Sam said not to put you in the main guest suite sir but to leave that for your guest so we've put you in the second suite. Is that alright? If not we can soon change it.'

'That's fine. I know the way. Has the electrical chap Liam been here?'

'Yes. I don't know what he's been doing exactly but I think he's been working on the hi-fi systems in the main guest suite and done something in the one he's using'.

'Right thanks. Ask him to pop along and see me will you please'. Soon Liam knocked at his door and introduced himself. The conversation didn't take long and Mark was satisfied that what he'd wanted installed had been done. 'Are you going to stay and work it?'

'Yes if that's what you want'.

'I do'. Is it easy to remove afterwards?'

'Yes'.

'OK when you've got enough, a good and varied selection shall we say, you can leave and send the stuff to BI. Here, first half of your payment' and he held out a medium sized padded envelope. 'Balance on delivery of finished articles'.

Dismissing the electrical man he showered, changed into slacks, sweat shirt and a pair of old loafers then walked back to the rear deck and asked the steward who was hovering in the background for a large gin and small tonic. It appeared almost immediately and sitting alone he contemplated the coming few days, tomorrow in particular. He thought of his father and wished that he could be present as the noose squeezed ever tighter on Charles Houghton. Soon he'd be able to tell his old dad what he'd done for him, but not how. His eyes glittered and stared into the night sky.

'Now sir what would you like for dinner? Chef recommends the sole, with new potatoes and a fresh salad. Perhaps some watercress soup to start?'

'Sounds fine thanks' and it wasn't long before he was enjoying his supper alone at the deck dining table. When he'd finished he asked for a phone so he could ring Abi with whom he had a long conversation. Finishing he asked for some fresh fruit and a bottle of chilled vodka to be taken to the cabin he was using that night and once there he hesitated a couple of times before picking up the phone and ringing Sam.

He wasn't sure what to say or why he'd rung except that he missed her and lying back on the large bed in this cabin wished that she was here with him. He didn't say that though and they spoke for a few minutes initially about work issues then more general matters.

Finally her voice going husky she asked 'How's the boat? I'm in bed having an early night but I wish I was with you on board. In fact I wish I was anywhere with you. Sorry. You probably don't want me to say that but it's true. I can't help it. I miss you, I want you and whether you like it or not you want me. Remember that. You do want me you know and I'm always here waiting for you, whenever or wherever'.

There was a pause when neither of them spoke before she added very quietly 'Good night darling. I bet you're missing me aren't you? Just think what we could be doing with each other…….. in that big bed…….. right now……..sweet dreams' and she broke the connection but when the line had disconnected and still holding the receiver she added 'I love you my darling' and a tear slowly ran down her cheek.

Damn. He shouldn't have rung her but she was right. He did want her and it wouldn't be long before he was unfaithful with her again but he couldn't help it. He was hooked like a drug onto her. Pouring himself an extremely large slug of vodka and topping it up with a small quantity of sparkling water he opened his briefcase, took out some papers and sprawling on the bed read and made notes until past midnight when he picked up the phone which was answered immediately by the night duty steward. He asked to be called at six thirty, undressed, got into bed and putting Sam out of his mind and thinking instead about Abi and Chloe went to sleep.

The next day dawned warm but grey and raining. Breakfasting on smoked salmon and poached quails eggs, orange juice, toast and coffee he settled down to wait for Sir Charles to arrive.

It was mid-morning when the Citroen pulled up on the quay and the large man sweating profusely heaved himself out of the car and walked heavily up the gangplank followed closely by another man who was shorter, medium build and carried two bulging briefcases.

Having been alerted that Sir Charles was arriving Mark waited at the top of the gangway surprised to see two visitors.

'Morning Charles welcome aboard. Good journey? And this is?'

'Good morning Mark. Yes thanks we took the early flight from Heathrow. Let me introduce David Lewis my finance director'.

The three men shook hands and made their way to the large saloon in the middle of the boat where a sizeable oval table was covered with a green baize cloth with notepads, writing paper, pens, pencils already positioned. A steward waited in the corner of the room who after serving coffee and mini croissants withdrew.

'Thought I'd bring David, to help with any complicated financial issues'.

'Ok no problem' replied Mark returning Sir Charles's look with an uncompromising unwavering stare which soon had the older man dropping his eyes and looking around the large saloon.

Mark continued. 'You still want to discuss some form of joint working or joint venture I believe? Well why don't you outline what form you think that might take so I can understand your thinking as on the face of it I can only see benefits for your Company and none for mine. I will however listen with an open mind'. A smile flicked across his face and he appeared quite relaxed.

The old industrialist opened one of the two briefcases and removed three folders. Passing one each to Mark and David Lewis he opened his own copy and started to speak.

'I'm glad you have an open mind as I think there are distinct possibilities for us both here so let me take you though them' and with that he launched into a long monologue which talked about the synergies of both companies and how they could work closely together, pooling skills and experience and building a strong partnership to attack their mutual competitors in Europe.

The more he talked and referred occasionally to the quite sparse folder the more Mark realised that in reality the old man had nothing to offer. His company was on its knees and all he wanted was a life line into the financial strength of Lovells which would keep his business afloat.

Smiling inwardly recognising the irony of what he'd just thought with Charles sitting on Mark's boat trying to find a way of keeping Houghtons afloat, whilst he the owner of the boat was trying to sink the old man once and for all. Too many metaphors about boats he mused to himself.

Sir Charles had stopped speaking and obviously having asked him a question was now looking intently at him.

'Sorry what did you say Charles?'

'I said what do you think of my plan? David here will fill you in a little more on the financial details'.

'Thank you Sir Charles. Mark this schedule here shows how we could share the proposed profit from this joint venture. You can see that we've allocated it on a slightly less than fifty fifty basis for you but that could be the subject of further consideration'. He passed across a single sheet of closely typed figures.

Mark realised that the whole thing was a farce in fact he considered it a complete bollocks. There was nothing here for Lovells, the only benefit was for Houghtons and there was absolutely no way that he was going to agree to it. However he couldn't dismiss it out of hand at this stage as he needed to get into discussion and pass over his own proposal for Lovells to buy Houghtons. If he switched Charles Houghton off too quickly he might just get up and walk away as he had before in his club. He had to keep the talks going for a while before he could introduce his own offer and then afterwards ensure the old man stayed on the boat, alone.

'That is certainly an interesting proposition and I'm glad that you've had the chance to explain it properly. Let me understand this part about joint marketing. Could you take me through your thoughts on that issue again please?'

Trying to look interested he played the game of pretending to consider Sir Charles's proposed arrangements but the old man's ideas for how it would be run were hopeless. He asked several more questions and slowly the discussions proceeded. At one point he glanced at David Lewis and thought he detected a look of desperation? No not desperation, ambivalence maybe? Not even that. It was a look more akin to disbelief. Yes that was it. So even Sir Charles's own finance director didn't think the plan was workable. What was more Mark knew that David Lewis was one of the first of Houghton's senior people when sounded out about selling who had said an enthusiastic yes. His amazing memory clicked into action to tell him why David Lewis was so keen to agree a sale.

He had four children, two at university and the other two still at extremely expensive fee paying schools. He had a large house, a huge mortgage and his wife was a profligate spender. It was as simple as that. He was overstretched financially, unusual in a senior finance man but he was clearly not only in financial debt, but emotional debt to his wife for whom he'd apparently agree anything. Yes you need me to buy Houghtons because you want my cash for the shares you hold which are currently just worthless paper. No wonder you hope your boss's crackpot plan doesn't persuade me to agree. He wished he could put the finance man out of his worry but he couldn't, not yet.

'There's certainly some thought provoking ideas there Charles. I'll need to think about it carefully so why don't we take a break and have some lunch then afterwards we could spend a little time on my proposition. You know what it's going to be but I think it is worth you reconsidering it and I'd like to hear David's view as well. So come on let's stretch our legs, break for now and start again this afternoon'.

Maintaining the initiative he stood and led the way onto the deck and towards the stern of the boat where he knew lunch would be waiting to be served as during the discussions with his enemy he'd kept a careful eye on the time. He'd planned the whole of this encounter with great care. Entering the dining saloon the steward quietly checked what each wanted to drink. Sir Charles ordered a malt whisky, David Lewis asked for dry sherry and Mark stuck to sparkling water ignoring the old man's snort of derision at his choice.

Back in England at about the time the three men were having their pre-lunch drinks a taxi pulled up outside one of the new stylish blocks of expensive apartments in Chelsea Harbour, west London. The cab driver walked into the reception area and spoke to the concierge who dialled a number and said that the taxi had arrived.

It wasn't long before the lift doors opened and an extremely attractive woman in her early twenties with her long blonde hair hanging loose walked across the foyer carrying two large suitcases. The concierge rushed forward, took the cases and loaded them into the taxi. She flashed him a dazzling "thank you" smile.

'Going somewhere nice Miss?'

'Yes, south of France for a few days. Staying with some friends'.

'Have a lovely time then Miss'.

Another smile and she slid into the taxi which Eve had booked and confirmed Heathrow as her destination.

'We've gotta pick up someone else on the way though' advised the cabbie.

'I know'.

The driver headed for Kew working his way through to a mews road where he drove slowly peering at the numbers eventually stopping outside a white painted house with a dark blue door. He rang the bell which soon opened to reveal another very attractive young woman of around the same age as his first passenger, although this one had dark hair and was a little shorter. She had two suitcases waiting just inside the door and a large grip in her hand. The cabbie took her two suitcases as she shut and locked her door then lugging her grip she clambered into the taxi smiling at the other woman.

'Hi I'm Annabel, you must be Penelope?'

The two girls took to each other straight away which was good seeing they were going to be working together on an extremely intimate basis for the next few days.

Arriving at Heathrow the check in formalities were soon dealt with and they made their way to the business class lounge. As they were a stunningly attractive couple of girls several heads turned to watch them. Annabel was wearing a knee length denim skirt and a tight thin jumper while Penelope had dressed in a loose sweater and skin tight jeans. They chatted quietly soon feeling quite like old friends.

'I wonder what our client is going to be like?' wondered Annabel.

'No idea but from what Eve said he's some big shot industrialist. Elderly I believe'.

'Oh good. He'll probably have difficulty in getting it up or if he does manage it he'll soon get knackered' giggled Annabel.

'Oh I don't know about that. I've found that some of these old boys are quite long stayers, able to keep it up for ages and can be really dirty bastards. Still we'll soon find out won't we?'

The object of their curiosity was at that moment draining the last of his whisky before sitting down to lunch. During the meal the three men talked about business, the economy, foreign affairs and a myriad of subjects but not about either Sir Charles's plan to work with Lovells or Mark's plan to acquire Houghtons.

'Must say that was an excellent meal' boomed the fat old man later as he sat back slurping his coffee from the cup he held in one hand while swirling his brandy around the crystal glass that he held in the other.

'Shall we re-convene then?' asked Mark maintaining control and leading the three of them back to the main saloon where clean glasses and cups, iced water and fresh coffee awaited them.

'Now Charles you know what I want to talk about, which is that Lovells should buy Houghtons. I know you disagree all I ask is that you listen to my proposal'.

'Mark you did me the courtesy of allowing me to talk my plan through this morning so the least that I can do in return is listen to what you have to say. However I warn you again that I am not inclined to agree to what you want as I do not want to sell Houghtons to you, or anyone else. With that proviso clearly established please proceed'.

Taking a deep breath and placing his hands flat on the table in front of him Mark looked hard at the old man sitting opposite him. This was the moment he had waited for all these years. This was the start of avenging his father. He started speaking, quietly at first but as he expounded into his theme his voice grew stronger and louder.

'Charles I completely understand your viewpoint and indeed if I was sitting where you are then I'm sure that I might have the same outlook and hope as you have. However hope is all it is as your desire is not realisable. Your business is in serious, and in our view terminal trouble. We know that your cash flow is unable to support your current working capital requirements and it is only a matter of a very short time before the cash runs out and your bank calls in the Receivers. Your European businesses have virtually collapsed. You are losing what little market share you have left in your UK business. You've cancelled virtually all your advertising and pulled out of some scheduled new product launches. I believe that you've even mortgaged your own large country house and estate and pumped those funds into the business, but it isn't enough. You simply can't go on much longer'.

Mark had seen from the corner of his eye that David Lewis was nodding to each point that he made yet old man Houghton had remained impassive so clenching his hands into loose fists and then pointing both forefingers directly across the table like gun barrels he looked at the old man as he continued.

'Why struggle on when if you are honest with yourself and your team you know that you can't succeed. Give up now while there is still something left to sell, while the business still exists and hasn't collapsed into the unfeeling and destructive arms of an amorphous Receiver. They won't help you, they'll dismember you. There is an alternative though. Let me buy your company'.

He paused, removed his clenched hands from the table and turning to his side extracted three thick folders from a case that had been sitting on a chair next to him. Two were slid across to the two men opposite and he retained the third.

'This is my proposal. In your folders there are three sections. Firstly there is a short synopsis of the benefits of a complete takeover. The second section goes into considerable detail of how the whole process will be managed and integrated, timescales, procedures, responsibilities, and costs. Finally the last section lays out for your consideration the specific details of our offer to acquire your business. We believe that our offer is fair and reasonable bearing in mind the considerable problems that exist in your company. I realise that it is complex and you two may require some time alone to study the matter or possibly talk with some of your other Board colleagues. If you want to call anyone back at your offices or your bank, the phone over there is totally secure so feel free to use it'.

He noticed that the finance man had gone straight to the third section to look at the terms of the offer and although saying nothing briefly raised his eyebrows, glanced at Mark then looked back down at the papers.

Sir Charles on the other hand opened the folder at page one, smoothed it flat, adjusted his half glasses and started reading slowly and thoroughly. The boat moved slightly as another vessel passed and its wash gently rocked the craft. Silence reigned as Sir Charles read each page until he came to the end of section one.

He topped up his glass with some iced water and missing out the second section turned to the last where he read expressionlessly through the detailed financial arrangements in which Mark had outlined the method he intended to employ to facilitate the purchase using a combination of Lovells shares, immediate cash and some deferred cash payments depending on the performance of the main acquired businesses post acquisition. It also outlined share options and the financial package that would be paid to the key people who joined Lovells, together with severance terms for those that were not required.

He then turned to section two but as it was nearly forty pages long and full of great detail he didn't do more than flick through it before looking up.

'You've done your homework thoroughly I'll grant you that, but I am not persuaded'.

David Lewis's looked horrified. Mark looked surprised. Sir Charles looked smug.

'I think it might be a good idea if David and I had a little time together?'

'Of course' and telling them to call him when they were ready Mark left.

Going on deck where the sun was now shining strongly and the deck steaming as the heat was drying everything, he gazed over the bustling marina as he walked slowly around the stern deck of the boat watching all around him whilst wondering if the document over which he'd worked so hard would sway the old man over. There was no doubt the finance director was persuaded, it was just Sir Charles to convert. He slowly pounded the ship's rail with frustration, anger even hate.

'Go on' he said softly staring into the distance. 'Agree damn you, agree'.

If Mark's staring could have seen all the way to Nice airport at that moment he would have observed two attractive girls walk through immigration control collect their bags and struggle for a moment to load them onto a trolley. A couple of men rushed forward to help and telling them that they were very kind the girls pushed their trolley through customs into the terminal building looking carefully for a man holding a board marked **LOVELLS.**

Seeing him standing to one side they introduced themselves then followed him outside to where a grey Renault which was stifling hot was parked where the driver said in heavily accented poor English 'We av to going at otel for wait on telephone calling to on go boat, comprendre?'

The girls nodded and in perfect French Penelope replied that they understood completely and to which hotel were they going?

'Hotel Carlton. Very big otel, yes you like'.

Reaching the hotel their driver led them inside and a porter helped with their luggage. Rapid conversation in French ensued between the two men until their driver beamed and said 'All ok, fixed'. He then spoke rapidly in French to Penelope who listened carefully before explaining to Annabel that the arrangements were that their luggage would be stored securely and that they should have a drink in the bar while they waited until the driver returned to take them to the boat.

Finding a corner of the bar they ordered some wine and swapped stories about how long each had worked in this business, how they got started and why, and clients they'd met working for Eve. They discovered that they'd both had dates with a certain very senior German Banker, a Kuwaiti Prince and a British Opposition Minister and found it fun to compare notes about them. They also established that they enjoyed each other's company.

Back on board David Lewis came and found Mark.

'Look he's going to turn you down. I think he's mad as we can't go on for much longer. I'm not being disloyal merely stating the obvious you know that as well as I do. Something however just stops him. I don't know what it is. Blind faith that something will turn up to put it right? He's been in tight spots before over the years and always pulled out so perhaps he thinks he can do it again. But he can't this time it's too serious and too far gone. Selling is the only option and your offer is certainly sensible but I'm sorry to say that it isn't going to happen. Not today at least. Maybe he'll just have to wait until it all goes bang around him and then perhaps he'll see sense. Sadly then it'll be too late'.

Mark and David returned to the saloon where Sir Charles Houghton was still sitting at the table. He looked at the Lovell's Chief Executive.

'Now look here Mark. Having thought about your offer at this stage I remain committed to trying to keep Houghtons independent. David here says that I won't succeed and that I should accept your deal. He may be right so I'd like to think about it for a few days and I'd also like time to read the second section of your document in much more detail and consider what a combined company could look like, its strengths and its weaknesses.

This does not mean that I'm changing my view but I will think about it. Furthermore I need time to discuss things with my advisers. So that is my position at the moment. At the end of the process I will probably still say no but I need the time to work through it carefully'.

'Take all the time you need Charles. Stay here. It's secluded, quiet and you can work in peace undisturbed. The boat is equipped with all the necessary communication systems, phone, fax, computer links, internet in fact everything that you could possibly need. Be my guest'.

'I might just take you up on that. As it happens I did bring a few clothes with me as I thought that I might spend a day or so down here in the south of France. Will you be staying on as well?'

'No 'fraid not. I've got to get back to Italy and then onto the UK' replied Mark grimly his mind now made up to implement the final stage of his plan.

The meetings at an end the three men shook hands. Mark asked Captain Stevens to arrange for Sir Charles to be shown into the main guest suite as he would be staying for a few days.

David Lewis bade his boss good bye and leaving the boat got into the black Citroen. Mark watched him walk down the gangplank and then went to the small office that he kept on board. Picking up his mobile he dialled a number and waited until it was answered.

'Apportez a bord le bateau aux filles' *(Bring the girls on board the boat)* was all he said.

He went to find his old adversary. Shaking his hand and saying that he had to leave he confirmed that the boat was completely secure and confidential and that the older man should avail himself of any amenity that he found on board which took his fancy. As he said these words he looked straight into his enemy's eyes and smiled.

'Give me a call when you get back to England and let's see what your view is then about my proposition. By the way here is some further documentation that may be of interest and might help you make up you your mind. It elaborates a little more on section two' and he lifted a further thick volume off a side table and handed it to the head of Houghtons.

'I'll read it with much care and interest and thanks for letting me stay on here on the boat by the way. Time on ones own is so difficult to find nowadays. Something as important as this needs careful consideration'.

'Absolutely. Enjoy your time here, good bye Charles' and with a further handshake Mark left the old man and returned to his cabin where he quickly threw some clothes into his bag and then walked along to the rear deck, reminded his yacht captain to ensure that Sir Charles had plenty of privacy, good food, lots to drink and was able to relax with the support of the Public Relations girls who would be coming on board shortly.

Carrying his bag he walked quickly down the gangplank to join David Lewis in the car and tapped the driver's shoulder. The car whizzed off to the airport on its way out of the marina passing the Renault driving in with Penelope and Annabel.

Shaking hands at the airport they headed for their respective flights, the Houghtons man on a British Airways flight back to Heathrow and Mark on an Air France flight to Rome.

On their respective flights they both brooded on the day's discussions. David Lewis was frustrated that Sir Charles still refused to see sense.

Mark felt the same but was pleased though slightly nervous of what he had put in process to hopefully become the final stage of his plan to get even with Houghton and avenge his father. Still he told himself he didn't have to use what he'd soon have if he really didn't want to.

True but he knew he would use it without hesitation if he had to and everything else failed.

CHAPTER 35

The girls walked carefully up the sloping gangplank and were taken to their adjoining cabins which although comfortable and nicely fitted out were small and only had single beds, a toilet and tiny shower cubicle, compared with the major guest cabins with their overt luxury of large king size beds, lots of space, long wide baths and big walk in showers.

'Ladies if there's anything you need just let me know' said the steward as he'd delivered their bags to their cabins.

'Unpack, quick shower and then go and meet our man?' queried Annabel as she wandered into Penelope's cabin.

'Yep. I feel all grubby after the travelling. Seeing the time I guess cocktail type outfits would be best. Give me a look when you're ready'.

It was about forty minutes later when Annabel walked back into Penelope's cabin wearing a black outfit the trousers of which were so tight that they looked like a second skin, matched to a sleeveless blouse top that was equally tight and so clearly showed her nipples through the material. Her face was carefully made up and her dark brown hair shone in its bob style.

'Give a twirl then' grinned the blonde and she smiled appreciatively as Annabel did as asked. 'Lovely. You'll knock his socks off. Now do I look alright?'

'Fabulous. He'll probably ejaculate just looking at you' Annabel laughed admiringly. Penelope looked stunning wearing an extremely short dark blue dress showing most of her long legs.

'Come on let's see what's been booked for us then' and linking arms the two walked down the yacht corridor making their way to the rear saloon where they walked unselfconsciously into the wood panelled room.

The tall large very fat man was talking to a ship's officer. They both turned when the girls entered and although the sailor's face remained impassive the other man looked delighted. Walking forward he held out his hand.

'Hello there. I'm Sir Charles Houghton but you can drop the Sir and just call me Charles. This is Captain David Stevens. He's in charge of this ship aren't you?'

'Something like that. Now if you'll excuse me I've a few things to attend to but I'll send in a steward and he'll look after you for drinks, snacks and anything else you might need'.

'Thank you' boomed Charles then after the sailor left leaned conspiratorially towards the girls smirking 'but I think most of what I want seems to be standing right here in front of me eh, don't you know?'

They laughed politely as they moved into their role which of course included laughing at the client's jokes. A moment later as they turned when Pierre the steward came in and asked what he could get them Penelope encountered another requirement of the role when she felt the old man's hand slide across her buttocks and give them a squeeze. Pushing herself back onto his hand she signalled that she didn't mind and was available to him.

He ordered a large whisky. Penelope asked for a glass of champagne and then he turned to Annabel.

'And for you my dear' he boomed starring at her nipples while she contemplated her choice.

'Well I don't drink very much really but I'm feeling rather naughty tonight so could I have a gin and tonic but just a little one please?'

'Ha ha feeling naughty are you well that sounds promising' he chuckled conspiratorially as he led the way over to the large dark green leather armchairs that were set on the other side of the saloon and in the process managed to give Annabel's bottom a rub.

'Ah thanks' he nodded to the steward when he brought their drinks, then told him he could leave them to chat and they'd help themselves to any more drinks.

'Certainly sir. Dinner is planned for eight o'clock if that's satisfactory to you but just press the bell if you need anything before that'.

'Well now come and tell me all about yourselves' smirked Charles Houghton. 'I must say you seem to be a very charming pair of young ladies and I'm sure that we're going to have a wonderful time together. We've got a few days together so there's no rush. We can savour the moment as it were, like a fine wine don't you know. Now I'll start by telling you about myself shall I?' and he launched into a long rambling explanation of his life accentuating the parts where he could show how clever he was at having built up his business and skipping over the current problems.

The girls made suitable "gosh" and "how clever of you" and "did you really" sorts of comments and after he'd refilled his glass he went and sat on the settee that ran down a long portion of one side of the room and patted the seat on either side of him.

Joining him Penelope made sure as she curled up next to him that her skirt rode up giving him a clear view of her long legs and knickers. Annabel sat next to him on his other side, gave him a little peck on the cheek and stroked his thigh.

Charles Houghton beamed and knew he was going to enjoy himself for the next few days. He decided he'd have the blonde one first and the brunette afterwards when he'd had a little time to recover. When he asked them why they did what they did for a living Penelope leaned towards him, placed her hand in his lap, felt for his cock and squeezed it before replying without embarrassment.

'I could tell you it's because I like to meet interesting people like you. Well I do of course but that's not why I do this. I could tell you that I want to travel first class, stay in wonderful hotels or lovely yachts like this and see the world. Well yes that's nice too but it's also not the reason. No Charles for me it's very straightforward. I do it because I adore sex in all forms. I'm very good in bed and I like earning heaps of money. The two seem to go together, sex and money. So nothing deeply intellectual or complicated, simply lots of sex and lots of money. That's why'.

'And you?' he grinned turning to Annabel.

'Oh similar really. I finished Uni, travelled the world a bit but not in luxury like this, went home got bored, so moved to London and spent my allowance clubbing and fending off blokes. I told you that I don't drink much and most of the blokes just wanted to get me pissed and into bed. I decided that if men wanted to screw me they could pay for it so when I was approached I jumped at the chance. I have to say I love it, getting paid and screwing. Now talking about screwing what do you want to do? We are here for you and as you said there doesn't have to be any rush but it is nearly seven thirty. With dinner at eight if you want to play before we eat we'd better get started'.

'No rush my dear' he said pinching her nipples through her top. She stopped herself from wincing and smiled instead. He continued 'Now I'm going to have a bath and change for dinner. Let's meet around eight and then we'll see how the night evolves shall we?' Turning back to Penelope he grinned, lifted her skirt to look at her knickers then wandered off to his cabin.

Watching him go they looked at each other and wondered if they should go and get into his bath to wash his back for him.

'No sod him let him wash himself' decided the darker of the two before adding 'but if you want me to give your back a wash, or anything else for that matter I'd be happy to oblige'.

'Not now but perhaps later' smiled Penelope.

Sir Charles realised he was in the company of two very classy professional girls. He'd hoped that his hint about a bath might have brought a response but as it hadn't he laid back in the large tub and thought about the evening ahead. Fleetingly he also reminded himself that he had to find time over the next few days to study Mark Watson's documents however that was for the future. Tonight he was with two stunning girls and lying there in the warm water a part erection developed as he speculated on what he might do with them and more importantly what they, unlike his wife of many years, might do for him.

Belinda had never been keen on sex having seen it as an unfortunate wifely chore that had to be endured when her husband needed to slake his sexual thirst. Not a prude but simply disinterested in the whole process she considered it something that was necessary to produce children, of which she had delivered three and then had to be put up with from time to time when it wasn't about producing babies.

He on the other hand realising that he couldn't change her attitude decided that it wasn't worth creating a fuss about the matter and had simply sought his enjoyment elsewhere. He thought she had probably guessed but said nothing and in return he ensured that she wanted for nothing in the big house and country estate that he'd bought many years ago.

So Mark's offer of a few days hidden away with sex on tap was a great incentive to pack his wife off to the health farm. Mind you it had been touch and go as to whether she would go there or want to come down here with him. Fortunately his description of hours of boring meetings over several days with no female company for her had finally persuaded her to ring her old friend Amy to accompany her to the health farm. Perhaps he mused, they had a resident young stud there to service all the older women? Well good luck to him if he tried it on with Belinda.

Deciding that the girls were not coming to join him he clambered out of the bath noting from the occasional movements of the floor that he was afloat and not in an hotel. He liberally splashed aftershave onto his face, chest and pubic hair, then dressed carefully finishing by pulling on his dinner jacket, checked his appearance in the full length mirror and made his way back to the rear deck where he'd been told that the dining table had been set. The girls were waiting for him.

Penelope was wearing the white low fronted evening dress that Mark had seen in her picture a few days before. Annabel was in a stunning bright green high necked outfit but which had a slit up each side almost to her waist. When she stood still they weren't visible and it looked like a full length close fitting dress but when she walked both legs seemed to leap free and were exposed right up to the very top of her thighs yet the centre portion of the dress managed to hide her crotch.

'Well ladies I must say you look charming, now shall we have a drink? There's some champagne over here so can I pour you both a glass?'

As he started to fuss around them Pierre the steward came and smoothly taking the bottle from the old man's hands dispensed the drinks. When they sat down to dinner Charles Houghton took the head of the table with the girls ranged on each side.

The first course was consommé and after he had slurped his first mouthful Annabel leant towards him and took his soup spoon out of his hand. Filling it from his bowl she lifted it to his lips where he obediently swallowed the proffered soup then she slowly licked both sides of the now empty silver spoon before refilling it from his bowl and presenting it again to his lips. Continuing this process until his bowl was empty, occasionally interrupting it to drink some of her own soup, she took his napkin, gently wiped his mouth then tucked the white linen cloth back into the top of his trousers where feeling around his crotch her hand squeezed him gently.

Watching with amusement Penelope waited until the brunette had finished feeding the old man before she reached for his glass of champagne. Taking a large mouthful and then half standing to lean over him ensuring that he had a good view down her low fronted dress, she used her little fingers to prize open his lips and push his teeth apart before clamping her lips onto him and slowly dribbling the fizzy liquid from her mouth into his. Sitting back down in her own chair she blew him a kiss and asked if he'd enjoyed his soup and champagne.

Pierre appeared from nowhere, removed the dirty bowls and cutlery then reappeared a few minutes later followed by another waiter. The salmon which was served with lightly steamed fresh vegetables was delicious and the three of them chatted quite like old friends, except that old friends probably wouldn't put their shoeless foot into his lap and rub him to an erection which Annabelle did while he was eating.

He wondered who to have first. The brunette certainly seemed a randy little bitch but the blonde was slightly prettier and had bigger breasts.

The dessert of light fluffy meringues made by the on board chef with fresh fruit and cream was delicious and he noticed that although both girls drank quite sparingly Penelope consumed more than Annabel. He drank less than he usually did as he wanted to be sure that he could perform with them both and didn't want to risk any alcohol induced droopiness of his manhood. Coffee was served and they chatted and laughed and he stroked their hands.

Annabel again put her foot in his lap and rolled it around so he rubbed her foot and ankle but when he tried to slide his hands higher she laughed and took her leg away.

Penelope then took charge. 'That was a lovely meal wasn't it, now it's time to play. I'm really feeling in the mood and I bet you're fantastic in bed so come on don't let's wait any longer'. Taking his hand she pulled him to his feet and led him away from the table and towards the cabin area. 'Coming to join us' she called back over her shoulder to Annabel.

'Just try and keep me away. You're not the only one whose feeling horny' and following the other two she saw the way his hand was fondling her companion's backside while he whispered in her ear.

As they entered the cabin both girls were impressed by the size and luxury of the surroundings. The large room was bathed in soft lighting and the bed, cushions, curtains, settees and other soft furnishings were a mixture of soft pastel shades. A fresh bottle of champagne was sitting in an ice bucket and the room had been tidied after Sir Charles had changed for dinner.

The carefully hidden sensor which was triggered by movements sent its electronic instruction to the tiny lens which was equally carefully hidden and it instantly started to started to transmit its information to the tape machine hidden in another cabin. Liam noted it click into life and checking the monitor to see that all was working well watched for a few minutes and then returned to his book.

Before Sir Charles could say anything Penelope put her arms around his neck to kiss him her tongue reaching deep into his mouth as he fumbled around in front to find her breasts.

'Hang on while I take this off' she laughed stepping back while reaching behind her for the zip.

'Let me do that Pen love' offered Annabel and in seconds the zip was run down. As Annabel helped her step out of the white dress Penelope turned back towards him her large and now unencumbered breasts swinging gently with the movement. He looked her up and down and saw that all she was now wearing was a pair of pretty white lacy French knickers.

'Would you like to take them off or shall I?' she smiled putting her hands on her hips.

'Or maybe you would you like me to do it?' chipped in Annabel as standing behind the blonde her hands appeared round the front of Penelope's waist, traced their way upwards to sensuously massage the large breasts before gently tweaking the nipples for a few seconds, after which the hands slid down to hook into the waistband then the knickers were slowly eased down the tall blonde's legs revealing a completely shaven pussy.

'There she's all ready for you. Now can you help me undress? Unzip me please'. Turning her back she waited while he undid the zip. 'Now slide it down and off' she commanded turning back to face him so breathing heavily he knelt and fumbled the dress down her legs before slipping his fingers into the waistband of her black thong which was soon removed.

He shuffled forward moving his mouth towards her carefully trimmed strip of dark pubic hair but giggling she moved away and stood next to the blonde with her arm around her.

'So which of us are you going to have first...... brunette or blonde, shaven or hairy?' queried Penelope swaying her hips from side to side. 'It's make up your mind time' and she walked over and helped him struggle to his feet. Leaning back she untied his bow tie then while she undid his shirt buttons Annabel knelt down unzipped him and slid his trousers down. He abandoned himself to their attentions and soon he was standing completely undressed except for his black socks and sagging white pants bulging with his erection. Annabel removed his pants and gave his penis a quick rub while Penelope having taken her evening bag over to the bedside unit turned to face the now naked old man in front of her.

A feeling of revulsion momentarily swept over her. This was the down side of what she did. Sometimes she was lucky and got a good looking man to sleep with but usually they were middle aged or older and unattractive like Charles Houghton.

When dressed although obviously overweight he was a large impressive looking man but naked it was quite different. Not only grotesquely fat and really quite ugly but he was covered with thick hair that had originally been black but was now substantially tinged with grey. It was all over his chest, back, arms and legs. His very large protruding and heavily sagging belly was also thickly covered with hair.

God he looks like an ageing gorilla she thought as she looked him up and down noting his surprisingly small but stiffly erect cock but smiling sexily she quickly got her feelings back under control.

'Well....... her or me first?' she asked licking her forefingers and running them around her nipples while slightly pushing her pelvis forward.

His voice dry with excitement went croaky as he said 'You........ please'.

'Good so let's try out that big bed shall we?' and she walked him across the cabin savouring the thick carpet that covered the deck.

A second lens silently watched and recorded the naked Sir Charles's surrender to Penelope's tongue and lips working on his penis before she manoeuvred herself into a position where she could reach her bag from which she extracted a condom, quickly opened the pack and popping the rubber in her mouth leaned down and expertly rolled it down his erection finishing with her hands to ensure it was properly in place. Kneeling astride him she gently lowered herself.

'Oh that feels so good' she groaned as she started to make love with him. Her movements alternated between slow and quick, long and short. 'Do you want me to stay up here or would you like me under you?' she asked taking his hands and placing them on her breasts a move which she instantly regretted as he pinched and squeezed her far too hard. 'Ouch, gently darling'.

He wanted to be on top so she climbed off but because he was so fat they had to wriggle around to find a position that enabled him to enter her being careful that the condom was still in place. He huffed and grunted as soon as he was inside and it wasn't long until giving a particularly loud grunt he stopped moving and collapsed on top of her.

Surprised that he'd come so quickly she gave a few moans to make him think he'd turned her on before wriggling out from under him. Pushing him onto his back she told him that it had been wonderful, pulled off the rubber and lay alongside him wiping drops of sweat off his forehead, neck and chin. The hair on his chest was also damp and she stroked his belly while watching his penis deflate.

For his part he lay still and gradually his breathing slowed as he relaxed to her stroking his body.

'That looked fantastic. Now it's my turn' giggled Annabel holding a towel as she joined them on the bed.

The old man thought that he was in heaven. Here on one side was a beautiful blonde that he'd just screwed while on the other side was a lovely brunette asking for it.

Annabel kissed him gently while drying some of the more sweat ridden areas of his body then she started to play with his nipples before stroking his chest and belly replacing Penelope's hand with her own as she moved down to his limp penis. Rubbing and squeezing had no effect and she resigned herself to waiting before he'd be ready for action again.

Leaving Charles's next sex mate to play with him Penelope went over to the champagne, opened the bottle and poured out three glasses which she took back to the bed. She and Charles drank deeply but Annabel only had a small sip. Later he started to grope Annabel's body and detecting a little movement from his penis she leant down and started to lick it from root to tip which soon stiffened it up.

'Woof woof' growled Charles and for a moment she looked blank. He "woofed" at her again and suddenly twigging what he wanted she swivelled round positioning herself on all fours with her bum pointing at his face. Muttering "miaow" and then making loud purring noises he leaned forward and buried his face in her pussy.

Penelope watching his animal antics with amusement grabbed another condom and slid it on him as he knelt up positioning his cock at the entrance to her pal's pussy. He thrust forward and giving several loud grunts and puffing loudly screwed away for a much longer time on this second occasion, stopping several times to get his breath until snorting loudly he thrust really hard a couple of times, exclaimed 'Yes' and clasping Annabel tightly, stopped moving. He stayed there bent forward gasping and dripping beads of sweat over her back until after a few minutes he collapsed flat out on his stomach as a smiling Annabel twisted round to lie down next to him.

The old man struggled onto his back chest heaving, red faced, unable to speak panting for breath. Eventually he calmed down as Penelope towelled the sweat off him while Annabel removed the rubber from his now wilted cock.

Slowly his breathing returned to normal and he relaxed then to the surprise of both girls he closed his eyes and it wasn't long before started to snore loudly.

Deciding that he was out for the count, or at least for some time they carefully got off the bed found a duvet and laid it over their naked client before picking up their clothes and creeping out of the enormous cabin back to their more modest abodes.

The hidden lenses had recorded everything.

'Perhaps we'd better leave him a note or something?' queried Penelope when they reached Annabel's little cabin.

'Saying what?'

'Oh I don't know. See you at breakfast?'

'Or if you wake up and want another fuck give us a call' giggled Annabel.

'Maybe. After all that's what we're here for though from the state he got into when he screwed you I thought his heart was going to peg out. Look I'll go back and prop up a note where he can see it and then let's you and I have a drink together'.

Collecting a negligee from the wardrobe in her own cabin the blonde walked back to where their client was still fast asleep and soon found writing paper, envelopes and pen.

We decided you needed your beauty sleep to get your strength back!! If you want us we are in a pair of little cabins down the corridor. Come out of your cabin, turn left and then turn right. We're just along there in Cabins 3 and 4. If you don't come to us then we'll bring you breakfast (and a few other things!!) in bed around 8 in the morning. Sleep well. Thanks for a great evening. Look forward to lots more fun tomorrow. Love and kisses

Penelope and Annabel.

Ps. You were a really fantastic lover tonight. Can't wait till tomorrow!!!

Looking at him still snoring she folded the note, put it in an envelope, wrote his name on the outside and propped it on the dressing table where he'd be sure to see it.

The unseen lens stared and recorded what she'd done.

Picking up the half empty champagne bottle she tiptoed back to cabin 3 glad that a couple of fucks were enough to knacker him for the night. Some of her clients were quite insatiable and wanted to screw her as many times as they could as if they were trying to prove their virility. Although it was what she was paid for nevertheless there was no pleasure in being pounded into time after time by the same client pretending that she loved every second of it.

Annabel who was stretched out naked on the narrow bed smiled when Penelope came back.

'All OK?'

'Yes sleeping like a log or based on the snoring noises like a hog might be a better description. Tell you one thing we are better off down here as if we were in there with him we wouldn't get a wink of sleep with all his snoring'.

'I think we're a lot better off in here' the brunette said softly reaching over for the other girl's hand and pulling her towards the single bed. 'Come here Pen' and kneeling up she kissed her companion softly on the lips before opening the negligee and tracing her tongue around the exposed full breasts and nipples.

'Nice?'

A nod of blonde hair confirmed the answer.

'Umm come here then' and twisting themselves onto their sides head to foot they were soon enjoying a classic sixty nine love making. Taking their time they both enjoyed their own climaxes, finished the champagne and then cuddling together went to sleep in each other's arms. No lens had watched them and their pleasure was their own.

In the morning Annabel looked in to the huge cabin but he was still asleep so the girls shared a shower in the little cabin before dressing and going to wake their man. Pen wore a pair of very skimpy shorts and a little bra top, while Annabel popped on a micro skirt and a boob tube. They woke him up then ordered and ate breakfast together but it wasn't long before the girls were undressed and being humped and sweated over by their client.

The unblinking lens watched and noted all that followed during the next few days. The girls had both brought several outfits with them so Sir Charles enjoyed the benefits of having sex with Penelope dressed as a leather clad dominatrix, a schoolgirl, and a nurse as well as considerable periods when she was completely naked. Annabel's outfits included a French maid, a police woman complete with handcuffs with which she shackled him to the bed, and a school mistress including gown, mortarboard and long swishy cane.

He had never been with such attractive girls who were not only so open and uninhibited about sex but seemed happy to spend as much time as he wanted doing whatever he wanted so he found it amazingly stimulating to be with these two highly inventive girls. When he was flagged out they would put on a lesbian show to arouse him again. On other occasions they produced vibrators which they mainly used on the outside of his body primarily his penis, balls and nipples but on a couple of occasions a buzzing plastic dildo was inserted into his bottom to restore a wilting penis to full strength or if it was already hard to bring an additional dimension to his sexual climax.

After the first night when they'd been tied up alongside the marina jetty, the Captain suggested that they cruise along the coast and so when they weren't in bed the three of them lounged on deck in the warm sunshine drinking and relaxing as they sailed past St Raphael, Frejus and Saint Tropez. He managed to find a little cove between these last two places and having anchored about a quarter of a mile off shore the three of them swam from the boat.

The girls swam naked but Sir Charles wore a baggy pair of swim shorts until one time as he started to climb the boat's little ladder that led out of the water Penelope still in the sea yanked them down and gave him oral sex while he held onto the ladder.

After that first night when he'd fallen asleep he insisted that from then on they both sleep with him in the huge bed and of course they agreed as he was the client and his requirements were what they were being paid to satisfy. The sex was usually quickly over and on no occasion did he give any thought to their needs, simply his own. When he'd ejaculated into the rubber he would withdraw and lie back gasping to regain his breath and strength, oblivious of whether they'd enjoyed it, had climaxed, or were satisfied.

But the camera lens saw everything and sent it all down the tiny cable to the recording machine.

Charles Houghton also found time to be alone and study Mark's documents which were detailed and comprehensive. The arguments for Lovells buying Houghtons made compelling reading and the more he studied what was in the folders the more he knew it was the right thing for Houghtons to do but every time he considered the point he just couldn't bring himself to say yes.

Surely he could magic up something that would enable them to stay independent and why did Mark want to buy Houghtons so much? There were other acquisitions that Lovells could make but it was almost as if over the years, indeed ever since Mark had joined Lovells he'd targeted Houghtons and set out to attack and destroy them.

He thought back over the years. The American business that Lovells had bought after forcing Houghtons to their knees over there; the European businesses that had been all but destroyed by Lovells; and the UK business that was now being so severely mauled.

Lovells had attacked Houghtons continuously and consistently. Sure they'd fought against others and won, driving up their market share but no-one else had been so constantly on the receiving end of Lovell's firepower. For whatever reason the old industrialist mused Mark Watson had targeted Houghtons and was clearly determined on a destruction strategy. Well he hadn't got it yet and he'll not get it while I'm running the business and retain a controlling share decided the old man. That was final. No, he would not sell. Not to Mark Watson. Not to anyone. He'd thought about it over and over again but his mind was made up and was not going to change.

Having made that decision he decided that he might as well enjoy Mark's hospitality to the full and so putting the files back into his briefcase and locking it he went in search of the blonde who was the prettier of the two girls, not that Annabel was in any way unattractive it was just that Penelope was better. They must be costing Mark a fortune he thought and that thought cheered him no end as he found Penelope and took her to bed again.

Eventually the few days in the south of France came to an end and the yacht sailed back into Cannes marina. A thoroughly sexually satisfied Charles Houghton left the boat mid morning after giving each of the two girls a wet slobbery good bye kiss while squeezing their bottoms. He thanked them for having given him such a wonderful time. The girls who told him the pleasure had been all theirs and that he was a fantastic lover, were pleased to see his chest swell at their lying compliments on his sexual abilities.

On Sunday afternoon they stayed on board having sex with each other in the big bed used by their client before catching an evening flight back to London. After landing they exchanged phone numbers, kissed goodbye and went their separate ways.

It was the Tuesday of the following week when Mark took two calls both of which had relevance to the few day's that had just passed on the yacht.

The first was from Andrew Spicer of B I advising that they had several tapes clearly showing the old man cavorting with two pretty girls and that he would send them over. Mark agreed but also asked for a couple of dozen large size prints taken from the film. He asked for the tapes and photos to be with him as soon as possible.

The second was from the unknowing subject of the filming. 'Good morning Mark. Just wanted to say that it was most useful to be able to sit in total peace and quiet and study your proposition on the boat. Gave me plenty of time to really get into the detail and I have to say it was a most comprehensive proposition. I've read it, thought about it, and talked to my team about it'.

There was a pause and Mark could feel his heart racing and his hands felt clammy as he waited for the old man to continue.

'The answer though I'm afraid, is still no. I have given this matter the greatest and most careful attention but I remain opposed to merger or takeover by Lovells on your terms, indeed on any terms. In my view it isn't in the best interests of our shareholders. I must however thank you for the hospitality by the way. All in all it was a most agreeable few days and I'm sorry that I don't see how we can do a deal'.

'Charles, you are making a mistake, a big mistake but if that is your decision so be it. I will have to find another way to force you to sell and believe me I will find that way. Selling to us is the only viable way forward for what remains of your business. There is no other solution that makes sense. Saying that you don't think it is in the best interests of the shareholders is crazy. The primary shareholders are you, Belinda, and the family trust you control plus the few directors to whom you've give some shares. And what about your employees? What about their best interests? How can it be best for them to continue in a business that is collapsing around them? If it finally,......no not if, when Houghtons finally implodes on itself and the banks call time then most of them will be out of a job and it will be you that has caused that. Is there nothing else I can say to you to persuade you to sell?'

'No, sorry Mark but no'.

'Goodbye Charles'. He put down the phone. 'Damn. Fuck it. Fuck, fuck, fuck. Why is the stupid old sod being so stubborn?' he exclaimed out loud and as the door to Sam's outer office was open she came in looking worried.

'Everything alright boss?'

'No it bloody isn't. The stupid old goat won't sell. Right that's it. I'll force him to sell you see if I don't' and as she looked at him and his burning eyes she knew that he would. She didn't know how he'd do it, or why it was so important, just that he would.

He worked furiously all day having meetings with Tim, Caroline some of his Directors, phone calls to their bank, phone calls to some of the big Institutions that he had so assiduously wooed and long telephone discussions with Colin Ringwood from the PR company, and Andrew Spicer from B I.

In addition he continued to run the whole Lovells business, held his normal review meetings, rang the head's of several of the Lovells companies who realised that for whatever reason this was an unhappy Mark and they did their best to avoid upsetting him in any way. Some escaped unscathed others got a verbal roughing up from their Chief Executive.

By six o'clock he was tired and still angry about Charles Houghton's decision so when Sam came in to check whether he wanted anything else that evening before she finished for the day, he said no but left his desk and walked over to the easy chairs arranged round the coffee table.

'Got a few minutes to chat?' he queried pouring two cups of coffee.

'You've had a bad day haven't you' she said kindly looking sympathetically at him as sitting down she tried somewhat ineffectually to tug her short skirt into a position of providing some modesty as she sank into the low soft chairs. 'Is it Sir Charles's decision not to sell?'

He looked vacantly at her legs and then swivelled his gaze to her face. 'Yes. I can't understand why he won't sell. If he'd said that he wouldn't sell to us but was going to do a deal with someone else, then I wouldn't like it but I could understand it......except that there isn't anyone else that's in a position to buy them now. Anyone else would take time starting from scratch. We're ready. We've done the work. We probably know more about his business than he does and we could quickly finalise a deal which would be best for his employees, give him and his family trusts a big chunk of cash, provide their Directors with some value for their presently worthless shares and strengthen our own competitive position. It's so obviously the right thing to do yet still he says no. Why Sam? Why?'

'Maybe he's frightened of selling, or too proud to sell?'

'Yes Caroline said some time ago that he'd be too proud to sell. He's stubborn and it's his stupid pride. He thinks he can pull the business round but he can't, not this time. Everyone knows that, his bank, his Directors especially his Finance Director and the press. I mean just look at the financial pages which are permanently speculating about when he's got to sell or go bust. I want Houghtons and I'm going to get it. I've one card yet that I can play and it will trump anything else he's got in his hand'.

His voice had risen. His eyes flashed. His face was tense. His fists were clenched. He was like a time bomb waiting to explode.

She would have loved to have gone and sat on his lap and kissed him, soothed him but here in the office she couldn't. That had always been the rule. Whatever went on between them was secret and only happened outside the office.

'Sam do you fancy a drink?'

'Here?'

'Well just a small one as we're both driving'.

It was so long since they'd slept together. He'd seemed to establish a barrier between them since little Chloe had arrived into the world. Sam desperately missed their intimacy so much so that she feared that she might have lost him again. Now was the time to find out.

'Why not come back with me to my flat, relax and have a drink there? You could tell Graham that we've got some work to do and we both want a break from the office'.

As he stared right into her eyes she felt goose bumps appear and her heart started to thump so loudly she was sure he'd be able to hear it. The tension was almost unbearable as she waited to see what he would say to her offer but he said nothing, just continued to stare deep into her eyes. Then his gaze moved to her breasts, her legs and back to her face as he slowly relaxed.

Standing he walked over to his desk picked up the phone and punched some numbers. Her heart thumped intensely as she waited to see what he would say and to whom.

'Graham leave my car here and take yourself home. A meeting's come up at the last minute. Bit uncertain when it'll finish so I'll drive myself rather than have you hang around all night'. His driver obviously said that he was prepared to wait but Mark firmly told him to go home.

Breaking the connection he punched another number and when it was answered said 'Hi Abi, how are the two of you today? Look I'm going to be really late. Something's come up on this Houghton business which could go on for ages. I might get a room and stay over if it drags on' and so saying he looked at Sam with an enquiring expression.

Nodding with a big smile she experienced such enormous relief. He did want her. She always told him that she was there for him any time but when he turned to wanting her as he'd just done she couldn't help feeling almost overcome. It came from being hopelessly in love with him she supposed but whatever the reason he was going to be with her this evening. She'd make it so good for him that he wouldn't want to leave but stay all night.

Hearing him start to ask about the baby and get into "daddy" mode she quickly left his office and started to tidy her own desk and outer office area. He was still talking to Abi when she put her head round the door and placed a handwritten note in front of him saying that she'd leave now to go and organise something to eat for them and that she'd see him at her flat in an hour or so. He nodded and carried on with the call.

After the call was finished he read through some more documents, dictated some letters for tomorrow and then sat for a moment and thought about what he was going to do. He knew he should go home to Abi and Chloe but he also knew he wanted Sam.

Life with Abi presently was fraught as Chloe was going through a difficult patch and not sleeping resulting in Abi having to get up several times a night to cuddle and nurse her. This meant that she was exhausted so when it came to the evenings she just collapsed into bed and fell asleep. Once or twice he'd tried to stimulate her but she'd said no and turned away. In the mornings she'd told him that she was sorry but he'd just have to grin and bear it for a while until Chloe got back into a regular routine when she'd be less tired and things would become more normal.

Muttering 'Sorry' more to himself than anyone else he put away his papers, closed and locked his desk and walked down to the car park from where he drove the Jaguar slowly to Sam's apartment.

He rang the bell. When she opened the door he saw she'd changed out of her day clothes and was wearing a loose fitting pale lilac silky outfit which he would best describe as fancy pyjamas. Barefoot with her hair tied back into a pony tail she held the door open to let him step inside. He smelt her perfume and could see from how her breasts moved under the lilac top that she was obviously not wearing a bra. Following her into the apartment he also noted no sign of a panty line as her neat bum cheeks moved sensuously in the pyjama bottoms.

Her heart leapt when she saw that he had a small bag with him meaning that he'd brought his shaving tackle and some of the clothes that he kept at the office and so was obviously planning to stay the night. Putting her arms round his neck and pressing her body into his she kissed him passionately to show how much he meant to her and how much she was his tonight. Forever if he wanted.

The next morning in the office he rang their bank and asked them to finalise the formal offer for Houghtons on which they had been working for the last few weeks telling them he wanted to despatch it to Sir Charles Houghton by the end of the week with copies for all his Directors and a copy to Houghton's bank.

A package arrived at the office in the late afternoon marked for Mark's personal attention and when Sam gave it to him he mumbled that it was something from an advertising agency that he'd been expecting. Alone he opened it and saw that there were three video tapes, and several dozen black and white photographs. A quick look through the photos brought a smile to his face. He put the entire contents of the package into his safe, locked it and returned to his desk.

Early Friday morning Graham drove him Caroline and Tim to their bank in London where they double checked the offer document then he signed the covering letter and asked the bank to get it delivered by hand that day to their target.

It had to get to Houghton's main offices in Leeds but the bank's lawyers had done a good job in preparing the document and so Caroline had only required a couple of very minor amendments before its despatch by courier. It had also been established that one of the Houghton's

Directors was out of the office that day so a copy was sent to his home so that it would be there for when he arrived home that evening.

Tim and Mark chuckled to Caroline on the journey back to Crawley that once the shock of receiving a formal offer for the business had worn off they imagined the Houghton's team and their advisers would be working on the document all over the weekend and wondered how long it would be before they got the summons to meet for serious takeover talks.

This time Sir Charles wouldn't be able to brush it away. With all his Directors having copies of the offer and a copy having been sent to Houghton's bank who were now known to be desperate to find a way out of Houghton's financial problems, collectively they would force Sir Charles into calling an extraordinary board meeting to discuss Lovell's offer. Tim and Mark were convinced that Houghton's bank would be pressing for a decision to sell to Lovells and get the bank out of the financial bind in which it found itself and from the ground work Mark's team had done with the Houghton's Directors then they should all vote to sell to Lovells. That just left Sir Charles.

The spring was sprung. He'd played his hand but in addition of course unknown to anyone else, if necessary he had one final trump card to slam the trap shut. He would have no compunction in using it if that meant the end of Houghtons and the revenge that he wanted for his father as whatever it took he was going to get Charles Houghton, and soon. It wouldn't be long before Houghtons ceased to exist and with that thought he leaned back and smiled.

Tim who happened to glance across at him at that moment was startled by the expression on his Chief Executive's face.

They were right in their assumption that the summons wouldn't take long in coming and it didn't as the next week several contacts were made.

Houghton's bank rang Lovells bank to say that there was a deal to be done. Three Institutions rang Mark to say that they understood that the well publicised possible merger between the two companies was likely to proceed and that it would have their blessing. Tim also received calls from other City people to support the move.

Finally Sir Charles himself rang Mark and said that his Board had asked that formal talks should commence and although he himself remained implacably against the idea nevertheless he was duty bound to hold such discussions and therefore would Mark and his team like to meet the Houghtons group to discuss the offer document that they'd received.

Smiling broadly but speaking graciously Mark said that he'd send his team up to Leeds for the initial discussions and then he'd join later.

That night at home with Abi he varied between being happy and relaxed or taut like a coiled spring. Whilst she knew that he had a lot on at work nevertheless she was worried that it might be because of her or the baby, not helped probably because they hadn't made love for so long.

Deciding that it wasn't fair on Mark to make him take second place in everything and as Chloe had for once settled down straight away after her ten o'clock feed she ran a deep hot bath poured in a liberal quantity of bath oil, soaked for a while, then got out, dried herself, applied a little makeup and a couple of dabs of perfume, slipped on a pretty pink nightie and went back downstairs to find him. He was working in his study.

'Darling I'm sorry that I've neglected you since Chloe arrived but any new baby is always demanding and she is especially so, a trait I imagine she got from her father. However that shouldn't exclude you from me. You've been so understanding and I want to make it up to you tonight so come to bed darling now ....please.'

He swung round in his chair and looked at her. Smiling he said that he'd love to go to bed so holding hands they walked side by side to their bedroom where they made love very slowly and gently.

It was the first time that little Chloe didn't wake at all during the night.

Next morning Mark woke at six when the alarm jerked him into life to tackle another day's challenges at Lovells of which the most pressing was hopefully finalising the deal with Houghtons. He showered, dressed and was soon in the car so he didn't hear the baby start to cry just after he left unlike Abi who padding quickly to the nursery bedroom picked up the tiny child cooing softly to her as she opened her nightie and settled Chloe to her breast.

Yes he thought the discussions with Houghtons should by now be well advanced. He was nearly there. Houghtons was nearly his. Fists clenched, his face set and grim he stared unseeing out of the car window.

CHAPTER 36

As he walked back into the other room to join the others he realised that it was going to seem a very long ten minutes.

He snapped 'I've given Sir Charles ten minutes to think about it. Why the fuck can't he make up his sodding mind? It's over for him. He knows that. It's just his stupid belief that he can work some sort of miracle. No way. Either he signs to us tonight or I'll bet the receivers are in pretty damn smartish'.

Sam produced a cup of coffee which he took without a word and leaning against a filing cabinet with one foot resting on a chair sipped the hot liquid slowly while staring blankly at the wall a few feet in front of him. His fingers drummed softly against his leg as he slowly drank the coffee. No-one spoke and they all waited for something to happen.

The time crawled by and the ten minute deadline passed. Still Mark waited and said nothing but everyone present could see how uptight he was as he regularly glanced at the wall clock. Nearly fifteen minutes went by before there was a knock on the door and when it opened one of the junior members of the Houghton's team stood outside.

'Sir Charles asks whether Mr. Watson could rejoin him please'.

Lovells Chief Executive gave a quick glance around the room but said nothing as he stood up slowly straightening his shoulders and followed the young man back to Sir Charles's office.

'Come in. Sit down, please'.

The bluster had gone. Alone sitting in his office holding the package of photos he seemed smaller, no longer intimidating or dominating. He appeared exactly what he was, a defeated man.

'You gave me your word. I am replying on that'.

'You can. I told you the photos will be destroyed. It's your business I want. If you'd agreed before to what is after all a sensible business proposition then none of this unpleasantness need have happened but I could see no other way to force you. If I'd allowed your business to collapse and go into the hands of the receivers then several of our competitors might have picked up bits of Houghtons empire. I don't want that. I want it all and I'm going to have it all, but especially Charles I want you'.

'Why Mark? Why is destroying Houghtons so important to you?

'It's not Houghtons it's you, because you are Houghtons and destroying you gives me Houghtons. You ask why? Many years ago there was a small wholesale company called Anderson and Watson. You probably don't even remember it, but I do. It was a nice little company that had been carefully built up by the two founders but you destroyed it through underhand pricing and unfair dealing. You ruined a good business. That business was part owned by my father Christopher. He was the Watson in Anderson and Watson and what you did forced the business into bankruptcy. The people all lost their jobs with no payout, no compensation, nothing was left. You didn't care. You weren't bothered at the effect on my Dad, my Mum, me, or the loyal people who worked there. To you it was just another little business to crush.

Well the day that my Dad came home and said that it was all over and that Anderson and Watson no longer existed because you'd forced them out of business I promised him that I'd get even with you. He didn't think that I would, or indeed could. He thought it was just boyish talk but it wasn't, not to me. For me it was real. It was a promise that I made to my Dad and now I am keeping that promise. You could easily have destroyed our family life but my Dad had been very careful with money and we scraped by until eventually he got another job. It was nothing grand but it was enough to support me and Mum and enable me to finish my schooling.

The difference between us is that I'm not going to destroy your business and your employees. Yes, I want the business and I want you out of it and by taking your business into Lovells then Houghtons won't exist, but most of your remaining employees will be saved.

So Charles that is what this has all been about. That is why I have stalked you and your business for all these years. I've got files and files on you and Houghtons. I organised my life and career so that I could get even with you for what you did to my Dad. Houghtons is finished. You're finished. It's over.

So go to your team and tell them that after due consideration of the best interests of your employees you have after all decided to sell your shares to me. I'll tell you what' he added seeing a stubborn look come on the old man's face 'we'll even agree to you keeping your company Rolls Royce for a few months and you can continue to call yourself Houghtons Honorary Chairman until the end of this year. Lady Houghton would like that wouldn't she? After all Belinda does like the trappings that go with your role as Chairman doesn't she? If that's a face saver you can have it but you must recognise that you can have nothing to do with running the company. No decision making, no authority, no power, no ability to do anything, and no rights to even come into the office. Think about it'. Mark's face contorted and his voice rose considerably as his anger exploded. 'You didn't give my Dad any face savers did you?' he yelled.

Sir Charles shook his head sadly. 'I don't know. I just don't remember. Sorry. So that's what this is all about'. Sighing he muttered 'All right Mark, all right. Now what about my people?'

'They are all taken care of' snapped Mark. 'Ask your team. Our terms are fair indeed generous in many ways. Now get on with it. Go to your lawyers and brief them. I'll talk to mine and let's get the deal done. The bulk of the work is complete so if everyone gets moving to sort out the final details we should be able to get signing within a couple of hours'. He looked at his watch and smiled. 'Midnight would be ideal. That's just over two hours away. Have we got a deal?'

Sir Charles nodded.

'Say it'.

'Yes Mark'.

'Tell me that you are selling your business to me. Go on tell me'.

'I will sell my business to you'.

'Tell me that you will sell me all the shares that you control. Go on, I'm waiting'.

'Mark you don't need to do this to me. I've said that I'll sell to you'.

'Oh but I do. I've waited years for this moment and for my Dad's sake I'm going to savour every second of it. Now tell me what I want to hear' he hissed his eyes flashing.

Sir Charles Houghton glared at his younger adversary, paused and then shrugging his shoulders spoke softly. 'Alright I'll sell my business, my shares, Belinda's shares and those in the family trust that I control to you. You've won. Houghtons is yours. I'll tell my team to finalise the arrangements'.

Mark pierced the older man with a stare that lanced deep into him then smiled before walking out of Sir Charles's office and back down the corridors to the small room where Caroline, Steve and Sam were waiting. They looked up as he entered trying to judge from his face what had been the outcome of the meeting with the head of the opposing business? Mark deliberately kept his face blank and looked slowly from one to the other saying nothing.

It was Caroline who broke the silence. 'Well come on' she queried. 'Do we pack up and go home or do we have a deal?'

Mark sat down and said so quietly that it was almost inaudible. 'We have a deal'. Then louder he repeated 'We've got it. He's agreed to sell all the shares that are his and that he controls to us. It's all done. DGH is ours, lock stock and bloody barrel. Caroline get in there and finish it off. I want to sign at midnight'.

'How the fuck did you persuade the old goat?' asked Caroline.

'Made him an offer he couldn't refuse' smiled Mark and explained about letting him keep the Rolls and the short term pseudo Chairman non-role that he'd offered his opponent.

'And that was all it took? I don't believe it'.

'Really Caroline, that was all. It appeals to his flattery and ego. That's what you didn't offer him'.

'Mark that's bullshit' Caroline jumped up and strode towards her boss. Thrusting out her chin and leaning towards him she glared stony faced at him. 'You said that it was a key part of the deal that he went. Get him out, you said. I don't want him around to interfere and fuck things up, you said. He's the old school who'll block every change we need to make, you said. He's too old, he's past it he's a problem, you said. I want him out and I want him to know he's out, you said. Now you keep him on? Well fucking hell Mark why didn't you give me the freedom to find him a sinecure role.'

'He won't interfere. It's a non-role but it sounds good. Now stop arguing with me and go and finalise the details. We sign at midnight and you're wasting time Caroline'.

'No special one off payments to his private bank account Mark?' she continued still furious with her boss.

'Nope, nothing like that'.

'Well what about........'

'Caroline' interrupted Mark, 'shut up, stop asking daft questions, stop bloody arguing and go and finish off the fucking legals.........now. Oh and Sam get me Hans in France please'.

'Mark it's late he'll probably be asleep can't whatever it is wait until morning?'

'No get him now' and he waited impatiently while she got the call.

Caroline glared furiously at him, paused for a moment, shrugged and then swung round on her heel and strode out of the room and into the Board Room where she called out to her team who were sitting in various chairs quite relaxed and just waiting for the top brass to decide what happened next.

'Right stop sitting on your arses doing bugger all. Am I the only one doing any work around here? We've got a deal to finish off'. She then started to issue instructions with the speed of a machine gun and the whole process swung into action. 'The boss wants this ready to sign by midnight so we've lots still to do'.

'No chance' muttered one of the more junior staff members of her legal team.

'Pete are you going to tell Mark that it can't be done because if you are I suggest you hand him your resignation at the same time? If he says midnight then that's what it's going to be. Got it?' she snapped.

'Yes got it sorry' replied a duly cowed Pete and the rest of the team hurriedly bent themselves to their own particular part of the complicated legal documents. There were pages and pages still to go through. They worked quickly but thoroughly and although each was skilled in a particular area of expertise they all regularly checked a point of detail or asked for advice from Caroline. She from time to time went and talked to Houghton's team to clarify or settle a particular issue and then find a form of legal wording with which both sides were happy. Around eleven thirty she asked how everyone was getting on and received progress reports which gave her the knowledge that they would make it. She walked over to Steve and asked him to go back to the anteroom where Mark was waiting to tell him to come through in about ten minutes for a final briefing before signing.

Meanwhile Sam apologised to the Dutchman for calling at this time but said that Mark wanted to speak to him right away and handed the phone to Mark.

'Hans hi there. Sorry to call you this late but you remember that special project on which you worked so hard for me? Well Houghtons is ours. We've achieved our Ambition. Just thought you'd like to know, goodnight' and he put down the phone.

In another large room on the other side of the Board room, DGH's Directors, several lawyers, a couple of senior managers, two bankers, one insolvency expert, several accountants from Slade Waters Morrison a high powered city firm of accountants and assorted junior staff were also working furiously to finalise their side of the deal.

Sir Charles had come in after his meeting with Mark and explained that after careful reflection in order to ensure the minimum loss of jobs and to continue the great work started by his father, albeit now to come under new ownership, he had concluded that provided for a little while he remained as Chairman of Houghtons and so was in a position to advise the Lovells people to ensure a smooth transition which Mark had agreed, then he thought that the best course of action was to sell his controlling shares in the business and so the deal was to proceed.

Thus caused considerable surprise among his side in view of his previous unmoveable stance that he wasn't going to sell and they all wondered what had really changed his mind. Maybe he'd done a side deal and got himself a lot of money on top of the share value. Maybe he had realised at last that the banks really would foreclose and the Board would have to call in the receivers.

They guessed that they'd probably never know but what they did know was that Simon Eggar the insolvency expert had warned them that if they didn't get a deal done tonight then they would have to call in the receivers tomorrow as the Company was effectively insolvent. Consequently as it wouldn't meet its financial liabilities then they as Directors would be committing an offence if they carried on the business and didn't cease trading immediately. Receivership would mean no payouts, no salaries paid to the staff, no wages for the factory personnel. Nothing. Finish. Shut up shop immediately and be run day to day by the receivers who would break up and sell the business piece meal. It was as stark and close to the wire as that.

The clock hands climbed slowly towards midnight and as they passed that magic witching hour the two sides reassembled in the Board room. There were a couple of last minute queries which resulted in hasty crossing out of certain typed parts of the sale documents replaced with hand written initialled by lawyers and the principles of both sides.

Finally all was ready and it was suggested that the two Heads of business should sign their respective copies and exchange them for the other's countersignature. Mark signed his with a flourish and pushed his thick bundle towards the older man who hesitated, pen poised over the paper. Time seemed to stand still. Mark felt the sweat start to run down his back as he wondered if his adversary was going to back out at the last minute but he forced himself to remain calm, smiled and nodded slightly to Sir Charles who looked sadly firstly at him then slowly around the room before reaching into his pocket for his pen.

The document was signed and passed to Mark. Both men countersigned the other's copy and then lawyers and other directors signed and witnessed. Countless other documents were also signed. The deal was done. It was all over. At twenty five minutes past midnight Houghtons no longer existed as a separate company. It was now wholly owned by Lovells. Houghtons was Mark's. Sir Charles Houghton was Marks.

Christopher Watson had finally been avenged by his son.

Both Caroline and Sam noticed the look of triumph on Mark's face contrasting so vividly with Sir Charles's miserable broken look.

Normally at the conclusion of a takeover, champagne is broken out and everyone toasts everyone else with lots of hand shaking, backslapping and mutual congratulations. This time it was different. Mark merely went up to Charles, shook his hand, looked hard at him for a few moments and then turned on his heel and walked out of the room feeling strangely empty. Caroline and Sam followed him.

'You staying on for a while Mark? Maybe someone will open some champagne' asked Caroline.

'No. You and the rest do so by all means but I've got to go and see my father first thing tomorrow morning as there's something rather important that I need to tell him. Then I've got an afternoon flight to Brussels so I'll leave it to you and your team to wrap it up. By the way you've all done a great job on this. Thanks. I'm going to get off to bed now. Sam, you staying here or do you want a lift to the hotel?'

She looked at him and saw immediately that he needed her tonight. Whatever had gone on earlier in the private one to one talks between him and Charles Houghton somehow Mark had played his trump card whatever that had been and won. The deal that he'd wanted to complete for so long was done. He'd got what he wanted, Houghtons.

Now he wanted her. From the look on his face she could see that there would be no soft gentle lovemaking tonight. He'd fuck her fast, furiously and hard, probably more than once. When he was like this he was totally thoughtless of her needs. Tonight would be all for him, not her, not even for them. Other times it would be for her or them but tonight it was just him and she loved him deeply for it.

She loved him for everything he said and did. She loved him whether he was angry or tender, kind or demanding, ruthless or sympathetic. Whatever, whenever, however, she loved him like she'd never loved anyone or anything before. The fact that he didn't love her didn't matter. She just loved him utterly, totally, absolutely.

Looking at her watch she smiled and said that as it was late and she didn't think there was much left for her to do here then yes a lift would be nice.

Caroline watched the two of them leave. Chief Executive and his secretary. Yes. Chief Executive and his lover? Almost certainly. A great team in business and with a twinge of jealousy she guessed they were a great team in bed.

Lucky Sam she mused wistfully.

THE END

Ambition is not a vice of little people. Michel de Mountaigne

EPILOGUE

Christopher retired eventually and lived quietly with Betty in a bungalow at Banstead in Surrey, where Betty tended the garden which under her care turned into a delight of colour. He watched Mark's career in business from afar and was incredibly proud of him and was simply staggered when he heard that his son had acquired Houghtons although he never knew how Mark forced the old man's hand.

Lionel had a number of jobs after Anderson and Watson failed but was unable to hold them down for any length of time. He and Amy who never had any children got divorced and he moved to South America where he made and lost money in various ventures eventually dying of yellow fever in Peru.

Colin Ringwood sold his PR businesses it to a larger competitor and then moved to the South of France to enjoy the sale proceeds.

Andrew Spicer continued to provide discrete intelligence information to various businesses and in so doing became a multi millionaire.

Sir Charles Houghton used the money he'd received for his shares to unmortgage his great house, paid off the rest of his debts and started to try and enjoy life. Needing to get away from Belinda he missed not being able to escape to the office so he played golf two or three times a week, went shooting as often as he could during the season and spent four separate weeks' salmon fishing in Scotland. He also secretly bought back the little house in Paddington and regularly went to London ostensibly to his club to meet old chums, but in reality to continue having secret meetings with various paid girls, but never found any as good as Penelope or Annabel.

Lovells continued to flourish. Houghtons was integrated rapidly as Mark instructed that no trace of them should remain and the combined business went from strength to strength. The acquisition was good for Lovells and made them what Mark had wanted – a truly multinational conglomerate whose share price reached nearly £12 shortly after the acquisition.

Caroline continued as Lovell's corporate lawyer for a few years before moving back into private practice as a senior partner with one of the big London law firms. She remained single for a long time finally marrying a lawyer from another top London firm with whom she had two children, a son who became a lawyer and a daughter who became a doctor.

Eve remained a provider of sexual services for several more years until retiring and selling her business to Jackie one of her girls who had a degree in business studies and with whom she'd once suggested that Mark might like to sleep. The business continued satisfactorily under Jackie's control.

Penelope and Annabel both continued servicing a variety of clients.

One evening before going to his hotel for sex Penelope was taken to an embassy drinks party by her client for that night, a Chilean diplomat. There she met and subsequently started to date an American banker. The romance blossomed so she decided to give up her life of paid sex and agreed to marry him. They moved to Chicago where in quick succession she produced three children and became the dutiful "all American" mother and wife constantly amazing and delighting her husband with her almost infinite variety of sexual techniques and experience. He never found out about her earlier life.

Annabel, who one night was booked by a Nigerian oil man stupidly ignored her usual little or no drinking rule and got very drunk while out with him. Returning late to the hotel in Hamburg and with her mind fuddled by drink, he had sex with her three times that night without using a condom. It was the only time she'd ever made that mistake but it was a fatal one. Many months afterwards having felt unwell for a while she was diagnosed HIV positive. Three years later reduced to mere skin and bone and a shadow of her former beautiful self because the various drug regimes had not worked for her, she died in her childhood bedroom in the white house near Winchester being cared for by her elderly mother and father.

Mark continued to run the now much enlarged Lovells business following the integration of Houghtons until eventually he was headhunted to become Chief Executive of Wilsons Oil, a huge multinational world wide conglomerate oil company competing directly with Shell, Esso and the other majors.

Abi was an excellent mother to little Chloe who grew up a happy contented child much loved by both her parents and her elder sisters. One night though having suffered a nagging ache in her stomach for nearly a week Abi collapsed with agonising pains and serious bleeding and was rushed to hospital where she underwent an emergency hysterectomy. She made a full recovery but was sad that now she would be unable to give Mark the son that she knew deep down he wanted.

Sam remained desperately in love with Mark and the two of them carried on their ongoing affair quietly and secretly. No one ever found out although Graham guessed as did Caroline but neither of them said anything. She also left Lovells and followed Mark to Wilsons Oil but progressively became ever more resentful of Abi and especially young Chloe with the obviously increasing affection which she could see that Mark had for the child so she decided to do something about it to make Mark more firmly hers.

It was several weeks after making that decision that she woke one morning and was violently sick. Surprisingly she smiled especially when it happened for the next two mornings. After a week and with some considerable trepidation she bought a home pregnancy test kit and later her excitement was intense when it turned blue. Hugging herself excitedly she waited until a visit to the doctor confirmed her pregnancy. That same night having persuaded Mark to come to her flat, after they'd made love she kissed him tenderly. 'Give me your hand' she whispered placing it on her tummy. 'Darling I'm pregnant. We're going to have a baby. Yours and mine'.

When he got over the shock and had accepted her explanation that she must have muddled up the start and stop dates for the pill on her monthly cycle as she didn't dare tell him that she'd deliberately stopped taking the pill, he realised that he had started to create another family separate from Abi and himself. Enthusiastically offering Sam every help and support that she wanted nevertheless he worried about what role he would or could have in the child's upbringing without Abi knowing, and how he'd manage two families.

Continuing to work until the eighth month of her pregnancy her final task was to find a replacement for herself which she did describing Mark's new secretary as 'efficient, old and ugly'.

She went to the same maternity hospital as Abi and after a nineteen hour labour the baby was safely born at twenty past three in the morning. Mark had managed to visit her twice briefly during her labour but was obviously unable to be present for the birth. Leaving home the next morning he rang the hospital and was excited to hear that the baby had been safely born during the night but irritated by the hospital's refusal to confirm the weight or sex of the baby as Sam had expressly forbidden the release of any information to anyone.

'Hospital now' he snapped at Graham. 'Sam's had the baby. I'd....... err like to go and congratulate her' and soon he was opening the door of her private room.

She was resting quietly and looked tired but happy. A plastic see through cot was beside the bed containing a small white bundle.

'Good morning' she said softly then turned to the baby. 'Sweetheart your daddy's come to see you'. She looked back at Mark.

'Darling come and say hello to your son'.

END OF EPILOGUE

Lightning Source UK Ltd.
Milton Keynes UK
UKHW01f0103011018
329749UK00001B/19/P